Published by Crescent Sea Publishing.
www.crescentseapublishing.com

Cover designed by Reading Transforms.
Image copyright © K.M. Robinson Photography.

THE SIREN WARS SAGA

CELENA'S TRILOGY

THE SIREN WARS
DARKER DEPTHS
BEYOND THE SHORES
with
SECRETS SURFACE

a Merrick Prequel Novella

by

K.M. Robinson

THE SIREN WARS

by

K.M. Robinson

Antaire
Metten
Shadare
Scylla

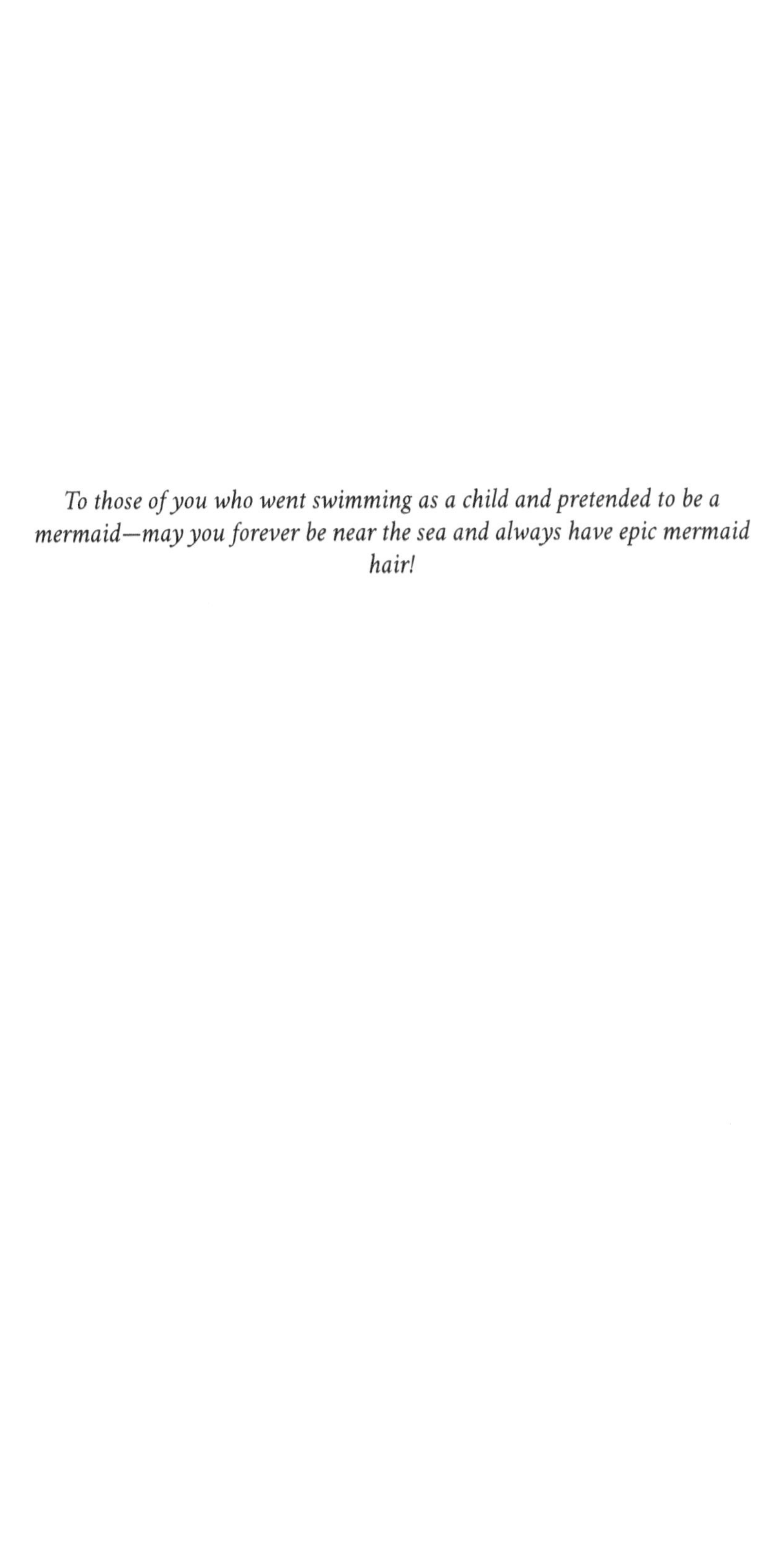

To those of you who went swimming as a child and pretended to be a mermaid—may you forever be near the sea and always have epic mermaid hair!

CHAPTER 1

A well-placed accusation—even a small, insignificant one—has the power to change the tides and start a war.

This is something I've grown up learning.

My kind have always been careful with our words…we have to be. For the last one hundred years, we've had to fight against the actions of one mermaid. Well, to be fair, one mermaid, her mother, and a group of followers, but that's just semantics. For a hundred years before that, we had to be careful too—we had an agreement with the humans.

"Are you intentionally trying to look like that?" I ask, flicking my tail flirtatiously.

"Like what, Celena?" Merrick glances up from where he's working on the sea floor against a rock, his brow low.

"Brooding," I reply.

His face lights up, realizing that he has been caught.

"Sorry, Len," he uses his pet name for me—no one else is allowed to call me that—as he moves the knife in his hands, cutting the rope.

He brushes his blue hair back with a smoldering grin before lifting himself off the sand, swimming over to me.

"Need a hand with that?"

"We're fine, Merrick," Caspian says. "Go back to not paying attention to the rest of us."

"I didn't miss *that* much," he mutters.

"*Sure,*" Caspian replies.

Merrick gives him a mock-annoyed look, rolling his eyes as he grabs the net, helping us to untangle the rock.

"How did we get stuck on clean up duty?" Merrick asks, using his most charming voice as he sidles up next to me.

"We volunteered," I remind him.

"Mmm," he murmurs. "*You* volunteered. I just followed."

"Nothing new there, brother," Caspian teases loudly. "Always following my twin around no matter where she goes."

Caspian has *no idea* why Merrick and I spend so much time together.

"Shut up, Casp," Merrick chides, winking at me.

What neither of the boys knows is that I didn't volunteer just to help out—I'm on a mission.

"It amazes me how the humans are still so intent on capturing us," Caspian murmurs. "It's been a hundred years since Persephone ruined the alliance for us."

"Be fair, Casp—it wasn't *just* Persephone. Chantay was instrumental in all of this—most say she was the mastermind and her daughter just followed along."

My fingers work to cut away the net waving gently in the current. The knife in my hand is far more effective than the broken shells I sometimes resort to using for cutting up the instruments of death that fishermen leave in the ocean when they snag on something like coral or rocks.

"It's a shame we can't just sing this work away," Coralie swims over, attempting to carry a large, round ball. She barely manages to roll it across the sea floor.

"That's not the way sireny works, starfish," I correct her. "And stop playing with that canon ball."

My little sister pouts, looking up.

"I'm not playing with it, I'm trying to help," she mutters.

"We don't need to collect human things, just remove the dangerous ones," I remind her. Coralie has only been out to help us a few times, but I'd rather she stay at home—she's too young for me to be able to sneak off and run missions while she's with us, and Caspian will start to catch on if I dump her in his care all the time.

"It would still be easier if we could sing it away," she grumbles, running hair hands through her blonde hair.

"We are not sirens, Cor, and don't even suggest that," I snap. Caspian and Merrick stop to look at me. I try not to blush as I lower my voice. "We are not like that, Coralie. Sireny has been outlawed since great-great-grandmother Aila caught Persephone sirening the prince."

"We're better off," Caspian mumbles. "We don't need the humans to survive. They haven't been able to find us in a hundred years anyway, so who cares what stupid stunt Persephone and her mother pulled?"

"You mean *aside* from hundreds of dead humans, the mer population splitting, our entire kingdom having to leave our home and move here, and—*oh, yes*—the entire human race hunting us for a century?" I chide him.

"Settle down, children," Merrick chimes in, playfully trying to quell an impending argument.

This is why Caspian has never been informed of my extracurricular activities over the last few years. This is also why Merrick *has* been on most of my missions with me.

"Well, maybe we could train the sharks to move this stuff for us," Coralie suggests.

I certainly have my hands full with this one.

"Coralie, it's all we could do to train them to act as a barrier for Scylla, *for coral's sake*. It's not like they're pets—they don't have the ability to open things like an octopus does. They're there to eat —that's all."

"Well maybe grandma Aila should have come up with a better plan," Coralie mumbles.

"Aila saved us all, Cor," I eye her. "Show a little respect. She prevented Persephone from destroying the entire mer population. She even managed to bring Persephone in from the open seas."

I idolized my great-great-grandmother and aunts—they were heroes. Aila even saved the humans, though they didn't *deserve* her help one bit.

"Princess Kailania helped," Coralie persists. "So did Ebba. And Chantay went on to live and cause destruction for *years* before she died."

"Coralie," Merrick interrupts, flicking his hand to send a small seahorse toward her. "You understand the sirens terrorize the mer *and* the humans, right? Your ancestors did a great thing when they set up the shark barrier to prevent them from attacking us here in Scylla."

Coralie has always loved the stories of our great-great-grandmother and always wanted to visit the old kingdom, so she's just being stubborn because she doesn't want to work.

"I know," she sighs. My sister tries to suppress her grin when the brown seahorse darts by her. "I just wish this were easier—or more fun."

"Tell you what," I smile, suddenly getting an idea. "Why don't you let Casp take you home and Merrick and I will finish up here. We're almost done anyway."

She cheers before my twin can protest. He grumbles, brushing back his hair.

"You two behave," he pretends to be serious, pointing at us. He wraps his arm protectively around our sister and guides her through the currents along the ocean floor.

When I turn back around, Merrick is working overtime to cut up the abandoned net. He nods for me to join him.

"I take it we have somewhere to be?" he asks casually.

"Yes."

"You weren't planning on taking me along, were you?" Merrick glances at me through his long, wavy bangs.

He caught me.

"It's not a big deal."

"Everything we do is a big deal, Celena. Every time we get near the shark barrier or swim up one of the reefs, it's a big deal."

"They wouldn't have trained us for this if they didn't want us to do it," I say, rolling my eyes at him.

"Just remember *which one of us* nearly swam into a bloom of jelly-fish last time we went out *alone*," he reminds me with a smirk.

"I only did that because you showed up and distracted me."

"You mispronounced *saved*." He grins wildly.

"Hardly, pretty boy."

We snap each rope on the net, making sure no mer or sea creature would get tangled in it. At least this one wasn't covered in barbs like the last one I found.

"I like your *iluse* today," Merrick adds, eyeing my chest covering. "Judging by those weapons you hid on it and called decorations, I'm guessing your little mission isn't as serene as you led me to believe."

Of course he'd notice the broken shells I hid in the netting and decor of my top—Merrick notices *everything*.

I slip my knife into the pouch tucked along my belt where it rests over my hips as my partner does the same. Belts were always traditionally worn by mermen a century ago to show power and prestige. The mermen would wear them specifically for special events or if they held a place of power. Now, most mer have a version they wear, especially when going to town or leaving the kingdom proper.

"So where are we going?" Merrick asks.

"This way," I reply, darting away.

I race around the seaweed gardens, swimming just high enough that their wispy tips don't touch me as I glide over them. A sea turtle swims off to the left, not bothering to take notice of us.

"There's been word that the sirens have found a way in on the west side of the kingdom. I just want to check and make sure nothing has changed since we've last been there."

"Did they *ask* you to check?" Merrick challenges me.

"She doesn't have to," I snip, flicking my tail to propel me faster, leaving Merrick in a trail of bubbles.

"*She* the queen or *she* your mother?" He easily catches up to me, having a far more powerful tail than I do.

"Take your pick," I retort.

"It's rough being princess to the entire mer kingdom, isn't it?" Merrick mocks.

"I'm barely a princess," I remind him, darting around a school of fish. Merrick pulls away at the last second, barely missing them as I smirk.

"You descend from royalty. Just because your cousin holds the official crown, doesn't make you any less of a princess."

"I'm a warrior, Merrick. I hardly sit around the palace all day."

"Neither does your cousin," he points out as we slow our pace. "You all work for this kingdom. *You* just take it more seriously than the rest."

"Aila did."

"You don't have to do everything Princess Aila did," he counters. "And if you'll recall, she didn't set out to do any of that—it just happened.

"Next thing I know, you'll be swimming to the surface to meet some human prince." He rolls his eyes at me as he brings up Prince Jarek, the human Persephone tried to siren when she caused the war.

"I have no intention of befriending a human, thank you very much. That would be a stroke in the wrong direction for sure."

"Ah, but speaking of a stroke in the *right* direction, looks like our rides just arrived," Merrick calls, rushing forward. His hand darts out, catching hold of a dolphin.

He quickly reaches back, grabbing my hand as the creature pulls us forward. Once he pulls me to him, I catch my own ride.

The coral barrier stretches up high toward the surface of the ocean, protecting Scylla from intruders. The barrier blocks larger ships from entering most of the territory, protecting us from many of the humans' attempts to find us.

While their searches have slowed, it's very clear that they are not done looking for trophies to take home. A year ago, I found a book that had fallen to the ocean floor describing the most absurd ideas the humans had about mer. One page detailed our bone structure—which, in fact, they *do* know from cutting up our ancestors—while another page contained information about how we cry pearls and dissolve into foam when we have our hearts broken.

Humans are curious creatures who *clearly* haven't learned much in the last two centuries.

When we finally let go of the dolphins, Merrick and I examine the coral. Nothing looks out of place, though it's been months since I was last here. I only make it out to this side of the kingdom a few times a year, just to check on it. We have mermen standing watch at all times, but I like to see it for myself.

"What I don't understand is how the sirens have been getting in," Merrick murmurs. "We have all of these barriers in place—we're protected. How are they slipping in?"

"We've only seen evidence of a few so far—barely enough to warn the people."

"We've never officially found any inside Scylla, I know." Merrick sighs. "But *how* is this possible?"

The few sirens we've noticed have disappeared before we could bring them in for questioning—the mer have only seen them from a distance.

Rumors have spread like seaweed that the sirens have changed in appearance—long, hideous noses, scraggly hair, and sea serpent-like tails.

I know that can't be true based on the books I've found from the humans. Sirens still look just like the mer—because they still *are* mer. They just cultivated their wicked talents while the mer forced it out of our offspring.

Once, we all had the ability to sing a human into doing our bidding. Now, only sirens hold that dark magic. Instead, we avoid humans and their destruction, leaving us no need for the deadly songs sirens have the ability to sing.

True, Marcelline—*the defender of the sea*—originally sirened King Leon into creating an agreement with the mer, but that only lasted a century until Persephone ruined that promise of safety for us. Marcelline's great-great-granddaughter, Aila, tried desperately to save the agreement and repair our relationship with the humans, but today we find ourselves living deep under the sea, refusing to venture to the surface where we once used our voices to save humans on the rough ocean surface.

Now, we wouldn't surface to save a drowning fisherman or guide a ship safely through a storm for any price. We don't associate with the population trying to murder us.

"Can you feel that?" Merrick asks, holding his arms out to his side. "The tide is changing. Just beyond the coral reef, the temperature drops. It's not a terrible difference, but just enough to be noticeably cooler."

I pause, giving Merrick his moment. Truthfully, I can sense the difference as the water drifts around me.

"I still don't see anything different," I finally announce.

"I don't either." He frowns. "We should go. We'll come up with another idea."

Instead of turning around with him, I flip my tail, propelling myself toward the surface. A moment later, Merrick is by my side, grumbling.

Careful not to touch the coral to avoid damaging it, I peer over the top of it, looking out into the blue ocean. Seaweed waves against the current while small fish swim in and out of the grass.

A shadow passes over the sea floor, stealthily gliding over rocks, sand, and seahorses. I gasp.

"Get down," Merrick commands, pulling me down below the top of the coral. I struggled to get away.

"No," I protest, prying his fingers off my waist. "We need to see the ship."

Reluctantly, he swims us both back up to the edge.

The ship drops a net that silently slices through the water. Fish dart out of the way as the fishermen search for dinner—or a mer trophy to string up on their mast before taking them back to land to show their people.

We watch as the net drags through the ocean, something shiny sparkling from the ropes. Suddenly, a figure darts out from behind the coral on the ground. She races toward the net, swimming as quickly as she can.

"What is she doing?" Merrick whispers as the mermaid catches up to the net.

The mermaid suddenly changes course, propelling herself straight up to the middle of the net. She tries untangling the shiny object from the rope. When she can't free it, she struggles against it, pulling as hard as she can to rip the object free.

It's hard to see her from so far away as she thrusts her hands deeper into the net, frantically trying to retrieve the object. After a moment, her movements change as anger and frustration shift to panic.

"She's stuck," I murmur.

"Celena," Merrick quickly warns, looking at me. "We can't."

"We can't let them take her," I plead with him.

"She's a siren. King Gaspar made it very clear we aren't allowed to help them."

"King Gaspar has been dead for nearly a century," I protest. "Even so, he did everything in his power to try to keep us all together."

"You realize that only one of us gets forgiveness if we decide to become a rebel, right?" Merrick remarks, giving me a look before glancing at the mermaid. The net lifts toward the surface and his face falls.

"Merrick," I shout. My worry was in vain—Merrick was already swimming over the reef.

I flick my tail, racing forward to follow him as we rush toward the siren. No matter how hard we try, we'll never reach her in time.

The last thing I see is her red tail lifting out of the water, her wrist still tangled in the net as she screams. Merrick never slows, pushing to reach her.

"Merrick!" My shouts don't deter him. He doesn't stop until she's gone. My friend pauses in the water, floating in the bubbles that trailed off of the mermaid's thrashing tail.

"We have to go." His voice is dark when he turns back to me. I stare at the bottom of the boat, far closer than it should be. "Len, *we have to go.*"

As quickly as a dolphin, Merrick dives at me, knocking me out of my trance. He pushes me back, tail beating against the water to move us away from the boat and out of siren territory.

"Merrick, we can't leave her."

"Oh, yes, we can," he says as if it's not an option. "I wasn't joking about this grace thing—we crossed a line just now. As a royal, you might be given leniency, but I certainly will not."

"Our mothers worked together, Merrick—you'll be fine."

Something sparkles above us, reflecting off the water. Red trickles down, slowly fading to where the sky meets the sea.

A firework—a celebration of a mermaid catch.

"Right now, they're tying that mermaid to the beams on their ship, Celena. I won't have them do that to you—we're leaving."

"Merrick, she's a mermaid. She's about to suffer the unthinkable. Maybe we can rescue her."

"You know that's been attempted before and hasn't worked," he argues. He's terrified for my safety and while I understand that, I can't just swim away.

"None of those mer know as much about humans as you and I do —we've studied them," I reply.

"From books. We've studied them *from books.*" He looks desperate, pleading with me to turn back.

"We have to," I whisper.

"Len," he whispers back. His fingers grip the shell necklace that rests on his chest. When he sighs, I know I've won.

He grabs my hand as we race after the boat. The water rushes against my ears, flooding my senses. We push harder, forcing ourselves beyond what any mer is normally capable of doing.

My hand slips to the knife on my hip. I fumble for it, unable to detach it as I swim toward the human boat—I doubt it would do any good, even if we *could* reach them.

"Stay below the surface," Merrick warns, grasping my hand tighter.

Bits of my pink hair float around me as we come to a sudden halt. We're far enough away from the boat that the men likely won't take notice of us, but close enough that I can see them trying to tie the thrashing mermaid to the mast of their ship. She struggles against them, trying to siren them into submission.

Her singing appears to be working as most of the men back away. Several untie her as she frantically sings. I'm mesmerized by her ability to control them.

"I didn't think that was possible," I murmur.

I know that we once all had the ability to control humans with our voices, but over the last century, that skill was taken away from us, trained out of our people until it no longer existed. To see sireny so strong was an incredible experience—I almost wish I could surface and listen to her song.

They pass her along the deck of the ship near the edge, close enough that we can see her moving. Not everyone is under her spell though—several men race toward her in anger.

The edge of the ship covers our view. Merrick holds me back. In my distraction, I had nearly surfaced to see the scene unfold.

"We can help her if she makes it into the water, but Len, we have to be careful. Your mother will kill me if you get hurt."

"You're more scared of my mother than you are of the queen," I snap back.

When the mermaid crashes into the ocean, red plumes around her, mimicking the color of her tail.

CHAPTER 2

Her blood fills the water, dancing beautifully around her. One of the men that was unaffected by her song must have cut her.

Her hair quietly floats around her as her body sinks toward the ocean floor, leaving the blood trailing in her wake—it's a horrific and beautiful sight.

Merrick is halfway to the mermaid before my senses kick back in and I move to follow him. He tries to scoop her into his arms, racing to the sea floor where the humans can't see.

I follow, trying to assess her injuries from afar—I don't think we can save her.

She lies lifelessly in his arms as he sinks onto the sand. I dart around, ripping seaweed from the sea floor to bandage her wounds, though it won't help the mermaid.

I reach her just as she opens her eyes. The mermaid's hand lashes out, clawing at Merrick. He jerks back, trying to avoid her talon-like nails as she hisses her strangled battle cry.

"Let her go!" a voice surprises us.

I turn to find three other mer facing us down. They hold knives toward us, sneering. The girl in the back looks terrified, but she keeps her trembling in check as she peers around us toward the nearly-lifeless girl.

"Give her back," the merman demands. He looks to be about our age.

"We saw them try to take her," I attempt to engage them, showing that we're not a threat.

"Give her back," the mermaid who isn't nervous says. She looks ready to slice me open like the humans cut her friend up.

Merrick releases the mer with the red tail and swims back. He makes a sound deep in his throat, indicating that I should join him. I appreciate his wisdom in leaving my name out of the conversation.

"What are you doing here?" the merman demands while the two mermaids rush to their friend, pulling her arms around their shoulders.

"We were near the coral and saw them take her," I explain. "We were just trying to help."

"We couldn't reach her in time," Merrick adds as I take my place by his side.

"Go back home, *mer*," the merman siren demands. "We don't need your kind here."

Out of the corner of my eye, I see the red-tailed siren's head tip back as her friends carry her away—she's dead.

Her body is covered in puncture wounds. The knives of the humans sliced through her tail and abdomen. There's a vicious gash along one arm as they tried to pin her down and prevent their trophy from leaving their ship—it looks like the knife went right through her. It must have been an incredibly painful way to die.

"What was she doing?" I suddenly question. "And if you were here, why didn't you help her?"

"*Don't*," Merrick hisses under his breath.

The merman siren advances on us. Merrick puffs himself up, ready for battle. Thankfully, the two mermaids keep their distance, holding the body of their friend as they try not to mourn her loss publicly.

"That's none of your concern," the merman sneers at us, twitching his tail in anger.

"We risked our lives for your friend, which is more than *you* can say," I snap back. Holding my tongue has always been a bit of an issue for me.

"They took her sister. She's been searching for her for days," the nervous one chokes.

"Shut up," the stronger girl glares at her.

"It must have been part of her *iluse* or belt that we saw," Merrick whispers.

"Swim home, little merfolk, before we send the sharks after you," the merman sneers. He holds his knife out menacingly. "This is your only chance to make it back over that barrier—I'm not feeling forgiving today after all this."

Merrick doesn't hesitate. He pulls me away.

I twist my body to face the sirens as my friend pulls me toward the reef. Merrick guides us while I protect us—this is the way we always operate in situations like this. He gets us to safety, and I swim backward, allowing him to drag me along, as I watch for attack.

The moment we're over the reef, I yell that we're clear. The sirens didn't follow us. As soon as we were far enough away, the merman swam over to the others and scooped up the red-tailed mermaid's lifeless body. The three turned, swimming toward the reef.

"Merrick, they're swimming toward the reef. Why would they do that?" I ask as he wraps his arms around me, hugging me.

"Are you okay?" he asks, still holding me. He pulls back just enough to brush my hair out of the water between us.

"Yes, you?" I struggle to see where the three are going over the edge of the reef.

"Are you all right?" Llyr asks, rushing to swim to us.

"We're fine," Merrick turns to our friend.

We've always had an understanding with certain guards. They know a bit about what we do and allow us a little more leeway than they should when we're running missions—for example, he didn't stop us when we approached the reef wall, nor did he stop us when we went over it.

"You saw something," he prompts. He takes a deep breath before reaching up to brush back his light-colored locks.

"Sirens," Merrick informs him.

"Sirens who are currently swimming toward the reef," I correct.

"No," Merrick quickly jumps in, calming the panic that fills Llyr's eyes. "They aren't following us. The humans caught one of theirs. She made it back into the water but didn't survive. They took her body, and they happen to be swimming along the reef—they aren't coming over it."

Llyr sinks back down in the water. He's familiar with swimming to the top of the reef to scout for us, so being this high doesn't frighten him like it would for most mer, but also like most mer, he doesn't want to spend too much time this close to the surface.

I peer along the edge of the coral, trying to float high enough to see, but not high enough to be noticed by the sirens below should they turn back. After a moment, they disappear from sight as they swim too close to the barrier as it curves around slightly.

"What were they doing?" Llyr asks.

"They said the mermaid's sister was taken. It looked like she had been tangled in the net from the ship, but we couldn't reach her in time. We think she saw part of her sister's *iluse* or something," Merrick answers. My fingers continue to hover near the sharp coral, but I avoid touching it.

Reluctantly, I give up, turning back to the conversation with two of my favorite mermen.

"Llyr, have you seen any sign of the sirens lately?" I redirect the conversation.

"No ma'am," Llyr replies as his hair floats back in front of his eyes. "I hadn't seen anything until today. In fact, I didn't even see them today—one of the other guys swam by and I didn't want to give you away."

If my mother or any of the aunts knew we had crossed the barrier, we'd be shut up like a clamshell for a few months until they had had enough of not being able to use us for missions. Llyr was hyperaware of keeping our bolder moments to himself to avoid getting us in trouble.

"Keep an eye out for them, would you? Something isn't right."

"I heard the rumors about the sirens slipping in somewhere," Llyr says, nodding. "They haven't come through here, but that's why they have extra mer on patrol."

"We just need to be careful," I proclaim, stating the obvious.

"Perhaps you should be getting home," Llyr gives me a look before glancing at Merrick. Llyr knows far more about our work than anyone else does. On occasion, he's helped with a mission for us.

"I think that's probably a wise choice," Merrick smiles. "Thanks for watching out for us, buddy."

The two shake hands, smiling. When in public, the two are a bit more formal, but when Llyr isn't on duty, the mermen are practically brothers.

"Take good care of our girl," Llyr calls as we swim away. "And watch out for Merrick too—you know how easily distracted he is."

Merrick rolls his eyes at the joke, motioning me along.

The swim back to the palace is quiet. A few schools of fish swim by, and a whale glides over our heads at one point, but we encounter less sea life than usual.

We chat on the way, trying to figure out where else the sirens might be getting into Scylla—assuming they're getting in at all. Telling a siren apart from one of us is extremely difficult because we're all mer—some of us just have the ability to control humans while others don't use that ability. You'd have to be able to recognize that they don't belong with us to tell at all.

Our only indicator that they've been here at all is the sireny book we found. It appeared to be older—it could have even come in with the shifting waters—but we'd rather treat it like a threat than write it off and be surprised later.

"See you tomorrow?" Merrick asks as we reach the palace district. I nod, allowing him to swim off.

The palace is grand, covered in jewels and fantastic doors made from the wood collected from shipwrecks of old. I swim inside under the cool glow of a bloom of jellyfish that sits high above near the ceiling, casting light down for us like a grand chandelier in the human books I've read.

I bend around the corners, making my way down the halls of the palace. The guards nod to me as I swim through.

"Celena, you're back," my grown cousin greets me as I swim into the parlor. She darts across the room, taking a seat on the lounging couch.

I settle onto the other half of the lounging couch, allowing the bump to sit between us. The couch itself is designed for mer to lounge on, propping their tails up to support their backs, but it also acts as a nice table between two mer, should we choose to use it that way.

"What did you find?" Marilla asks.

"We saw sirens over the reef barrier, but we didn't see how they would get in. I think we need to explore more," I inform my queen. Even though she is my mother's cousin, I try to keep a few lines drawn when handling kingdom business.

Dylana floats into the room, surprised to see me.

"Cousin!" she smiles, swimming over. "Have you brought us news?"

She takes a seat at my tail, resting her hand on my scales. I absent-mindedly stroke her hair. She closes her eyes at my touch, listening for me to explain what I saw.

"Not much, I'm afraid. We cut up the nets that the sailors left. After I sent Casp and Coralie home, Merrick and I went to the west reef barrier," I inform my cousins. "We saw sirens—one of them got caught in a net and taken to the surface."

Dylana's face pales as her eyes pop open. She's a year older than me, but when she looks up at me like this, she appears much younger —though it could be her fiercely pink locks. Hers is a much deeper hue than mine are.

"What happened?" She demands.

"I assume she sirened her way back into the sea, but I don't think she commanded *everyone* because she didn't return whole." I look away sadly. "She didn't survive. Three other sirens—a merman and two mermaids— took her body and swam along the reef until I couldn't see them any longer. We came straight home after that."

"Did you inform your people along the west barrier?" Marilla asks, hand lifting to her crown to adjust it.

"We did," I confirm. "They'll be watching."

"You'll be attending the meeting tomorrow?" Marilla changes the conversation. I nod. "Good, we need to discuss our next moves. I wouldn't put it past Persephone's sirens to find a way into Scylla— they've been trying for a century to get back inside."

Our eyes all narrow at Persephone's name—if only my great-great-grandmother Alia had let the fishermen take her back to the human queen to face punishment, we wouldn't be in this mess.

"Should I bring my collection?" I ask, inquiring as to whether Merrick and my other contacts should join us.

"No, family only tomorrow," Marilla answers. "We'll bring the others in on the next meeting. I think we need to keep the discussion small this time—just the cousins. Bring your mother."

While we're all decedents of King Gaspar, our families are removed enough that the current generations are no longer close. Marilla and my mother are only as connected as they are because I descend from Aila's line. The other princesses that grew up with Queen Kailania, Aila, and the others went on to have their own families and *those* lines have stayed close to one another. While we see the other family groups and refer to each other as cousins, the rest aren't as close—with the exceptions of the mermaids like me who work for the Queen.

"Go home and get some rest, cousin," Dylana adds. "I think tomorrow is going to be a long day."

I nod, smiling as she retracts her hand from where it rests on my tail. She floats up, hovering in the same level as me.

"Actually, let me swim you out. I have something I want to show you before you go."

Dylana guides me to her room—the same one my great-great-grandma Aila occupied when she first moved into the palace. Shell crowns cover her dresser in hues of coral, pink, and purple. Gold accents sparkle on some of them. An *iluse* lies on her bed, a mixture of netting, seaweed, and shells.

"Come sit," Dylana motions to her bed. She waves her hand toward a pesky crab and it scurries out of the way.

Next to the head of her bed, several seahorses use their tails to grasp onto strands of seaweed. They watch her move around the room like little pets.

"I was in the vault yesterday and I found this." She unwraps the seaweed from around something in her hand. "I think it belonged to Persephone."

A drawing of a human stares back at me from inside a necklace.

"Is that the prince?"

"Jarek, yes, I believe so." Dylana nods. It looks similar to some of the other drawings we've seen of the human prince who helped destroy the human-mer agreement. "Though, it could also have been Aila's."

Both Aila and Persephone were good friends with the human prince and helped keep the alliance between our kinds before Persephone fell in love. When she tried to siren him to her—fully believing that her love could give him the ability to breathe underwater—she nearly drowned him. My great-great-grandmother saved him several times before Persephone's mother, Chantay, got involved. Together, they sought revenge on the human queen and prince, murdering hundreds of their men and causing a division so great that not even Aila and Persephone's grandfather—the king—could fix the damage they had done.

"It's possible King Gaspar brought some of Persephone's things with him when the mer moved to Scylla, though I doubt he ever let her have this again after she was captured and sentenced."

Referring to our relatives by their titles and names was easier than figuring out how many times we needed to add the word *great* in front of grandparent.

"Which is why I was wondering if perhaps it was Aila's," Dylana hands me the necklace.

"Mother never said anything about it," I frown, turning it over. "Neither did grandmother."

"I suppose it isn't anything too terribly important," Dylana answers. "I thought you might like to see it though."

"I appreciate it," I reply, taking another moment to study it. "He *is* fairly handsome. I suppose I see why Persephone was interested—the whole leg thing just doesn't make sense to me though."

"No," Dylana turns, running her fingers through my hair. "I suppose it doesn't."

She works her hands around my hair, braiding tiny strands back for me while I examine the drawing. Untangling a hair comb from my mane, she works it back in to hold the locks she braided out of my face.

"You should let me do your hair more often," she teases. "Maybe we could find you a merman that way."

I pause, willing myself not to roll my eyes.

"Yes, because I see *you* so happily partnered," I joke.

"I'm the princess, dear," she reminds me. "Every eligible merman in this kingdom wants me, and likely every eligible merman in the surrounding kingdoms too."

"Are you saying," I grin, "that you have to swim all the way to the Arctic to find a merman? Or perhaps to the warm waters?"

"Why," she says innocently, "that would require me leaving the barriers. Celena, I would never do that!"

With each passing generation, the royal mermaids became bolder. After Aila and her cousins moved to Scylla, they lived in enough fear that they kept their children very protected. The next generation was filled with nervous mer. After that, though, our people wanted the chance to live again.

Our grandmothers organized a secret group of mermaids to scout and run missions for the Queen and King of Scylla. It was a slow process, taking one forbidden mission at a time, but by the time our mothers were old enough to partake in the missions, they had worked out a system.

Duties are passed from mother to daughter, keeping all other family members out of the collection of spies. Like my mother, I am trained to do things no ordinary mer can do.

On occasion, we bring in other members—like Merrick—to assist us, but even they must have the proper connections. My father, brother, and sister know nothing of what my mother and I do for the queen—though I suspect my father knows more than he lets on.

Typically, the reigning royals are not involved in anything but overseeing the missions, but Dylana isn't like her mother. She's taken on plenty of missions. Her mother found out, but Dylana talked her into allowing her to continue working with us, though she's not supposed to venture as far out as I do.

"No, never." I place my hand over my heart and nod with wide eyes. "You always follow the rules, Princess."

"Oh, stop that. You know I don't like when you call me that." She waves her hand playfully at me. "You're just as much a princess as I am."

"Yes, but I'm not a reigning princess. Besides, can you picture *me* as the reigning princess? I don't have the grace and patience for it."

"Grace, yes. Patience, no," she laughs.

"Speaking of patience, I should probably get home."

My cousin sighs floating up from her bed. She swims me to the door.

"Wear your pink *iluse* tomorrow. I love how it sets off your eyes and hair," she mentions. I have a sinking feeling there's a reason she wants me to wear my attention-drawing *iluse* to the meeting, and I have a feeling it has to do with one of the merman scouts she occasionally has floating around the palace when she wants to try her fins at matchmaking.

"Good night, Dylana," I shake my head at her, handing her the necklace.

"Good night, Celena," she calls after me, giggling.

The swim through the palace is quiet. I wave hello to a few of my other cousins as they float through the halls but don't stop to talk. A midwater squid swims alongside of me for several minutes but branches off when I reach the exit.

Outside, the world dips down, expanding into a courtyard that extends out into the palace district. Life slows as people close up shop for the day. Mermen and mermaids swim back to their dwellings. Small children play with schools of fish. A few collect shells. One mother pulls her mer baby away from a starfish on the ocean floor.

I make my way through the town toward my own home. I may not live in the palace, but the granddaughters of Aila and Troy still live in an extravagant setting not too far from the palace, just far enough outside that we aren't watched too closely.

We're isolated just enough that people don't take notice—which is why when a merman's voice echoes in my ear, I nearly ink like an octopus.

CHAPTER 3

"I'm sorry," Llyr gasps.

My heartbeat falls heavy under my hand as I clutch my chest.

"For *coral's sake*, Llyr, *don't do that!*" I shout.

"Sorry," he smirks with a shrug.

"What do you want?" My hand knocks into the pouch at my side when I put my hands on my hips.

"Can't a guy just miss his friend?" Llyr quips.

"Do I *look* like Merrick?"

"A guy can have more than one friend, you know," he laughs. "And...*definitely* not."

He tips his head, examining me from head to fin before grinning at me.

"Why are you here, Llyr?" I chuckle at his banter.

"I did a little extra exploring after you left today. I might have found something helpful."

He twists around, reaching into the pouch strapped to his belt.

"The current brought it over," Llyr says as he hands me a shiny trinket. "I believe this is what you were looking for?"

The object the siren was trying to retrieve.

The silver starfish glints in the light. Bits of netting stick out from behind it on one side where it was woven into the design of an *iluse*. A single pearl is attached to the remainder of the netting.

"I would say so." The starfish is cold under my touch. "You reached through the coral for this?"

"It's possible I trained one of the dolphins to fetch things for me," Llyr grins.

"Which explains all of your other finds as well," I smile appreciatively. "Nice work."

"Just make sure the queen knows how helpful I've been. She's been good about giving extra rewards out, and *coral knows*, my dad and I sure can use it."

"You're a good merman, Llyr," I reach forward, placing a kiss on his cheek. I pat his shoulder as I pull back. "Thank you for getting this for me."

"Anytime, princess."

"I—" I begin to protest before he cuts me off.

"I know, I know, you're not a princess—*Dylana* is the princess. We *all* know, Celena." He rolls his eyes looking eerily similar to Merrick and Caspian. He swims backward, darting away. "Tell your brother I said hello."

"Can't, then he'll know I did something fun without him," I shout as he swims off.

"Maybe he'd think we were off kissing in a grotto somewhere." He wiggles his eyebrows at me flirtatiously.

"If he thought *that*, he'd kill you, Llyr. You'd be thrown to the sharks."

"Eh, I'll risk it," he blows a kiss to me before turning to swim away at full speed, playfully waving over his shoulder as he goes. Between Llyr and Merrick, my friends might be the death of me—especially since we're *all* keeping secrets from my twin.

I tuck the starfish away in my pouch and swim home.

"Where have you been all day?" Caspian asks the moment I swim in the door.

"Celena?" My mother's call rescues me from an interrogation.

I swim through the halls until I reach her in the parlor.

"I thought I heard you come in," she says without looking up.

I flip the door shut with my tail before swimming over to her to give a report.

"Marilla wants us all for a meeting tomorrow," I inform her.

"I know, she sent word earlier. Did you find anything?"

"Merrick tagged along. We went to the west reef barrier," I pause, unsure of how she will react. "We saw a siren get caught in a net."

"What happened?" she sets down her shell work on the *iluse* she's hand creating for the Pearl Festival.

"We…" I draw my words out, trying to decide if I should plunge in and tell her or beat around the kelp bed.

"You went over the barrier, didn't you?" she asks calmly.

"We did," I reply solemnly. "We had to try to help her."

"You know that's against King Gaspar's laws, don't you?"

"I do, but I couldn't leave her. Merrick just followed to protect me," I add quickly, trying to keep any of this from falling on him.

"I won't tell Marilla if that's what you're thinking, nor will I ban you from scouting. I don't like that you disobeyed a direct mandate to stay within the kingdom confines, but I've had moments where I've broken the rules too for good reasons." She picks up her shell work again. "Will Merrick be there tomorrow? I'd like to have a word with him."

I swallow.

Thank goodness Marilla called for family only.

"No, just the cousins," I inform her.

"Very well. Go get your sister ready for dinner. Tell Caspian to fetch your father—he seems to have become lost on his way home this evening." She waves me off.

I duck under an octopus that has taken up residence in the corner of the hallway entrance, tentacle stretching from one side of the doorway to the opposite corner. I consider tickling the orange thing, but I know he wouldn't like that.

"Coralie," I call. "Time to get ready to eat."

My twin swims up to me, putting his face near my ear. I push back, creating some distance between us.

"Go find father," I instruct him before he can speak.

Caspian has always asked too many questions so I relish the moments I can avoid them.

"What are your plans for today?" Casp asks the next morning.

"I'm going to see Dylana," I reply, placing the clamshells back in the cupboard.

"Will you and mother be wearing your crowns?" he teases. "I hear she's going to see Marilla today."

"We are, and no, we have no need for crowns today. It's not like it's a ceremony or festival. We're just going to visit."

"For as frilly as you are, I'd think you'd be one of those mermaids who wears seashell crowns *all* of the time," he remarks.

In truth, I would if I could—those crowns are gorgeous—but unless you're full-time-royalty, you make do with hair combs, wreaths, and other accessories, leaving the fancier headwear to the queens and princesses for everyday looks. I have a trunk full of crowns though that have been passed down over the years. I also have a number made just for me—though those are not as ornate as great-great-grandma Aila's crowns.

"You don't wear your shoulder armor all the time, do you?" I question. "You're supposedly a dashing young merman—shouldn't you wear that fancy stuff all the time?"

"You've got me there, sis. Then again, *I* have no one to impress."

"Neither to do," I counter.

"Not even Merrick?" My twin grins at me, leaning back onto the lounging couch.

"I've never tried to impress Merrick…" *with the way I look.*

"*Sure,*" he drawls.

"Did you want to come with us today?" I try to change the subject, exasperated—I gave him exactly what he wanted.

"Maybe I will, I haven't seen Dylana in ages."

Panic sets in.

"I'm sure she'd love to see you. You don't have anything else to do today?"

"Nope," he replies.

"He's watching Coralie," mother swims into the room.

"I don't need a mer sitter, mother," Corlie complains, swimming behind her.

"I'm sure you don't, dear," mother pacifies her. "You know he's not the one actually doing the mer sitting, don't you?"

She winks, making our little sister giggle.

Coralie settles on the lounging couch near Caspian and I swim up behind her to do her hair. A box of pearls sits on the table next to the couch within reach, waiting for such an occasion. I work my fingers through her hair, taming the knots. Picking up a shell comb, I untangle the snarls.

Caspian reaches over, assisting. When we're done combing her locks, Casp braids back two long strands and clips them with one of the jeweled combs from the box while I decorate the front with pearls.

He whips his hand in the water, creating a large bubble for Coralie to examine herself in.

"I love it, thank you," she chirps. Darting up so quickly, she nearly knocks the box of hair accessories off the table, she rushes off to show our mother her hair for the day.

Caspian smiles at me, gently pushing me down onto the couch. Floating behind me, his hands work their way through my hair, delicately braiding back pieces into an intricate design.

"If you're going to the palace, you should at least pretend to look like we belong to Gaspar's children."

I close my eyes as he works, adding pearls to my braids and twists. He pushes my head forward slightly so he can manipulate my long strands of light pink hair. My twin carefully creates a masterpiece out of my hair, leaving the majority of it to float behind me, while the top portion swirls around in a crown of greatness.

"Bound and determined to get me to wear a crown today, weren't you, brother?" I tease before wrapping an arm around his shoulder and kissing his cheek. "Thanks."

He winks.

"What are brothers for?" He quickly does a backflip, pulling away from me. "Have fun at the palace today. Tell Dylana I'll come visit soon."

"I'm sure she'll believe that, since you haven't been there in months," I call after him.

"What can I say? I'm a busy merman!" He darts out the door.

Caspian likes to play tough, but he's as soft as a hermit crab's torso when it comes to his sisters.

"Ready?"

My mother swims into the room—Caspian must have seen her from the hallway and been given the release to leave before I could see them. Coralie follows behind mother, I assume to come to the palace with us—she must have talked mother into letting her show off her hair and Casp won't mind not having to watch her. Several of the younger girls will be there as well and I'm sure someone will entertain them during our meeting.

Coralie swims up next to me, tucking herself along my side as we leave the house. Merrick catches my eye as I swim toward the palace but neither of us acknowledges the other, going about our tasks.

I turn to look back at Coralie in order to catch another glimpse of Merrick in the distance, just in case he needs to communicate with me. He doesn't, but it gives me an excellent opportunity to stare at his muscles as he lifts a heavy anchor for his father.

Not that I meant to stare.

"There it is!" Coralie says, breaking my attention on Merrick's back and shoulders. I pull her a little faster toward the palace, hoping no one caught me.

The meeting takes longer than I assumed it would. I sit on the palace floor, listening intently to every word, hoping to find some direction for my search.

A roascea colony floats overhead, casting a blue glow over the grotto. Their tentacles delicately float in the water, moving just slightly every time one of us moves and makes a wave.

Eventually, Marilla dismisses the cousins, sending them off with new missions. She holds us back.

"Almeta, stay." She nods to me as well. Dylana swims across the room to join us.

"Tomorrow, we have the Anchor Marketplace. I want you two to monitor it carefully. You can bring in a few of your people, but I want to make sure everything is crystal-clear—nothing fishy is going on."

"You're worried about these siren rumors, aren't you?" my mother asks, putting her hand on the queen's elbow.

"I'm not sure if I should be," Marilla admits. "I'd rather be cautious though."

"As you should be," my mother assures our cousin.

"I'll be there, of course," Marilla continues. "I just want all of you paying attention too. Spread out and see what you can find. Hunt down any rumors you hear."

"We will," I promise. My tail twitches, anxious to go find Merrick and see if Llyr is available to help tomorrow.

"You'll stay with me tomorrow," Dylana whispers, floating up next to me. "Bring the boys, of course, but I want to stay close to each other."

I nod, reaching up to brush back a piece of my hair as it floats in front of me. She smiles—she always did like pairing up together. I can't say that I mind it either.

"Are you ready to go, dear?" my mother asks, breaking away from the queen.

"Yes, Mama."

I say goodbye to my cousins and swim to find my little sister. She's in another grotto, talking about the mermen with the younger cousins. Coralie blushes when she realizes I heard her talking about a certain mer boy in her class.

The collection breaks apart, all swimming to find their families now that one of us has intruded on the conversation—it wasn't long ago that I was one of them.

"What do you and mother talk about every time you're here?" she questions. "You're gone for hours and then you never talk about it."

"Grown up stuff," I reply. "It's pretty boring."

"Why doesn't Natale have to go?"

Because Natale's mother didn't train her to be a spy and she's not invited to the meetings.

"She was lucky enough to not get netted into it," I say instead. "She must have wished on the right starfish."

I bump against her, making her giggle. I might not be as cool as Caspian in her eyes, but I could always make her chuckle.

"Let's go home and get Caspian," I announce. "I think we need a bit of an adventure."

"Ugh, we're going to play bull shark again?"

I gasp.

"You love that shell game."

"Not when we play it once a week," she rolls her thirteen-year-old eyes again.

"What else do you expect the three of us to do?" I say in a haughty voice. "It's the only thing Casp can trounce us at."

"Ha, because he flounders at everything else," Coralie says sarcastically.

Our brother is basically perfect at *everything* but we like to *pretend* we have a fin up at some things.

"Do you want to play or not?" I demand.

"Fine," she says, clamming up when we round the corner and see our mother.

She smiles at us, waiting for us to catch up. Together, we swim home.

The sensation of scales against scales is a frightening one when it is not expected. Every time a merman or mermaid brushes against me, I worry about losing scales.

Of course, it's not detrimental—I won't die if I lose scales, but I certainly don't like the sensation of it. Occasionally they grow back with a different color—sometimes even a different shape—and it changes the pattern on my tail.

I prefer keeping my scales in place.

"Careful," Dylana warns as a younger mermaid nearly crashes into me clutching a silver trinket someone must have found in a shipwreck.

Some of my favorite vendors are the ones who explore the shipwrecks and gather human items to sell at the market. Half my *iluses* are decorated with shiny human items.

The young mermaid turns around, eyes growing wide when she realizes who Dylana is. She nods sharply—a sign of respect—before rushing off to her mother's side a few tables down.

"I kind of wish we could shop," my cousin says wistfully.

"Me too," I reply, eyeing netting that I'd *flip* to add to one of my festival outfits.

"Have you seen anything out of the ordinary?" Dylana asks, swimming through the crowd to a less densely packed area.

"Not yet," I remark. "Unless you count Llyr over there."

Llyr flirts with a mermaid at one of the tables where she's trying unsuccessfully to sell pearls. It's not easy talking to other mer while Llyr is flashing his electric eel smile.

Dylana rolls her eyes, smirking at his antics. Llyr was always good at talking information out of unsuspecting targets.

"Where is Merrick?" she asks before gasping. "Caspian! Where did you come from?"

"Why is everyone so set on asking about Merrick all the time? I'm clearly the more interesting one of the two of us?" Caspian rolls a gold coin over the back of his knuckles, catching it between his fingers as it rolls off the tips.

"He's a little less of a puffer fish," Dylana snaps playfully, swimming back out of range.

"I am *not* a puffer fish," Caspian shouts, offended at the accusation. In response, he inadvertently puffs out his chest. I bite my lip as hard as I can without drawing blood.

"No?" Dylana teases, swimming even farther away.

"Should I ask?" Merrick sneaks up behind me, whispering in my ear.

I shudder in shock, accidentally slamming my shoulder into his chin.

"Ow, watch it, Len," he chides.

"Don't sneak up on me, for coral's sake," I retort.

When I turn, he's rubbing his chin. I momentarily feel bad for injuring him, but then I see it behind him—the sirens from beyond the barrier.

"Merrick," I whisper, never taking my eyes off the merman in the crowd.

My friend stills, dropping his hand. He eyes me warily, trying to decide if he should turn to look or wait for me to give him some kind of signal.

"They're here," I murmur.

He swallows, turning slowly to take in the sights of the marketplace.

People continue to call out to one another, going about their business, making sales and trades. The sirens never notice us as we blend in with the crowds.

"I'd say we officially have confirmation," Merrick mutters. "Go find Marilla."

"*You* go find her," I grumble back. I have no intention of leaving my mark.

"You're more recognizable than me," he protests.

"*You* have blue hair," I challenge his assessment.

"And you have pink hair, now move," he commands. "*You're* the one that got in that guy's face yesterday. They'll remember you."

"What are you two doing?" Caspian swims up behind us.

Merrick turns on him.

"Go find Marilla," he instructs.

"Why?" Casp snaps, eyes narrowed.

"Just do it, Casp," Merrick's voice is angry, snapping my twin to attention. He hovers in the water for just a moment before taking off to find the queen.

"What just happened?" Dylana demands, swimming over to us quickly. I nod toward the crowd.

"Sirens."

From the corner of my eye, I see her inhale sharply, eyes growing wide.

"You're certain?"

I nod again, trying to remind myself to keep a pleasant look on my face instead of the scowl I usually wear when I'm concentrating.

"Which ones?"

I point them out to her.

"I'm going to get a little closer. You two keep an eye on them, I'll see if I can listen in."

She moves into the crowd, pretending to look through tables of goods until she reaches the sirens. Brilliantly, she keeps her back toward them, listening in without engaging with them.

When the angry mermaid siren splits off from the other two, I inform Merrick that I'll follow her while he watches the others. She slips away, a few tables down and buys something at the booth —a knife.

"Great, now she's armed…if she wasn't before," I mutter.

I float a few feet away from Merrick, watching the siren girl, trying to figure out how she got into Scylla in the first place.

"What happened?" The queen's voice is low and dangerously close to my ear, but I felt her presence before she reached me and didn't fright.

"Sirens," I answer quietly.

"What?" Caspian shouts. I hadn't realized he was here.

"Quiet, child," the queen scolds.

I risk a glance at Caspian. His face is a cross between shocked and infuriated. His eyes dart around looking for the subject of our conversation.

"Caspian," I hiss at him, drawing his attention so he doesn't give us away. I quickly find my mark again in the crowd—she hadn't moved far.

"What is going on?" Caspian demands.

"Caspian, go get your mother. Now," Marilla instructs. She pauses, muttering, "What is Dylana doing?"

Horror mixed with admiration fills her voice. Her daughter floats in and out of booths, pretending to take notice of the wares.

"Which ones?" she asks. I point them out to her discretely.

When my mother arrives, we fill her in quickly.

"We now have our proof," Marilla says when Dylana swims back to us. "Did you learn anything?"

"Not a thing." Dylana shakes her head. "They were smart and kept quiet—they blended in perfectly."

"They're moving!" I interject. Everyone spins to look at them.

"Follow them," Marilla commands. "See where they go, but don't cross the barriers and don't engage with those barracudas."

Dylana and I are the first to dart forward, Merrick quickly taking off after us. Llyr notices our rapid movements and descends on us as well.

"You can't come," Merrick hisses behind us. I turn to find Caspian flicking his tail, trying to catch up.

"I don't know what's going on here, but you are not going without me."

"We have orders," Merrick protests.

Caspian looks hurt that we're all in on something he clearly wasn't meant to be a part of—I guess there's no avoiding telling him about my spy work now—so much for mother's decision to keep him safe from all of this.

"Caspian, go back—mother will explain everything," I plead with him, earning the most pitiful look I've ever seen from my brother.

"If you're going, I'm going," he states, fully prepared to protect me in any way that he can.

I hold my hand out beside me, waiting for him to catch up like when we were little. He darts ahead, scooping my hand in his. I squeeze it, communicating silently that I'm sorry for keeping secrets. When he doesn't squeeze it back, I know he's upset.

We quickly swim around the large anchor resting in the middle of the marketplace—it was too heavy to move when our grandparents originally found it, so now we use it as a marker for the market. It rests heavily in the sand as we swim around it, making our way toward the perimeter of the marketplace.

When we're close enough to the sirens, we slow, hiding behind rocks and seaweed, staying far enough back that they aren't likely to notice us. Eventually, the three swim away from the collection of mermaids and mermen, acting like they're taking their purchases home.

Instead, they branch off, making their way to one of the kelp forests.

CHAPTER 4

They blend in with the plants swaying in the water.

The light floats in through the murky water, giving a yellow haze to everything as particles from the kelp float in the water. I use my hands to move the water in front of me, brushing the bits of decaying plant away.

The kelp forest is quieter than the marketplace, cutting off the sounds of the chaos that mer create when being social. Caspian stays attached to my side, though he relinquishes my hand.

Merrick trades a glance with me—we both know we're in trouble now that Caspian has found out. Llyr might be let off the hook for keeping his involvement from my brother since they aren't as close, but Merrick and I are in for a lecture.

Dylana slows, holding us back.

Deep in the kelp forest, the sirens change direction. We follow them at an angle, trying to stay hidden without losing them.

"Where are they going?" Caspian asks to no one in particular.

"Isn't this the way toward Metten?" Merrick remarks.

"You don't think..." I trail off.

"They can't be," Dylana objects, her opal tail paling in the murky light.

"I think that's exactly what they're doing," Llyr replies, glancing at the princess.

"What would they want from the old kingdom?" I interject, trying to figure out their plan.

"They could be staying there," Merrick suggests. "If the sirens really *have* breached our barrier somehow, they'd need somewhere to stay.

"It's been a century—I'm sure the humans have felt that Metten was fully explored as an option for locating mer and have moved on from the area. *We* certainly haven't been back in a century for fear that we would be found there. What if the sirens know all this and have moved in?"

"You think they're *all* there?" Dylana gasps. "How did they get in without us knowing?"

"How did *any* of you know about *any* of this?" Caspian finally interjects, exasperated.

"We'll explain later," I tell him, brushing back my hair as it tangles with a piece of kelp.

"I suppose mother knows about this too?" he asks indignantly, huffing at me.

"She does."

"And is Dad in on this too? What about Coralie?"

"No," I snap at him. "Now clam up until we figure out what these sirens are doing."

He looks like he wants to ask how I know the sirens but he doesn't say another word.

After a few minutes, we reach the far side of the kelp forest. It would have been easier to swim around it, but I assume the sirens are trying to conceal their movements and are using precautions such as swimming through the murky waters of the kelp forest. The water clears up, offering us better visibility but also less covering.

We hang back, hiding behind whatever objects we can—rocks, coral, seaweed, giant sea turtles. We have to stay so far behind them that we eventually lose them.

"Now what?" Llyr asks.

"Now we go home," Dylana announces, doing a backflip to correct her direction. "We have a general idea of where they might have gone —we can have a team of scouts investigate for us."

"Or we could do it," I add.

"No, if we go, no one will be available to report back," Dylana protests.

All heads swing toward Caspian.

"No," Dylana proclaims. "He is not going back alone. Turn your tails around and let's go."

She swims away without waiting. I frown but follow her lead. The mermen eventually follow us.

This time, we swim *around* the kelp.

"Metten was our home for a very long time," Marilla explains. "It's likely that the sirens would have knowledge of it, especially under the guidance of Chantay after King Gaspar imprisoned Persephone. It's possible that they are there—I just don't know how they got in."

"It's important to know how they got into the kingdom, but it may be *more* important to know where they are while they're here," my mother suggests.

Caspian broods in the corner, clearly annoyed that he has been left out of this conversation his entire life—I can't say that I blame him.

"I'll go," I volunteer.

The adults all look at me. Merrick stills along side of me, trying not to cringe over the fact that I spoke.

"I'll go too," Dylana offers—she's always wanted to see the old kingdom.

"I volunteer," Llyr interjects, earning himself several glares.

"I'll go," Merrick quickly swims in, redirecting the attention off of Llyr.

"I'm tired of being left out, so I'll go," Caspian announces, floating up from the floor.

Marilla considers our proposal before sighing.

"Take Morgen with you," she gives a pointed look at her eldest daughter. "Don't approach the sirens if you find them. Watch them for a few hours and then report back.

"If we find that Persephone's collection really has inhabited the old kingdom, we will bring our fiercest warriors back to Metten and remove them from our palace."

Someone leaves to find Morgen. He swims in, bejeweled in the shoulder armor he prefers to wear all of the time. Most mermen only use it on special occasions...or when trying to impress someone.

Marilla quickly explains the situation to him—he looks like he's been slapped. While he hasn't been trained like Dylana has, Morgen is still a royal and has been educated to protect himself should the need arise. He fingers the sword on his belt.

"You're not taking that," Marilla instructs.

"But—"

"No." Her words leave her son grumbling. "Go, pack your things. We'll work on a strategy for you and meet you back here in an hour."

The queen waves us off to pack a few supplies in our pouches. I don't like the idea of Caspian and Morgen joining us on the mission—they aren't trained for this and could get hurt—but we don't have a choice.

Dylana lectures her brother on what to bring as they branch off into their wing of the palace, Morgen still arguing the benefits of bringing the human sword that has been passed through the generations.

"*I heard,*" Casp grumbles before I can say anything.

Merrick nods to me before taking off toward his home. A dolphin swims by and Merrick flicks his tail faster to catch the dolphin's dorsal fin, speeding his trip up.

Caspian and I rush to swim through the crowds toward our house. The iridescent glow of the outside of our home greets us.

"What are you doing home so early?" Coralie asks, sitting up on the lounge couch.

"Mother will explain later, we don't have time," I inform her, swimming quickly to my room.

Unlike my brother, I already have a bag ready to go. I add a few extra weapons to it, buried inside the designs of my *iluses.* Thinking it might be wise, I add my own shoulder armor—a more feminine, less intricate version of Morgen's—and a chest plate, should I need it.

I tuck it into my bag and race to the galley to pack some food so that we don't have to stop on the way.

Caspian is already there.

My brow furrows without my permission as he hands me several items from the cupboard. He has a bag in his hand.

I have no idea how he packed so quickly, but perhaps it's a merman thing.

"Parlor hutch. Right drawer, second shelf," he informs me, waving me off with a flick of his tail.

I retreat, not knowing what else to do.

In the parlor, I swim to the hutch, opening the doors that once belonged in a captain's room on a ship from long ago. Glancing over the shelves, I discover my brother has sent me to my grandmother's shelf. On it sits her shiny hair combs and glittering necklaces. There's only one reason I could be here.

I pull out the silvery necklace held together with pieces of tan rope. Metal detailing sits in the front, encrusted in several seafoam green gems. Each piece is different, detailing unique aspects of being a mermaid.

My grandmother used this necklace to defend herself. Its secrets have been long held in my family. We all know what it is and what can be done with it, though only mother has ever worn it in public.

I lace it around my neck, pulling my pink hair up and out of the way. It floats above me as I fasten the necklace around my throat.

"Ready?" Caspian asks, slinging his bag over his shoulder.

"Yes," I nod as he reaches for my bag. I shake my head and he lets me carry it myself. Ordinarily, I'd allow him to take it for me but it's heavy and we have a long way to go.

Coralie tries to get more information from us as we leave but we quickly kiss her on the head and dart out the door.

Merrick is already waiting on the palace steps when we arrive. Caspian glares at him, betrayal lingering between the mermen.

"Are we waiting for Llyr?" I ask, hoping to distract the boys from their feud.

"Yes," they both answer at once.

I sigh, setting my bag next to Merrick and take a seat on the steps. Why a mer palace has steps is beyond me, but I assume we originally fashioned them after the human castles above the surface…perhaps they actually *are* from human castles that had fallen into the sea.

The mermen say nothing as Caspian floats in front of the palace steps and Merrick sits next to me. We wait for Llyr in silence until my mother bustles out the door.

"Oh good, you're here." She reaches out, snatching Casp's arm in her hand as she drags him away for a conversation. My eyes are as wide as his are.

"How bad do you think this is going to be?" Merrick murmurs once my mother has pulled Caspian far enough away.

"I think he's going to hold this against us for a long time, Merrick," I mutter. "I'm pretty sure a blue whale has a shorter life expectancy than this grudge will."

"That's what I was worried about," he says, clamming up as my family approaches.

Llyr swims up just as my mother pulls me away.

"You protect him," she hisses, getting in my face. "He is not trained for this. You watch out for him and don't let him get hurt."

"I would never let anything happen to Caspian, Mama," I reply, pulling my wrist back.

She eyes Grandmother Tama's necklace around my neck. She

nods sharply, approving of my choice. Mother leaves me with final instructions before kissing my cheek and returning home.

Dylana and Morgen greet us at the door and we swim toward the northwestern side of the kingdom.

Caspian and Morgen bond over both being left out of the loop. The two swim behind us, pointing out every instance we must have mishandled the truth when we swam off on missions.

Llyr swims to a halt, turning back on them.

"We might as well get it out of the way," he announces with wild hand gestures. "I am not listening to the two of you try to bicker with your siblings the entire way to Metten. Whatever this is, handle it."

I've never seen Llyr so frustrated and outspoken in his entire life. He swims ahead, trying to stay out of hearing range. Merrick flicks his tail, choosing to abandon me to my brother's anger.

"You lied to me," Caspian growls, putting enough distance between the royal siblings and us that we can't hear each other. Morgen looks furious.

"I didn't," I correct him. "I just didn't mention certain things."

"So that's why you and Merrick spent so much time together. Here I thought he liked you or something ridiculous like that. Instead, the two of you were just working behind my back."

"Casp, be reasonable. I didn't have any say in this—"

"Didn't have any say?" he roars, baring his teeth like a shark. "You had *every* say, Celena. I'm your twin—you couldn't trust me with this?"

"It wasn't an option, Casp. Grandmother Tama started this and passed it down from eldest daughter to eldest daughter. That's why Dylana and I were both involved. Mother warned me not to tell you —she was protecting you."

"But she could sacrifice *you*?" He glares at me, brushing his hair back angrily. "I'm the oldest—why wasn't it me?"

I don't say anything—I don't have answers for him. All I know is that I was chosen to live this life and take up this mantle and he wasn't.

"I'm sorry," I finally say.

"Why didn't you ever tell me?" he asks with a sigh.

"For the same reason I'll never tell Papa or Coralie—it's dangerous."

"Secrets are always dangerous, Celena," my twin mumbles. "I could have helped you."

"Dolphins," Merrick calls from ahead. My brother scowls at him.

"You're not off the hook yet, sister," Caspian grumbles as we swim faster to catch the pod of dolphins.

Llyr turns them in the right direction, and we catch a lift for a while, letting go temporarily only when the dolphins decided to surface for air. They took half a day's swim off our schedule at least.

In the massive ocean, the sound of the silence waves in my ears as we swim. It's different when the water isn't rushing around you at dolphin-speeds.

Below us, the seaweed waves in the water. The anemone looks stunning, but from this height, it's hard to make out details.

"How did it go?" Llyr sinks back to match my strokes.

"With Casp? *Charming*," I inform him. "Let me guess, Merrick wants to know how much trouble he's in?"

"I always knew you were a smart mermaid," Llyr teases.

"Probably as much as me," I reply. "Now swim along and tell him he should probably find us a good cavern to sleep in tonight without any light so my brother can't easily find him."

Llyr chuckles, pulling ahead.

"You know, I can command them to forgive us," Dylana makes her way over to me. "I have that kind of power."

"*Sure*," I quip, knowing she'd never exercise that kind of influence over any of us. "At least we got it handled."

"Kind of," she corrects, frowning.

"*Kind of*," I agree with a sigh. "Maybe if we find them dates with the siren mermaids, they'll leave us alone."

"Oh, that sounds like a great plan—infiltrating the enemy."

"They'd probably siren them away," I comment.

"Suddenly our brothers are human now?" Dylana mocks.

"They're certainly as moody as humans," I joke.

"Yes, and *we'd* know…" she rolls her eyes at the idea of knowing a human to compare our brothers to.

Eventually, we come to the first marker of the trip—a sunken ship.

Algae covers the sides of the vessel. Barnacles grow everywhere. The mast—terrifyingly tall—makes me picture the dead siren strapped to it, her blood mixing with the color of her tail.

"We need to make sure it's safe," Merrick takes charge. "I'll go."

Caspian looks like he's going to protest but my hand on his arms stops him.

We watch as Merrick quietly swims toward the ship. He takes a few moments to swim around it, checking the perimeter. When it's cleared, he swims to the top of the ship toward the deck.

Merrick disappears inside the boat. I hold my breath, waiting for him to return with all of his limbs attached—anything could be lurking inside the boat.

Moments pass.

A few bubbles trail up from the boat toward the surface. They float like tiny crystals against the expansive blue sea. The light catches them as they move, making them twinkle in the purest of ways.

"Is something wrong?" Dylana asks. "Why isn't he back?"

"Should we call to him?" Morgen swims a little higher to get a better view.

"No," we all answer at the same time.

"We don't want to give him away if something is happening," I explain quickly.

We wait in silence, bobbing on the water.

I notice his fingers before anyone else sees them.

Merrick climbs over the edge of the ship, hand over hand as if he's dragging himself up. I relax when I see the first bits of his blue hair appear over the edge.

He makes eye contact with me, raising a finger to his lips. He looks as worried as I feel—something is wrong.

I dart forward when his head whips back, looking at whatever terrifying thing is behind him.

CHAPTER 5

"**G**o," Merrick shouts as he rushes away from the ship.

A young shark whips through the water, aggressively moving toward Merrick. Everyone gasps, lurching back in the ocean.

Before any of us can help, the shark changes course, veering away. It's sleek body cuts through the water, furiously swimming away.

I reach Merrick first, taking his arms in my hands.

"Are you okay?" I look down at his tail, examining his fins. When I don't find any damage, I look back up.

He's breathing heavily, looking shaken.

"I'm okay," he confirms. "I scared the thing."

"Looks like he scared you too," Llyr jokes, trying to lighten the mood. "You good, man?"

Merrick nods, chest rising and falling heavily. My fingers tighten around his wrist, silently lending him my support. He squeezes his fist together, tightening the muscles under my fingertips, letting me know he's okay.

"Was he the only one in there?" Caspian asks, bringing everyone back to the task at hand.

"I think so. He was in the last place I checked—I *thought* I lost him when I swam up the staircase, but apparently not."

"Let's get inside," I pull away, swimming toward the ship.

Rays of light stream into the ship, making the walls dance. Sea plants grow on the walls and ceilings, looking like fireworks from one of the human books I read as a mer child. I watch them carefully as they pulse with the moving water.

Particles float in front of us, reminding me of the kelp forest. Some glitter as brightly as the silver starfish Llyr handed me two days ago. My fingers absentmindedly reach toward the pouch on my belt where it's tucked away.

We pick a place near the top of the ship, just under the deck. The holes in the boat allow light to filter through, giving us enough visibility to see each other as we settle in for the night. Caspian sulks in the corner next to me.

"Tell a story, Morgen," Dylana prompts. Her brother has been studying mer history his entire life, and he never fails to produce a good story from our past.

"Like what?" Morgen glances at his older sister.

"I don't know, pick one."

"Well, since Merrick was nearly bitten in half, let's talk about dissection," he announces as we groan.

"I don't want to hear that one," Dylana protests.

"You said to pick and I did," he lectures his sister. "Now clam up and listen."

I tip my head back against the wall of the ship, careful to avoid the sea life cluttering the area. Merrick raises an eyebrow at me from across the room, unamused at Morgen's antics.

"Centuries ago, long before the human-mer agreement, long before Marcelline sirened King Leon into the treaty, before Persephone ripped us away from the surface and Aila saved the human prince, the mer had their first encounter with humans."

Morgen waves his hand through the water, creating a whirl of bubbles. He uses the back of his hand to create a wave, pushing the bubbles out from his chest, toward the rest of us. They vanish into the ocean.

"A *simple* merman with a *simple* dark green and brown tail was swimming through the ocean. He looked toward the surface and saw what we now know was the underside of a human ship.

"We had never been so close to the human kingdoms, you see, so he didn't know what awaited him when he surfaced."

The water feels colder, though I'm sure it's just my own dread manifesting in my veins.

"The ship had cast a net into the water, and by chance, it scooped the merman out of the water, depositing him onto the deck—to this day, no one ever says the poor merman's name, for no mer family should have to suffer the image of what happened next."

I dig into my pouch, pulling out the silver starfish. That siren girl —and likely her sister—had experienced what was coming next. Somehow it feels right to remember them at this time.

"When the humans saw him, they mistook him for a human—they had no idea what a merman was. They assumed his tail was a fish that had tried to swallow him.

"They attempted to pull the fish off of their comrade, but try as they might, they could not remove it."

Caspian notices as I cringe and scoots over next to me. He reaches up, tangling his hands in the ends of my hair to comfort me. I tip my head toward him, wanting to rest on his shoulder, but I also want to give him the space he just gave up to take care of me.

"They used their knives to try to cut the fish away only to discover it was no fish at all. The merman's spinal chord ran all the way down his tail, shocking the humans.

"He, of course, was dead. They mutilated him despite his cries of pain and loss of blood."

I shudder, imagining my tail being ripped off of me like that.

I've cut myself on coral before, but I imagine the knives of twenty men make that seem small in comparison.

"He became a trophy to the sailors," Morgen continues. "They strung him up on the boom of their ship, blood dripping on the deck as they sailed for their kingdom."

"*And then they went after mer for generations until Marcelline sirened the king into the treaty. Thank you, moving on,*" Llyr concludes swiftly. "We get the picture, Morgen, we don't need all the graphic content."

"Here I thought I was giving you the tame version," Morgen chuckles.

In fact, he *was*.

"Other sailors saw," Morgen insisted on adding one last bit to the story. "They wanted to discover what the creature was and went searching in the same area.

"Other mer were there to look for their friend and were ultimately caught and strung up as well—and are to this day. Though, admittedly, the humans have taken less interest in us recently, so it appears."

It was something to be grateful for, at least.

I try to think of something else—*anything* else—so that I'm not haunted with pictures of the red-tailed siren mermaid as I try to sleep.

"What do we know about Metten?" I ask, changing the subject. Llyr looks incredibly grateful.

We spend the next hour talking about what we'll find when we arrive. Sleep comes quietly as we all doze off in the safety of the sunken ship.

The next morning, I find a conch shell outside the ship. I whisper my mother's name into it, leaving her a message that we had reached the ship safely.

Attaching it to a passing turtle, I send it toward Scylla. A mer would find it and listen to my mother's name being whispered over and over again until they deliver it to her and it releases its message.

She, in turn, would inform Marilla and our families that we are safe. I just hope the turtle hurries up.

Back in the expansive blue ocean, we start out toward Metten, keeping a look out for sirens lurking about our waters.

Over the years, we've sent scouts out beyond the barriers, but we try not to risk the lives of our mer simply to gather intelligence. While we have some ideas on the locations of humans and sirens, overall, we're swimming blindly. Perhaps I could talk with Dylana about expanding our scouting missions once she takes over as queen.

Caspian tugs at my tail as we swim. I look back to find him giving me a sad smile—he forgives me. I flick my tail, breaking the grip he has on me as I dart forward to swim with Morgen.

"You realize Metten is incredibly close to the human world, don't you?" Morgen remarks. "It's only a few hours' swim."

"Less than that, if what they say is true."

"We've never been so close to the human world before."

I can't tell if he's interested in seeing it or if it frightens him. His voice changes pitch as he speaks but I don't know him well enough to figure it out.

"We can't go there, of course," I add. "It's far too dangerous. The last thing we need is to fight both the sirens *and* the humans."

"We're staying *far away* from the surface," Merrick commands, joining the conversation.

"I didn't say we weren't," Morgen snips. "We're close—all I meant was that we needed to be careful. We don't have to be *as* careful in Scylla, but Metten is a different story."

Aila once swam in these waters. The realization washes over me like waves on the shore, slapping against the sand. She once made this journey in reverse, traveling from her home in Metten to Scylla.

"Here's where the water changes," Llyr announces, shivering.

The water temperature drops against my scales, though only for a moment—it must be a cold current. The other side is warmer, though not as warm as it was a moment ago.

Aila must have loved coming to warmer waters.

"Here," Dylana says, swimming up to me. She hands me a few strands of seaweed and some shells from the sea floor.

She waits for me to slip the shells into my pouch before we both begin to fashion a wreath out of the seaweed. Dylana and I twist the green stuff into loops, wrapping extra pieces around it to hang down over the back of our hair.

The shells are tied on with the loose pieces of seaweed. We help each other adjust our wreaths, placing the shells perfectly in our hair.

"I feel *much* better now," Dylana announces.

Mermaids are rarely without some kind of trinket in their hair—it's just no fun without something to draw attention. The mermen nod appreciatively, admiring our inventiveness.

The wreath gives me a sense of calm as I swim with it tangled in my locks. Something about the way it lightly rests against my head is soothing—but then, so is *everything* when it comes to our hair.

A stingray glides over the sea floor beneath us, gracefully floating over the sand. When it sees us, it darts up, flapping its fins to reach us. It looks like its wiggling in pure joy.

The soft creature hovers over our hands, looking for food. When it finds nothing, he turns, swimming away to hunt for his own meal. I assume it must have been one that frequents the palace district to be so friendly.

We swim through the day, darting in and out of rays of light filtering down from the surface. The light refracts off of our tails, illuminating them brilliantly. Dylana's opal scales sparkle.

I look back at my own lavender and purple tail, catching Merrick in the background. He purses his lips, reaching up to brush back his blue hair. Somewhere along the way, he fashioned himself a *sarasa* of seaweed, lopping it over one shoulder, over his chest, and around his waist.

He looks stunning.

His gold shoulder armor and navy tail are striking against the blue depths of the sea. He's tried all his life not to stand out so he could handle missions easier, but I don't know how he's ever managed to accomplish anything with looks like those.

"How long are you going to stare, Len?" he calls, making everyone turn to look at me. I try not to blush.

"Nice *sarasa*," I throw back like barbs. "I see you didn't want to be left out."

I pat the wreath in my hair.

"When have I ever?" Merrick shouts back.

He does a backflip purely for attention before speeding up to catch me. My partner grins smugly.

"Just admit it, you were staring."

"I was staring at myself, thank you," I realize how ridiculous it sounds as I say it, but I can't back down. "I was admiring my tail in the light."

Before he can throw out a snappy remark, Dylana comes to my rescue.

"I was admiring it too! You always look so pretty in the light, cousin."

Merrick's *sarasa* dangles off his chest as we swim, hovering a mere inch away from his flesh. My hand goes to the netting on my *iluse* as it too dangles toward the ocean floor. My finger brushes over one of the broken shell pieces I have attached strategically in case I need to rip it off and defend myself.

"There," Merrick points ahead. "I think that's the cavern."

"Are you sure this time?" Llyr asks. "You thought that an hour ago too."

"It looked big enough from the outside," Merrick complains, hand moving to his *sarasa* as he adjusts it.

"It has to be," I add. "We can't swim much further today anyway, so even if it's not, we should find a place to stay."

Merrick swims ahead, once again checking our resting place before we enter. With the exception of a rather annoyed octopus crawling out of the mouth of the cavern, we find ourselves clear.

Once we set our things down, Merrick and Llyr announce that they're going to look for food. Reaching the mouth of the cavern, Llyr turns to invite me along. I dart out quickly before my brother can object.

We swim far enough away from the cavern that we can't be overheard before we dive to the ocean floor to look for clams and oysters.

I gather the shelled creatures in my arms, wishing I had brought my pouch with me.

"Here," Merrick offers, opening the pouch on his belt. I had taken mine off once we reached the cavern, not thinking I would be exiting again for a while. I drop the food into the pouch before bending to collect more.

"Want some help getting those shells out of your hair when we get back?" Llyr asks, scooping up a muscle.

"Please," I nod.

All mermen are skilled at working with mermaid hair—it's a sign of respect and honor. It's also incredibly comforting to have someone brush out your hair for you. Assuming there is no bad blood between two mer, it's common for friends and family to work on each other's hair.

Mer have very few boundaries.

"We should reach Metten by tomorrow night," Llyr comments. "Those dolphins were very helpful yesterday."

"I think we should stay outside the city," Merrick remarks, bending down to catch an oyster as it buries itself into the sand. "Then we can enter at first light."

"That's a good idea," I reply, playing out both scenarios—it made the most sense. "I think everyone will agree to that."

"Conch," Merrick says, nodding a few feet away.

I scoop it up, cradling the shell in my hands.

"I should probably let Dylana send this one," I sigh. The mermen nod.

When the pouches are full, we return to the rest of our collection. They sit inside, draped over the rocks that rest inside the cavern. Dylana perks up when we enter.

I smile handing her a clam and the conch. Her eyes widen in delight as she sees the shell. She hands the conch back to me for a moment while she pries open the clam, quickly eating it. The princess darts outside to send her message to her mother while I settle down beside Caspian.

Digging my knife out of my pouch, I pry open an oyster, relishing my dinner. We open shell after shell.

"Here," Merrick says, breaking the silence as we eat. He flicks something toward me. I catch it in my hand. "For the Pearl Festival next month."

When I open my hand, I find a large, white pearl. I smile.

"Thank you."

He could have taken it home for one of the women in his family, but Merrick was always good about sharing with me.

"This will look perfect in my new shell crown."

"I thought it might," He smirked, turning back to his food. He'd heard me talk about the crown I was creating for the festival enough times that it shouldn't surprise me that he had tucked that bit of information away.

"She can wear it assuming the sirens haven't figured out a way to sing the sharks into doing their bidding—then we're all sunk," Morgen chatters.

"Good news, Morgen," I add in a cheery voice. "If they *do* send the sharks, they're coming for *you* first."

He looks shocked for a moment before cracking a smile.

"They'll come for Dylana first, and then for you. You know the only thing sirens hate more than the reigning royals is decedents of Princess Aila."

He makes an ink-worthy point.

"No one will ever touch you," Caspian whispers next to me, growling. His back arches up like an angry stingray.

"If we *do* come across the sirens, they must never find out who any of you are—especially Celena and Dylana," Merrick quickly adds, looking worried. He brushes the hair out of his eyes. "If anyone asks, we refer to them as Len and Lana."

We all agree, also creating fake names for Caspian and Morgen should the occasion bubble up. Until recently, I'd say the sirens have no way of knowing who we are, but now that we're sure they've been inside Scylla, they very well may know our roles in the kingdom.

Sleep comes easier as I sprawl out on the cavern floor, building a resting place out of sand.

A pod of dolphins greets us the next morning, shortening our trip again. I'm sure Aila wishes she had been able to catch a ride with one when she was leaving Metten, but she had all her trunks and chests with her.

We arrive in late afternoon, much earlier than we expected.

The abandoned city sits in the heart of what was once a mighty kingdom. Even from the outskirts, we can see the glorious palace in the distance—this was Aila's home.

Entranced, I swim forward slowly, mesmerized by the radiant

glory of Metten. Merrick pulls me back, sharply jerking on my wrist. His raised brow and judgmental eyes are all I need to realize I was swimming toward the old kingdom like a squid to an anglerfish's bioluminescent light.

I put my hand on his shoulder and let him guide me into the remnants of Metten.

We carefully swim into the old kingdom, checking the first homes we find on the edge of the city. Our goal is to get a feel for the area, but not actually enter into the main part of the kingdom until tomorrow.

No signs of life can be found in the dwellings, but we're leery to believe the entire kingdom is empty based on a few homes. We carefully swim around the outskirts of the area, looking for a place to spend the night where we won't be seen should the sirens be in the area.

"Any idea where your family used to live while we lived in Metten?" I ask quietly. Dylana, Morgen, Caspian, and I already know we come directly from the palace, but Llyr and Merrick don't.

"Some idea," Merrick sounds undecided.

He knows *exactly* which ones belonged to his family.

"Relatively," Llyr mimics his casualness. Similarly, he also knows but is being noncommittal.

After an hour or two of searching, we decide it's best to sleep away from Metten and backtrack into the sea. We find a quiet cavern to hide in for the night.

Morning floats in quietly, dancing as usual with its mystical rays of light from the surface—I wish for a moment that I could feel the sun on my skin. Mother has told me so many stories that Aila passed down about the surface and how different the world up there is—I can't help but imagine how it would feel.

I've only been to the surface once or twice, but never when the sun wasn't hidden from view by the clouds in the sky.

We decide to split up, checking different areas of the kingdom for sirens. It isn't safe for the royals to travel alone together, so Morgen and Dylana split. Caspian works with Morgen, which terrifies me since neither of them are trained like we are.

For a moment, I consider working with my brother, but that's also a bad idea since sirens hate my family more than they hate Dylana and Morgen's. I branch off with Merrick while Llyr works with the princess.

We swim in and out of dwellings, checking for signs of life. The closer we get to the palace, the more my body hums.

"Calm down, Len," Merrick criticizes, only his smile giving his teasing away. He drops his voice to a whisper. "We'll get there soon."

Lounging couches and tables remain in nearly every home. It's like the mer packed everything they could fit in their trunks and left the rest. After centuries of abandonment, the dwellings are overgrown with anemone.

"It looks cute, but you wouldn't want to sleep on that," Merrick jokes, swimming up behind me as I stare at the waving polyps.

"When was the last time one of those things stung you?" I counter.

"Nothing stings me, Len." He grins.

"No? Not even the jellyfish when we were ten?" I remind him.

He opens his mouth to speak but no words come out.

"That's what I thought." I grin triumphantly. "Now, clam up and start searching."

He rolls his eyes dramatically, spinning toward the door. Something about the small victory is so freeing that I do a backflip before following his bubbles out.

"Where are we going?" I ask quietly when we reach the door.

"What do you mean?"

"Where are we going, Merrick?" I cross my arms, waiting for him to tell me where his family used to live in Metten.

"We'll get there eventually," he sighs. "It's more important to finish scouting and make our way to the palace."

My body hums like a shock from an electric eel...at least that's what they say—I've never actually seen one this far north. Anticipation floods through me.

The closer we swim toward the palace, the stronger the sensation grows. *Home, home, home.*

A shadow passes over the sand as we swim out of the home covered in sea life. Merrick and I look up toward the surface as a dark object passes over—a ship.

It seems to be small—not a fishing vessel or a pirate ship.

Still, we hover in the doorway, floating in the shadows as we're trained to do. Boats rarely make it over the barriers in Scylla, but we know how to react if one does.

Even if this boat had dropped a net or its anchor, it never would have reached us at this depth. Our training, however, is so ingrained in us, that at the moment of a shadow sighting, we retreat into what-ever darkened safety we can find.

It passes quickly, leaving the area in peace. Merrick lets out a breath as I sag against the frame of the door.

"We're never going to get over doing that," he informs me as if I didn't already know.

"Aila's training runs deep," I credit my ancestor.

"I think Gaspar had more to do with it than his granddaughter."

Not long after, we find ourselves in the palace proper. This is the area I would currently be living in if we had stayed in Metten.

The homes are just as grand, encrusted with jewels and wide, looming doors, though the colors here are darker than they are in Scylla. I dive in and out of dwellings, checking for signs of siren life.

My heart hammers into my chest when I glide into a completely empty house. There are no anemones, no coral, no seaweed. It can only mean one thing—sirens.

CHAPTER 6

I back up so quickly that I slam into Merrick's chest. His chest plate rattles as it clinks against his shoulder armor—a wise choice for doing battle with sirens, but a terrible choice when the partner you're spying with is having an involuntary meltdown.

Merrick wraps his hands around my upper arms, steadying me. He's solid enough that even if I were trying, I couldn't get him to back up.

Over my shoulder, he sees what I saw—evidence that the sirens have made their way to Metten.

His fingers bite into my flesh just enough to let me know what he's thinking. Slowly, we swim back. I watch the inside of the room in case any mer come swimming out while Merrick turns and watches the expansive ocean for possible harm.

When he doesn't see anything, he drags me away as I watch behind us, swishing my tail as hard as I can to help propel us forward.

"They're here," I seethe once Merrick tucks us around a corner.

"I know," he breathes, holding me close.

My back is tucked up against the wall of another dwelling as Merrick uses his body to block me. My tail is far easier to see than his dark one, so he frequently helps hide me in times we do not wish to be seen.

"Get your knife out," he instructs. "We don't know what we're swimming into here."

Suddenly I'm grateful for all the little braids Caspian wove into my hair this morning—it won't float into my face while I'm handling whatever we may encounter. I reach up, touching the comb he embedded at the back of my skull, ensuring it's not tangled should I need to pull it out and use it as a weapon—Coralie would be horrified that the majority of my wardrobe doubles as something to save my life.

"Ready?" he whispers. I nod, swimming boldly behind him out into the open waters.

We quickly check more houses, finding most covered over in a century's worth of sea life. Several appear to have been used recently though.

I nod to the seaweed floating a few feet from us, remembering Merrick's *sarasa* from yesterday. Blending in with our surroundings is probably a good idea, and in this instance, that means looking like plants.

He gets my drift and starts pulling the plants from the sand, wrapping them around his wrists and arm, dangling them from his shoulder across his chest. I tangle a mess of them in my hair, hoping to hide my pink locks. We wrap bits of the seaweed around our waists, hiding the top of our tails and stomachs from easy sight.

Around the corner of the palace, I spot Dylana and Llyr. I wave them back, motion that we found something concerning. They signal that they haven't found anything, but heed our advice and stay back.

Noticing our attire, they conceal themselves as well, creeping back only once they are covered in greenery.

I look around for Caspian and Morgen but can't find them anywhere.

Merrick takes the lead, gesturing directions to Llyr. He nods back to us, pulling Dylana away from the front of the palace to enter from another location.

All thoughts of Aila and her grand palace exit my mind as I tune out my childhood fantasies of seeing her home. I focus in on the task at hand, turning the knife over in my palm.

Merrick enters first, blocking my view of the entryway as I slip in behind him. A bloom of jellyfish sits at the top of the room, as I imagine they have since the days of King Gaspar's reign. The room glows blue.

A small sea turtle swims through the water across the room, gliding easily through the palace. An octopus tentacle sticks out of the corner of another doorway, having taken up residence on the other side of the wall.

I know the palace by heart from the maps I've studied over the years. If they're here, there will probably be signs of them in one of the parlors or grottos.

"Left," I whisper swimming alongside of my partner.

We turn down the hallway, swimming slowly as we watch for signs of the sirens. I suddenly wish we had brought tridents with us, but we're here to spy, not to fight.

"If anything happens, you get out of here, Len," Merrick warns me, refusing to say why it would be worse for *me* to get caught by the sirens out loud.

I nod, having no intention of leaving him.

A flash of color invades my peripheral vision as something darts by the doorway. Merrick and I turn together, ready to confront the siren. We're fully prepared to break our promise to observe only if we have to.

"Tiko!" A voice shouts, raising the alarm.

The mermaid faces away from us, her long, black hair trailing down her back. Her tail twitches as she yells, a mix of orange and brown with hints of white mixed in indiscriminately.

"Already ahead of you," the merman that must answer to Tiko says. He enters the room holding Dylana captive.

She struggles against him, trashing against his periwinkle tail. Throwing her head back, she crashes into his nose, drawing enough blood to be noticeable, but it disappears before it reaches his blond hairline.

I wrap my hand around Merrick's arm, holding him back from rushing in to help Dylana—we still have the advantage. Llyr must be holding back too.

The knife Tiko digs into Dylana's arm is the last crab leg. Merrick reaches forward, dragging the mermaid siren back. Once she's against his body, out of the way, I immediately recognize Tiko as the merman who carried away the body of the red-tailed siren.

"Let her go," Tiko commands loudly, forcing the knife to draw more of Dylana's blood. She refuses to scream.

His eyes narrow as he examines first Merrick and then me—it must be hard to recognize us through the seaweed.

"What's going on?" the weaker of the two mermaid sirens I met a few days ago swims in the room, backing up the instant she sees the standoff.

"Nir!" she screams at the top of her lungs.

Tiko stares us down and Merrick holds a knife to the mermaid's throat. I assume she's the other siren from the reef barrier judging by the markings on her tail.

"Tiko, do something," she pleads, attempting to dig her nails into Merrick's forearm.

"Hands down, siren," I sneer, holding my knife toward her pretty fingers. I'd have no problem cutting them off if I needed to. I'd happily feed them to a baby shark.

She eyes me, releasing her grip.

"Who are you?" Tiko demands.

"Metten belongs to the mer," Merrick challenges. "You shouldn't be here."

"You weren't using it," Tiko fires back, words dropping like a cannonball from a pirate ship.

A massive merman rounds the corner, trident ready.

Now I wish even more strongly that we had brought bigger weapons.

Nir is tall, with one of the longest tails I've ever seen on a merman. His scales are as black as night and just as deadly looking— they practically pulse under him. With his dark brown hair, he's the perfect shadow spy, able to sneak through the waters without anyone noticing. It wouldn't surprise me a bit if he had been in the room, blending into the shadows the whole time.

"Release Roni," he says calmly, trident posed to strike.

"And if I don't?"

I could slap Merrick.

"Tarni, get back," he says without flinching, waiting for the mermaid with the peach tail and quivering lip to swim out of the way. His muscles twitch as he prepares to attack.

"I wouldn't if I were you," Llyr hovers behind him, knife at the base of the siren's neck. "You release that and I'll drive this into your spinal chord. You might survive, but you'll never be able to swim again."

Not being able to swim was a death sentence to mer.

"We're offering a fair trade—your mermaid for our mermaid," Llyr continues, trying to negotiate Dylana's release. "No one has to get hurt here."

"*Someone* has to get hurt," Tiko growls, looking at Roni as she seethes under our knives. So far we haven't drawn blood, but her mere presence begs me to remove a scale or two just to teach her a lesson.

The dark merman decides to risk it, launching himself forward so quickly that Llyr can't keep up with him. His knife slips away, falling out of his hand. He catches it mid water and lunges at the hulking merman.

Roni lurches forward, trying to escape. I clamp down on her so hard that I likely leave marks. Tiko attempts to drag Dylana backward, further into the palace, as Tarni cowers in the corner, trying to decide which of her friends to help.

Out of nowhere, a flash of mer drops down. A second figure joins him, holding on to the edges of a seaweed net. They swim toward the sea floor, dragging the net over Nir.

The mer screams in pain.

Caspian looks up at me, still holding the net. From the edge of the seaweed, long tentacles stick out—jellyfish.

Morgen forces the net to the floor, nodding to Casp to let go and help the rest of us. The two of them had captured the stinging jellyfish in the loose net they made of seaweed and used it to take Nir out of the equation temporarily. I have no idea how they managed that.

Caspian darts toward Dylana, taking on Tiko himself. Dylana bites down on Tikos hand, forcing him to release her as he yells out. Morgen subdues Tarni while Merrick and I handle Roni.

We misjudged Nir, however, and he rears up, still reeling from the red welts on his body. He throws the net off his shoulders, eyes smoldering.

He races toward Caspian, throwing him into the wall before turning on us. Merrick sucks in a breath, ready to defend me, but unable to let go of the mermaid, he can only prepare to be struck.

Tarni screams in fear.

The giant merman slams into Roni, pummeling her and Merrick into the wall. I dig my knife into Nir's shoulder, slicing into the meaty part of his flesh to avoid any real damage.

He reels back at me, setting Merrick into motion.

I'm propelled backward, faster than anything I've ever experienced. The breath is knocked out of me long before I hit the wall. I wait for the bone-crunching sound of the impact against the palace support system. Over his shoulder, I see all four of my mermen racing toward me, trying to stop what they can never stop in time.

Pain radiates through my body, down into my tail as everything vibrates inside me. Blackness fills my vision as tiny bioluminescent spots dance in front of me.

I slip down under the weight of the merman as he tries to crush me into bits of sand and broken coral.

I register the sound of a scream as Caspian, Merrick, Llyr, and Morgen attack the merman trying to kill me. His hand slips around my throat, pushing on my vocal chords.

Dylana claws at me as the mermen rip Nir away. I blink back to life as she shakes me. Tiko is in the corner moving Roni and Tarni out of the way before he races into the brawl.

I gasp several times, shuddering as I try to regain my balance.

"Go," I croak knowing they need help against the sea monster masquerading as a merman.

I claw my way up the side of the palace wall, wondering if Aila had ever had to do that.

I'm dizzy as I swim forward, but I don't have time for that right now—we're in a whirlpool of trouble. I swallow, gathering myself before swimming as fast as I can at the collection of mer.

I take Tarni out—an accident, as I was aiming for Tiko—and whip myself backward to elbow Roni. Everything spins around me. I nearly hit Morgen but he ducks, quickly recovering from the near collision.

Surprisingly, Caspian and Morgen fight just as well as the rest of us, if not better. I blink, wondering if I hit my head harder than I thought.

Llyr manages to get his hands on Nir's trident and turns it on the group, taking aim. A weapon in any of our hands is a good thing, but a weapon in Llyr's is the most helpful thing of all.

"Back up," he commands, forcing Tiko back.

Tarni darts out of the room and Dylana and I take off after her, racing through the halls of the palace. The grotto is incredible, but we're only there for a second before racing away.

Roni follows us, pulling Dylana back by her tail. She digs her nails into Dylana's fins making her shriek. A damaged tail could be just as deadly to a mermaid as a broken spinal chord.

I flip around and launch my knife at the siren. She shrieks, letting go of the princess as she darts out of the path of my blade. Dylana scoops it up for me as it floats down, hitting the sand. The siren flees.

We follow her back through the grotto and hallways toward the sound of the mermen clashing.

Blood floats in the water, dissipating somewhere above our heads. I wish on the silver starfish in my pouch that there are no sharks lurking within the palace walls.

Tiko attempts to go after me the second I swim in, but Caspian pushes me away, taking the hit. A small mark on his arm is proof of his brotherly love for me.

"You don't honestly think Dad didn't train me, did you?" he smirks, lifting himself off me.

I had always believed my father knew a little of what my mother and I did in secret and turned a blind eye to it. Never once had I considered he had also been trained...and had trained my brother.

"*Someone* had to protect you," he adds. "You and Mom may have kept us in the dark, but we never once were *completely* clueless, sis."

Seventeen years of my life had gone by and only just now did I realize that my brother was trickier than I was. His skills amaze me.

If Caspian is trained, then I also assume Dylana's father had taken it upon himself to train Morgen too, thus their dramatic entrance. Our brothers had been trained to protect us whether we knew it or not.

Suddenly, I am no longer worried about my brother surviving this war.

A merman cries out, forcing me to whip around. Merrick's arm bleeds. Llyr has a harsh cut running along his jaw. My twin and I rush forward to help.

I use my tail to deliver a powerful slap to Tiko's shoulders and back, knocking him off balance. He topples forward into Roni. Llyr uses the trident to slam into Nir's skull, temporarily knocking him out.

"Go," he shouts, motioning for us to swim away.

When we reach the palace door, leaving Tarni trembling in our wake, we split up into our original teams.

Merrick grabs me with his uninjured arm, pulling me backward. I attempt to help us swim, but I'm still reeling from Nir's attack. Merrick holds tighter, sensing that something is wrong.

We dart in and out of shadows and light, making me more sick than I've ever been. I don't know where he's taking us but I have to assume he has some semblance of an idea on which route to take.

My mind slams to a halt as I remember something—Caspian.

I don't know where my brother is—I don't know where *any* of our people are. All I know is that Merrick is taking us away from the palace—away from Aila's home—and we're evading the sirens that have taken over and forced our kind away from Metten.

Tiko and Roni leave the palace, searching for us. They split up, going different ways.

Since no one else got involved with the fight, I think it's safe to assume that it's only them in the palace.

But sirens don't play games alone—where there are four, there are many.

CHAPTER 7

"Hold on," Merrick murmurs gently, still swimming at dolphin-pace. I cling to his arm, afraid to let go. "There. There's a cavern up there."

He swims faster pushing us toward safety as I pitifully flick my tail in hopes of assisting.

He slows as we reach the mouth of the cavern.

"You'll like this place." I can hear the smile in his words. "It's called Scur Caverns. Not many people knew about it, but the ones that did, passed it down in incredible stories once they left."

"What's so special about it?" I mumble, trying to turn to see it. He keeps me tucked under his arm.

"Aila and Troy didn't pass it down?" He sounds surprised. "Well, maybe they wanted to keep it secret—I hear it was a favorite among the royals."

He chuckles warmly as we enter the looming mouth of the cavern.

Everything grows dark as he finally lets me turn around. For a moment, everything is pitch black. Merrick's hand on my back is the only thing that assures me that I haven't slipped into unconsciousness.

Quietly, as if by magic, the entire cavern lights up, glowing enticingly.

"They say it mimics the storms above the surface," Merrick informs me.

The lights swirl above us—and all around us—looking radiantly endless. I'm not sure if the motion is real or if it has to do with my injuries, but it's breath-taking.

"Len, let me see you," Merrick says quietly.

When I turn to face him, I get a good look at his injury.

"Merrick, your arm." I reach up to touch his skin, examining the wound.

"I'll be fine." He waves me off. "We need to make sure you're okay first. You took a pretty hard hit."

I shake my head.

"We need to check your arm," I protest, gently pulling the seaweed away from his skin.

He stills, allowing me to care for him. I silently pull off one strand of seaweed at a time, revealing his muscular arms and torso. Merrick reaches up to unclip his shoulder armor, letting it sink off his shoulders to the cavern floor.

He watches me work, floating in front of him. I use a bit of the seaweed to clean him up, brushing away the bits of sand and debris that got caught in his open flesh. His eyes close momentarily as I wipe it away, catching the edges of his skin.

I move slowly—slower than usual—I blame it on my injuries. Everything seems to be moving like the still waters on the surface of the sea when the wind doesn't blow, bobbing back and forth.

"Len," he catches my hand. "I need to look at you."

Merrick looks at me earnestly, willing me to stop. I give up, dropping my shoulders as he guides me to sit on the cavern floor.

The space glows blue and purple. Deep, dark colors invade the cavern, bathing Merrick in the strangest light.

Once I'm seated on the ocean floor, Merrick begins his examination, studying my eyes, looking for bruises or marks, and moving my limbs to check for damage.

He focuses on my tail, making sure my fins aren't damaged—I can't blame him with the way I was swimming earlier. His hands glide over my scales slowly, checking my bones and muscles. He's careful not to hurt me as he locks eyes with me and tests my fins.

"Okay, let's take a look at that head of yours, pretty mermaid," he mutters, floating up in front of me.

Merrick swims around to untangle the braids and comb from my hair. His fingers feel incredible as he works them up through the underside of my locks, inching their way from the base of my skull to the crown. Slowly, he brings them back down along the sides of my head, resting just over my ears.

"Close your eyes," he whispers, inviting me to relax.

I block out thoughts of the sirens that are still searching for us, forbidding myself from wondering about my brother and the others, and let my partner work a little magic into my aches.

With steady hands, he untangles each braid. My hair comb rests in my hands as he works. I breathe in and out, watching the colors of the glowing cave dance behind my eyelids.

I remember a story my grandmother once told me about a glowing cavern from the old kingdom. It was a romantic place all the royal couples visited with their partners. I can easily see why they liked this spot.

"Mmm," Merrick grunts, cringing, but continues to work on my hair.

"Merrick," I say, eyes flying open as I turn to face him.

His arm is bent slightly as he cradles it.

"You don't need to hurt yourself for me."

The look I give him silences him before he can speak.

I rest a hand on his arm below his injury. Merrick is one of the most stubborn mermen—he never asks for help and he rarely accepts it.

I swim behind him and touch his wavy hair. Working my tired fingers into his scalp, I massage the worry away. He tips his head forward allowing me to work the knots out of the back of his neck. I work quietly, trying to calm his beating heart.

Just when I think we're both soothed enough to have a rational conversation about what happened in the palace, Merrick turns to me, disturbing the peaceful balance of Scur Cavern.

He's close—so close that the shells on my *iluse* press into his chest. Merrick breathes heavily as he stares down at me. He smiles softly, still bathed in the light of the glowing cave.

His hair floats quietly in front of him, dancing in front of his eyes. Mine matches his, swirling around us, almost as if it's enclosing us in some kind of circle made just for us.

His lips part slightly, and once again, I find myself drawn to something to which I should not be drawn. I lean in, this deadly sea creature calling me from a pocket of darkness, and he is the one and only light I must swim to survive.

Merrick gravitates toward me too, rocking his body toward mine.

Until he pulls back.

A giant lobster backs out of the cavern entrance, frightened by our presence.

"We should go," he murmurs.

I bite my lip, unsure of what just happened. He blinks, rubbing the back of his neck with his good hand. We swim toward the mouth of the cavern.

"It's beautiful here." I sigh, taking one last look. There's a very good chance I'll never see anything this beautiful ever again, and certainly not *this* cavern.

Merrick can sense my hesitation and pauses an extra moment to look at it with me. I think we're both aware that this moment is special and won't ever be replicated—at least not in our life times.

Merrick slips back into his armor, checking to make sure the water is clear before we swim back into the light. Somehow the beams of light dancing in the water look a little less spectacular now.

Silently, we set off toward the cavern where we'll meet the rest of our team.

Merrick slips an arm around me, monitoring how I'm swimming. When he's positive I've recovered after being attacked, he gives me more space to swim.

"Jellyfish?" I ask, breaking the silence.

"Hey, it was a good plan," Merrick defends my brother's decision to drop the stinging creatures on Nir's head.

"How did they even come up with that?" I shake my head.

We both flinch when we see the shadow pass over us. A large swordfish swims above us—not a human or a siren—and makes it's way to the surface. It leaps out of the water high above us before dropping back down into the water. It's long nose reminds me of the trident Llyr took away from Nir. I wonder if he still has control over it.

"How much trouble do you think we're going to get in when Marilla finds out we didn't stay out of it like she instructed?" Merrick muses.

"I think we're going to let *Dylana* explain it," I stretch out my words, hoping our friend can smooth things over on our behalf, but not really believing that she can.

"I didn't see any sign of other sirens. Did you?"

The swordfish passing over has made me extra nervous. Every twitch of seaweed along the ocean floor, every school of fish that appears in my peripheral vision, every strange ray of light coming from the surface makes me tense.

"Nothing that I saw, but I also didn't get a good look," I admit. "Logically, we know they were hanging out in the palace, but we also know that someone has been living in some of the dwellings long enough that they cleared them out."

"Which means that it can't just be the four of them," Merrick concludes.

"Six if you count the red-tailed siren and her sister."

"That's a good point."

"What kind of a group would send a bunch of teenagers into enemy territory alone?" I mutter.

"Seriously, Len?" Merrick turns to me.

I am a teenager and *I* have been sent into enemy territory…even though it's still *technically* under our control. I have also been highly trained—but then, so have they.

"The point is, if the sirens want back into mer territory, they wouldn't send a collection of six mer. There have to be more of them somewhere."

We swim up to the cavern we had been staying in—this one far less grand than the glowing cave we just left—and find it empty, save for four conch shells.

The first two are meant for Dylana and Llyr. The third and fourth are for Merrick and me. I lift mine to my ear and Caspian's voice reaches out to me.

"The sirens swam by here. We're following them. Just keep swimming home and I'll try to leave signs along the way. If you don't see any, get back to Scylla and warn the others—we'll meet you there when we can. Don't worry about us—Morgen and I have this covered."

The shell crackles out like sea foam.

"Let's go," Merrick flips to face the door as soon as his message crackles out a few breaths after mine. He nearly slams into Llyr and Dylana.

"Grab your conch shells and listen on the way," Merrick directs.

"The guys found the sirens," I add. "They're following them and we need to catch up."

Dylana grabs her shell, desperate for word from her brother. Llyr takes his too, though he already knows everything it says. A massive trail of bubbles lingering in the water is the only proof that we had ever been in Metten.

My eyes scour every inch of the ocean floor, looking for a sign from my brother. It isn't long before I see a strange pattern in the seaweed. A path starts to take shape, but only noticeable from a higher height. Patches of seaweed seem to be missing—it could be a coincidence, but because I know to look, I see Caspian's message. It was something he used to do when we were children.

I point it out to the others and we race ahead, swimming as fast as our tails will allow. They can't be too far ahead of us—we only had a few minutes between the time we left the palace and the time we returned to the cavern.

The seaweed bends out of the path we would take to get home, a sharp angle in the missing seaweed notifies us that we must veer off course.

Dylana finds a conch and sends it with a passing squid, hoping it reaches her mother so she knows that sirens have been found and our people should prepare themselves. I would have sent one to my mother, but I couldn't find another conch.

We track our brothers until we run out of seaweed and find ourselves lingering where we never thought we would end up—near the shark barrier on the south-west side of the kingdom.

"This can't be good," Llyr mutters as we gently swim into shark territory.

Our ancestors had been so careful to set up the shark barriers, creating feeding grounds for the creatures to ensure they would stay in the area where they were well fed and deter unwanted visitors from trying to invade their space. For a century, we have avoided going near the grounds, with only the occasional mission to make sure the feeding grounds were still active. Now, we're swimming right into the heart of it.

The mermen take it as their task to watch for predators while Dylana and I search for places to hide should we need them. When I find seaweed inappropriately growing out of the top of a grotto, I know it must be our friends.

We swim over to the rock formation, carefully checking before we enter.

"This way," Caspian hisses, motioning us to move quickly. "They're on the other side."

He guides us through the grotto—which is *much* larger than it looked from the outside—so we can see through the other exit. I expect to find sharks roaming the waters. Instead, I find a collection of sirens, all covered in shark skin.

"What's happening?"

We watch them for a few minutes as they listen to Nir and his group of sirens. They look concerned.

A few of the older sirens swim up higher than the rest. Their arms move in big, grand gestures as they give orders to their people. I count fifty sirens, but I imagine reinforcements are on the way as they send a few of their sirens back into the expansive ocean, away from mer territory.

The remaining collection turns, swimming directly down the shark barrier without any fear.

"This makes no sense," Morgen says, trying to wrap his head around what we're seeing.

We follow behind them, keeping to the far left of the barrier—we don't want anything to do with the sharks. Even Llyr and Merrick look worried.

Ahead, we can see the sirens swimming toward Scylla. They move straight toward a shark.

Suddenly, as if the creature is trying to evade a much larger predator, the shark panics, throwing its body back and forth as it tries to escape. I've never seen anything like it, nor have I seen anything move so fast in my life.

The sirens never flinch.

They swim on as if the shark had never been there. A few of them watch the gray creature swim away, but most seem ambivalent toward the scene.

"For coral's sake, they really *do* know how to siren sharks," Morgen says, horrified.

"If we had the ability to siren sea life, we would have been doing it for centuries," Merrick comments. "Something else is going on here."

"How did they kill that many sharks??" I ask. "A bunch of them are wearing shark skin on their armor. How did they get close enough to kill them? Maybe that can offer us some clues."

"I think we'd have to get our hands on one of them to find that answer," Llyr responds, eyes fixed on the leaders of the sirens as they swim with tridents in their hands, leading their collection safely through what used to be shark-infested waters.

"Now we know how they got through though—they broke the shark barrier," Dylana adds, hand resting on her knife hanging in her belt. "At least we know they didn't damage the reef."

"Although, that might be easier to repair at this point," Caspian points out, pushing us to swim slightly faster. "I don't know how long it will take to create something to replace the shark barrier. We might need all of our mer to take turns creating a mer fence around our territory for the next couple of centuries until we can grow more reef barriers."

"I don't see why they feel the need to invade our kingdoms," I gripe. "They're free to siren the humans all they like out there—that's what they wanted. Why do they care about us? We aren't even close enough to do any real damage to the human world out here in the middle of the ocean. If they move in here, they'd have to take a ton of extra time to travel back and forth to the surface to claim their human victims."

Caspian looks as exasperated as I do. It's just not logical for the sirens to want control over Metten or Scylla. It would be more believable for them to try to take over one of our sister kingdoms like Dariah or Ambra—those are far more strategically placed to carry out their mission to destroy the humans.

Coming to Scylla can mean only one thing—they still want revenge for Aila ruining Persephone's plans a century ago. Chantay had been furious when her daughter lost a chance at a crown. Perhaps this was their way of getting it back—even though Chantay's line ended with Persephone.

It's said that Persephone didn't last long in captivity. When King Gaspar locked her in the cells below the palace in Scylla, Persephone withered away. She died well before my mother was born. Now her bones rest in the royal crypt below the palace along with those of Aila and her sisters.

We follow the sirens until they take shelter for the evening, though they seem to have no fear as they sprawl out on the sand in the open waters. A few sleep inside rock formations, but the majority of them just lie down and rest. A handful keep watch.

I float in the water behind a small coral reef, hovering just high enough to see over it as I watch the sirens rest. The water is quiet as darkness settles in.

"You know you won't be able to see them," Caspian remarks, swimming up next to me. He rests his elbow on my shoulder lowering his head.

"What, Dad didn't train you to see in the dark?" I tease, tipping my head on top of my twin's.

"No, did Mom train you?"

"Not for that, I'm afraid."

"We have to get better at our twin-communication skills," Casp. "We could have avoided a lot of drama *and* secretly learned some new skills from each other."

"Oh, you mean like a jellyfish attack?" I quip, bobbing in the water.

"That was effective and you know it, little sister." He tips his head to face me more. "And that guy is going to have a reminder not to mess with us for the next week or so."

Caspian laughs quietly.

"He got *tangled* in those monsters."

"I can't believe he stayed upright after all that," I snicker.

"If sea monsters were real," Caspian says, laughing quietly, "that guy would most certainly be one of them."

"Agreed." I pause. "Hey, maybe *that's* how they're handling the sharks—Nir's really one of them and he can command their every move."

"Oh, wouldn't *that* be lovely?" Caspian jokes, lifting his head off my shoulder.

"That merman is so massive that he could make *anybody* ink."

"We probably should have brought a bloom of jellyfish with us in case he comes back."

The moon filters down through the waves. It glitters off the surface high above us as the waves roll along their path toward the land. Below us, I can see our friends sleeping on the sand, tails stretched out as their hair moves gently in the water. It's a shame that the moonlight is only strong enough to see the area around us and not the siren collection in the distance.

"Should we send someone ahead?" Caspian asks, thinking practically. "The rest of us can stay and watch the sirens, but maybe we should have someone swim ahead."

"What if they get caught? What if there's no way around the sirens and we give ourselves away?" I question. "We sent the conch. Hopefully, Marilla is getting everyone ready. We need to be sure the sirens are headed toward Scylla and not back out to sea."

"You really think they're headed anywhere other than to find us?" Caspian challenges. "I love you, Celena, but you're not thinking logically. Those sirens are headed straight toward us and they're going after you and mother first."

"Well, *one of us* isn't there to be found," I remind him.

"Which means they'll go for Coralie."

His words sting, leaving unseen welts all over my body as if *I* had been tangled in a bloom of jellyfish.

The sirens would be going after my sister.

"We can't let them hurt her," I say urgently.

"I know. We'll protect her. Mother and Father won't let them touch her."

"You two okay?" Llyr asks, swimming up from below us. Somehow I had missed his movements as he woke up and swam up to us.

"We're worried about Coralie," I supply.

"Ah. That makes sense." Llyr nods, his seafoam green hair, swirling above him. "You two ready to switch?"

I nod, letting him take my position at the coral. Caspian guides me back down to the sand, settling next to me as we stretch out and try to sleep.

When I wake up, Dylana is shaking me. Merrick hovers at the top of the coral, bathed in soft white light—*day.*

"Time to go, sis," Caspian informs me from a few lengths way, adjusting the pouch on his belt.

I quickly float up from my place on the sea floor and hurry to help him fasten his shoulder armor and chest plate. The chains that dangle from it make it nearly impenetrable. We were lucky to have found that ship with all that human metal work on it a few generations ago. We've been passing it down through the years.

I'm grateful I brought one of my heavier *iluses* with me. Hidden beneath the decorations are rows of metal chains that will act as protection for me if I'm attacked.

Following the collection of sirens is harder than following Tiko and the others to Metten—there's far more of them that could accidentally spot us. We stay as far away as possible, trying to keep coral and kelp forests between us.

This time, we take a more direct route home, avoiding the twists and turns that Tiko, Roni, and Tarni took to avoid mer seeing them. These sirens are bold and unafraid of the fight to come.

After a few hours, Dylana leads us into a kelp forest, staying on the very edges of it so that we can still see the sirens. It stretches on forever.

At one point, we end up in a denser part of the kelp as it spirals upward, dancing in the water. I don't worry much when I lose track of the siren collection, assuming the others have kept them in their sights.

Reaching the end of the kelp forest, we hover for a moment, looking at options for our next cover. I lurk further back—the last in line as I watch over my collection—letting Llyr and Merrick take the lead.

Something tugs hard on my tail, dragging me back through the kelp. It happens so quickly, I don't even have time to scream as I'm pulled through the kelp.

Nir has me by the tail, dragging me away form my friends.

"Nope," Tiko's voice says quietly from above as I look for an escape.

I look up just in time to see a net wrapping around me.

CHAPTER 8

Tangled in the net, I fight to reach the shells on my *iluse*. Tiko descends on me, catching the ends of the net, pulling them sharply toward his chest. I'm dragged with the motion.

For coral's sake, we just can't seem to shake these sirens.

Tiko glares at the others.

"I knew you'd never see me sneak up from behind you—you were far too busy looking ahead—I've been waiting for you to go through the dense part of this sun-forsaken kelp forest."

Nir digs into my tail with his nails just above my fins. If I struggle, he could damage them. Tiko pulls on the net, trapping me even more. He bunches up a smaller fishing net that ended up in the sea—one that we might use as part of an *iluse*—and forces it around my mouth so that I can't speak. He carelessly ties it in back, catching my hair as he pulls it into the knot.

Tears sting at my eyes, and, for a moment, I wish the human myth about crying pearls was true so that I could aim them at my captors and free myself. Instead, I growl through the netting in my mouth.

"Calm down before you rip a fin off, *mer*," Tiko advises.

Water glides over my skin and scales as they drag the net and me away from the kelp forest. I twist, trying to see behind me.

The moment Merrick sees me in the distance, his face bleaches like coral.

"No," he swims for me, but we're too far away.

Stretching my hand out, I try to get him to stop. Only Morgen and

Llyr manage to bring him to a halt, yanking back on his arms until they can control his tail. Together, they drag him back to the kelp.

Dylana looks like she's going to be sick, but she murmurs quietly to Caspian who looks ready to murder every last siren in the ocean to get me back.

"Aww, looks like your friends are sad," Tiko sneers as he pulls me. His finger grazes my tail through the netting accidentally and I cringe. "They're smarter than I thought though. At least they kept their distance."

The entire collection of sirens surrounds me, cutting me off from my friends. They watch helplessly from the edges of the kelp forest.

"Swim along now, and tell the queen we're coming for Scylla," a merman calls to my collection. I assume he's one of their leaders. "Don't worry, we'll bring your friend home soon...she's just here to ensure you do as we ask. If you don't...we'll give her to the humans."

He turns his back to my collection.

"Follow them," he instructs, waving Tiko, Roni, and two others toward my mer. They swim off, waiting for Caspian and the others to swim home without me.

I try to lock eyes with anyone from my collection, but making out facial details is hard at this distance. My own expression morphs from one of sadness and fear into one of shock as I'm lifted higher in the water. Making good on their promise, Nir takes off toward the surface.

I barely hear my collection call out as the water rushes passed my ears. I struggle against the ropes, but it's hopeless as we draw danger-ously close to the surface.

They start to move, swimming away from the kelp forest, but Nir doesn't stop. I gasp as we reach the glassy top of the water, breaking out into cool air.

Pushing, I try get my hair out of my eyes so that I can see. The cool air stings my skin.

Admittedly, I have been to the surface before. I've felt the wind and seen what the waves look like on the other side of the water. I shouldn't have, but I did it while hiding behind the secrecy my missions have offered me.

This is different though. This is raw and rough and unwanted. I don't want to be in the human world.

The more I struggle, the more tangled I become.

"Calm down," Nir instructs me, for the first time looking into my eyes. "You will behave or I will swim to the nearest human ship and attach you to their anchor so that when they pull you up, they'll skin you alive and tie you to their ship. It is a cruel and painful way to die."

I try to reply, but the net in my mouth muffles my words. I breathe sharply through my nose and anger floods through me.

Nir looks familiar—dark brown hair, dark tail, eyes I nearly recognize.

I study him another moment before I figure it out—he's one of *us*.

I try to speak again as he ducks under the water, allowing us to rest close enough to the surface to touch it if we wanted to. Bubbles follow us down.

He reaches through the net, removing my gag.

"Who are you?" I demand. I shouldn't be so bold this close to the surface, but I have to know.

"I'm not important."

"Clearly you *are*, Nir." I use his name, trying to unsettle him. "Who do you come from?"

"From mer you've never met."

"You come from the royals, don't you?" His eyes twitch as I ask the question.

"How do you know that?"

"You have features from the royal line. I can tell. You look like the queen and her siblings."

"I see," he nods knowingly.

Please don't let him get a good look at my eyes.

"I come from the siren queen's line."

He finally begins to lower us in the water, returning to the ocean floor.

Chantay must have named herself queen after King Gaspar banished her. Unlike Persephone, Chantay built another life for herself, including, so it seems, new children to take up her mantle— we were wrong to think her line ended with her eldest daughter.

"That makes you a prince?" I ask, trying not to show fear.

"That makes me the merman who will sit on the throne after my father takes Scylla. Oh look," he changes the tenor of his voice, "there go your little friends. I guess they took your death seriously—you should be flattered. Sirens know better than to abandon their mission."

"Is that why that red-tailed girl Tiko and Roni carried off died? Her mission was to untangle a silly little shiny thing from a fisherman's net and die in the process?"

"She was stupid and unfit to siren," he counters, lifting the net over his shoulder so I'm resting against his broad back. His skin is warm against my scales and completely uncomfortable. "Anyone dumb enough to get themselves tangled in a net for the sake of a trinket deserves what they get."

"She got sliced to pieces," I point out over his shoulder. "They peeled back her skin and scales and cut her into shark bait."

"Which is exactly what I'll do to you if you don't clam up, *mermaid*."

I work my hands toward my *iluse*, going after my knife that I have hidden inside. I quietly begin to snap the net open as I wiggle around, trying to conceal the fact that I'm close to escaping.

Of course, figuring out what to do once I'm free of the net should *also* be high on my priority list.

I reach through the net, putting my hand on Nir's shoulder to try to get a better look at where Caspian and the others are. They're so far ahead that I can only see Tiko's periwinkle tail flipping away. My heart sinks like a book thrown into the ocean—though those are more fun to collect.

We travel for a while as I remain tucked away in the now-loose net. The older merman from before swims up to us, having a conversation with his son around me—he's Nir's father and king of the sirens.

Shark skin covers his shoulder armor, trailing down his chest and back. His long, dark hair is snarled and bits of shells are tied into it at different heights.

"Why the shark skin?" I ask, prompting the older mer to look at me.

"We don't waste things," the older mer replies curtly.

"So you kill sharks?"

"When needed," he scowls at me. "It warns our enemies."

They think the skins will impress the mer? Hardly.

The muscles in Nir's arms are taut as he transfers the net to his other shoulder, bumping me along his back. I grab on to the netting, ensuring I don't accidentally slip out before the time is right.

"You disrespect sea life the way you disrespect human life," I say judgmentally.

"We were created to be superior, child," he growls. "We wouldn't have been given the gift of sireny if we weren't supposed to use it."

"The humans weren't hurting us," I spit back.

"They were going to kill us one way or another. Persephone knew that and tried to position herself into a place where she could control what they did to us—it was only a matter of time."

"Persephone fell in love with the prince. Her intentions were less than noble—she wanted someone to command. She wasn't trying to help the mer—that was Chantay's line once she discovered what was happening."

"How do *you* know? Were you there? Did you see it?"

"You come from Chantay's line," I admit what I know, making the muscle's in Nir's neck tighten in anger. "You believe whatever she told you. You believed her lies."

Several sirens turn to watch the exchange as they swim. My back is killing me after riding around in the net for the last hour. My tail needs to be stretched out and I'm desperate to free my arms. The sirens eye me warily.

We pause and Nir lowers me to the ground.

"*Don't move,*" Nir punctuates his words, glaring at me. I hold still on the ocean floor, trying not to breathe heavily.

I'm safer on his shoulders than I am on the ground.

The sirens all float to the sea floor, resting their fins for a few minutes. A scout darts back after a little while.

"Sir, sharks up ahead. There's an entire shiver of them."

"Do it," the older mer nods.

The scout moves over to a group closer to the front. Inside of a large pouch one of the sirens had been carrying on his back is a baby shark.

I watch in horror as it wriggles trying to get away. They stop the small thing, slicing it open.

The scout holds it in front of him, swimming full speed toward where the sharks must have been sighted.

The sirens all nod appreciatively over the death.

"The smell of death," one of the sirens murmurs in reverence to my right as he watches the scene over top of me.

So sharks fear the scent of dead sharks—that's how they broke the barrier. It all makes sense. It also explains the skins the sirens wear.

I glance up, hoping they don't realize I overheard and put it together—this information will come in handy when I make it back.

If I make it back.

"Tarni," the older mer says harshly.

The mermaid with the peach tail and trembling lip swims up to us.

"Yes, father?" she asks, voice quivering slightly.

So I'm distantly related to *this one* too—for coral's sake, how many of these sirens share my blood?

"This mermaid talks too much. She needs to be taught a lesson." He hands her a knife as her eyes grow wide.

My body involuntarily trembles.

"Nir can hold her down while you work," he turns, swimming away to handle other matters.

"Please, Tarni," I beg, trying to hide my fins under me as I wriggle on the ocean floor. "Please don't."

If she touches my fins, I will lock her in a treasure chest and leave her inside the darkest cavern I can find until she's nothing but a pile of bones like Persephone.

"Hold still," she says more confidently. Nir presses down on my hips as his sister swims toward the end of my tail.

"Please!" I plead.

I can't let her take my fins. I'll die without them. Mermaids can't survive if they can't swim. I can't let her hurt them.

I thrash, trying to evade the knife.

"Clam up!" she commands. "I'm only taking some scales. It could be worse—he could make me cut off your fins."

She holds the knife carefully, eyes running the length of my tail as she picks a spot to remove my purple scales. I sob uncontrollably— I've been taught better.

She grimaces before closing her eyes, concentrating.

"Tarni, *please!*"

"What's your name?" she asks, pausing.

I blink, confused at her words.

"Len," I finally answer.

"Len, just hold still. It will be over soon," she promises as she digs the knife into my tail, peeling up a scale from the underside. Her face twitches.

I scream, frightening several nearby sirens. They gather around to watch.

I can't pretend I don't have a way to escape—she's peeling off my scales. I give up my secret, bursting from the net. Nir's shock leaves him frozen for a moment before he races after me.

In the frenzy, I knock Tarni back, snatching the knife from her hand. The older siren turns, watching how his children react as I hold the knife out to them.

My training flips on, quiet and fierce. I wait for them to approach me, dropping my shoulders down. When I strike, I draw blood.

Ripping the knife across a siren's shoulder, he reels back in pain. Nir smirks at the siren's reaction, the giant welts still covering his face from the day before.

Reaching up, I remove the silver conch shell off of my grandmother's necklace. I swipe it toward another siren, slicing him across the arm. His entire body goes into shock as the poison runs through his system. I quickly reattach it while they're all watching him twist and turn involuntarily.

As I am distracting them, none of the sirens notice the pod of dolphins swimming our way near the surface. Just as Nir approaches me, I thrust my tail, propelling myself up. The knife sinks into his shoulder, giving me enough time that his fingers barely graze the end of my fin as I latch on to a dolphin.

We dart away, the pod surrounding me protectively as we jump in and out of the water on the surface of the ocean. Each slap of wind horrifies me, but anything is better than staying with the sirens.

After a few minutes, the dolphins slow, returning to lower depths.

"I have to get to Scylla." I will them to understand me. "I have to warn the queen. Take me to Scylla."

They chatter at me, clicking and nodding their heads as if they understand. I supposed they do, as they take me toward my home.

I cling to the dolphin's dorsal fin as he races through the water playfully. As a mer child, I always loved swimming with the dolphins. A number of them adored the palace and frequented Dylana's home enough that we gave them names and they swam to us on command for the fish we would give them.

My entire body aches from being trapped inside the net. It tingles like a million tiny shocks from a baby jellyfish.

Once, when I was young, my tail brushed against one. I regretted it for an entire day.

We glide through the water higher than I'm used to swimming when traveling. It gives me a different view of the ocean.

We quickly come upon the sirens that the king sent after my friends, their backs to us as we approach.

Tiko and the other sirens hold tridents out to my friends who are preparing to take them on to get back to me, daring them to swim closer. Llyr holds his up too while the others threaten with only their knives. Dylana sees me first over the shoulders of the sirens. She uses her tail to slap Caspian quietly. The rest of my collection notices the pod of dolphins swimming toward them. I wave wildly, trying to get their attention.

Similarly to how I escaped, they bide their time, waiting for us to get close enough.

Dylana brilliantly holds her hands up in surrender, pretending to convince the mermen to turn around and leave instead of fight for me. They swim toward Scylla slowly—it's almost painful to watch. Tiko, Roni, and the others don't move as they try to put a little distance between them and the mer.

It's their downfall.

Merrick and Caspian dart up at the same time, flicking their tails to out swim the sirens. There is a pause between the time my collection races toward us and when the sirens realize what is happening—they're not used to being in situations that they can't control with their voices.

Dylana, Morgen, Caspian, Llry, and Merrick grab onto the dolphins that immediately speed up, dragging us higher in the water. We leave the sirens behind us, Merrick laughing over our victory.

We cling to the dolphins until they slow an hour later. When they pause to feed, we sink to the ocean floor, knowing they won't stray far. I believe they really *do* know what I said and will take us back to Scylla.

My friends don't even have to ask this time. They simply look at me.

"I'm okay."

"Your tail says otherwise," Dylana replies, voice flat.

They all glance down to my missing scales.

"I can't catch a break." I try to play it off. "Oh, good news, Casp, Morgen, and Dylana—we have new cousins."

"Excuse me?" Dylana asks, crossing her arms.

"You want to explain that?" Morgen doesn't sound impressed.

"Celena?" Caspian waits, swimming up next to me as he runs his hands through my hair to soothe me.

"Apparently Chantay had at least one child after King Gaspar kicked her out of Metten. She has decedents."

"Please be Roni, please be Roni, please be Roni," Morgen mutters.

One of the dolphins swims down to check on us, bumping Llyr with his nose. Llyr pets his side as he swims back to his pod overhead.

"Nir and Tarni," I answer.

"We're related to the sea monster?" Caspian doesn't sound surprised. "I'm shocked."

"I'd like to say it could be worse, but can it?" Dylana asks.

"Their father commanded Tarni pry up my scales. I had cut the net they were holding me in and decided I shouldn't wait any longer. The dolphins were a happy accident." I motion to my saviors.

"Celena," Dylana says cautiously. "We saw Nir drag you up to the surface…"

"I'm okay, Dylana. Really."

She doesn't look convinced.

"It's horrifying," she finally responds.

"Cousin," I reply gently. "I've been up there before. It's really fine."

Caspian's eyes grow wide. Everyone but Merrick looks shocked.

"It was only twice and never around humans," I try to back swim.

It doesn't work. They look at me disapprovingly.

"Your scale will grow back." Merrick changes the subject. "It looks like our ride is ready to move on. Shall we?"

We swim up, positioning ourselves in their slipstream to make traveling easier.

They take us as far as they can before night falls, then further.

I'm exhausted by the time we stop. The dolphins slowed while some of them rested, taking short naps while swimming at a slower pace. I am grateful they don't need to stop to rest.

The others look nervous when we surface, catching bits of air as the dolphins breathe. The first time, I panic, worried about humans possibly being in the area. After that, I'm too tired to care.

The air continues to sting, but it's a good kind of pain—it means freedom.

Merrick and Caspian laugh the second time we rise out of the water, enjoying the new sensation. Morgen looks horrified but his sister only glances at me to get a read.

I tip my head back as the water drips off my hair, breathing in the smells of the surface. We almost instantly retreat under the water.

"I think we've learned a valuable lesson here, mermen," Merrick announces as we dip under the water. "Mermaids look *very* different above the surface."

"Hey," Dylana and I protest tiredly.

"You can't blame a guy for noticing the difference in your hair," he points out.

"You're a jerk, Merrick."

"And you looked like a slicked-back sea lion," he retorts.

"Merrick!" Caspian and I shout together.

Maybe he was doing it to help us stay awake, maybe he was trying to be funny. Either way, I wanted to slap him with my fins.

At some point, we decide to take turns sleeping. In pairs, one stays awake and makes sure we hold onto our rides while we rest and then we switch.

Morning comes far too quickly, and with it comes disaster.

CHAPTER 9

The dolphins put us within swimming distance of Scylla. By the time the sun filters through the water, we can see the outskirts of the city.

Our conch message had arrived and we are greeted by our best-trained warriors. They part in the water, allowing us to swim through. Marilla floats at the back of the mass of mer, planning our next move with my mother and the other cousins who act as her advisors.

"You're back?" Marilla asks when she sees us.

"We arrived a day early," Dylana explains. "Dolphins."

"Thank goodness for those gorgeous creatures," Marilla adds quickly. "What do we need to know?"

The princess details everything we have experienced, skipping the part about breaking the surface. Marilla and my mother listen to every detail, turning to their maps to figure out where the sirens will be coming from to attack.

We show them where the shark barrier is broken before I realize I hadn't told anyone *how* the sirens broke it. They're shocked to learn the sirens' trick, though their shock is reasonable since we only kill sea life if absolutely necessary and haven't witnessed the impact it has on the other creatures.

"We'll need to remember that," Marilla remarks, nodding to one of the cousins who is in charge of keeping histories for the mer.

"We have one day to prepare," Marilla announces to the crowd.

"We will be breaking you into teams to give you assignments. The sirens want to take Scylla—we will not let them.

"Take all of the mer children and get them to safety. Our most skilled fighters will be put in place to protect them. No matter what becomes of us, they are our future and will be our priority in this campaign." The collection nods in agreement.

For mer, the future is more important than the past. If our city should fall, we can recover. If we lose our hope for the future of our society, we lose everything. Nothing has meaning without them.

"Prepare yourselves," she shouts. "War is here."

Mercifully, the queen keeps us all together. We spend the day resting to regain our strength.

The sirens will not arrive until tomorrow, so now is the time to let our bodies heal.

My mother sighs at my missing scale and the other injuries I suffered at the hands of the sirens.

"We haven't engaged with the sirens in a century and *you* had to be the one to go and pick a fight."

"They came after me, Mama. I didn't go looking for this." I wave at my bruised body.

"Mmm." She purses her lips as she hands me something. "Swallow it. It will help."

I do as she asks, regretting it the second it touches my tongue—it tastes awful.

"And you—" She turns on Caspian. "How long have you known about this?"

"I knew less than father knew," he reports. "I just assumed you were involved somehow. I knew it was my job to know how to protect you, Celena, and Coralie—that's all."

"And you, Morgen?" the queen demands an answer from her son, crossing her arms to match my mother.

"The same, Mother."

Our fathers will have a lot of explaining to do later.

The queen and my mother shake their heads before retreating from the house we are resting in, leaving us alone.

"I guess we're not the only ones who are bad at communicating," Caspian muses, tipping his head back on the lounging couch.

"Celena, come over here and let me handle your hair," Dylana waves me over. I settle on the floor in front of her.

War isn't something the mer have dealt with much aside from generations ago. The most we've seen is when sea creatures act aggressively toward the mer, which isn't often.

Still, we're familiar with how it works. We've always been prepared for fighting—sirens, humans, or the seas. The mer are used to pageantry and war is no exception.

The mermen polish their shoulder armor. When they finish, they move on to shine ours while we braid our hair back. Dylana's hands are skilled as she works my locks back into an intense set of braids. She weaves broken shells into the strands to prevent the sirens from trying to pull me back by my hair.

When we switch places, I start at the crown of her head, twisting her long, dark pink hair back. I pile it into a twisted design that wraps around her skull, creating a look that mimics the design on her shoulder armor and chest plate.

In war, the rules are different than when we are acting as scouts. We do not hide our positions—we display them proudly.

Dylana's crown is short to avoid weighing her down. It wraps around the front of her head, crystals standing straight up. With any luck, they will catch the light just right and blind her attackers.

Like Dylana did for me, I weave shells into her hair to complete the crown, making the top layer look like a wreath. I add bits of broken coral for added pain should someone touch her.

My hair is uncomfortable while back in its massive braid comprised of many tiny braids rather than floating free, but I've suffered through it for festivals before. I reach up to brush it back, remembering at the last second that I should avoid cutting my fingers before the battle has even begun.

Though we don't sleep, the quiet does us good, restoring our strength. In the corner of the dwelling, a starfish sits, minding its own business. I hope it will survive whatever becomes of Scylla tomorrow.

"I vote that we all stay together tomorrow, no matter what," Caspian breaks our concentration.

"I'm fine with that," Morgen replies, polishing his small-but-magnificent three-pronged crown. I smirk, realizing it looks like he's wearing a trident on his head. It matches his tail.

"Do you honestly think we're going to be able to just magically stay together?" Merrick says realistically. "We can try, but I doubt it's going to happen."

"You and I are not separating," Caspian informs me. "Mother and Father already have their assignments. They'll be together. Coralie is safe with the younger mer—"

"She's going to hate that you just called her that," I interject with a teasing grin.

"She's thirteen. She *is* young. She's not even allowed to date yet."

"Neither are you," I counter on her behalf.

Merrick snorts next to Caspian, earning an elbow to his stomach. I think it hurt Caspian more than it hurt Merrick through the chest plate.

"She's right, Casp," Merrick laughs. "You haven't found anyone yet."

"Neither have you," he retorts, "Unless you count my sister, and now that the truth is out there, we have an explanation for why you two were always together."

"Can't get anything past you…" Merrick mutters, rolling his eyes.

Outside the dwelling, shouts rise up. We instantly float up from our seats and swim toward the door. Mer turn to each other, passing the word along.

Llyr swims outside, leaving the rest of us floating in the doorway. When he returns, his face is grim.

"The scouts haven't been able to locate the sirens," he reports. "We don't know where they are."

"They can't find them?" I repeat, questioning what I had heard.

"No," Llyr confirms. "We have no idea where they are."

"They were clearly on their way here," Caspian jumps in. "They couldn't have just disappeared."

"Maybe they swam out to sea and will be back," Merrick suggests. "It wouldn't be unreasonable for them to circle around and enter somewhere that we aren't expecting."

"It could take *days* for them to arrive, if that's the case." I frown as I speak. I guess we didn't have to get dressed for battle so early.

"I'm sure Mother is already planning to spread us out to watch for them," Dylana adds. "And we have the guards watching the barriers *anyway*…they could probably use some reinforcements though."

"Should we go out there?" I question, not even sure myself how I feel about that idea.

"So that they can lord you and Dylana over us if they find you? Haven't we been through that once already?" Merrick snips.

"You're already going to be on full display—let's not make it easy for them to get to you," Caspian continues. "You two and our mothers are going to be their biggest targets once they arrive."

"I personally vote we lock all four of you up in separate locations and keep you under guard until this is over," Morgen comments, adjusting his crown.

"That's *ridiculous*," Dylana complains.

"We're *not* going into hiding," I add. My body tenses at the thought of not being involved.

"You're also not going to the barrier," Caspian says defiantly.

I hadn't planned on it, but now that he forbade me from going, my tail twitches to swim straight there. It doesn't matter which barrier, as long as it was a barrier.

Or maybe it did.

"We need a map," I proclaim. "We need to figure out where these sirens are going to enter Scylla. Or…*maybe…that's it!*"

I backflip in excitement, spinning around the room.

"Why wait?" I grin at my collection of mer. "Why just float around and wait for them to come to us on their terms?"

"What are you getting at, Len?" Merrick asks.

"I told you, you're not going to the barrier," Caspian repeats himself, thinking my intention is to meet the sirens before they reach us.

"We need to stop thinking like mantis shrimp and start thinking like angler fish." I wait for them to catch on. "We need to bring *them* to *us*. Why try to guess their opportunity for entry when we could create one?"

Merrick's lips part in a smile.

"How far could they have gone and where would they need to loop back?" I ask. "If their plan is to go wide and come back around on us, then there has to be a point at which they will swing back toward Scylla. We need to figure that place out and make a way for them."

"If we can drive them in through a point we already know they will be entering, we can be prepared," Merrick nods appreciatively.

"We need maps," I prompt again. "After Persephone was captured, Lanika spent the next year mapping out the kingdom to protect her daughter from Chantay's retribution. Aila spent years referring to them after but ultimately gave them to Queen Kailania to hold in the palace. We need those maps—they're the most precise things we have and our best chance at finding weaknesses."

"Lanika spearheaded all of the barriers—she knew everything about each one of them," Dylana adds. "I'll send for them."

Swimming to the door, she calls someone over to fetch the maps —the ones Marilla had been using don't contain enough information.

I can't contain my nervous energy. All I want is to swim around the room rapidly, making everyone dizzy.

Merrick takes a place beside me, calming my nerves. He's always has a way of doing that. His fingers twitch beside mine, letting me know that he's aware of my current state, but the tides are changing and I need to handle this myself—I can't always count on him or my friends to take care of me.

We wait for a merman to return with the maps from the palace and spend the rest of the day figuring out where the sirens will be entering.

There's a spot on the southern barrier where the coral doesn't connect. It's not a large area, nor is it one that is easily seen. Mixed in the pinks and peaches of the reef, the gap is big enough for a few mermaids or mermen to slip through at once. The coral overlaps just enough that the only way to see the hole is by being right next to it on our side of the reef. From the siren's side, it's easier to see—when there isn't something blocking it.

From my vantage point, I can't even pick out where it is in the giant wall of the reef.

The beauty of the location is that once you make it through the gap, there's still a maze of coral to wind your way through—it would be easy to wander aimlessly, staring at the creatures on the reef, if one didn't have a mission to attend to.

Today, we have a mission.

We've spent the entire day waiting—they *have* to be coming through here. It's the only thing that makes sense.

On the far side of the coral sits the only barricade between the sirens and us—a wooden boat that sank long before Aila's time. Nothing about it is modern, making it easy to pry apart.

Our collection had worked on it all through the night with only the midwater squid light mixed with the rays of the moon by which to see. Board by board, they took it apart and moved it inside the reef barrier. We hid it inside the cavern. With the boat gone, the sirens have a crystal clear view of the opening in the coral, which, I assume, they too already know is there.

We haven't seen any sign of sirens here in a generation, which should lend itself to them not being aware of when we dismantled the ship—if they realize we did it overnight, they'll know it's a trap.

Merrick's shoulders sway up and down in the water next to me as we wait. Despite floating in the same place all day, he's hyper-aware of everything happening outside of the cave we're hiding in. It's amazing how attentive and disciplined he is—my mind began wandering hours ago.

The rest of our collection is hiding below us in the tangles of seaweed that has overgrown the area. There's enough space between the reef and the seaweed that the sirens should feel secure—we're going to let them inside our borders before attacking—though I don't like the idea of not being permitted to get involved unless its absolutely necessary.

Dylana sighs next to me.

That's when I see it—a flash near the coral.

It darts in and out so quickly that I can't tell if I actually saw it or if it was a piece of debris catching the light that is about to start to fade away for the evening. I stare at the spot, elbowing Merrick.

A shoulder peeks out from behind the coral, followed by a head of shockingly red hair—the sirens have arrived.

She moves quietly out into the open, several of her friends in her wake. One of the sirens has the most beautiful coral and silver tail that reminds me of what my great-great-grandma Aila's tail must have looked like—though hers was gold and coral.

We move further back into the cavern, letting Llyr stand guard at the mouth of the cave. I fixate on his hand, waiting for some kind of signal. Caspian places his hand on the end of my tail, letting me know he's there before swimming a bit closer. He rests his hands on my shoulders as he floats above me, watching over my head.

Noise rises up outside. Llyr quickly holds his hand up, forcing us to stay put. Dylana doesn't care and slowly moves forward toward the entrance. Sinking to the ground, she crawls forward, letting her tail hover just far enough off the sand and rocks that she doesn't scrape her scales as she pulls her body forward.

She peeks up over the edge of the cave, one shoulder jerking back at the sight. The rest of her holds steady as she watches the scene. Her chin tips up in defiance, tilting her crown back just slightly.

Maybe she shouldn't be by the entrance where the lights can catch the crystals on her crown and give us away.

"We've got to go," Llyr announces, not bothering to look back at us. Dylana shoots straight up in the water before throwing herself out of the cavern's mouth.

My eyes widen in surprise but Merrick's quick motions compel me to follow. We leave the shelter of the cave and dart into the blue ocean. Below us, the mer and sirens fight.

The sirens still wear bits of shark flesh on their armor, though I think that's more for show. With tridents in hand, they attack our mer as they hover above the seaweed they had been hiding in.

Somehow, the sirens moved around the mer collection, positioning themselves between the barrier and Scylla. They're attempting to force our collection back toward the reef as we join them.

"Well, look who it is," Roni sneers, flicking her orange and brown tail as she swims toward the reef barrier. "Come and get me…"

Her eyes grow wide when she notices our crowns—there's no hiding our identities anymore. The rules of war under the sea have given us away.

"Good luck, *princesses*," she calls, bending herself in half as she swims backward, mimicking a bow. She holds her trident out to us as if she means to defend herself despite the distance between us—her face assures us that she thinks she has the upper hand.

She grins, darting through the opening in the coral.

"What do we do?" Caspian asks. "We don't know what's on the other side."

"Our people are on the other side," Merrick responds. "They forced them through and whether it's a trap or not, we can't leave them there."

He's gone instantly, his blue hair a mere flash before he disappears. Without thinking, I follow, leaving Casp to protest behind me.

"Get her out of here, Morgen," Caspian quickly instructs.

Only Caspian and Llyr follow through the barrier as the prince removes his sister from the scene. I'm sure they'll fight together on the Scylla-side of the barrier, but we can't afford to lose royals to the sirens' territory—especially both of them. Dylana's sisters aren't ready to take the crown yet and if anything happens to her, it falls on Morgen to lead.

"They have the queen," Llyr informs us as we tangle our way through the reef and swim into the open. "That's what we saw."

"*Swordfish*, that's bad," Casp mumbles. "So much for staying back."

"Did you honestly expect Queen Marilla to *stay back*?" I snap.

Ahead, several sirens hold on to Marilla's wrists and tail, preventing her from resisting against them. They pull her back in the water, further and further away from the barrier. She bucks under their grip, but they have her tail and she can't fight without being able to move it freely.

"About time you showed up," Roni taunts us, floating far enough away that even if we swim full speed at her, she'll be able to easily escape. "I take it this isn't Mommy…which means…*auntie?*"

She appraises the crowns Caspian and I wear, a clear indicator of our royal heritage, but not as grand as the ones the reigning royals wears. The mermaid grimaces when she notices the jagged shells woven into my braids.

"Well now, that won't do. I guess there's no taking you home to the king—I'll just have to stab you instead."

If I could put my spear through the base of her fin and pin her to the sand, I would.

Llyr gasps quietly beside us. I look beyond Roni and discover the sirens have used a chunk of coral to knock the queen unconscious. Her body sinks toward the ocean floor, but they lift her back up—bleeding—and swim away with her.

"Where are you taking her?" I demand.

"Control the queen, control the kingdom," Roni sings but her eyes spark—there's more to this.

If Marilla falls, Dylana instantly takes over. They can take a queen, but they'll never remove the crown from power as long as even one royal exists in this sea.

"Bye, mer children." She flips backward, twisting in the water as she moves. Several others join her, rushing after our abducted queen.

They have a head start on us, but the entire collection of mer on this side of the wall swims after our captured queen and friends. Several other mer are dragged backward by their tails. They reach for us, calling for help. I can't tell how long we swim—minutes or hours —but we're far enough away that the barrier can barely be seen on the horizon of the ocean floor.

Everything stills around us as the sirens slow.

My scales prickle.

"This isn't right," Merrick whispers.

We pause in the water, watching the sirens. They turn to face us, holding Marilla and the others in the middle of the ocean.

The water goes icy as a shadow passes over us. I look up to find a single tail floating down from the surface, it's blue color nearly matching the water as we look up.

The boat moves closer, directly on top of us. The nets quickly move behind us. A mermaid screams as she finds herself entangled in it—she didn't notice it was behind her.

The humans cast more nets, sending spears plummeting into the water. One hits a merman's tail, piercing him. Blood clouds around him, dyeing the water a pink tone as the life fades away from him.

I turn back as the sirens smirk—*they had planned this all along.*

They keep a safe distance between the mer collection and themselves as their companion sirens the humans from above, directing them where to catch us.

The water is shallow enough here, that should the humans dare to enter the water, they could swim to the bottom and return to the surface on a single, skilled breath.

The sirens had forced us into the shallows—it's the humans' hunting grounds. Their ships must be compact fishing vessels rather than large boats made for transportation and long distances. These humans only had one mission—catching fish and mer.

Merrick moves forward first, rushing toward the net, knife in hand. I swim after him, reaching for his trident to give him the freedom to move without restriction as he cuts our mer free. Caspian's hand darts out, handing me his as well.

I balance the tridents in the crook of my arm, fumbling for my own knife as I hack at the nets that are quickly being pulled to the surface with our screaming friends.

Llyr takes off toward the sirens.

A net catches my tail, setting me off balance. I nearly drop the tridents, catching them just in time to find myself being rapidly propelled toward the surface upside down.

Merrick and Caspian's horrified faces are the last thing I see before I breach the waves and dangle in the cool air.

CHAPTER 10

Water drips off my scales, down my stomach and across my face. Something about the water running over my scales backward in little streams makes me cringe as much as the kiss of the salty air does.

The blue siren sits in the water, singing her vicious song as she directs the humans to catch and murder us. She nearly looks like she's in a trance the way she stares back and forth between the fishing boats. She never makes eye contact with me.

The other mer that have been caught are forced onto the decks of the boats after dangling in the air. Some hang upside down like me, others fight to turn themselves sideways as they fight against the rough ropes of the nets.

I keep silent, knowing screaming will not help me. I look around as much as I can, trying to understand what I'm about to face.

The waves look different from above the surface—choppy and merciless. Under the water, everything looks far more gentle and refined.

My tail burns from rubbing against the netting I'm hanging out of precariously. Unlike many of my friends, I was not captured inside a net, but rather am tangled in the edge of one, only my fins holding me in place. If I struggle, I could rip them off—a fate nearly as bad as whatever the sailors will do to me.

A shattering scream makes me jerk around anyway. I find a sailor —old and tattered—ripping his knife into a mermaid. She thrashes under his violent touch as blood pours from the gash in her hip. He peels her scales back and I vomit.

I crash hard against the wooden deck of the boat. Several humans grin down at me. I crawl backward on my elbows, trying desperately to escape but there is no hope.

Above me, a firework bursts against the sky. Another follows—another mer caught and killed.

They step toward me, murmuring things as they follow the siren's commands.

The siren.

It's my only chance.

I clutch at one of my tridents, casting the others to the deck alongside of me, hoping the humans can't reach them.

Then I sing.

For a moment, the men only stare at me, still under the command of the blue-tailed siren. They blink for a moment, watching me as I sing.

"Celena!" Caspian screams from somewhere below—the clownfish came to the surface after me. I'm sure Merrick is by his side as well.

The sailors converge on me and I raise my weapon, ready to stab their pathetic little hearts—humans have always had fragile hearts and I intend on taking advantage of that if I must.

Suddenly, they back away. Just one step, but it's enough to tell me I'm winning. I didn't know if I held the voice to siren after so many generations without it, but it's working.

I sing louder, hoping my brother and partner can hear me and will join me in sirening the sailors away from our enemies.

My voice surprises me. We sing all the time in Scylla for festivals and events, but I've never heard myself so powerful before. I wonder if it's because I'm above the surface and things are different here or if it's because I'm motivated to survive.

I sound powerful and strong—my voice even higher than usual.

The humans listen to my melody and I force them back another step.

I've never sirened before—I don't know how it works—but if Persephone could siren Prince Jarek, then I can certainly siren a bunch of murderous fishermen and not regret a thing.

The sky glows pink as it hovers between day and night. It might match the sailors' blood had they been in the water instead of on a boat when I make them turn on each other.

Now their blood glistens red—bold and nauseating.

It runs down their necks, their hands, their chests, their stomachs. It trails from their wounds to the planks I sit on as I wait for them to kill each other under the command of my siren call.

I am worse than Persephone, but a perfect match for her mother, Chantay, as she once sirened all the queen's soldiers to a watery grave in retribution for shackling her daughter to the land until King Gaspar arrived to settle the matter.

The one thing mermaids are not supposed to do is to siren a human. Not only have I sirened many, I've also caused their deaths.

I will take whatever punishment there may be after I get the other mer back into the water.

I command the remaining sailors to lift the mermaids and mermen over the edge of the ships. The mer panic until they realize I am in control. They plummet into the water.

Pieces of dismembered mer are thrown back into the sea making me so unsteady that I nearly lose my siren song.

The blue siren realizes what I'm doing and fights back, calling more to assist her. Together, they can over power my voice and take back control of those that she lost.

I pull myself to a barrel after tossing my other two tridents into the water. I'm heavier on land than in the waves and maneuvering myself is incredibly hard.

Once on the barrel, I can see over the edge of the ship. Sailors remain alive, making their way around the bodies of their fallen comrades as they follow my orders in a daze.

I command the humans to release the rest of the mer, screaming my song loud enough to be heard on most of the ships. Forcing them to move the boats close together is easy as I fight against a group of sirens. When I force the sailors under my sireny to climb from one ship to the other, they obey without question and release the rest of my collection from their procession.

I , however, have no way of reaching the edge of the boat.

Losing control of the humans means they will surely mutilate me, stringing me up on the boom of their ship. I'll bleed all over their deck as the life slips away from me while they watch and mock me.

My only hope is to allow them to do the one thing I can't bring myself to do—I have to let them touch me.

A young man stands nearby. He looks strong enough that I think he can hold me.

"Celena!" Merrick screams in the distance. Caspian's voice sings, attempting to gain control of the humans with me. He seems to be having a harder time than I am at controlling the humans.

The young man, dressed in a light shirt and dark pants lingers in the doorway. He looks as though he just woke up, stumbling to the door to see what the commotion is about on deck.

I sing to him.

I call him to me, making him stop in front of me. I hold my trident to his neck to be sure he really is under my spell.

When I can wait no longer, I lower my weapon and siren him to pick me up.

His hands are gentle as he wraps an arm around my back, the other slipping quietly under my tail.

Tears spring to my eyes, burning and clouding my vision.

Terror courses through me as his skin touches my scales.

This is wrong, this is wrong, this is wrong.

I just want to see Caspian and Merrick again. I just want to go home. If I make it to the sea, I'll never come to the surface again, not even on my silly missions to gather information for the queen.

He grunts as he lifts me into the air, taking away the only stable thing I had in my life—a wooden barrel on the deck of a boat, surrounded by humans that mean to kill me. I hover in his arms as he stands in place, staring straight ahead.

Whether he recognizes that he has a mermaid in his arms or not, I do not know. He waits for my command.

I lower my song, singing for him to take me to the side of the ship.

He poses me on the railing. I linger between air and sea. For a moment, I wait there between two worlds.

His fingers twitch against me, making me worry that he might be waking up from my sireny song.

A small boat has been cut free from the side of the fishing vessel. It bobs in the rough waters. One oar sits in the bottom of the boat while another rests outside, only the very edge still remaining in the metal contraption on the side of the boat meant to keep it in place. We occasionally find missing oars at the bottom of the ocean—they make excellent shelves for our grotto walls.

"Release your love into the sea and wait by your boat-side until she returns," I sing, deciding to spare him the certain death I committed the rest of the sailors to—I could have easily told him to throw himself into the sea with me.

He leans forward as if to kiss me—perhaps using fancy words was not my best choice, but I didn't want him to remember too much of this when he comes back around and filling his head with romantic stories of lovers by the sea was the first thing that came to mind.

I push away, falling backward off the ship.

Plummeting to the water, it knocks the breath out of me when I crash against the surface. I see bioluminescent spots in front of my eyes as everything clouds black for a moment.

I feel sick as someone pulls me through the water but I don't have time—or stomach contents—to be sick again. Instead, I force my eyes shut and hope I survive.

"It's me," Merrick croons quietly, assuring me I haven't been caught by a siren. I whimper in reply.

My tail aches. My body shudders against the water resisting against our movements. I concentrate from behind the darkness of my eyelids, trying to discern if my knife is still on my hip.

"Celena!" Merrick commands, realizing that I'm not with him. "Come back to me!"

I force my eyes open. The sea isn't spinning as much.

"We have a job to do," he says harshly, trying to activate me to help him instead of acting like a barnacle on the hull of a sunken ship, clinging to his strong arm as he pulls me through the water.

Caspian catches up to us, eyes wide as he swims behind me. Focusing on him helps.

When we slow, I release Merrick's arm. Caspian dives to the ocean floor, retrieving the tridents I had discarded while still on the ship. He hands one to Merrick, keeping the other for himself. Miraculously, I managed to hold on to my own during my fall.

"You sirened them," Merrick says quietly, looking disappointed in me.

"She had no choice," Caspian protests. "She had to survive...and she saved all those mer."

"I'm not criticizing her, Casp," Merrick says sadly. He looks at me dismally.

"I know," I whisper. "We can't right now though, we have to end this."

"Llyr," Caspian whispers harshly. He takes off around us.

It's days like this that make me think we can't ever move slowly—we always have to be rushing around like the waves slapping against the side of the boats still floating above us.

"Nets," a merman yells somewhere. The sirens must have control of the humans again. I should have killed them all while I had the chance—too bad Aila was in my head while I was above—she worked too hard to preserve human life for me to callously take more than I had to for survival.

Nir hovers near Marilla. She's conscious now, watching us intently. His father stands with a sword above Marilla's neck—he's going to behead the queen.

Llyr floats nearby, trident posed to strike at least one of the sirens. His rage is checked, but I can see the tenseness in his shoulders from all the way over here.

Overhead, the sirens start calling the humans into the sea, assuming we will take up Aila's heart-cry and save them—they're wrong, of course. The sailors fling themselves into the ocean, swimming toward us. We ignore them, turning on the sirens.

"What do we have here?" Nir's father calls, remaining next to Marilla. "A princess, I see. How quaint. Whom do you belong to?"

Marilla glares at me, instructing me to keep quiet. If I admit I'm from Aila's line, I may suffer a worse fate than Marilla will.

"Release the queen," Merrick calls, taking the focus off of my crown.

"And who are you?" the siren king replies.

"He's one of the ones from Metten," Nir mutters, glaring at us.

"Shocking," Nir's father rolls his eyes.

Of the entire collection on this side of the barrier, Merrick and I are the most likely to be able to save Marilla. I flick my tail, moving forward with the current.

"What about a trade?" I ask.

"Why would we do that?" the siren king eyes me.

"Why wouldn't you?" I counter, being vague on purpose.

Marilla glares at me, lips tightening.

"You're one of Aila's..." he muses. Nir stiffens next to him, pupils dilating slightly.

"Why now?" I ask, swimming forward slowly. They watch as I approach.

He tips his head, looking at me thoughtfully.

"My wife is dead. She has no female heir to carry on Chantay's legacy. Revenge ends now because it can not go on another generation."

I squint at him. He sees me glancing toward Tarni in the crowd.

"She's not blood. We took her in as a baby when my brother died."

"You live the life you want," Marilla interjects. "Why change things now? We've gone generations without harming each other."

"Not for lack of trying," the king responds, tightening his hold on the rope wrapped around Marilla's upper body. Rope will be far easier to remove than chains at least.

Sirens…always holding a grudge.

Marilla breathes deeply, moving her entire body as she does. She uses the distraction to slip a hand up into her *iluse* and returns with a broken shell. She quietly begins cutting away at the rope, allowing us to be her distraction.

"And you think this war won't go on after this generation?" I call out.

"My father and I will honor my mother's wishes. We will see to it that the mer pay for what was done to Persephone," Nir snaps, glancing at his father.

"Persephone did that to herself," Merrick counters. "She didn't use her head. She messed up and played the game wrong."

"You want to try to end this, little mer girl?" The king shouts to me. "The only way is for one of Chantay's to battle one of Aila's."

I am to fight Nir.

"*I'm* one of Aila's," Caspian pushes in front of me. "Son against son…*since you have no daughters.*"

Caspian's taunts don't help the situation.

He puffs his chest out like a puffer fish, making himself look as menacing as possible. I understand that our father trained him, and that he's trying to protect me, but this is getting silly.

"Her," the king says, requiring that I take on his son in battle. "If she succeeds, we'll consider going our own way. If she fails, you concede to us in a harmless transfer of power."

His hair floats in front of him toward the queen.

"You'll only kill me in the process," Marilla warns everyone.

"We'll spare your children though…maybe," the siren king's lips tick up just enough to let us know he's enjoying the exchange.

Nir swims forward, clutching his trident.

"You have to go through me first," Merrick interrupts, forcing his way in front of my brother and me.

"No," I counter loudly. "This is my fight."

"If you interefer, mer boy," the king adds, "you will secure your queen's very painful death."

I look around. There are more sirens then there are mer. Should we engage with them, it will be a tough battle.

I eye the shark fins resting on Nir's shoulders. The skin of the creature covers part of his chest. I imagine he has armor on under that. Stabbing him might prove to be rather difficult. If, however, I can take out his tail, I have a chance of winning. It's a cruel reality, but he wouldn't hesitate when it came to me. In fact, he's likely going to go after my fins in the first place—I'll have to watch that.

Nir lashes out before anyone can move, striking at Merrick. His trident hits, tearing Merrick's arm open. He grunts in surprise. Our enemy reels back, preparing for another attack.

I flick my tail, darting in front of Merrick as I take the second strike. I thrust my trident up, locking it with my distant cousin's. The metal clashes.

Nir's eyes grow large, anger overtaking him.

Nothing about the fight is easy. He doesn't care that I'm a mermaid half his size. He's fighting for his mother's dying wishes—to destroy what is left of Aila and Kailania's blood.

Tarni shrieks next to Tiko and Roni. The two chant, encouraging Nir to violently destroy me.

No one comes to my rescue—they don't have a choice—they can't interfere.

I feel like I'm reliving that moment in the Metten palace, though, there are no walls for me to crash into this time. Nir grunts, lowering himself in the water as he levels his body with the ground and swims straight at me.

I hold my place, waiting for the impact. I attempt to keep my tail behind me while holding out the trident. In the background, I hear someone helping Merrick to stop the bleeding.

At the last second, Nir changes directions and veers off, positioning himself to hit my partner.

CHAPTER 11

My scales prickle as I dart toward Nir's dark tail. I'm positive I look like a fish caught in a net, struggling to find an escape as I attempt to save my friend.

A shout resounds through the water—the queen is free and fighting back.

I latch on to Nir's arm, attempting to pull him off course as he swims toward Merrick and Caspian. My brother pushes our injured friend behind him, ready to take the brunt of the attack.

Unable to use my trident because I'm so close to him, and finding everything else proving ineffective, I do the only thing left that I can think of to do—I bite him with what I pray contains the sting of a thousand jellyfish.

He screams, attempting to move away from me but I dig my nails into his arm. He drags me with him, scratching at my face. Nir clips me, leaving what I assume will be a nasty gash down the length of my neck and part of my shoulder. I wonder if he feeds my skin that is now under his nails to the sharks, will they learn my taste and come seek me out? I wouldn't put it past him to try.

When I finally let go, he isn't expecting me to do anything else. I take the opportunity to punch him in the nose, right next to the horrific welts the jellyfish left. Blood clouds around him as I desperately swim to my mermen. They blink at me in surprise.

"Okay then," Merrick says, still in shock over my display of unique defense. "Time to move."

He regains his balance, cradling his arm. He, Caspian, and several others turn on Nir as I swim back to help Marilla. She fights against the siren king with Roni and Tiko at his side.

I poke Roni in the back with the long end of my trident. The moment she turns to find out what knocked her forward, I whip my trident around, crashing into her torso with the flat side of my weapon. It knocks her into Tiko. I jab at his abdomen, not intending to actually hit him. He shoots back, trying to avoid contact with the points.

I slash the trident down toward Roni's tail and she screams in surprise as I nearly brush some of her scales. Marilla grapples with the siren king, nearly gaining control of his trident—if she can take it from him, she can escape.

A body drifts by me—the sailors sirened into the water didn't make it. I push it aside with my trident, angling it toward Tiko and Roni as they grimace. The merman grabs the body and shoves it aside.

The light above me wanes as a ship floats overhead. The shadow is cool to the touch but I shouldn't take the time to notice.

A loud cry fills the area from behind me—mer reinforcements have made their way through the barrier to aid in our fight. Marilla uses the opportunity to strike at the siren king as I face off with Tiko and Roni.

The two converge on me, attempting to surround me—they've forgotten that unless there is a wall or barrier, two mer can't adequately block in a third—there's always a way out. I back up in the water as they approach, though I don't back down.

The two attack, clashing against my trident. Roni attempts to rip at my tail once I knock her trident out of her grasp. I pull back, trying to avoid her talons. One quick jab at Tiko's eyes gives me a little space in the water.

The others reach us after a few moments, making it a more fair fight. We tangle with the sirens, injuring each other in the process. Roni grins as she scrapes her nails along the end of my tail, just before my fins. I cry out in pain and retaliate, cutting her hand open with my trident.

"Celena!" my mother cries as she approaches us.

She drives a knife into Nir's shoulder as I turn around. Merrick quickly darts away from the merman, joining me in my fight as my parents assist Caspian.

Merrick's arm looks stiff as he tries not to use it, though clearly he hasn't had that luxury. He tries to hide the pain in his eyes, but I can tell he's suffering.

I won't let Tiko or Roni cause any more damage.

Before Merrick can lash out at them, I flick my tail, moving as quickly as I can to take them by surprise. Turning my trident sideways, I hold it level to the ground in front of me. When we collide, it sweeps both of them back, knocking them off balance.

I use the opportunity to grab hold of Tarni. I wrench her around, wrapping my arm across her chest. Balancing my trident with my tail, I pull my knife and hold it to her throat.

"Stay back," I warn.

Tiko and Roni look furious but hold their ground.

"Cooperate and you won't get hurt," I hiss in Tarni's ear.

I glare at her friends, daring them to disobey me.

"Remove your sirens," I command. "Now."

"You know that won't happen," Roni protests.

"Get your king and tell him to leave," I instruct her, moving the knife near Tarni's neck. "If *he* won't, then get Nir."

Tarni cringes against me, knowing that my unspoken point about her uncle's compassion toward her was true. At least Nir seemed to care about her.

"Back," I direct her. Merrick quickly joins me, taking my trident so I can swim.

"He saw," Merrick mumbles, nodding toward Nir. His blue bangs drift up in the water majestically.

"Tarni?" Nir calls. He sounds upset—I assume it's his version of desperation, considering how little he cared in the Metten palace—he doesn't want his cousin to die. I wouldn't want Caspian or Coralie to be hurt either, so I understand his fear.

"Get them back," I call to him.

"You'll pay for this," he yells.

"Probably," I shout over Tarni's shoulder. Her lavender hair floats in front of my eyes and I make a face.

Nir's face goes slack for a moment. I can't help myself as I turn to look at what he's watching.

Marilla has killed the siren king.

His body floats in the water, long hair hovers in front of his tipped over body, shells catching the light as they float in his locks.

The sirens turn to Nir—their new king—and race toward him. They know they must rescue him before we get him. They pull him away, but in their haste, we overtake them.

I cling to Tarni as the battle takes a turn for our side. Those that survive swim as quickly as they can, protecting their injuries. Nir disappears, as does the body of the slain siren king.

I can't imagine this will end well for us now that Nir's father's blood is on our hands.

But then, we've also crushed the siren forces. They no longer have the strength to come after us.

Our collection is wounded, but many of us are still alive. Once we regroup, we can go after Nir's remaining forces.

We take our captive sirens and swim back toward Scylla, blocking the barrier entrance and posting guards everywhere that Nir might try to access the kingdom.

Tarni struggles against me, a sobbing mess of a mermaid.

"Let's go," I force her forward.

The captive sirens are placed in the cells below the palace—a fitting place since that's where Persephone lived out her days after betraying the collection. They fight against us, eventually begging for mercy.

I swim away as Marilla's soldiers question them. She nods to me from her place in the hallway, watching the interrogations.

"Celena," Dylana glances at me when I enter the grotto. "Here, let me help."

I settle on the floor in front of her and she quickly moves her fingers through my hair, removing the broken shells before unbraiding my locks. Llyr floats behind her, working her hair out of its war-design.

"Len," Merrick says softly, floating up from his seat in the corner.

"Did you have that looked at?" I question, eyeing his injury.

"I'm fine," he informs me.

"No, he's not, and we've been telling him that for the last half hour," Dylana protests, accidentally pulling my hair in frustration.

"Is Casp okay?" I ask, glancing around for my brother.

"He's with your dad," Llyr replies. "They went to get the kids."

"Good," I nod, realizing I had completely forgotten the mer we had in hiding. "I'm sure they'll be happy to come home."

"Are we learning anything?" Dylana asks.

My mother and I had interrogated several of the sirens and had learned quite a bit about where they were staying and how they were making their decisions, but nothing that would help us at the moment.

"Some, but nothing useful for right now."

Dylana sighs, clearly disappointed.

"Did Tarni tell us anything?" Merrick asks, settling on the ground next to me. His injury looks even worse up close.

"Merrick, you need to get that taken care of," I insist.

He looks at me, not speaking.

"She hasn't said anything. She's too busy shaking and crying," I finally respond.

"I have a feeling Nir won't let this go."

"If he wants her back safely, he's going to make a treaty," Dylana proclaims from behind me. Her fingers tug at one of my small braids. "He can have her back, but that means the war is over. They stay on their side of the barrier and we stay on ours. They have to stop sirening humans—though I doubt they will, even if they agree—and we live our lives ignoring each other. It's as simple as that."

"Do you honestly think he'll do that after your mother killed his father?" Llyr asks.

"I think that he only has one living relative left and *she* is in our cells," I interject. "If he wants her back, he has to give up his vengeance. He's lost both his parents. If it were me, I'd want my cousin back, especially since they grew up more like siblings."

I would do anything to protect Coralie and Caspian, even if it meant giving up everything else.

Of course, sirens aren't good at giving up what they want.

"Merrick, would you *please* get that looked at?" I beg.

He sighs, annoyed.

"Fine." He floats up and swims out of the room.

"I am convinced you are the only mer in existence that could convince that merman to get his injuries looked at," Dylana murmurs after he's gone. A few moments later, Llyr settles on the ground next to me, having freed the princess' hair.

"At least he's going," I roll my eyes.

"Dylana," Morgen interrupts, swimming into the room. "Mother wants you. We're sending out the conch messages."

He turns abruptly, flipping in the water.

Dylana and I follow.

"I'll go check on Merrick," Llyr says, knowing he's not welcome for the family event.

We swim to the queen's parlor. She waits inside along with my mother and several others. Marilla is surrounded by one hundred conch shells. She floats in the middle of them, waiting for us to enter.

She nods and everyone else backs out of the room, giving us quiet. The queen quietly speaks the name of the reigning kings and queens of our sister kingdoms to the north and south. Once she has delivered her message, informing them of what has transpired, she waits for another batch of shells to be delivered.

We repeat the process, helping to move the shells until enough communications have been created to send to Dariah, Ambra, Keldori, and the other mer kingdoms. We remove groups of one hundred shells after each round, handing them off to mer guards. They will attach them to different sea creatures—dolphins, turtles, squids—at different times, and send them off in the direction of the kingdoms in hopes that a few will reach the kings and queens.

"Celena, Dylana, go help send off the shells," Marilla instructs. "We'll finish this last group for Ambra and be out to join you in a few moments."

I lead the way through the palace, conch shells spilling out of my arms.

"Sometimes I think it's a little much to send so many," Dylana murmurs as we exit the doors. "But then, how many do *we* receive from Dariah?"

Not many.

"And even less make it from Keldori, so I suppose I see why it's necessary."

"You're just jealous because you want to use the conch shells to send your own messages," I tease. "Some merman is going to be heartbroken not to hear from you tonight, I'm sure."

She flicks her tail haughtily.

We attach individual shells to passing sea creatures. Many of the guards have taken their shells to different locations where the sea creatures are known to frequent. While we have sea life roaming around the palace, the ones that travel more tend to be further away from the kingdom.

When we run out of options near the palace walls, we help pack the remaining shells into baskets and hand them off to two mermen with very long tails. They grin at us, running their hands through their hair—they aren't much older than Dylana and me.

The mermen turn, glancing over their shoulders as they swim away. Dylana smirks, trying not to giggle.

"Popular, aren't we?"

At least it's not the one Dylana is always trying to match me with when she's bored.

"We should talk about finding you a mate soon, Dylana," Marilla says, swimming up from behind.

"Mother!" the princess gasps out of surprise and embarrassment.

"She's right, Dylana. You're getting to an age where you should be thinking about that," my mother adds. "You too, Celena."

"Maybe we should find Caspian a date first…" I suggest.

I refuse to turn around to see my mother's face.

"If you don't like any of the mermen here, we could always have a conversation with one of the other kingdoms," Marilla offers.

"No!" Dylana and I yelp at the same time. This was *not* how I saw my evening going.

"Now that the messages have been sent off," Marilla redirects. I can hear the grin in her voice, "we should discuss the celebration."

"What are we doing about a treaty with Nir?" Dylana inquires.

"There will be one if he wants his sirens back," the queen confirms. "I'm confident we will reach out to him and he will accept our terms. I've already sent a few conch shells out to him."

"It should be over," my mother adds.

"A century and little more and it's finally over," Marilla muses quietly. "I didn't think I'd see it in my lifetime."

"I'd like to talk to Tarni again," I finally comment.

"Do you think that's wise?" Mother asks. "She seemed pretty terrified of you earlier."

"I held a knife to her throat—of course she'd be terrified." I shrug.

"Go, if you like," Marilla says, wrapping an arm around her daughter's shoulders, staring at the last bit of light leaving the kingdom.

I swim back inside. The rooms are lit with rosacea colonies, glowing blue near the ceilings. The water sparkles with the tinted light, bathing everything in a sense of calm.

Down in the cells, sirens huddle against the rock walls, their glances a mixture of fear and hatred. I make my way down the row, swimming slowly as I look for the mermaid. Her peach tail twitches in the corner as she quietly cries.

I wave one of the guards over and motion to the siren. Turning, I leave before she can notice me. She's horrified when she's brought into the tiny room for questioning.

The guard closes the bars over on the room, preventing her from escaping. She turns back, swimming over in her shackles. I consider using the one grounded to the rock to clamp her tail in place, but I don't want to frighten her anymore than she already is.

"Have a seat, Tarni," I address her, motioning to the ocean floor.

She trembles as she stares at me through her hair.

"I just want to talk," I encourage. "I want to talk about your brother."

I use the term the siren king had used, hoping it means something to her.

"We want to end the war, Tarni. We're hoping we can make a treaty with Nir for your safe return and the safe return of the others here." I pause. "You want to go home, don't you?"

She nods.

"I'm going to need you to help me, Tarni. Will Nir agree to this treaty?"

Her bottom lip puffs out. If this mermaid actually cried pearls, we'd have enough to stock the entire Pearl Festival already with what she's cried *just* since she arrived in Scylla.

"Tarni, I need you to stop crying. We won't hurt you. I told you earlier that if you cooperate, you'll be fine. That's all I'm asking for here. Help me to help Nir make this treaty so you can go home."

Waiting doesn't seem to be helping so I plunge forward.

"What does Nir need to make this agreement?"

"I don't know," she admits quietly.

"What can we do to persuade him?" I ask again. "Is there anything that will help tip his decision in the right direction? He's going to want to get you back, right? You're like a sister to him..."

"I'm sure he'll want to get me back," she mutters, not looking at me.

"And Tiko and Roni will too, I'm sure," I bend my tail up, resting my elbows on it. Merrick has always been jealous of how flexible I am and how easily I bend in half—mermen can't bend as much.

Tarni looks away.

"What can I do to help you get out of here, Tarni? I don't want to keep you in here any longer than we have to. I know you've already been through so much—if there's anything you can think of, I can help you."

"He'll probably want to see you dead more than save me," she hangs her head as she speaks. "His mother hates you because of what that witch, Aila, did."

"Aside from my death," I chuckle, "what can I do?"

"I'm not sure, Len. I'm trapped in here—I have no way of knowing what he's thinking."

"You can call me Celena," I reply, watching the light shift on her skin. "I'm sorry you're trapped here."

"Being confined is my worst nightmare," she whispers.

I can't blame her. Being forced into a tiny cell and shackled is horrifying to me—nearly as bad as being caught in the fishermen's net. Unlike being dragged to the surface, she has the assurance of continuing to live, even though she is confined.

"Tarni, if you can help me, I can get you out of that cell. You'll be under constant supervision, but you won't be down here in the cell."

She instantly perks up, floating up slightly from the ocean floor.

"You can get me out?" Her words are eager and willing.

Desperation creeps into her face, pulling the corners of her eyes back. Her hand brushes her hair behind her so she can see better.

"I can get you out," I promise, hoping Marilla will go along with it. "Just work with me, Tarni."

She takes a deep breath before meeting my eyes.

"Okay."

CHAPTER 12

"Celena, hurry up," Coralie's voice filled the house.

"Calm down, Cor," Caspian shakes his head.

I was up for most of the night talking to Tarni—turns out that we don't have too much to fear—the sirens can't take us on with their remaining numbers and convincing Nir to form an agreement should be easy.

My eyes are heavy as I adjust my *iluse* and swim out of my room.

"*You* look lovely," Caspian teases, eyeing me. I brush my disheveled hair back and glare at him.

"*Clam up,*" I retort.

"*Celena,*" Coralie judges me. "You have to look nicer than *that*—it's a celebration. Go put on something sparkly."

She twirls in the water, her blue and green scales glimmering with the movements. I try not to roll my eyes but exhaustion leads to failure. Thankfully, she doesn't notice. Caspian smirks.

"A little more effort, sis," he chimes in, swimming toward the door. "I heard Nir sent a conch back considering our terms."

It's not surprising, but it's incredible to hear anyway.

Now I really *do* need to dress up more.

Back in my room, I rummage through my chest of *iluses.* I have one made entirely of pearls that I typically wear for the Pearl Festival, but this requires a different look.

I dig out one of my net *iluses* and switch it out for the one I'm wearing. Blue shells adorn the covering, setting off my tail. I haven't found the occasion to wear this one yet, so it's been sitting in my room for ages. Crystals and a few pearls are strung over parts of the *iluse.*

I add a belt covered in pearls to my hips, tightening it to conceal the knife I always keep tucked between it and my back. Somehow it feels right to wear an ornamental shoulder armor piece, so I add the silver chains to finish my outfit for the event. Strands of pearls mix with the metallic silver that stretches from my shoulders almost to my elbows.

"Much better," Coralie appraises me when I return. "Add a crown and you'll be ready to go!"

I hold up the crystal crown, the pointed spikes settling onto my head when I drop it on my hair. It matches the large necklace I added before I swam out of my room—a crystal sitting inside black netting, resting just below my collarbone.

"Perfect!" she replies. "Casp already left with Dad, and Mom is just about ready.

"Do you think Marin will like this?" Coralie pauses.

She glances down self-consciously at herself. I take in her beautiful blonde hair, her striking tail of green and blue, and finally rest on her best *iluse* that our mother gave her—it's been passed down for the last two generations, making Coralie the third to wear it.

"You look incredible, starfish, and if he doesn't notice you looking like that, then he's lost in a kelp forest." I smile at her, giving her a wink.

She blushes and looks away.

"Ready, my mer babies?" Mother asks, swimming into the room. One of Aila's crowns sits on her head, her royal heritage on full display.

The city is filled with excited mer, relief written all over their faces. They make a way for us as we swim through the festivities that appear to have begun earlier than planned.

Merrick catches my eye when we arrive at the Anchor and I quickly say goodbye to my mother, knowing I likely won't be at the event long if I'm being summoned already. She nods, seeing my partner.

"You look striking," Merrick compliments me as I take a place beside him.

His *sarasa* stretches from his right shoulder to his left hip, tucked carefully under the shoulder armor that gracefully rests against his skin. I've only seen him wear the ornamental piece for the Pearl

Festival over the years, so to have pulled it out for this, his family must be emphasizing the day.

"Thank you," I reply. "Where are we going?"

He looks at me mischievously.

"We have somewhere to be," he says.

"How is your arm?" I ask, reaching out to touch it. I pull my hand back at the last second, realizing that it might be painful.

"Better than it was yesterday. Speaking of which," he grins at me, ready to revisit the topic. "You *bit* Nir."

"Don't look at me like that, Merrick," I say in feigned shock. I clutch my hand to my chest, touching the shells on my *iluse.* "I had to do *something* so he didn't kill you."

"Do you honestly think that merman could take me?" he jokes.

"He's the size of a whale. Yes, I think he could destroy you."

"I'm hurt, Len," he lifts his hand to his heart as we turn, swimming around a corner.

"Did you hear we've released Tarni?" I ask casually, knowing what his reaction will be.

"What?" The word comes out rushed and high-pitched. Merrick slams to a halt, lifting himself straight up in the water, hovering in front of me. I slow, turning around dramatically in a big arch, ending my loop mere inches from his face.

"She's still under guard, but she's able to move around certain areas of the palace. She's helping us convince Nir to sign the treaty. I believe Marilla had her send out a conch this morning right after I left."

"You were there all night?" He looks concerned.

"I'm fine," I reply.

"Are you?" Merrick examines me, searching me from head to fin.

"I'm fine."

"After the battle yesterday, and then staying up all night to talk to a siren girl...that worries me, Len. I know you—you need your rest to function properly."

I wrap an arm around his elbow, turning him to continue swimming.

"I have *you* to take care of me if I need it, Merrick." I bat my eyelashes at him, making him smile reluctantly. "Seriously, where are we going?"

"To the palace, actually," he informs me. "Llyr sent word that we're needed."

"He's already been to the palace today?"

"*One of you* didn't spend the night out, Len," he smirks as he corrects me. "Besides, this is probably Morgen's idea—you know he rises before the tide does."

"Oh!" I gasp, darting to avoid being crashed into by a mermaid with an orange and purple tail. She twirls in the water, apologizing quickly before spinning back into the celebration, tail shimmering as she leaves.

"Okay, so the word of the day is *careful*," Merrick comments, lifting his tail higher for an extra powerful flip.

We hurry through the crowd, making our way to the palace. Merrick and I duck low in the water, swimming under the path of a baby sea turtle. I almost scoop him up into my arms and take him to the palace where he can roam within the walls of the structure, but if I did that for every sea creature I found, the palace would be overrun. I can't imagine Marilla would be pleased, even though she's known to have a rather large herd of pet seahorses living in her chambers.

"Where is your brother at today?" Merrick changes the topic.

"He left with Dad this morning, so I don't actually know." I frown.

"How do you feel now that you know that Caspian is nearly as well-trained as you?"

"A little shocked, honestly. I haven't really had much time to think any of this through. How did he do when you two took on Nir?"

"I was impressed. I had a feeling he always knew more than he let on—*I'm guessing* that was to protect *you*—but your brother has skills, Len."

Knowing his actions in Metten were not an anomaly is certainly reassuring.

"How do we proceed with this? Will he start coming on missions with us?"

A warm current flows over my arms, down my body. I shiver in delight.

"I don't know—maybe that's what this is about," he suggests. "Maybe we'll get our orders and find out how things will be restructured now—especially since the pearl's out of the clam for Morgen."

We swim up the palace steps. A guard nods, showing us where to go. Morgen greets us before his mother and sister can.

"There are rumors that a siren has made it into Scylla without anyone knowing. We don't know who this is and it would be a *sea witch hunt* if we inform the people to watch for someone they don't know..."

"We need to find this siren," Dylana interrupts, swimming up from her seat on a lounging couch, "or at least determine if the rumors are true.

"What's the plan?" Merrick asks, straightening his shoulders.

"The two of you," Dylana answers. "*We* have to handle the ceremonies today. We need you two to handle looking for answers."

"Llyr is back at his post for the day, so he won't be able to help you," Marilla informs us.

"What about Caspian?" I inquire, hoping she will allow us to inform my twin.

"You can ask him to join you, if you like," she nods with understanding. "He's already involved at this point anyway."

A stingray glides over my head, swooping gracefully into the room. It swims toward the queen eagerly. She raises a hand and the creature glides under it, excited to be pet.

It turns, swimming toward me. I hold out my arm, allowing it to glide under my hand, it's soft body floating next to me. The creature turns, ready for attention from my partner. When he has no food for it, it moves on to Dylana and Morgen.

"How do you want us to question people?" Merrick asks, redirecting the conversation.

"We're not sure," Dylana informs us. "We don't want to alert anyone that we're searching, but it will be hard not to and still get information."

"Actually," I interrupt. "I have an idea that might get us around that."

They look at me curiously. Marilla brushes her hair back as it floats in front of her face.

"What if we don't need to ask questions because we can identify any sirens floating among us?"

"How do you propose we do that?" the queen questions.

"By using a siren to find another siren," I offer. "We have Tarni and she's cooperating. We promised her a bit of freedom for helping us, so why not use this as a dual opportunity?"

"You want to take her out of the palace?" Marilla asks calmly. Morgen looks shocked, blinking as he stares.

"Do you see a more effective way to find hidden sirens?" I counter politely.

"I suppose you're right. Do you honestly think she'll cooperate?"

"It's freedom—I think it's what she craves more than anything right now. You saw how she responded when we took her out of that cell. Imagine what she'd do to cooperate if she got to escape this palace for a few hours..."

"Do you think she'll obey you? We can't have her misbehaving on us," Dylana asks.

"We can't exactly take her in shackles—everyone will know," Merrick points out, flicking his tail—something he always does when he finds a problem with one of our plans.

"You think they won't know anyway?" I remind him. "They all saw her yesterday—at least *some* of these mer will recognize her.

"So how do we approach this?" Merrick turns to me as if the others aren't in the room.

"I say we dress her up and take her out into the festivities. She won't leave our side and if she tries anything, we immediately shackle her hands and fins together and drag her back to the palace where she will be promptly returned to the darkest cell we can find. That should frighten her enough to make her comply."

"And if someone makes waves about her being out in the open?" he bounces off my idea.

"We move her."

"Really? *That's* your master plan?"

The stingray returns to confirm once again that I have no meal to offer him. Merrick waves his hand at the creature, motioning him away.

"Do you have a better one?" I challenge, crossing my arms. I add sarcastically, "Do you want to drag a jellyfish after us and threaten her with it?"

"I'm not questioning her willingness to work with us, I'm questioning the reaction of the collection. Don't you think this will upset some of them?"

"*More* or *less* than sirens swimming around posing as mer?" I counter.

Like a school of fish turning in the water, Merrick's face changes.

"What if we disguised her?"

"Excuse me?" I ask, taken back.

"If they can't easily identify her as the siren from the battle, what can they do?"

"She has peach hair and a purple tail, what do you expect to do to hide that?"

"Well, we can't do much about her tail," he reaches into the pouch on his hip and pulls out a broken shell he keeps as a backup weapon. "Her hair is a different matter."

"Shells?" I ask, bewildered.

"Cover her in shells." he nods. "It's excessive, but *today* of all days, mer will be taking their wardrobe to the extreme."

I grin as his plan hits me. We could cover her locks with so many shells, no one could guess her hair color if they tried. She might look a little ridiculous, but the young mermaids are likely to wear too many accessories today anyway—she could possibly fit in.

We quickly start planning how to make it work, talking over each other, but still responding to each other's words, carrying on two conversations at once with each other.

He swims closer to me as we plan, hands waving in the water. When we reach the part of the discussion about how to balance it on Tarni's head, congratulating each other when we come up with a brilliant solution, we're interrupted.

"You two want a moment?" Morgen smirks as Merrick leans in close enough that his bangs brush against my forehead as we quietly discuss our next move.

"Morgen!" the queen and princess gasp, chastising him as we turn, realizing that we aren't alone.

"You didn't see *me* getting that close to Celena," he shrugs, making things more awkward. Dylana rolls her eyes, pursing her lips playfully as she glances at me, approving of what Morgen was hinting at —Merrick and I.

"May we?" I ask, hoping to divert their attention.

Marilla blinks.

"May you...*what?*"

Fins, she's not sure if I mean be with Merrick or take Tarni out in public.

"May we disguise Tarni and take her out siren searching?" I clarify what apparently seems to be rather murky waters in the discussion.

"Oh. Yes, of course. Just don't lose her, and *don't* let her talk to anyone."

"Yes, ma'am," I reply. Everything inside me itches to go work on Tarni's wardrobe immediately.

"Take whatever you need from the pieces in the guest grotto," Marilla instructs. "We need to go, but if you need help, the guards are at your disposal. Please consider taking at least one of them with you while you're out."

Consider.

That doesn't mean it's mandated.

We nod, waiting for the royals to swim out first.

"Feel free to use my room if you need," Dylana whispers as she swims out last.

I won't invade her space if I don't have to, but she *does* have the best tools for creating customized *iluses,* so I may have to take her up on that. I thank her and turn to follow her out.

Merrick grabs my arm, slowing me.

"Are you sure this is going to work?" he asks, still holding on to my arm.

"What's the worst that can happen?"

"I'd say a shark could eat us, but we all know *that siren* controls them all," he teases.

I consider punching his arm, but it's still injured and that would be cruel. *Technically.*

He sees my change in posture and darts back out of striking distance.

"Wow, you have a bit of a bite yourself today, don't you?"

"Want to find out?" I threaten, swimming toward him.

"How about you just go get your things and work on Tarni's *iluse* while I handle her hair?"

I swim after him, grinning at my victory.

We split off once we reach the guest grotto, each looking for the materials we will need to create a new Tarni. Merrick collects shells while I search for netting and seaweed to make her a top. I'm careful to only choose supplies that she can't turn into weapons, though I doubt she even has the knowledge to do so.

"Ready?" Merrick asks after a few moments.

I glance at the octopus in the corner of the room. For a moment, I consider hiding Tarni's hair under *that,* but shake my head at the ridiculous idea—no one in their right mind would wear a living creature as a hairpiece.

"*Really?*" Merrick teases when I swim to his side.

"*I didn't do it,*" I insist.

"But you thought about it." His voice gets low when he ridicules me playfully, glancing at me from under his bangs.

"*Clam up,* Merrick, you would have considered it too. Don't forget, I know the way you think."

We find Tarni under the watchful eye of two of Marilla's best soldiers. They move to the side of the room to give us space.

"Tarni, are you ready for a little extra freedom?" I ask, swimming up to her. She eyes the basket of supplies I'm carrying, but brightens as soon as she realizes she might not have to be restricted to the room where she's being supervised.

"What do you want?" she asks.

"There are rumors floating around that there may be a siren hiding in Scylla. If it's true, we want you to identify them so we can bring them in without anyone getting hurt."

"They'll be released with the rest of you when Nir finalizes the treaty," Merrick adds.

"You'll be able to spend the day with us in the city."

"What's that for?" Tarni nods toward what we brought.

"It will be easier if you aren't recognized," I explain. "We're going to dress you up a little and cover your hair as best we can."

She stares at us.

"In or out, Tarni? We don't have time to wait around," Merrick snaps, hoping to motivate her to make a decision and stop questioning us.

"Fine," she growls, dropping down to the ocean floor.

I hold out a basic *iluse* bodice and she swims back up, snatching it from my hands. She shrugs it on over her own *iluse*. I can't imagine it's comfortable, but who am I to question another mer's wardrobe choices?

Resting on the sand once again, she waits for Merrick and I to take over. My partner expertly styles Tarni's hair back into braids, attaching them to her head while I weave seaweed and pearls around her *iluse*. By the time I finish, Merrick is positioning the shells around Tarni's braids, covering as much of her purple locks as possible.

I swim up to where he floats, helping him weave the pink shells into her hair. Examining her, I decide it's as close as we're going to get, nodding to my partner.

"You look good," I inform her, trying not to flinch when I say the words.

Pink and white shells cover her head like a knight's helmet in the human books I've found over the years.

"Now, Tarni," I add. "You need to act like you're excited to be a part of the festivities. You're all dressed up and you're actions need to match. You look young, so act young. It's okay to look around at everything because it will look like you're taking in the event."

"In reality, we need you to be watching for other sirens. Understood?" Merrick chimes in, looking at her.

"I understand," she mumbles quietly.

We guide her out of the room.

Mer mix with fish as we take Tarni deep into the heart of the city. It seems as though the fish have come out in full splendor for the event, creating a rainbow of colors swirling around the celebration. I don't know if I've ever seen this much sea life in the center of the city at one time—freedom demands attention.

"Do you see anyone?" Merrick mumbles. His face morphs into a smile as he raises his hand to wave to Keone. The merman waves back, nodding with a grin toward the mermaid floating next to him—apparently, he found a friend for the event. When she turns, I discover it's Natale. She and I might need to have a conversation later —though that might not help since she and I aren't very close.

Merrick flashes him a smile, congratulating him. Keone notices the two of us swimming with Merrick and he returns our conspirator's appreciative grin. I fight not to roll my eyes, instead doing a backflip as I show off my tail.

Mermaids love attention and if Keone is going to stare, I'm going to command his attention.

When I right myself, I place a hand on Tarni's upper arm and propel her forward. I catch a quick view of Merrick out of the corner of my eye as he grimaces.

During the Pearl Festival, vendors are usually set up with food and commemorative items in the center of the city. Surrounded by music and laughter, they make enough profit to last them several months.

On days like this, when the celebration isn't planned, everyone comes together to create a festival unlike any other. Next year will be different and the vendors will own the seas, but today, the mer have collected everything on display this morning to celebrate and freely share with each other—the free oysters have never tasted so good.

I reach down, scooping one up from a pile on the table. I motion that Tarni can try one as well and her hand darts out greedily as if the queen hadn't been feeding her well all along.

I smile as a group of mer children wiggle by me, attempting to dance in the water. One day they'll learn how to control their tails so they can move gracefully, but today is not that day.

I wink at Coralie, lifting a finger to my lips to tell her not to ask questions. She squints at me, but finally looks away, running her fingers over the shell necklace that has miraculously found its way to her neck.

A large mermaid swims in front of me, thrusting a shell necklace at me. She towers over me, her tail much longer than mine.

"Here, for the celebration!"

Before I can react, she forces the necklace over my head. Eyeing Tarni's shell sculpture, she hands a necklace to her instead.

"A handsome necklace for a handsome merman," she chuckles, dropping a string of shells over Merrick's head.

"Thank you, ma'am," Merrick replies.

"Tell your mother I expect to see her at the market next week," she murmurs as she turns away to give out more necklaces. "No more skipping to do other things."

"I will," Merrick laughs. He turns to me. "Don't ask."

"Wasn't going to, *handsome*."

"You two are gross," Tarni says, swimming ahead. I give her one tail flick of space, knowing I can easily overtake her if I need to.

I duck under two brightly-colored fish, glancing around the area to see what else is going on. Merrick and I take turns watching our charge.

"What is *that*?" Tarni asks, stopping abruptly.

"The Anchor," I reply. "It was dropped here long before any of us existed."

I avoid telling her exactly when it was dropped.

"We use it as a central location now—it's rather hard to miss."

"I see that," she comments.

"What is *she* doing here?" a voice demands.

My heart sinks into my tail when I turn.

CHAPTER 13

"She can't be here," the merman insists. "Why is she even out of her cell?"

"Calm down, Murdoch," Merrick cautions. "She needs to be here. Just go over there and enjoy the party."

"She's going back in her cell." He darts forward, latching on to Tarni's wrist. "You think you can dress her up and drag her out here? You're wrong. The queen will hear about this."

"Let her go," I command, hoping I sound more in control than I feel. Tarni shrieks as he pulls her, struggling to get away.

Murdoch takes off, propelling them toward the palace. Merrick and I chase after them, swimming above the crowd.

Caspian glances up in the distance and notices us swimming high in the water. His eyes track our path as we move toward him and he casually positions himself to take Murdoch out. At the last second, he darts up in the air, knocking the merman off course.

Before I can call out, he realizes who the mermaid is and spins her around, pulling her into the crowd. Murdoch turns, searching for them. I split off, diving into the crowd to make my way to my brother and our charge while Merrick handles the confused merman.

"Are you okay?" I ask.

Tarni rubs her wrist, glaring at me.

"This is unexpected," Caspian announces, looking to me for an answer.

"Searching for sirens," I inform him, keeping my voice down. "Apparently not our best idea."

"Sanctioned?"

I nod, my hair floating in front of my face. Living in the sea means never having a bad hair day, but it also means we have to tolerate our locks drifting in front of us all the time.

"Len!" Merrick shouts, warning us just before Murdoch crashes into us.

When I can see again, Tarni is gone.

A crowd forms around us as Murdoch clings to me—he got the wrong mermaid.

I shriek, letting the crowd think what they will.

If they assume Murdoch is attacking me, who am I to change their mind.

Caspian rips him away from me, pulling on his tail. I'm jerked backward until the merman releases his grip. A number of mer swim between us, blocking his path to me. I use the opportunity to swim away.

Frantically, I search for the siren I'm supposed to be supervising. Merrick swims alongside of me, darting in and out of the tables the mermaids and mermen have set up to celebrate.

"This is bad," I hum.

"Should we split up?" he asks, eyes darting around quickly.

I dive low into the crowd, not wanting people to take notice of us searching overhead.

"No, together," I reply. He follows my lead, sinking into the crowd.

We swim for fifteen minutes, searching for the siren. My heart hammers against my chest as hard as it does when I end up on the surface.

"What do we do?" I ask finally.

"She can't have gone too far," Merrick comments. "If you were a siren being held captive in a mer kingdom, what would you do and where would you go?"

"I'd flee. I wouldn't stay. I'd try to get back to the sirens. I'd even risk taking on the sharks if it meant freeing myself."

"Tarni isn't you. What would *Tarni* do?" he poses.

"She's scared and meek. She's not brave enough to escape, nor is she strong enough to take on a mer, but she wouldn't just wait around. We've only searched for her on the ocean floor—do you think it's possible she went somewhere other than *over*?"

"You think she went *up*?"

"I think she's a fish in a net…she's going to swim in any direction she can to escape capture."

"But we would have seen a mer that high up near the festivities, wouldn't we have?" Merrick questions, playing out the scenario.

"If it were me, my first instinct would be to blend in and not be seen. If she managed to swim into the crowd—if she eluded us—she could swim upward later, when she was far enough away to not be seen."

"Which way did she go?" he asks, trusting my line of thought.

Mer have an innate sense of direction. No matter where they are or what they do, they can tell you the direction of another kingdom.

"She wants to get over the barrier. It's easier for her to find her friends once she's out of Scylla. She would go to one of the reef barriers."

"We can see coral from here, but it's not the barrier," Merrick glances through the water.

"No, but I bet she doesn't know that. Come on."

As we swim, the visibility in the water decreases. Everything is filled with white haze. We can only see things that reside closer to us until the water clears, making towering coral reefs a surprise as we swim upon them.

"We need to go faster," Merrick says, pushing his tail harder as we swim around the coral that used to look like the barrier from a distance.

"We can't see," I remind him.

"We can't afford to wait around, Len. I'll go first if you're worried."

He darts ahead of me, leading the way. I struggle to keep up with him.

Everything looks empty as we reach the barrier. I'm sure there have to be guards around—perhaps even Llyr—but we can't see them. The coral looms before us, stretching high toward the surface.

"We have to check," Merrick says, not waiting for an answer.

We swim to the top of the reef, though I don't know what we'll be able to see. Surprisingly, the water is a bit more clear near the top, but not much. The coral feels abnormally high, but that might just be the water as the cloud starts to dissipate.

"I don't see her—" Merrick's words are cut off as he's launched toward the surface.

"Merrick!" I scream, racing after him.

"No!" he commands, trying to wave me off.

With a powerful flip of my tail, I reach him, grabbing onto the net that surrounds Merrick. My tail drips as we're lifted out of the water.

"Let go," Merrick begs, desperately trying to pry my fingers off of the net.

"Knife," I yell, trying to reach my own.

Merrick fumbles for the pouch attached to his belt. He pulls out his weapon and quickly cuts near my hand.

"I've got this," he informs me as he snaps the rope that's holding me in place.

I slam into the surface of the water, having an eerie flashback to yesterday. My ribs ache again as I hit the waves and sink below.

Flipping my tail back and forth as hard as I can, I pop out of the water, glaring.

The boat sits right next to me—the reason I thought the coral was so high. It was really the ship covered in barnacles that blended in with the reef in the murky waters. The humans pull Merrick's net toward their deck.

I have no way of saving him from the water and he's too tangled to free himself. I only have one choice.

Taking a deep breath as a blue firework sparkles overhead, I focus on producing a sound loud enough to carry to the deck of the ship. My voice is high on a normal day, but today it's piercingly shrill. The notes come out unsteady at first, but I find my pitch and wield it against the humans.

At first, they spot me, pointing at me in the water. Several of them prepare to throw another net on me, but my haunting words stop them as I seal their fate.

Merrick thrashes in the net, still dripping fiercely. I move to be closer to where he will fall if it comes to that. He struggles until he hears me. Turning, he watches me quietly from the net.

I sing the sailors into a false sense of security, convincing them that they don't see us. They stare as if captivated by my voice. It's frightening watching their eyes latch on to me as if I'm the most important thing in their worlds, while simultaneously looking right through me.

I convince them to lower the net and Merrick starts to descend from the sky.

A sharp pull on my tail stops my words as I am forced back under the sea. I have no control over my body as I'm dragged backward. Someone is holding my tail, preventing me from being able to swim.

"You're sirening them," Murdoch accuses. "The queen will shackle you in shark territory for this."

He pulls harder.

"Murdoch, stop!" I beg. "They have Merrick."

"He deserves whatever fate he gets for sirening them. It's against the law of the sea, Celena. Royal blood or not, you can't go against our laws—not even the queen can."

"We can siren to protect ourselves if a human catches us," I protest, trying to climb down my own body, using my tail as a chain to pull myself on until I can reach his hands above my fins.

"Where is the siren?" Murdoch demands.

"Let her go!" Caspian demands. Several mermen, including Keone, swim alongside of him to back him up.

I finally reach Murdoch, scratching him. He digs his nails into my scales before releasing me in pain.

I turn, not waiting to explain.

The wind has picked up on the surface, the skies dark and gray.

I sing at the top of my lungs, fast and unyielding.

Merrick flops around in the net, attempting to siren his way out of the situation, but it's been trained out of us for so many generations, that he doesn't have the control he needs to win their thoughts over.

I screech at the humans, forcing their hand.

Several of the mermen propel themselves over the waves just as I convince the men to drop Merrick's net into the sea slowly enough that he isn't hurt.

Everyone swims to him, ripping the net apart as I continue to sing. The moment he is free, we dive.

CHAPTER 14

"She's a siren," Murdoch protests.

"She is not," Caspian yells.

The palace is crammed with some of the mermen from the rescue mission, all floating around me as I hover in front of the royals.

"I was rescuing us," I angrily inform them.

"She was helping that siren girl escape," Murdoch cries.

"That *siren* girl is back in her cell," Marilla informs him. I'm sure she means that Tarni is under guard somewhere in the palace—we had a deal, after all.

"How was she out of her cell in the first place?" Murdoch demands.

Marilla appraises him for a moment.

"We were using her as a spy," she finally informs the group. "We heard rumors of a siren hiding in Scylla and they were using the mermaid to determine if it was true without starting a sea witch hunt."

"So she tricked you into releasing the siren so they could set her free?" Murdoch presses.

"Of course not." Marilla barely keeps her face straight. "They were working on my orders."

"Then how did she get away?"

"She escaped because *you* interfered," I challenge.

"Everyone saw you sirening those humans, Celena. You did all of this on purpose and I demand you be put on trial for this."

A collective gasp fills the room. Even the turtle that was roaming around the room realizes it's his cue to leave.

"On trial for what?" Merrick says in a low, dangerous voice as he rises in the water next to me.

"For sireny. For working with our enemies."

"Then I should be on trial too," Merrick insists. "I sirened them too to save my own scales."

"No one saw you siren," Murdoch folds his arms over his chest. "You're lying to save her."

"But I did," Merrick repeats his claim.

"No, he didn't," I interject. There was no way to escape a trial now, but we certainly don't need to put both of us through it.

"Enough," Marilla silences us.

She has no choice but to put me on trial, but it's really just a waste of everyone's time. Murdoch will never let it go though, and to clear my name, we must go through with this.

"Celena has done nothing wrong, but if you insist on this ridiculous conversation, she can prove it before the council, because I don't want this outrageous claim hanging over her head for the rest of her life." She looks apologetically at me. "And *you*...Murdoch, is it? I want you to remember this—if we turn on each other without fully investigating first, we are no different than Chantay was."

He grimaces at being compared to Persephone's mother.

"I encourage you to think things through better before you do something like this again, because if you falsely accuse someone like this, you'll be the one to pay the price."

Marilla flicks her tail suddenly, swimming up in the water before exiting the room quickly to prove her point.

"The trial will be tomorrow afternoon, concluding tomorrow evening." Dylana slices her hand through the water to silence Merrick and Caspian. "You will all attend and none of you will speak a word of this until after the trial tomorrow."

She follows after her mother, leaving Morgen in her wake. He puffs out his chest imposingly as he rests a hand on the sword attached to his belt.

"Not one word," he repeats, looking directly at Murdoch.

The grotto clears out, the mermen swimming home for the evening.

"How in the seven seas did this happen?" Caspian demands when we're alone.

"This is the most ridiculous—" Merrick says sharply.

"It doesn't matter," I cut him off. "It happened. We just have to get through it.

"Marilla will bring in Tarni, and the rest of you will speak, and I'll be fine. She'll announce that we're siren-free and that I was never associated with the sirens."

"And you have to sit through the indignity of a trial," Caspian adds harshly.

"*And I'll look fabulous while doing it*," I shake my head at him. I huff. "It's fine—we'll just get through it and move on. But apparently, I won't be able to talk to Tarni now to find out what happened."

"And talking with the royals is out of the question until the trial now," Merrick adds.

"What happened with Tarni anyway?" I turn to my brother, hoping he knows something.

"I sent Morgen after her when I saw Murdoch chasing after you two," Caspian admits. "Kind of wish I didn't have to stop to explain to Morgen—we wouldn't be in this mess because I would have caught Murdoch before he reached you."

"It's fine, Casp, it's not your fault."

"But it is. I'm supposed to protect you and I didn't. Now we're in this mess."

"We'll be fine, Caspian," Merrick assures him. "No one is going to touch Len."

"We need to get you home," Caspian swims to my side, wrapping an arm around my shoulders. "It's late and we haven't had the proper amount of sleep that we need in a very long time."

Weariness drags over me like a jellyfish pulling a fish into its mouth. Every muscle in my body hurts. My tail feels numb.

I lean into my twin, allowing him to guide me.

Merrick swims us home, leaving us once we reach our dwelling to continue on to his family.

"You look tired," Coralie says, swimming by me.

"You would too if you'd done all I've done in the last few days," I mutter. She doesn't hear me as she darts into the hallway.

"Should I ask?" our mother asks.

"I'll tell her, you go rest," Caspian advises me.

I don't resist, floating to my room.

The last bit of light dances through the water as I swim inside. The jellyfish glow overhead, illuminating the room.

Slipping out of my *iluse*, I put on a simple piece meant for sleep. My crown sparkles against the light of the bioluminescent glow that lights my room, distracting me. Lifting myself out of bed, I snatch it from my shelf and hide it away in my chest.

I can't get my brain to turn off as I lie in the near dark.

Whether or not we hear from Nir tomorrow, I have to endure a trial, though I hope we hear back from him. I'm more than ready to have Tarni and the other sirens out of Scylla.

I spend the next hour shifting on my bed, trying to quiet my thoughts. Defeated, I work out my defense for the trial before eventually falling asleep.

"Wear this," my mother's voice wakes me. She hovers over me in the water, strands of pearls in her hands. A single shell sits on the pearls, a stark contrast to them.

I sigh, trying to clear my mind as I sit up.

"It will be fine, Mama," I mumble, frustrated that she didn't let me sleep longer.

"You need to go to the palace, Celena."

"I will," I protest.

"No, now. You slept all day, Celena. You have to be there soon."

I dart upright.

I couldn't have possibly slept in late—I never sleep in late. My body wakes me up at the same time every single day, there's no way I could have overslept.

"Time to go, sis," Caspian calls from the hallway.

"Get dressed, Celena—something royal. You have to be there in an hour and you should arrive early." She exits the room.

My father always tells me I never look more royal than when my *iluse* reflects my scales, so I choose one with purple detailing. I slip into it, grabbing the pearls my mother left on my bed. I settle them over my hair, letting the shell rest in the center of my forehead. It feels cool and reassuring against my skin as two of the strands of pearls sit directly above my eyebrows. Once it's balanced, I secure it and swim out to meet my brother.

"Take care of each other," my mother calls as we leave.

"Worried?" Caspian asks.

"When am I ever?"

"Good point," Caspian nods approvingly. "This really is ridiculous though."

"I'm aware." I roll my eyes.

Merrick is already waiting at the palace when we arrive. His eyes grow wide as we swim into the room.

"We might have a problem," he whispers, turning us. "I think some of the others have been talking."

"Which means?" I lead.

"Which means we could be in trouble," he replies.

"Oh good, everyone is here," Marilla says, swimming into the room. "We can get started early."

I glance at the two mermen floating next to me.

Time to decide my fate.

"We all saw her siren those sailors," Murdoch yells. "And she sirened them during the battle too. Did any of the rest of us try that? No! We fought them, like we've been trained to do!"

He swims across the room, hands waving wildly.

"A siren's first reaction is always to control and manipulate—the rest of us were protecting ourselves," he adds.

"Celena saved every mer on those ships during the battle, Murdoch. Your father was one of them, I believe," Merrick reminds him loudly.

"I had no other choice—they were filleting our friends. I wasn't going to just let them continue to mutilate mer."

"And if you'll remember, she came back to the ocean too after she ensured the others we returned to the water." Caspian glares across the room.

"Then why did she kiss that human?" Murdoch counters.

Everyone's face falls.

"I did no such thing!" I yelp.

"We saw you." Murdoch tips his head up triumphantly.

I turn to the queen.

"I did not kiss a human. I was instructing him to put me back in the water and he tried to kiss me. I pushed myself away from him and ended up falling over the side of the ship and slammed into the water so hard, I couldn't breathe."

Everyone is quiet for a moment, letting that information sink in—a human had tried to kiss me.

A siren would have sung the sailor to his death for that—or maybe they would have agreed to it and used it to control the human even more—but I had been nothing but horrified in the moment. Now I almost wish I hadn't let him escape death at my voice.

I'm sure the young sailor didn't meet a kind end once the siren got control of him after I entered the sea again, but his blood isn't on my hands.

"She was the one who found the sirens in the first place," Murdoch continues. "Then she was the one sirening humans. Then she took the siren mermaid out of her cell in disguise and paraded her around Scylla without warning people they were in danger, and then she *set her free and returned to the humans?*"

Tarni trembles in the corner, terrified of what might become of her.

"The siren mermaid is working with us to bring peace to our kingdoms," Marilla speaks over the merman. "Celena has been working under my command."

"You're going to ignore the fact that she's in love with a human?"

"I'm not in love with a human!" I scream in frustration.

The council quietly murmurs.

How could this go so wrong?

"She needs to be locked up," one of Murdoch's friends presses. "We can't trust her. She has *everyone* under her spell."

"Clam up, Relo," Merrick growls.

"You worst of all, Merrick," Murdoch hisses back. "You follow her around like a guppy."

Merrick draws back his shoulder like he might hit the merman. Murdoch takes it as a challenge and rises to the occasion, preparing to strike.

"Enough!" Marilla shouts.

Murdoch looks at her in surprise before reeling around to turn on me.

"You did all this, *siren*. You've put us all in danger and we're all going to pay because you fell in love with a human."

He moves toward me suddenly but Merrick wrenches himself between us. Hi arm must still hurt a great deal, but he hides it well as he moves.

"I'll rip every last scale off of you if you touch her," Merrick threatens.

I consider threatening to hand him over to the humans, but I doubt that will help my case. I stay quiet, watching the water spark between the two mermen like the shock from a jellyfish.

The light shifts in the room.

More and more ships have been making their way over Scylla, though I'm not sure if that's the sirens' doing or if the humans have just figured out something is going on and are searching aimlessly for us. I'm not sure how they managed to find a way around the barriers, but apparently, they have.

"I witnessed it—what more do you want?" Murdoch growls.

"I'm sure you weren't the only one on the surface when all of this was happening, Murdoch," Dylana comes to my defense. "We're adjourning until we have more information."

My eyes dart around as I try to think of who might have seen me on the surface.

"Len?" Merrick asks quietly as Caspian swims over from his place against the wall.

"Keone," I say, remembering a flash of his face at some point during my time above the waves.

"I'll go," Caspian swims away before Merrick can stop him.

"How did this get so out-of-hand?" Merrick whispers.

Even Dylana looks worried from across the grotto. I wish I could speak to her, but we can't talk until after the trial is over.

Marilla seethes from her seat near her daughter. She never intended for the trial to got this far, but Murdoch's fear of sirens convinced several of the mermen to fall into his trap and label me an enemy.

"We need to get you out of here," Merrick murmurs, pulling me away from the crowd.

I let him drag me through the palace, removing me from the trial area—we had thought this would be so simple.

As soon as we were out of sight and safely tucked away in Dylana's personal parlor, I started to shake.

"It wasn't that bad." Merrick swims over to me, wrapping an arm around me. "Caspian will find Keone and bring him here—that will help that we have a witness."

"I don't understand." I continue to quiver. "Why Murdoch is pressing this so much? What did I ever do to him?"

Merrick shakes his head.

"It seems like genuine terror of sirens, Len. I don't think it's you personally."

"He didn't go after you," I point out.

"He didn't hear me sing." He offers me a sad smile. "If he had, he definitely would have been pushing to shackle me in shark territory."

He laughs quietly.

"You have an amazing voice, so don't pull that, Merrick," I answer.

"Oh, yeah?" He leans in from the side, ducking his head to see me.

I try to push him away, but he holds fast.

"You like my voice, huh?" he asks, dropping an octave.

"I said you had a good voice, not that I liked it." I continue to struggle away from him, unable to hide my grin. "I hear it way too much to ever *like* it."

"You'd whither away and turn into sea foam with me, Len, admit it," he teases, wrapping his far arm around my waist to pull me closer.

"Shove off, Merrick," I giggle, unable to help myself.

"You will be fine, Len, I promise." He grows serious, encircling me with his arms. We still in the water. "I will not let Murdoch or Tarni or any of the others beach you. You will be perfectly safe and go on to live a long and danger-filled life with me by your side."

His face goes slack when he realizes his words came out wrong.

"You intend on being partners our entire lives?" I yelp, helping him to cover.

He smiles softly.

"What if I do?" he asks.

Light sparkles in through a hole in the parlor ceiling. It glitters against the rock of the wall, dancing with the water above. Fish swim by, adding a colorful presence to the room.

"Fine, but only so I don't have to break in a new partner. I mean, Caspian shows promise, but it's taken me years to get you in working order for all of this..."

"Did that human actually kiss you?"

His ocean blue eyes cloud over in dismay.

"He tried, but he didn't."

He closes his eyes, breathing out in relief.

"You really scared me during the battle, Len," he admits. "I didn't know how we were going to get you back."

"I heard you singing, Merrick." He opens his eyes to find me smirking at him. He grins, blushing slightly.

I feel safer than I have in days. I almost wish we could just hide in the parlor for a few years and let all this wash over.

A seahorse swims across the room, finding another piece of

seaweed to wrap its tail around, distracting me. When I look back, Merrick is still staring at me.

"I would have tried anything to get you back, Len—even sireny."

"And so you did," I purse my lips, trying to suppress my grin. My cheekbones don't get the message and rise up so I can see them in the foreground of my vision as I watch Merrick floating inches from me.

His hair waves in the water, slowly moving in front of his eyes but he never looks away. Merrick reaches up, tucking my pink locks behind my ear.

I shiver.

"You're needed," a hand slams into the door, making us both jump. My heart slams against my chest as I pull away from Merrick. His hands trail down my arms, grasping my fingers before we separate.

My entire body feels like I slammed into a coral reef, cuts running down every part of me when he lets go.

"Okay," I call, turning to leave.

Merrick follows close behind, grumbling.

"Caspian can't be back this soon unless Keone was in the courtyard," I murmur, hoping to distract Merrick from our moment while trying to figure out what is happening that we are being summoned so quickly.

I start to move the door but get pulled back inside, Merrick roughly pulling on my hand. I collide with him, hand instinctively wrapping around him to stabilize myself. He feels amazing under my touch.

A school of fish bursts through the slightly opened door, swirling around us as Merrick presses his lips against mine. I close my eyes, falling into the moment.

His hand moves up my back, skimming over my *iluse* until he reaches my hair. His fingers knot in it, pulling slightly. He's as hungry as the stingrays gliding around the palace, begging to be nourished.

Merrick crushes his lips against mine again and again. My arms reach around him, dancing up his back, pulling him closer to me as I reach the shell necklace around his neck. He shudders under my touch.

He backs me up against the wall as the fish swirl around us. They dart out of the way as Merrick pins me, barely pulling away long enough to notice them.

My fins twitch against his, rippling in the water as he kisses me, careful to avoid the injury on my neck and shoulder.

His shoulder blades are sharp under my hands. I drag my fingers down them, making him gasp against me. I smile for a moment before reaching a hand up to brush back his bangs as they sweep across my cheek.

A strangled giggle escapes my lips as I run my hands through his hair. I become obsessed with touching his locks, moving both of my hands to his blue fringe.

Merrick complies, letting me mesmerize him as I move my fingers through his hair. He lowers his hands from my mane and rests them on my hips and the small of my back just over my tail.

I push him back away from the wall so that we're both floating.

"*Hey!*" a voice shouts, pounding on the door to remind us that we were called for already.

"Coming," I shout, lips still attached to Merrick's.

"No, we're not," he murmurs just loud enough for me to hear.

"We have to go," I object, pulling back.

"I see no reason for that," he retorts, moving one of my hips forward toward him.

"Oh, well, my life just hangs in the balance, that's all," I remind him.

"*No one* is touching you..." he tips his head at me. "Well, no one except for me."

He pulls me toward him, slamming me into his chest. His seaweed *sarasa* crinkles between us as he kisses me quickly.

"Now can we go?" I ask, refusing to break eye contact.

"If we must," he taunts, brushing my hair back again—I'm never going to be able to let him do my hair again for missions because his touch holds an entirely different current now.

His fingers trail mine as he swims away from me, opening the door. He motions for me to go out first.

The hall is empty so we swim toward the council meeting.

Inside, Tarni is floating in the middle of the room, looking petrified. Her eyes plead with me when she sees me.

"What is going on?" I demand.

"The point was brought up that we don't really know much about where Tarni was between the time she swam away and the time I found her," Morgen informs me. "I tried talking to her about it on the way back, but we thought it might be wise to not waste time while we're waiting for Caspian and the others to return with the witnesses."

"I told you, I didn't know where to go. I just tried to stay out of the way," Tarni cries. "I was near the palace when you found me—I was trying to get back so I wouldn't get in trouble."

She brushes back her hair, hands still shackled.

"Tarni," I swim up to her, hoping to calm her before she dissolves into hysterics. "It's okay, just tell us where you were."

"I don't know," she whispers urgently. "I don't know, I just swam and tried to avoid people."

"Tarni—"

"No! They're blaming you too! You can't help me—you can't even help yourself!" she shrieks, taking away any hope that I can stop her outcry. "They're going to feed me to the sharks as soon as Nir signs the treaty and say I tried to escape and they had nothing to do with it."

She sobs, sinking down in the water.

"No, of course not, Tarni. They wouldn't do that, not to anyone!" I protest, trying to lift her up so that she'll look at me. "They're not going to hurt you. They're just trying to figure out what happened."

"See?" Murdoch encroaches on the conversation. "They're in this together—look at the way they're talking! They're *friends*."

Shouting erupts in the room. Marilla tries to calm the conversation but Merrick and Murdoch have had enough, and it takes all of the guards to hold the two at bay.

I can't tear my eyes away from Merrick.

This is going to change everything, apparently.

"What is happening? Caspian shouts, entering the room with Keone and several others.

Merrick and Murdoch growl accusations at each other.

"I saw what happened," Keone attempts to yell over the crowd. "I saw!"

"Enough!" Marilla swims to the center of the room. She gently stretches her hand in Keone's direction. "What did you see?"

"When I was on the surface, I heard Celena sirening the humans. She got all of the surviving mer in the water before even considering saving herself," he replies as I hold my breath. Keone and I have never been close. "She instructed the sailor to take her to the side and drop his lover in the sea.

"He placed her on the edge of the ship but then he tried to kiss her. She pushed herself away and fell the entire length of the ship down into the water before Merrick got to her." He looks around the room. "She rescued all of us and only barely made it out herself. She's not at fault here."

"She still sirened the humans yesterday," Murdoch protests.

"*Oh, for coral's sake*, Murdoch, let it go," Marilla snaps. "She was rescuing Merrick. We've already established that."

She darts up in the water, holding both hands out to her sides.

"I find these accusations to be baseless and prejudicial, what say you?" she asks the council.

They nod in agreement.

"I proclaim this trial over. Celena, you are free to go and we apologize for the inconvenience you have suffered today. Thank you all who have participated. The public will be made aware of what has transpired today."

Marilla leaves, swimming out of the room quickly to set up the public address.

Dylana and Morgen swim to us, eyes blazing like the sun reflecting off the surface of the water directly overhead.

"I say we put him in a net and leave him out by the Anchor all day," Dylana scowls. "Come on, it's time to feed the stingrays."

We turn to follow her, knowing she wants privacy from the crowded room. Merrick lingers next to me. His fingers brush against mine as we swim—I try not to blush.

Tarni screams as the guards try to remove her.

"We'll take her," I say, swimming between them. "Come on."

I tug on her, not giving her a choice, though I suspect she would choose us over the guards at the moment.

Dylana doesn't look pleased when I turn back but she doesn't stop me. We swim to her parlor—the one Merrick and I were just in—and I'm certain I turn seven shades of coral. Merrick risks a glance at me, making it worse.

The fish are still there, swimming in circles.

"Who let them in?" Dylana mutters. She lets a breath out when she sees her seahorses and swims over to greet them.

A guard taps on the door, offering a basket of shrimp. Morgen carries it to his sister as the stingrays flood into the room. Tarni's eyes grow wide.

Caspian and Morgen keep a watchful eye on the siren while the princess and I feed the stingrays. Merrick's hand brushes against mine as he reaches into the basket to help. He's much better at looking non-conspicuous than I am—he doesn't let on at all. I press my tongue against the roof of my mouth, hoping no one notices how jumpy I am. I suppose I could always play it off on the trial if I need to.

The light shifts again as rays of sun filter down through the waves above. The room is filled with streams of light, catching every piece of debris floating in the water and setting them alive. Everything glitters around us, bouncing off the thrashing stingrays as they collect their dinner. The light glares so brightly off the tiny winged creatures that I have to squint.

I'm surprised when I see one of them slam into the sand well below us. It thrashes as a trident sticks out of it, sand pluming around it. I look up in horror, finding Tiko's face staring back at us through the hole in the ceiling.

"Miss me?" he calls cruelly.

The sirens are here to attack.

CHAPTER 15

We dive for the edges of the room as Tiko aims a spear into the parlor.

"How did they get into Scylla?" Dylana shrieks.

I can't look away from the hole where Tiko had been.

"Guys!" Merrick's voice is sharp.

When I turn to look, Tarni is holding the trident to Merrick's chest, running the tips of it down his skin just enough to leave red lines. Bits of the stingray are still attached to it.

"Tarni!" I warn.

"Oh come off it, princess," she says powerfully. "If you were too stupid to catch on to my little act, I can't help you.

"*You*, however," she eyes Merrick. "You can come with me."

"Spear me," Merrick mocks her.

"Oh, big tough merman doesn't think I'll hurt him," she pretends to pout. "What will your *girlfriend* do when I skewer you and put you out for the sharks? Or, perhaps…I should skewer *her* instead."

She backs up as she speaks, pretending she might turn toward me.

"I dare you to try, Tarni," I taunt.

A spear floats through the water hitting another stingray.

"Let's go, Tarni," Tiko warns. He looks shocked at her transformation.

I'm grateful the hole in the ceiling isn't big enough for a mer to fit through, but I also wish I could crash through it and take Tiko out.

"There's five of us and one of you, Tarni," Caspian says. "Merrick can handle himself."

Caspian moves forward. From the corner of my eye, I can see Morgen draw his sword just out of Tarni's sight. I'm thankful at least one of us has a weapon. I nod to the spear in the dying stingray, hoping Dylana will get the message and retrieve it while I help to distract the siren.

"I wouldn't do that if I were you, princess," Tiko warns, reappearing as Dylana goes for the weapon.

Tarni jabs her weapon at Merrick but he deflects it, tipping it up above her head. Turning, Tarni doesn't have time to adjust her stance. Instead, she flicks her tail, darting toward Dylana instead.

The princess shrieks but moves away. The trident breaks the skin on her arm but does no real damage.

In the hallway, a war seems to rage. The door bursts open and Tarni uses the opportunity to push past a guard and rush toward the other sirens.

"Stop her," I shout, racing out the door behind her. The guard crashes into me, slowing me down as he attempts to avoid me.

I expect to find Nir, but he's nowhere to be seen as his sirens attack the palace.

I crash into a siren, knocking her against her partner. She growls at me, ready to engage. Not having a trident or spear on hand, I resort to the only thing I have available—the knife I always keep hidden in my *iluse*.

She bleeds as I beat her to striking. The siren hisses at me menacingly. Her partner comes after me, holding his trident out.

Morgen appears, holding a trident of his own. He battles against the siren, stabbing him in the shoulder roughly enough that the siren flees. Morgen hands me the weapon before darting away to get another one for himself.

I quickly swim around the fighting, knowing it's more important to get outside where the queen had been preparing to address the collection. Merrick, Caspian, and Dylana follow.

Marilla—looking entirely done with the situation—floats on the top of the palace steps with pursed lips. I catch a flash of Llyr's mint hair in the crowd and know he's on his way to assist.

The rest of the collection is kept at bay by the threat of their queen being hurt. They all look ready to attack.

In the crowd, sirens hold tridents up to the mer collection, threatening to hurt them if they swim out of line. I recognize some of the faces—I've seen them before. The sirens have been planning this for months—their mermaids and mermen have been floating around

Scylla gathering information and fitting in with the rest of us—no one had any idea.

They must have also planned to only reveal a small number of themselves when they breached the barrier—they wanted us to think they wouldn't be able to fight back if their first plan hadn't been successful.

Still, how did they get that many sirens into Scylla with us watching so closely?

Dylana glances at me, trying to figure out a plan. Tiko descends from over the palace where he had been spying on us, crashing into the princess from overhead. Caspian launches himself at them, assisting our cousin in battle.

"We're not here for our sirens back," Nir informs the crowd, yelling over their angry shouts. "We're here for your palace. We were run out of Scylla a century ago—"

"Your collection chose to leave," Marilla corrects him gracefully. Even in the face of danger, she's incredibly elegant.

"You forced us out," Nir growls in her ear.

"King Gaspar gave you all a choice. Sireny was not welcome here, nor is it now. Chantay made her choices."

"Don't speak about my great-great-grandmother."

Something sharp drags across the back of my arm, slicing through my skin. Roni pulls her broken shell back, ready to strike again. One of the nice things about living in the sea is that hair floats—she missed cutting my locks.

"She was my blood too, mer boy," Marilla reminds him.

The light shifts again, waning from the glittering gold to a dull gray color as the sun fades from the human sky—it will be night soon and our war will be taken into the darker parts of the waters.

Sirens spill out of the palace to assist their friends, rushing toward the crowd as they overlook us on the landing.

I slam my trident toward Roni but she quickly darts away. Tiko moves away from Dylana and Caspian, grabbing my trident from my hands. I try to hold on but fail.

Even the fish dart out of our way as the fighting continues. Red tails move the water just enough to leave whispers against our skin.

Before Tiko can strike, Merrick hits him with the long end of his trident in the small of his back, just above his tail. Tiko gasps for air.

I launch myself at Roni, propelling my tail as fast as I can. I grab her tail and hair, hauling her back into the mostly-empty palace, separating her from her collection. She bucks under my grasp but I've clamped down so tightly on her tail that she can't move it.

Without hesitating—or thinking it through—I slam her face first into the palace wall. She sinks down in the water slowly, a trail of blood slowly trembling from her broken nose.

I could do it right now—rip her tail off and remove her from the war altogether—but even the idea of tearing off fins renders me useless. I pull off part of the netting on my *iluse*, using my knife to cut it free, and tie her hands to her tail behind her. When she wakes up, she won't be able to move. I drag her to the closet and lock the door for an extra terrifying touch.

I wish I could see her when she wakes up in a dark closet, bound and unable to move.

The fish in front of me turns sideways in the water, swimming at an angle so he can turn around. I nearly collide with him as I rush by him. If fish could glare, I'm sure that would be the look I'm getting as I rush away.

If we can get the royals back in the palace and hide them, we'd have the advantage. If the sirens find a way in, they can easily locate us in the glow of the blooms above me.

I need to remove the jellyfish that light the palace.

For that, I need help.

Outside, I try to wave any one of my friends over to assist me without drawing the attention of the sirens.

"What are you doing?" Morgen hisses in my ear from behind me.

I jerk in the water, pulling away from the door.

"What are you doing?" I whisper harshly, repeating his words.

"Fighting inside, what are *you* doing?" he demands, brow furrowed.

"We have to move the jellyfish," I say as if he should have guessed. Really, it is rather unfair of me, but I don't have time to be nice about things if my plan is going to work. "It needs to be as dark as possible."

The moment he understands, his face changes, eyebrows shooting up.

"Okay." He nods. "I'll get the nets, you get the mer. Meet me in my grotto."

He darts off, racing through the palace to find supplies. I turn, preparing to swim back into the fighting.

Caspian grabs me by the wrist as I exit.

"We're making the palace dark. We need to hide the royals inside. Morgen's getting nets. I need your help."

"Merrick," Caspian calls. "Handle this!"

Without waiting for an answer, Caspian pulls me back inside. Over my shoulder, I see Dylana defending her mother, ready to take on Nir herself if she must.

"Where is Morgen?"

"His grotto," I reply.

We nearly collide with the walls a few times as we take corners too fast, swimming as quickly as our tails will let us.

"Go," I finally tell Caspian. "I'll catch up."

He hesitates for a moment, but he thrusts his tail and propels himself through the water faster—it must be nice to have such a powerful tail.

I try to take note of everywhere I see the roascea colonies as I dart by rooms. There are hidden places in the palace—locations only the royals and those closest to them know about—where we'll hide Marilla and her children.

It hadn't occurred to me until this moment that Marilla's other children must be hidden somewhere in the palace. I'm sure Morgen saw to their safety—as did their guards who likely gave up their lives protecting them—but we will have to be mindful to keep Marilla and Dylana away from them. Should the sirens find one of the reigning royals, we cannot afford to let them find the others.

"Here." Caspian drops the nets in my arms the moment I enter the grotto. "We're going to have to do this together. You and I will capture them and Morgen will remove them."

"It's going to be a pain getting these guys back in here when this is all over," Morgen grumbles.

"Let's go." I turn, leading the way to the closest room as Morgen drags out the first bloom.

Caspian and I each take a side, holding the net far out from our bodies. I eye the jellyfish carefully, trying to avoid their long tentacles as we scoop the net around them. Diving down, we catch the creatures inside the ropes, giving enough space at the end for Morgen to drag them out of the palace walls without getting stung.

We hand the net off to him as we swim to the next room. My twin and I systematically work our way through the palace, removing as many as possible. Thankfully, not every room has a colony—just the ones frequently used at night.

I'm terrified over what is happening outside the palace walls and why Tiko hasn't made his way inside yet. Nir, I'm sure, is attempting to terrorize the collection.

"Celena," a quiet voice calls out as we enter one of the grottos.

That's not right. That voice shouldn't be here.

"Coralie?" I ask.

Caspian whips his head around, looking for the source of the voice.

She lets out a strangled cry, racing out from under a chair made from the wreckage of an old ship. She releases the stingray she had been holding, blocking her from sight. It reels back into the water, angry enough to strike. Caspian quickly stops it from hurting Coralie.

Our sister races into my arms, sobbing.

"What are you doing here?"

"Mama told me about the trial. I snuck in to see what was happening but Natale was here and saw me. She made me wait with her and when the sirens attacked, we got separated. I hid," she confesses, pointing back toward the seat. She glances to the door, clearly worried about Natale.

"I'm sure she's safe," I assure her. "We need to get *you* safe."

"What is this?" Morgen gasps as he swims into the room.

"Don't leave me," Coralie begs.

"Hide her," I beg Morgen, holding Coralie's hand out to him in mine.

"*You* hide her, Celena," Caspian cuts in on the conversation. "Morgen and I will get the rest of the colonies. Then get back outside and help Dylana and Marilla."

"Come on." I don't have time to question our brother.

I spin Coralie, praying she stops sobbing.

"You have to be quiet," I tell her harshly.

"What are we going to do?" Coralie begs for an answer.

"We're going to hide *you* and then *I'm* going to stop the sirens," I inform her, darting around the corner in the dark as she clings to my arm.

"But if they find out who we are…"

"They will not find out who you are, Cor," I promise. "They already know me, but you need to keep quiet. Tell them you're Natale's sister if you need too—she'll back you up. They won't care about *her* nearly as much as *us*."

"Why did Aila have to do this?" Coralie cries.

"Aila protected us all. It was Persephone and Chantay who betrayed us. They're the ones that caused all this."

"But couldn't it have been one of the other princesses?"

"Aila did what she had to do. She saved the collection and she tried to stop a war," I defend my great-great-grandmother unnecessarily.

"But it started two," she protests more out of fear than anything else.

"Starfish, you love great-great-grandma Aila for what she did. Don't question that now."

Coralie has always had more of an affinity for the old tales than I have, and considering how deeply invested I am, I have no idea why she's questioning things now. Fear does that, I suppose—it makes us question what we know is true because it gives us something to grasp onto in the moment.

"I know you're in here," Nir's voice sings.

I crash to a halt, pulling Coralie back with me. The darkness offers us protection, but even Coralie's place under the chair in the grotto was safer than clinging to each other in the hallway.

I feel Coralie tense against me as she straightens her shoulders. She casts her tears aside and prepares to fight alongside of me—I couldn't be prouder—or more terrified.

Reaching into my *iluse*, I pull a broken shell out. Taking her hand in mine, I carefully trace the shell with her fingers, gently explaining without words what she needs to know. She turns her hand, squeezing mine to tell me she understands.

I let go, reaching up to weave the shell into the underside of her hair where the sirens won't be able to see it. Coralie's hand floats up, locating the shell in her hair should she need it.

"Don't make me get my pet sharks to find you," Nir taunts. Someone struggles near him.

I place a hand on Coralie's shoulder, forcing her to stay in place. Quietly, I make my way to the edge of the hallway, hoping to figure out who Nir is traveling with through the palace.

The visibility is dim in the foyer, a bit of light coming in through the ceiling giving off our only visibility. Nir's figure swims toward the shaft of light and I wish on all the starfish in the palace proper that he swims *through it* instead of going around. He's either grown an extra tail since I last saw him or he has someone pressed against his body.

She squirms again, grunting around Nir's hand.

Her opal tail flips into the light, shining enough to catch my attention. Bits of her dark pink hair follows next as she struggles against the siren king's son—the *new* king.

Dylana looks frantically around the room—I'm sure the lack of light in the palace surprised her.

"I'll feed your princess to the sharks if you don't come out," Nir calls, still singing to us.

Dylana tries to yell, but her captor's hand muffles her cries. I push Coralie back, tapping her frantically to get her to move. She backs up, giving me enough room to turn around without flipping my tail out into the middle of the hallway.

I take us slowly at first, trying not to makes waves, but as soon as we reach the end of the hallway, I pull her as fast as I can back to the mermen.

"Nir has Dylana," I announce, nearly crashing into Morgen.

"What are you doing back here?" Caspian looks horrified.

"They have Dylana?" Morgen shouts.

"Cor has to come with us," I inform them, flicking my tail impatiently. "We can't get by them."

"What did you see?" Caspian asks.

"He has Dylana." We all flinch at the sound of Merrick's voice. He swims into the room looking radiant. "I saw you in the hallway and followed you—sorry."

"Did Nir see us?"

"No, he was too far beyond you at that point but I was still near the door. I saw him bring Dylana in."

"My mother?" Morgen questions, eyes wide.

"She's hurt but she's alive last I knew," Merrick replies. "Nir had Tiko and the others bring her in first, but he's been parading Dylana around like a prized seahorse."

Our future is in our children.

Merrick sounds furious by the time he's finished speaking.

"We need to get her back." Morgen's frustration spills into the rest of the group. "Do you know where he took her?"

"You're not leaving me here," Coralie interrupts, crossing her arms.

"Oh, yes, we are." Caspian crosses his arms to match her. "You will go back under that chair in the other room, or so help me, I will net you and lock you in a closet myself."

"You need help," Coralie insists. "I can help."

"You will get yourself filleted if you go out there, Cor," Caspian protests. "No."

"I'm with him," I declare, nodding to my twin. "No way in the seven seas are you going out there with us."

"You either take me or I'll sneak out once you're gone, and I can't imagine that's going to be helpful to anyone, especially if I get caught, because apparently, I'm the only guppy that didn't bother to learn how to do this."

"It's not safe," Caspian replies.

"Nothing is," Coralie responds, pouting.

"Coralie," Merrick draws her attention. My sister has always had a fondness for the blue-haired mer. "We need you to be safe."

"I will be," she cuts him off. "I'll be with all of you. Now, let's go."

She swims to the door, trying to be brave, but her movements are hesitant. I swim after her, knowing it's pointless to argue. Working against Coralie is as silly as trying to remove an octopus from where it wants to be, or worse—trying to keep it in.

"Come on, mermen. We have work to do."

"Oh, not yet, you don't," a merman calls from overhead.

CHAPTER 16

We quickly look up—we really need to start checking for the holes in the ceiling before we start talking.

"Can you get me in?" Llyr calls down.

"Not through there," Merrick calls back up sarcastically.

"Funny," Llyr whispers. "I can't get in the front. I swam all the way around and ended up here, but I can't fit in anywhere."

"Below," Morgen says. "Adjacent to the cells is an underground escape. We've got the others waiting down there in case they need to flee, but you can access it from the outside."

"Where?" Llyr asks.

Morgen quickly describes the route, telling him where the secret panels are to access the tunnel dug into the sand and stone under the palace. The merman nods down to us before swimming away.

"Now we just have to get down there to help him in," Merrick comments. "You know he's bringing mer with him."

I glance out the door and notice the body of a mer guard floating by. His embellished hair trails behind him, nearly as long as his arms. I recognize him from my visits to the palace—he was a kind merman.

A sea turtle swims into the room. Coralie watches it for a moment, fixated on it before turning back. It loops the space, moving just enough to propel it forward.

I lead the way, swimming through the halls. Caspian holds Coralie's hand, guiding her through the palace that she's less familiar with than us.

We approach the hallway that leads to the foyer where we left Nir with Dylana. I slow, checking for signs of them.

The school of fish in the room suddenly turns at once, swimming in the opposite direction together as if warning us that danger lies ahead. They dart down our hallway, wiggling their bodies to move in the water. Their scales catch the tiniest bit of light the hallway holds and reflects it like a phantom cloud devouring the ocean, sweeping through the sea and changing everything in its path until the waters clear and all is right again. The water whispers over my skin in their wake.

I swim through the foyer, guiding us down another hall. Murmurs fill the water from one of the grottos. I pause, trying to peek inside but the door is closed over at the wrong angle for me to see anything.

I wait, biding my time until I dart by to the other side. Each mer does the same, Caspian bringing Coralie with him. Merrick hovers just off my shoulder, waiting for me to take the lead again—I know the palace better than anyone except the royals.

When we reach the last room, Morgen guides us into the grotto, carefully checking for enemies hiding within. When the room is clear, he opens a closet and removes a secret panel, revealing the doorway to the hidden entrance.

We guard the door as the prince swims inside to help Llyr and whomever he has brought along with him. A few minutes later, they return, nearly the entirety of the wall guards with them.

"How did you—?" I ask.

"We have our ways of communicating quickly, Celena," Llyr grins, brushing his hair out of his face. "Don't question, just accept."

I want desperately to question.

Merrick backs up, making way for the mermen to exit the hidden passageway and enter the palace. His back presses against me. I hold my hands up to let him know I'm there and he settles back into my palms, calming under my touch.

To be mean, I gently run my fingers up his shoulder blades to his shoulders, making him shiver involuntarily. Coralie notices and looks shocked. I shake my head quickly in the dim light, barely able to see her—though her eyes have always been better than mine in the dark.

She smirks, turning back to our brother.

I will *never* hear the end of this.

Coralie suddenly shrieks, making the entire room turn toward her. She bats at the water, shaking her head back and forth as a fish darts away—it hadn't noticed her and swam right into her face.

Caspian and I turn on her, grabbing at her hands. Casp clamps a hand over her mouth, stilling her.

"It's fine, you're fine," he croons, trying to calm her. Our brother wraps our sister in his arms, running his hands over her hair. He pulls back when he feels the shell.

"Defense," I hiss before turning to the crowd and adding a bit louder, "Let's go."

I've never witnessed the palace this dark. I know every turn, every twist, every rock by heart, but I've never experienced it in such vast emptiness.

The moonlight shines in through small holes in the ceiling catching the debris as it filters by in the water. It does nothing to change the luminance in the room, only to give hope that somewhere out there, there is a place not cast into hopelessness.

The small beam of light makes me realize that we only have a few hours before the sun comes up above the waves again and the palace will once again be beautifully lit—and our cover of darkness will be taken from us. We have mere hours to free Dylana and Marilla and take back the palace.

After that, we still have to free the rest of Scylla.

I wonder what the sirens are doing to them beyond the walls of the palace—they can't let them leave. Darkness must make them hard to control, so what is their plan?

"What did you see out there?" Merrick asks Llyr.

"The back of the palace is empty. There are no entrances back there so I don't think they thought to post anyone there because there's no perceivable means of escape."

"Good thing the sirens didn't stay long in Scylla when the war started," Merrick comments.

"Good thing none of the royal sided with Chantay," Morgen adds. "They would have known the palace at that point and would have been able to tell them. I don't think Chantay was ever in the palace at Scylla—no one had lived here since King Gaspar was a mer boy at that point, and only during certain times of the year."

All the books I've read indicate that Chantay had never seen Scylla before she and Persephone tried to capture Aila from outside the palace proper. She wouldn't have any knowledge of the secret escapes.

"I don't think she was ever here," I agree.

"Good, that means the tunnel is available for use," Merrick says, a grin in his voice. "Change of plans, mer. We're rescuing the mer children first."

"And doing *what* with them?" Caspian asks.

"Sending them to Metten," Merrick replies.

It's brilliant, really. If we can free the royals and other mer children, their guards can sneak them through the back of Scylla. If they hide in caves and move in darkness, they have a chance of reaching the old kingdom without being harmed.

It will take longer with the mer children than it took for us, but if they can find a pod of dolphins, they stand a better chance of getting there without incident.

"There's a royal journal with a map of Metten in Dylana's room. That will show them where to hide when they get there," I announce.

I instruct one of the wall guards on where to find it in Dylana's chambers. Llyr assures me the merman is the best spy they have on the wall. I trust his assessment and let Morgen guide the group toward the secret chambers where the mer children are hidden well past the vault that houses historical treasures—I hope the sirens don't find that either.

We cling to the walls, the sides of the rock comforting under our touch. Each flick of our tail brings us closer to the hidden room, but we move so slowly to avoid detection that we end up pulling ourselves across the rock with our arms.

Coralie hovers just off my tail, her hands touching it each time she reaches out. Caspian is wrapped around her, pinning her between himself and the wall to protect her should anything happen.

She doesn't know it yet, but we're going to force her to go to Metten with the others.

As soon as the palace in Scylla is secured and the collection is free from the sirens, we'll go to Metten and take care of the mer children. I imagine we'll stay there with them until we're positive its safe to return—moving them again could be dangerous.

The mer children won't like being kept away, but it's for their own safety, and I doubt anyone will argue with the queen's assessment—once we get her back.

The line of mer pauses, waiting for Morgen to proceed. He motions the guards off to go in search of the sirens while our small collection continues to the hidden chamber.

I'm not sure how the mer children and guards will be able to see once they leave the palace—they can't take the midwater squids with them or they risk being caught—but they'll have to find a way. Perhaps they'll swim blindly in the right direction until the sunlight deigns us worthy enough to join us again.

"We're here," Morgen whispers swimming up to the door.

He knocks a specific pattern—his royal signature—and we wait for the guards to let him in.

The room is small and empty as we swim through the door. It quickly latches behind us. Once the guard confirms Morgen's identity, he moves to a second concealed door.

The first room is a ploy, meant to trick unsuspecting trespassers. Should anyone make it this far, they would only find an empty room and move on to another location in search of the mer children or other royals. A mere guard resides in the room and would be the only one injured if it ever comes to that.

The guard opens the concealed door, revealing a room lit with bioluminescent algae to avoid the possibility of jellyfish stings. A few squids also light the room, hovering by their royals—over the years, we've trained them to stay close.

"You're leaving," Morgen informs his siblings and the others that happened to be caught in the madness of war inside the palace. Several adult mer nod. The guards quickly straighten, ready to obey their commands from the highest-ranking ruler in their midst.

The mer children look terrified. A chorus of questions is silenced with Morgen's hand in the air. He looks to the guards.

"No one is guarding the back of the palace. It's dark, so visibility is limited, which will make this harder for you, but *also* harder for the sirens. You need to take everyone here and go to Metten."

The guard from the first room joins us, slipping the journal into my hands—the wall guard we sent for it must have returned. Morgen had told the guard to watch for him.

"This will guide you," I say, holding it up. "Inside is information about the palace at Metten. Take the mer children there and hide them until we come for you when this is over."

"You will protect them," Morgen instructs.

I hand him the journal and swim back, giving him the space he needs to direct his guards. Coralie twitches beside me.

"Swim as far as you can tonight. Don't stop, even when they're tired. You need to get as far from here as possible.

"Take turns resting." He continues to explain what the mermen and mermaids must do to protect the little ones.

When he's finished, we check the hallway, letting Merrick swim down first. Once he returns, we use Caspian's technique, shielding the mer children with our bodies. The adults in the group do the same, quietly keeping to the walls to move their charges to freedom.

We crawl along the rocks again, though this time my forearms don't hit the wall now that a petite mer girl with red hair is nestled between the wall and me. Her brown tail twitches against me, fighting to take small flicks instead of large ones to avoid slamming into me—she should have just let me drag her along.

At the end of the hall, we follow the path back to the hidden tunnel, acutely aware of the noise in the grotto. Caspian taps my fins letting me know we need to come back—this is likely our next battleground.

The mer girl is braver than I expect her to be. She doesn't even whimper when some of the others do. Perhaps Marilla should enlist her as a future spy when this is all over.

Morgen opens the door for his siblings and the others to escape.

"No!" Coralie says harshly to Caspian. "I won't go."

"You have to, Cor. You have to stay safe. Mom or one of us will come for you as soon as we can, but we need to you to go with them and help them protect the mer children," I insist. "It's our job as Aila's blood to protect the royals."

"You have a job to do, Cor," Caspian adds. "Ours is here, yours is with them."

"Mine is here too. I'll protect the palace."

"Go to Metten, starfish," I refuse to let her stay. "It's beautiful there —you'll love it. You've always wanted to see Metten—this is your chance."

"I also wanted to see the inside of an octopus' mouth and a shark up close," she argues. "I'm not going."

"*You are* if I have to drag you outside," I threaten again.

I pull her along as she fights me. If I have to drag her by the tail, I will, and I'll instruct the guards to do so too if I must.

I swim out with the collection going to Metten, leaving Llyr, Caspian, and the other guards to watch the grotto. Merrick and I check to make sure there are no sirens in sight before releasing the younger mer and their caretakers.

I hug Coralie and push her out into the crowd. I almost instantly lose sight of her in the dark waters as they swim away—a blessing that means the sirens can't see them either.

Merrick and I wait, floating in the waters.

"Do you think they'll be okay?" I ask, turning to look at my partner.

"They'll be okay," he promises. "Those are the palace's best guards with them and a bunch of other mermaids and mermen who really care about them. They'll be safe. Metten will be good for them."

The water swirls behind my back and I float forward into Merrick. He catches me in his arms.

"We should go in," he says.

I take one last look at the royal mer children and Coralie swimming somewhere in the distant dark waters before letting Merrick guide me inside.

He closes the door, blocking it.

In the dark, his lips brush over mine, as light and fleeting as a stingray's kiss.

Bubbles float up from the tips of my fins through my entire body. His hand holds my chin as he pulls away, refusing to give me more than a single kiss but it's as exhilarating as our first—even without the swirling fish.

He hovers there for a moment, inches from my face. I can barely see him in the dimly lit tunnel, but the blue glow of algae gives me just enough visibility to see that he's grinning uncontrollably.

I bite my lip and he smirks at me, one corner of his mouth stretching high on his face.

"Like that, huh?"

I'm positive I blush, but at least in the blue bioluminescent glow of the tunnel Merrick can't tell.

"We should go," I say curtly, swimming away, hoping I'm leaving him in shock.

His hand reaches out and strokes my fins, making me jolt. He chuckles deeply, making me giggle like a mer girl waiting for her mother to finish a meeting with the queen.

We're back to business by the time we reach the end of the tunnel. Merrick drops my hand—he picked it up when he swam alongside of me—and we exit into the hidden grotto.

"Still clear?" Merrick asks.

Caspian glares at us.

"What?" I ask.

He turns, glaring at…

"Coralie!" I shout louder than I mean to say.

"Apparently she swam back in after you sent her off," Caspian snarls.

Which would explain the wave of water I felt. If I hadn't turned to look at Merrick, she wouldn't have been able to swim by me—she also might have been trapped outside alone.

"I can't believe—"

"Yes you can," Caspian corrects. "We both would have done it too."

"Did someone instruct you on how to do that?" I ask, realizing that if our parents had kept our family in the dark about training me and my twin, we also might not know if they trained Coralie.

"What?" she wrinkles her nose, pulling her head back slightly.

Apparently not.

"Fine, you're staying here." Before she can protest, I hold up a hand. "We need all of our trained people to fight in this battle, but we also need someone to handle this tunnel. You're in charge of letting us in if we need to get in and escape."

Casp quickly sees the merits to my plan and shows her two knocks—Morgen's and one we create for the rest of us to use. We position her behind the door and show her how to secure it, practicing several times while the others swim ahead to locate Dylana and the others.

"You're sure about this?" Caspian mumbles as we float outside the door, waiting to make sure our sister locks it properly.

"We have to let her grow up sometime, Casp."

We promise to return, and check to see Coralie is really locked in before we swim away.

When we arrive at the grotto we passed before, we find it empty.

"They've moved," Merrick says, waiting for us with the information. "We're spreading out to find them."

A stingray sails through the water overhead, oblivious to the danger lurking in the palace. I almost reach out and pet its underside, but I refrain from disturbing it.

"This is the last crab leg," Caspian mutters. "Time to take these sirens out."

"Don't beat around the kelp bed, Casp, tell us how you really feel," Merrick replies sarcastically.

"Where did the others go?" I cut them off.

Merrick points to the right. We swim to the left. Mogen and Llyr wait a few hallways away.

"Anything?"

"Nothing yet," Llyr says. "Let's keep going."

Trusting the mermen I'm with, I use the swim to think things through. I still don't understand how all of the sirens got in, nor how they slipped into the palace.

Guards are posted at every entrance and should have prevented any unknown mer from entering. Even if they took one of the guards out, they'd still need to get past more unless they had someone from the palace with them.

The mermen guarding the royals are very unforgiving when it comes to knowing who mer are and aren't. They go through rigorous training and know nearly as much about the different mer that spend time in the palace as they know about themselves—they would know the instant someone was out of place.

The sirens had to have someone inside the palace to get in—I don't think it's plausible to assume they just swam up to the door and knocked a guard out. What I can't figure out is how they got someone in place that the guards trusted enough to let get close to them.

"There," Llyr whispers.

We all stop in the water, waiting to see what he noticed.

A figure swims out of the room slowly, checking the dark hallway. We move further back, hoping the merman doesn't notice us. The mer swims toward us, deftly moving through the water until he's right next to us, his partner by his hip.

Llyr lashes out, restraining the merman. Caspian's hands dart out, wrangling the mermaid.

"Let go," the merman hisses, sounding familiar.

"Keone?" Merrick asks, swimming closer.

"Merrick?" he replies, still struggling.

"What are you doing?"

"Saving the queen, what are you doing?" Keone challenges.

"Let him go," Merrick commands. He faces Keone. "Same thing."

Keone settles as Llyr releases him.

"Sorry, buddy," Llyr apologizes.

"Don't ever touch me again," Natale's voice fills the space.

"Oh," Caspian says in reply. "Sorry, cousin."

"Caspian, lovely," Natale says, realizing who had a hold of her.

"What are you doing here?" I shake my head. "Natale, we need to get you to Coralie. You can't be out here."

"I'm not going anywhere, Celena."

"Natale, you're not trained for this—"

"Except I am, cousin," she responds curtly.

"What are you talking about?"

"I'm trained for this, Celena—you just never knew it. I wasn't quiet for no good reason—I'm very, very good at what I do and you and the collection need me. Keone too."

"It's true, friends," Keone adds smugly. "She's terrifying and she's currently very, very annoyed, so that's going to work to our benefit."

I shake my head.

"You need to help Coralie."

"Coralie should be in hiding. I tried to get her to the hidden room but we got separated, but right now, she can't be my priority. Go take care of your sister if you need to—I have work to do."

She starts to swim down the hallway.

"Natale—" I call to her.

She flips around to face me, annoyed.

"Don't be so naïve, Celena, You sound just like Aila. Ebba took up the lead secretly when Aila backed down. Your ancestor was so busy obeying the rules that she forgot that mer can't back down from a war.

"My family has been working to help you for generations. Once a royal, always a royal," Natale informs me. "You think I don't know what was going on here? Why do you think I always happened to be in the palace at just the right times? Hmm?

"It wasn't for fun, Celena. I didn't enjoy spending all my time with the children, but it turns out they know more than they think they do. I learned all sorts of information from them—your sister included. That's how I was able to support you."

Her fin flicks in the water, annoyed.

"Ebba's line wasn't welcome to spy for Kalania's line, so we handled it ourselves. We were always thought of as the softer line, but *all* jellyfish can sting, cousin—some of us just keep it better hidden."

"When this is all over, you're going to have to tell me how you *supported* me," I say softly, trying to keep it bubbly. The fact that Natale has been working alongside me without me knowing for years is concerning.

But then, what else is new?

"Anyone *else* have secrets?" Merrick asks.

"Don't look at me," Keone replies mischievously. "I'm just here to look pretty next to this one."

He nods at Natale, grinning.

"Don't be inky, Keone," she snips. "He's perfectly capable of taking care of himself."

"She's trained me well," Keone answers, wrapping an arm around her.

"Off," Natale orders, all business. She pushes his hand away, smiling at him to soften her rebuff.

He makes a kissy face at her, winking flirtatiously.

"So the smarmy guy façade is just an act, huh?" Merrick asks.

"No, he's really like that," Natale informs us. "He only *just* convinced me to spend time with him."

"She's always spent time with me—just not the fun kind. This mermaid is all about business."

"I have a job to do," she protests.

I wonder if Merrick and I will ever sound like that.

We all turn when we hear a siren swimming our way.

CHAPTER 17

The siren yells for assistance, notifying the others of our presence. He prepares to engage with us, holding his trident out. The squid at his side casts the hallway into a dull blue color as the light bounces off the rock walls.

My fingers drift to my *iluse*, double-checking to make sure my knife is still there. I tighten my grip on my trident.

A school of fish I know truly have yellow detailing on them, swims by, a blue color in the bioluminescent light. They don't seem to mind us.

Tiko flips around the corner, rushing straight at us. His eyes widen when he sees us, grin spreading across his face.

"Of course it would be you," he says. "Where is Roni?"

I consider telling him that we filleted her and put her outside for the sharks, but I imagine that would only make him reckless.

"Where is our princess?"

"Dead," he answers bluntly.

"No!" Morgen gasps quietly.

"No, she's not," I reply. "You need to control her if you want power."

"We already *have* power, *princess*," he answers. "We don't need any of *you* to run Scylla. We're in control. Nir owns this palace and everyone in it. We may allow some of your mer to stay, but we don't actually want them here—you can go wander the seas like we had to.

"Well…" he slows. "Not *you*. *You're* going to die. But your collection will probably be allowed to leave if they don't give us any trouble.

"In fact," Tiko continues. "I have a suggestion on where they can all go. The shallows are lovely this time of year and the humans find it the perfect time to hunt mer."

"You'll never find her," I interrupt, bringing the conversation back to Roni. "Shame."

"I will take your tail off scale-by-scale if I have to," Tiko replies casually. "You don't get to tell me no on this. You're too weak to hurt her—"

"You did see what I did to the humans, right?"

"You wouldn't touch her. You tried to help Durdania when she went after her sister's starfish—"

"Oh, you mean *this* starfish?" I pull it out of my pouch.

"Where did you get that?" he seethes.

"Where is our princess?" I counter, hoping to throw him off.

I move the silver starfish around so that it catches the light. It bounces the muted blue tones back at Tiko just enough that I can barely see it on his face.

"Give it to me," he growls.

"Take us to Dylana."

"Easy, Len," Merrick murmurs without moving his lips just loud enough for me to hear.

More sirens round the corner, assessing the situation. We all sink back in the water, leveling ourselves with the ground before flipping our tails to propel ourselves toward the sirens.

Our attack surprises them—the sirens that have just arrived aren't prepared to engage in battle with us and we easily strike first.

Merrick and I take on Tiko as he lashes out at my fins.

"Who is Durdania to you?" I demand, trying to distract him with the memory of the red-tailed siren that died in front of us. The image of her lifeless body floods my thoughts.

Tiko's trident rips over my tail, cutting the edge of my fin. I double over in pain.

"No!" Merrick shouts, driving his trident toward Tiko.

A siren catches Merrick's tail in his hand, pulling Merrick back just enough to jerk his trident out of alignment. It slams into the rock, drifting toward the floor.

Merrick scoops it up, turning to lash out at the siren behind him. He strikes, stopping the merman.

Tiko growls, striking at Merrick. Straightening, I dive between

Merrick and Tiko, successfully knocking the trident away before it sinks into Merrick's back.

I turn on Tiko, knowing he's coming for me. I dropped my trident in the struggle, so I reach for my knife on my hip to defend myself. In turn, Tiko grasps his knife as well, ready to destroy me.

Caspian cries out from somewhere behind me. My instinct is to turn and help my twin but Tiko doesn't plan on showing any mercy—turning my back on him would likely result in my death.

I slam into the wall as another siren collides with me. Tiko uses the opportunity to grab my hair—I wish I had buried broken shells in it before the trial.

He jerks my head back to look up at him as the other siren uses his full weight to pin me against the wall. The knife falls from my hand, drifting quietly to the sand.

"Where is Roni, *princess?*"

"I don't know," I lie.

He wrenches my hand out from where it's pinned between my hip and the siren merman crushing the life out of me. He smiles when he notices I've dropped my weapon.

"It's time you learned a little lesson," he says, holding up his knife.

I can hear the others clashing with the sirens around my captor's body, but I can't see around him. Tiko's knife glints in the glow of the hallway.

He holds my wrist, but struggling does nothing to help me—the siren merman has me pinned. My lungs feel like they're being crushed from the sides, snapping in on themselves as he pushes.

The siren jerks around, swimming against the wall, trying to hold me there. I can't reach him with my far hand to try to hurt him so my next option is to distract him just long enough that I can force my way out from the wall.

Tiko brings the knife down toward my skin as I use my tail to wrap around the siren pinning me. My scales against his tail fluster him enough that he pulls back for a moment just as Tiko is about to start carving off chunks of my flesh.

It disrupts the siren intent on injuring me. His periwinkle tail flashes as he flips it in anger as I pull backward, flipping my fins toward him to escape.

His hand darts out, slicing at my fins—he barely misses.

I could cry, I'm so happy to not have endured another slice in my fins. As it is, I'm going to have to learn how to swim with a split in my fin now—I don't know if it's long enough to affect me yet, but I'll know as soon as we leave the hallway's limited space.

Caspian slams his trident into the back of Tiko's shoulder. He screams in pain, spinning to face my brother. Next to him, Llyr adds his as Tiko spins around, stabbing the same shoulder from the front.

"Natale!" Morgen shouts, shock ringing in his voice.

I turn, unable to help myself, and find the body of a siren floating in the water next to my cousin.

"I told you," she says. "I know what I'm doing."

She turns, snarling at another siren who backs away from her.

"Hold your place or Nir will feed you to the sharks," Tiko snarls through his pain.

The siren swims away anyway.

At least we have *one* advantage.

The merman that had pinned me against the wall turns back to me, ready to slam me into the hallway rocks once again.

What is it about sirens and slamming mermaids into walls?

My knife is still on the ground. I had moved back enough that I can't reach it even if I *do* manage to swim past the siren. I try to position myself to be able to swim to the side as he races toward me.

Before I can move, the siren crashes upward. A dolphin flips its head up, butting the siren again. He quickly floats toward the roof of the hallway, the dolphin continuing to slam into him.

A second dolphin enters the hallway, clicking.

Relief floods over me. These dolphins have frequented the palace as long as I've been coming here—they're here to help us.

The sirens eye the dolphins warily. When one of the dolphins swims to me, I take the opportunity to grab its dorsal fin and allow it to move me to safety.

He darts past the sirens, carrying me over their heads in the water before circling back once in the foyer. Outside, I wait for the others to join me.

The dolphins communicate back and forth, actively blocking the sirens from following us. Morgen reaches me first.

"There's a trap door," he informs me, waving me over.

Swimming is painful with a split in my fin, but I force my way over to the wall just outside of the hallway entrance. A tiny sea turtle crosses the room, moving out of our way.

Hidden high above the outline of the door is a wall of rocks. It's attached to the wall of the palace and blends in so perfectly that unless you know where to touch to release it, you'd never know it existed. Even *I* didn't know it was there.

"There have to be at least a few secrets, Celena," Morgen comments. "We've all seen how easily one of our own can turn on us.

"Don't be offended," he continues, pointing to where I need to slide my hand between the fake wall and the real one. "Dylana knows things I don't know and I know things she doesn't know...just in case."

He darts to the other side of the wall, ready to move his lever.

A third and fourth dolphin swim into the foyer as our friends burst out. The first dolphin carries Llyr. The rest swim out on their own.

The dolphins in the foyer hover in front of the exit, blocking the sirens.

"Now!" Morgen yells, indicating that I should release the wall.

I move the lever and the entire wall starts shifting so quickly that I barely have time to move. The water sucks me down as it moves with the motion of the rock wall. Morgen swims quickly, guiding the wall down faster than it would normally travel in the water.

The last dolphin pops out of the hallway just before the rocks slam into the sand.

"Everyone okay?" Morgen yells, righting himself in the water.

All four dolphins click in answer. Caspian looks a little beat up and Natale seems to have taken some abuse, but they're all in the foyer and the sirens are not.

Morgen locks something on the rocks. He nods for us to follow him.

"There's a lever on the other side to free them—it's in case we ever get trapped—but they'll never find it buried in the sand," he whispers. "They won't be getting out any time soon."

"Do we have any idea where Dylana or Marilla are?"

"One of them said something about the queen's grotto," Natale informs us. "I don't know who is there or if they're using the room at all, but it's a good place to work toward."

The dolphins swim with us, trailing behind as we move through the palace. When we stop at the end of a hallway, I put my hand on one's nose, guiding him to a halt. He flips his nose in my hand playfully.

Noise stretches out to us, indicating someone is inside the grotto. The piercing yell that follows confirms it.

"Where are the others?" Nir yells.

Silence follows.

"Where are they?" he repeats.

"From what I hear, you don't look like Chantay at all," Marilla finally responds. "How can anyone be sure you are who you say you are, mer boy?"

"He is the siren king," someone answers. "He is of Chantay's blood."

"But not Persephone's," Marilla replies. "The crown is passed to the eldest. Your ancestor is not that, Nir. You have no rights here, but even if you did, there is a line of succession and you do not reside in it even if you *had* come from Persephone's line."

"You murdered Persephone," Nir calls.

Llyr slowly swims toward the door, trying to get a look inside.

"Persephone was locked up for her transgressions over a century ago, Nir. Her actions led to this, and even then, King Gaspar did all that he could to take care of his granddaughter, despite her nearly getting everyone killed for nearly drowning that human prince."

The dolphin nudges my back, forcing me forward. I glare at him but he doesn't care, smiling back at me. I put my finger to my lips, warning him to stay quiet.

"And we've paid the humans back for what they've done to us. We've drowned so many of them that we've built our homes with their skulls and bones. They sit in our caverns and rest on our sea floor.

"The humans are paying for what they did to Persephone and Chantay, and the rest of us in turn," Nir informs the queen.

I picture a palace made entirely out of skulls.

It's not uncommon to occasionally uncover remains of humans and mer along the ocean floor, but to create an entire structure with them—it's not possible that they've sirened and drowned so many sailors.

"Now it's time for *you* to pay. Aila, Kailania, and Ebba's lines all need to suffer."

"They stopped Persephone from hurting innocent mer," Dylana objects.

We all straighten at the sound of her voice.

"Don't touch her!" Dylana growls.

Llyr struggles to see around the door as the queen tries to muffle her cry. He doesn't need to look though—I know what's happening.

Nir is taking her scales.

"Stop!" Dylana begs, trying not to sob.

"Tell us where Aila and Ebba's lines are and your deaths don't have to be painful," Nir insists gently.

"But it's far less fun that way," Marilla taunts, having trouble getting her words out.

She and Dylana scream at the same time—one in pain, one in protest. I cringe at their reactions, my own tail tingling where I had a scale pried up.

"Ebba had nothing to do with this," Dylana shouts when her mother quiets. "Persephone dragged Ebba out into the sea to draw Aila out. She's already paid a price that had nothing to do with her."

At least Dylana was trying to save as many of her cousins as she could. I'd still have to answer as Aila's great-great-granddaughter, but Ebba's great-great-grandchildren wouldn't.

We didn't need to confess that Ebba's line took up the fight even more than my line did in the time after Chantay's supporters took their collection of mermaids and mermen and left Scylla—let them see her as weak—at least there will be a resistance when this is all over and we're long since dead.

"Queen Kailania kept us out after Gaspar died. As her descendants, you are responsible for her actions," Nir continues his speech.

"Isn't that why you're mutilating my tail?" the queen asks casually through her pain. It sounds like she's gritting her teeth.

The light shifts in the room as if perhaps the sun is slowly revealing itself through the hole in the ceiling of the room. It spills out into the hallway, separating Llyr from us by a muted ray of light.

"Where is Celena?" another voice asks—Tarni.

"Why do you care?" Marilla asks. "She's the one that tried to help you."

"She's the one that nearly got me caught," Tarni replies spitefully. "It's a good thing she didn't keep a tight grip on me during your little party or I wouldn't have been able to sneak away and get the others in."

"*You* helped them in?" Dylana shrieks, angry.

"Of course. It was an easy distraction, and your silly little brother didn't find me right away. You all fell for my little teary act," she gloats. "It wasn't that hard."

"I admit," Marilla replies, "you fooled us. We didn't see you coming."

"Nor should you have," Tarni replies. "I was flawless."

"We've kept Tarni a secret her entire life," Nir adds. "My mother trained her well. No one but my father and I knew what she was capable of."

A stingray floats past the door quietly, distracting me for a moment.

"Stop!" Dylana screams.

"We have to go in there," Morgen begs. Llyr looks like he's going to burst through the door whether we back him or not.

"Go," Merrick instructs, knowing it's best to move together.

The dolphins move with us, bursting into the room. A few fish swim the perimeter, but the grotto is mostly devoid of sea life.

Nir floats over Marilla as she's tied to a lounging couch on the right side of the room. Several fierce-looking sirens surround them. Surprisingly, none watch the door.

Tarni hovers between Marilla and where Dylana is tied down a few feet away. She uncrosses her arms, tilting her head at us, looking ready to bite.

Nir glares at us from beyond the welts from the jellyfish on his face. They've only just started to fade slightly. He holds a knife in his hand, poised to pry up another of Marilla's scales. Several sit at awkward angles, still barely attached to her tail.

Morgen races toward Nir but one of the dolphins beats him, slamming its nose into the siren. Nir jerks back, but not far enough.

He holds his knife out as Morgen approaches, but the prince uses his trident to slam into the siren's wrist. The spear-ends of the trident move around Nir's wrist, the points moving to either side of his skin. I should feel bad wishing it had struck him instead of gone around him, but I don't.

Morgen pulls it back, attempting to slice Nir's wrist open anyway. As he moves, Nir slashes his knife at Morgen, burying it in his side.

"No!" Dylana screams, fighting against her restraints.

Tarni swims at me, trying to knock into me as Llyr swims to free Dylana. Caspian works to break the ties binding the queen to the lounging couch as Tarni crashes into me.

We grapple as she tries to reach my tail. A dolphin comes to my aid, knocking into her. She slams into the side of the lounging couch. If it hadn't been so solid, she might have toppled Dylana off of it.

The siren quickly rises back up, knife in hand.

Her *iluse* is made of netting and seaweed. Thankfully, no shells or decorations were permitted to a prisoner—or else I could be in trouble.

I hold Caspian's extra knife in my hand, ready to fight against the sea-witch-of-a-siren. She lashes out at me, attempting to slice my stomach.

Dylana struggles next to us as Llyr continues to work. Tarni turns quickly toward my cousin, intent on destroying her tail. I move forward as Dylana tries desperately to free her tail.

Tarni attempts to bring her knife down on Dylana's beautiful tail but I catch her wrist with mine. We crash together as I try to force her hand up, keeping my knife far back from her with my other hand so she can't take it. I force her arm above her head as she struggles against me.

"Hurry," I instruct between gritted teeth.

I wish I had Merrick to back me up, but he's taken on Nir alone now that Morgen has been injured. We need to help him but each of us is locked in our own battle as Keone and Natale attempt to hold off the other sirens.

I grunt as Tarni tries to force her hand away from me. In response, I dig my nails into her wrist, hoping she drops her knife. The siren screams as I pinch her even harder but she doesn't let go of her weapon.

My stomach burns as her free hand claws against my skin. She snags my *iluse*, nearly pulling it with her. The net slips free of her talons just as she swipes her hand away.

She attempts to punch me, connecting with my hip as I twist to try to avoid her swing. Tarni grabs the pouch on my hip and rips it away from me. The contents spill out on the floor, the starfish belonging to her friend, Durdania, settling in the sand on full display.

She stares for a moment, mesmerized by the way it catches the light that is now streaming in through the hole in the ceiling. A few reflective waves trickle over the walls and on the sand from the sunlight filtering through the water.

Colors start to become brighter as the light grows more intense, erasing the dull, gray, lifeless colors of early morning under the ocean's surface. The fish seem to revel in the light as they dance around the room, ignoring the screaming.

The dolphins seem to know the greatest threat is the sea-monster-of-a-siren and they assist Merrick in his battle against the creature that can't possibly be a merman. Their clicks fill the room. One darts out of the room—likely to swim to the surface for air—they've been in and out the entire time they've been with us, taking turns returning to the surface to breathe.

I try to use the opportunity to knock Tarni off balance as she stares at the silver starfish on the ground. Llry manages to free Dylana and she pushes herself up in the water before immediately turning to attack Tarni.

Llyr rushes to help Keone and Natale with the other sirens as my cousin and I wrestle with Tarni. Dylana pulls the knife from Tarni's hand where I continue to dig my nails into her flesh—she's going to have a nasty scar from that when this is all over.

The room freezes as a merman sounds like he's being sliced in half.

CHAPTER 18

Nir roars from across the room as Merrick injures his tail. A trident sticks out of Nir's black scales, wiggling in the water as the siren thrashes in pain.

"That's for hurting Celena," Merrick grunts. He moves forward to retrieve his trident, but Nir hurls himself away.

A siren rips at Merrick's shoulder. He cringes in pain as he turns to fight the merman off.

Nir looks like he might pass out from pain as the trident moves with his every motion. Tarni's gaze is concerned but only lasts for a moment as Dylana brings the hilt of my knife down on Tarni's head, knocking her out.

For a moment, it looks as though Dylana considers slicing the siren up as she lies in a heap on the sand. Finally, she orders me to restrain the mermaid as she races to her injured brother.

"I'm here," Caspian whispers next to me, having released the queen.

"Where is Marilla?"

"She passed out from the pain," Caspian says. "They did a lot of damage, Celena."

I don't have time to worry about that now—we have far too many other things going on in the room.

A herd of seahorses clings to seaweed growing in the corner of the queen's grotto. They stare at their queen, waiting for her to come feed them for the morning as the sun glints through the water even brighter, filling the room with intense colors.

"No," Dylana pleads as she looks up from her place next to her injured brother. She focuses on the doorway as a fever of stingrays swims into the room, looking to be fed.

They overtake everyone, rushing to them in search of food. The sirens bat them away, using their weapons to remove them if they approach.

Nir rips the trident out of his tail—something that would cause any other merman to pass out from the agony—and jabs it into one of the stingrays.

More winged-creatures pour into the room in search of the mermaids that feed them every morning. Dylana shouts a warning to them, but it's no use. The sirens destroy them, attempting to get away from the creatures creating a blanket that blocks everyone's vision as we fight.

When the stingrays finally start to clear, Nir is gone. Several of the sirens seem to be missing as well, having used the stingrays as cover.

Tarni rests in the sand, still unconscious. I leave Caspian to watch her as I swim to Dylana to help with Morgen.

Marilla blinks awake as I swim by her. I stop to help her up—sitting looks painful.

"Everything is wavy," she whispers. She quickly pulls herself together when she spies Morgen's wounds.

She beats me to them, caring for her son's injuries with her daughter at her side.

Natale and Keone restrain the remaining sirens. We quickly interrogate them, learning that they haven't freed the sirens in the cells yet. We knock them out to allow Keone, Natale, and Llyr to clear the rest of the palace.

"Llyr," Dylana calls. "Are you okay?"

"I'm fine," he calls back. "Are you all right?"

"I'm fine. Morgen will be okay."

"I'll be back," he informs us, swimming after Natale and Keone.

"Merrick?" I ask, not sure how he faired during the fight.

"I'm fine," he says, swimming up to me. "Is your tail okay?"

He leans down to examine my ripped fin.

"I think it's okay. It hurts to swim," I admit.

Dylana drags herself across the sand to examine my torn tail as her mother continues to help her brother. She waves Merrick off to watch the sleeping sirens as she works. I flinch when she touches me, but it's no worse than any of the other injuries I've acquired over the years.

After a while, Keone returns with a number of mer at his side.

"The palace is cleared," he announces. "Natale is organizing everyone outside with the king.

"Apparently Nir fled, taking a few of our own with him as captives to control the collection. He took all of his sirens with him."

"How is he moving at all?" Merrick questions.

"They're helping him. I honestly don't think he can swim at all with the damage you did to his tail," Keone replies.

"Coralie!" Caspian yelps, darting out of the room. I let him rescue our sister alone, too exhausted to move.

"We need to get you all to a better location," Merrick insists. He looks like he wants to scoop me into his arms and carry me across the palace, but Morgen needs more help than I do at the moment.

Reluctantly, he turns, slipping Morgen's arm around his shoulder. Dylana takes the other side while I help Marilla up. The other guards see the queen struggle and rush forward to help. I let them take her from me, swimming her to the infirmary where she and Morgen can be looked at.

The remaining mer remove the sirens from the grotto, taking them down to the cells where they will be questioned. I swim out quietly after them, following them toward the cells to make sure Tarni is locked up tightly enough that she'll never be able to escape.

The hallways are light again, filled with colorful fish swimming in and out of the spaces in the palace. A school of small fish pops into the foyer through the hole in the ceiling as I eye the rock wall we blocked Tiko and his friends in with—once the mer return from locking up Tarni and the others, they are to remove the wall and fish out Tiko and the sirens behind it.

"Hey," Merrick's voice is deep as he swims up to me.

I think about holding back for a moment, waiting, but there's nothing I want less. Flipping my tail is painful, but I don't care—I swim as fast as I can to Merrick.

He grins as I dive toward him, opening his arms to catch me.

My lips brush against his, refusing to leave like a barnacle on a ship. I pull back after a moment, but Merrick isn't finished yet. He kisses me over and over, hands making their way to my hair as I sigh into him.

I run my hands down the sides of his scales, making him tighten his grip in my hair. I graze over the pouch on his belt, taking me back to Tarni's reaction to the silver starfish that had spilled from my pouch not too long ago.

"What do you think the silver starfish means?" I murmur.

"Hmm?" Merrick grunts as he continues to kiss me.

For a moment, I lose my train of thought. My fingers move over the muscles on his abdomen as they climb toward his chest. He breathes faster.

"The starfish," I repeat, realizing I had been talking. I pull back slightly. "Why is it so important?"

"It belonged to their friend," Merrick offers, still distracted. "Do you think it's something more than that?"

"I don't know," I look away. A stingray floats on the sand below us —at least one got away. "I would probably react the same way if it had been one of my friends."

Merrick watches me quietly, wrapping one of his hands around my waist.

"Should I give it back to her?"

"If she lives longer than today, I think it will be a miracle. This has been the highest loss of life we've ever had, Len, and it's her fault. If Marilla doesn't shackle her with the sharks, I'm not sure the collection won't break in and do it themselves."

"Honestly, I don't even think she'd ink in the face of sharks," I reply, smirking at the thought of her looking like an octopus.

"I'd say we have a better chance of using that silver starfish against Tiko and Roni once we fish them out."

"Roni," I gasp. "She has to be awake by now—I locked her up last night."

"Hold still," Merrick says as I try to swim away. "We'll tell someone else to go get her out of wherever you hid her."

He holds me in place, refusing to let me swim away. I settle back into his embrace.

"Celena!" Coralie shouts, darting into the foyer.

Caspian looks horrified as he stops swimming. His eyes are wide as he stares at Merrick's arms around me.

My sister crashes into me, knocking me away from Merrick.

"Merrick!" Caspian's words are sharp.

Merrick looks to me to see what he should do, but Coralie tears me away, babbling about what happened while she was in hiding.

"They were there, Celena," she gasps. "The sirens were right outside the door. I stayed quiet and they didn't find me, but they could have and it was terrifying."

"I want you to stop talking to Natale for a while, starfish," I redirect her.

"Why?"

"We just need a little distance from her, that's all."

"But I like Natale," she whines.

"I'll explain later, just don't talk to her until I tell you about it, okay?" I wait until she promises. "Now are you okay?"

She continues to tell me about her time in the secret entrance.

"Where is mother?" she finally asks.

"She's probably helping everyone outside the palace," I tell her, stroking her blonde hair. "I'm sure she's fine."

With Marilla inside the palace and injured, my mother is likely one of the mers to take charge and help the people alongside the king. They're also very likely to respond to her since she's from Aila's line.

The mermen arrive to remove Tiko and the sirens from behind Morgen's trap door, so we swim toward the foyer at the front of the palace to check on the other mer.

The foyer is empty when we arrive. Roni bangs against the door of the closet, fighting to free herself despite being tied up. I shake my head at Merrick when he raises an eyebrow to ask if we should retrieve the siren.

"Calm down," I shout through the door. "We'll get you out in a few minutes."

She struggles again, flopping against the door. I roll my eyes.

"Who is that?" Coralie asks.

"Siren," I shake my head. "You don't want to know."

I wince as my tail starts to sting from the ripped fin.

"What happened?" Coralie asks, realizing that I'm injured.

"I ripped my fin a little, that's all," I tell her as we move toward the door.

Roni slams into the door louder, trying to shout.

"Oh, *fine!*" I shout, flipping around in the water. "For coral's sake, calm down, *siren.*"

I open the door to find Roni glaring up at me through her squid-ink-black hair.

"You're going to the cells," I inform her, pulling her out by the binding around her wrists and tail. She floats out of the closet sideways, her back toward me as I tug on her.

She flails against me, trying to move.

"I said to calm down," I direct her again. "You don't want to get hurt at this point. We've already won, so cooperating with me is the best thing you can do."

Coralie screams behind me.

"Let her go," Tarni demands. She holds Coralie by the tail, knife to her throat.

"How did you get out?" I shout, pulling Caspian's blade on Roni.

"You shouldn't have sent all your mer guards away, pretty mermaid." She tips her head.

"You just slipped through the bars on your cell?" I counter, watching her hand hover near Coralie's throat as she rights my sister.

Several sirens swim up behind her.

"Oh," she smiles. "No, I had help."

Without removing the knife from my sister's throat, she reaches out to the side with her other hand. Grasping a merman's hand, she pulls him alongside of her.

Our faces fall when he swims over. A look of guilt crosses Murdoch's face for a moment before he glares at us.

"You shouldn't have treated the sirens so badly," he informs us defiantly.

"*You?*" Merrick questions, furious that one of our own betrayed us. "How?"

"Oh you stupid merman," Tarni taunts. "The sirens have been in your midst for months. We've seen each other a few times now."

She turns to bat her eyelashes at Murdoch.

"We met one day when I was at your little Anchor Marketplace. I was collecting oysters to take back with me—I had to buy something, so it might as well have been decent food—and there he was, grinning at me."

She turns back to face us.

"Why, he couldn't take his eyes off me, could you, Murdoch?" She giggles like Coralie and her friends do when talking about Marin and the other mer boys. "*We're in love.*"

Amazing—mer can't siren each other, but it appears Tarni found a way around that.

Murdoch looks at her, holding her gaze until she turns back to us, tightening her grip on Coralie. My sister looks terrified. She clamps her teeth together, trying to keep her lip from trembling.

Caspian places a hand on Roni, ready to tear her apart if Tarni touches our baby sister.

"Let her go," Tarni commands.

Roni struggles against me, attempting to buck with her limited ability to move.

"She said to let her go," Murdoch repeats, siding with the sirens for good. I wonder how much his family knows about his relationship with our enemies.

I cut the ties between Roni's hands and tail, freeing her to stretch back out. She instantly uncurls herself, frantically moving to make sure her tail still works after being bent for so long. She groans with the motion.

"Now her hands," Tarni advises.

Slowly, I snap the binds around her wrists. She instantly darts away, returning to her conspirators.

"Congratulations, you're one step closer to getting out of here alive," Tarni announces. "Here's the tricky part. We need to leave and the entrance is blocked. Handle it."

"What do you mean?" Caspian growls, fists clenched at his sides.

"I mean all of your mer folk are out there," Tarni nods to the door. "Get rid of them so they don't see us leaving."

She sighs when we don't move and starts to dig the knife into Coralie's neck. A red line starts to form and we all dart toward the door.

"Go," Merrick whispers, pulling the door open. Llyr follows with me, leaving the others inside.

The collection is still there, save for the young children who have been sent home for their own protection. They back up as I swim out. Llyr quickly shuts the door behind us.

"Back," I command.

"Is the queen safe?" a merman calls.

"She is alive and in the infirmary," I call to the crowd.

"We couldn't get in," someone yells.

"No, the palace was locked up to protect against any more sirens getting in," Llyr informs them, looking regal in his shoulder armor.

"They took twelve of our mer," a mermaid calls.

"We know—we're going to do everything we can to get them back," I shout to be heard. "The royals are all safe but we need you to leave and protect your homes now. We need to make sure the sirens really have left and aren't still hiding in Scylla."

They stare for a moment.

"By orders of the queen, you all must return home. We'll send word for you once our spies have returned with information, now go!" I shout, trying to convince them to leave.

I catch my mother's eye in the crowd. I jerk my head toward our house, willing her to help me get the collection to leave the courtyard. She moves into action, forcing our friends to turn and return to their dwellings.

Llyr convinces several mermen to check the back of the palace to make sure no sirens have found their way back there. They swim off, happy to have a mission.

"We need you to swim away," Llyr quietly informs the king. He nods, not sure why, but he follows our lead.

"Good thinking," I praise him.

"We'll make sure Coralie is safe," he promises.

"We just need to get these sirens out the door. Once they're gone, we can follow them and skin them alive before they reach the barrier."

"At least Nir is out of the way," he reminds me.

"It's a good thing Tarni didn't free Tiko," I roll my eyes as we wait for the collection to swim away.

My mother glances over her shoulder in the crowd. I hold my face still, letting her swim away.

After a few minutes, the waterways clear, leaving us alone. We turn back to the door, pulling it open.

"They're gone," I announce. "You can leave."

"Perfect," Tarni gloats. "Open the door, princess."

I pull the door back for them.

"Let her go," I hold a hand out to stop her from leaving.

"No," she smiles. "That's not how this works. She's coming with us until we're safely away or else you're sad little collection of hot mermen will follow us and try to kill us. No, she's coming with us."

"You're not taking her," Caspian spits.

"Mmm," she sighs. "Pretty little merman...so brave, so strong."

She looks like she wants to run her hand up my brother's chest.

"Swim away, little one. If you want the mer child to live, you'll let us take her."

She pushes Coralie forward in the water. A fish darts out of the way, swimming through the partially open door.

"We'll send her back when we're done," she grins. "*Probably* in one piece."

"*Back*," Murdoch commands as Tarni swims through the door. He snatches a trident away from Caspian. "I'll take that."

He backs out of the palace, following Tarni. The others quickly follow, making their way out into the open water.

We follow behind them, watching the sirens drag Coralie away.

"Good luck finding her in the open sea," Tarni calls. "If she survives the sharks, she might have a chance at getting back to you!"

Merrick reaches for my fingers when he feels me move away from him, but he doesn't catch me. Caspian attempts to rush after me, but Murdoch stops him with a trident aimed at his throat, forcing him back as I dart by them.

"Celena!" he calls.

One of the sirens reaches out to stop me. I scratch at him but he holds fast, clutching me to his chest as his hair floats into view—it might be prettier than mine. Roni swims over, quickly forcing my hands behind my back as she ties me up like I had tied her up—binding my tail back behind me so I can't swim.

Coralie screams but can't do anything with Tarni's knife at her neck.

"Bring her along," Tarni grumbles, not wanting to waste time.

Murdoch thrusts the trident at my brother before returning quickly to us. I struggle against Roni and the merman siren.

At least I'll be with Coralie to help her escape.

I catch Merrick's eye—a mixture of fury and fear.

"I'll come back to you," I mouth, hoping he knows what I'm saying from so far away.

"We'll find you!" he shouts, fingering the shell necklace around his neck.

"Stay strong," Caspian calls, rallying with his friends.

The sirens drag me backward in the ocean.

"It's okay," I murmur to my sister.

We swim farther and farther away, our friends unable to save us.

The longer we swim, the darker the water becomes—a storm raging on the surface above us.

"Where are we going?" I demand. Laughter is my only answer as Roni flips Caspian's knife in her hands. My pouch, along with the silver starfish, sits on her hip.

Through the long strands of my hair floating over my head as the sirens pull me backward, I lose sight of the palace. Scylla disappears completely.

When they finally flip me around, all I see are darker depths as we descend into the unknown.

Find out what happens next at
darkerdepthsinfo.kmrobinsonbooks.com

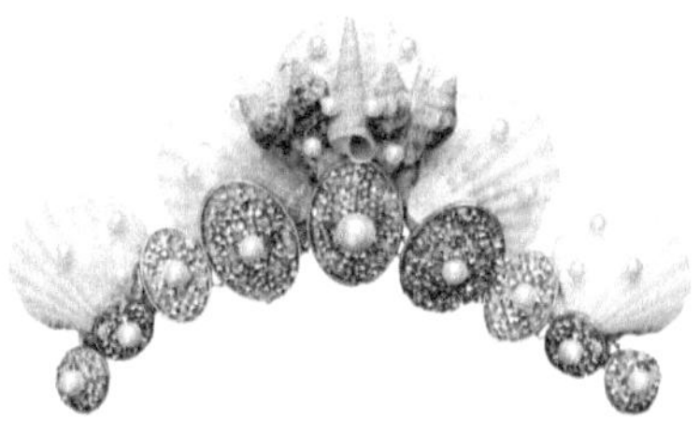

Acknowledgements

When I was a little girl, I would always pretend I was a mermaid any time I got near water. I loved spinning and letting my long hair float out behind me! I've never lost that love for all things mermaid, so when the opportunity presented itself to write a mermaid "tail" (yeah, I'm hilarious) I had to dive in.

If you want more of Celena and Merrick's story, fear not, the next two books are being released back-to-back. In fact, you can read the first chapter of Darker Depths right after the acknowledgements!

If you're interested in Aila's story, you can check it out in Origins of the Siren Wars which will be part of the Of The Deep mermaid Anthology this summer and then released individually this fall.

I'm also planning more in this series beyond the original trilogy, so if you're ready, I've got a brand new take on all of this coming soon!

One thing that I learned while writing this series was that there aren't a lot of resources out there for mermaid culture. I knew there were specific words for things like a mermaid bra, but I couldn't find them anywhere. As it turns out, different authors made up their own words and you can't use their words. If you're a writer, I don't want you to struggle with your mermaid stories, so over on my blog, you'll find a collection of mermaid phrases and objects that I used in my mermaid books that you're welcome to use in yours as well (if we all do it, that makes it official, right?)

Special thanks to my parents who constantly took me to the beach for vacations and inspired my love of the ocean! Extra special thanks to them for giving me the opportunity to play with dolphins, belugas, orcas, stingrays, sharks, and more—it really helped!

Thank you to my marvelous editors for all of their help with Siren Wars and all of my books! They would have lots of typos without you ladies!

To Elle, long live the Sarcastic Fringehead! (It's a fish, my friends, and a creepy looking one at that—look it up ad you'll be amazed!)

Thanks to everyone who tolerated me during he cover shoots for this series—I know it wasn't super fun to have me take over everywhere with a billion handmade mermaid shell crowns, but it was *so* worth the effort!

To each and every one of you who played mermaid as a child, and especially to those of you who still do, thank you for coming on this journey with me. I have loved telling Celena's story and I can't wait for you to see the rest of it! Keep being mermazing!

Stay inspired!

-K.M. Robinson

DARKER DEPTHS

by

K.M. Robinson

Antaire
Hontan
Waterfalll
The Ropes
Abandoned
Dwelling
Brine
Pool

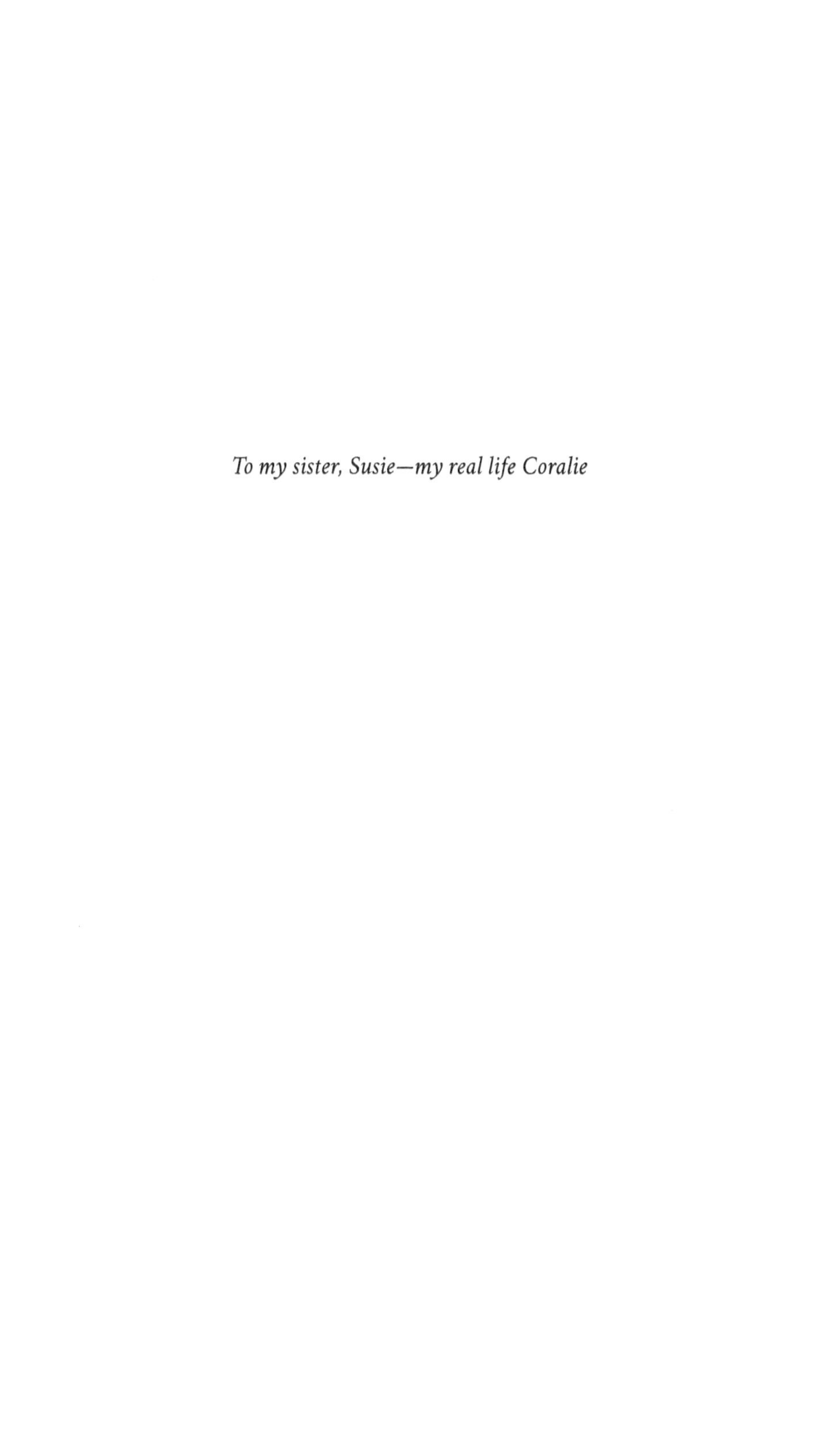

To my sister, Susie—my real life Coralie

CHAPTER 1

Even the best intentions—those well thought out and planned —have the potential to end in disaster.

This is one of those disasters.

Then again, this was *hardly* thought out.

"Just stay quiet, Coralie," I instruct, her head on my lap. I pet her hair as if our life depends on it.

My finger grazes over the shell I tucked away in her hair while we were still in the palace in Scylla—*it's still there*. When Murdoch turns away to face the love of his miserable little life, I dart my fingers toward my *iluse* and pray no one notices.

I dig a small hole in the sand beside me—once they realize I have a weapon, they're going to look for an explanation. They swept the area before letting us sit, but if I can convince them that I found it under the sand, maybe they'll let me keep my *iluse*. I wouldn't put it past them to take my covering and make me swim around without one.

The light filters down through the water, giving everything a muted look, but at least we can see again—the moonlight hardly gives enough light to swim by under the waves.

"Sit up!" one of the sirens demands, holding a trident out toward my little sister. I grab her shoulders before she can move and drag her to a sitting position.

"She's up," I inform the siren.

"Don't touch," he snarls, turning back away.

"What are we going to do?" Coralie asks quietly. "It's been two days."

"You heard Caspian and Merrick—they're coming to get us," I remind her. "At least they're letting us talk now."

The sirens had spent the last two days dragging us through the water. It's a miracle I can move my tail at all after being bound together backward.

"You're not getting any ideas in that pretty little head of yours, now are you?" Tarni asks, feigning innocence as she floats over to me. She drops down onto the sand, leaning back on one arm to support herself.

If only mermaids could be drowned.

She eyes the gash on my neck and shoulder. I nearly reach up to rub it but that's likely exactly what she wants—to see that it bothers me. My captor sighs, sweeping her gaze over to my sister.

Drown her—yes, that's *exactly* what I want to do.

"I suppose it's time I learn a little bit about you, don't you think, tiny one?" She swims over to Coralie and lifts a lock of her blonde hair. "Are you one of Aila's descendants too?"

Tarni smiles, looking back over her shoulder at me menacingly.

"Good thing you're older, Celena," she taunts. "We'll offer you up to the humans before we send your sister to the surface."

Coralie bleaches whiter than coral.

"You still need us, Tarni," I retort.

"Oh? Why is that?" she asks. "It seems to me that we've accomplished what we wanted—to get away from Scylla. We're safe now, and your friends aren't close enough to catch us, so we could siren you out of our lives and into the hands of the sailors, and it would actually speed our trip up—*and* get rid of the witnesses."

"There are three mermen coming after you. They're more powerful than any of you here and they're smart enough to bring reinforcements. They're going to catch you, and the only leverage that you're going to have is being able to trade the two of us."

"Fine," Tarni sighs. "I'll keep you around for now, just in case your merman shows up, but don't forget that at any time, I can drag either of you to the surface and destroy you."

She tugs harshly on Coralie's hair, jerking her entire body forward. Coralie tries not to gasp, closing her eyes to focus herself.

"Time to move, mer children," Tarni says motioning for the other sirens to pick us up off the ocean floor.

The siren that stopped me from rescuing Coralie outside of the palace two days ago swims over to me. He's slightly bigger than Merrick and Caspian, but not so much so that it will throw me off balance when we inevitably fight. I've practiced with Merrick so many times that it's become second nature to me—I know right where to hit this siren merman.

"Let's move," he says gruffly. He picks up the chain attached to the shackles on my wrist. I'm loosely bound between my hands and my tail. A secondary chain runs from the middle of those links to my captor's hands, allowing me to swim—difficult as it is to move with heavy chains around my tail—and if I try to escape, he can pull the chain and restrict the use of my tail.

I could curse the seven seas that the sirens got us far enough into their territory that they could find supplies they had hidden in the cave.

I glare at Murdoch. He almost looks apologetic for dragging us into this disaster, but he's following the lead of his partner, and Tarni controls it all. Murdoch sucks in a breath and brushes back his hair —it's a deep red with a purple sheen to it—and narrows his eyes at me.

I swim slightly behind Phorcys, keeping a careful eye on Roni as she oversees my little sister. Thankfully, they didn't chain her up the way they've constricted me, though Roni is much stronger than Coralie and could easily hold her back by the chains on her wrist, even with her tail free. I, on the other hand, might be a tough match for Phorcys.

Tarni brushes her hand over Murdoch's shoulder, reinforcing her manipulation. She's brilliant really—sirening a merman is as easy as making him fall in love.

"Where are we going?" I ask loudly. It's been two days of them dodging my questions—I've had enough.

"Does it matter?" Murdoch mumbles.

The rest refuse to speak, though Roni snickers at me, looking back over her shoulder as she dangles my sister's chain from her fingers for my benefit. I use the silence to look around.

I keep a careful eye on the route ahead of me, but my eyes bounce over the sea floor, looking for anything that might help me. I try memorizing what I see in case Coralie and I can escape—I'll need it to guide us home.

We swim over a seaweed garden that hasn't been maintained in years. It looks like this used to be a dwelling place for sirens at one point, but they've since moved on. I wonder if all the sirens stayed together after they left the mer collection or if they branched off and formed smaller groups.

We're close to the seaweed, hovering just far enough above it that I can't reach down and touch it. The further we swim, the more something nags at my brain. We nearly reach the end of the garden before I realize what it is—a message.

Swimming so close, it's hard to tell, but I'm nearly certain the gaps between the seaweed aren't random. It looks like a path has been cut into it.

Caspian has been here.

I perk up the second the thought crashes over me like the waves on the side of the human ship I sirened not long ago. Phorcys notices my shoulders jolt and glances at me out of the side of his eye. I wiggle, trying to make it look as though I'm attempting to adjust the shackle around the bottom of my tail.

"Couldn't have picked a lighter cuff, could you?" I snip.

He rolls his eyes at me, tugging just enough for me to feel it through my chains. I risk a look back, pretending once again to fuss over my tail. In the distance, I can vaguely see part of a division in the seaweed—definitely a path.

If my twin has been here, that means the others are here too. There's a chance that Caspian, Merrick, and Llyr out-swam us, going the long way around.

But do they know where we are or are they searching for us and just went too far?

I glance around, looking for more clues.

If I can find them—or if they can find me—Coralie and I might be able to survive this. I just have to make sure to position Coralie correctly so that they can ensure her safety.

A fever of stingrays glides by effortlessly in front of our path. Tarni hesitates for a moment, allowing them to cut us off. Several have their wing-like fins up in the water, not moving them at all as they propel themselves forward. I wish swimming were that easy for me.

Coralie catches my eye, looking pitiful. Her blonde hair hangs down over her face. I haven't been able to slip the necklace off of her neck yet, but she miraculously wore our grandmother's jewelry to the palace during my trial—the one with the secret weapons in it that I used when we chased the sirens the first time. If I can transfer it to my own neck, I'll have at least a few resources on my side. It's a shame Coralie doesn't know what hides inside the necklace, nor does she know how to use them.

We swim to the left, avoiding a wall of coral that stretches halfway to the surface. The collection of sirens and mer could have easily gone over it, but it seems that Tarni likes to keep us low in the water.

"Princess," one of the other sirens says. "Would you like me to—"

"Yes," she cuts the merman off. "Go."

I watch his movements as he swims ahead of the collection, likely to scout the next place we'll stop. It would be nice if Merrick could take him out before we arrive, but I know the mermen won't hurt the scout until they're certain that they know where we are.

A sign. I need another sign.

The sirens haven't left us alone long enough for me to leave a conch shell message for anyone—even if I *did* have the time, which one would I leave it for? The message can only be listened to by one mer and I have no idea which of my friends would find it or if they'd even be together. It's practically pointless to leave a message like that.

Coralie sighs ahead, dropping her head down slightly in the water. The poor thing has been through so much.

"Can I swim with her?" I ask quietly, hoping Phorcys has some kind of heart.

He grumbles but knows it will make it easier if I calm Coralie down. We position ourselves so that I can swim next to my sister.

"Hey," I say, announcing my presence.

She sucks in a breath and sighs, turning with a small smile.

"This is the worst," she responds.

"Yeah, I know," I say ruefully. "Let's play a game."

Roni and Phorcys both lecture me, but I don't care—Coralie needs a distraction, and *I* need another set of eyes to help me look for clues.

Cor just doesn't know what the stakes are yet.

"Do you remember that spy game we used to play with Casp when we were little? Let's try that," I encourage her, hoping she remembers the real reason we played that game—Caspian had hidden a baby sea turtle, and we had to sneak it in without our mother looking, and the clues he left were the only way to find where he had hidden it before returning home that day.

"Which one?" she asks.

"The one where we had to find the baby sea turtle and other things."

She frowns for a moment and I pray she wasn't too young to remember.

"Oh, I remember," she adds. "I'm Thinking Of…"

"Yes! That one," I cheer. "I'll go first."

She nods, but I'm not sure she fully understands.

"I'm thinking of…something red," I say, spotting a school of red fish swimming at us.

"The fish," Coralie replies.

"Yes," I chuckle. "They remind me of Caspian."

"Isn't your brother's tail teal?" Roni criticizes.

"Yes, that's not why they remind me of him." I keep my words pointed, hoping Coralie starts to process all my clues and pieces this together.

"I'm thinking of something dark," Coralie says, doing a terrible job of hiding where she was looking.

"The cave," I reply.

"It reminds me of Merrick's tail," Coralie responds with a smirk. It reminds *me* of Merrick too, but for an entirely different reason.

"So this whole game is about your pathetic little friends?" Roni asks, flicking her tail impatiently.

"Oh, well excuse us," I retort. "We just won't say why things remind us of them anymore."

Good, now we have a focus, but we don't have to discuss the connections out loud.

Coralie glances at me from under her hair, nodding so briefly that I can barely tell. I think she understands.

We continue to play for a while, pointing out rocks and jellyfish. Phorcys starts to pay attention, glancing around to see if he can spot the items before the guesser does. Roni continues to frown.

"I'm thinking of something green and long," Coralie says, sounding more excited than she has the entire game.

"Seaweed?"

"Kind of," she replies. "But not from the bed over there."

I keep looking around, trying to see what my little sister noticed.

"The fish?"

"Nope, better hurry," she informs me.

I look straight down, swinging my gaze up just a little to see what is in our direct path that we might be leaving behind soon.

There, on a rock a dozen lengths away, is what appears to be a *sarasa*.

Merrick.

Coralie tips her head at me when she knows I've seen it.

"Too late," she pretends to gloat. "It was a dead jellyfish tentacle floating over there."

She points in the opposite direction.

"Do I get to go again?" she continues.

My sister might be brilliant.

"Yes, Cor, you can go again," I say dramatically.

She makes a show about searching for something else to point out while I desperately look for another clue. I spot a second *sarasa* draped over another rock on the left. Not long after, another appears, though none of the sirens take notice of them.

"We're here," Tarni finally announces.

Ahead, a cave looms in the water, dark and dangerous. I have no doubt if the scout hadn't gone ahead, they'd shove me into the darkness of the cave first to test for sharks or other dangerous creatures lurking in the depths of the shelter.

The scout hovers outside of the rocks, nodding to the siren princess. Tarni takes Murdoch's arm as she smiles at him like he's the whole sea to her—I'm positive she'd leave him for dead if he ever becomes unuseful to her.

Murdoch wraps an arm around Tarni's waist and guides her into the cave. Phorcys pulls on my chains, moving me away from Coralie. For a moment, I panic, thinking they're going to separate us, but Roni follows, allowing us to swim into the cave first.

Phorcys moves me to the back of the cave and lets me settle on sand against the wall. Roni swims away before Coralie curls into me on the ground.

"They're here," I whisper into her ear around her hair as she adjusts her position, moving enough to cover my words.

She ducks her head slightly, indicating that she understands.

"Follow my lead and do whatever I tell you to do. No questions."

She nods, settling her head on my shoulder. Roni looks over, rolling her eyes at us, but she lets us stay curled up together.

Murdoch eventually brings us some oysters to eat. I take them hungrily, helping Coralie to hold them.

The midwater squids light up the cave as they swim slowly around the room. The light entering from the doorway adds some visibility as well, though it will be significantly less within the next hour as the sun vanishes entirely from the sky above us. I stare at the space, waiting for a dark figure to conceal the light, but Merrick never arrives to block the sunlight.

"How long?" Coralie whispers while the sirens are distracted with their meals.

"Probably morning," I reply. "Just try to rest."

I touch the necklace clasp on the back of her neck as I stroke her hair. I'm sure my hair is a disaster too after days of not being able to brush it.

"Can I brush her hair?" I ask loudly, making all of the sirens look at me. "I just want to brush her hair out."

The sirens scoff at me, but not Murdoch.

"Murdoch, please. You can sit here and make sure I'm not doing anything, but let me fix her hair. Don't let her turn into—"

"Fine," he cuts me off before I can bring up the old mermaid in town that hasn't taken care of her hair in three years.

He swims to Roni's belongings and digs a comb out of her pouch. She protests, but Murdoch can apparently get away with things now given his connection to the siren princess.

Handing it to me, he sinks down to the sand.

"It was nothing personal," he says.

"I get it," I reply, starting to brush through Coralie's hair. I'm careful to avoid knocking into the shell I have hidden there.

"Ow," Coralie complains when I hit a knot in her hair.

"Sorry," I murmur.

"I kind of wish you two had stayed out of the way," Murdoch informs me.

"Well, I'd love to get out of the way *now*," I reply, pretending to be sweet.

His face goes slack before his eyes narrow.

"Hurry up," he snaps.

"Love to," I reply, brushing Coralie's hair a little faster. I work my way through her locks. She sinks back into my hands as I work.

I intentionally clip her necklace with the comb, making her flinch.

"That looks heavy, starfish," I say just loud enough for Murdoch to hear. "Do you want me to take it?"

I unclip it without waiting for a response and Murdoch stirs from where he watches us.

"It was our grandmothers," I explain softly. "It's the only necklace we have from her."

He reaches a hand out, and I drop the necklace into his waiting palm. Murdoch inspects it, flipping it over, but Grandma Tama had concealed her secrets perfectly. My sad story proves effective when he reaches around my neck and clasps it on for me, instructing me to hurry with Coralie's hair.

When I finish, I look to Murdoch to see if Coralie can help with my hair. He frowns, taking the comb from me. He shifts so that he's sitting behind me and quickly rips through my hair with the brush. Unlike Merrick and Caspian, this does not relax me. Every moment is filled with as much tension as Murdoch is putting on my hair.

"Thanks," I mumble as he swims away, taking the comb with him.

"That looked painful," Coralie says with wide eyes.

"It was," I glance down at the necklace.

Coralie quirks an eyebrow up, but doesn't ask questions.

We take turns sleeping, one keeping watch while the other rests. So far, I've been able to make sure Coralie has had the majority of the sleep—she'll need it on this journey to wherever we're going—but my body needs to rest soon. It's a miracle I haven't turned to foam already.

I wake with a start as Roni screams in the cave.

My eyes blink quickly as the mermaid swims directly at me. She rips Coralie away from me—Cor's nails dig into my tail as she panics.

"You signaled them!" Roni accuses.

"Who?" I shriek, trying to get to my sister as Phorcys holds me back.

"Your mermen!" she shouts. "They're here."

Swordfish, they found them.

"How would I have signaled them?" I screech. "You've been watching me this entire time—we haven't been out of your sight!"

"I don't know how you did it, but you did." She attempts to slap me, but I dart out of the way, leaning into the merman holding me.

"It doesn't matter," Tarni interrupts. "We have to move."

"Good thing we know how to avoid the mer," Phorcys says harshly into my ear as he digs his nails into my upper arm, pulling me roughly toward the door.

CHAPTER 2

Once again, I'm relegated to staring at the path behind us as Phorcys carries me over his shoulder. My hands are attached to my tail behind me, bending me uncomfortably in the wrong direction.

Murdoch has taken Coralie from Roni's oversight, carrying her on his back. Thankfully, he bound her in the front, so she's not in much pain.

I bounce against Phorcys' back each time he flicks his tail to move us forward—the merman has muscles for days.

I look for any signs of Merrick or Caspian in the dark. I'd even be grateful for a sign of Morgen, but there's no way he will be involved in this rescue mission with the injuries he suffered in the palace when Nir attacked.

I wonder what's happened to Nir. Merrick damaged his tail badly during the battle, but he *is* three times the size of a normal merman, and he *did* manage to escape the palace somehow.

I hope Tarni isn't taking us as a gift to her cousin.

We travel quickly through the water—faster than we have the entire escape from the palace. Tarni has a plan to avoid Merrick's wrath, and whatever it is, it can't be good.

Despite the sun starting to come up, we find ourselves swimming into darker and more dangerous waters. A boat passes overhead, casting a dim shadow on the sea floor. Instinct tells me to hide, but siren hands tell me not to move as Phorcys readjusts how I'm sitting over his shoulder.

I wish on every starfish in the sea that Merrick and Caspian are hovering just beyond the light behind us where I can't see them.

Yet, they don't appear.

"Are you sure this is a good idea?" Murdoch asks, still carrying Coralie.

"It's our only option," Tarni says. "We have to lose them, and they'll never suspect we'd risk going in there."

My head jerks toward the sound of her voice. I wish I could see her around Phorcys' body, but I have as much luck as I did seeing around Nir the last time he moved me this way.

"Is it safe?" Murdoch continues, setting me on alert. Whatever we're swimming into, it must be bad.

"We've done it before," Tarni replies.

"Successfully?" Murdoch sounds nervous.

As a mer who has never been outside the kingdom of Scylla, I imagine this is even more terrifying for him than it is for me—at least *I* have some experience.

"I'm *here*, aren't I?" Tarni chastises him.

I wonder if Tarni really *has* done what she's claiming though. If Nir's mother trained her to be a secret weapon in hiding, then would she have gone out on her own to face the terrors of the ocean?

I realize that Tarni has been trained to fool everyone—*including the other sirens*—but she's played the part of being fragile and weak her entire life. Would she really have gone into the darker depths of the ocean at any point?

"You've been out here before?" Murdoch whispers, clearly concerned over his girlfriend.

"*I* have," Roni interrupts. "Now get over yourself, *mer*, before I tie you up with the other *mermaids*."

Murdoch huffs, angry over being called out.

The light around me brightens just enough that I can see a few lengths behind us—still no sign of my friends.

I pull a piece of driftwood from my *iluse*, hoping I can pick the lock on my shackles. It attached itself to my attire last night in the cave, but I made sure it didn't slip away, looping it in the netting until it was wrapped securely in back of me. As the last in the line up of sirens, no one can see me working at the lock.

We swim into a kelp forest, debris dancing in the water all around us. There's something eerie about a kelp forest in the dark. Once, I thought kelp forests were beautiful, but that was before the sirens tried to take over Scylla.

The water changes around us, getting cooler. The kelp whips back and forth and I wonder if perhaps there is a storm on the surface causing the change in the water below. It would explain the darkness as well, but I can't see through the kelp to tell what's happening above us.

A flash of blue above me gets my attention, though.

It moves so quickly, I wonder if I'm seeing things.

A shell floats down through the water, getting tossed in the waving kelp, but I catch just enough of it to be certain—there is a merman overhead.

The sirens don't notice Caspian's tail high above us in the water. He holds back, letting us swim away. I imagine it's harder than when he had to let us go outside of the palace in Scylla.

If I can see him, we can figure out a plan—there will be some way to communicate—but he's too far away and out of reach.

But if Caspian is here, so are Merrick and Llyr. I imagine some of the others are as well. It wouldn't surprise me if Keone and Natale had raced after us with them.

They had to wait until we were far enough away that the sirens couldn't spot them. *I* had been watching the entire journey and hadn't seen my friends, so the mermen had to have had enough time to form a plan. The king had been with them when we were taken from Scylla —it's possible he went to Marilla and secured some of her guards to come with them to rescue us.

Regardless, it doesn't matter—they're here. They know where we are. Even with Tarni's plan, they can't escape my collection.

Working on the lock, we swim further into the kelp forest. I stop searching for my brother as I try to pop my shackles open while resting on Phorcys' back—Caspian wouldn't have backed off if he planned on setting us free inside the kelp forest. Whatever he, Merrick, and Llyr are planning, it will happen on the other side of the massive strands of kelp.

It takes time, but I manage to break the lock inside the shackles, popping it open. I'll have to move quickly when the time comes to free Coralie, but even if we just get her away from Tarni and her collection, we can free her of her chains after.

"This way," Tarni suddenly announces, darting sideways out of the kelp forest.

We race after her, out into the open waters still consumed with dim light and shadows. Phorcys is struggling to catch his breath by the time we slow—I might have maneuvered myself to slam into his back extra hard while he was swimming to keep up with the siren princess.

I'm not sure what Merrick's plan is, but I assume I should probably help to distract the sirens so they can sneak up on them and help free us. I consider my topics of choice, wondering which will get the best reaction from Tarni.

"Where are we going?" I ask, leading into my line of questioning.

"It doesn't matter," Tarni replies, swimming low to the ground. Everyone sinks down, following her lead.

"Are you taking us to your brother?" I ask. She cringes as she uses the connection her uncle gave her to their family when he took her in. Tarni is really the former siren king's niece by his brother, but she was raised by the siren king and queen as their own, effectively making Nir her brother.

She turns to look back at me.

"Do you think he's still alive?" I ask casually. "If he's dead, does that make *you* their queen? Or does that title fall to the one who stabbed him after we did and ended it for real?"

Tarni launches herself at me, knocking me away from Phorcys. She grapples with me, trying to hurt me. I use the metal still wrapped around my wrists as protection. Miraculously, I manage to angle them, so they stay on despite having popped the lock.

She yelps as her knuckles collide with the heavy metal. Tarni reels back, arm over her shoulder as she prepared to scratch my face with her nails.

I use the metal clasped over the end of my tail just above my fins to injure her again, crashing into her tail with mine.

"Enough, Celena!" Murdoch shouts, dropping Coralie and rushing to push me away from Tarni.

One of the other mermen grabs Coralie as she floats toward the ground, keeping her from crashing into the sand. She holds her feelings in, bravely facing our captors as I provoke them.

"What if we're swimming into a trap," I protest. "What if there's a new siren king already and he's going to dispose of you as soon as you return? What then?"

"Nir is fine," Tarni hisses at me. "They barely touched him."

"They stabbed his tail," I reply in horror before switching to sarcasm. "Didn't you see it? Oh, no, maybe you *didn't*—you *were* knocked unconscious, after all."

If Merrick weren't nearby, I wouldn't risk taunting Tarni so soon, but if this is my last chance to terrorize her, I'm going to do all I can to destroy this siren.

"Move," Murdoch directs, forcing everyone into action.

Phorcys scoops me up, tossing me over his shoulder again. Murdoch takes Coralie from the siren and leads us forward, swimming quickly once again.

"He could barely move the last time I saw him," I call out, making the situation worse. "He *pulled* the trident out of his tail. They must have had to carry him out."

"Enough!" Tarni shouts, racing toward me. She rips her hands through my hair, pulling my head violently to the side.

I barely hold back my scream, knowing that if I make a sound, Merrick will descend on us so quickly that it will ruin whatever plan he and our friends have created to save us.

Bits of pink hair pull out of my scalp, remaining tangled with Tarni's fingers as she pulls them away. She drops my hair in the water, and the pieces float away.

"Nir is *alive*," she hisses at me, seething. "You couldn't kill him if you tried. Who was it that hurt him—that little boyfriend of yours? I'll see to it that he *dies* before all this is over."

"You can't touch him," I whisper fiercely. I try not to grin too smugly.

Even if for some reason Tarni beats me, she'll never be able to hurt Merrick—he's too smart for her.

"No, but I can hurt *you*," she sneers. "You're being awfully bold for someone who is trying to protect her little sister."

Her face begins to shift, realizing that I *wouldn't* be this bold unless I knew something was coming. I over-played my hand, and she's caught on.

"To the pool," she shouts in horror. "Go, go!"

We dart once again through the water, pummeling our bodies forward in the expansive dark ocean.

"I don't know where they are, but you *will* tell them to stay back," Tarni growls.

"I don't know what you're talking about?" I reply innocently. "The only mer here are you and us."

"I doubt that," she mutters. "You *will* play by my rules, Celena, or your sister pays the price. Remember that."

Threatening my sister is nothing new, but I should probably be careful.

"I still don't know what you're talking about."

"You will," she promises.

As we continue to swim, strange things start happening. In our wake, a trail of dead shellfish litter the ocean floor, their tones a mixture of dark blues, grays, yellows, and tans.

It's like something swept through the ocean floor, killing everything in its path, and left the carcasses to rot—only they haven't. It's almost like they've been perfectly preserved.

Trails etch their way through the ocean floor, leaving swirling designs covered in—crystals?

A large crab body sits at an odd angle. Underneath it, an extra leg sticks out, noticeably a different color. It's like the creature was trying to eat the dead crab and died on top of it. It's a horrifying color—both of them.

More tiny crystals sit on top of the shells and dead creatures that lie in a strange pool. It almost looks like the pools of water sitting on the deck of the fishing vessel I was trapped on when the sirens coerced the fishermen into killing the mer they caught in their nets.

I try to get a good look at the crystals in the pool sitting on the ocean floor. They aren't like the ones we wear on our crowns or *ilueses.* These are short and strangely shaped. They cover everything.

"Remember what I said, Celena," Tarni sings.

An eel dips into the pool, diving into the strange-colored water. When it comes back up, it twitches, diving back into the darker water. Suddenly, the creature spasms, twitching and rolling in on itself. It jerks mercilessly, bending and twisting its shape.

"It's a brine pool," Tarni explains viciously. "It's four times as salty as the ocean. If a creature swims in there, it goes into toxic shock. It convulses, and if it can't escape, it dies."

She grins as she swims close to my face.

"All those crab bodies you see in there...they're probably older than either of us."

I look away, eyeing the muscles forming walls to contain the brine pool. I've never seen anything like it. It's haunting in all the wrong ways.

The eel continues to twitch, convulsing violently as it bends around its own body in unnatural ways. Suddenly, it stops moving, sinking down to the bottom of the brine pool.

"Get back!" Tarni screams to something beyond us, drawing my attention away from the brine pool. She holds a trident out toward the darkness. "*Get back!*"

From the shadows, a figure emerges—our savior.

I don't know where the others are, but Merrick's shape fills my vision. He's backlit, and I can't see his expression, but I'm sure it's murderous.

"I said, *get back*," Tarni punctuates her words. "Or else."

Coralie is shifted off to Roni so that the merman can take a place beside Murdoch for the impending fight. She holds Coralie in front of her, letting her dangle in the water.

"Or else *what*?" Merrick's voice is threatening and still the most lovely thing I've ever heard in my life. He swims slowly toward us.

His moves are precise as he closes the distance between us. I adjust myself so that I'm ready to break free of my shackles—my hands will be free, but my tail will not be. I'll have seconds to pop the lock before I'm out of time and they use it against me to pull me back.

Control a mer's tail and you control the mer.

"Or this," Tarni says, flicking her hand in the water toward Roni.

With horrific force, the siren throws Coralie into the brine pool, submerging her in the toxic saline.

CHAPTER 3

"**G**et back!" I scream, knowing my job is to remove Merrick. Coralie fights under the water, twitching under the influence of the toxic shock to her system. Roni hovers above her, ready to pull her chain up when Tarni approves.

"Merrick, get back!" I scream, sobbing. "Tarni, pull her up."

"No," she says in a voice so quiet, only I can hear her.

"Tarni, please!" I plead, body shaking with tears that leak out into the water.

"What's happening?" Merrick shouts, swimming a few lengths toward us, losing all bravado in his concern for my reaction.

Caspian rushes toward us from the side, trident in hand. He swims straight toward Tarni, ready to take the siren out.

I use the opportunity to pop the shackles off of my tail. It sinks to the sea floor, but I hold the ones around my wrists in place, knowing any movement away from Tarni would earn me a trident in my side and then I'd never be able to pull Coralie up.

Tarni barely has time to react to Caspian's movements.

"Merrick, stop him!" I shriek.

Without knowing why—knowing it's against everything we're trying to accomplish—Merrick listens to me, swimming straight at my twin. The mermen collide as Merrick knocks Caspian off course.

"Pull her up," I beg, dropping the rest of my shackles. I race toward Roni, attempting to pull my sister out of the pool as she convulses.

Surprised, Roni can't withstand my assault and accidentally relinquishes the chain to me. I pull as hard as I can, swimming toward the surface.

Coralie coughs, popping out of the brine pool. Murdoch catches her, pulling her back from me. He panics as the saline touches him, but it barely has an effect as it brushes off my sister.

I swim down to them, slapping at my sister's skin to remove the toxins. My system tingles but I ignore it as I try to help Coralie recover.

All of the sirens surround us, tridents poised to force us back into the brine.

"Get back," I shriek at Merrick and Caspian. "Go!"

Both mermen are breathing heavily, shoulders visibly moving. I pray Llyr is here and staying hidden—if they don't know he's here, maybe he can come after us even if Merrick and Caspian can't.

Coralie shudders against me, sobbing as she attempts to catch her breath. I brush her hair back to ensure it's not hindering her recovery.

"Are you okay?" I ask quietly. "Coralie, look at me. Are you okay?"

She continues to choke against me, and I pull her closer. It's probably not helping her ability to breathe, but I would wrap myself entirely around my little sister if it would protect her from the sirens who are obviously willing to kill us if it comes to that.

Murdoch looks horrified, but he sides with Tarni—he will not help us escape. He clutches at the chain around Coralie's wrists and tail.

"Take it off her tail," I demand. "She's in trouble, Murdoch, and whatever happens next is your fault."

"No," he growls, eyes fixed on Tarni as she holds a trident out in the direction of my friends who are slowly backing away at my insistence.

"Murdoch, please, I need her free," I plead, still trying to clean her tail off as she sporadically spasms.

He finally relents, unshackling Coralie's tail. I drop in the water, using the entire length of my arms to hug around her waist, sliding down her tail to clean her off. Coralie clings to Murdoch's shoulders, curling into him. I don't even care if it means she's safe. Mercifully, he holds her up while I work.

Tarni challenges Merrick and Caspian in the background, but I don't have time to listen. I will do whatever I have to do to protect my sister, and if that means staying as a hostage to the siren princess, I'll do it.

I take Coralie back from Murdoch, holding her against my body. Her convulsions turn to shivering as she slowly recovers.

"Deep breaths," I murmur, willing her system to cooperate.

"Celena?" Merrick yells in the distance.

"She's alive!" I call back, trying not to shake Coralie as I yell.

"Get back," Tarni roars. She drops her voice so that I can't hear but I assume it's a threat.

The mermen start to retreat.

"Actually," Tarni adds. "Stay there."

She nods to Phorcys. He bends down, scooping up the shackles I left on the sea floor when I escaped. She trades with him, taking the chains herself as the two of them approach Merrick and Caspian. Roni joins her with another set of shackles—they must have brought a spare in case I broke mine.

"Turn," she demands, eying my boyfriend and brother as they slowly spin. Her eyes linger over them as she appreciates what she sees. My nostrils flare and I'm sure Coralie can hear my heart beating furiously in my chest.

They comply for the sake of our safety. Phorcys holds them in place with the trident while Tarni runs her hands down Merrick's arm slowly. I cringe as she slips the shackles into place. Just as the sirens did to me, she binds the mermen with their hands behind them attached to their tails.

Caspian and Merrick rest on the ocean floor, struggling to free themselves. Tarni leans forward and says something that makes both mermen snarl at her.

Spinning, she and the others swim back to us.

"They're hot when they're mad," she taunts me. "Let's go."

Leaving Merrick and Caspian is heartbreaking. I'm no longer in shackles since they gave mine away, but keeping Coralie bound is enough to keep me in line now that I know what they're willing to do.

My vision bounces between Coralie ahead of me, and Merrick and Caspian behind me until I can no longer see them.

I force myself to stay quiet and forbid my shoulders from shaking as I cry into the ocean—at least the sirens can't see.

After a few hours, they finally let us rest. Coralie hasn't been able to swim on her own since we left the brine pool, but she huddles on the sea floor anyway as if she had raced all the way here.

"Cor," I'm nearly in tears again as I pull her against me.

"It's not as bad as it looks," she croaks. She looks up and winks.

My eyes grow wide. Coralie may not have ever been trained by my parents, but the mermaid catches on quickly, faking worse symptoms than she actually has.

I squeeze her shoulder to let her know how proud I am of her and try not to snort.

A shark starts to swim by—it's small enough that we don't have to worry about it—but one of the sirens pulls out a bottle from their bag. Inside it must be parts of a dead shark because the creature swims out of range so quickly you'd think it had been stabbed as we continue our journey, swimming away.

It's several more hours before we're able to stop and rest again.

"Can you swim?" I murmur into Coralie's hair as I hold her.

"I think so," she replies. "Are Caspian and Merrick okay?"

"I'm sure they're fine. They're probably free by now."

If Llyr was around—and I'm sure he was—he probably had them free within minutes of us leaving. Unless, of course, they split up. Then it might have taken longer to find them.

"Can we do that?" Murdoch mumbles from across the cavern where we stopped for the rest of the day. The sirens' plan was to stay hidden until well after dark and swim through the night, hoping to catch anyone else who might come to free us when they swim by in the light. Darkness will be our companion now, I suppose, as will the midwater squids be if they insist on traveling under the cover of night.

"Try to rest, Cor. I'm going to listen."

She puts her head down, desperately needing sleep to recover.

"But can we really go there?" Murdoch takes Tarni's hand in his.

"We'll be safe, darling," Tarni hums. "I'll keep you safe like you kept me safe. We'll just siren them into doing what we need them to do. They can't harm us if they're under our control."

If Tarni is talking about sirening, she must be planning to take us near the humans. My fingers still as I pet Coralie's hair.

I can't let her near the humans.

"It will be easy. I'll teach you how to do it too, so you'll always be safe," Tarni says, leaning her head to rest on Murdoch's shoulder. She wraps herself around his arm, tail twitching in the light streaming in from the cave entrance.

Phorcys turns around from the gaping hole in the rock.

"Still clear," he murmurs before turning back around. He makes a face when he sees Tarni latched on to the merman under her spell.

"Can we make it that far that quickly?" Roni asks, leaning forward to wrap her arms around the bend in her tail. I still have the urge to claw some of her scales off, and after what she did to Coralie, I'd happily hand her over to the humans and watch them skin her.

"As long as we don't have any other setbacks, we can make it," Phorcys assures them. "I've been there enough times to know."

"They wouldn't dare come after us up there, would they?" one of the others asks, looking to Murdoch.

"They'll do anything to get Celena and her sister back." My former collection mate sighs, "but if we use them to leverage the situation, I think we can control it."

He points up when he mentions *them.*

"And they can remove us from the situation anyway," Tarni chimes in, looking relaxed as she nestles closer to Murdoch.

Roni looks disapprovingly at Murdoch before turning to stare out the entrance of the cave. At least I know I can play Murdoch against them if I need to later.

"What, the big tough merman is afraid of a few humans?" Roni says without looking back. "Haven't been to the surface yet, guppy?"

The muscles in Murdoch's back tighten at the sound of her words. Tarni sits up, still keeping her fingers wrapped around her boyfriend's arm.

"He'll be fine, Roni," Tarni addresses her friend. "He'll probably end up being the best siren of us all. You saw how good Celena was and she hasn't done it until just now."

She drops her voice when she speaks my name, not wanting me to overhear. It's amazing that she doesn't think I can hear any of her conversations at this point.

"But the others didn't, from what I hear."

"Murdoch is better than those other mermen anyway. You saw the way he deceived them. He's skilled at this." Tarni tucks a lock of her hair behind her. "We should rest. We need to leave soon."

"Tell me about it?" Murdoch asks, changing the subject.

Tarni pulls back to look at him. She sighs before answering.

"There's an inlet. It's almost like a bay. The deeper ships can't get in, and most of the sea life stays out. We can hide under their docks and in the underwater caverns there. There are even waterways that take us into land.

"If we need, the humans can move us from one location to

another. It's something we've only tried once, but it works. We'll be able to survive."

"The mer will have no idea where we are if the humans take us to the other side of the peninsula—and they wouldn't have time to reach us even if they *did* know," Phorcys calls in over his shoulder.

"It's flawless…as long as you don't screw it up, *mer*," Roni adds.

"How will they move us?"

"Ships? Carry us? Does it matter?" Tarni asks. "They'll be under our control. We can command them to kill the mer brats and then we can return to Shadare."

"Do we have a plan if something has happened to Nir?" Murdoch asks Tarni as if they were alone.

"He's fine," she insists.

I open my mouth to harass her and suddenly realize that's a bad idea while trapped in a cavern. An octopus crawls against the wall, looking for a new place to nestle in—if only I could be like that—I could flatten myself out and slip along the edge of the cave, sneaking out without Tarni noticing. It's amazing what an octopus can do to survive.

Without warning, Tarni turns around to look at me. Her eyes grow wild when she sees me staring back at her—too late to look away.

She swims up off her seat on the ground and moves toward me.

"How much did you hear?"

I consider my options but know I'll only pay for it if I lie. If I confront her with what I know, maybe I can get more information.

"Everything…*mostly*," I inform her. "Where is it that we're going to deal with the humans?"

I wait for her to give the name—any name—of a human kingdom, as I try to figure out where we're going. Over the course of our travels, I've figured out the general direction, but it would be so easy to move to different kingdoms with the change of the current here—we could be headed to anywhere.

Mer have always had an innate sense of direction, but predicting the future isn't in our skill set.

"So many questions, so little cares," Tarni croons at me, but it's her grin that terrifies me. "Good night."

She raises her hand, bringing a rock down on my head.

CHAPTER 4

When I wake up, it's nearly dark. Coralie is across the room, looking at me with seaweed wrapped around her mouth as a gag. She tries to swim up when she sees me stir, but Roni forces her back down to the sand.

"Next time, I suggest you mind your own business," Murdoch hisses in my ear, scaring me. "Keep your mouth shut, Celena, or you'll pay."

He was willing to label me as a siren to the collection, but suddenly he wants to help? If I could bite him, I would.

"Time to go!" Tarni announces, swimming into the cave. "Our ride is arriving."

Murdoch drags me outside.

"Behave, or your sister will be making this trip by being dragged by her chains, understood?"

I nod as the dolphins approach. Phorcys signals them over, grabbing on to one's dorsal fin. We all catch a dolphin, allowing them to swim with us as passengers. Phorcys oversees Coralie, nestling her between him and the dolphin. He uses his powerful tail to assist in the swim so the dolphin doesn't have to do all of the work on its own.

My fingers on one hand quietly pet the dolphin, allowing myself small strokes that won't be seen by the others as I try to make friends with the creature in case I need her later.

Unlike the mer, the sirens don't let go when the dolphins need to surface to breathe.

"Cor, it's okay," I call as I realize her dolphin is about to surface.

She tries to turn to see me, but Phorcys tightens his grip as he says something into her ear.

"Up," I whisper, urging my dolphin to follow.

She does, crashing out of the surface of the water as the moon glitters down on us.

Coralie catches sight of me over the dolphin's back.

"It's okay," I promise her before she sinks back down into the water. After a moment, we follow.

We continue to swim through the night, bouncing over the waves in the moonlight every so often as the dolphins carry us away. By morning, I discover that we're in a part of the ocean so deep that I can't see the bottom no matter how low we swim.

"You don't want to go down there," Phorcys says, glancing over at me. He turns to Coralie. "You either, little mer. Remind your sister you don't want to find out what's in the depths."

Coralie's eyes grow wide, but she stays quiet. I can see she wants to make a biting remark—wisely, she holds it in.

Partway through the day, we find a coral reef to hide behind. I'm careful not to touch the edges of the coral as we sit. At some point, we swerved away from the unknown depths of the ocean, coming to a place where colorful fish once again grace the waters.

We don't rest long before continuing on, the dolphins leaving us to our own fins.

My tail hurts less now, thankfully, as we pick up our journey, though the first few days on a split fin were merciless. The sirens allow Coralie to swim on her own, still forcing her hands together at the wrists. If I could take the shackles for her, I would—I'd even accept being cuffed at my tail if it meant she wouldn't have to wear the metal around her wrists, but in order to control *me*, they need to control *her*.

We travel through the night again, putting another day between Merrick and me. The bioluminescent squid help light our way through the waters.

In the distance, other creatures glow, calling their prey to them. It's eerie as we swim through the water. Coralie is close by, though I wish I could tuck her under my arm for safekeeping. I may not trust Murdoch, but I think he is looking out for my young sister as much as he can. He stays close by in the dark.

"Ow!" one of the siren yelps. "What—?"

A second yell cuts him off as another siren is disturbed in the water.

"What's happening?" I ask, swimming to Coralie.

A piercing scream frightens us all into action. I wrap myself around Coralie, pulling her away from Murdoch. He pulls out a knife, ready to defend himself. Tarni and Roni lift their tridents, having carried them in their hands instead of on their backs.

When the screaming merman turns, something is sticking out of his arm. It's long and slender with a nose like a knife. It twitches, still embedded in the siren.

"What is that?" Tarni gasps.

Roni screams as a similar creature attacks her. In the glow of the midwater squid, I see an entire school of the creatures with long bodies and noses.

They crash into the sirens, accidentally inflicting wounds. The creatures swim wildly in the water, swarming around the squid.

"The light!" I shout. "They're drawn to the light."

The creatures race toward me, drawn in by the nearby squid.

With all the force I can muster, I shove Coralie down in the water, pushing her into darkness.

"Get down," I command, pulling the shell from my *iluse*.

So much for saving it.

I slash at the creatures, narrowly missing being struck by two of them. They look like Morgen's swords in the palace in Scylla.

The school looks like a storm raging in a kelp forest, throwing everything around wildly as they twist and turn in the water in a horrifying blanket of reflective scales picking up the color of the bioluminescent glow.

I bat my hair back as it floats in my face, wishing I could braid it back for battle with the creatures of the night.

Everything happens so quickly as the fish huddle together, following their instincts. They don't mean to attack us—it's not their intent—we're just in the way.

Coralie screams as one of the creatures comes toward me, but Murdoch's trident knocks it out of the way, spearing it. He turns without acknowledging me.

"It's the light," I say again. "They're drawn to the light."

I drop down into the darkness, away from the squids floating in the water. The sirens follow, cradling their injuries. The merman whose name I still haven't learned isn't quiet about his pain.

We swim lower in the water, trying to put distance between us and the needlefish still swarming the squids.

"You're hurt," Coralie whispers. She touches my arm, and I reel back—I hadn't realized I'd been injured.

"I'll be okay," I assure her.

Swimming in the dark is difficult. The collection stays close together to avoid losing each other. Once we're safely away from the needlefish, we move closer to the surface to see by moonlight.

I hope Merrick, Caspian, and Llyr don't run into those things on their way to find us.

The siren merman has suffered a number of wounds. I can tell even in the dark that he should have them looked at soon. Inside my necklace, I have something that could help him heal but I'm reserving that for Coralie if she needs it.

"You should look at that," I inform them. "That's only going to get worse if you don't take care of it."

"And what makes you the expert on that?" Tarni snaps.

I don't say anything.

"She's right, it should be bandaged," Murdoch informs them. "I've seen injuries like that before, and you don't want to know what happens when it's not taken care of."

The injured siren looks horrified, thinking about all the possible scenarios he might face. He won't die, of course, but the scars won't be pretty if they don't take care of it.

Sirens often use their looks to manipulate humans, drawing them in before they use their voices. I can't imagine that scars would help his case.

"Fine, then you handle it, *mer*," Tarni replies, annoyed. She leads the group to the sea floor as the water brightens a bit. I look up, noticing that the sun is starting to lighten the sky, even though we can't see it yet.

I tug Coralie along behind me, keeping her against my back as I examine the siren's cuts.

"I need seaweed," I inform Murdoch, giving him a list of items I need to help repair the merman resting on the sand. He glares at me as I lift his arm to get a better look.

Murdoch returns after a few minutes, dropping my supplies on the ocean floor near my tail. I twitch as his hand brushes against my fin.

"I saw that little trick you pulled back there," Murdoch whispers in my ear. "The next time I see you, your *iluse* had better be cleaned off or we'll do it *for* you."

There it is—the threat of taking my *iluse* away.

I pick a few pieces of driftwood out of my *iluse* as I work on the siren's arm. Knowing he'll be looking, I take away the tiny decorative shells as well, leaving only the netting in place.

I wrap the siren's wounds, covering them as best I can. The cut in his abdomen is subtle, but I wrap it to be safe. By the time I'm done, he looks like Merrick and I did before we entered the palace in Metten the first time we met Nir.

"We should go," I push, knowing if I add greater strain to the sirens now, it will work in my favor later.

The sea starts to come to life again as we swim, the sun now clearly in the sky above us. Schools of fish glide by in an array of colors.

"It's cooler here," Coralie murmurs as we swim beside each other.

"It is," I answer, noticing a stingray swimming by, the debris in the water near it glittering fiercely in the sunlight streaming through the ocean.

"We're going to Antaire, aren't we?" she asks miserably.

"I'm not sure, starfish, but we're definitely headed in the direction."

"You don't think they've moved back yet, do you?"

"The queen moved Prince Jarek out of the palace when Persephone and Chantay tried to drown him a century ago. From the sounds of it, I doubt the royal line will *ever* return to the palace by the sea."

"But there will be others, won't there?" she asks nervously.

"Yes, I'm sure there will be."

I keep my arm around Coralie as if I'm helping her swim, still acting like she's recovering from the brine pool.

"I've always wanted to see the human palace, but not like this," she murmurs.

"I know, starfish, so have I." I never *actually* thought I'd see it though.

My heart half tugs on me, wanting desperately to hope we're actually going to Antaire. The other half chides me for wanting to see where the fall of the human-mer agreement came to take place.

The surface is dangerous. I shouldn't want to go, no matter *what* is up there.

Yet, I do. *I desperately do.*

If I didn't have Coralie with me, I might not even protest until I had seen it—I'd have to destroy the sirens at that point, but at least I would have seen the steps Aila sat on over a century ago with Persephone and Prince Jarek.

I wonder what it would be like to see the things my great-great-grandmother saw over a century ago. To be fair, I've seen the palace at Metten where she spent her entire life until the war, but I haven't seen the human world through her eyes.

What must it have been like to sit on the palace steps with the human prince, her tail half in the water, half resting with him on the steps?

Was it easy to talk to him? It must have been—they were friends—at least until Persephone tried to drown him.

Aila used to watch the sunrises and sunsets from the steps that were built down into the water. My scales itch to sit on the steps and watch the world from there.

Her time was when worlds overlapped. Mer and humans respected each other. King Gaspar and the human queen intentionally worked together to preserve both mer and human lives.

Now we all live in fear of the known.

"We'll find out soon, I suppose. We'll have to turn at some point if we're not."

We swim for hours, keeping up a grueling pace as Tarni leads us forward. I wonder how often she's been in this area, and if the sirens ever resided near here that she's so confident with where we're going.

Coralie and I are both exhausted by the time we reach the next resting place. At this point, I give up keeping watch, letting us both sleep tangled in each other's arms so we'll know if the other moves.

Darkness is our guide once again. While we were resting, one of the sirens acquired more midwater squid to see by, though this time, we try to keep our distance to avoid any more attacks. We swim near the surface, using the moonlight to guide us.

As the sun rises again, we slow our pace. Just before I swim into the mouth of the cavern we will be resting in, Tarni pulls me back by my hair.

"Mission time."

"What?" I reply, pulling at my hair to get her to release me.

"Let's go, mermaid," Tarni tugs harder on my locks.

"I'm not leaving her," I proclaim as Phorcys tries to push Coralie inside the cavern.

"She'll be fine as long as you cooperate," Tarni assures me. "Now, let's move."

I struggle against her.

"I'm not leaving her," I yell loudly, disrupting a school of fish. They swim away quickly, changing directions.

"You are. You don't have a choice." Tarni nods to Murdoch. He lifts a knife and swims toward Coralie.

"Murdoch, *don't!*"

Coralie holds her space, not flinching as he moves toward her.

"You're coming with us, princess," Tarni decrees. Murdoch and the others will stay here and watch her, and you can have her when we return. The faster we swim, the faster you get back to your sister."

"Where are we going?" I growl reluctantly.

Coralie bites down, clenching her jaw. She watches me intently as I glare at the siren next to me.

"I'll be back," I look to Coralie. As I turn, I tap the back of my head as if I'm adjusting my hair where the siren had pulled it, hiding my message to my sister—use the weapon I hid in your hair if you need to, and be merciless if you must.

I don't know if Coralie can, but if it comes down to her safety, I hope she can do what needs to be done to survive.

Tarni and Phorcys guide me away. I wait until we're out of sight and they can't easily swim back to warn the others if I become problematic for them before I speak.

"Where are we going?" I demand.

Phorcys' fingers wrap around the trident when he hears my voice. His shoulder shrugs up just enough to indicate that he's displeased with me.

"We're running a little mission for my brother," she says referring to her cousin. "There is something of his mother's that we need to retrieve. You're going to help us."

"And what is that?"

Tarni smiles but doesn't answer. When I open my mouth to speak, Phorcys holds the trident up to my arm, threatening to knick me if I don't stay quiet.

I let them guide me through the waters, around a kelp forest, directly into the heart of a decaying city.

"What is this?" I ask.

"Dwellings, you foolish mermaid," Tarni snips at me.

Siren dwellings look like a convoluted version of mer dwellings, though these appear to have been haphazardly put together—perhaps the others are better. It looks like the sirens aren't ones for long-term locations, meaning my guess was right—they travel, wandering the seas.

"When did you live here?" I inquire.

"*We* didn't. This was before our time," she corrects me. "My aunt moved us closer to Scylla before Nir and I were born. We've been moving for years, scouting our revenge on the mer and finding the best locations to control the humans."

"I see you've done so well for yourselves," I murmur as we swim up to the coral reef blocking most of the temporary siren city from view.

Phorcys uses the opportunity to scratch his trident along my upper arm, leaving a line that's anything but straight. I grit my teeth to avoid grimacing, though my nostrils flare, giving him the satisfaction of a reaction anyway.

"You, Celena, get to go retrieve a necklace for us," Tarni replies. She quickly describes which of the dwellings I'm going to be looking for inside. "Bring it back and we'll let your sister keep all of her fingers."

Tarni holds her trident in the crook of her elbow, balancing the end in the sand below us. She holds a knife in her hand, spinning it so the tip rests against her left pointer finger. When she looks up, she smiles.

"Good luck."

Phorcys forces me around the coral reef's edge toward the main part of the city. Instead of seeing the same dwellings that rested on the other side of the reef, I find that the entire city has been overtaken with jellyfish.

They dangle everywhere in the water, their long tentacles flowing in all directions. I've never seen anything like this. Some are so large, they could likely eat me.

"What is that?"

"It's not a monster, if that's what you think," Tarni replies. "They just get really big out here. Swim along now. We have to be back within the hour."

"If we're not," Phorcys adds, "you don't want to know what Roni will do to your sister."

That's all the incentive I need.

I swallow hard as I swim forward. The first bloom of jellyfish is easy to swim under. I hover over the sand as I lightly flick my tail in the water to propel myself forward. They're floating high enough their tentacles rest at window level on the homes I swim by as I make my way through the abandoned city.

When I make it several lengths into the city, the blooms seem to sink lower in the water. I take a deep breath and hold it as I attempt to swim under them. One tentacle touches the back of my tail for a moment, sparking against my scales.

I try not to cry out.

I make my way through them, finding an opening between two dwellings. Flipping over in the water, I sit on the sand, looking up to get my bearings.

If I'm careful, I can swim up in the water at full height to try to determine where I am.

"Better hurry," Tarni calls from her place by the coral. When I turn to look at her, she's backing up in the water, avoiding a jellyfish that is swimming at her. She makes a face as it darts up in the water, over her head.

Without waiting, I swim up, turning my head quickly to see what is around me. A jellyfish moves and I dart back down.

Two dwellings over, I see the monstrous jellyfish that I saw from the reef. It's so large that it could practically be a dwelling. Making a note to avoid that, I chose to go the longer way around it.

Of course, Tarni had to pick the home in the middle of the small city, making me work incredibly hard to retrieve a stupid necklace.

Necklace.

My hand darts to Grandma Tama's necklace around my throat.

Is there anything that can help me here?

A weapon or two may be of use, but I doubt there will be any reason for me to get it out. Shells litter the ground, and I can easily use one of those to defend myself if I need to.

Phorcys will probably search me when I return, so I don't even have any hope of smuggling the broken shells back with me when this is all over. I risk a glance over my shoulder and find them both trying to see me.

The jellyfish pulse around me, moving slightly in the water. They dip up and down in a massive cloud of toxic tentacles.

I round the corner, hoping to remove myself from view of the sirens so I can think more clearly. Another clearing allows me to see the central dwelling place I'm looking for—the home where Nir's mother left her belongings once when the sirens left in a hurry.

Unfortunately, to get there, I'm going to have to swim directly through a bloom of jellyfish. There's no way around it.

I drop to the sand, hoping to crawl as much as I can under the tentacles floating in the water. It stings as I brush by the first few, tingling fiercely against my back.

Using my arms, I dig the sand out in front of me, trying to create a deeper trench to drag myself through. My fin stings as I flick it in the water to help me move forward—I stop instantly, opting instead to drag my body through the sand.

Like a crab scurrying under the ocean floor, I pull myself through the bloom, crying out when the stings are too much.

"Still alive?" Tarni yells in the distance.

I'm sure this is payback for Caspian and Morgen dropping a net full of jellyfish on Nir's head in Metten.

"Ow," I moan quietly, hoping the sirens can't hear me. I don't take the time to look back.

The water moves around me—my first hint that I should look up. Above me, a jellyfish approaches, it's bell longer than any merman I've ever known. Its tentacles could stretch to the coral reef, and I'm sure beyond it.

It quietly makes its way to me.

CHAPTER 5

My body radiates with pain as its tentacles touch my body. I scream, unable to help myself.

My hand digs helplessly in the sand, trying to cover my body to avoid the pain. I'm sure Tarni is torn between panicking that I won't succeed in retaining her gift to her cousin and being thrilled that I'm suffering.

I can feel where every mark and every line will stretch across my skin. If I survive this, I'll end up looking like Nir for weeks, covered in red welts. At least my face and stomach are somewhat protected against the sand.

Picking up a shell, I slice at the tentacles, trying to force the giant creature away. Another scream escapes my lips as it catches my forearm as I move.

Tears leak out into the ocean as I swat at the jellyfish.

I'm doing this for Coralie, I remind myself. *Her safety is at risk—don't mess this up. You can handle this.*

The sand feels gritty against my stomach as my *iluse* shifts below me. I push myself forward, trying to gain ground on the creature.

I know I'm just making things up, but it seems like the jellyfish is descending on me even further. Glancing up, I see it's giant bell still hovering over the dwelling, not moving since I last saw it.

Tentacles wave in the water over me, dancing along the skin on my back and tail. They tangle with my hair. Occasionally my locks offer me protections—and occasionally they trap the tentacles against me, forcing me to endure more stinging.

I reach up, brushing my hair back toward my tail, cringing as another tentacle moves along with it. I have no choice but to remove myself from this situation.

I gather my strength, forcing myself to do what I know needs to be done.

"Go!" I instruct myself, knowing the only way *out* is *through* this mess. I push myself off the sand, flipping my tail as powerfully as I can. I dart through the large jellyfish tentacles and the surrounding bloom, refusing to stop until I'm away from the monstrous creature.

I try not to cry out as pain slips through my entire body. Darting inside a dwelling, I find it free of jellyfish. I sink to the ground, trying to assess my injuries.

"Celena?" Tarni shouts, almost sounding worried. After a moment, Phorcys lends his voice to the inquiry.

"I'm here," I finally respond, still not moving. I didn't mean to sound so pitiful, but it's all I can manage in my current state.

Remarkably, the stings aren't as bad as they felt, though I can only see a few on my arms and hands—those should heal in a few days. Even more miraculously, I appear to have found the dwelling I was searching for—the former home of Nir's mother during her travels.

I drag myself the first few lengths until I can swim again. I twitch in pain with every flip of my tail, but I keep going—I have to get back to the sirens immediately, and then we all have to get back to the cave or Roni will hurt Coralie.

"I'm in the right place," I scream to let them know I'm coming and not to leave without me.

I hurry through the small dwelling, tipping crates and boxes, dumping their contents out onto the floor. Most of the pieces look like they had been collected from sunken ships or lost during storms.

The dwelling appears to not have any furniture, though if they were just passing through, that makes sense. I have a vague idea of where she slept in the small dwelling, but with the amount of possessions she left behind, who can really tell.

I look for anything that could be of use getting back to the sirens as I search for the necklace, hoping for something to make the return trip easier—I don't know if I can survive the toxic sea creatures again.

Tarni screams for me to hurry up, earning a nasty reply from me.

A strange device is tucked away in the corner of the room, barely sticking out from under a pile of useless trinkets. It appears to be a tool of some kind. Two bars, almost like oars, connect at a curved metal piece at the top. When one of them shifts, I realize they're similar to the scissors we use to cut fabric for our *iluses*—my cousin, Dylana has the most beautiful golden pair in her room that she lets me borrow when I'm in the palace.

Thinking of her prompts me to look down at my *iluse*. I'm a complete disaster and would be ashamed to let other mer see me in such disarray, but I don't have time to do anything about it now.

I pull my hair back again, wondering if I should quickly braid it to avoid having it tangle with the jellyfish again. Finding a small piece of rope, I reach back, nearly fainting from the pain of moving my arms and shifting my injuries, and quickly braid my hair just enough to keep it close to me as I swim.

I look back to the device I found on the floor of the dwelling. The metal snaps together powerfully when I move the two ends—this will be coming with me.

I tuck it under my arm as I continue my reckless search of the room. Inside a bag meant to be strung over a mermaid's chest, I find the necklace. I grab a few other useless items that can't be used against me and cram them into the bag, hoping it will earn me a little grace with Tarni if I deliver extra.

Taking the tool I found, I slowly slip out of the dwelling.

Not knowing how the creatures will react, I quietly lift the tool, making sure the end is open. Slipping it around a small tentacle on the first jellyfish I see, I close the device around it as quickly as I can. It recoils, moving away from the pain of losing an appendage.

The tentacle floats in the water, drifting away as gracefully as a large stingray. Nodding, I move forward.

I snip away, clearing a path for myself as the blooms scatter around me, lifting higher in the water when they sense danger. It's slow going to get around them, but I manage to swim under a number of the creatures, cutting off a bit of the time...along with a few tentacles.

In the distance, Tarni looks shocked. I wish on all the starfish that I could hold up the bag around my chest and see her reaction, but that will have to wait until I survive my current trial.

My body aches, still stinging from the jellyfish, but I eventually find myself clear of the vicious creatures. Tarni looks like she wants to rush to me to claim her prize, but she's smart enough not to get too close as the lionmane's tentacles continue to float nearby—the giant jellyfish continues to hover over the dwellings, unaffected by my assault.

"You did it," Phorcys sounds impressed.

Sagging in the water, I try to lift the bag from my shoulder. I drop the bladed tool to the sand, knowing I couldn't wield it against the merman even if I tried. The last thing I need is for him to take it and turn it on me—or worse, Coralie's fingers.

Phorcys eyes it curiously in the sand but lets it sit as Tarni rips the bag away from me. My fingers trail after it, pulled with the force of her movements.

Phorcys notices me slipping and swims over to me, ripping the end of my braid out so that my hair hangs loose once more. His face is hard and unrelenting, but he slips under my arm, supporting me with his shoulder. We float in the water together.

Never have I been so grateful for a siren in my life.

I wrap one arm around him, refusing to give him the satisfaction of knowing I need him by curling around him like I want to.

If Merrick were here, he'd take me in his arms and carry me all the way back to the cave.

I want his safety.

"We need to get back," I croak quietly, concerned about what Roni might do to Coralie.

"Come on," Phorcys instructs Tarni. She looks euphoric when she pulls the necklace out of the bag. Surprisingly, it looks exactly the way she described it to look.

As we swim, she fishes around inside the cloth pouch, looking to see what else I retrieved from her aunt's former dwelling.

I barely remember what I shoved in the bag—mostly trinkets—but she considers each piece carefully before returning them to the pouch. Tarni slips the strap of the cloth pouch over her head, pulling her lavender hair free after settling the bag across her *iluse,* down to her hip.

The sirens leave the metal tool behind, deciding it's too heavy to bring with us. I don't bother helping Phorcys swim—he carries me under his arm back to the cave.

Yellow fish swim by us, reminding me strangely of the rays of sun cascading down through the ocean's surface. A turtle glides by in the water, curiously turning toward us for a moment before veering away.

Phorcys is warm under my touch. His long hair trails out behind us as we move through the open waters. He holds his trident at his side, keeping it as far away from me as possible, though I pose no threat in my current state.

I want desperately to lean my head against the merman's shoulder to rest. I allow myself enough grace to let my head hover halfway between his shoulder and where it should be if I straightened my back while being carried.

A stingray swims close, nearly colliding with us. I don't have the energy to avoid it, so I duck my head against Phorcys. At the last second, it pulls up, gliding over our heads. It's tail bumps against me in the process.

Phorcys swallows, jerking my head as it rests against the side of his neck. I pull away, trying to untangle our hair without him noticing. He shifts his grip on me, and I gasp as he brushes against the stings on my back. The merman releases me slightly, loosening his grip. He drops his hand down to my hip from my waist to support me without hitting my injuries.

Tarni looks at me when I gasp, and I quickly tip my head up, looking at the stingray swimming away. She rolls her eyes and continues toward the cave where we left Coralie.

"Is she going to be okay?" I whisper, hoping Phorcys will swim faster.

He refuses to answer.

"Tarni, is Coralie going to be okay?" I repeat louder.

"We should make it back in time," she replies carelessly. "You kind of took forever in there."

"Knowing I was walking into the valley of the jellyfish, why did you schedule such a short amount of time?" I attempt to growl.

"You needed the proper motivation," Tarni replies. "Just be glad I gave Roni strict instruction not to touch her while we were gone before the time ran out—she's still incredibly mad that we left without Tiko."

"I'm sure he's rotting in the cells in Scylla with Persephone's bones."

Phorcys cringes against me. Tarni turns to glare.

"I can still cut her fingers off and feed them to a shark if I want, Celena," she offers. "Don't tempt me."

I take a deep breath, stretching the skin across my back. I blink back my tears. If mermaid tears really were pearls like the books the sailors dropped in the sea said, our collection wouldn't have to worry about finding new pearls for the next two Pearl Festivals just from the tears Coralie and I have cried since leaving Scylla.

"I'm really tired of listening to you, *mer*," Tarni adds. "Keep talking, and I'll start pulling scales up again."

"I had a feeling you enjoyed that," I murmur.

"Had to keep up the act," she replies. I can hear the grin in her voice.

As we continue, I try to figure out a way to get enough strength to steal the trident from Phorcys and take Tarni out. If I pin her tail to the sand, she'll never recover enough to swim on her own again. If I miss, it could cost Coralie.

I'd have a lot more confidence in my plan if it were Caspian being held hostage with me—at least my twin has been trained to protect himself. Mother and father did us all a disservice by keeping our training quiet from each other.

If only we'd all been aware, the three of us could have been trained to a more advanced level. Instead, Mother trained me as passed down by Grandma Mara and her mother before that all the way back to princess Aila. Father had quietly trained Caspian, keeping it hidden from the rest of us—something all of the men in our line have apparently done.

I wonder if the king has suffered Marilla's wrath yet for quietly training the prince, or if she, Morgen, and Dylana are still recovering from the injuries they suffered at the hands of the sirens.

My parents must be beside themselves—all three of their mer children out in the darkest, most dangerous depths of the seas, far out of their reach. I imagine it would be terrifying for any parent, but even worse for them since Caspian, Coralie, and I come from Aila's line—the only one the sirens hate worse than the reigning royals because Aila was the one that interrupted Persephone and Chantay's plan to control the humans.

I'm sure my parents found out shortly after Caspian and the others left to find us. There's no way Casp, Merrick, or Llyr would ever wait around to come and find us. There must be a whole team looking for us though—my mother and Marilla would never let it stand if the best mer weren't out looking for us.

With any luck, the rest of the collection is on their way to Metten to bring back the royal mer children after we helped them escape the palace during the siren attack. I hope they made it safely through the dark—though, the more I travel at night, the easier it has become. I almost don't mind it now except for the terrifying things that come out at night that you can't see in the dark waters.

In the distance, I spot the cave. Afternoon is shifting into evening and the rays of light dance in the open waters, shifting and crashing into each other as they overlap. A few starfish crawl across the sea floor below us, catching the light as they move.

Anemone wave in the current, tiny fish darting in and out, using them for safety. I've always wanted to wear an anemone in my hair, but I know better. Instead, I mimic their look in other ways.

I watch the cave carefully, looking for any sign of the sirens or Coralie. The mouth of the structure is wide and dark, preventing me from seeing inside.

Phorcys notices me taking a breath to yell to the sirens, and he squeezes me against his hip.

"Don't," he warns quietly enough that Tarni doesn't hear him. My breath catches as I still against him, tensing my muscles.

"I can swim," I whisper.

"No, you can't," Phorcys objects.

"I can do it," I defy him. "Let me go, I'm fine."

"She's going to know when she sees you anyway, so there's no need to make it worse," he replies. "That will just make it more difficult for us to transfer you anyway."

"She doesn't need to know how bad it is, now let me go, and you go tell Roni to get away from my sister. Tarni can guard me."

He's shaped similarly to Merrick, though slightly taller. This reminds me of swimming backward with my partner, checking for dangers following behind us, though the siren isn't nearly as comforting.

I wiggle, trying to get him to release me, but he holds fast. I purse my lips, defeated.

"What—?" Tarni mumbles, jolting up in the water to see better.

I follow her gaze as I see someone shoot out of the cave.

Coralie turns around, screaming at the sirens that follow her out.

My sister is free from her shackles and holding the shell from her hair. She spots us and screams my name.

I don't have time to think, I only have time to act.

Coralie is free and defending herself, and I need to swim.

This is our only chance at escape and if they stop us, they'll kill us.

CHAPTER 6

Coralie screams again, slashing the shell at Roni. She connects with the merman whose name I don't know, slicing across his arm and chest. He reels back, knocking into Tarni.

I squeeze Phorcys' neck, pinching tightly enough to knock him out after cringing in pain. I catch his trident as it floats down in the water and attempt to race to Coralie's side.

On my way, I slam the trident against Tarni's head—she didn't see me coming from behind while she was busy trying to figure out how Coralie escaped.

Roni pushes the merman off of her and charges at us.

"Go!" I instruct, trying to swim while looking over my shoulder to see where Roni and the others are.

My world spins a little between the pain of the jellyfish stings and the loss of my equilibrium as I continually turn around to look while I'm swimming.

"What happened?" Coralie shouts.

"Jellyfish, keep going," I answer.

"I used the shell," she informs me, swimming as fast as she can.

The water streams over my body as we move and I can't tell if it's soothing my injuries or making them worse.

"I saw," I reply. "Cor, I need you to guide me."

"What?" she yells, glancing back at me.

"I'm hurt, and I can't swim backward to protect us like this. I need you to be Merrick."

"I don't understand," she shouts as we whip through the water. Roni is quickly gaining on us, two of the other sirens right on her tail.

"Grab my arm," I instruct her. "You swim forward and guide us while I swim as fast as I can backward and protect our tails."

Coralie slows, letting me catch her. She loops her arm through mine, ready to follow orders.

"Your only job is to swim as hard as you can and get us out of here. I'll help as much as I can, but my job is to keep us safe—I'll have no idea where we're swimming to."

"I can't do this," she cries. She lowers her head and swims faster anyway.

"You can, Cor, just don't stop," I shout above the rushing water. "And if anything happens, keep going. If we get separated, I'll find you. Just swim until you physically can't swim anymore and then find a place to hide. I'll find you."

She doesn't answer but hesitates slightly before pushing ahead even stronger, attempting to be Merrick for the moment. I flick my tail up and down, desperately trying to help my sister swim faster—I don't think we have any hope.

Now would be an incredible time for our mermen to show up and save the day. Instead, we'll have to save ourselves.

"Sharp turn right, Cor," I call, directing her. The wise choice would be to go left—toward mer territory, but turning left puts her directly in between the sirens and me, meaning I can't protect her. If we go right, I'll be wedged between them and able to defend her—we can find our way back later.

I turn my tail, using it to steer us hard to the right as Coralie angles her body to turn us as well. We pull quickly away from the path we were on, shocking Roni and the others for a moment.

Realizing I can easily steer us with my tail, I use the opportunity to take control of the situation.

"Is it clear?" I ask, hoping the path is open for us.

"Coral ahead," she shouts.

"How far?"

"Twenty lengths," she replies, still pushing her tail as hard as she can go.

"Tell me when we're one length away," I yell back to her. I flip my tail, trying to help as Roni begins to catch up to us. "We're going down and then back around."

"Are you sure we can do that?" Coralie sounds like she's struggling.

Focusing on escape is giving me temporary relief from the jelly-fish stings—I wonder if that's how Nir still had the ability to nearly kill me in the palace in Metten after Caspian and Morgen's plan slowed him down.

"Now," Coralie gasps, clearly in pain from the strain this is putting on her body.

I flip my tail, sending us into a hard dive. Coralie shrieks, indicating it's time to swerve. I move my tail again, turning us to the left sharply. I look straight ahead and see the end of the coral ahead of us. I dive around it just as Roni pops over the edge.

"Did she see us?" Coralie gasps quietly.

"Probably, I don't know," I reply. "I couldn't tell that quickly. I only saw her for a moment."

"Where do we go?"

"Around and back toward Metten," I say. Our best hope is to hide in Metten and pray that all of Scylla is there to back us up. If they aren't, we could be risking the royal family. If nothing else, I hope Marilla has sent people to recover her mer children and bring them home before we arrive.

At least in Metten, I'd have the advantage of knowing where to hide and where our ancestors might have hidden supplies for us over a century ago should they ever return. I have no clue out here.

The light is nearly blinding as I look up, pumping my tail to aid our escape. When I look back down, I see the end of everything.

The collision knocks us down in the water. I lose my grip on Coralie as the siren slams into us. Using the stolen trident, I attempt to fend them off, but I'm too weak to do any damage.

My world spins like a whirlpool. Colorful fish form a beautiful blur. The water makes me wavy. I sink, unable to control myself.

"Nice try," Roni remarks, knocking the trident from my hands so that it snaps my wrists. "Too bad you weren't fast enough. That's the brilliant part about trying to escape while injured—it never works, does it?"

Coralie looks miserable when I regain the ability to comprehend my world again. Her idea was good, but her timing was off, and she knows it.

"She was going to take my finger," Coralie announces. I'm the only one that cares.

"Still might, *mer baby*," Roni reaches toward the pouch on her hip, ready to pull out Caspian's knife again.

Tarni swims up, arm around Phorcys. Murdoch stares in obvious discomfort.

"We have to go," Tarni announces. "You'll pay for this tomorrow. I'm not sure how yet, but we have the entire rest of the night to figure it out. Now let's swim."

By the time the sun drifts down in the water, we find ourselves staring at the underside of a small kingdom in the distance. Boats fill the inlet far ahead of us, and even Phorcys seems nervous of the number of humans that must be nearby.

Murdoch attempts to hold a brave face, but I can tell he's shaken by the way his eyes pull back to his ears further than usual. He stays close to Tarni as we turn to the left, swimming away from the human world.

A boat seems to be following us as we swim parallel to the land. The vessel is long and dark and doesn't appear to made for fishing.

"What's that?" I ask, hoping to get a better idea of the types of humans we might be facing here.

"A boat," Phorcys answers.

"What kind?" I try again.

"We *siren* humans, we don't *talk* to them." He bristles, brushing his hair back as it floats between us. He keeps a firm grip on his trident—I didn't do myself any favors by knocking him out.

The water grows shallower as we swim adjacent to where the humans walk on the land far above our heads. Being in such a shallow depth makes me nervous. Finding places to hide isn't as easy as Tarni made it sound while we were traveling.

We swim closer to wooden columns in the water, drawing dangerously close to the ships in the water in the quieter part of the inlet. Rounding a piece of land that sticks out into the ocean, we come to what appears to be a quiet bay. Three ships bob in the water, tied to the docks.

"Tarni?" Murdoch asks.

"It's fine, Murdoch," she encourages him. "You'll learn quickly enough. All mer have the power to siren—we just need to wake it up in you, that's all."

"Don't you think we should do this slowly?" he replies. "Maybe practice first?"

Something bad is coming—I can feel it in the waters.

"I see that you need proof." She puts her finger on Murdoch's lips before he can speak. "I'll show you."

She swims a length away before turning around to face us. Tarni latches eyes with me.

"Hold her." Her words come out dark.

Phorcys and one of the other sirens grab onto my arms, prohibiting me from moving. Tarni and Roni grab Coralie and drag her toward a large wooden column in the water.

She says something to Coralie before they pull her to the surface.

"Murdoch!" I scream at him, knowing he's my best hope at stopping this.

He turns to me, shocked at the turn of events. Tarni's tail twitches happily as she holds Coralie above the surface.

"She can't siren," I shout, pulling viciously against my captors—it hurts me more than it hurts them.

In the water above us, the sirens move closer to the dock until they're right against the wooden column supporting the structure blocking all the light. When they dip back down into the water, Coralie isn't with them.

"Where is she?" I scream as Coralie's tail flicks back and forth, barely in the water.

"She's proving a point," Tarni calls down. "She'll figure it out."

"Maybe," Roni adds.

"They'll kill her," I shout in horror. I turn to Phorcys, hoping he'll listen. "Please, they'll kill her, let me save her."

He holds his expression, staring straight ahead.

"Phorcys, please, she's a little mer girl, don't do this." I turn to Murdoch. "Please, you might have turned your back on the collection, but please don't do this. She's only thirteen."

Murdoch shifts to look at me. When he does, Phorcys loosens his grip. I take it as a sign to move and beat my tail as hard as I can, ripping my arm away from him.

My movements surprise the other siren, and I escape his grasp as well, racing toward the surface despite the pain crawling over my back.

Coralie screams, begging for the humans to leave her alone as they reach for her chains with a hook. Tarni and Roni managed to lift my sister out of the water enough to string her up on a metal hook sticking out of the column holding up the dock.

The bottom of her tail is still in the water, but she's out far enough that the sailors have taken notice. They call down to her as they attempt to catch the chains binding her wrists over the hook and pull her up.

I swim for her on the surface, the waves crashing around my chest and abdomen as I move. Singing, I try to ensnare the men in my melody. Coralie quiets, eyes round with shock—she doesn't know the extent of my skills with sireny.

The men drop their hook into the water, and I let it sink to the ocean floor as I continue to sing. I try to think things through as I lure the men into my trap—do I kill them or let them live?

Holding them still, I swim to Coralie and struggle to free her. I have to stop several times to continue my song, leaving my sister hanging in the air longer than she should be.

I position myself under her tail so that she can sit on my shoulder. Gathering my strength, I push myself out of the water with everything I have, lifting her high enough that she can use her tail to push off of me and extend her hands over the end of the hook suspending her.

We crash down into the water, Coralie dunking me under the waves. I pop back up over the surface immediately, singing so that the humans don't fall out of my sireny and attack before we can escape.

My hair is plastered against my face, and I rush to move it back enough that it doesn't hinder my words as I lull the humans into my sireny again, keeping them at a distance.

If I make them jump into the sea, they could fight off the sirens for me, or at least get in their way and prevent them from stopping our escape. Tarni once said that the humans could move us if necessary—I consider letting them lift us into their boats and allowing them to sail us out of Tarni's reach, but I don't trust my voice to hold out that long, nor do I trust what will happen to our bodies if we remain out of the ocean for more than an hour or two.

I look around, trying to find Coralie. She's not on the surface with me, nor is she below me in the water near my tail as I expect her to be. Panic rises in my chest as I use my hands to try to clear a path in the water to see her—an impossible task.

I look back at the humans, not wanting to release them from my sireny, but also knowing I have to find Coralie immediately.

I dip under the water, finding Tarni once again holding my sister.

"Come back down," she directs in a casual manner, holding a knife to Coralie's throat.

"But—"

"Now." Coralie rolls her eyes as Tarni speaks.

Ducking all the way under the water, tail flipping up into the air as I maneuver myself back down into the sea. I hear the humans already starting to come out of my sireny as I make my way below the waves.

The hook that the humans dropped into the sea sits on the ocean floor, too far out of reach to be of any use to me. Tarni and Murdoch are arguing when I arrive.

"She didn't though, did she?" he protests. "Her sister did it for her."

"Oh, but she will," Tarni retorts. "She'll learn just like her sister did, because there will come a day when Celena can't save the little princess."

She glares at me as I approach.

"What's the matter? Grandma Aila didn't teach you mermaids how to defend yourself?"

"Aila didn't have to. She took down sirens without even trying—it's in our blood," I growl.

"Unlike you, though, Aila didn't siren," Tarni challenges me.

"Maybe not like *you* siren," I approach her threateningly. "*She* sirened to help the humans, but she most assuredly did siren."

"You wouldn't be caught dead helping the humans, though, would you?" Tarni releases Coralie to me.

"No."

"Then why not side with us?" Tarni replies with a knowing smile. "Not that we'd ever trust *you*, but I see no reason why the mer and sirens can't work together. We already command the humans when we need to. With all of us, we could control them all of the time, not just when we come across them."

"We're in Hontan, not Antaire," I remind her. "Just what do you plan on doing?"

"We're going to end them all, Celena. Don't you see? Nir is on his way with the entire siren army. We're going to destroy the humans and rid the ocean of them once and for all, and you're going to help."

"The royals have always been better at sirening than the rest of the collection," Phorcys adds.

"That's why you were able to siren the humans away from us outside of Scylla." Murdoch swims into the conversation, earning glares from Roni and Tarni.

As a royal, my sirening skills are stronger than the others'—which is why Merrick couldn't control them outside the reef barrier in Scylla but I could.

It *also* explains why Nir didn't kill Marilla and Dylana when he had the chance—he needs us.

But as the descendant of Chantay, Nir should have the same skills we have. Maybe one royal voice isn't enough for whatever they have planned.

"You *want* them to follow us," I murmur, realizing there was a reason behind leaving Merrick and Caspian alive. "You want the royals."

"We'll let the others join us if they cooperate, but we don't really need them if they don't want to do as they're told," Tarni replies.

"This was always your back up plan if taking over Scylla failed," I point out as a fish swims between us.

"It was. *Smart* mermaid," Tarni taunts. "We just had to accelerate our plan, that's all. We'll get the humans to help us get the mer royals and then we'll use them to destroy the humans—if the royals happen to come to us, that just makes it easier.

"Nir should be here soon," she concludes, pulling her hair over her shoulder as she turns to bat her eyelashes at Murdoch. "If *we* can siren, *you* can siren. You'll see."

"I'll go check for Nir," Roni announces, swimming off without waiting for permission.

"We have a few things to check on before they arrive," Tarni tells Murdoch. "Want to see the most magical place you've ever seen in your life?"

She takes him by the hand, leading him away. I watch them swim through the water until I can no longer make out their details.

"We have things to do too," Phorcys says, grabbing my arm.

Having no choice, I swim alongside of him in his slipstream. My body aches, battling between the pain from the jellyfish and from what I did to save my sister.

He guides us in the opposite direction, swimming away from the humans, still parallel to the land. We keep a safe distance between us and our tail-less enemies, but we could easily spy on them if we rose to the surface.

"We're going to scout the area," Phorcys informs us, glancing back at Coralie as she follows. "We won't go near the humans though, don't worry."

On occasion, it's like Phorcys actually has a heart.

A few sirens swim behind Coralie, watching us to ensure we don't attempt to escape—even if I wasn't so broken, now would not be the time to attempt an escape.

Coralie swims under my arm, helping to make sure I swim straight without veering off course or crashing into anything.

"Casp will have something to say about all this," she murmurs so no one else can hear her.

The ocean is still and unmoving around us, not even a hint of light dancing through the water as if everything above us is perfectly calm. An octopus sits on the ocean floor, slowly moving one tentacle across the sand and rocks below. Fish swim by as if nothing were wrong in their lives.

I note several caverns as we pass, but Phorcys guides us forward. Soon, we find ourselves nearing the surface again, though the sea floor is still just as far below us—the shallows. Coralie doesn't say anything, but I feel her tense up under my arm when she realizes where we are. It makes my skin prickle.

"We need to fix her injuries," Coralie suddenly protests. "She won't be able to make it much longer if she doesn't rest."

"She'll be fine," the siren merman answers.

I glance at him, worried that he'll try to carry me again.

"You're on your own this time, *mermaid*," he mutters, realizing what I'm thinking. "I have too much to do to haul your tail around."

He darts ahead of us, letting Coralie guide me. The sirens behind us perk up, knowing Cor and I are their responsibility now as the merman swims away.

Ahead, Phorcys darts low in the water, gaining speed. A cold terror washes over me as he launches himself out of the water, jumping like a dolphin. Coralie's fingers bite into me where her arm is wrapped around my waist to help me, and I cry out softly.

She darts her head toward me, eyes wide from the sight. My sister releases her grip on the edge of my scales before looking back to where Phorcys is crashing down in the water.

He dives low, flipping over so that his back barely misses the sand on the ocean floor as he races toward us. The merman pulls up at the last second, twisting to face us. The rush of water sends our hair floating above our heads.

"You're going to want to see this," he grins, eyes narrow.

Turning, Phorcys grabs my hand, dragging me along. I yelp, but he doesn't stop. Coralie tries desperately to keep up while I let the merman drag me, refusing to help swim.

I take a deep breath right before we break the surface of the water. We bob on the waves together as Coralie and the others join us.

Most land that I've seen has been covered with sand and rocks.

There have been some plants, but the majority of the colors were tans and grays. This is like an explosion of color.

Green fills the hill, rolling all the way down to the rocks at the edge of the water. The cliff is raised high above the waves, over-looking it dangerously. I imagine if any human stood on the edge of it, they might be perilously close to falling off it.

"You're going to need to remember this," Phorcys murmurs just loud enough for me to hear.

Sea urchins speckle the side of the cliff, swaying in the breeze in a multitude of colors—I think they call them flowers. In the sky above, the blue is miraculously bright, etched with white clouds in the distance. Looking straight up, I can't find a single one.

A single line of water makes its way down the cliff, cascading into the ocean at the base of the land. I'm sure it's bigger up close, but it looks so tiny from our distance.

Birds fly overhead, crying out in obvious pain. Over and over, they shriek. A few land in the distance, picking at things on the sandy shore next to the cliff.

A stingray brushes against my hip, scaring me. I look into the water and notice him gliding to one of the sirens to check for food, which makes no sense since mer don't live this close to the shores—unless they do.

"There are more sirens here, aren't there?" I ask Phorcys quietly while Coralie is distracted by the sights.

"Once, not anymore." The muscles in his arms tighten. "Speaking of, it's time to go home."

He dives under the water.

"Time to go, Cor," I say, tugging at her hand.

We slip under the water, diving to the sand below. A crab scurries across the ocean floor, guiding our path for a moment until we over-take it, leaving it angrily in our wake.

Swimming further, we find ourselves back in an area covered in ships again—another harbor. The collection stays low to the ocean floor, moving under the dangerous-looking boats.

An anchor drops in front of us, surprising even Phorcys. He reels back, pausing in the water.

"Around," he announces, moving us out of the path of the boats.

Swimming through the harbor is as terrifying as entering the shark barrier without anything to scare them off. Even when scouting for the queen, if I left mer territory, I always went around the reef barriers instead of daring to venture into the feeding areas.

"Scared?" I taunt the siren. "I thought you could just siren them into doing your bidding…"

He glares to me from under his brow.

"You'll see," he mutters.

Flipping his tail, he directs us around the boats and humans, keeping enough distance that he doesn't bother to watch their every move. I, on the other hand, mind them very carefully.

We swim into a cavern that looks like a giant shelf. The rock stretches above the surface, forming part of a new cliff. The dark rock moves down into the water deeper than the human boat's sit, hiding the entrance from sight.

Surrounded by darkness, our only guide is Phorcys' voice as he instructs us to continue straight ahead. I hold my arms out, looking for any obstacles in the way as we swim slowly into the shelter.

When we venture back into the light again, the cavern is bathed in a bioluminescent glow. The cave rises up overhead, opening into a grotto that rises out of the water.

We surface. A long ledge sits just above water level—the perfect place for a human to sit by the water. I wonder if this is what the cave looked like where Persephone sirened Prince Jarek a century ago.

Glowing algae covers the bumpy rocks. I've never seen a cave like this before, with its strange angles and smooth edges.

"Stunning, no?" Phorcys asks coyly. He swims so close that he could reach out and touch my face. "Look closer."

His words have an icy edge, and the spark in his eye sets my scales prickling. I swim back, not taking my eyes off of the terrifying siren. His skin is tinged blue in the bioluminescent glow of the cave, making him look even more menacing.

I bump into the wall of the cave before I turn.

Phorcys moves toward me again, and I turn, quickly trying to follow his command. Examining the rock, I find that the legends are true—the sirens built their kingdom with the skulls of their victims.

CHAPTER 7

Bones litter the ground below us and over the water's edge. Skulls piled on top of each other form walls and barriers, strengthening the rocks already in place.

Some blend with the rocks, old from age, while others look only a generation old. Sediment has filled in the gaps over time, covering the secrets the skulls once held, allowing only their hollow eyes to communicate now. They watch us, judging our every move.

"You see, mermaid, the thing about sirens is that we always do exactly as we say we're going to do. We built our kingdoms on the deaths of our enemies. We took over Scylla. We're going to use the mer royals to control the remainder of the humans, and when we're done, you'll either be useful to us or you won't. Time to make up your mind."

Phorcys motions for me to swim to the ledge.

"Now is a great time to start." He grabs my hips and forces me into the air. I land heavily on the ledge, rock biting into my scales. "Crawl over there."

He points across the ledge to the back of the cavern. In the corners, I can see where two doorways lead out of the cavern—a human entrance.

"Against the back wall is a hidden partition. Find it and open it." The merman points to the right side.

I steel myself and crawl away from the water, grateful he didn't put Coralie through anything else.

"Be careful," Cor warns. "Don't catch your scales on the rocks."

I look down, realizing I should be more mindful.

Hand-over-hand, I pull my entire body weight across the flat rock, wishing I had the water to keep me warm. Despite the cooler temperatures, the water was much more agreeable than the cool chill of open air.

Skulls clutter the higher rock formations on the mainly flat surface. My finger accidentally reaches inside an empty eye socket when I reach forward. Knowing I can't recoil, I keep my cringe to myself and use the skull to pull myself forward.

Old and fragile, it breaks, dropping a cheekbone into my hand.

There's something more horrific about finding skulls on the *surface* than there is when finding them under the sea.

I worry I've gone soft in the presence of the sirens—a few days ago, I never would have hesitated or been squeamish about any of the things I've faced since being dragged away from the palace in Scylla.

For a moment, I consider ripping the skulls out of their places in the ground and using them as weapons against Phorcys and the others, but Coralie is still in the water. The sirens were the ones that did this to the owners of the skulls—I'm sure the people they came from wouldn't mind getting one last word in as my weapon of choice.

"Move it along, mermaid," one of the sirens calls.

A few more arm lengths and I reach the back wall. Hidden partially behind a rock formation, I use the opportunity to look at the doorway near me. It appears to be a tunnel, and though dark, I can see that it takes at least one turn. Faintly, I can hear more water— perhaps another room? It doesn't sound like the ocean waves though, it's more of a consistent noise instead of the pulsing waves.

"Did you find it?" Phorcys interrupts my thoughts.

"Not yet," I call back, running my fingers along the wall. An indentation so small that I can barely feel it appears under my touch. "I found it! How do I open it?"

"If I knew that, I would have told you," he calls back.

"Are you okay?" Coralie calls.

"I'm fine, Cor, I'll be back in a minute."

I trace the outline, carefully gliding my fingers over the thin line. When I can't reach the top, I drop my hands to the ledge and push myself into a sitting position. Once up, I can barely see over the rock formation between the sirens and me, but I have just enough visibility to see that Coralie is surrounded by sirens.

Reaching back up, I continue my way around the outline of the hidden partition of the cave.

"I think I need to pry it open," I shout. "I can't find any other way in."

I hear a loud smash, turning to discover pieces of bone skidding toward me.

"Try that," Phorcys calls, expecting me to pick up the shattered skull he just threw at me.

"Lovely," I mutter, picking up the cracked bones.

I wedge it between the wall and the small door. The bone starts to crumble in my hand—age mixed with the pressure I'm putting on it—but the majority of it holds while I work to pry open the panel.

When it finally pops open, I set the bone down and use my fingers to open it the rest of the way. Air moves quickly through the tunnel leading into the cave, rushing past me. My hair moves over my shoulder and I realize that I probably look ridiculous with my wet hair plastered down my back and the sides of my arms—I'm sure Merrick would have a snarky comment if he were here.

It opens silently, swinging to the side away from me. I scoot my tail over to avoid colliding with it, making me twist at an odd angle to reach back into the dark space.

I give myself a moment for the light to fill the recess—it's so dark inside that the glow of the cave barely helps.

"Well?"

"I letting my eyes adjust, just a minute," I shout angrily.

"There should be a box inside," Phorcys shouts back. "Bring it back."

I deftly reach in and scoop the box out, setting it next to me. Chances are that the sirens know exactly what is inside the box, so snooping won't help me. Instead, I use the few precious moments I can steal from them to search the rest of the hidden compartment.

Knowing I don't have time to be cautious, I scrape my hands along every bit of the inside of the partition until I find another hidden panel. Inside sits weapons. One slices the end of my finger like a piece of coral. I retract my hand, wiping the blood away quickly—blood on land isn't like blood in the water—it smears on the rock.

I can't sneak a weapon by Phorcys. There's no way he wouldn't see it tucked in my hair and I have nowhere else to hide it. I shut the door quietly, hiding it back in the dark recesses of the compartment. A second hidden door reveals a set of shoulder armor—also helpful, yet unavailable to me.

I pick up the box again, dropping it heavily to the ledge so that the sirens can hear it. Pushing it forward, I move away from the hidden compartment and close it again.

"I'll be back for you," I whisper to the contents locked safely inside.

I ensure that it's closed firmly so that no one else can access it easily and then push the box forward again as if it's heavy—the sirens won't lift it outside of the water, so they won't know it was light enough for me to move without much struggle.

The box drags across the ground as I push it, then pull my tail to join it, only to mimic the movement all over again. Moving this way requires much more effort than merely dragging myself to the back wall had, but between the split fin and the jellyfish stings, this doesn't seem nearly as bad.

When I reach the edge, Phorcys rises up in the water to help move the box. I intentionally push it past him, knocking it into the water.

By the time I sink into the ocean again, relief washes over me with the water, calming my scales. I hadn't realized how on fire they felt from dragging myself over the sand and rocks.

"What's in the box?" I demand.

"Maps," he answers truthfully. One of the sirens holds the box under the water for him while he opens it, proving his point. "You've just uncovered all of the details we need for fighting the humans. Time to go back."

We make our way out of the cave, back to open waters as the sirens carry the box with maps. Phorcys pages through a few of them, attempting to organize them before we reach Tarni and whoever might be with her—I hate to think what she's been doing this whole time.

A plan starts forming as we swim now that I know where weapons are hidden. I'll need to know as much as I can about the area when Coralie and I try to escape. I assume by the time I'm well enough to fight in a day or so, Merrick, Llyr, and Caspian will be nearby, but they won't have the layout of the ocean here—I'll need to do some intelligence gathering for us.

I swim alongside Phorcys, glancing over his shoulder at the maps.

"Is that where we are?" I ask bluntly, pointing to the sketches.

"What do you care?" he challenges.

"If I'm going to be swimming around helping you, you're better off letting me know how to avoid the humans, *you eel*," I counter.

He looks amused at my resorting to name-calling.

"So the princess wants to learn her way around, huh?" He grins. "What are you willing to do for it?"

He's flirting with me, I realize in shock.

Fine. If Persephone could siren a human and Tarni could siren a merman, I'll do what I have to in order to siren a siren.

"I won't kill you when this is all over, how about that?" I say in a low voice.

"You honestly think you're going to win?" he counters.

A stingray swims by, cutting through the water between us. I pull back to avoid it.

"I think there's only one way this ends and it's with most of your sirens' skulls being added to your little collection back there."

"If you thought *that* was bad, wait until you see Shadare." He shrugs. "I'm sure we'll take you back when it's all over—assuming I can save you during the battle, that is."

"Like you saved me from the jellyfish?" I bat my eyelashes innocently at him.

Coralie pokes my stomach as I swim. When I turn to her, she looks horrified. I smile and turn back to the siren.

"So you *did* want me to save you from them. Here I thought you'd rather be eaten by that monstrosity than spend more time with us."

I sniff at his words, trying to be mysterious. After a moment, I point back to the map.

"Where are we? There, right?"

"We're here." He uses his finger to trace a route from where we left to where we're going.

"What's that?" I scrunch my nose as I lean closer, trying to decipher what the picture means.

Phorcys follows suit, pulling the map closer to his face.

"Oh." He lowers the map, looking at his companions. "Around, mermen—to the left."

We change course slightly, following his directions, though he doesn't take us far before correcting our path. Eventually, we swim upon what I saw in the drawing—a dark, terrifying stretch of ocean covered in all the waste the humans have left to the ocean's devices for a century or more.

Anchors lay on the ground, kelp growing quietly around them. Ropes twist in the current, caught on anchors and rocks. Chains litter the ground, much as the skulls had inside the cave. Light filters down, finally dancing again in the water—this time adding a dangerous edge to the dark, isolated place.

"Remember this sight, mermaids," Phorcys insists. "I have no problem chaining you up in there if you don't cooperate. I doubt you'll ever make it out, even if your friends *do* show up to help you.

"Swimming over the top would be easy," he continues, motioning to a bit of open water over the stretch of destroyed sea. "Dropping you into the middle of that mess wouldn't be difficult. Good luck surviving *that.*"

The loose ropes sway in the water. Some lay coiled on the sand below. A few chains snake out like jellyfish tentacles, quietly resting on the outskirts of the area.

Bones of creatures long since dead rest mixed in the middle of the disaster. Most of them are fish skeletons that got caught while floating through the water, but some are from larger creatures that got trapped in the ropes and floating netting.

One catches my eye as we skirt around the dangerous area—mer.

"Is that—?"

"I told you, princess, it wouldn't be hard to drop you in there. We know this from experience." He glances at me before shifting the map to the next in the pile. "She didn't want to cooperate."

If there were mer bones entangled in there, that meant the sirens had sentenced one of their own this way. A siren had died there at the hands of her collection.

"Don't worry, that was two generations ago," he says loudly. "But if you think you'll need help remembering this little lesson, I can assist with that."

Phorcys swims away, diving down to the sand. He crawls toward the edge of the ropes and chains, fishing out something before returning.

"Obviously I couldn't reach her, but this will serve as a reminder for you." He holds up a fish skeleton between his fingers. Breaking off the bone, he lets the rest fall. "Now, just in case you get any ideas, I want you to think about this moment."

He swims dangerously close to me.

"Turn around," he whispers, growling at me.

The siren reaches under my hair, tangling the bone in the underside of my locks as I had done with the broken shell in Coralie's hair.

"This stays," he reminds me, giving me a warning look. "And when you think about doing something stupid, remember this and be glad it's in *your* hair and not your sister's."

Beyond him, on the far side of the ropes and broken pieces from ships and cargo, a bit of blue flashes in the distance. I try to keep my focus locked on Phorcys as he floats in front of me, but it catches my eye again.

"Are we going to go?" Coralie is quick to ask.

Phorcys turns to face her, angry at the interruption.

"Yes, little mermaid, we are," he sneers. "No need to waste any more time at The Ropes."

Behind him, Merrick ducks behind the debris in the water.

Coralie nods to me as we swim away.

Our mermen have arrived.

"Come with me," Tarni grabs on to Coralie's arm the moment we swim into the cave where we're supposed to be meeting them.

"Tarni," Phorcys says forcefully. "A word."

Tarni scowls but swims out of the cave with him to talk in private. Murdoch takes Tarni's place by Coralie, guiding her outside to join Tarni and Phorcys.

"Murdoch, let her go," I warn him as he tries to take her away. My skin stings again as I move in the water.

"Tarni needs her," he replies.

"Murdoch," I growl.

"No, Celena. You don't get a say in this."

I glower as he takes my sister to the entrance of the cave. He pauses while the others hold their tridents on me to keep me in place.

If the fishbone in my hair were stronger, I'd slice their throats open with it and start the battle early—Merrick and Caspian could catch up.

Perhaps it was my decorations that made me brave—my shells and knives, and things I wound into my *iluses* to protect myself. Suddenly a single hidden accessory is making me ready to destroy my enemies again instead of just survive them.

Tarni and Phorcys swim back into the cave. Roni follows behind them, forcing Coralie and Murdoch back into the shelter.

"They'll be here tomorrow," Roni sings enthusiastically. All of the sirens smile.

She clings to a siren merman who looks like he's been racing here for days. Their collection must have sent him ahead to scout for them.

"They're in Rochay now, but they'll be here before the tide tomorrow."

"Which means we have work to do," Tarni announces. "You all have your assignments—go."

Several of them swim away quickly.

"Behave, Celena," the siren calls to me as her counterpart takes a place by my side, "Or Nir will do a lot worse to you tomorrow than I will."

"Where are they going?" I demand once she's gone with my sister and Murdoch.

"Celena," Phorcys says with a sigh. He shakes his head. "I have a mission. That means you have to stay here so that you don't interfere."

He rushes toward me, strong arms grabbing my shoulders as he propels me back into the wall of the cave. I can't breathe for a moment after slamming into the rock, the pain worse because of the jellyfish stings.

He pins me, dropping down to the floor to pick up a shackle. He attaches it to my tail while I'm crumpled over on myself, unable to deflect his hands from chaining me inside the cave.

"You won't be alone," he informs me.

I consider taking the fishbone to his eye just to make a point.

"You're leaving?" I ask in a sad voice.

The merman immediately perks up, straightening to face me for a moment with a blank stare.

"Behave," he instructs, repeating Tarni's words.

The moment he leaves the cave, another siren swims in front of it. He looks in, only to turn and hover outside, leaving me somewhat alone inside the cave. After a moment, he moves over so I can only occasionally see his tail as he floats to the side of the entrance.

I turn, trying to examine the shackle. The fishbone is too thick to do any good picking the lock, but a piece of driftwood nearby might be up to the job.

Unfortunately, it's out of reach. I tug relentlessly at the shackle, trying to claw my way to the driftwood.

If I can escape, I can knock the guard out and find Merrick or my brother to help me locate Coralie—I'm terrified Tarni might take her back to the humans.

The sand collects under my nails as I attempt to scrape my way to the driftwood. No matter how far I stretch, I can't get close enough. Nothing in the sand is close enough for me to reach to extend how far I can stretch.

A gasp sounds outside. I reel back, shooting straight up in the water, worried the siren might see what I'm attempting to do to free myself.

The siren guard struggles with something, clearly panicking.

"What's happening?" I call.

More strangled sounds filter into the cave.

"Hey!" I shout. "What's happening?"

The siren grunts and I press myself against the back wall, unable to escape whatever is lurking outside. My eyes dart around, begging for something to float close enough for me to escape the shackles with to escape..

All goes quiet.

A minute goes by...

Then another.

Finally, the siren turns, hovering in the entrance of the cave, backlit so that I can't see any of his features, just his outline against the strong light of the open waters.

"It was a shark—a small one—but I had to get rid of it."

"You killed it?" I ask in horror. I didn't want any more baby shark deaths in my presence.

"No, you stupid mermaid, I scared it away. We always carry the scent with us. Now clam up! I don't want to hear you until Phorcys gets back."

He turns, floating out of the entrance, back to his post.

As he does, someone else slips in.

The siren hurries toward me, taking up the light again. I press myself against the wall once more as he rushes foward.

"Quiet," he hisses.

No, *not* a siren—*Merrick*.

CHAPTER 8

"How did you—?"

"Shh," he hisses. Merrick leans in, pressing his lips against my ear. "He didn't see me swim up beside him. I gambled that he would turn back to his post without looking and I slipped in. He's still out there listening."

His lips are warm against my skin. Merrick quickly risks kissing me behind my ear, nearly sending me into the sporadic twists the brine pools cause. I clench my body in place, hoping he doesn't notice, but my insides twist and writhe under his gaze as he pulls back.

Without thinking, I reach up and tangle my hands in the very ends of his hair, scooping up his jaw in the process. Smiling, he quickly grabs my waist, pulling me toward him as he kisses me properly on the lips.

Merrick reaches around, running his hands from my hips up my back. I yelp in pain, mumbling into his lips, as he comes into contact with the welts striped across my back.

He pulls back, shocked.

"Celena?" he gasps, hoping he didn't go too far by kissing me—he should have known he *wasn't* by the way I was kissing him back.

I gape, not wanting to explain.

He looks at me cautiously before moving closer to me and running his hands over my sides again, fingers brushing the edges of my back. I wince, and he immediately swims behind me, moving my hair out of the way.

"*Len!*"

When he swims in front of me, his narrowed eyes demand an answer. My jaw opens and closes, trying to figure out how to explain.

"Celena," he says harshly, "what is this? What did they do to you?"

"They needed something from an old siren dwelling," I whisper, hoping the siren outside can't hear me. "It's been overtaken by hundreds of jellyfish—the biggest ones I've ever seen. Tarni wanted me to collect something from Nir's mother—"

"The siren queen?" Merrick murmurs. "Anything that could help us?"

"A necklace," I inform him. "I don't think so."

I pause for a moment, suddenly remembering the revelation that Nir's still alive.

"Nir is on his way—he'll be here tomorrow."

"How did *this* happen?" Merrick punctuates his words, motioning to my injuries.

"I had to swim through the jellyfish to get the necklace for Tarni."

"When?"

"Yesterday," I admit.

"Len, how are you even functioning?"

"I'll be fine." I rest a hand on his chest just below his shoulder.

"We have to get you out of here." He looks like his wants to shatter every jellyfish and siren in the sea.

"Tarni has Coralie."

"I know, Caspian and Llyr are following them, but she took half the collection with her."

"So you came to rescue me?" I whisper against his cheek, making him shudder.

"You're shackled," he surmises, looking down.

"Driftwood." I nod. "Over there."

He darts back, scooping up the possible pick that is still just out of my reach. Expertly, Merrick works to free me, attempting to break the lock from around my fin.

If Caspian and Llyr can save Coralie, and Merrick and I can escape, we can bring the collection back to stop the sirens once and for all—and keep the royals far, far away from them.

I twitch as he works—both anxious to be free and nervous to be near him for the first time since we changed our relationship.

A small gasp escapes his lips as the driftwood breaks.

"I don't know where they got this, but I've never seen a lock so small," he mutters as he tries to find something else to break my bindings with before we're caught.

We both freeze when a second voice approaches the siren outside. They murmur together, only a few words drifting in.

"They're going to move you," Merrick looks up at me.

"You have to go," I tug at his hair—the only part of him I can reach as he fumbles with the lock around my fins. He hesitates, but I pull harder on his tresses and force him to swim up to me. Merrick buries his hands in my hair protectively.

"What is this?" he asks as his fingers find the fishbone in the back of my hair.

"A lesson from Phorcys."

"Who?" Merrick's brow furrows.

"One of the sirens," I say hurriedly. "Oh, I might try to siren him, just ignore anything you see."

"*Excuse me?*" Merrick's voice rises.

"You need to *go*," I push at him as the siren's squabble grows louder.

"I'm not leaving you," he hisses, shocked.

"Then we'll both be trapped inside this cave, Merrick," I respond, thinking practically. "Go help them save Coralie. Once she's safe, I can fight back and we'll get me away from the sirens."

He sighs, annoyed at my point.

The two sirens get into a heated debate outside, my guard not wanting to release me until Tarni or Phorcys return, the other wanting to take me…*somewhere.*

"Promise me, no matter what," I say in a rush of words, "Promise me that you'll get Cor out of here, no matter what happens to me. She is priority."

He grimaces, but I grab his neck, demanding his attention. Merrick will do as I ask though, if it comes to that. He will always protect my sister and let me take care of myself if the choice is between helping me or protecting someone that can't protect themselves—as it should be.

"Promise me she comes first."

"I promise," he whispers but looks like he wants to argue.

"I have my orders," one of the sirens shouts.

"Please, Merrick. We'll handle my escape later, just don't get caught or we'll be in an even bigger mess," I beg.

His hair looks especially blue in the light filtering into the cave, making his eyes pop fiercely. Merrick wraps his arms around me.

"Merrick, please, you have to go," I repeat, attempting to push his arms back even though that's the last thing I want to do.

The corners of his lips tug down as he studies me, taking the corners of his eyes down with them. I'm sure his face matches my own as I wrap myself around him quickly, clutching the muscles in his back under my hands.

"This isn't fair."

"You need to go, Merrick," I insist. "You'll get caught."

"I'll risk it," he replies, slowly leaning into me to catch my lips in his.

Merrick's kiss is slow and deep—nothing like the frenzied, passion-driven kisses we've shared before. Every movement is painfully slow and perfect.

He pulls me closer to his chest, running his hands through my hair while he avoids bumping my injuries. Somehow he works a hand between us, cradling my chin before tipping my face up to look at him.

"I will come back for you," he promises.

I pull on his seaweed *sarasa,* dragging him back to me for one more kiss a moment before the sirens turn to enter the cave, still arguing.

Horror washes over me—they're about to find Merrick.

I push him, forcing him away from me. His hand reaches out, clutching mine as long as he can as he flings himself toward the wall of the cave and slides along it quickly.

Without any other choice, I start screaming, hoping to distract the sirens. I wail as loudly as I can, bending down to claw at the shackle around my tail as if it's hurting me.

The two stare at me, unsure if they should rush to me or if I'm tricking them and will kill them the instant they get too close like the human books claim. I consider playing into that delusion for a moment, bending my fingers enough that I could use them like claws against my captors, but instead, I still.

"Please," I whine. "It hurts."

They approach me cautiously as Merrick slowly slips around the wall of the cavern, watching my performance. One of the sirens moves as if he might turn around or back away so I gasp, recovering his attention.

"I'm injured—this is too heavy," I whimper.

"Then sit down," the second siren sneers.

I pause for a moment as if the thought had just occurred to me. Sinking to the sand, I keep my focus on them.

"It's still too heavy," I complain. "You *do* realize I just swam through a jellyfish bloom for your princess, right?"

"The chain stays on," my guard snips.

Merrick pauses in the entryway—a final goodbye—then he's gone, lost to the open waters outside the cave.

"I thought I was supposed to leave," I comment flippantly.

"You are—"

"You aren't—"

They glare while they talk over each other.

"We're going to move her," the second objects.

"Tarni didn't say to move her."

"But Phorcys *did*."

If Phorcys sent for me, that can't be good. I consider my options— Merrick can't be too far away—if he hears them screaming when I attack them, he could easily come back to assist. I need to know what the siren's plan is though, and I can't do that while swimming for my life—I need to play along.

"I'll go."

They both turn to look at me.

"Well?" I look down at my tail, indicating that they should hurry up. "I've learned it's best not to keep you eels waiting, so let's hurry up, shall we?"

The second siren looks triumphant as the first unshackles me. I'm thrilled when none of Merrick's attempts at freeing me caught inside the lock. The siren merman pops it open, freeing me, while the other cuffs my wrists together.

I follow them out of the cave like a queen would—head in the air, shoulders back, unyielding even in capture.

Marilla and my mother would have been proud.

The swim is longer than I expect, but we eventually reach Phorcys.

"Our job is to move the humans toward one central area," he explains. "Once your friends arrive, we need to make the transition as easy as possible."

"And I am to *sing* them into submission?" I ask dubiously.

"You are to sing them to the west side of Hontan."

Near Antaire, where the remnants of Prince Jarek's former kingdom still sits on the cliff next to the sea.

"You can't do that on your own, *siren*?" I question, running my fingers through my hair.

"Why should I? We have *you*. Your voice holds more power than ours—it will be faster this way. We might even beat Tarni and your sister back if you hurry up."

I open my mouth to ask where they are but he silences me with a hand in the air.

"You belong up there." He points to surface. "There are a hundred men out on the docks. Get them to the west side or we'll kill them all. I know you don't like humans, but I also know you don't want their blood on your hands, so handle it or I will."

The way he looks at me with a sharp glint in his eye tells me he's more than willing to siren the sailors into the sea. He'll probably use their skulls to build his new dwelling when this is all over too.

Reluctantly, I swim up.

Perhaps I'll siren the men into the sea myself and allow them to kill Phorcys and the other two mermen with us. If my voice really is as powerful as the sirens believe, even if the three of them work against me, I still have a chance at winning.

Phorcys stays right by my side.

"See those sailors over there? Start with them." He puts a hand on my forearm as he points with his other hand.

His hair drips down his back, much as I assume mine is doing as well. I was conscientious about how I exited the water this time, brushing my long bangs back as I surfaced.

I look to the west where the sun sits low in the sky. It glares off the surface of the water with harsh orange tones.

"They need to go there?" I confirm, nodding to the distant shores.

"Beyond," he replies. "They need to bring their royals back."

I whip around to face him, regretting it the instant my muscles scream in pain as I move.

"What?"

"They need to go and bring their king back. He needs to be here when we siren them all."

"How do you expect me to get them there—follow them?"

"You're creative, Celena. Find a way. Suggest they do it and make it so compelling that even once you're gone, they'll follow through because they believe there is no other choice. Make them follow your commands."

"That won't work—"

Phorcys opens his mouth to sing. Though not as lovely as mer voices, Phorcys quickly produces a sound that makes the sailors near the shore turn to us.

I panic as they lay eyes on me, but Phorcys holds me in place at his side while the other sirens hover below us in the water. He tightens his grip on me and propels us closer to the shore. My instinct is to whimper in the presence of the humans, but I choke it down, summoning the strength my mother has trained into me.

Phorcys glances at me as if it's my cue to take over. I hesitate, and he turns cruelly away. As his voice rises, the sailors walk quickly toward the dock. After a moment, they start to run toward the end, keeping in step with the siren's voice.

"Stop."

I pry at his fingers around my arm.

"Stop, I'll do it. Stop."

"You had your chance," he pauses long enough to say. He doesn't bother to face me.

The men reach the end of the dock as more clamber over the terrain to rush onto the wood planks that rest quietly above the water.

My voice surprises me, though it shouldn't—I have to prevent the men from jumping to their deaths.

The siren doesn't stop, attempting to overpower my voice. My fists clench at my sides, but I won't give him the satisfaction of a reaction. I close my eyes for a moment, focusing on my song. When I open them, I raise myself out of the water to be higher than Phorcys and sing as loud as I can.

It takes a moment, but some of the men fall under my command. They reach forward, lashing their hands out to rescue their fellow sailors as they attempt to walk off the dock, plummeting perilously to the water below.

I pitch my voice higher, hoping to project my words louder than Phorcys, though if what he says is true really is, I should be able to siren them away from him without too much effort.

I will the humans away from him, instructing them to force back the men that they can on the dock until every last man standing above the water is under my control. Manipulating them back, they slowly start to turn as they listen to my guidance.

A few men splash in the water, unsure of whose command to follow. The rest turn on the dock, walking back toward the land.

Phorcys continues to sing, miraculously still controlling a few of the men left in the water. He instructs them to dive under the surface to meet their fate.

I work harder, changing the song so that my words have more of an impact on the humans. I command them away from the siren next to me, lowering myself to his tactics to gain control.

Still, a few remain under Phorcys' power. Willing to risk the lives of the men in the water under my control, I send them after their counterparts below the surface, instructing them to return them to the air above the water.

Several dive below, pulling the other sailors up with them. The men come up choking—coughing and spitting until their lungs are clear enough to breathe again—still under Phorcys' siren song.

Frustrated that the men in the water are so torn between us, I push down on Phorcys' shoulder, submerging him as far as my chains will allow me.

With the men's attention, I sing them back to shore and command them to rush toward the western shores to retrieve their royals.

The siren stays under the water, but his anger is unfurled in the form of nails piercing into my tail. I cry out, disrupting my song, but my own nails in his shoulder encourages him to release me.

Desperately, I issue my final orders and drop back under the water before my captor can do anything else to injure me.

"Happy?"

"I would have been if you'd done what I told you to immediately," he huffs.

"At least they're going," I snap. "I doubt *you* could have made them do that."

"And look at you, little mer princess, you saved the humans. I bet you'll regret that in a few days," he counters.

He swims back up to the surface. I join him to ensure he doesn't try to undo my work—I'd rather have the sailors walking to the western shore to eventually return with a king with the *hope* of surviving whatever will be coming along with the sirens' wrath rather than to have them drown today.

The thought makes another resound in my head—I sent the men to retrieve a royal.

Any *royal* must be a descendant of Jarek's, must they?

Soon, I may be face-to-face with a man tangled in this war because our great-great-grandparents broke an alliance together. The lines of Aila, Chantay, and Jarek will all be present for another battle, and I will be at the center of it, commanding fates and changing lines.

"What did you tell them to do?"

"I instructed them to go to the western shores and to return with their royals."

"That's it? You think *that* will work?" He blinks at me, hair flowing out behind him majestically. Phorcys would make an attractive mer if he hadn't made such bad life choices.

"I think if the royal mer have any chance of doing as you asked and controlling the humans even while not in their presence, that was your best shot. If it doesn't work, it never will."

What he doesn't know is that I added in a little instruction of my own to the song while he was underwater—the humans will do as the sirens want, but they'll also hopefully be activated to do my bidding as well when the time comes. Now I'm left to wish on all the starfish that my song really *does* work.

"It will work," I insist, taking the lead. The sirens quickly follow behind me as I swim away.

I instantly regret my burst of speed, slowing to prevent the welts on my skin from crinkling as I move.

I hadn't realized as I was singing that the sun had set and a dingy gray color filled the world around us while on the surface. Now, under the water, everything was growing dark.

A large fish swims by us, swaying its body back and forth until it veers off from us, abandoning our shared path. For a moment, I want to follow it as it swims into the darkening water.

"You're not so lucky," Phorcys mutters, seeing my gaze traveling away. "At least you've got your sister to go back to."

I cast a look at him, asking without words. He sighs.

"Tarni is teaching her to siren." His words cut into me. "Don't object. If she doesn't learn now and we throw her into the fray with the rest of you to command the humans, she could die because she doesn't know how to manipulate her voice yet. Tarni knows what she's doing."

As much as I hate it, he has a valid point. Coralie needs to learn how to protect herself for the battle to come.

We dive deeper, following the ocean floor as we make our way back. I don't have long until Nir arrives with his sirens. I can't even begin to surmise what condition I'll find the monstrous merman in when he graces us with his dark presence.

Ahead, several squid—or possibly jellyfish—glow in the water in the distance. The sirens around me frown, squinting to see what creatures lay ahead of us.

The sea life twinkles in front of us in group formation long enough to distract us—the same trick most bioluminescent fish use to capture their prey—and we're drawn to the mysteries that they hold.

Our careless stares betray our safety and we find ourselves surrounded, an attack eminent as a vicious cry fills the water.

CHAPTER 9

I move quickly, thrusting my hands in front of me to protect myself. The chains dangle around my wrists, swooping in front of me as I launch myself toward the merman.

With the chain wrapped around Phorcys' neck, I pull back. Caspian and Llyr rush to assist me.

The siren struggles against me, but I'm at the advantage having caught him off guard. I pull back forcefully on my restraints, attempting to subdue him.

He pulls against the chain, trying to slip his fingers between it and his neck. He grimaces, twitching against me as he attempts to overtake me. A strangled laugh escapes his lips as if this amuses him.

"You can't—" he grunts out before Llyr slams his trident into the siren's skull. He falls limp in my arms.

"Coralie?" I demand, attempting to keep the siren from sinking to the ocean floor.

"Not now, Celena," Caspian yelps as he turns to collide with my guard.

The second siren rests on the ocean floor nearby—Merrick took him out. His face is hollow as he stares at me.

"Celena, are you okay?" Llyr asks. I turn to face him.

"What happened?" Caspian shrieks, noticing the injuries on my back. "*Merrick?*"

When I twist around, my twin is glaring at Merrick, demanding an answer as to whether he knew about my injuries or not.

"There wasn't time." Merrick holds up his hands.

"Where is Coralie?" I demand again, eyeing the sirens at the bottom of the moonlit sea.

"We have to get you unchained," Llyr interrupts, darting down to the sirens to look for a key to release me.

"*Caspian!*" I shout, ready to loop my chain around *his* neck until he answers me.

"We couldn't get her," Merrick answers quietly. My body stills, only my eyes turn to him.

"What?" My whisper comes out as a growl.

"Tarni and Murdoch were teaching her to siren. We couldn't reach them without risking Coralie's life, Celena," Caspian sounds heartbroken as he swims slowly toward me.

Merrick darts up in front of me, making the water rush up my tail uncomfortably. He reaches for my hands, trying to stay low enough in the water to not obstruct my view.

"Merrick?" I can feel a bubbly sensation crawl it's way up the inside of my tail, working its way through my stomach until it flushes in my cheeks, making me dizzy.

"I promise we'll get her back, Len."

"We'll rescue her, Celena," Caspian adds. "But we couldn't get to her, so we got to you instead."

"But I can protect myself," I argue. "She can't. You should have stayed with her."

"Well, we didn't," Caspian snaps, making me drag my accusatory gaze away from my partner. "Stop fighting against us and start fighting with us."

The moonlight flickers in the water as the surface grows stormy. I look up, noting the rough waters overhead.

"What do you think they'll do to her when they discover I'm gone?" I ask. "And what happens when the sirens wake up?"

"We could take them with us," Caspian suggests. "Make a trade, maybe?"

"They won't do it," I sigh. "They wouldn't trade Cor for their entire collection—it's our voices, Casp. Royals have stronger sirening abilities than other mer. They didn't just want Scylla—they wanted the royals. We aren't the reigning royals, but we still come from the same line. That's why I sang those sailors away from the blue-tailed siren outside of the reef barrier when they dragged Marilla out.

"Fine, then we take them so they can't cause any more trouble," Caspian declares.

Llyr breaks the lock and the shackles slide off my wrist. I grab my wrist, rubbing it with my thumb.

"Been a while, huh?" Llyr mumbles quietly enough that the others don't hear.

I let out a soft snort.

"Where are we taking them?" I ask, louder.

"We can probably get away with having you disappear for the night." Merrick brushes his hair back. "I'm sure Tarni will be worried, but a few hours will probably be tolerated before she does something irrational. The mermen will be with us, so for all she knows, you're still under their control."

"We'll incapacitate the sirens, and then we'll get in place to rescue Coralie at first light. Dylana and the others should be here tomorrow —they weren't far behind us," Caspian adds. "They won't see us coming."

"They already know you're coming, Casp—they've been waiting for us to arrive. They made sure you were never too far behind."

"And Nir is set to arrive tomorrow as well," Merrick reminds us.

We swim down to the sirens, using rope that Llyr was carrying on his belt to tie their hands to their fins. I glare at Phorcys as Caspian restrains him.

"Do we have any intelligence on what state Nir is in?"

"Nothing," Llyr replies, tightening the rope around my guard. "We came straight after you. Dylana only stayed long enough so she and her father could plan the rescue and get the collection together."

"Everyone else moved to Metten because they thought it would be safer for the time being."

"*Perfect*," I mumble. "Now they're closer to this war."

"We'll send someone to warn them when they arrive tomorrow," Llyr assures me.

The mermen lift the sirens off the sand, letting them dangle in the water as they guide me to wherever we're dropping them off. Silver light flashes off Phorcys' long hair as we swim through the sea.

The water grows darker as the storm intensifies overhead. I'm grateful we don't have to deal with the storm aside from our loss of moonlight below the waves.

"We're close," Merrick says, eying me as my body sags under the intensity of my jellyfish stings. All three of the mermen look like they want to scoop me up and carry me back to whatever cave we'll be residing in for the night, but none of them say anything, knowing I'm likely to have a biting remark.

"Up ahead," Caspian murmurs, floating closer to me as the cave's mouth comes into focus in the dull water.

"Keone and Natale came with us, but we separated yesterday, trying to find you faster. They'll join us soon, but don't be surprised if they show up tonight."

I nod, tired.

Llyr hands off the siren he's carrying to Merrick and swims inside to make sure we still have control of the location. After a moment, he exits, glowing squid in tow. He waves us in.

The floor of the cave looks so inviting that I nearly tumble onto it the moment I make it to the center of the small cave. The boys let me sprawl out, hair flipped over my head and arms as I stretch them above my head on the sand, my back facing up to protect my wounds.

"Len." Merrick breathes, seeing my injuries better in the blue glow of the cave.

"Celena," Caspian sounds like he might cry. He lowers himself to the ground next to me and brushes the underside of my hair with his hands. I arch into his touch, tears springing to my eyes.

"It hurts," I whisper.

"More or less than the pried-up scale?" he asks with a small, sad chuckle.

"She's endured a lot in the last two weeks."

Looking at how far I've come, I realize that less than a month ago, we weren't even sure sirens were in our midst, and now we are so far into siren territory that we were practically on land.

The water moves slightly along the sand as Merrick settles down on my other side. He hesitates before touching my skin, tracing the welts with his fingers. I suck a breath in, hissing at the pain.

Through strands of my hair, I see Llyr turn to look at the sound I made. He sits near the sirens, trident in hand as he wraps his arms around his tail, waiting for one of them to wake and challenge him. I have no doubt he will take an eye out and *then* ask questions.

My eyes are too heavy to keep open any longer. I let them flutter shut under the cover of my long locks while the mermen talk. I interject occasionally, telling them what I've learned over the last few days. I explain the cave made of skulls and how we were attacked by needlefish in the night. I can practically feel them cringe as I recount the jellyfish to them.

Caspian flips over next to me, staring up at the top of the cave.

"I'm sorry, Celena. I should have been here."

"Don't be silly, Casp," I say sleepily. "One of us needed to be here to free Cor. I clearly can't do it in this state.

Merrick's hand quietly finds its way to mine, surprising me. I nearly yelp as his skin touches mine, but I manage to hold it in. His thumb rubs circles around the fleshy part of my hand, soothing me as much as my brother combing my hair had.

"Rest now, Celena," Merrick encourages as I finish my harrowing tale of surviving the jellyfish bloom.

"What, you don't want to hear about how Phorcys had to carry me back, and Coralie tried to escape just as we arrived?"

"*What?*" all three mermen demand. One of the sirens stirs—Llyr takes care of it before I can even lift myself up to see which one.

"Coralie decided to try to break out. She used a shell I gave her." I smirk as I tell them the story, occasionally yawning. I want to curl into Merrick, even though I'm still furious with him for returning for me instead of staying with my baby sister.

"Sounds like something *you* would have done," Caspian says in a smug voice.

"Except *I* was trained. *I* would have incapacitated at least one of them and escaped."

"And likely would have found a dolphin somewhere," Casp adds. "You have an affinity for finding those right when you need them most."

"There's something else," I add reluctantly, telling them about how Tarni strung Coralie up and offered her to the humans, and what I had to do to save her.

"You're becoming a natural at this sirening thing," Llyr tries to joke. "Looks like we may have to change some rules in Scylla and Metten so you can come back to us."

"Who says I want to do that?" I try to tease back. "Maybe I'll move into the skull cave and spend my days there."

Merrick squeezes my hand, making me jump out of my scales.

"Somehow a dwelling built out of the skulls of your enemies makes you even more fearsome, Len," he laughs. "Now, rest. We have to go save Coralie soon, and you need sleep."

"Yes, partner," I sigh, nestling my head against my arm, trying to get comfortable.

Merrick releases my other hand so I can pull it under my head to rest on it. One finger runs over the curve of my side from my *iluse* down to my scales before he swims over to Llyr to help keep watch.

Caspian stays by my side as I fall asleep, allowing them to watch over us until morning.

"*There* she is," a merman's voice interrupts my thoughts as I wake.

I take in a deep breath as the world floods in around me, filling my senses once again. It's like everything inside of me wakes up at once, jolting me into consciousness.

"Stop speaking," Caspian growls at the siren.

I lift my head, still surrounded by blue light.

"It's time to go," Caspian says, swimming over to me and lowering his face to mine. "It's almost first light and we need to get in position before they can see us approaching."

"What are we doing with *them*?" I motion to the siren that just crooned at me. "I vote we stab their tails and take them out of the picture."

Momentary horror washes over Phorcys' face, but then he grins, knowing I wouldn't subject him to a fate like that. Pushing myself up, I swim over to him, getting dangerously close to his face. His eyes widen in surprise.

"Behave, Phorcys." I level a cold gaze at him before allowing the smallest smile to transform my face as I bat my eyelashes.

His breath comes in a short gasp, pulling back from me slightly. The other two sirens turn to him, evaluating his response. They snarl at me, looking every bit like the deadly sea creatures the human books describe our kind to be.

One of them hisses at me, jerking toward me in the water. Merrick and Caspian dart toward us, but Phorcys' glare stops the siren. Phorcys angles his shoulder to block him from me, but his stare is enough to end his short-lived tirade.

"Control them," I whisper. His pupils dilate—maybe this sirening thing really is working.

"He won't have to," Llyr announces. "The advanced team is here."

Several mermen—Marilla's personal guards—swim into the still-dim cave. They nod sharply to me, respecting my title, even though I'm not a reigning royal.

Three of the mermen float over to the sirens, taking a place where they can watch over them, while the remaining two prepare to join us in the rescue mission.

I turn to leave. Warm skin caresses mine, but the fingers are foreign.

Phorcys smirks as I whip back around to him. I dart toward the door, pulling away. My body says to destroy him, while my brain reminds me that I might need to keep him under my influence.

I swim past the mermen, refusing to make eye contact. Caspian leads the way to where the sirens have Coralie.

"Want to explain that?" Merrick attaches himself to my side.

My hand floats back to tap the knife on the makeshift belt we created out of seaweed—the boys didn't have time to bring me armor in their race to find us. The weapon brings me security as I touch the blade.

"You know as much as I know," I remind him. "Just trying to use every advantage we have."

"Look!" Llyr's voice interrupts. He points up and behind us where a pod of dolphins swims our way.

My breath exits my lips as a loud sigh that I instantly regret. I clamp my lips shut, cutting off Merrick's snide comment about my current condition. He closes his mouth, and suddenly I wish I could press my lips against it.

"Here we go," Caspian warns us as they approach.

I swim with them, refusing to show any weakness despite the pain in my back.

Like the ones from Scylla, the dolphins seem thrilled to see us, allowing us to latch on to their dorsal fins as they race through the water. I suck in the human air as we surface, releasing it when we dive back under the water.

It's still dark when we arrive at the cave where I had been held.

"You think she's still here, right?" I murmur.

"I'd say so," Merrick mutters as something catches the light by the cave entrance. "Is that Murdoch?"

"I think," I reply, squinting to see through the dark waters.

"That means they're here. Time to stage a rescue." Merrick grins at me as he releases the dolphin carrying him. Reluctantly, I do the same and drop down in the water next to him as the pod continues forward.

Quietly, we swim through the water, coming at the cave at an angle so the watch mer can't see our approach.

"Your job is to get Coralie," Merrick directs. "We'll take care of the others."

"Once you get her out, swim as far as you can—we'll catch up," Caspian promises.

"You sure that's a good idea? Nir is set to arrive today—what if we run into him?"

The group gets quiet for a moment.

"Don't go too far, then. Just hide nearby and we'll find you," Caspian corrects.

They quickly form a plan that involves me waiting at the mouth of the cave until they engage with the sirens. The plan is for me to slip in and free Coralie—assuming she is chained—and escape while they hold the enemies off. As we approach, I fall back, allowing the mermen to sneak up first.

Tarni has joined Murdoch outside the cave. I can't see her around the rock formation, but I assume she's clinging to his arm as she speaks to him.

"But where are they?" she pouts. "Even if they *had* trouble, they should be back by now."

"Do you want to send some of them out to look?" Murdoch counters with a sigh.

"No, they couldn't do anything in the dark anyway. Phorcys can take care of himself, even against that stupid *mer princess*."

"They probably met up with Nir and are on their way here."

"I suppose," Tarni replies. I can picture her pursing her lips in annoyance as she speaks.

Merrick darts forward around the rock while Llyr holds his trident. He drags Murdoch back so fast by his tail, I'm sure Tarni is left to believe he disappeared with only the water rushing by her as evidence. Caspian quickly holds a knife to our former collection member's throat, threatening him to stay quiet.

His terrified eyes meet mine, and I see a flash of concern for Tarni's wellbeing before hatred fills them. I hold a finger to my lips, reminding him we're in charge, and if he gives us away, he will pay, and so will his girlfriend.

"Murdoch?" she screeches.

Sirens stir inside the cave at the sound of her panic.

When she rounds the corner, she's clutching at her trident. In the dark, it's hard for Tarni to see, though the storm above seems to have cleared enough to allow the muted gray light of morning to start filtering through the water. She's greeted by the tridents of Llyr and Marilla's guards while Caspian and Merrick hold her lover in place.

Merrick expertly uses the shackles that were once on my wrists to bind one of Murdoch's wrists to his tail, preventing him from swimming. A piece of rope ties his hands together behind his back as he struggles.

"Tarni, go!" he shouts, earning a knick in his neck.

"Get the girl!" Tarni shouts into the cave. My head jerks up, knowing she means Coralie.

The others surge forward as Merrick and Caspian drop Murdoch. He sinks, still bound.

"Cooperate," I hiss at him. "Marilla might just let you spend your days in the cells instead of tied out for the sharks."

He struggles to free himself, but quickly realizes it's pointless, settling himself on the sand below the cavern.

I move around the rock, hovering in the entrance.

The siren with the injured arm from the needlefish attack holds Coralie by her throat, knife raised. Her eyes are locked on Caspian as he grapples with Tarni.

"Cor!" I call, trying to get her attention so she can assist me in freeing her.

The siren whips around to face the entrance.

"Don't even think about it," he cautions.

"Kill her!" Tarni instructs. "We don't have time for this. We need you to help us!"

"No!" Coralie screams.

"Don't!" I caution from the entrance.

Darting down in the water, I pull on Murdoch with everything I have. He grunts as I pull his arms backward, separating them from the sockets enough to cause discomfort.

"Tarni!" I challenge from the open waters.

Light spills down through the water—morning has arrived. Fish come alive, filling the ocean with dark flashes of color.

Llyr's arm pulls back viciously as one of the siren blooms pink. A vicious gash runs from one shoulder, across part of his neck, down to his armpit on the other side. His head lolls forward, lifeless.

"So, what—you want to trade? Is *that* it?" Tarni growls, slashing her weapon at my twin. Caspian twists, attempting to roll her wrist. She moves, avoiding his maneuver.

"That's exactly what I propose."

"Len!" Merrick warns as one of the sirens pulls away from him, darting toward me.

I push Murdoch down in the water. He grunts as his face scrapes along the side of the cave accidentally, but I don't have time to correct my course. I duck just before a trident is thrust at me. Dropping Murdoch, I fling my hands above my head to twist the trident away from the siren.

I cry in pain as I rip it away from him, pulling tightly on my injuries. He loses his grip and the trident slams into me, crashing into my side.

"*Celena?*" Llyr yells, terror in his voice as he realizes what happened.

I look down, checking to see if I had skewered myself. A little blood escapes a small scrape, but on the whole, I'm fine. The pointed weapon had missed me, much to the chagrin of the siren merman.

"I'm fine!" I shout, rushing to get Murdoch before I accidentally lose control of him to a siren—it's not like he doesn't have enough of them in power over him.

I drop him on the floor of the cave and pull his head up to expose his neck.

"Celena," Murdoch gasps as my knife pokes into the side of his throat.

It's adorable that he doesn't think I'll slit him open right now.

"You made your choice, Murdoch. I even gave you the opportunity to make a different choice, and you didn't," I murmur dangerously into his ear. I realize how much I'm looking forward to do the same thing to Phorcys at some point—threatening sirens might become a new hobby of mine.

I raise my voice, ready to take on Tarni.

"How much do you really care, siren?" I taunt, quickly realizing that that question might not work in my favor.

Tarni moves to Coralie, relieving her siren of his duty. He slinks back, still cradling his injured arm. Based on the injuries I'm pushing through, I come up with several names to throw at the *baby octopus* that looks like he's about to ink.

The siren's knife drags down over Coralie's shoulder and back, leaving a trail of blood bubbling up from the thin cut.

"Please, don't," Murdoch begs as Tarni squares off with me.

"She won't have to," Tarni calls, looking over my shoulder.

"No, she won't," a new voice booms behind me outside the cavern.

CHAPTER 10

Someone hovers in the water behind me so close that I can feel the water pulsing as he moves his tail to stay in place.

I throw my elbow back, colliding with the merman's chest, refusing to relinquish my hold on Murdoch.

"You better hope I save you and they don't get their hands on you," I hiss at him.

Turning, I discover a siren mermaid floats next to the merman behind me. She has long, elegant hair in a soft white color. It dips gracefully down to her waist, curling softly in the water. Her tail is a dazzling blue that matches her eyes. Gentle pink lips are the biggest feature on her face— they pick up some of the colors from the objects she wears in her hair.

Holding her face calm, she looks serene enough to be a royal portrait from Aila's journals. Her expression doesn't change when I lock eyes with her, recognizing her as the siren that killed all of those sailors outside of Scylla.

The merman wraps his hands around my waist harshly as Coralie screams for me. He pulls my hips back toward him, forcing a collision between us.

The blue siren silently lifts her hand toward Murdoch, curiously tipping her head at him. The knife lays silent in her fingers making him shudder when he realizes it.

"Nir!" Tarni calls, seeing the scene unfold.

"Fine," a voice responds from outside.

He's here.

The blue siren lowers her weapon, instead, raising her other hand to cup Murdoch's chin in her fingers. He looks at her uneasily as I drive my knife into my captor's tail.

He shrieks in pain, releasing me.

I push the blue siren out of the way, knocking her into the open waters as I drag Murdoch out with me. I hear Caspian grunting inside the cave as he fights to get to our sister.

The blue siren retreats to hover by her king.

Nir sits on the upper part of what was once a chair, lost from some ship into the ocean. Several sirens hold onto poles that have been placed under the seat to help move him across the open waters of the ocean. He looks like a king making his servants carry him around.

His tail is badly damaged, though its dark color hides many of the blemishes on his scales. When the light catches them at just the right angle, they glint off his twisted scales, showing the injuries he suffered at Merrick's hands.

The siren prince—now king—glares up at me from where his sirens hold him in position. His shoulder armor glares in the early morning light.

"I see you survived," I break the silence.

"No thanks to you," he yells back. "Why don't you come down here so we can even the score?"

He sits up on his makeshift throne, trident teetering to the side in his hand. He looks vicious enough to attack from where he sits.

"I don't think that's how this is going to work," Natale says from behind me.

Relief floods through me as she swims around in front of me, Keone right behind her.

"Bring me the princess," Nir commands.

Caspian bursts through the entrance behind me.

"Here," he gasps. Something collides with me, nearly making me release my hold on Murdoch. Arms wrap around me, dissolving into sobs.

"Celena," Coralie cries, burying her face into my hair and the welts underneath it.

Tarni rushes out of the cave past us so quickly that Keone can't catch her.

An invisible line is drawn between mer and siren, and neither side dares cross it yet. Only a few of Nir's sirens are with him—just enough to keep the king safe while coming to find his cousin. The rest must be nearby.

I stare down the siren king as he broods, watching us. Tarni reaches him and whips around to face us. Her pouch sits on her hip, and I imagine she's dying to give Nir his mother's necklace.

In my peripheral vision, something catches my eye below us. Nir sucks in a breath from his seat far enough away that I can't hear him unless he yells to us, but his chest swells with the movement.

Looking down, I discover several corpses floating to the ground, Murdoch's entire body shakes as he notices them.

"They didn't make it," Merrick says softly as he approaches.

Caspian throws himself at Coralie, prying her off of me as he wraps her protectively in his arms. He brushes our sister's hair back, murmuring to her to keep her calm.

Llyr forces two sirens out of the cave, handing one off to Merrick now that his arms are free of bodies.

"Perfect timing, looks like our rides are here," he murmurs as dolphins show up at the perfect time once again.

Natale and Keone growl viciously at the sirens, holding their tridents menacingly toward them, though none of the sirens move—most are busy holding Nir's throne. The two mermaids wait by his side, poised to follow his commands, though neither holds any power over other mer.

Nir watches us as we swim up to the pod of dolphins, captives in hand. Tarni looks ready to murder us, but there's something different in Nir's eyes—this wasn't his battle, and he knows it—his time will come.

His face morphs into a one-sided smile as he watches us dart across the ocean with our dolphin rescuers, chilling me to my fins.

"Let me take that, Celena," Keone says, leaning over from the dolphin he's swimming with to me.

I stretch my arm out, handing Murdoch off to our friend. With a flourish, he moves Murdoch away from me, looping his arm through the shackles between Murdoch's wrist and tail. He winks at me as he *accidentally* digs his nails into Murdoch's flesh.

"Oh, I'm sorry, buddy. Did I inconvenience you? I'm usually so good about protecting mer...oh, that's right. You're not mer—you're a traitor. I forgot." He smirks. "We don't take kindly to those, you know."

Natale takes the opportunity to poke at the siren Merrick is holding.

"That goes for you too." Her voice is terrifying. She recoils her hand, pulling it to her chest.

I'm going to have to take some serious time to find out just how much my cousin knows about interrogations and terror tactics—she might be able to teach me something my mother and the queen haven't already taught me.

Once we're far enough away from the sirens that they can't reach us, we release the dolphins, swimming the rest of the way to the cave. We pause far enough away for Llyr and Keone to check to ensure Nir's other sirens haven't found the rest of our collection.

They return after a few minutes, waving us in.

"Miss me?" I swim up to Phorcys. I can feel the entire room stop to stare.

He grins wickedly, enjoying the game.

"You can't stay away too long, can you?"

"I brought you a little present," I bat my eyelashes. Turning, I glance to the boys. They take that as their signal to drop the captured sirens on the cave floor.

Phorcys' face falters just enough for me to notice as I turn back.

"I saw your king," I address him as if I cared about Nir's title. "He didn't look so good—they're carrying him around on a makeshift throne. He'll probably be thrilled to get you back so you can carry him around—well, he will be *if* he doesn't find out how helpful you've been to us."

"I'm sure he'll love hearing how you betrayed him," Merrick adds, flicking one of the sirens with his tail to make sure he's listening.

They all snap their heads up, stretching to see Phorcys.

"I did no such thing." His voice is gravelly.

"How else did we know where to find Tarni?" Caspian asks. "You clearly have a thing for my sister, it wouldn't be that difficult to get information from you."

Casp shrugs as he swims away from the sirens bound on the sandy cave floor. They swing their heads from Caspian back to Phorcys, considering our well-placed accusation.

Coralie swims behind Caspian, holding her head high. They sit in the corner as Caspian examines her injury. I want desperately to join them and take care of my sister, but I know my place is with the sirens, sewing the seeds of discourse among the mermen.

I sink down in the water to be on eye level with Phorcys, smiling sweetly, thinking of what Tarni would do. I reach out, brushing the tips of my finger under his chin, lifting his jaw just enough to be noticed before I pull away. Swimming away, I exit the cave followed by Merrick and Llyr.

Once we're around the side of the cave, I turn back to them. Llyr looks shocked.

"Perimeter," he commands Merrick. Llyr doesn't give him a chance to argue, pushing him away from us.

Merrick complies begrudgingly, swimming around the cave.

"What is going on?" Llyr demands. "I thought you were with Merrick?"

My heart crashes into my tail as I realize it's not a secret.

"Don't give me that look, Celena, of course, he told me. It's all he and Caspian talked about while we were chasing after you. I'm pretty sure the only reason Merrick is still alive is because Caspian knew we needed his muscle to get you back."

My brother and my boyfriend discussed my relationship. Lovely.

"I am," I frown, contemplating my relationship. "I think. We haven't really talked…"

"Yeah, too busy kissing," Llyr cuts me off. If my eyes weren't wide enough to freeze my entire face, I might have warned him before I slapped him. Fortunately, my hand missed the memo too and instead of hitting him like my head told me to do, I hover there, gaping at him.

"He didn't tell your brother, *but don't worry*, I heard you're a great kisser." He looks at me with a blank face, trying not to make his comment worse as he realizes he said too much. Llyr tips his head to the side, smiling slightly. "You're messing with his head now, Celena, and you need to stop."

"I—"

"*Yes*, you are. Stop messing with Phorcys, because it's also messing with your boyfriend."

"But it's working—"

"I'm aware of that, *princess*, but you need to have a conversation with him because from what I can tell, you haven't talked to him since all this happened."

"When exactly would I have had time for that, Llyr?" I roll my eyes at him as a school of fish catches my eye, nearly distracting me from my subtle insult.

Llyr wraps his hands around my elbows, willing me to listen to him.

"Celena, please. I'm looking out for both of you here. If I had to *lose you* to someone," he grins, joking, "I'm glad it was Merrick, but you two are my best friends, and if you hurt each other, I'll give you to the humans myself."

He releases me and swims away, leaving me floating outside the cave. After a moment, Merrick's arm settles across my back, just over my tail as he clutches my hip.

"You know I'm just trying to mess with the sirens," I say, turning into him.

He opens his arms, pulling me to him.

"I know." He nods, but his eyes are dark.

"Merrick," I sigh, reaching up to brush back his blue bangs.

Why does he have to be so darn cute?

I don't finish. Instead, I reach a hand around his neck, resting my forearm on his shoulder, my other hand on his collarbone. I pull his face toward me, kissing him.

It's slow and tender as he gently reassures me of his affection for me. I'm freer to use my hands than he is, not restrained by having to avoid any injuries like the ones covering my back—he has to be careful of where he touches me. He doesn't seem to mind as my hands roam from the base of his skull, down his shoulders and back, learning his curves and planes in a whole new way.

He tugs my hair back, tipping my head up to him as he stares at me, looking amused.

"Apparently, I'm jealous," he murmurs.

"I noticed." I smirk. "But I'm going to do what I need to in order to defeat the sirens, and if that means throwing Phorcys off his game—"

"I know." He sighs deeply, dropping his shoulder back.

"What is this?" a voice gasps.

As fast as the sharks running from the sirens when they pull out the scent of a dead shark to scare a live one off, Merrick takes off, whipping me around to face the threat as he propels us out of its path.

Dylana stares back, looking horrified.

"Merrick." I tap on his arm, trying to get him to slow. He whips around, releasing me to float on my own, holding his trident out to my cousin.

"Oh," he admits his mistake with the simple word. "Sorry."

I blink, trying not to laugh. Dylana is definitely *not* the enemy.

She swims over to us, raising her hand in front of herself, using her body to block her motion from the others. She points between us and smirks.

The others follow behind her, overtaking the cave when I point.

"So this is new." Dylana grins wildly.

Merrick wraps his arm around me in response as Dylana's eyebrows shoot up. She purses her lips, trying not to laugh.

"Admittedly, I didn't think you two would ever get around to this." She turns to me. "I was definitely going to force you to date—"

"Stop," I interrupt, cutting her off before she can mention the guard she wanted to set me up with before.

"Fine, but I was." She bobs her head victoriously. "I like this better though. Now, tell me what's going on."

"Nir's alive," I inform her, making her face fall.

"How?"

"I don't know, but he is. We just left him. His tail is damaged, so the sirens are carrying him around on some throne-type creation," I reply. "Tarni is with them, but we have Phorcys and a few of the others."

"Phorcys?" Her eyebrows are up again.

"Long hair," I say, motioning behind me as if I were brushing hair back off my shoulder. "Orange tail."

"Ah."

"There's something else you should know," Merrick adds, spinning me.

"Celena!" Dylana shrieks as she sees my injuries. The water shifts around me as she rushes up to examine me.

"I'm fine," I insist, trying to turn. She doesn't let me.

"*Hardly.*"

"How is Morgen?" I try to change the subject.

"Recovering," she rushes. "What is this?"

"They made her swim through a giant bloom of jellyfish to retrieve a necklace that belonged to Nir's mother," Merrick supplies.

"Celena," her voice comes out as a lecture.

"We have bigger problems, cousin." I stop her. "The sirens need us. Royal lines have stronger sirening voices. They want all of us so they can force us to control the humans and destroy them—they didn't just want the palace."

"Perfect," Dylana grumbles, finally letting me turn back around.

"It gets worse. They made me siren the humans already—not all of them, just some of the sailors. I had to send them to the western shores to get their royals and return here for the battle."

"Royals? As in…?"

"Jarek's line, I assume."

"Oh, beautiful. Not only do we have to take on Chantay's lines, but now we get Jarek's too. It's like we crossed the barrier and swam back in time to Kaliania and Aila's lives."

"Except Ebba's line got fierce." I laugh ruefully.

"Oh. One point for *us*." She rolls her eyes.

"When will the others be here?" Merrick interrupts our moment.

"We left an hour before them to scout and make sure it was safe," Dylana brushes her hair back as it floats in front of her. "They'll be here soon."

"Good, because we're going to need all the reinforcements we can get."

"Gaspar should have handled Chantay when he had the chance," Dylana growls, turning to face the cave. "I'm done with this nonsense."

"Dylana," I call her back. "How is Morgen?"

"He'll be fine." She gives into my persistence. "They're moving him to Metten, which I'm worried about, but he'll survive. They're just going slow and protecting him."

"Your mother?"

"She's okay, but she's on her way. I forced your mother to stay with her though—she wasn't happy about that."

"I imagine not," I reply.

"That would be like telling the two of *you* not to get involved in something," Merrick adds, pulling me closer to his side. I nestle under his arm, feeling every breath he takes.

"Are *you* okay, cousin?"

"Better than you from what I can see," Dylana remarks. "Merrick, go inside. I need a word with my cousin."

Merrick hesitates, looking to me for confirmation. I nod, and he flicks his navy tail to give us space.

"I figured you wouldn't say everything in front of him." The princess turns back to me, and I quickly explain everything that's happened.

"Caves made of skulls, lovely." She glares into the distance.

"It's a shame Morgen isn't here to see it—he'd appreciate the history in it," I offer her a sad smile. "Dylana, you know what we have to do, right?"

"Move the humans?" she surmises.

"They aren't a part of this war. This started under the water, and now we have to finish it. The sirens have been murdering humans for a century—it ends now."

"And is your plan to take everyone with us for this?"

"Do you think it should be?" I ask, unsure of how I would answer.

"I...I don't know," she admits. "If you and I can move them on our own, we can protect the collection. We still have to fight the sirens whether we move the humans or not and if the humans hurt our mer while we're trying to relocate them than the sirens will overpower us."

"So we do this alone?" I ask.

"I think so. Are you ready for that?" She bites the bottom of her lip as she waits for my answer. Unlike the princess, I've been sirening humans for the last week and a half—this will be her first experience, and she's unsure she can do it. It will be her first time face-to-face with humans too—a terrifying experience.

"I'm ready," I say confidently, trying to encourage her.

"And, if I die, there's always Morgen."She shrugs casually, as if it's unimportant. I shake my head at her. "Do you have a weapon?"

I glance down at the knife on my hip.

"If I go back in to get a trident, they'll know," I murmur. Dylana grimaces but nods.

"Let's go," she sets our plan in motion.

"Where are you two going?" Natale asks, swimming up behind us as we try to sneak away.

Dylana and I glance at each other.

"I'm coming too." Natale sighs. She swims quietly beside us, trident in hand. When we're far enough away, we inform her of our plan.

"You realize you had three other royal voices in that cave, don't you? You think the two of you—the most powerful and irreplaceable two—should be doing this alone?" she argues, clearly annoyed.

"You said *we're* the most powerful," I retort.

"You're also covered in injuries, cousin. Just how did you plan on protecting the princess?"

"*Still here,*" Dylana jumps in.

"That was a stupid plan, and you know it," Natale finishes. "Don't leave me out of things next time—I've already proven that I can help."

She spins in the water as she swims, her mossy green tail sparkling in the light. For as much as I overlooked my cousin, she was always one of the more stunning royal descendants with her neutral colored tail and brilliant brown locks.

"Isn't this something?" Dylana remarks. "Kaliania, Aila, and Ebba —off to war again."

"And *Chantay*—back as the sea monster she always was," I add.

"Time hasn't served her well—I hear she used to be quite the beauty," Dylana smirks.

"How are we playing this?" Natale asks, focused on the mission.

"We have to get the humans to move away from where we can reach them—they have to move inland. We don't know where the sirens are, so at least one of us needs to watch for them," I reply. "I did well sirening them yesterday—the sailors all left the docks and went to find their royals."

"So maybe you should do the sirening, and we'll protect you," Dylana replies, looking to both of us. "Then if you need help, one of us can assist you."

"You," Natale interjects. "I'll hold off the sirens, and you can help her."

Dylana nods, sending her dark pink hair waving behind her in the water as we swim around a sea turtle that decided to cross our path.

"How long do you think we have before the boys notice we're gone?" I wonder out loud.

"Based on the way Merrick was looking at you, I only give it a few minutes," Dylana says matter-of-factly.

"It isn't *that* bad."

"Yes, it is," both of my cousins reply.

"You've seen us together for all of two seconds—you know nothing," I pretend to snap.

"*Sure*," Dylana teases.

"Even *I* noticed, and I don't even spend time with you," Natale adds.

"Wonderful, so I'm the only dense one." My mind floats back to the brine pool and how the density of the saline held it down in the water—I'd need to warn them about that soon.

I point out everything possible as we swim, noting where different locations are for my cousins. They grimace when I describe the Ropes to them and point out the general direction for the cave of skulls, informing them of the weapons I left there.

"Guess we don't have time to go get those first, do we?" Natale grumbles.

"Not if we want to handle this without getting caught," Dylana answers.

"We'll be fine."

"We'd better be." Natale frowns, letting her hands sink behind her.

"We're about to find out," I reply. "We're here."

CHAPTER 11

The docks are just as I left them—tall and dangerous. Sailors walk out along the boards, preparing their ships, moving cargo, and fighting with each other.

"And we're sure we want to save them?" Natale asks as we watch a sailor slam his fist into another's face, nearly knocking him off the dock.

"I'm sure we want one less enemy to fight with," Dylana says, chin just above the water.

The sailors haven't noticed us yet, though I'm not sure how—Dylana and I both have pink hair— a stark contrast to the blue waves. The fight seems to be distracting them.

Natale pops back under the water, checking for any oncoming problems.

"Are you ready for this?" The princess sounds nervous.

"I'll be fine. If you have to help me, just sing your instructions—don't get fancy about it—I learned that the hard way. Tell them what to do and move on—or repeat yourself."

"And you really think they'll follow our commands after they're out of range?"

"They seem to." I shrug, bouncing the water around me.

"Did you both decide to siren, or…?" Natale pops out of the water.

"No," Dylana shakes her head. "I'm coming. Good luck, Celena. I'm right here if you need me."

My cousins dip below the surface, tridents in hand. I pull my knife out of my makeshift belt just to be safe.

Swimming forward, I approach the docks. A giant ship rests near one of them, and I take great care to avoid it. Ropes dangle down into the water. A net falls carelessly near the back of one of the small ships, partially in the water.

A cry rises up as a few of the sailors notice me—it's now or never.

I lift myself out of the water higher, allowing my shoulders and chest to be seen enough to confirm that I am indeed someone in the water. The sailors call to me, assuming that I'm no human in need of rescue.

"Here, dearie," an older man with a scruffy beard calls. "Come here and we'll help you."

He reaches a hand toward me far enough that if the breeze kicks up, it will likely knock him over into the water. From that height, I don't know what kind of damage the surface of the water will do to his face. If it's anything like what I experienced when I fell off that boat outside Scylla, it will be painful.

"Hello, little mermaid," another calls over the first. He's younger and stronger looking. Dirt covers his pants and shirt, and his greasy hair hangs down in his eyes as he crouches on the dock.

"Pretty mermaid," another says, trying to stroke my ego as if all mermaids cared about their looks and sit about preening all day. "Why are you so far from home?"

I silently continue toward them as they watch me, calling out to me. I can see how sirens use this to fascinate men—they track my every move.

One sailor runs onto a boat. His footsteps fall heavy as he darts across the ship to the side closest to me. He grabs a rope hanging from the boom and leans out off the ship, dangling over the water.

"Hello, beautiful," he calls down to me. I have to fight to avoid glaring at him. "Pretty pink girl, look up here."

"Oy, lads," one of the more sensible sailors cries out. "Get back! She be the reason all the other lads disappeared!"

He confirms that the sailors I sirened yesterday really had obeyed.

"You said they abandoned their posts, Cap!" another man challenges him.

"Aye, but I didn't know *she* was around. She'll kill you dead if you don't get back boys—*get back* I say!"

I raise a hand, catching all of their attention. They fall silent as I wave a hand in the air, bringing it back down to the water's surface gently as I move the ocean in front of me. They watch as if I'm mesmerizing them.

Once they're silent, I open my mouth to sing. They all rock back on their feet, waiting for something horrible to happen.

I spin a song about danger coming toward them and the need for them to find an escape. When I'm sure they're all listening, I test my power over them, having them all return to the sand to face the water.

Swimming closer feels like a mistake, but I have to ensure that they can hear me and will follow my requests. It's a scary thing to float forward, getting so near to the shallow depths that a human might be able to swim down to the bottom and linger there on a single breath before returning—I'm too close to them.

I send them through a few tests, making their collection look ridiculous as they squat down and stand back up—Merrick would appreciate my inventiveness.

The men obey when I instruct them to return to their families, get their wives and children, and the other people in all of the nearby towns, and flee the city, traveling inland for the next year. I hope I've given enough time to end the war—assuming it doesn't end later today—though I'm unsure my sireny will last more than a few hours.

"We have a problem," Dylana slices through the water, nearly overshooting me as she surfaces in her haste to reach me. I lurch forward in the water, frightened by her appearance, voice warbling. "They're here."

"Who?" I ask, already knowing the answer.

"The sirens."

I screech at the top of my lungs, enforcing my earlier commands. The humans turn, ready to walk away.

Dylana disappears under the water. I duck, looking to see where she and Natale are. I can't leave my post yet—I have to make sure the humans are gone—but I need to know where to go once I can return to the water.

Through the choppy waves, I can see a blur of color as Dylana swims toward a figure I assume is Natale. I risk a moment away from the humans, sticking my face under the water so I can get a clear view of my cousins and enemies.

Dylana and Natale prepare to engage with a small collection of angry-looking sirens. They need my help, but if I leave, I can't ensure the humans will escape the shores.

When I lift my head out of the water, my long bangs fall over my face, impeding my vision. I struggled to pull it away, silently lecturing myself for forgetting to control my hair when I ducked under the water.

I'm more startled than I should be when I hear another voice. Her icy blue song captivates the humans—*my* humans—and calls them back to the sea.

The sailors start walking into the water, drenching their boots. The ocean laps at their feet, splashing high each time they break the surface with their feet.

Her white hair nearly looks pearlescent in the sun with the waves writhing about her shoulders. The sailors are mystified by her beauty as she sings to them. She occasionally rises out of the water to hold her long, slender arms out to them, beckoning the men to her embrace.

Anger washes over me as she tries stealing the men I've already sirened. Once again, she and I plan on attempting to best the other.

She glances at me, serene face breaking into a coy smile. She dramatically turns back to the sailors walking toward her and dips into the water, hands out to them. The blue siren calls them to her side, promising them love and riches for all eternity.

I could use my knife and gut her now, slicing open the exposed part of her abdomen just over her tail. I could do it and rid the ocean of her forever.

But that would take time away from saving the humans and sending them as far from the bays of Hontan as possible.

Instead, I grip my knife at my side and turn back toward the shore. I consider swimming farther in again, but I won't risk getting beached. The blue siren doesn't seem to mind—she floats toward the sailors, welcoming them with open arms.

I sing, sirening them away. A few of the men start to twitch, turning their attention to me. The blue siren glances over, frustration overtaking her.

Her voice screeches as she commands a small group to drag me out of the water. I hold my place, refusing to put any more distance between us—her voice can't overpower mine.

"Celena!" Dylana screams to me, too far away for me to reach if I needed to. "We have to go!"

The blue siren's smile is eerily calm as she deftly moves just enough to see me out of the corner of her eye.

"Not yet," I call back.

Behind me, I can hear my cousins clashing outside of the water with the sirens. Their tridents slam into each other—metal against metal—as they fight to protect me while I struggle to win the humans back.

"Celena!" Natale calls.

My song spills out of me as I win more of the sailors back. They turn, rushing to the shore as I command them to take their families and leave, following my earlier instructions.

The siren's fists pound against the surface of the water as she loses control of more sailors to my song. She bares her teeth at me, turning.

The majority of the sailors are racing away, far out of reach of our voices, though a few still linger, hanging between our commands. The blue siren works tirelessly in her attempts to win them back. She demands they murder me—though she knows it won't come to that. *She* couldn't kill me even if she wanted to—Nir's orders say otherwise.

She splashes toward me until something under the water catches her attention.

I duck under the surface too, where I discover Marilla and my mother have arrived. They swim quickly toward Nir, his back toward them.

The siren screeches under the water, warning him. His small collection—the same ones I saw yesterday—turns, staring down a matching collection of mer lead by our mothers. The group must have been out scouting.

I don't have time to wonder where the rest of the mer and siren collections are—the blue siren lifts her head back out of the waves, hair arching strikingly in the air as bits of water fly off in all different directions.

My hair hangs down plastered against the sides of my face and shoulders again. The remnant of the two-siren lead war-on-land stares back at us. I direct the men further back, sending them to the left toward the docks.

The blue siren reaches me, pushing me under the water. I struggle against her as she tangles her hands in my hair, forcing me to stay down. The siren knocks the knife from my hand before I can plunge it into her scales to free myself.

Instead, I push at her with my hands, raking my nails down the side of her. She cringes away, accidentally giving me enough space to wriggle out of reach.

I whip my hair out of the way as I exit the water this time, keeping my face clear of my locks so that I can fight back with my song. A fish pops up out of the water at the same time as it attempts to eat something, making it look like we planned the exit.

The blue siren has coerced the remaining sailors onto a boat. They hang over the edge on ropes like the greasy one did earlier, reaching toward us.

The men lower a net into the water as the blue siren swims to them. I stare in horror for a moment, wondering why she would risk getting close to them. She aims herself directly toward the net.

She's a few lengths away when I figure out her plan—she's going to have them drag her up into the boat so she can direct them. I can't let that happen.

Diving under the water, I race toward her. Dylana and Natale follow a few lengths behind.

"What are you doing?" Natale shrieks, swimming wide as she tries to catch me.

"We can't let her on that boat!"

"What?" Dylana snaps, realizing what's happening.

I reach the siren first just as she grabs hold of the fishing net. The men lift her out of the water, droplets falling to the ocean surface in streams as she rises into the air.

With no other choice, I throw myself at her, catching her tail. The wind kicks up, whipping against my tail as it's exposed to the air. Dylana grabs on to my waist as Natale latches on to the net by the siren.

"Hold on," Dylana says through gritted teeth as she attempts to drag herself up my body to the net.

Once her hands are secure, I fight against the siren. She thrashes against me, angry that we've spoiled her plan. Slapping her with my tail throws her off balance, and I use the opportunity to pry her hands off the netting.

She slashes at my arm, missing. Her hand catches the net as I free the other one just in time to catch herself. Dylana delivers a powerful blow with her tail from the side, sending the blue siren careening down into the water.

"*Cassidia!*" a siren shouts from the water as she splashes below the surface—I hope it hurts as much as it hurt when I fell from the deck of a ship because of her.

The humans start to snap out of their trance, and I realize both siren songs have stopped. They drag the net up greedily.

"Don't let go," I command, knowing it won't do us any good to injure ourselves. "Sing with me."

The mermaids pause, listening to the first lines of my instructions to the humans. After a moment, they pick up the words with me, helping me to enchant the sailors into doing our bidding. They look like they're going through shock as the men swing us over the deck of the boat, gently setting us down on the wood in desperate need of a cleaning.

I look around as I continue to keep the men at bay, looking for anything that might help us in the fight below. A cannon sits on each side of the cargo ship to fend off unwanted company, but sending a cannonball into the bay could easily mean the death of a mer instead of a siren. I've held a cannonball before under the sea—I don't want to risk the kind of damage I know it can cause.

The blue siren screams in the water below us. There's no way she could keep her serene face calm and still sound like that, but I can't peek over the edge to see how her features have twisted.

"What do we do?" Dylana asks, pausing her melody for a moment.

She picks it back up so I can answer.

"We have to move the boat."

"Move it where?" Natale asks, the last part of the word morphing into the notes she sings.

"West. We have to stop the humans from coming back here with the prince. We need to block them from returning from the western shore."

"But our mothers—"

"Will lead everyone here," I cut Dylana off. "There's nothing we can do to help at this point."

"She's right," Natale stops singing again. "This is our best shot at stopping this and prevent more death."

Dylana nods, not bothering to pause her vocals.

I use my hands to turn myself on the dock of the ship. The net grinds under me uncomfortably. I locate the old man—the one they called Cap—and instruct him to set sail.

The boat lurches forward. We sail away from the dock. Dylana's eyes grow wide as she pulls herself to the side of the ship.

"She's mad," the princess reports back on the state of the blue siren. "We haven't seen the last of her—unless our mothers kill her. She'll be out for our blood when we return.

"We'll have a new plan by then," I remark, allowing Natale to continue singing while I rest my vocal chords for a moment. "And, apparently, a ship. Keep going, Natale—I'm going to see what else is here."

A man standing nearby eyes me curiously even in his trance. Lowering my voice, I call him over to me as I once did to a cabin boy on the last ship I visited. He stoops down and slides his dirt-covered hands under my tail, supporting my back painfully as he lifts me up.

I wrap an arm around his shoulders and neck for extra support should something happen. Quietly, like a whisper, I instruct him to carry me around the ship.

I glance at his face as we walk from one end of the boat to the other and I picture the skulls in the cave piled on top of each other. I could shudder as I picture it, but I hold myself together.

Trying to wipe the image from my memory, I focus on his skin. It's light, but dark at the same time. I've read in books about how sailors have different skin than most from working outside all day and night, but I hadn't thought it would be like this. His hands are rough, full of calluses.

The sailor's hair is longer, resting a bit above his shoulders. The collar of his shirt is off-center and smudged with dirt and blood. Hair pokes out on his chin and cheeks curiously, looking brittle.

Much like us, his chest rises and falls under the workload of carrying a mermaid across the length of the ship. A heart beats somewhere in his chest just enough for me to feel it.

The men are quiet, only producing noise when they move heavy objects as they handle the mechanics of directing the ship, giving the boat a sullen mood.

I direct the man to place me at the front of the ship on a raised area where I can see everything that is happening, then send him back for my cousins. They look as nervous as Coralie as he lifts them one at a time, but knowing it is per my instructions, they allow him to carry them across the deck.

I had searched the deck twice before choosing this location to stay in for the remainder of our trip, finding nothing helpful. Piles of rope and nets sit everywhere, cluttering the space, but unless we decide to tie the sailors up, I doubt that will be useful to us.

Dylana turns, facing the front of the ship while Natale and I stare at the sailors under our command. The princess looks for the men I sent away yesterday and oncoming threats, while Natale watches the waters behind us and to the sides. I watch over the sailors as we each take turns singing to protect our vocal chords.

When we feel dried out, I instruct several of the men to haul buckets of ocean water to pour over our tails, cooling us down as we sit in the sun that looks perfect, but scorches the deck of the fishing vessel.

We pass the area where the skull cave is located, and I point it out to my tiny collection of mermaids so they know where to find it should they need it. We sail beyond it as the sun rises higher in the sky.

I pick up singing as Natale taps my tail, passing off the responsibility of maintaining our captives for a while. I sing softly, testing to see if there's any change in the men. I consider pausing all together to see if they'll continue doing our bidding, but decide the middle of the ocean with no help in sight probably isn't the best time to test the waters.

"There," Dylana points. "There they are."

I turn without meaning to. Along the base of the cliff, a row of men march in a line toward the main docks in Hontan, a young prince and princess in their possession being held against their will.

CHAPTER 12

"I'd like to say I don't mind seeing humans in chains, but that's just depressing," Natale murmurs.

"I didn't tell them to do that." I stare blankly at the sailors dragging their royals along in chains.

The prince struggles against the chains, keeping a careful eye on the princess in her ornate dress. She looks nervous and too young to fight back. She reminds me of Coralie, but my sister is far more capable than the young girl on the cliff surrounded by brutish sailors.

"Turn the boat to the cliff," I sing, instructing the humans to change directions.

"It just seems wrong going to all this trouble for them after what they did to our ancestors," Dylana sighs. "I get it—we don't need to make the situation worse—but we're on a human boat, sailing toward the enemy to…turn them around? What is our plan here?"

A sailor with light brown hair carefully pours a bucket of water over our tails, dousing us in a tiny bit of the sea. I run my hand over my scales, moving the water around to cover the spots it missed.

"Yes, we'll turn them around. I'm sure they'll wake up and restore their *prince* to whatever throne they plucked him from."

My tail twitches as I speak.

"She doesn't look happy," Natale comments, mimicking my motions to spread the water around on her tail.

"Would you be if you were chained and being dragged along?" I reply thinking of the last few days.

"Sorry." She cringes, realizing.

"Let's have them unchain her," I look to Dylana. "It's the least we can do after forcing them to drag her out here. *He* can stay chained though."

I have no remorse for Jarek's great-great-grandson—I assume it's his descendant anyway. From here I can't see any similarities, but we're too far away to really see anything.

"He doesn't look like the picture in Aila's locket," Dylana frowns, reading my mind.

"We don't know that was Aila's," I protest, "and the only thing we can make out from here is that his hair color is different. You and *your* mother don't have the same hair, so they might not either."

"True," Dylana concedes. "Still, I'd like to know if that's what we're facing."

"We're not getting close enough to find out," Natale points out. "We're staying on this boat until we can't anymore."

"How long *are* we staying on this boat?" Dylana asks. "If we're sending these men away, are we planning on swimming back?"

"Oh, umm," I stumble over my words. "I'm not sure."

Suddenly, the boat shudders beneath us, pitching us forward. I topple into the deck, nearly slamming my jaw into it.

"Everyone okay?" Natale yelps.

"What was that?" Dyalan gasps, pushing the entirety of her hair back over her head.

"We hit something, I think."

I turn, singing a man to my side. I command him to explain. Just as I thought, we hit a sandbar, running the boat ashore.

"We sing from here, I guess," I shrug.

Opening my mouth, I call out to the men on the side of the cliff. They stop to listen to the haunting refrain. My cousins join me, instructing the men to free the princess and return the royals.

My heart stops when they misinterpret our song. They unwind the bindings from the princess' waist, leaving them on her wrists, and throw her into the sea while the prince screams on the cliff, miraculously immune to our song. The sailors hold him back and prepare to march away, back the way they came.

The girl crashes through the air, slamming into the water. We all crawl forward on the boat to see if she comes back up.

She doesn't.

The prince thrashes against the sailors as they restrain him. He elbows a man in his attempts to escape and save his sister, but they hold fast, refusing to relinquish their grip on him despite their bloodied faces.

"We can't let her drown." I scramble to the edge of the ship.

"You're not going over the side, are you?" Dylana shrieks.

"Yes, follow in the net. Natale, you come too, but keep singing."

I dive off the edge of the ship, feeling the pain course through my body before I even hit the water. The water surrounds me as I point my fingers up, changing my direction to propel me toward where the girl crashed into the water.

Looking around, I desperately search for her. When I find her, she's struggling to swim, not knowing which way is up.

I reach her before I hear Dylana yell that she's on her way. Dragging the girl up is difficult, as her dress blossoms in the water around her, tangling with my tail. We push through the surface, choking.

I attempt to throw my hair back before desperately wiping her long, dark locks away from her mouth and nose so she can breathe. The girl panics, flailing even though I'm holding her up.

"Are you okay?" Dylana asks. The human princess' eyes grow wide.

Up close, I can see that she has a tiny nose and high cheekbones. Her dark brown hair is matted against her face and shoulders. Her lip trembles, partly out of shock, partly out of fear.

"You're okay," I assure her. She doesn't look convinced.

Noise rings out low on the cliff as the prince escapes. A rowboat sits on the small shoreline and he throws himself in it, ripping something off that was wrapped around his head—maybe a blindfold or something to keep him from overhearing the sailors' plans. He paddles as hard as he can toward us. The prince keeps checking over his shoulder, threatening us as he steers the boat in our direction.

"You'll be fine," I tell the girl as her brother hurls vicious words at us. "Your brother will be here soon."

I nod to Dylana.

"Get back."

She shakes her head, worried over leaving me alone with the humans.

"I've got this, just get back."

Dylana hesitates again.

"You can come help if I need you, but for now, just get back, princess." I use her official title, hoping to get her to realize that she needs to protect herself for the sake of the kingdom.

The human girl's eyes dart toward Dylana as she shrinks back in the water, disappearing before the girl's brother arrives.

The prince glides up next to us quickly, his face twisted in anger.

"She's safe," I inform him. *"She's safe."*

He glares at me but slows the boat so he can retrieve his sister.

Reaching down, he grabs the chains between her wrists, tugging her away from me. The young royal drags her to the rowboat, his sandy brown hair flopping in his face with the motion.

I slowly approach, wanting to assist.

"Stay back," he yells, grabbing an oar to swing in my direction.

"Let me help you get her in the boat," I say, trying to calm him.

He locks eyes with his sister, and though they don't say a word, she convinces him to stand down.

"I'm just going to push her up while you pull and then I'll leave," I say, hoping to avoid trouble. Though, I think if he had a weapon, he would have already used it.

The prince moves slowly, watching me as I swim toward his sister. I don't make sudden movements so as not to upset him.

"Ready," I announce, giving him a moment to prepare himself to pull his sister up.

I attempt to lift her by the waist as he hauls her up. She topples into the boat as I flop backward in the water. The rowboat rocks viciously as the two fall inside it, nearly tipping over.

My hand darts out before I can stop it to steady the contraption—swimming is so much easier than flailing around in a boat—and I calm it in the waters. The prince's head pops up over the side, glaring down at me while my hand still rests gently on the side, fingers spread out as I stabilize their transportation.

I pull back quickly, recoiling as if he were about to cut my hand off while still attached to the boat. He looks as if he's about to lash out but takes a deep breath and quiets himself as he stares at me.

I move back in the water, lowering myself until only my face is above it. Just as I'm about to submerge myself, he speaks.

"Thank you."

His hair frames his face as he leans forward in the boat. His sister works to right herself beside him, but he doesn't notice her struggling. His fingers wrap over the edge of the boat.

Up close, he shares Jarek's eyes from the portrait, but his nose and chin are all his own.

"You're not safe here," I warn him in a small voice.

My words force him out of whatever strange state he's in, and he pulls back, jerking away like I bit him. He grabs the oars, commanding his sister to sit as he jerks the rowboat into motion.

I watch for a moment as he steers them away. When I duck below the water, I wonder if I've done the right thing.

He rows his sister away from the sailors, deciding to stay on the water rather than risk losing her to the sailors again—probably a dangerous choice if the sirens manage to find him this far away.

Natale continues singing to the crew of the ship beached on the sandbar in the water of the bay. Dylana joins me, and we swim to finish our mission with the sailors.

Together, we convinced them to return to the western shore. We stop singing for a moment to ensure they'll follow through even when we're gone. The men respect our wishes, and we feel free enough to escape under the water.

The swim back is short-lived. We barely make it to the cave full of skulls before we discover the war has come to us.

Both the sirens and mer have gathered reinforcements, clashing along the shallow waters of Hontan's coast. Several sirens appear to be hovering above the surface, calling to humans that aren't there.

Much like a pod of dolphins, the three of us jump out of the water, raising our heads above the waves just enough to spy on the sirens. They call to the land, but no one is close enough to hear their cries. Under the water, I check their tail colors only to discover that the blue siren—Cassidia—isn't among them.

Sirens attempt to wrap netting and ropes around mermaids and mermen, trying to drag them to the surface. A boat sits on top of the water, the humans under siren control as they help pull the mer from the waves. Our collection fights back, trying to drive the sirens away from the boat they are protecting so the humans will stop obeying them.

Nir directs the sirens nearby in a net at the surface. He holds on with one hand, wielding a trident in the other. A magnificent crown sits on his head—the detailing would make any royal jealous. He raises and lowers himself on the net, giving instructions in dual locations. Cassidia hovers near him, reinforcing his words while she sirens the humans for him.

"Looks like we're going siren hunting," I mutter.

A line of sirens blocks the fighting from extending to Nir, only allowing sirens with captive mer to pass by just long enough to drop their victims off to be taken onto the boat—they planned this well.

In the distance, Marillia is surrounded by her guards as they attempt to fend off a nasty-looking group of Nir's mermen. If their goal is to capture the royals, Marilla will likely be their most sought-after target. The king is by her side, taking on as many sirens as he can.

"Mother," Dylana whispers.

"We have other things to worry about, cousin," Natale says, grabbing the princess' arm.

"Who should we take out—Nir or the blue siren?"

"Cassidia," I reply, moving to dive around the ship. "She's controlling them all for Nir."

"But Nir is the royal—his voice is stronger." Dylana's eyes dart between us, looking for an answer.

"It's going to take all of us to hurt Nir." My fingers move with the current, nearly dipping me in the water. "The boys tried to take him on, and they had trouble. If we try to take him on, Cassidia could rally the humans. We need to get rid of her first."

"The princess!"

We turn, searching for the voice. A siren points up in the water as we try to quietly make our way around the boat where Nir and Cassidia can't see our approach. The sirens surrounding them swing around to face us as one tugs on Nir's tail.

He lowers his face below the waves, spotting us.

"Get them," he instructs, not even bothering to stay below the surface long enough to watch. We must not be that much of a concern to him.

Dylana and Natale block for me, swimming in front of me. They use their tridents to attempt to fend off the sirens while I use my knife to defend myself.

A merman tries to collide with me, working to knock me off course. My knife digs into his forearm, making him yell as blood blooms around him, dissipating into the water. He jerks forward, trying to hit my tail with his trident.

I feel a second siren approaching behind me, prohibiting me from escaping that way. Taking hold of the trident, I wrestle for it, clawing at his hands to force him to release his grasp.

He pokes the weapon at me again, but with my hands on the metal, he can't angle it enough to reach me. Twisting, I duck under it, changing the trajectory of his assault. The trident slams into the other siren, piercing him in the stomach.

Horror washes over the first siren just long enough that I succeed in taking his weapon. Having no other choice, I rip it out of his friend's abdomen, pull back, and lash out at him, striking his tail.

The merman flinches, roaring in pain after he realizes what happened. I pull it back, taking several of his scales along with it. When he sees me prepare to go after him again, he hurries back in the water using his arms to propel him since his tail is now damaged.

"Celena, behind you!" Dylana calls, tucked around where I can't see her.

Whipping around in the water, I discover Cassidia has taken notice of my arrival. She slowly wraps her hands around sirens' forearms as she glides through the water, allowing Nir to do her job while she does his.

"You didn't bring my ship back," she says quietly, for the first time speaking to me rather than singing or hissing.

"They had somewhere else to be," I reply.

"So do you—a grave."

Her hair floats around her ethereally. White strands fill the ocean, surrounding her as she gently moves toward me. Her presence alone is so overwhelming that I see why Nir selected her as his lead siren.

She holds her weapon in her hands next to her chest, but she and I are too similar for me not to realize what she's doing—she's attempting to trick me into thinking she's not as much of a threat as she really is.

Beyond the siren, in the foreground, I see several figures swimming toward us.

Caspian and Llyr angrily handle the line of sirens blocking us from the rest of our collection while Merrick rushes toward us. I try to conceal his approach by making grand motions to keep Cassidia's attention. Her eyes are fixed on me as I move forward to strike.

Before I can reach her, Merrick swims up behind her, slamming into the back of her skull with the flat end of his trident so hard that I'm positive everyone on the ship can hear it. Sensing trouble, Nir reappears in the ocean.

"I just can't kill you, can I?" Nir bellows.

The mermen must have been looking for us after we disappeared because they aren't coming from the main part of the fighting.

"Do you *really* think the sirens want a king who can't kill their enemies *and* can no longer swim?" Merrick taunts. He grins at me, throwing an overly-dramatic wink and kiss.

I have every intention of slapping him later for the theatrics—the last thing I want right now is for him to make himself a target. Isn't it enough that Dylana and I are where the sirens are focusing?

Behind his taunting, I can see the frustration in his eyes before he tears his gaze away. I'm sure he's upset that we swam off without any warning.

"You're very confident that you're going to live through this, *mer*," Nir sneers at him.

"I have a feeling only *one* of us will," Merrick retorts. He shrugs casually.

Llyr suddenly darts away from the siren he's fighting, racing past us in the water. His tail moves as quickly as a kelp forest during a storm as he rushes by us. Beyond me, I hear Dylana and assume he's on his way to help her and Natale.

"I actually need your princess, *mer*, but I can hurt her in other ways—like you, for example. If you die in front of her, she still lives long enough to do what I need her to do, but..."

He leers at us in a failed attempt to scare us.

"I'm pretty sure even if you let go of that net *right now*, Nir, you still wouldn't be able to reach him. Why is that?" I taunt him, attempting to torment him in any way I can. "Oh, yes, because he speared your tail. How is that going, by the way?"

Tipping my head casually to the side, I smile sweetly, waiting for an answer.

Nir smiles back, pausing just long enough to make my blood go icy to the point that I wonder if I was magically transported to the kingdom of Keldori in the north. He leans forward, still holding the netting.

"About as good as this." He shrugs quickly before launching himself away from the net and swimming as quickly as he can toward me, suddenly able to use his tail.

I scream.

Nir had fooled us. While still injured, the giant merman is still able to swim, having recovered remarkably fast for his injuries in the week since it happened.

He slices through the water so fast that I barely have time to react before he's within an arm's length of my body. I flick my tail, trying to move before he can reach me.

Nir grabs hold of me, clutching me to his chest as he twists in the water. We spin as if he's attempting to drown me by forcing me deep under the waves. Each time I move, he moves with me, propelling us forward.

I cling to my trident—though it's useless to me with my arms pinned against my sides. His trident rests in his hand, running parallel to my tail.

The welts against my back collide with the muscles in his abdomen and chest, but flinching isn't an option. Using my tail, I intentionally try to get in his way, slowing him down as he spins us away from the other sirens.

He grunts as he moves, but doesn't have the ability to speak easily while he's busy trying to kill us both.

Llyr flashes by me again as I move. I barely see him start to come after us when we spin by him and Dylana.

When Nir finally stops twisting around, he pushes his tail as hard as he can to move me away from the boat. As easily as if he were holding my tail, he forces me through the open water without much resistance.

He's prepared for me to bite him this time, jerking his hand out of the way only to move it back, grabbing my chin. He pinches my jaw bone, forcing his fingers to poke my cheek between both rows of my teeth painfully. My mouth is forced open so I'm unable to close it. His fingers are gripping me so tightly that I wonder if he will break through the skin and touch my teeth.

"Don't," he commands.

After a painful moment, I nod, hoping it will alleviate the pressure. He pushes hard on my jaw before releasing me.

Merrick and Llyr call out after me, and I realize just how fast Nir was actually swimming. It will take a moment for the mermen to reach me.

I consider flipping my trident around but worry I might hit my own tail by mistake. The only thing I can do is wait for help.

Nir slows, starting to tire. He pants as he swims, but refuses to loosen his grasp on me.

"Nir, let her go!" Merrick calls, catching up to us.

"I'd rather have my cousin by my side for this," Nir calls over his shoulder. The muscles in his torso shift dramatically as he turns to call over his shoulder.

We continue slowing down—Nir is unable to keep up the breakneck pace with his injuries, even if he has healed a bit. I shift, trying to work my hair out from between us in hopes that it will block his vision and slow us even more.

"Len, careful!" Merrick yells just a breath before Nir and I go careening toward the ocean floor.

Nir relinquishes control, needing his arms to guide where he swims. I twist, looking up to see Merrick turning over his trident—he had struck Nir's tail with the end of it to knock us off course.

Realizing my mistake in pausing, I quickly use my arms to course correct and attempt to swim away. Nir is fast, grabbing on to the end of my tail. Before his fingers can close around it all the way, I flip it powerfully, slamming through his fingers into his face. He reels back as I dart away.

Merrick catches me as I throw myself into his arms, attempting to grab his waist to spin myself behind him until I can get my bearings. Instead of letting me slip past him, he wraps an arm around me, and I bury myself in his chest for a moment.

When he doesn't scoop me behind him, I turn to see what we're facing. Nir swims away from us, joined by two of the other sirens.

They slip under his arms and help him swim through the water, as he finally starts to suffer for swimming before he should be.

His tail slips up high, revealing the front of his scales as he moves. His injury looks like it may have ripped open, but it's hard to tell.

"We can't let him get away." Keone swims up behind us, not stopping to wait. Llyr takes after him, Dylana close behind.

Natale puts her hand on my arm, questioning if I'm okay as she swims with Merrick and me through the open waters away from the boat and fighting.

Nir and his sirens swim toward the caves, darting into a small kelp forest to try to lose us. We stay to the edge, looking from the outside. When they exit, assuming we've haven't found them, we aren't far behind.

We lose sight of the battle, dropping behind a coral reef to track the sirens as they flee. The waters shift, and the colorful fish quickly disappear from sight as the light starts to retreat—a storm is taking over the early evening.

"He can't escape again." Llyr sounds frustrated as he rakes his hands through his seafoam green hair. "We can't keep this war up."

"We'll find him." Dylana's words are determined.

Tarni screeches at us not too far away, trying to get our attention in an effort to save her cousin—she found us. We have to choose which one to chase—the king or the princess who started this mess.

"It's going to take all of us to stop him," Merrick decides for us. "Someone else will take care of Tarni."

When we turn back from her outburst, Nir is gone, hidden somewhere in the caves. Tarni sees us leaving and takes off after our collection, a small group of sirens trailing behind her as she attempts to stop us.

"Let's move," Llyr says, speeding up. "If we're going to stop him, we need to reach him before Tarni catches up."

We dive low in the water, swimming along the ocean floor, avoiding the storm brewing above the surface. Rain pelts the ocean's waves, mixing with the movement of the turbulent water.

"Which one?" Keone asks, matching Natale's movements closely.

"We have to check them all," Merrick announces, looking at the different caves. "We can't risk it."

"Can we afford to stop that long?" Natale asks, picking up speed.

"I guess we'll find out," I comment, tipping my fingers ahead of me so that my body swerves and cuts them off. "First stop."

I don't slow until I reach the side of the cave. Merrick, Llyr, and

Natale are right behind me while Dylana and Keone watch Tarni's approach, prepared to warn us if she advances too far.

I take the lead, prepared to strike if Nir is hiding around the corner. Leaning around the corner, I find the cave empty. Merrick and I sweep the cave quickly, confirming it's the wrong one.

The collection darts out, racing to the next cave several boat lengths away. We follow the same pattern, sweeping the cave. When we exit, Tarni is drawing near, but the light is so muted that we can barely see her racing toward us like an angry swordfish.

"She's too close," Natale proclaims. "We need to do something."

"Come on, I have a plan," I say, intentionally skipping the next cave.

"Celena, where are you going? We need to check that—" Merrick starts to argue as I set a course for the second cave ahead.

"That's the skull cave, it has weapons and shoulder armor," I reply. "And better than that, it has a secret."

The others look skeptical, but follow my lead, pulling around the next cave. The darkness envelops my friends and I, making it nearly impossible to see the sirens behind us—a perfect covering for our escape.

I dip low, as if we were going to rush into the cave we're really darting around just in case Tarni has better vision than I do. I careen around the edges of the cavern, hiding behind it so that it blocks us from view.

Quietly, I guide my collection into the skull-covered cave. When we surface, it still glows. The others look around, taking in the sight of the skulls ground into the walls and floors.

"I need you to trust me," I say, surfacing. "We have to go up there. That's where the secret tunnel is."

"*Excuse* me?" Natale asks.

"Come on." I fling myself as high as I can go, dragging my body up the rest of the way. "Watch your scales."

I pull myself along the ledge, making my way over to the secret compartment where I left the weapons. The others start to follow and I point to the tunnel to the right.

"Merrick, go first," I encourage him, knowing he'll protect us best if he takes the lead, leaving Llyr to protect the end of the collection while traveling through whatever we might find inside the tunnel.

When I turn to Llyr to tell him my plan, I notice lines of water running along the ledge from where we dragged ourselves.

"Llyr, splash water up here, we have to cover our tracks."

He looks at me quizzically for a moment before realizing what he needs to do. As he and Keone shower seawater over the entirety of the ledge, I tuck myself along the wall as Dylana and Natale slide past. Thrusting my hand inside the compartment, I pull out everything I had left behind the day before.

"Time to go, princess," Llyr addresses me as he and Keone arrive at my side.

"Got it." I hold up the armor, passing the knives off to Keone to help move.

We maneuver ourselves toward the exit, sliding as quickly as possible across the ledge's rocky surface. I will never get used to the feel of sand gritting between my scales and the rock beneath me.

The tunnel is dark and echoes strangely as we slip through it. I wish on all the starfish that this leads us somewhere safe where Tarni and her sirens won't find us.

The lapping water of the cave fades away as we continue to drag ourselves down the tunnel. I can only see flashes of Dylana as she rounds corners—Merrick and Natale are too far ahead to see.

Occasional streams of water grace the walls of the tunnels, tricking down in the darkness. My eyes begin to adjust to the difference in the light the deeper into the tunnel we crawl.

When we reach the second turn, I hear Tarni in the main part of the cave, yelling to the others, and I'm grateful we slipped into the tunnel when we did. Keone and Llyr speed up, remaining as silent as possible as I lead us to where I last saw Dylana ahead of me.

We follow every bend in the tunnel until it starts to get brighter. The dripping sound gives way to the lapping of water once again—I assume it's about to open up into the sea once again judging by the coloring of the light.

Instead, I take the last corner and promptly drop straight down.

I grit my teeth together as I fall, trying not to make any noise that the sirens might hear, though I doubt they can be heard clearly from this distance. I crash into the water, nearly losing my grip on my trident and the shoulder armor I'm carrying.

The second I go under, I propel myself back up, trying to warn Keone to be careful. He sits on the edge, staring at me.

"I'm aware," he smirks. I relax my lips, having twisted them up to inform him of the drop. Keone leans forward on his tail—knives in hand as he watches me.

"Len?" Merrick asks behind me.

I turn and see an incredible cavern dancing with cool colored lights reflecting off the water. Steam fills the room, and I'm suddenly aware that the water is warmer than what I left in the main part of the cave—I hadn't realized it since I was still catching my breath from the fall.

"A hand?" Keone draws my attention back.

I pass the shoulder armor and trident off to Merrick and back up enough that Keone can drop the knives into the water one at a time, blade up. Once it begins to sink, I catch it and balance it in the crook of my arm until I've collected them all. After I move away, Keone drops into the water.

Llyr follows, and we all press ourselves up against the wall under the drop in case we have any unexpected visitors. On the far side of the cave sits another ledge—this one without a tunnel.

When we finally feel comfortable enough that we believe Tarni has moved on, we spread out, dipping below the steam. We sink to the bottom, resting on the ground of the shallow pool.

"Now what?" Keone asks, setting his trident down.

Examining the shoulder armor, I pass it off to Dylana and Natale —its more important that they have it during battle than the rest of us since Dylana has to survive and Natale will be the one to ensure that she does.

Merrick tips his head back against the cave wall, his blue hair dipping down in front of his eye for a moment before swaying back up into place. I scoot over and curl against him, resting my head on his shoulder.

"Ow." Llyr rubs the back of his head, leaning forward. "What is this?"

He turns making us all perk up. His hands run over the wall, examining something.

"Well," he mumbles as if it's an answer.

I watch him curiously. He pulls back, revealing a hidden door.

"Is everything a secret around here?" I blurt out.

"Everything but your relationship," Llyr mutters making Keone snort.

"*Careful,*" I warn him—*I know things too.*

He quickly clams up, not wanting me to reveal his secrets.

"Looks like this will take us back into the sea," Llyr murmurs, examining the door.

"Tomorrow," Dylana says. "We need to rest first. We're safe here."

Llyr shuts the door, turning to rest against it once more. He offers Dylana a small smile as she nestles onto the floor beside him.

"We can take turns keeping watch," Merrick offers.

"You just want us all to sleep so you can kiss your girlfriend," Llyr teases. Once again, he stops talking when I eye him.

"Is that a problem?" Merrick asks, wrapping an arm around my shoulder.

"No, she and I already had a conversation about this," he teases.

"*Sleep*, Llyr," I command, rolling my eyes.

I can't help myself as my eyes drift shut and I fall asleep on Merrick's shoulder, his fingers brushing against the skin on my arm, lulling me into rest.

When I wake up, Merrick is resting his head against mine, sleeping quietly. My hand is wrapped around his arm uncomfortably, and it takes a moment for me to untangle our limbs.

My movements jostle his head, luring him out of sleeping.

"Go back to sleep," I whisper, hoping he can drift off again. He blinks twice before yawning.

"Never," he whispers, eyes still closed.

I bite back my smile and lean onto his chest. My head rises and falls as he breathes.

"How are you feeling?" he asks quietly, stroking my hair.

"I'm pretty sure I'll survive long enough to end this with Nir and Tarni, and that will be the end for me," I reply dramatically.

"You're just going to leave me after all this?" he jokes.

"Well, I mean, a couple of good kisses don't—"

"Excuse me, *good*?" His eyebrows shoot up in shock and offense. "Those were nothing short of incredible, *princess*."

"Fine, incredible kisses—"

"Which we need to repeat," Merrick smirks.

"Sure," I reply, deadpan. "But I—"

"Talk too much?" Merrick interrupts playfully again. He reaches up, brushing back my hair.

"You know the second we do this, one of them will wake up," I whisper, leaning in, tempting him.

Natale moves in her sleep and I jerk back, biting my lip in annoyance. I point to her as if to prove my point.

Merrick sighs, disappointed. He settles back against the wall, beckoning me to return my head to his shoulder.

I slowly move toward him, acting like I'm following his lead. My hand reaches up, grabbing his chin while he's busy watching me smile and I surprise him. I pull Merrick's face to mine and taste his lips, making him smile.

He shifts, making it easier to reach me. Merrick's hand settles on my hip, and I shift all of my weight onto my hands and locked elbows as I lean on the ocean floor between us.

Slow kissing Merrick is just as incredible as our original kiss. He holds still, letting me do most of the work—if he doesn't, his hands will be in my hair, and staying unnoticed by our friends won't be an option.

We keep our hands mostly to ourselves as I support my weight between us and he casually rests his hands on the top part of my scales. Merrick tips his head to avoid hitting my nose as I control the rest of our kiss.

"See?" he asks when we pull back. *"Incredible."*

Merrick licks his lips quickly before grinning, half of his face stretching toward his ear in a smoldering half-smile. He's always been good at getting attention by being flirty, but it's entirely different when it's focused on me and not meant as a joke.

"Putting that spy training to good use, I see," he murmurs in my ear. "I didn't see that one coming."

"Did you mind?" I slowly close my eyelashes once, opening them back up to a rather intense look.

"Not at all," he says softly.

"And if you two are done now…" Llyr snickers.

Merrick groans, rolling his head away as he puts some space between us.

"You clam up, Llyr, or I'll tell her—"

Just then, the rest of the group starts to stir, and *I* clam up, not wanting them to catch on to my threat.

"Llyr, check outside," Dylana instructs, sitting up to stretch. "We need to get moving."

"Looks like the storm died down," he answers, closing the door back over after checking. "It was a nightmare last night. I'm glad we weren't swimming in that."

"We need to get going," Dylana presses. "We don't know what the others have been through, but we need to get back."

"So, Celena… Where would Nir be?" Natale looks to me.

"I have no idea."

'You've been here longer than any of us. You've seen more of the area. Where would they be?"

"Well, he wasn't in the caves we checked." I try to think through where he might be. "He could be in the one we skipped. It's possible some of the caves have hidden places like this."

"So should we go back and check all the caves?" Keone questions.

"I'm going to check…" I point up, not bothering to finish as the group discusses our next move.

I quietly slip up through the water, leaving them to sit on the floor of the heat spring. The world above is suffocating as I emerge into the steam. I feel like I'm choking on the moisture that clings to my face.

Backing down a bit, I propel myself through the water, launching into the air as I grab for the entryway I fell out of last night. My ribs slam into it, and I cling on to the rock, trying to listen for voices.

Climbing through the tunnel won't do anything but give me scratches from the sand against my tail, so after a moment, I drop back down. A cloud of bubbles floats around me, trickling to the surface quickly.

"Nothing." I shake my head as I settle back on the ground.

"Don't get comfortable," Llyr informs me. "We're headed out."

I nod, floating up to follow.

Llyr leads the way, this time leaving Merrick to bring up the tail of the group. I follow out after Keone, my cousins in my wake.

The water is clear and blue as ever. There are no sirens or mer in sight. We loop around, deciding to check the cave that we skipped before moving on with our search. We cautiously enter and find nothing helpful.

We turn to leave, but Merrick darts back in the water, arm stretched out to prevent us from continuing. I reach behind me, stopping the rest of the collection as I bump into Merrick's arm.

I push my hair back, preventing it from floating out of the cave as I peek around him. Tarni and her collection swim through the water, just past the cave.

Nir is nowhere in sight.

"He had to have gone back, right?"

"I don't know where else he would be," Tarni replies. "We looked everywhere."

She sounds exhausted as they swim a little slower than they would typically swim. I glance at a starfish crawling along the ocean floor and silently wish on it that Tarni is too tired to fight well once she returns to the battle.

We hold still until they're far enough away that we're sure they can't hear us.

"Do we honestly think he went back?" Merrick asks the group.

"Here," Dylana grabs my hand, slapping something into it. I look down to find an oyster in my hand. "We're not prepared for today. If we keep going like this, we're going to look like Tarni, and then we'll be no help to anyone."

Her focus is always two steps ahead, but Dylana has always liked to take care of her collection. She motions to me, insisting I eat something.

"She's right, we need to eat," Llyr adds. He darts around the cave, picking up a few shells with breakfast inside.

We eat quickly. As soon as we're done, the mermen move behind us and wrangle our hair back into simple braids so that our hair isn't in the way as we enter the battle again.

Merrick tolerates me as I move around the cave while he's working, stretching to collect broken shell pieces to weave into our hair. He still manages to finish my braid before Llyr and Keone finish with my cousins. My hair is sharp to the touch—perfect for throwing my head into Nir's face the next time he tries to catch me.

I almost hope he tries, just so I can do a little damage.

Merrick's fingers drag along my neck before we separate, swimming to the entrance of the cave. I shudder, rolling my head back toward my shoulder to control it as my shoulder rises up to my ear.

"I feel more prepared now," Dylana announces, shaking her head from side to side to ensure her braid is sitting comfortably on her back.

"Good," Merrick says, glancing back in the cave over his shoulder. "Because it's time to face Nir."

The siren king has arrived.

I'm suddenly extra grateful for the broken shells wrapped in my hair. I raise my trident to my chest before glancing down to ensure my knife is still resting on my hip.

Merrick holds his hand up to signal us. We wait for Nir and the two mermen to swim by the cave. Once Merrick's hand drops, we silently dart out in the open water behind the sirens.

Nir's arms are looped over the mermen again, accepting help for the swim, probably trying to save his strength for when he returns to the fighting.

Llyr and Merrick dart forward, grabbing Nir's tail, and pull him back while we prepare to take on the other sirens.

Nir turns, roaring as he attacks our mermen.

CHAPTER 14

The sirens turn around to face us as their king is ripped away from them. Angry scowls quickly fill their features as they glare at us, flipping in the water to attack.

Phorcys dives at me—I hadn't realized he was one of the sirens that helped Nir escape last night in the darkened light of the sea. How did he escape? His hair waves around him brilliantly just before the merman lurches forward in the water, pinning it back as he moves.

He nearly crashes into me, but I use my trident to collide with his, setting him off balance.

"How did you get out?" I demand, preparing to crash into him again.

He whips around in the water, facing me once more.

"I have my ways, *mermaid,*" he glowers, curling his lip.

"You were under our watch, how did you escape?"

"I didn't." He grins. "It was a rescue. Your mermen are dead. Good thing for you, your little sister and your annoying brother got out right before it happened."

Marilla will be heartbroken when she hears of this. I'm sure Dylana is seething too, assuming she overheard.

"Great, we'll add you to the body count," Natale says, attempting to stab at Phorcys' tail.

Phorcys turns, catching Natale's arm with his trident. It rips her skin back as he pulls, making her cry out.

I return the favor, slamming my trident into him enough that it punctures his forearm, poking out the other side. I twist it before pulling it out, adding a little extra pain for what he did to the guards.

He turns on me, ready to fight. I don't have time to watch the other sirens or consider helping the rest of my collection—my job is to take Phorcys out of the game.

Something flashes across his face before he squints at me, but I can't quite read it. He grits his teeth, and I follow suit as we both flick our tails in the water, preparing to engage.

At the last second, he swerves away from me, dipping in the water until he slams into Merrick. Before I can say anything, Nir turns on me. Llyr attempts to stop him, but Nir rushes past him, slamming into his shoulder so that his flips around in the water.

Llyr turns back, rushing after the siren king as he attempts to slow him. I use the opportunity to swim, getting the siren king to chase me.

There's only one way I can win this, and I know exactly what I need to do.

Darting through the water, I guide us away from the collection while Merrick handles Phorcys, and my cousins deal with the other siren. Glancing back, I can see that Keone is chasing after Llyr as he follows us in our race to the skull cave.

I rush inside, Nir right behind me. Before I can enact my plan, Nir catches my tail, forcing me to a halt. He pulls cruelly on my tail, propelling me back into the wall.

A skull crumbles under the force of my head slamming into it. A chunk of the bone bounces down in the water, pinging off the side of the wall until tiny fragments of bone fall into my hair as part of the forehead drops into my lap. I pick it up, tossing it aside.

Nir grabs my shoulders, slamming me again into the wall. Llyr and Keone tug on him, attempting to remove him from pinning me against the cave. I shout for them to use their tridents, but once again, they don't want to risk hitting me. If they damage my tail, I'll be of no help to anyone.

As another skull crumbles above me, I use the rounded piece of shattered bone that falls between us to slash at Nir. I cut his cheek, leaving a nasty gash on his face. He reels back just enough for Llyr to latch onto his shoulder, pulling the siren king away from me.

I struggle out of his hold, nearly hurting myself as he lets go and turns on Keone and Llyr.

"Go!" Llyr instructs, trying to get me to leave the cave.

"No!" I shout back, unable to tell him about my plan without giving it away. "I won't leave you!"

"Celena, go!" Keone yells, fighting to hold back Nir's thick arm when the siren turns on me.

As they struggle, I notice the necklace around Nir's neck that I retrieved three days ago. He must have put it on as soon as Tarni gave it to him yesterday.

For my plan to work, I had to get the mermen to release Nir.

Llyr and Keone work together to slam Nir against the wall, making more of the skulls cave in on themselves, crumbling down the side of the rock. Nir shakes his head, trying to recover.

He slips his arm away from Keone just as yelling fills the water outside. I do a backflip, darting outside to make sure everyone is okay. The boys allow Nir to follow me, likely because it's wise not to be trapped in a tight space with a sea monster.

Phorcys and Merrick collide, their tridents slamming into each other as a school of fish angle themselves to swim around the mermen. Once I see that Merrick and my cousins are still alive, I do the stupidest thing I can think of to do—I swim over Nir's head and race back into the cave.

He tears himself away from Keone and Llyr, pushing past them roughly, and follows me back into the cave, threatening me.

"Len!" Merrick calls.

When I look back, Nir is gaining on me, but Merrick is nearly close enough to latch onto the siren's tail. I swim faster, pushing myself through the water—I only have one chance at this.

I lift my hands in front of me as I swim, slicing through the ocean as I prepare to lift myself out of the water. Like a dolphin, I arch myself out of the water. Slamming into the ledge knocks the breath out of me, but I don't stop.

I scramble across the ledge, dragging myself through the gritty dirt on top of the rock. Pebbles grind into my scales and poke into the flesh on my hands as I scurry away from Nir.

He follows me without hesitation, launching himself onto the ledge. Without being able to use his injured tail to propel himself out of the water like I had, he has to resort to using his arms to drag himself up, slowing him down just enough to give me a lead.

Merrick follows behind him, but Nir evades him by the width of a piece of kelp. I slip into the tunnel as Merrick calls a warning to me. I don't stop.

Turning around, I face Nir, moving myself backward through the cave. I use my tail to push me along, while my arms pull me. He struggles to keep up, not used to his weight above the water. Nir grunts, growling horrifying things as he chases me.

I look over my shoulder frequently to guide myself so that I make the corners and don't slam into the walls. Intentionally looking panicked, I let him believe he's cornered me.

"You will die here today," he warns. "You'll pay for what Aila did."

"You've really got to let that go," I throw my words back at him like a weapon. "They were our great-great-grandparents. They've been dead for years."

"You're right. We'll all move on from this after today…once you're dead."

I drop my trident, leaving it behind. Nir drags himself over it, unable to avoid it as we move quickly. He cringes as the barbs hit his scales, but he keeps coming toward me.

Merrick, following behind, slows enough to move around the trident. When he looks up, he catches my eyes and figures out my plan, realization creeping over his face. He nods, yelling at Nir to keep up the charade.

"I won't let you hurt her!"

"You can't stop me," Nir shouts, finding a new depth to his rage. He turns, trying to wrap his hands around Merrick's throat. "Especially since you'll be dead. You'll be a good lesson for anyone that tries to take me on in the future."

I scream a battle cry, launching myself at Nir. Wrapping my arm around his neck, I pull back in an attempt to stop him. Merrick manages to get his trident back far enough to slam it into Nir's shoulder—the tunnel only has so much room and clearly wasn't designed for fighting.

Nir roars in pain, reaching around to flip me over his head. My hair drags across his skull, the shells cutting into his face as he pulls me upside down into his lap—I barely avoid crashing my face into the floor as I slide.

Merrick grabs at me, trying to get me upright before Nir can react. I slap Nir with my tail and he bats at me, eyes closed. His face twitches as the sting from my slap starts to burn into his skin, taking him a moment to notice. He holds a hand to his face.

"Wrong move, cousin." He bares his teeth, trying to launch himself at me.

There's nowhere for him to go though—I'm too close for him to get any speed. His chest bumps into me as his arms reach around my waist. I duck my head, allowing the underside of his chin to crunch against my hair.

I snicker as the broken shell pieces in my hair cause more damage.

"Fine, you were right," Merrick sighs, pretending to have lost an argument we never actually had. "It was worth following you around this morning."

"I'm always right," I remind him as I toss my head back, colliding with Nir again.

My head throbs from the collision, but that doesn't stop me. I angle myself to do it again, but Nir pulls back, adding space between us.

I take Merrick's trident and jab it at Nir. He lurches back, trying to put more space between us as Merrick turns to retrieve the weapon I had discarded a few moments ago.

Able to move faster than the giant siren king, I crawl toward him menacingly. The edge of my trident strikes the ends of his fins, tearing little holes as he struggles to avoid me.

"Come back, Nir," I say in a gentle voice. "We're not done with our reunion yet."

"You're insane," Nir replies, still dragging himself back. He bumps into the wall, but I give him a moment to collect himself, turning to move down the hall.

Each time he reaches forward to try to spear me, I slam the barbs on my trident into his fins. He doesn't have much left of his tail to use, but shredding his fins really could be the end of him.

Realizing that he's allowing me to control the situation, he sits up, stopping his retreat. Using his trident, he throws it toward me, catching the end of it at the last second so he doesn't lose the only weapon he has. I slash at him with mine, barely managing to deflect the blow.

Merrick's trident flies over my head, sinking into nearly the same place he had already hit. Blood pours from Nir's shoulder. It cascades down his chest, over each of his muscles, forming a river much harsher than the ones trickling down the sides of the tunnel as it drips onto the floor.

All we need is one more turn and we'll be near the end of the tunnel. If we can get him back far enough, we can push him over into the hot spring, and if we don't give him enough time to look around, he won't find the hidden door to escape.

"Don't let him back there!" Llyr's voice fills the tunnel as he follows behind us. He must have caught on to the plan.

"Go get help," Merrick instructs, playing along to get Llyr out of the cave to block the hidden door while simultaneously getting Nir to go exactly where we want him.

"Clam up!" I shout, sounding even angrier than I meant to. "Don't move, Nir."

Nir takes another jab at me, but Merrick grabs the trident from my left hand, deflecting Nir's attack, while I reach out and rip the trident from Nir's shoulder.

The tridents collide next to me, and Nir whips his arm around, knocking Merrick's trident into the wall. He nearly loses his grip but hangs onto it enough that he can regain his hold.

Nir moves toward the last part of the tunnel, and I act flustered, which only encourages him. Merrick pushes me behind him, acting as if he's trying to protect me—I'm sure he actually is.

The siren king hovers near the edge of the tunnel, taking the last turn as he teeters on the edge. Instead of falling in, he reaches forward, grabbing Merrick. He lifts him into the air, throwing the merman over his head.

Merrick careens through the air, arms waving as he tries to catch himself even though nothing is there to save him.

"Merrick!" I screech. My hands fly to my mouth, knowing I shouldn't have called out, but I can't take my eyes away from him.

Nir had twisted around at some point to see Merrick's flight. His movement to turn back to me catches my attention, giving me just enough time to take advantage of the situation. Using my tail, I kick as powerfully as I can against his hip.

He falls over the edge, crashing into the hot spring below. The slapping sound he creates fills the space, echoing off the walls as the steam rises around him.

Beyond him, Merrick lays on the edge, having skidded across the rock. It looks painful to breathe, but I'm hoping that's because of the shock of the collision and not because it caused any real damage.

"Merrick?" I scream as Nir hovers under the water, not moving.

Merrick flinches, trying to prop himself up on his elbow. His back is to me and the muscles in his side ripple as he shifts his weight.

"I'm okay," he grunts, obviously in pain.

The sharkskin on Nir's shoulder armor rises out of the water before the rest of him does. The steam swirls around him as he lifts his body up on the ledge. The siren pushes up on his hands, rising out of the hot spring, moving toward Merrick.

"Behind you!" I shout.

Merrick turns just as Nir grabs his tail, pulling the merman toward him. Nir picks up the trident that Merrick dropped on the ledge as he fell and flings it into the water where Merrick can't get it. His own trident lays a few feet away.

The siren latches on to Merrick's wrist, dragging him close enough to dig his nails into Merrick's shoulder. The movement makes Nir's wound bleed profusely, dripping onto the ledge.

Merrick tries to fend him off, slamming his fist into the side of Nir's head. The siren reels but doesn't relent. He forces Merrick back, crashing him backward onto the ground.

I suck in a deep breath before I push off the ledge, dropping into the water with my trident in hand. Diving to the bottom, I pull Merrick's weapon off of the hot spring floor.

I'm louder than I think when I surface. Nir hears me, whipping around. He crawls toward me dangerously, eyes locked on mine.

"Celena!" Merrick shouts. "Get out!"

"Not a chance," I mutter quietly as the steam rises around me.

Nir crashes down on top of me, bent on destroying me however he can. He doesn't care that we're stuck in a small hot spring from which we seemingly can't escape. It doesn't matter that Merrick could come after us in an attempt to defend me—the only thing that matters is that he has me cornered.

"Sing, siren," he mocks me when the water clears. His hands are on my shoulders, forcing me down in the water.

"I have yet to sing for you, Nir," I reply, digging my nails into the back of his hands. "Aila wouldn't let Persephone get away with her treachery and I won't let you get away with yours."

"Too late, little mermaid. I've already won. My sirens have already taken your family hostage. They'll siren the humans whether I'm there or not—Cassidia will see to that. We will wipe them out and own the seas—they'll never work against us again. The ones we leave alive will live to serve us."

"You're really okay with dying for all this?" I snarl.

"To fulfill my family's wishes? Yes. Tarni will carry our legacy on once we've repaid Jarek and Aila for what they did."

"Well, good news. I think we can help you with the dying part."

I flip my tail, wriggling away from him as Merrick crashes into the water. He carries the trident I left for him on the ledge, driving it into Nir. The siren whips my weapon away, but I grab for my knife.

Nir's trident jerks through the water, knicking my side as it slams into the warm walls of the hot spring. I claw at him as I swim to the side, out of reach.

"Go!" Merrick instructs as the two grapple for control of the trident.

I race to the door, trying to open it—it's stuck.

"Llyr!" I scream, banging against it. After several attempts, the door loosens. I throw it open.

"Celena?" he gasps, looking through the unassuming exit.

Merrick yells for backup, and I flip in the water, swimming toward them. I crash against them, driving both mermen into the wall.

Nir makes a strangled noise, and I realize Merrick's trident is still protruding from his back—when I slammed into them, I wedged it between him and the wall.

He holds my gaze as he slips away, sinking in the water.

Merrick grabs my waist, moving me back until he's sure the siren is dead. His eyes flutter open and shut, hovering between life and death.

"Come on," Merrick whispers to me as he pulls Nir by the tail.

We exit, the bottom of the trident scraping along the ocean floor as we move the fallen siren king. Llyr's face is pulled taught, eyes wide with surprise as I pull the trident out of Nir's body.

"Nir?" Phorcys' voice rings out in the water. He has apparently followed Llyr around the cave, as have the others.

Nir bucks, blinking.

We all lurch back in the water—Nir isn't dead yet.

Phorcys and the other siren rush toward us as I skirt the half-dead siren to take them on.

CHAPTER 15

Overcome with rage, Phorcys attacks, trying to injure me. The mer collection spaces themselves out, each taking on different opponents as Nir lets out several strangled cries, trying desperately to cling to life—or take one of us into death with him.

Knowing their king is dying, the other siren attacks mercilessly in revenge.

Phorcys and I collide, tangling in a frantic battle. He uses his trident to sweep my tail out from under me, turning me upside down just long enough for me to do the same to him, pulling out his tail from under him.

I flip around crashing the broad end of my weapon against his arm, not nearly strong enough to force him to drop his trident. He reaches around, yanking my hair only to discover the shells. He pulls back, angry.

I can see Nir bucking out of the corner of my eye as Phorcys growls at me, clashing against my trident once more.

The waters grow still despite the fighting—Nir is dead.

Furious, Phorcys raises his trident in both hands, preparing to hit me with the long end in an attempt to force me to drop my weapon. At the last second, I release one of my hands, blocking his strike with my trident as I grab my knife with my dominant hand. Turning it quickly in my hand as I dart through the water, I plunge it into Phorcys' side.

His eyes grow wide as his head jerks forward. His jaw looks like it may fall, but shock quickly overtakes him. Still holding the trident in place, he glances down at his side as I pull my weapon from his flesh.

For a moment, I feel terrible when he looks at me—he looks so helpless. He breathes in a shuddering breath before he starts to sink.

With my hand still on my trident, I free three of my fingers and quickly snatch his weapon away, holding them both awkwardly in one hand. He doesn't fight me.

I pass the tridents off to Dylana. In the distance, the siren she was fighting swims off—the only one to escape.

I help Phorcys to the ground. Natale joins us while the mermen check Nir to make sure he really is gone. My cousins strategically block their view of me as I help Phorcys.

His long hair moves in the water gently as he holds a hand to his wound. His eyes hold accusation, but more than anything, he looks surprised.

"I told you not to fight me, Phorcys." I instantly regret saying it. "I didn't want to hurt you."

"Of course you did." His voice cracks as he grimaces. "You've wanted me dead since the brine pool."

"You shouldn't have hurt my sister."

"I didn't, if you'll remember. That was Roni," he points out.

"She'll pay for that, too," I assure him. "And I won't go easy on her like I did with you."

"I helped you."

"If you mean carrying me back from the jellyfish attack, you didn't have a choice." I cross my arms in front of my chest, covering my *iluse.*

"I could have let you swim." He blinks in pain.

"I wouldn't have made it. I was slowing you down, that's why you did it."

He looks like he wants to say more. When he doesn't, I continue.

"I can't tell how bad it is."

"Bad enough," he mumbles as I try to lean around him to see how badly he's bleeding.

He reaches up as I stretch over him, grabbing my waist. Phorcys pulls me to his chest, inches from his face. I push back, trying to hold myself away from him.

The merman stares at me without speaking.

"And now we leave him to die alone," Natale says loudly, burying the end of her trident forcefully in the sand.

The siren lets go of me, and I struggle to push away.

"I doubt he'll make it." Dylana motions to the injury she can see better from her side of the conversation. "And even if he did, we'd have to kill him for that little stunt."

"You couldn't have me if you tried, Princess," Phorcys addresses Dylana. "Don't be jealous."

Dylana makes a face, but I can tell it's forced. Under other circumstances, she might actually develop a crush on the merman—too bad he's slaughtered far too many people she cares about.

"I have a feeling I'm going to like you better dead anyway," Dylana snips. I'm overwhelmingly proud of her insult—she's usually so nice.

Phorcys cringes, folding in on himself as a wave of pain washes over him. I touch his arm, trying to get a better look at his injuries as he gasps.

"Just go," he begs. "Just let us die."

"He's already dead," Natale points out, motioning behind her to where Nir is stretched out on the ocean floor. "He's not coming back."

"Just let us be," Phorcys requests again, tail folding up toward his chest as he coughs. He latches on to one of his necklaces as he moves, running his finger over it. "I don't want you here for this."

He makes eye contact with me, pleading with me to remove my collection so he can die alone. I hate the idea of anyone dying alone, but I also understand not wanting to be surrounded by enemies when the time comes.

"We should go." I nod, looking up to my cousins. "We can give him this. He made sure I made it back in time to save Coralie from Roni, so I can offer him this much."

Natale and Dylana grumble as I start to float up, but they turn to tell the mermen it's time to go. Phorcys catches my wrist once they aren't looking.

"I really wasn't trying to hurt you," he murmurs.

"Could have fooled me, Phorcys."

"I'm sorry about your sister." He sighs.

"So am I."

I'm not going to give him the satisfaction of letting him know I care that he's in pain. Despite everything we've been through, he's right—he did help me a little, even when he didn't have to.

"I hope you don't suffer," I tell him, swimming over him. "Much."

He snorts, and I turn to find him stretching himself out on the sand, arm reaching toward his king. His eyes lock on the merman's body, and he mumbles an apology before closing his eyes.

His chest still rises and falls with shallow breaths, assuring me that while the end is near, it hasn't arrived yet.

Merrick holds his arm out to me.

"She would have been better with me," Phorcys calls, finding some semblance of strength to speak.

Merrick flinches, turning toward the dying merman, but doesn't say anything.

We swim away, leaving Phorcys to die by his king.

Nir's body looks just as imposing in death as he did in life. His dark hair and darker tail shimmer in the light streaming down through the water. The fish, already curious, hover near him.

I point to the merman, motioning that they should take the necklace from around his neck as proof of his death. They covertly follow my instructions.

If Nir's mother hadn't died, Nir would have made the perfect shadow spy—something I've said since the moment I met him—as he worked for the siren's cause. There are days I almost wish I could trade my pink hair and purple scales to be able to conceal myself better when working for the queen, but seeing him lie there on the ocean floor makes me grateful I have something a little more dazzling for when people look on me after I'm gone—I don't want to stay hidden in mystery forever.

"Are you okay?" I ask harshly as Merrick wraps his arm around me, leaning heavily on my shoulders.

"I'll be fine, Len." His voice is hushed. "He did a number on you too, are you all right?"

"I don't know at this point," I admit. "We need to get back though, it sounded like Nir has a plan in case anything happened to him, and Tarni and Cassidia are probably enacting it already."

"Cassidia?" His eyebrows dip down as he asks.

"The blue siren."

"Oh." Merrick's eyes widen, smoothing out the little lines between them from his frown. "Great, we got rid of Nir, but we still have to deal with Tarni and her friend."

"It could be worse," I remind him. "Tiko could be roaming free."

"Considering everyone else seems to have gotten themselves free," he grumbles.

We spend the swim back trying to come up with a plan.

We swim around the coral only to find the fighting has moved. A trail of bodies leads the way closer to Antaire—perhaps this really *will* end where it all began.

"If the fighting has moved toward Jarek's kingdom, that also means it's closer to Metten." Dylana's worry invades the waters, trailing out to each of us. "We sent everyone there to be safe—now the fighting is coming to them *again.*"

"This time, we might not be able to protect them," Merrick mutters.

"Oh!" I gasp as I see one of my neighbors lying on the ocean floor beneath us. His body is marred with gashes. He lays randomly on the ocean floor—proof of the vicious fight.

"Don't look." Merrick tries to stop me from seeing the carnage.

"If our families are down there, we have to know, Merrick," I whisper.

It isn't too much longer until we come across another body. It's getting difficult to tell mer apart from siren.

We pause, stopping to collect armor from the fallen sirens, covered in pieces of sharkskin for the boys to wear. It's strange to see them wearing siren attire, but as long as it keeps them safe, we don't invest much time worrying about it.

The closer we swim toward Antaire, the more the feeling in my stomach transforms into something hard, convincing me I'm part shellfish and producing a pearl inside of me. Merrick squeezes my hand, alleviating some of the dread.

"Metten is over there," Llyr points. "What should we do?"

We turn to Dylana—the highest-ranking royal we have.

"What would you do, cousin?" she addresses me.

I take a deep breath. My head swings back and forth between the human kingdom and the mer one.

"I would go to Antaire. Tarni's mission now is to end the humans —she already has all the royals she needs here in the battle, so unless our mothers somehow snuck to Metten, they're here somewhere. And if they *did* sneak off to Metten, then our collection there has already been warned and are making plans to survive any possible attack."

"I was thinking that too." Dylana nods.

"As was I. We need to stop this war now and we can't do that from Metten," Natale joins the conversation.

"Halt!"

We whip around to face a small collection of mermaids and mermen. They hold their weapons out to us, ready for a fight.

"Wait...Celena?" one of them questions. "You're Celena, right? And you're..."

The mermaid trails off, catching herself.

"What is your name?" She stiffens—trying not to give away too much information without getting some in return—and nod at Dylana.

"Dylana, princess of Scylla and Metten, daughter of Queen Marilla," Dylana answers, straightening her shoulders.

The mermaid breathes a sigh of relief.

"Good. I'm glad we found you."

"Who are you?" I demand.

"I'm Larina," she replies, resting her weapon at her side. "We're from Ambra. We came to help as soon as we got your mother's message."

Dylana raises her eyebrows.

"There's a whole collection of us here," one of the mermen says. "I'm Quilo, by the way. We were just with your families."

"Your sister told us about you, Celena," Larnia informs me. "I recognized you and the princess because of your hair. It's amazing you're still functioning after everything you've been through the last few days—I guess you really *are* as strong as she said you were."

"Where are they?" I snap, fingers flying to my grandmother's necklace. "Are they safe?"

Their faces grow dark, and my body goes cold. Merrick takes my hand, preparing for the worst.

"Coralie is fine, she's with your father," Larina informs me, her hair floating in front of her. "But the sirens have your brother and mother. We think they're going to try to use them against the humans."

"That's *exactly* what they're planning," I reply.

"What about *my* family?" Dylana interjects.

"The queen and king are safe—or at least they were when we left."

"The mer outnumber the sirens now that the collection from Ambra has arrived," Quilo says. "It's just a matter of time now, assuming they don't get to the humans first."

"The blue siren is leading them, isn't she?" Merrick looks for confirmation.

"Yes, and that other mermaid siren," one of the Ambra mermaids says from the back. Her hair and tail are striking.

"Where are *you* all going?" Llyr asks skeptically.

"The fight swam through this area pretty fast. The fighting has tapered off a bit now that the sirens control Almenna and Caspian, and everyone separated to regroup." I cringe as she says my mother's name wrong. I bite back the urge to correct her as she continues. "They sent us to come look for survivors, just in case the collection missed any during the battle."

It's logical that Marilla would send part of the collection from Ambra to look for surviors—she wanted to protect the mer that self-lessly came to assist us, even when they didn't have to.

"You should hurry," Quilo announces, looking at me. "They're planning what to do about your mother and brother—at this point, the only royal left that can help is the queen."

Dylana, Natale, and I are the only other royals that can handle taking on the sirens and humans with our voices—aside from Natale's mother. I hadn't considered it yet, but it would make sense for her to be as skilled as her daughter is. Perhaps she's secretly launching a counter attack as we speak—assuming she's still alive.

I wonder what's become of Merrick's parents and siblings, and Llyr's father. I realize I don't know that much about Keone's family, but I know he has one that I'm sure he's worried about too. We need to find everyone's family when we return.

"Will you be okay?" Llyr asks, making sure we remain friendly with the group.

"We'll be fine," Larina replies. "You should hurry though. Did you see anyone alive on your way through?"

"No, none that we saw," I reply, itching to go.

"Okay, you go ahead. We'll finish checking back to where we left off, and then we'll be back. Keep a careful eye out—we hear there are sirens hiding in caves."

"We haven't seen any yet, but just be aware as you travel," Larina adds.

We thank them, swimming away quickly.

"We'll get them back, Len," Merrick assures me, not bothering to mention his worries about his own family. A bruise is starting to form on his ribs where he slammed into the ledge—it looks painful.

A pod of dolphins swims overhead as if the world below isn't falling apart. A turtle glides through the water, swimming past a small fever of stingrays. The ocean faces death every day and holds no remorse for us as it continues on in the wake of our destruction.

The trip doesn't seem to take as long as I think it really does, but that's because I'm lost in my head, already formulating a plan to rescue Casp and my mother. I keep Merrick in my peripheral vision, letting him guide me as we swim. My eyes are focused somewhere ahead of me, but by the time we arrive, I have no idea what we passed or where we had been.

We hurry through the collection, looking for the queen. When we find her, Dylana rushes forward. She quickly pulls back after hugging her mother, requesting an update.

"Celena," my father's voice erupts behind me. "Where have you been?"

I spin in the water and rush to him.

"We were chasing the siren king. He's dead."

"Nir is dead?" Marilla's voice is high-pitched as she faces me.

"He's dead," Dylana confirms. "We left his body and came straight here."

"Which just means we have to deal with Tarni and Cassidia."

Marilla shakes her head, waiting for an explanation as I release my father.

"Nir's cousin—the weak one," I inform my father. "Cassidia is the blue siren Nir has been using to control the humans."

"How is that mermaid controlling the humans? She's not related to us, is she?" Marilla ponders out loud.

"Not that we can tell—Nir was his mothers only child and the last of Chantay's line. As far as we know, she's just a siren who practiced really, really hard over the years. We don't know more than that," I reply.

Coralie reaches around my father, grabbing my hand. She clamps down on me but knows it's not her place to interrupt while I'm speaking to Marilla.

"They have your mother," Marilla informs me quietly.

"They took Caspian while he was trying to stop them." Coralie sounds like she's going to cry.

"We'll get them back, Cor." I swim around my father to scoop her into my arms.

"Celena!" Marilla sounds horrified as she sees my back. My father's jaw tightens, but he doesn't say anything.

"Where did they take them?" I inquire, still holding on to my little sister. She rests her head on my shoulders.

"Toward Antaire." Marilla points toward the distance. "There's a line of sirens we'll have to get by first in order to reach them."

"There has to be a way around them." My eyes dart around,

looking for an answer so far over the horizon that I can't see it, even if it *does* exist. "The caves maybe. The one we were in had a secondary entrance. Maybe there's one hidden that we don't know about."

Between us and the horizon, mer swim back and forth, preparing for the next stage of the battle. They all look anxious as they speak, working out a plan.

A mermaid catches my eye, holding my gaze for a moment before flicking her mauve tail to propel herself back into action. Her light brown hair picks up hints of copper as the light catches it and for a moment, I'm jealous of her beautiful color combination. She glances back at me, reminding me of how worried I should be.

"You really think we wouldn't know about that if one existed?" Marilla reproaches me. "Lanika worked exquisitely hard to create all of our maps—"

"*After* King Gaspar moved everyone to Scylla. Her maps of Scylla are flawless, but she had to design the Metten maps from memory, and she wasn't one of the ones who would know the area so well. Aila or Kalania would have been better suited for that."

"What makes you think they didn't help?"

"Maybe they did," I relent. "But that still doesn't mean they might not have missed something. Right now, it's our best shot."

"She's right, Mother." Dylana comes to my defense. "We should go."

"Absolutely not." Marilla rises up in the water. "We'll send a collection out to search, but you two are staying here."

"There's no way I'm waiting here," I protest, horrified at the thought.

"If you go out there and get caught, they can use you against the humans. It's too risky. The others will get Almetta and your brother back."

"I'm not leaving my mother and brother out there in the hands of the sirens when I can do something about it. I'm the one who's had the most experience with the sirens—especially Tarni and Cassidia. I nearly got Murdoch on our side while we were with them—"

"And she basically sirened Phorcys like Tarni did to Murdoch," Dylana adds, cringing the moment she says it.

"*Excuse me?*" My father's voice is the last one I want to hear right now.

"Of everyone here, I'm the best one to take them on," I continue. "I've already proven that I can overpower Cassidia, and Tarni has yet to do me in."

"Celena, I forbid you." Marilla crosses her arms. Her crown sits at an angle as if it had been knocked off balance during the fight and she forgot to adjust it.

"You know she'll just sneak out while you're not looking," Natale pipes in. "You might as well send her with a team so at least she has a fighting chance."

Marilla looks conflicted, opening her mouth several times to speak before she actually does.

"Take Marrick and Llyr." She sighs angrily. "Do not get caught."

She motions for a decent-sized collection of mer to join us. They quickly prepare themselves to go.

"They'll be fine," I promise Coralie. "Just stay safe until we get back."

I hug her and my father goodbye.

"*No*," Marilla raises her voice to her daughter when Dylana tries to join me. "You and Natale are staying here. We can't risk it."

I swim up to Dylana and hug her quickly.

"Be careful," I warn her. "I'll be back soon."

"Take this," Marilla insists, pulling her armor off.

"I can't—" I start to protest, knowing the queen shouldn't be exposed to attack.

"I'll only be without for a few minutes—we have extra. Go before you lose any more time."

I quickly shrug into the armor, long pieces covering my arms as it trails off my shoulders. Coralie double-checks it for me, hugging me before I go.

Dylana and I share a look before I swim off with Merrick, Llyr and our back up in my wake.

CHAPTER 16

The caves are quiet—they almost feel forbidden to enter.

Skulls line some of them—many still intact in their original, unbroken state. The mer guards with us look horrified for the first few caves we check, but they quickly grow accustomed to the sight.

The first three caves we check are simple caves with no possible hidden exits, but the fourth holds the promise of more. We check several times before leaving, not locating any hidden panels to escape from the cave.

"Are we sure this is the right idea?" one of Marilla's mermen asks. "We're getting awfully close to the sirens, and if they catch us, our plan is over. Should we start searching for another way to get around them—a distraction maybe?"

I consider his words as a school of fish moves around our collection, darting by us in a flash of red before we angle off to check the next cavern.

"A few more," I instruct, taking the lead. He sighs, following behind me.

This cavern has a ledge much like the one in the skull cave. Merrick and Llyr perk up on either side of me.

"Promising," Llyr mutters.

"I'll go," I say, preparing to launch myself out of the water again. "I—"

"No, Merrick, you are not doing this one. Ledges didn't work so well for you last time," I try to joke.

"Nope," Llyr cuts in, grabbing my arm. "You're not throwing yourself out of the water this time, princess—I'll help you."

I let my hand sink back down to my side while I close my mouth —I had been prepared to argue, but he wasn't telling me I couldn't be the one to go—he was volunteering to help.

Llyr puts his hands around my waist, and we both swim up. With the combined force of our tails, I pop out of the water, and he boosts me up so that I'm sitting on the ledge.

Not slamming into a flat rock is the highlight of my day.

"You okay?" Merrick asks, floating above the water. The other mermen look nervous.

"We've been doing this for days, it's fine," I tell them. "I'm going to look around."

The mermen float in the water, watching over me. We leave one merman down below to monitor the entrance, so there are no surprises.

I crawl around on the rocks, searching along the walls. There are no tunnels in this cave, but that doesn't stop me from checking every inch.

"Merrick, check below."

He hesitates, but follows my orders, diving below to check along the wall.

"Is there a particular reason you sent him and not me?" Llyr asks.

"I just thought staying under the water might be good for him." I shrug. "He's already injured enough—I don't need the air drying him out or something."

"You think the air will dry him out in five minutes?" He speaks as if it's preposterous.

"I don't know, Llyr," I snipe back, running my hands down a crevice in the wall. "I'm just worried. I'd do the same to you if *you* had collided with a rock."

Something clicks under my fingers.

"What was that?" Llyr splashes up in the water to see. His hand taps on the surface, indicating that Merrick should come back up.

The water separates as Merrick breaks the surface. The waves lap along the edge of the rocks, slapping softly.

I work my fingers into the tiny line in the wall I have created, feeling gently for another lever to open it fully. After a moment, I find it.

"Well, well, boys, what do we have here?" I grin as I speak.

The door opens up, revealing a small tunnel—this one just big enough to swim through horizontally.

"What is it?" Merrick shouts.

"You're not going to like it," I call back. "It's a tunnel, but it's tiny. We should all be able to fit through it, but it's going to be slow going because we won't be able to move our tails very far."

The tunnel immediately dips down, leaving only a hand's width dry at the top. We'll have to slip down into it and then pull ourselves through the space.

"Can you see the end of it?" Llyr sounds skeptical.

"Barely, but yes. It looks like it goes right back out into the ocean—not a hot spring this time."

"All right, boys, you heard the lady. Time to move," Merrick directs.

Merrick turns around to help the others up on the ledge while Llyr comes to examine the tiny tunnel. I wish he wouldn't push himself like that—he's already injured enough.

"I'm going to check it out, block for me," I whisper.

"Celena," he tries to discourage me.

"One of us has to, Llyr. I'm the least likely to get stuck, and I'll have the easiest time coming back if I need to. Besides, do you really think you mermen can flip around in there? You're not nearly flexible enough. I'm the only one who has any hope of getting back up here, so let me do this."

Without waiting, I turn and dive into the tunnel.

The water splashes around me as I drag myself through the tunnel. I was right to think there wouldn't be much space for flipping my tail to move me forward—the mermen will have an even worse time.

It's uncomfortable crawling through the exit, but after a moment, I reach the end of it. I hover near the opening, pausing long enough to get my bearings.

"Len?" Merrick whispers loud enough for me to hear, obviously having discovered my plan. His tone tells me we'll be talking about this later.

I slide out into the ocean, finding it empty. Double-checking, I give it a moment before calling up to tell the boys to follow me.

I guard the exit as the mermen work their way down the tunnel. Llyr appears first, apparently having convinced Merrick that he was in a better condition to help me if I needed it.

"Good luck handling this one later," he mumbles, taking a place beside me.

Once everyone is free of the tunnel, we set out toward Antaire—the site of Marceline's original sireny that prompted the human-mer treaty, *and* the place where Persephone and her mother destroyed it. Nerves wash over me as I realize what's at stake.

We swim up to one of the caves, and a few of us peer around it. In the distance floats a line of sirens—we've passed them. Llyr nods to me, commending me for a job well done.

We stay shielded behind anything we can find—coral, kelp, caves. Occasionally we find small siren collections swimming our way, and we hide until they pass by us. Engaging them now will only lead to us being found out before we reach Tarni and the others.

I glance over at Merrick, noting he's no longer having trouble swimming. While most wouldn't notice it, I did—I would be a terrible partner if I didn't.

He catches me staring and offers a smile that makes me blush every shade of coral under the sea.

"So I assume this doesn't count as our first date?" His smirk makes me forget to breathe for a moment, and I have to turn away to conceal my next large breath, using my hair to block it from him so he doesn't tease me. It's remarkably hard to hide behind my hair while it's braided back so beautifully, but I manage.

When I turn back, he's still watching me. Llyr peers around him, grinning smugly at me.

"Your hair looks nice, Celena," he compliments, even though he's been with me since Merrick braided it back.

"It's sharp," I reply, tossing my braid playfully.

"Looks like you did a number on Nir's face with it…"

"I assume so." I forgot to look—I was so busy dealing with Phorcys.

"It looked like that other guy gave you some trouble," Llyr guides the conversation. "Want to talk about it?"

I realize that this is the first time any of us have stopped talking about defeating the sirens long enough to have a conversation about anything else that has happened.

"I don't." *What was I going to say?*

"He seemed pretty bent on harassing you until the death," Llyr surmises. "Merrick too."

"Seemed that way."

"He really is dead, right? It's not like he's going to come back to haunt us…" Merrick's voice trails off.

"I don't see how he could have survived, I stabbed him in the abdomen. I'm pretty sure he has to be gone by now. We should have ended him before we left though."

If by some miracle, he survived, it would be my fault. I instantly run through every scenario where Phorcys could have lived—if another siren found him, if a mer found him and took pity on him, if a jellyfish drifted over and zapped him back to life. This line of reasoning is ridiculous, but it lingers at the forefront of my mind as we travel.

"Come back to us, Len," Merrick murmurs after a while. "Everything will be okay. You need to focus on fighting Tarni and Cassidia now."

"Now that Nir is gone, does that make Tarni their queen?" I try to focus on other questions to get Phorcys' death out of my mind.

"I don't know, I suppose we don't know much about how the siren's hierarchy is structured. Chantay wanted to be in charge, so I'm sure they put measures in place to make sure her reign lasted." Merrick brushes his hair back as he speaks. "It would make sense that if something happened to her direct line, any other connected living sirens would be eligible to take over."

"Tarni *was* running the show with Nir, and Nir definitely protected his cousin—she was like a sister to him—so I would imagine Tarni is in charge unless someone else swam in and took power from her," Llyr adds.

"Do you think Cassidia would try to take power away from her?" I ask as we duck behind coral, peeking out as we check for sirens.

"Do we know anything about her?" Llyr questions quietly. "I haven't been close enough to get a read on her."

"She's incredibly calm—unless she's not," I answer. "When I slammed into her while they had Coralie and I, she barely flinched, but when I steal the humans away from her, she actually hisses at me like a sea monster."

"She *hisses*?" Merrick checks to see if he heard correctly.

The light bounces down through the waves, shifting in the water as the sun rests high overhead. It sparkles off the fish swimming by, and for a moment, I want to rise to the surface and bounce through the waves like a dolphin.

"Every single time she's angry, she bares her teeth at me, hisses, and comes after me," I confirm. "If it weren't so strange, it might actually be funny."

"Maybe we can get her to focus that rage on Tarni and let her take the siren out *for* us," Merrick jokes. He gives me a sympathetic look.

"Splitting them up doesn't sound like a bad idea," Llyr remarks, adjusting the shoulder armor that's slightly too big. He cringes when he accidentally touches the sharkskin.

"How would we turn them against each other though?"

"Tell her Nir told you the blue one would be in charge," one of the guards behind us interjects—I had forgotten we weren't alone. "If she thinks Tarni is taking a job away from her that Nir meant for her to have, I doubt she'll take kindly to that."

"That's brilliant." I sound more surprised than I meant to. I rush to speak, trying to cover it up. "If we make her think Nir meant for her to be his heir and she confronts Tarni about it, there's bound to be some kind of fight.

"And," I pause dramatically, "I know just how to make that happen.

I nod to Merrick's hip. He looks at me quizzically for a moment before his face brightens. Reaching around, he pulls the necklace out.

"We were the last ones to see Nir alive—what's to say he didn't tell us as he was dying that Cassidia would take over for him and destroy us in his name? She'll have no idea, and if we do it strategically, she won't even know we're planting a fight between them."

"How do you plan on doing that?" the same guard asks.

"By engaging in battle with her." I turn back to look at him while speaking. "I'll wear the necklace so she can *accidentally* see it and then while we're fighting, I'll make some flippant comment about how Nir was wrong and how she can't defeat us. She'll force me to explain myself and I'll let the whole story slip."

"If it's in front of Tarni, all the better," Merrick adds. "That makes it easier to ensure Cassidia will actually tell Tarni and not just murder her when she isn't looking."

"Do you honestly think Cassidia would do that?" I'm shocked at the idea, but it wouldn't actually surprise me, especially when I consider her past behavior—after all, she *did* murder all those humans. If Tarni is seen as a threat, she might be considered the enemy.

"I think she's one of the most capable sirens we've faced—yes, I think she would consider it."

"I do too at this point," Llyr adds his opinion to the conversation. "Whatever they do, we're just the catalyst for it—we didn't cause it.

They make their own decisions, just like we make our own decisions. Our goal is to divide them."

"We can't take it on ourselves if something else happens."

I'd still feel guilty, but that's not going to stop me from ending this war. I don't think Tarni is strong enough to hurt Cassidia in any way. I wouldn't put it past Cassidia to offer Tarni to the humans though. I'll just have to try to keep my eye on her when the time comes in case I can prevent it. I don't mind seeing her suffer, but I'd rather not have her filleted on the deck of a boat.

I reach out to take the necklace from Merrick. He drops it into my hand, carefully avoiding touching me. He raises an eyebrow, pulling his hand back.

Pretending not to notice his attempts at flirting, I turn back, reaching around to clasp the necklace behind my neck. A piece of my hair gets caught in the clasp, and I struggle to untangle it—usually, it would just slide right out, and I could try again, but with my hair in a braid, there's nowhere to slide it.

"Want some help there, princess?" Merrick smirks, delighted to have a reason to come to my rescue.

I struggle for another moment, unable to work it out of my hair.

I sigh, allowing him to swim over and lift my braid, reaching under to set me free from the clasp. He works it through my hair, flipping my braid over his arm so he can use both hands to disconnect it.

After a moment, the necklace comes loose, and Merrick dips it down in the water so he can get a better grasp on both ends. I reach up, holding the medallion in my hand so it doesn't fall while he fiddles with the clasp.

Quietly, he clips the necklace around my neck and lets the chain fall against my skin where it can be clearly seen round my other necklace. He lingers for a moment before taking my braid off of his arm and replaces it on my back as we continue to swim.

"Thanks," I mutter.

"You're welcome," he replies, swimming back to his position between Llyr and me.

"*Adorable,*" Llyr sings. "Now when we get there, are you two going to *cute* them to death, or...?"

"*Clam up,* Llyr," we both say at the same time, nearly identical in tone.

"We probably *all* should—it looks like we're here."

In the distance, we see the under side of the ship Llyr is pointing to. It sits in the water next to a wall of rocks that almost looks like the underside of an island formation, not too far away from the shore that somehow snuck up on us. Several other ships bob in the water too—mostly larger ships, but various rowboats litter the water as well.

"Wait, is that—?"

"It is," I breathe. "It's the steps. We've reached the castle."

CHAPTER 17

ntaire is an incredible sight from under the ocean. I imagine it's even more beautiful above the waves. Aila's stories always mentioned the opalescent castle she would sit under as she rested on the steps that cascaded down into the ocean when she spent time with Prince Jarek and her cousin, Persephone.

If I can get above the waves far enough away to have time to look, there is said to have been the most magnificent light in the highest window of the palace. I'd love to see it, especially if this is my only chance.

"Metten is a short swim from here," I remind everyone. "We have to be careful. If anything goes wrong, we need to warn them, but we also have to be sure the sirens don't follow us."

"Do we know anything useful about this place?" Merrick asks.

"Aila passed down stories about the human palace, but they were mostly about its grandeur. I know about the queen and the prince, and what the palace looked like from the steps, but nothing about the waters below, aside from the cave Persephone sirened Jarek in, and the fact that they were able to chain her to the shore until they arrived to rescue her."

"Any chance the cave could help us?" Llyr huddles with us, but we turn to make sure everyone is involved in the conversation.

"I don't think so. Jarek was able to run out on the ledge, so it sounds like the tunnels would only lead to land, which wouldn't help us in this case."

"So we're on our own…" Llyr trails off, looking over his shoulder at the boats.

"It looks that way," I agree.

"Okay, so what's our plan?" Merrick defers to me.

"Find Tarni and Cassidia. We need to get me in front of one—or both—of them so I can show them the necklace. That means one of *you* will have to be in charge of rescuing my family." I look directly at Merrick. He grits his teeth but nods at my instructions. "Llyr you will help him—he's in no condition to be doing this alone right now. The rest of you will split up between supporting us."

I motion with my hand, dividing the group in two. They separate slightly, indicating that they know whom they're going to be following into battle.

"I think it would be wise for the three of us to go in first—they already know we were traveling together, so they might not expect us to have found reinforcements on the way here."

Everyone nods, agreeing with my assessment. The mermen and mermaids keep a careful watch over my shoulder as I speak.

"Let us swim in first to see if we can learn anything quietly before revealing ourselves. Just stay close and pay attention to what we're doing. If it looks like we need help, give it another two minutes, and then join us if it still looks bad."

They grimace at my words, but I know they'll follow through. They hover behind us as we swim toward the boats in the water, pausing far enough away that they might not be noticed as they watch us.

"We stay together until we can't," Merrick commands.

"Agreed."

"No arguments here," Llyr responds, gripping his trident harder.

The face of the rocks holding up the palace drops straight down into the water. The staircase extends from the rocky land out into the water, making it easy for mermaids to crawl up them to socialize with the human royalty we had first befriended two centuries ago.

The boats grow in size as we approach, taking up more of the waters than I'd like. Unlike most of the boats I've seen, these do not have nets in the water. Suddenly, the boats start to move in the water as if they're about to go out to sea.

"What are they doing?" I whisper to myself.

"Are they sending the ships out?" Llyr voices my concern louder.

"I think so."

"That can't be good." Merrick glances at me, knowing we can't save everyone. If the ships are headed to their death, we don't have the ability to stop them right now, but we *can* help the human collection standing on the shores, surrounding the steps.

"Is that Caspian?" Llyr points in the water where a blue tail appears to be struggling.

"I can't tell from here," I say nervously. I don't want to expose our position too early and risk not finding Caspain and my mother.

"I think *that's* your mother." Merrick points in a different direction. "And that looks like Cassidia's tail next to her. If that's Almetta, than *that* has to be Casp over there."

"Which means they aren't together. That changes the plan."

"We'll get Casp, you get your mother." Merrick decides for me. "We'll go at the same time."

"How do we plan on getting past the guards up there?" I ask, nodding to the sirens doing a terrible job at keep watch for us.

"By causing a distraction." Llyr grins, pointing up as a pod of dolphins swims our way. "You good on your own, Merrick?"

"Go." Merrick grins back, releasing Llyr to be our distraction.

He shoots up in the water, mixing with the pod of dolphins before steering one toward the sirens. The dolphin dives in the water, taking Llyr with him.

They swing by the sirens as Llyr acts like he doesn't have control of the creature. The sirens shoot up in the water, chasing after him, but they're no match for the dolphin's speed.

As soon as they're facing away, we turn, swimming toward the surface where my family is being held captive. I wave our backup forward, encouraging them to get on this side of the siren wall while they still can. They find places to hide behind large rocks on the ocean floor.

Merrick and I split off—he goes to the left to help Caspian, while I go to the right to save my mother from Cassidia. The blue siren is singing to the humans, trying to force my mother to do it *for* her.

Tarni holds a knife to Caspian's throat. She sees me, but Merrick is nowhere in sight.

"I'll kill him if you don't," Tarni shouts to my mother, ignoring me.

"You need him just as much as you need me, Tarni," my mother calls back.

"I'll kill your daughter too!" Tarni amends her threat.

Cassidia whips her head around, locating me. My mother's eyes grow wide when she sees me. I lock eyes with Cassidia, making sure the necklace is on full display, but I don't point it out yet.

My mother recognizes Marilla's armor, giving me a brief nod but I don't acknowledge her. I need to keep the focus on me, not what my mother is quietly doing while Cassidia isn't paying as close of attention as she should be.

The ships start to leave the area, clearing the waters for a greater war. Cassidia opens her mouth again, instructing the humans to enter the water. The first group splashes in and quickly disappear under the water as the sirens pull them down, just as Chantay and Persephone once drowned Jarek's guards a century ago in this very place.

Foam laps along the rock wall each time the water crashes against it. It jumps along the shore, leaving the off-white film to skitter across the grass and rocks. Pieces tumble along in the breeze. Miraculously, the foam avoids the steps.

"Do you honestly think you can control the palace, Cassidia?" I point to the palace that is just as opalescent as Aila described it to be, though dingy with age.

"We will, though there won't be much left when we're done, I'm afraid." She smiles. "We were so lucky your brother fought so hard to save your mother back in Hontan—we might have left him behind."

"You left my sister though," I remind her. "I guess you really *don't* have what it takes."

I finger the necklace resting on my chest under my grandmother's necklace just long enough to draw her attention to it.

"What's your plan, Cassidia—take over as the reigning siren queen?"

"Nir will be here soon," Tarni yells. She screams as we hear a loud splash. Cassidia's face goes white, and I whip around to see what happened.

Caspian is no longer in her grasp, and Tarni looks shocked. She ducks under the water where Merrick has pulled Caspian to safety. I see their outlines through the waves and assume they're safe.

"Are you really trusting *her* as your right hand?" I turn back to Cassidia, mocking her choice for council. "I thought Nir had trained you better."

Tarni pops back up in the water, swimming toward me.

"What happened, Tarni?" I ask in my most innocent voice. "Lose something?"

"You're boyfriend pulled your brother away, but don't worry, my sirens are getting them back. Good thing we only need *one* of them alive."

I'd quake if her threats scared me at all—we've survived the sirens this long.

"Honestly, it's not them I'd be worried about though—it's you. This time, we're going to kill you."

She pulls out her knife, prepared to take a chunk out of my tail. Tarni arches her back, leaping out of the water in an arc before she dives down in front of me, bent on cutting my scales.

I dip under the water, pulling my own knife as she swims toward me. I jerk my tail to the side and Tarni swipes at the water where I had been.

"I only pulled off one scale last time, Celena—time to take them all," she growls.

Above us, Cassidia's tail thrashes in the water as my mother tries to escape to help me. When neither appears under the waves, I assume Cassidia has the upper hand in the situation.

A tidal wave of humans pours into the water, jumping off the side of the palace grounds. They swim over us, covering the waters, blocking out much of the light. The men surround my mother and Cassidia, but don't appear to be hurting them.

Tarni slashes at me, barely missing. I drag my own knife across the top of her wrist, cutting her with a shallow motion—I should have tried harder, but I was hoping to avoid detaching her hand from her arm. She moves quickly in retaliation. Blood bubbles up on the top of my hand, but she doesn't do enough damage to deter me from fighting.

The light shifts as the humans swim above us. Their bodies hover above us, occasionally dipping down into the water. A boot nearly kicks me in the head as a man moves over us. I push it away, shoving him roughly—he barely notices under Cassidia's trance.

Suddenly, the entire group of humans plunge beneath the waves. Their heads dart around as they search for something. The men's eyes lock on us—on *me*—and the entire collection of humans turns to try to attack me.

Tarni grins wildly as she realizes what is happening. She swims up, double-checking that Cassidia has only sent them after me. The men swim by her as if she's not even there. As soon as she's free, she surfaces.

Having no choice, I attempt to siren the men as they swim toward me. In between hands and feet groping the water to get to me, I see my mother's face under the water. Cassidia's hand grips her hair as she fights to get her above the waves.

My mother's voice fills the water as she tries to assist me. Caspian and Merrick nearly collide into me as I swim to the ocean floor.

"Sing!" I command.

Caspian looks unsure, but he follows my lead, his voice blending with mine. Merrick makes a move to swim under the humans, trying to get around them to reach my mother while my twin and I attempt to move the humans away from the area.

Hands touch my sides, brushing against my waist and hips as the humans surround me. They shove Caspian aside, desperately trying to drag me to the surface.

I push at them, trying to beat their hands away—they drag me toward the waves anyway. My tail flips against them, trying to remove the people from me. When I can't pull away, I use my knife, trying to avoid doing any major damage.

A man reels back at the touch of the blade, but only long enough to display that instinctual reaction before the sireny takes back over. He continues swiping his hands toward me, attempting to follow orders.

Slowly, the men in the water stop, latching on to our siren song. Caspian filled in the gaps as I paused to attack the men coming after me, and between us, the men have turned to listen. They slowly swim to the surface and move back toward the land.

"No!" Tarni screams as we surface. She wheels around to face Cassidia. "Do something."

Cassidia attempts to sway them back, now forcing my mother's head under the water so she can't lend us her voice above the waves.

"Separate them," Cassidia says between lines. She nods at us.

Tarni turns, choosing to take on Caspian. She races at him, slamming into his chest. Murdoch would be furious if he saw the way she threw herself at my twin.

Where is *Murdoch?*

Caspian and Tarni disappear under the water. Cassidia holds my mother's tail in her hands, preparing to slice off her fins.

"He said you wouldn't flinch if it came to that." I raise an eyebrow, trying to act casually. I nod to my mother's tail. "I supposed *that's* why."

"Why *what?*" Her voice is low and dangerous as her hand twitches near my mother's fins.

"Why he left you in charge instead of his cousin."

She quirks her head at me, studying me as I float in the water.

The water breaks as Tarni surfaces without Caspian.

"You have more friends, I see," she snips at me, swimming over.

I ignore her, turning back to face the blue siren.

"I'd like to say you're going to live to see your days as queen, but I'm not convinced you're going to survive *today*."

"Queen?" Tarni sounds offended. "Nir isn't taking a wife anytime soon."

"And it certainly wouldn't be *me*," Cassidia adds, taken back by Tarni's words.

I allow my eyes to widen, mimicking shock.

"You don't know?"

Cassidia squints her eyes at me, leaning forward as she temporarily forgets she's holding my mother's tail.

"Know what?" Tarni growls.

"Cassidia is queen now." I have to fight my smile.

"What do you mean?" Cassidia hisses at me, lurching forward as she bumps into my mother.

In the water behind her, I see the shadow of Merrick's blue hair slipping through the water under the surface—I have to keep Cassidia distracted.

"He left you in charge," I reply, reaching for the necklace.

"How did you get that?" Tarni seethes in the water a few lengths from me—I have both of their attention.

"I took it to bring it back as proof."

"Proof of what?" Tarni shrieks, hair flopping in front of her she slams her hand on the surface of the water.

Behind the sirens, the humans are climbing into small boats and are rowing back toward us, no longer under anyone's siren spell. For now, I have to deal with one problem at a time—and I still have a few minutes before the humans reach us again as they row back from the palace steps Caspian and I sent them to.

"Nir is dead, and Cassidia is the queen," I inform her.

"He can't be dead!" Tarni gasps, preparing herself to wail over the loss of her cousin.

"He's gone, Tarni," Cassidia says quietly as if she has confirmation of it.

"We were just as shocked as you are that he would pass the crown to Cassidia and not you, Tarni," Llyr calls as he swims over to us. He and Caspian slow their crashing approach, releasing the dolphins he has apparently used to rescue Casp from Tarni's grasp—which also explains why she surfaced without him.

When they turn to look at them, Cassidia is pulled beneath the waves. I dart forward, grabbing onto her wrists, squeezing so hard that she releases my mother's tail.

Merrick drags her down in the water so quickly that she can't fight back. I dart up, telling my mother to swim. Llyr smacks the water, directing a dolphin to my mother.

"Go! Don't stop—we'll catch up. Find the guards!"

She grabs onto the dolphin's dorsal fin, letting it carry her away to get reinforcements. I imagine her tail is quite sore from being pulled on like that. I can't be sure, but she might have had a small encounter with Cassidia's knife as they were pulled under—I hope they didn't split her fin like they did to mine.

I careen back into the water in search of Merrick, but Tarni is on top of me, trying to rip my hair back.

"Give me that necklace, you eel!" Her shout is overtaken by the pain she feels when she latches onto my braid and rakes her hands across the shells Merrick wove into it.

"Nir said the exact same thing," I yell back. "Only it was his face, not his hands!"

I laugh cruelly as I taunt her, trying to throw her off focus.

"I will murder you," she screams, unable to come up with a more creative threat in the moment.

"Not going to let the humans handle it this time?" I throw back over my shoulder. "They're coming for us, you know."

I point up as I swim, noting the humans are drawing closer. I hear her startle behind me, gasping at the sight of the small boats coming for us.

"You'll pay for this!"

"I'm sure I will," I mutter as I continue to dive toward Cassidia. She and Merrick are locked in battle—she somehow freed herself of his grasp. They circle each other, knives in hand.

"Come to watch your boyfriend die?" Cassidia calls, noticing me.

"Go handle the humans, Celena," Merrick says without looking at me. The two continue to spin in a wide arch, waiting for the other to strike first.

"Tarni, do not let her get control of them," Cassidia instructs. "Go to the surface."

"You're not queen yet, Cassidia. I'm the next in line for the throne, and I'm staying to kill this *mermaid.*" She spits the word out like it's toxic.

"We have to work together, Tarni," Cassidia calls. "If Nir's plan is going to succeed, we need them all under our control. I'll kill both of them, and then join you so we can start the ceremony."

"What ceremony is—?" My words are cut off as Tarni screams again, this time in agony.

Tarni is jerked through the water, a harpoon extending out of her arm. Blood clouds behind her as the humans pull her toward their boat. She screams, knowing her fate if they catch her.

The siren princess attempts to rip her arm away, but the barbs at the end of the spear prevent her from ripping it from her arm. They pull her so quickly that she doesn't have time to free herself anyway.

Cassidia races away from Merrick, attempting to help her princess as the sailors drag Tarni into their rowboat. Their tiny boat shifts under their weight. Several humans move to the opposite side to balance it out while two men haul Tarni out of the water.

"Help me!" Cassidia shrieks before she reaches the surface. She pulls herself out of the water, slamming into the side of the boat as she reaches for her friend.

"We can't let them kill her." Without any logical reason, I race toward the surface to help save her.

The air feels heavier when I surface as if everything is weighing me down. Screams sound overhead as creatures move in the sky above us. I ignore them as I make my way to the boat where Cassidia is attempting to siren the humans as she claws for Tarni.

The siren princess sits in the center of the boat as the men attempt to bind her, wrapping ropes around her arms to pin them to her sides. One of the men breaks the harpoon, pulling it from her arm as she cries out.

Cassidia's song drops as she screams for Tarni, only fragments of notes escaping her lips as she bounces between trying to siren the men and direct the princess. I open my mouth to sing, but something hits me in the back of the head, sending me pitching forward. My face slams into the water but I bob right back up, knife in hand.

A man glares at me, ready to hit me again.

"We won't let you siren *us*, you sea witch," he sneers.

I duck under the water, darting toward the boat in an attempt to tip it. It's heavier than it looks and I only manage to rock it as I collide with the underside of the vessel. The oar dips back into the water behind me, and I turn, pulling as hard as I can, flipping the man into the water.

I swim away, trying to return to save Tarni. On the surface, I start singing, attempting to sway the sailors into leaving. The men shout directions to each other, passing along orders from closer to the shore.

A figure stands on the top of the steps leading to the palace in the distance—he looks like he's giving the orders. If I can get the men over there, they could silence him.

I lurch forward as a boat collides with me, striking the middle of my back enough to toss me forward again. Arms reach around me, lifting me out of the water.

CHAPTER 18

The edge of the boat scrapes over my scales painfully as the men haul me into the rowboat. I fight against them, looking for Merrick, but he's nowhere to be found.

Several boats over, I see Llyr grappling with a human in the water. Caspian is a few lengths away, trying to turn a boat away from coming to help the humans with Tarni and me. Cassidia pummels the boat, darting away each time they reach for her.

Tarni's cries turn to pleas for mercy as they go after her scales.

"Leave her alone!" I scream before bursting into song in an attempt to free myself.

One of the men pulls at my arm, forcing it over my head as I'm positioned to lay flat against their knees as they hold me between them. I try to pull my hands back as his knife dances over them, taunting me.

"We're taking you to his majesty," the man informs me. "Hold still, so we don't have to take you in pieces."

I sing louder, finally latching into their consciousness. The men slow, starting to fall under my song. I order the man to throw his knife into the sea, and he releases it quickly—I hope it doesn't hit anyone on the way down.

At my insistence, they gently lift me into the air, leaning over the side of the boat to set me in the water. When Cassidia sees me, she calms, trying to gather herself enough to siren the humans.

Cassidia is a smart mermaid—she knows Tarni is next in line for the crown, and if the princess is gone, there's nothing stopping the bigger, more brutish sirens from moving in and disposing of *her* so *they* can rule. She's wise to keep Tarni alive as the only siren that has a possible claim to the crown—it's written all over her face. She could care less about Tarni, but her safety and position are at stake.

I glance over while they're moving me. Tarni is in tatters, her tail being slowly shredded. They pull at her scales, each wanting one as a prize. One man takes a knife to her fins, slicing them into strips.

Tarni passes out from the pain, quieting as they rip her apart. My voice jumps an octave as I throw my words at them, stilling their hands.

The men set me in the water, allowing me to float on my own. I stretch my arms out to the side, continuing to lean back to stay in the same position, preventing my song from breaking or changing while I'm sirening the men with Tarni.

"Tarni!" Murdoch's voice is clear and strong above the yelling of the humans from the other boats as they attempt to catch more mer and sirens.

He rushes toward the boat, bent on saving her. I have no idea where he's been all this time. Cassidia blocks his path, holding a hand up.

"We have to save her!" He tries to counter the blue siren's moves.

"She is," Cassidia says calmly, looking at me.

From the corner of my eye, I can see Murdoch still, watching me. I carefully direct the men to pick Tarni up, and Murdoch raises himself up in the water, nostrils flaring as he prepares to murder me if I do anything to his precious siren.

The men in the rowboat lower the broken siren into the water. Her blood washes away as the water claims her body back from the human world.

"Take her." I slip the words into my song. "And don't ever come after the mer again or I'll give you all to the humans. The war is over."

Cassidia takes Tarni's unconscious body and dips below the surface. Murdoch hovers, and I lower my voice so I can hear him over my notes.

"Why did you save her?"

"No one should die like that," I tell him, adding a few notes to keep the humans at bay. "I tried to save Durdania too."

"They said Nir is dead."

"He is. I killed him."

"You killed Nir, but not Tarni?" He swims as close as he dares to me.

"Nir attacked me. I couldn't save him even if I tried. Tarni attacked me too, but I wasn't going to let her die at the hands of the humans—but so help me, Murdoch, if I *ever* see you, Tarni, or any of those sirens again, I will personally feed you to the human king and his family."

I sing quickly, my anger nearly rousing the men out of my trance. Calming, I sing lower, lulling them back under my command.

"So we're free to go?"

"Assuming you can get past the mer, yes. I'm sure they've arrived by now."

"They have—it's a bloodbath."

"Then might I suggest finding an alternative route?" I'm not sure why I'm telling him how to escape the wrath of the mer queen after all he and Tarni have done to us. I don't think they'll ever come after us again after we killed their king and rescued their—temporary queen?

"Thank you, Celena." He ducks his head, not looking at me as I right myself in the water. "I'm sorry for what I did to you."

"Just go, Murdoch."

He starts to turn away but spins back around.

"Relo didn't know. I know he stood up for me during your trial, but he didn't know what was going on. He just trusted me when he shouldn't have."

"Relo won't be punished for your mistakes," I promise him. "Now leave before I change my mind."

"I don't think there are many sirens left at this point, Celena. I think it's between the mer and the humans now."

He dips under the water, rushing away to find Tarni and Cassidia and extricate them from the situation before my collection finds them—bad things would happen if they did. I shake my head as they go.

If the sirens are disbanded, that leaves the mer to clean up their mess. I wonder if we could escape back into the sea and live another hundred years without the humans finding us.

I doubt that the humans will allow us to remain in the ocean at this point—they'll probably do everything in their power to hunt us down.

"Celena!" Caspian calls, searching for me around the boats.

"*Here*, Casp!"

I start turning the boats toward the shore. If I drowned them all now, I'd know for sure these men wouldn't come after my collection today.

"Celena, the collection is here," Caspian informs me, swimming up to me and grabbing my hands. He pulls me into a protective hug.

"I know, Murdoch told me."

Caspian's face grows cold.

"Where is he?" His whisper sounds vicious and deadly.

"I let him go." I hold a hand up between us as his eyebrows shoot up. "Tarni is practically dead—though I don't think Murdoch realizes that yet—I caught a look at her side before Cassidia took her away. Cassidia isn't planning to lead their collection, and Murdoch told me that there aren't many left anyway. They'll wander, but I don't think they'll be a problem. Murdoch knows I'll kill him if they are."

"That was stupid."

"Probably," I reply, smiling as he purses his lips in understanding annoyance.

"Llyr is bringing the dolphins back around. The humans frightened them off, but they didn't get too far. Where is Merrick?"

Merrick.

"He was right behind me." My eyes grow wide again, and I'm convinced my face is going to start thinking it belongs that way. I whip around, searching for Merrick in the water. Caspian shouts for him as I duck under the waves, quickly searching for him.

"Casp!" I shout, surfacing. "*Phorcys* has him."

"*What?*"

I stare at him for a moment, gaping.

"Do sirens *never* die?" Caspian throws his hands in the air.

"Apparently not, because he's down there." Tears spring to my eyes, leaking out. They drip down my face, causing a tickling sensation—I don't like it.

The inside of my nose feels heavy as the tears drip off my cheeks. Caspian looks horrified.

"Is that what those look like?" He mutters under his breath before grabbing my shoulders. "We have to stop Phorcys."

"Phorcys?" Llyr splashes us as he races by on a dolphin. He looks at me like I've lost my mind.

"He's alive," I tell him. "He has Merrick."

"Let's go." He motions to the pod before diving under the water and racing toward where Phorcys is dragging Merrick back in the water. He's so far away, I can only tell it's my boyfriend by his brilliantly blue hair and the way he's struggling to get free—Phorcys must have knocked him out to have bound him like that. Merrick bucks against the restraints tying his wrists to his tail.

I hold onto a dolphin as we dart through the water, leaving the humans to their own devices on the surface. We slice through the water, rapidly approaching Merrick and Phorcys.

Merrick shakes his head violently, trying to warn us off.

Llyr motions next to me and a dolphin breaks away from the pod, headed straight for the mermen ahead of us. It slams into Phorcys, knocking him off balance. Another dolphin counters, also striking Phorcys as we arrive.

I don't know how Phorcys is moving, let alone controlling this situation. But then, Nir surprised me as well. I flash back to when we left the two sirens for dead—Phorcys has a necklace. Maybe it was like the one I'm wearing from Grandmother Tama and holds secrets that he used to survive. I doubt I'll ever know though—I'm going to kill him before I have a chance to ask.

I urge my dolphin not to stop, mimicking its friends' attack on the siren. We slam into him, and I use the opportunity to pull Merrick out of the siren's reach. I don't have time to remove the gag.

"You shouldn't have left me alone," Phorcys taunts. "The smart ones never die, Celena."

"How did you manage to fix that injury?" I angle myself between Merrick and Phorcys, hoping one of the boys will untie the blue-haired merman behind me. His body rests against the small of my back as he struggles to free himself.

"You're not the only one with friends, Celena." He refuses to say more. The way his eyes narrow in a challenge, I can tell there's something to this story that I don't know yet.

It doesn't matter though—the entire mer collection—or what's left of them—swims up behind us. Our reinforcements form a wall Phorcys can't escape. He looks around for a moment before pushing himself to swim up in the water, headed toward the surface. His wound looks incredibly painful.

The collection starts to follow him, ready to take him back to Metten with us for question. I spot Marilla with my mother near the middle of the group. My father and Coralie swim nearby until the nets descend.

I've already started swimming when I notice the ropes. I'm two lengths away from the surface as I try to flip in the water and go back to help. I call out, but it's too late. The nets start scooping up mer.

They swim away, collectively trying to escape. The boats above rock as the mer pull against the ropes.

I'm stopped short, tangled in a net. It pulls me up—something I'm growing accustomed to now. I fight against it, attempting to cut the ropes so I can slip out.

I bump against the side of the boat as I snap the last rope I need to create a hole big enough to wriggle out of it. Merrick races toward me—now free—Llyr and Caspian behind him. I throw myself into his arms.

The mer that escape rush to the surface. I sing, trying to stop the madness while they surround the rowboats and larger ships that arrived from somewhere while we were under the water, attempting to free our friends and sink the ships intent on harming us.

Phorcys flops in one of the boats as the men try to subdue him. The larger boats approach—some huge, towering above the water, some just long enough that we couldn't capsize it if we tried.

My voice stops the men again as I command them to return any stolen mer to the waters below their ships. My hold over them lasts long enough to drop most of the collection to the ocean, including Phorcys. His wound bleeds as they move him—I'm still not sure how he's able to move with an injury so deep. The siren flounders in the water, trying to get away, but he's functioning about as well as a fish with one fin.

"Coralie!" Caspian yells, rushing past me.

I turn to find Coralie in a boat far enough away that I must not be reaching the men with my siren song from where I am. She's tangled in a net as my father tries to reach her. The men beat him back as he tips their rowboat in the water, desperately trying to pull Cor out of their grasp.

One man raises some kind of weapon to my father, preparing to strike him. I shriek as I race through the water, unable to duck below the waves where it will be faster because the men will fall out of my sireny.

The man looks to me as I slice through the water toward them. His expression is cold as he moves his shoulders back, building up momentum to hit my father.

Whatever the weapon is, it's effective.

It slams into his face, producing the most horrific sound I've ever heard. He crumples under the blow, sinking against the edge of the boat before driting down in the water.

The men turn back to Coralie, and I can see them prepare to fight for pieces of her like they did with Tarni. Caspian pushes ahead of me, determined to rescue our sister. I push as hard as I can, but I can't keep up.

They raise a knife to my sister, preparing to cut her.

I won't let them.

They will never touch my precious little sister.

I stop in the water, freezing on the spot. The entire collection of humans turns to look at why I suddenly halted. I open my mouth and without hesitation, I command the human with the knife to plunge it into his own heart.

He does, toppling over onto the side of the rowboat.

Caspian turns around, horrified. He shakes his head to clear his thoughts, spinning around to get Coralie while I systematically command the men in her ship to throw themselves into the water and swim to the bottom. If they make it, perhaps they'll have enough time to swim back up. If they don't.

The men take turns leaping out of the rowboat, rocking it so hard that Coralie is nearly pitched out into Caspian's arms.

He reaches her, throwing himself as far into the nearly empty boat as he can get. My twin scoops Coralie up, pulling her back into the water. The body of the dead sailor rocks in the boat. His head tips over the back edge of the boat, dangling in above the water, head lolling back—the sight is horrifying.

Caspian nods when he turns back to me, telling me I did the right thing. I don't have time to consider it either way—the humans are still attacking.

Whipping around, I continue sirening the men as I try to get them back to land. If I can separate them from us, we can disappear into the ocean and figure out how to proceed.

Caspian darts below the waves to hand Coralie off and, hopefully, find my father and see if he's still alive.

Merrick had attempted sirening the humans while I was saving Coralie—he managed to keep them under his control, but it took a great deal of effort, even with others joining in. I raise my voice up, commanding the men in the boats far easier than he had.

The vessels turn, heading back to land. For a moment, I consider having them tear down the steps leading to the sea with their bare hands, but I'm not willing to risk losing any time—they need to abandon their posts here in Antaire and flee for the country further inland, far enough away that they can't hurt the mer.

The man on the steps shouts, oblivious to my siren call—*something isn't right.*

I swim closer, hoping it's just the distance between us. More men rush from the shore, carrying small rowboats over their heads. They splash into the water, rowing toward the mer collection, clashing with their fellow humans as they try to take them away from my control.

"Fall back!" I shout, realizing something is wrong.

"What's the matter?" a human calls to me from a boat to my left. It drifts dangerously close as all of the men eye me.

They watch me thoughtfully, clearly not under my control.

"Oh, that's right," he shouts loudly. He points to his ear. "We can't hear you."

CHAPTER 19

The man grins as he reaches for me.

"Fall back!" I scream again, realizing that I can't siren the humans if they block out my voice.

I lose control of the situation quickly.

Weapons are raised, maiming and killing my collection. Bodies float in the water—both human and mer—almost instantly.

Llyr clashes with the men in the boat next to me. They use their weapons to try to injure him, jabbing at his shoulder. He ducks under a harpoon aimed at him, and it slices through the water. Llyr reaches up, grabbing hold of the weapon the man next to him is holding and flips the human into the water.

"They can't hear me!" I shout, frantically searching for another way to fix the situation.

"I got that!" Llyr yells back.

All around me words swirl from the humans, blaming us for the deaths of their family, friends, and the men they work with every day. They scream obscenities at us—at least I assume that's what those words are by the way they're saying them—as they blame us for the destruction of the seas.

They speak to each other with their hands, waving them wildly and pointing because they aren't able to hear each other either—they must have something in their ears to stop the noise from entering. The men are surprisingly good at reading each other's lips—probably from being out at sea and needing to know what people are instructing them to do from across the ship or over the roar of waves and storms. Merrick and I have become good at doing this too while we're on missions.

"We have to stop their leader," I murmur.

"What?" Merrick asks, arm flinging out in front of me to stop an oar from hitting me while I turned to look toward the palace. The impact jars me out of my thoughts. I whip around to face him, face slack with shock as I realized I wasn't paying attention.

"Merrick, we have to take out their leader—he's on the steps." I point to the distant steps leading into the ocean. The man still stands on the top step, as far from the water as possible. More boats launch into the water, traveling toward us.

"Llyr, get them back!"

I swim toward the boats coming for us.

"Celena, do *not* go over there!" Llyr shouts, starting to follow me as he splashes loudly through the water.

"She's right, we have to stop the man leading them. Get the rest of the collection back to Metten, Llyr. You have to," Merrick insists.

"Can you do this by yourselves?" Llyr hesitates, still following us.

"We'll join you as soon as we can."

Ahead of us, Keone ducks under the water, swimming in the same direction we are.

"We'll help them!" Natale shouts, waving for Llyr to take charge of reaching Marilla and getting the collection back to Metten before we flee for Scylla and make plans on how to escape the wrath of the humans.

A few mer stay with us, willing to fight to help us escape the humans. It's incredible how many mer are willing to die to protect the others.

Llyr turns, diving under the sea as he races back to Dylana and her mother. We could use his help, but the collection needs him more. Besides, if we don't survive this, Marilla will still need trained spies to keep the collection safe—at least Llyr will be there to support them.

I dive under the water, trying to avoid the fighting until I can make my way to the steps. If I can gain enough speed, I can dive out of the water and land halfway up the steps. Crawling fast enough, I could potentially reach the man giving direction and pull him into the water with me. All I need to do is silence his commands, and his people won't know what to do—they're under his siren spell just as much as they were once under mine.

A leader is nothing more than a siren with intentions of good or bad outcomes and all those that hear their directions fall under their command, whether it is desired or not.

Their human siren stands on the palace steps ordering our deaths.

He looks even more imposing as I draw near. Still, several boat lengths away, I can start to make out more than his basic shape as his arms fly from his sides, shouting orders to the men under his siren call's control.

Looking up, I find the men in a rowboat motioning to a group of sailors in a longer boat sailing up alongside of them. They're pointing to their ears.

Not all of them are blocking us out yet—they're trying to warn them.

"Merrick, up!"

He follows my lead and we swim to the surface. As soon as I'm free of the water, I start singing. The men start to turn toward me, falling under my song, but the ones trying to warn them quickly catch on. They turn to me, prepared to end my control over the other sailors.

"Get down," I warn Merrick. "I have to stay above the surface, but if they reach me, you'll need to save me, and they can't know you're here."

My point rings true, and he scowls as he darts below the water, moving far enough away that they can't easily see him once they approach. I work as hard as I can to force the men under my control to stop those that blocked out my voice, but it isn't enough.

I swim quickly, making my way toward the steps as the boats not under my siren song chase me. Seeing what I'm doing, they work to block me. I can't swim under them while sirening, so I have to swim around, taking me on a strange path through the water to reach their leader on the steps.

Someone figures out what my course is and moves the figure—a man I assume is their king— off of the step to higher ground. As I continue, determined to take him away from them, they rush the king back into the palace. Running off, he looks exactly as Aila described Jarek running off after his mother rescued him from Persephone's sireny when she attempted to drown him.

Inside the palace, I know there is no way to reach him, but I have accomplished my goal—the human sireny has been stopped for the moment—he no longer controls the men in the boats.

Another man *does* though. He's tall as he stands on the deck of a boat that's long enough that we couldn't tip it if we tried but low enough to the ocean's surface that if he lowered himself over the edge and I dove out of the water, perhaps I could pull him in.

I have to stop him.

Swimming quickly, I make my way back to his boat, darting around bodies in the water and gliding past boats under my control as they float in my way.

All I have time for is to keep the men at bay—I cannot use them to help me, nor can I siren them out of my way. My only mission is to get them to listen and stay motionless in the water.

Water laps in my face as I sink lower in the ocean, trying to blend in, even though all eyes are on me. My mouth hovers above the waves just enough so the crests don't block my words.

Just as I reach the boat, I feel Merrick tug on my tail below me. Before I can see what he wants, a giant net snaps around me as the humans catch me. It had been hidden closely along the side of the ship, waiting for me—Merrick's warning had been too late, and I was too busy locking eyes with the prince I met yesterday as he stares at me from where he commands his subjects on the long boat.

His face is stony as I struggle against the net, but his men leave me dangling in the water. He walks forward, examining me. The prince kneels down, balancing between the toe of one foot and his other knee.

The young prince places a hand on the side of the boat as he studies my movements. The man behind him looks worried, staying close to his side. He looks to be about the prince's age.

"Do you know who I am?" he asks, not shouting like the others.

"The prince," I reply. I can feel Merrick struggling with the net below me.

"If you try to siren me, I'll have you killed immediately, and it won't be pleasant."

The man behind him leans forward, something in his hands—he's holding something that will block out my voice. The same thing sticks out of his own ears—he's safely protected from my words and his job is to also protect the prince should I try anything.

The prince has nothing blocking his ears at this point so that he can speak with me, but his friend can easily fix that if I try to siren the royal.

"We knew you were coming," the prince explains. "*We* left the ocean a century ago, but our men couldn't leave—the ocean is our way of life. It's out survival. The fishing trade is what allows us to survive. When your kind started attacking more frequently, we knew it was only a matter of time."

He glares at me as if I was the cause of all his problems.

"My sister and I weren't supposed to be here—we stayed inland while my father came to oversee the battle—but you dragged us here. We were supposed to be safe, but you sent sirened men to capture us and bring us to you."

When I sent the man to fetch the human royals, they took the prince instead of the king because they weren't in the same location—I should have been more specific. Then again, how could I have possibly known what the royal family looked like now.

A sailor raises his spear, prepared to plunge it into my skull while the prince watches. I struggle against the ropes wrapped around me. Terror controls my body as I jerk to escape.

"Please don't do this," I plead with him. "We didn't hurt your men, the sirens we were fighting were. They're gone now. Please!"

The guard behind him leans forward, ready to protect him if I try to siren his prince. The prince waves his hand.

"I can't trust you. Your kind have killed our people for generations."

"It wasn't us," I promise, fighting against the ropes. "We've lived in the middle of the ocean, as far away from you as we could get since Persephone tried to siren Prince Jarek. I'm from Aila's line—she tried to help your prince."

He lurches back at Jarek's name. I push forward, trying to convince him to leave us in peace.

"Please, we haven't done anything but try to avoid you for years. It's Persephone's followers that did this to you."

"You're all like them. I haven't seen a single mermaid not act out against us." I open my mouth to protest, but he cuts me off. "*You're* not innocent, *mermaid,* I've watched you try to control us twice now."

He has a point.

"I've only sirened to protect us from you," I shout. "I saved your sister."

He pulls back at my words again, contemplating what to say next.

"I haven't figured that out yet—*it doesn't make sense*—but just because you rescued Analia doesn't mean I trust you. I'll never trust you—I saw you hurt all these sailors. I saw you force a man to plunge a knife into his heart."

"To save a thirteen-year-old mermaid they were bent on ripping to pieces!" My shrieks are in vain—the prince has no intention of saving me.

The noise dies down around us as the mer collection tries to escape, disappearing under the waves as Llyr forces them away, leaving only the remaining warriors to help us fight—I'm not sure many of them have survived this long. Merrick works quietly below me, snapping the net around me as I block him from sight with my tail.

The moment the net breaks, Merrick pulls me down, but the men are ready—they throw ropes around my torso. Most catch around my arms, but one loops gracefully around my neck.

I slam my hand into the water, making Merrick stop before the men snap my neck. Merrick freezes, following my commands. His hand presses against the bottom of my tail as he realizes what is happening. He pushes me up in the water enough that the rope loosens, putting slack into the line.

"I told you, we're prepared for you," the prince informs me, rocking back on his heels as he balances on one knee. "We've known you were coming for us since your sea witch tried to drown my great-great-grandfather. We were smart enough not to come back to the sea until now, but now that you've dragged us back here, you're going to pay for what you've done to our men over the generations."

I shake my head, not daring to speak.

A rumble races across the group of humans as they yell instructions to each other—*kill the sirens...kill them all.*

The boat jerks, knocking a few of the men off their feet. The rope around my neck tightens as they move. I force my eyes shut, trying not to gasp.

Everything pauses for a moment. The men stare at the water as if a dangerous predator might appear, creeping out of the depths of the ocean—too bad none of them had seen Nir—they'd be terrified.

They lean over the edge of the boat, looking into the water.

Natale's mother launches herself out of the water in a brazen attack against the men holding me. She twists in the air, lashing out as the men ready their weapons to use against her.

I had assumed Merrick had caused the boat to lurch—though I don't know why since he hasn't let go of me in all this time—instead, I discover it was Natale's mother.

Natale appears, throwing a knife at a human near the prince. It sinks into his chest, knocking him back. The prince looks horrified as he darts back in the boat to avoid being hurt.

"Pull her up," the prince instructs. "Pull her up *now* and don't hurt her!"

Merrick wraps his arms around my waist, still trying to remove the ropes. The men lift us out of the water. Miraculously, the one with the rope around my neck lets go, preventing me from being strangled as they lift us.

"Merrick, please," I beg. Attempting to remove his fingers from around me is an impossible task as I try to drop him back into the ocean like he had once done to me when I tried to rescue him from being dragged onto a ship.

"Celena, I will *not* leave you," he growls viciously, fingers biting into my waist so hard that I think I might break.

A human raises a spear to us, preparing to kill the blue-haired merman attached to their captive.

"Merrick!" I scream, unable to say or do anything else.

"Take them both," the prince instructs, holding up a hand.

The men swing us onto the boat and drop us *hard*. We collide with the deck painfully. I land partially on top of Merrick, and he instantly pulls me into his arms, trying to free me.

I know this merman, and I know he's going to try to rip the ropes off of me and push me into the water, fully prepared to pay the price for setting me free.

It doesn't matter though—the men are on us before Merrick can even attempt to remove the ropes.

Natale's mother launches herself out of the water again as the humans bind Merrick. She screeches as they spear her. Twisting, she convulses violently in the air. It's nearly as terrifying as watching Coralie in the brine pool had been. She collides with the water, disappearing from sight as Natale dips below to help her.

Merrick attempts to sing, hoping we can siren the men, but one of the guards slams into his skull with an oar, knocking him out. He flops onto the boat deck. All I can do is scoot closer to him and nestle against his head with mine—my hands are tied behind me making it difficult to even push myself to sit upright. My braid flops over him, and I carefully angle it to ensure the broken shells won't hurt him.

"Back to shore," the prince commands. "We're going to study these two."

A loud commotion sounds from the far side of the medium-sized vessel.

"Three, sire," a man informs him.

I turn to see which other mer they caught. My chest tightens when they drop Phorcys onto the deck. He struggles against them, but it's a losing battle with his injuries getting the better of him.

"I tried," he murmurs when he makes eye contact with me just before passing out from the strain on his injuries.

I look up into the eyes of the prince as he puts something into his ears to block noise out.

I can't turn as I hear the voices, but I can clearly hear Caspian and Llyr screaming that they'll find us and rescue us in the distance—they must have returned to assist in the fight and were too late.

"Time to see the palace you were so intent on ruling, *mermaid*. I'm sure you'll find it rather interesting."

They row us back to the steps. Men on the shore hold the boat in place as the guards pick us up—four sets of uncomfortable hands on each of us—and lift us out of the boat.

They carry us up the steps Aila and Persephone once sat on with Jarek before our worlds were divided. The men take the bumpiest course possible as they walk up the path.

The palace shimmers in the setting sun. The light glares off the opal-colored walls—a fierce, blinding orange color. It towers over us, both beautiful and terrifying.

A tear leaks out of my eye and down my cheek as the giant doors open. Merrick and Phorcys are still unconscious in the arms of rough, angry sailors working for the prince.

Our war with the sirens is over, but it was nothing compared to the one we face with the humans. This battle has only just entered into our lives, and it has no intention of releasing us until one side or the other is destroyed completely.

The king stands inside, appraising the situation, hands behind his back—he looks like the picture of Jarek in Aila's locket. He's terrifying as he points, directing the guards.

The palace doors slam shut behind us, trapping us within the human walls.

Acknowledgements

You are a completely fabulous person for sticking with me on this journey! I love, love, love Celena's tale (tail?) and the fact that I got to go darker in this one and really explore a lot of different themes is just such a gift for me.

I feel like a lot of this particular story has to do with family—specifically with siblings. As an older sister myself, a lot of my experiences with my little sister influenced Celena and Coralie in this story, though, to be fair, the mermaids aren't based off of my sister or I in any way. But that protective spirit Celena has is definitely something I've experienced with my sister.

I'm *so* excited for you to see what happens next in the Siren Wars, and while we're wrapping up Celena's story in the next book, you actually met some characters in Darker Depths that you're going to want to remember...because the spin-offs are in the planing stages! I can't wait!

Special thanks to Elle for all of your support and guidance while I was knocking out this series—you're amazing.

Thanks to Jess for all the effort you put into helping me flourish in this industry—I'd be lost without you!

Thank you to Yentl for being the fabulous person that you are—you make the dramatic times far more fun than they have any right to be!

Thanks to Susie for being my little sister so I could create this awesome relationship between Celena, Caspian, and Coralie!

Thanks to Julie for always being there to encourage and support me on my trips down the rabbit hole (oh, the jokes) on this series.

Extra special thanks to the aquarium cams I had in the bottom of my computer screen while I wrote this series—I appreciate the visuals which I immediately wrote into the story whenever I saw something cool out of the corner of my eye.

Most of all, thank you to YOU, oh fabulous reader! You are the most epic, awesome, lovely person and I'm truly grateful to get to hang out with you through these pages.

I'll see you in the final book in Celena's story (but not the final in the Siren Wars Saga) soon!

Stay inspired!

-K.M. Robinson

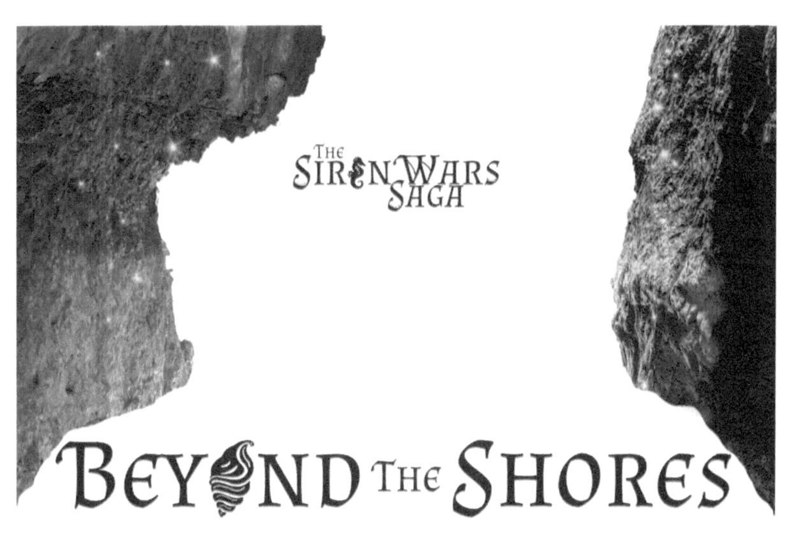

BEYOND THE SHORES

by

K.M. Robinson

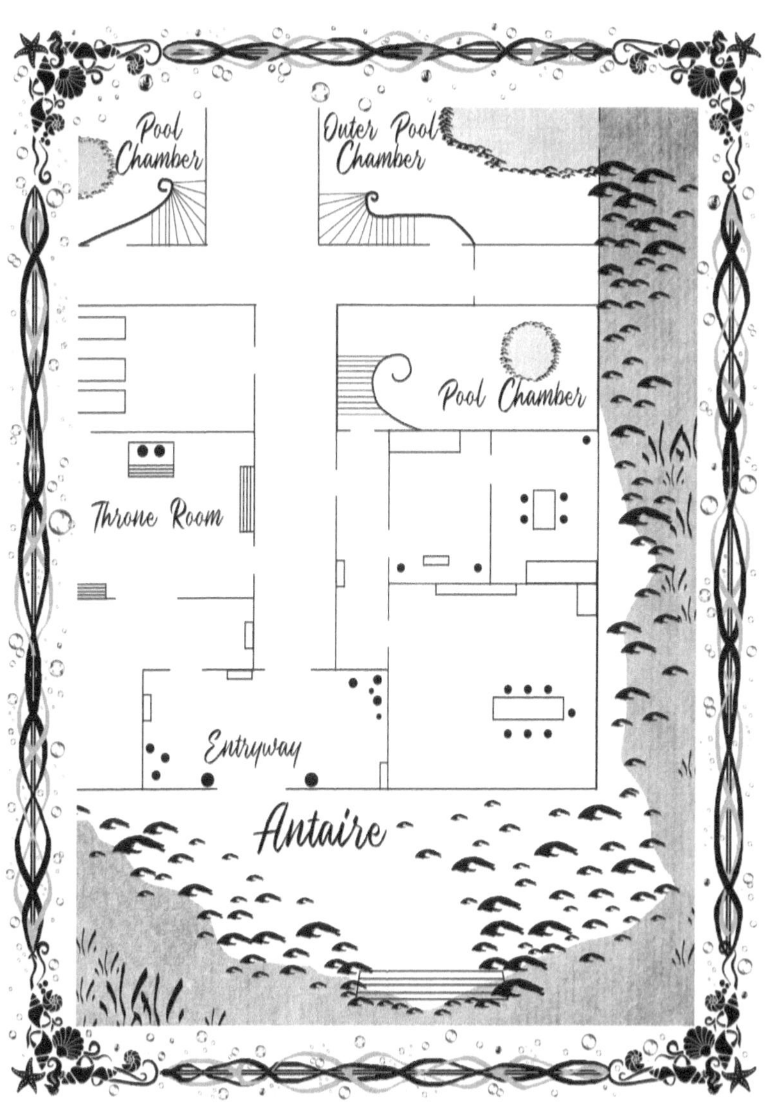

Pool Chamber
Outer Pool Chamber
Pool Chamber
Throne Room
Entryway
Antaire

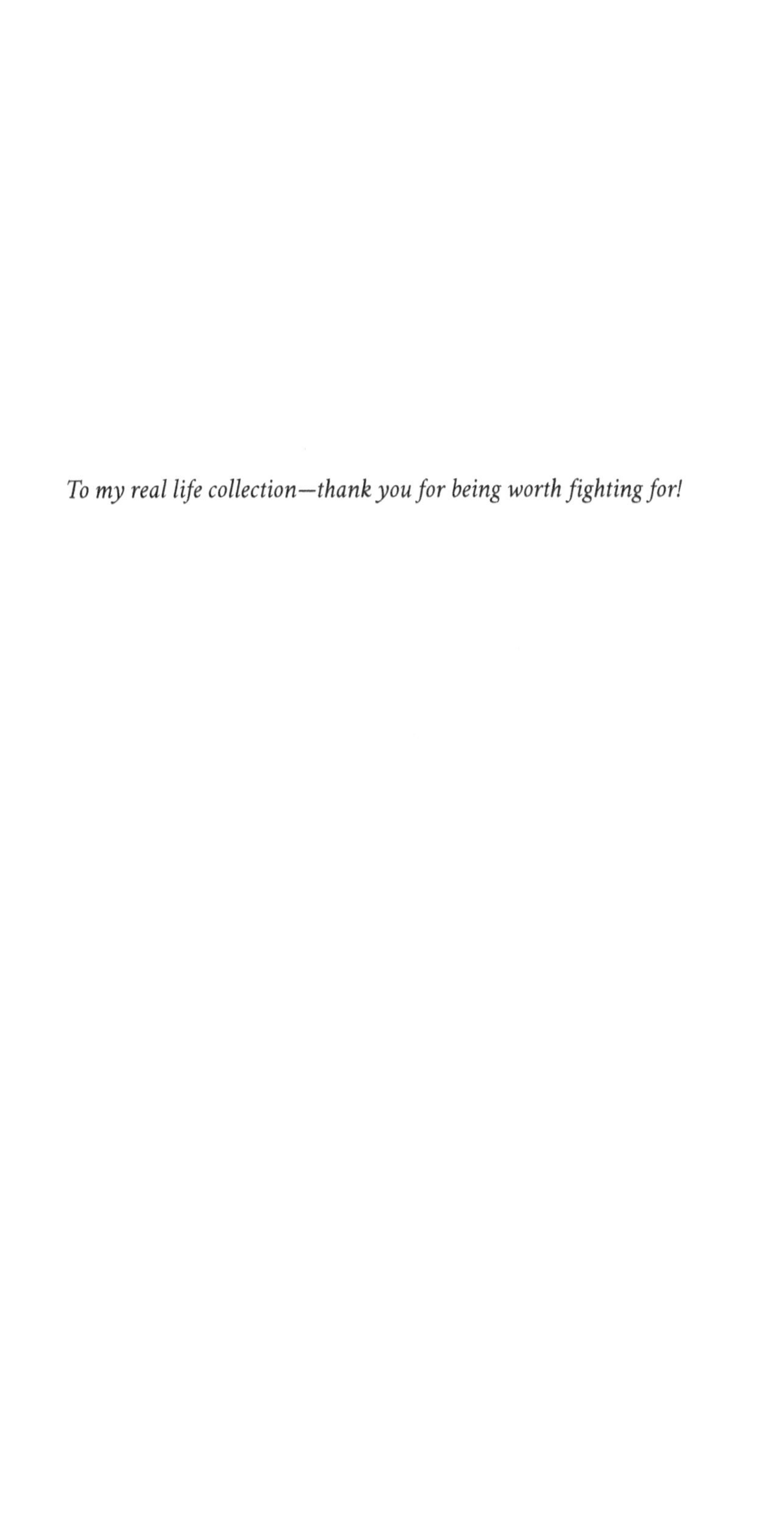

To my real life collection—thank you for being worth fighting for!

CHAPTER 1

In the darkest hours—those where everything seems lost and hopeless—we often find our redemption.

This is where I have learned to survive, even as my world falls apart.

Noises are something I've always identified my life by—the sound of my little sister's breathing when she snuck into my bed in the middle of the night as a mer child, the noise a dolphin makes when it glides through the palace hallways, the atmosphere of a kelp forest during a brewing storm—no matter where I am or what I'm doing, when I hear those noises, I'm taken right back to the first time those noises made an impression on me.

The sound of the palace door slamming behind me is one that will haunt me for the rest of my life.

Phorcys starts to stir as the humans carry us through the halls of the palace. I know better than to speak and upset our captors, but I try *willing* the siren to look at me.

His head lolls back, but he takes in the sights around us, quickly becoming alert. He attempts to sit up, but the humans forbid it. When Phorcys connects with me—upside down as he's pushed back—I shake my head quickly.

Like it or not, the siren is in this with us, and we're going to need to work together to save ourselves.

Merrick wakes but holds deadly still. I've seen him pretend to sleep enough times to know he is alert and listening to everything happening to us. His eyelids twitch, confirming that he knows what's happening and that he's taking advantage of the situation. I let out a quick breath of air from my nose, louder than the rest to assure him that I'm still with him.

The palace glides by me as easily as the ocean does. We slice through the hallways, flipping around corners in the air as the men carry us, doing all the work on our behalf.

Perhaps Nir had it right when he forced his sirens to carry him around the ocean on a makeshift throne. Then again, Nir is dead, so perhaps he's not the best merman to get ideas from at this point.

The hallways are an internal representation of the outside walls, casting an opalescent shine onto the floor as the light bounces off of them. The harsh sunset makes everything glow orange as light streams in through the window.

The chandelier my great-great-grandmother, Aila, had told our family about is even more stunning in person. I look up as we pass under it. Aila had never seen it up close—only through the window from the ocean outside the palace—but I imagine she would have loved this. If I were in the sea, I would swim up and touch the crystals.

I check on Merrick again as he continues to pretend to be knocked out. His breathing is steady, and he doesn't look to be in any more pain than the last time I saw him before the sailors hit him on the head with that oar when they pulled us into the boat, but I'm not entirely sure considering the beatings we've been taking the last few days.

"Let go," Phorcys insists, shattering the quiet. The men threaten him, hoping it will silence his rant. When it doesn't, they move to gag him.

"Phorcys," I say in a hushed voice, trying to still him. If the humans get too close to his face, I'm positive he will try to bite them, and there's no telling what they'll do in retaliation.

He bucks a few times but remains quiet.

Large tapestries fill the halls, dangling from the roof nearly to the floor in shades of gold. Fine, white sand appears to be covering each of them, though it looks like some of it has been swiped away by someone brushing against it, revealing a more brilliant shade of whatever gold it is made out of—perhaps threads of spun gold from the books I once read.

We walk by a throne room, and I peek inside as we brush past the door. The thrones are covered in jewels that sparkle as the sunlight glints off of them, entering through a high window positioned perfectly to bathe them in light. We rush by so quickly that I can't see anything else in the room.

We wind down a set of stairs, and for the first time ever in my life, the stairs I'm encountering are actually *needed*. It's uncomfortable as the men bump down the stairs, jostling me with each step.

"Over there." A man with a sharp nose points down a hallway. "Take her over there."

He points to the right, scribbling on a piece of paper in his hand.

He's separating us.

"Merrick!" I react without thinking it through.

His eyes fly open as he tries to sit up. Merrick reaches for me, his blue hair flopping in his eyes. It's amazing how quickly his hair dried, while *mine* is still mercilessly dripping down my sting-covered back.

"Don't take her," he begs, stretching as far as he can. The men cling to him, refusing to let him reach me.

"Merrick!" I lean toward him, trying to grab his hand.

"Celena!" He struggles against them.

"Please, just let us stay together," I try to negotiate with them. "We'll do as you ask, just let us stay together."

The guards pull us apart. Merrick and I shout to each other as he and Phorcys are taken down the opposite hallway.

"Shut up!" one of the guards orders, lifting a hand as though he might strike me.

I cower, letting them think I'm more scared than I am—much like Tarni spent her entire life doing until her cousin became king and she came out of hiding. The humans don't need to know I'm capable of killing them *before I actually do it.*

Little things stick out of their ears, blocking the sound of my siren song—not that I'm attempting to siren them right now. It looks like maybe they used pieces of rolled up fabric to block me out, but I can't be sure.

I'm close enough that I could reach up and pull whatever it is out of two of the guards' ears. I could siren them quickly enough to disrupt their plan, but at least two would be impervious to my song, and retribution would be swift.

They carry me down another set of steps and around a wall that doesn't reach the ceiling of the room. When we round the corner, an oval-shaped wall sits in the middle of the room with water in it.

I'm dropped into water that's barely big enough for me to do a flip in. I could sit on the bottom and be fully submerged, but this contraption is designed to keep me where they can get to me. If a human were to crawl in, they could stand and their heads would easily be above the surface.

The water is still—I've never seen the surface of any water so calm in my life. It ripples when I move or when the men tap on it to get my attention. They leer at me as I assess my situation.

"Like your new home, pretty?" one of them asks.

"Do not taunt the siren, you fool," a man who has clearly worked for the king his whole life addresses the grubby sailor. His voice is more proper than the sailor's, as is his ensemble.

I look at him, pleading with my face, afraid that if I open my mouth, he'll take it as an attack and hurt me.

He wrinkles his nose in disgust and backs away. Motioning for the others to follow, they leave the room. I'm alone.

I try to climb over the wall, but there's nowhere for me to go. The floor is massive. By the time I crawl to the stairs where the men brought me in, I'll be discovered—or dead from the exhaustion of dragging myself across the stone. Even if I made it to the stairs, I'd have to climb up them.

There is no escape from this room.

I dart around the water, checking every angle and side. When I find nothing useful above the water, I lower myself under—*unable to dive*—and search the walls for an escape, hidden message, or anything that can help me. Finding nothing, I return to the surface.

This room is different than the others. The walls are a bright white color but hold no opalescent shine to them. The floor looks like smooth rocks have been positioned to create intricate designs, though the entire floor is a solid white, sculpted only by the shape of the flat stones. It swirls around the room.

A window sits high above me, nearly reaching the ceiling. I can see bits of the pink sky as it fades into night, but the ocean is out of my sight. Soon the stars will be out—I might even be able to catch a glimpse of the moon one last time before my death.

The water bounces off the walls of my prison as I swim around in circles, trying to learn my limited surroundings. I grow to hate that sound.

The color fades from the sky, pulling all references to its hue from the room as it goes. The room grows dark until the moon appears, casting a pale glow through the opening. The light from the window bounces off the water of my prison and reflects on the ceiling and walls. It dances in eerie lines, shattering and moving as it consistently changes.

I breathe out, trying to slow my heart rate. Leaning against the wall, I wait for one of my captors to come fish me out of this place. Every so often, I dip under the water, cooling my skin and hair. I refuse to stay under long though—I don't want them sneaking up on me.

The toll of the last few days weighs heavily on me. I still haven't recovered from most of the trauma I've been through—the jellyfish stings, the beatings, the fights, even the brine pool—but as I'm forced to be still in the water, it all comes crashing down on me. My muscles scream, and I feel like bending in on myself to try to stop the agony. The welts on my back from the stings burn, even though they shouldn't at this point. My cuts pierce into my skin, a constant reminder of the war I was just ripped out of against my will.

I hurt, and I can't help myself to feel better.

Spreading my arms out over the top of the wall, I try to keep myself upright out of the water as I face the steps. I watch, waiting for them.

Eventually, exhaustion wins out, and I slip beneath the surface and curl up on the floor of the mini ocean as the moonlight dances over me.

I wake with a start. My eyes dart around the tiny space, checking the walls and surface above me before I lift myself out of the water. The room is still empty, but the moon is gone, replaced by the very first rays of morning.

The sun is still too low in the sky to be seen, but its pale reach graces the room. Not too much longer and the sunrise should appear, and I imagine, the room will be cast into many colors again.

"Well, well, look who is up."

I start at the voice, whipping around to face the steps as a figure rounds the corner. Last night I could hear men walking on the steps, but I was so focused on the window that I let my guard down, and he snuck up on me.

A second man follows the prince, much like he did yesterday on the boat. His ears are blocked once again, prepared to rescue the prince if he needs it. He scowls at me over the prince's shoulder.

I stay on the far side of the water—if he wants to reach me, he'll have to jump into the water or walk around to the other side, giving me time to change my location. I stay quiet as I watch him.

"If you try to siren me or any of my men, I will have them separate you from your tail, and no questions will be asked." He levels a cool gaze at me. "I haven't talked to your friends yet, but they're next, so don't make me angry."

He walks around the length of the wall, examining me. His servant follows along behind him. The prince pauses back where he started, leaning forward to rest his arms on the wall at an awkward angle as he leans toward the water.

"Who are you?"

"I am Celena, great-great-granddaughter of Princess Aila, daughter of King Gaspar."

"You're royalty?"

"Distantly, yes."

"So you don't rule the ocean?" One finger taps on the side of the wall as he tries to glean information.

"No, my cousins do."

"Why were you sirening my people?" He blinks through his sandy brown hair, dark eyes snapping at me.

"There is a war under the sea between sirens and mer—"

"You're all sirens," he snaps.

"What?" I ask after a moment, taken back by his outburst.

"There is no difference."

"We all have the ability to siren, yes, but some choose not to use it unless we have to—that's why we had the treaty."

"You broke the treaty."

The light shifts in the room as the sun starts to come up, tingeing everything yellow. The prince doesn't seem to notice.

"The treaty was broken." I nod my head in agreement. "But not by my grandmother. She tried to prevent that from happening."

"The mermaids tried to kill my great-great-grandfather."

"*Not* Aila. She and Jarek were friends," I insist.

"Do *not* speak the king's name," the prince growls at me.

"The royals from both of our kingdoms were once united in friendship. The king and my grandmother were friends, and when her cousin tried to hurt him, she saved him. She told us all about him—"

"What did she tell you?"

He looks angry, so it puzzles me that he's still talking to me. The prince watches me like I might leap across the water at any moment and attack him, but also like I'm a riddle to figure out.

"She told our family many stories that have been passed through the generations about how she, Persephone, and your grandfather used to sit on the steps outside and watch the waves together. He would pet their hair, and they'd tell him about life under the sea.

"Aila told us about the chandelier in the palace window that she always longed to see. She told us about Prince Jar—about the prince's mother, and how she was always looking out for him.

"She also told us *in great detail* about the destruction of the treaty, and what Persephone and her mother, Chantay, did to ensure there was a division between us."

He purses his lips, taking in the information, but doesn't look convinced.

"Aila said after she discovered that Persephone and the prince were together, she found them in a cave where Persephone was attempting to siren the prince. She convinced him to dive into the water, and Aila saved him from drowning.

"Your Highness," I begin. "After the human-mer treaty was dissolved, the mer split as well. Those that wanted to hurt you were banished, and the rest of us tried to avoid the humans' wrath. We moved far away from our home and never left our borders until now."

"And just why did you leave, *mermaid*?"

"The sirens—those that wanted to hurt you—also wanted to hurt us because of Chantay's banishment and Persephone's imprisonment. They've waited a century for revenge, and this was their last opportunity."

"Why is that?" The prince leans back, standing on his own.

The prince is looking for information, and I'll gladly give it to him. If I can be helpful, perhaps he will listen. If nothing else, I need to position myself to not seem like a threat to him and his people.

"The last of Chantay's line died without a female heir. Her son and husband were fulfilling her wishes to make both the humans and mer pay."

"That explains why *they* were here. Why were *you* here?"

This prince is nothing like what Aila told us Jarek was like in her stories. That boy was weak and passive—a dreamer. The prince before me looks like he will kill first and ask questions later.

His face has some similarities to Jarek's, but his hair and eyes are different. The prince's chin, cheekbones, and nose are close enough that I feel comfortable believing this is one of Jarek's descendants.

"They attacked us first," I explain, brushing back my hair as it floats in the water in front of me. "They tried to take over our palace and lost. They kidnapped my sister, and when I tried to save her, they took me too. My collection came after us to save us, but when we arrived, the rest of the siren collection was on their way, intent on using us to hurt the humans."

"I thought you said you didn't siren." His eyes narrow at me like I'm lying.

"The mer collection doesn't, but we still have the ability to. Most of our collection has lost it because it hasn't been used in a century, but those of royal blood have more powerful voices."

"And their royals are dead, so they wanted *yours*…" he murmurs.

He turns, starting to walk away, his servant rushing to keep up.

"Wait!" I call. Realizing I shouldn't have, I sink back against the wall, waiting to suffer for it.

The prince flinches but slowly turns.

"You're leaving?" I ask in a small voice, hoping to convince him that I'm not a threat.

He raises an eyebrow, turning again to walk out.

"What's going to happen to us?" I call, braver.

"Answer my questions and we'll see," he calls over his shoulder. His words echo around the room, setting my teeth on edge. The only time I've ever heard an echo was on the surface, and I don't like it. Even so, I can't let him walk away yet.

"Where are my friends?"

"They're in their own little pools," the prince answers.

My prison has a name.

"I need to know they're okay," I call. "Please!"

"They're fine…for now. We'll see how they cooperate." He turns to glance at me as he mounts the stairs. "If you behave, you'll live—for now. If you don't, we can make things very difficult here until we get the information we need and then we'll split you in half. Remember that, Celena."

"*Princess*," I snap.

"What was that?" He takes a step back off the stairs.

"*Princess* Celena," I correct him.

He appraises me, considering my words.

"Very well, *Princess* Celena."

The prince nods before ascending the stairs once more.

"We'll see how long you last."

Their footsteps fall heavy as they finish climbing the long stairs, turning once they reach the landing, and exit the room as an overwhelming feeling of dread washes over my body. I sink back into the water, waiting.

CHAPTER 2

An hour passes, and still no one returns to the room. The sunlight changes again, making the room bright. The light bounces off every surface—I'm sure by noon, I'll be blind.

Swimming in the tiny pool is infuriating. All I can do is move in small circles. Eventually, I duck under the water and swim laps back and forth, touching one side, then the other, as I try to think of something I can tell the prince to gain his trust.

Merrick and Phorcys are somewhere in this palace, but I have no way of reaching them. If I can convince the prince to put us together, at least maybe we can help each other cope—though I doubt we'll all fit in one of these tiny pools.

By the time the light starts to fade, I've devolved into thinking about my collection out in the sea. I don't know if my father survived being struck in the face by that sailor. I'm sure Caspian got Coralie to safety, but that still doesn't account for where my mother is. I know Casp and Llyr saw us being taken away—I'm sure they're working on a plan now—but who knows which of the mer survived and which didn't.

At least I'll never have to see Tarni, Murdoch, or Cassidia again.

The pool is decidedly empty, and I wish there were some seahorses swimming around or clinging to seaweed. My stomach makes a noise, reminding me I haven't eaten since early the day before. I wonder if they plan on feeding us here or if we'll wither away from starvation and the stress of whatever questioning they put us through.

"You're a lucky mermaid," the prince says, waltzing into the room behind the wall, feet tapping against the stairs. "Your lover sent you dinner."

He rounds the corner, coming into view. His servant carries a small tray. Once they reach the pool, he hands it off to the prince who looks like he's deciding between throwing it at me or setting it on the side of the wall.

Cautiously, he places it down on the side of the pool and steps back so I can swim over. The silver tray holds three oysters. Next to it sits a dull piece of metal that I suppose I'm meant to use to open the shellfish with.

I reach out cautiously, taking one in my hand. It's difficult to open it, but I don't stop trying.

"He refused to eat them—he sent them to you instead."

I look up at the prince, registering his words—Merrick sent me his meal, which means he hasn't eaten either today.

"Take them back to him," I reply. "He needs to eat."

"He won't take them back." He tips his head, studying me.

"Take one of them back," I respond. "I'll eat the other two. Just don't let him starve."

I hurry to open one of the oysters—a sign of good faith. Inside sits a small pearl, and I can feel the tears burning behind my eyes. I drop it quickly into the water, covering my movement, and eat the oyster.

The prince and his servant watch me as I eat, making faces at my lack of human social graces. I don't have the time—or desire—to care.

"Take this last one back to him."

"We can try again tomorrow with him, but if you don't eat this, *Princess* Celena, it will be thrown back into the sea—your friend had his chance."

I purse my lips, but open up the oyster—it's better for me not to waste an opportunity to gain a little extra strength, than to have both of us suffer for not eating it. I'll lecture Merrick later—if I ever get the chance.

"Now, I suppose we should talk." He tips his head at me again. I've never seen anyone do that so much. "If you're not the princess in charge, then where is she?"

"In the sea somewhere." I blink as I reply. "I would guess they're on their way back to our home kingdom or traveling far beyond that."

"They're not waiting for you?" One side of his lips tick up as he unconsciously snarls—it's not aggressive, but more like he's disgusted.

"They know better than that."

"Oh?"

"Her job is to keep the collection safe—they aren't safe here."

"Do you know how many mermaid bodies we dragged to shore?" He pauses, waiting for me to answer. When I don't, he continues. "We easily dragged fifty corpses out of the ocean on our boats—even more sank, I assume. How do you feel about your group's survival now?"

We lost well over two hundred, but I don't tell him that. All those lives just to save Coralie and me—it wasn't worth it. Coralie's, perhaps, but not mine.

"I think it's wise for them to leave," I reply, waiting for him to lash out.

"I doubt that's going to matter." He sounds almost sad.

"Why is that?"

My tail twitches in the water—I hate being so closed-in. I bump into the side of the pool and have to remind myself not to cringe.

"It doesn't matter." He shakes his head. "Tell me more about the princess."

"I still don't know your name," I say in an attempt to throw him off.

"My name isn't important," he counters.

"Oh? I thought you were a prince. Aren't you important by nature?"

He perks up, my sarcasm catching his interest.

"Tell me about your princess, and I'll consider it."

"Do you want to know about the princess or the queen?"

The prince's eyebrow shoots up, and he squints slightly.

"You have a queen?"

"When your father dies, will you remain a prince or will you become king?" I point out. "Of course we have a queen."

"Fine, tell me about the queen."

"She's lovely. She takes very good care of us. She's protected us for many years."

"What is your queen's name?"

"Almeta," I lie, giving him my mother's name. I won't have him searching out Marilla and my mother has trained me well.

For a moment, I panic, wondering if Merrick was asked the same question. If he gave them Marilla's name, any advantage I have will be taken away. Merrick is smart though—smarter than anyone I know—and he would have thought ahead to what I would have said. I trust he gave my mother's name too.

"Your turn," I add.

"I am Prince Edmund." He tips his head as if he's bowing slightly to me. "I am the prince of Antaire and the surrounding kingdoms."

"Nice to meet you, Prince Edmund." I brush back my long hair, revealing more of my face. "When can I leave?"

"You're not leaving, Princess Celena."

"So you're just going hold a royal hostage?" I snip at him, moving back in the water slightly.

"What do you expect us to do, trade you?" He puts his hands on his hips, stepping forward. "We can't exactly negotiate with people that aren't here."

People...because that's *another name for mer.*

"You could always let us go," I suggest, waving my hand in the air. Water drips off the back of my knuckles into the pool.

"That's not an—"

"Edmund," a voice echoes in the room, loud enough to make everyone duck. The king's head appears over the top of the wall protecting the stairs from the rest of the room. He stomps down the steps, rounding the corner as he approaches his son with his servant trailing behind him. "I thought I'd find you in here."

The king stops a few feet away from the prince. His dark hair is a stark contrast to the light room, despite the fading sun from outside. He appraises me as I float in the tank, his gaze making me uncomfortable.

"She is a beauty, isn't she?" he murmurs to his son.

"She's fine," Edmund replies, pursing his lips.

"Have you ever seen such vibrant hair?" The king tips his head like his son does, staring at my mane.

He's obviously never met Dylana—*her* hair is vibrant. Come to think of it, so are Merrick and Llyr's hair colors.

"No, father."

The king looks like he wants to examine me closer, but is afraid to change his proximity to me. I wonder what would happen if I swam forward quickly right now—his servant might accidentally crush his head in from trying to slam whatever those things are into his ears to protect the king from me.

"She might be worth something when this is all over."

I try to keep my face still as he speaks, but horror washes over me like the waves I create in the tiny pool every time I try to swim.

"We're not going to decapitate her, father, don't scare the princess." Edmund gives his father a look.

The king looks to his son for a moment before turning back to me.

"I apologize, I didn't mean to frighten you. We won't hurt you unless you give us a reason to do so."

"And I won't hurt *you* unless *you* give me a reason to," I reply, full of bravado. He cringes slightly at my words. The king's lips tug up in a closed-mouth snarl.

"Come, son. We have things to do."

"But I wasn't finished—"

"Let's go," his father interrupts.

Edmund glances back at me once before following the king toward the stairs. His servant quickly rushes up to the pool, snatching away the tray—good thing, because I would have used it against them had they left it unsupervised.

The group hustles toward the stairs, ducking behind the wall. I hear them murmuring as they leave, but with all of them muttering at once, I can't make out most of what the men say.

I consider dragging myself out of the pool once again, but as with before, I find no merit in the idea. The fall would likely be painful anyway.

Moving to the bottom of the pool, I search for the pearl I dropped into the water. It takes a moment to locate it because it blends into the bottom, but I retrieve it and sink against the wall to examine it.

With everyone gone, the place is quiet...but the water also helps with that.

The pearl has a slight pink tint to it. I'm sure Merrick didn't know it was inside the oysters he sent to me, but it's a nice gift from him all the same. I open up the backside of one of the metal shells on my necklace and pop the pearl inside to keep safe until later when I can show Merrick.

I finally give up and sleep on the bottom of the pool.

"It *is* you," a feminine voice scares me to death when I surface the next morning. I clutch a hand to my chest as I whip around to face the girl —the princess. "My brother said you were here."

She looks at me expectantly.

I stare back at her, but she doesn't say anything as she hovers near the side of the pool. I look around, trying to determine if this is some kind of trap.

"Princess," I regard her quietly.

"I'm Analia," she announces, tossing her dark curls.

I look at her cautiously from the middle of the pool.

"Why are you here?"

"To meet you, of course." She shakes her head as if I'm being foolish. "You're the one that rescued me when those awful men threw me into the sea."

"Okay…" I trail off as if it's a question.

"Your hair is pink." She changes the subject, moving closer.

"Yes," I reply, still leery of her.

"Why is it pink?"

"I've always had pink hair." I blink.

"You were born with pink hair? Do all mermaids have pink hair?" The princess tips her head, but not in the same way her father and brother do.

She's likely only ever seen Dylana and me, and since we both have shades of pink hair, I can understand why she might reach that conclusion.

"No, we have different hair colors. Some have hair like yours."

"Oh." She frowns. "Well, I like your hair."

"Thank you—" My words are cut off as the prince runs down the stairs.

"Analia, get back!" Edmund shouts. He races over to his sister and drags her away, his servant chasing after him as he chastises the young princess. "Do not go near her without one of the servants."

"She won't hurt me, Edmund. She saved me."

"You don't know that, Analia." His voice grows quieter as he tries to be gentler with her. "She's trapped in here, we don't know what she'll do at this point."

"You separated her from her friends, of course she's going to be upset, Edmund." The princess pouts.

I swim to the edge of the pool, resting the edges of my fingers against the wall as I watch the two interact. It's not unlike Caspian and Coralie when she was younger.

"Go back to your room," he instructs. "Father has been looking for you, and you don't want him to catch you down here."

She grumbles before stalking over to the steps and disappearing behind the wall. The prince turns on me.

"If you *ever* touch her—"

"I wouldn't ever hurt her," I cut him off. "She's a child. I didn't even know she was here until I surfaced and she surprised me."

The prince seethes a few lengths away, glaring at me. His face is an odd shade of red, but after a moment, it starts to fade as his shoulders sink back down to their normal height.

"You stay away from her," he threatens again.

"I can't exactly go anywhere." I motion to the walls around me.

"And it's going to stay that way."

"I'm sure," I bite back.

He looks unamused at my willingness to take him on.

"I'm going to protect my sister, no matter what the cost is, *mermaid*. I'm sure you wouldn't understand—"

"How do you think I ended up here?" I snap, crossing my arms. "I have loved ones to protect too. Aren't you lucky I took the time to protect *yours* as well?"

Edmund deflates as I make my point. He takes a deep breath before speaking.

"Thank you for saving my sister," he grumbles.

"You're welcome." I look away as I speak.

"I suppose it's not entirely fair to treat you like this after you saved Analia." He takes a step toward me. "Is there anything I can do to make you more comfortable?"

"Take me to my friend," I reply instantly.

"Is there anything *else* I can do?" he refuses.

"I want to see Merrick."

He sighs, locking his jaw.

"I'll try." His words surprise me. "What can I do in the meantime? Are you hungry?"

"Yes, but I'd rather you make sure Merrick has food."

"He will be seen to." He examines me again—not even Tarni and her sirens watched me this closely. "Do you need a pillow or something to make sleeping more comfortable?"

"I'm fine." I frown, trying to think of something small he can do for me—if I can start by getting him to do little things, it will be easier to convince him to do harder things for me later. "I would like a new net and some seaweed for my *iluse*, please."

"Your what?" His eyes narrow in a question.

"My *iluse*," I respond. "My covering."

"Oh. *Oh.*" He glances down at my chest, noticing how bad my *iluse* looks after all it's been through. "Certainly. I'll have someone bring them to you at once.

"I'll need something to cut it with," I tell him, cringing. "You can have it back as soon as I'm done fixing it though."

"I can't give you a weapon," he looks at me skeptically.

"I can use a broken shell if I can't have a knife. I'll throw it out when I'm done, and you can collect it."

"What if you don't?"

"Then your men will descend on me with spears and harpoons, I would assume," I offer. "I just need to fix my *iluse,* that's all."

He purses his lips but finally nods.

"Fine. I'll get you your things."

"Thank you." I smile softly to show I'm not trying to be a threat. "And I need to know that Merrick has eaten."

"And what exactly should I tell him to get him to do that?" The prince tips his head in annoyance, toppling his bangs over one eye.

"Tell him…" I think for a moment, glancing around the water. "Tell him that it's his turn to swim backward."

Edmund's face scrunches up in confusion.

"What?"

"It doesn't matter, just tell him," I command, waving my hand.

"Fine."

"Thank you. Please tell me once he's eaten." I turn to swim away and dip back under the water, dismissing him and ending the conversation.

"What's wrong with your back?"

"How do you know anything is wrong with it?" I ask coyly. "Perhaps all mer are like this."

"I've seen more than enough of you to know that isn't normal. Besides, my great-great-grandfather painted enough pictures of you mer to know that's not something passed down through the royal line either."

"Jellyfish," I reply.

He assesses me as I lift the hair off my back.

"Jellyfish did that to you?"

"They had overtaken a community, and I was sent in to retrieve the siren king's mother's necklace. I couldn't escape the creatures, so I had to endure the stings."

"Sounds painful," he muses.

"It was." I turn back to him. "It's starting to heal though—it's not as bad as it was."

"It must have been *awful.*" He walks toward me again. I swim back to the wall, leaning my elbows against it.

"It was," I smirk. "Not too long ago, the siren king attacked us in the palace in the old kingdom, and my collection dropped a net full of jellyfish over his head—you should have seen his face after that. I'm sure my back is *nothing* compared to the welts that covered his top half."

Edmund's eyebrows quirk up in surprise as his lips twist into a smile.

"Sounds interesting. What did he do to deserve that?"

"He nearly killed me." I shrug. "Seems that's harder to do than I thought. Good news though—he's dead now, and the sirens have disbanded, so at least you won't have to worry about them coming after you now—you might run into a small individual group now and then, but the collection as a whole is gone."

"Good to know, Princess Celena." He nods. "I'll also remember not to get on your bad side—or at least, not to get on your bad side when you have access to jellyfish—I hear those things are awful."

He turns to walk away, smirking.

"Have you really never been in the ocean?" This time, I'm the one who tips their head. Edmund swings back around to face me.

"The only times I've been on the water were when I rescued Analia, and then again when I fished you out. It's not safe—especially for royals."

"Shame. The water is lovely." I splash just enough to make the waves rock against the side of the pool, slapping into the side of it.

"All the same, I think I'll leave that to you." He grins, eyes sparkling as he turns to leave again. "I'll be back when your boyfriend has been fed."

I watch him go, sauntering back to the steps, his servant scampering behind him.

"I'll send in stuff for your…*covering*," he calls over the wall.

I grin smugly, knowing he forgot the word I used.

It seems I've made a little progress anyway. I should have asked for some seaweed or kelp to hide under though—I didn't think that through well.

After a while, a group of men steps into the room, each carrying something in their outstretched arms. They look wary at they step up to the side of the pool and deposit their offerings on the wall before quickly stepping back.

"You are to throw this on the floor immediately upon finishing. We will be watching from over there," one of the men yells, over-compensating for his inability to hear around whatever is blocking his ears. I nod to let him know I understand.

I swim to the side of the pool, frightening them all. They quickly dart back as I reach out and pull everything toward myself, dropping it in the water.

I duck under the surface, ready to make myself a new *iluse*. I use the broken shell to cut apart the netting the men brought me. Pulling the old netting off, I tuck the new ropes around my chest.

Thinking things through a little better this time, I secure it on so that it shouldn't fall off if I find myself in a fight with the humans. I carefully weave the shells back into place and break off part of the large shell to hide inside my *iluse*—I'll smash it later to cover up that I stole part of it.

I work quickly, knowing I won't be given much time. When I finish, I have an entirely new look—it surprises the men when I surface to return the broken shell.

The net is woven tightly around my chest, with a removable piece wrapped around my neck like a halter. I attempt to look as regal as possible, even fashioning a crown out of several of the shells that had been woven into my hair.

My hair flows free, released from the braid it has been in, framing my face. I tucked the rest of the shells into the design on my *iluse* covering it so much that it nearly looks like one of my pearl bodices from a distance.

On the surface, I hold the large shell used for cutting the net up in my hand, careful to cover most of it so they can't see a piece is missing. The men watch in silent fear, slowly stepping back with unease. I turn, nodding to the ground near the wall, far from where the men stand. Looking back, I toss the shell, aiming for the wall. It hits, shattering as it falls.

Motioning with my hand, I invite the men to pick it up. They poke at each other, volunteering anyone but themselves to walk toward me.

"You won't be harmed," I promise.

They finally force three of the men forward, cowering as they watch near the steps. The men tremble as they approach me.

"Princess Aila didn't hurt Prince Jarek, and I don't intend on hurting you," I murmur as they approach like timid seahorses. They glance up at me as they attempt to scoop up the shell pieces, inadvertently leaving several small shards of shell on the ground before rushing back to their friends.

"I didn't hurt you," I call as the men dart away. I roll my eyes as they scamper off.

Sinking into the water, I fall back into my routine of swimming from end to end of the pool, waiting for the prince to return.

A few hours later, a slap against the water nearly startles me as I move in my limited loop. Edmund pulls his hand out of the water, grinning playfully at me.

I swim to the surface, acting annoyed. Exiting the water with my arms crossed, I raise one eyebrow.

His eyes grow wide when he sees my new ensemble. He roams over me with his gaze, looking at my temporary crown, long, flowing hair, and my fixed up *iluse*. I'm sure the shoulder armor has the same effect it's always had, but my new accessories highlight just how fierce the armor really looks.

"How did you do that?" he gapes.

I smile politely, reaching up to brush back my hair regally.

"We're all skilled at this. We tend to create our own outfits for our festivals," I inform him. "You should see what I could have done if you had given me pearls and a week to work."

Batting my eyelashes seems to wake him up from the trance he's in, and he stands straighter. He opens his mouth to speak and closes it twice before getting any words out.

"Yes, right, well..." he sputters. "Your boyfriend ate."

"He did?" I perk up, swimming to the edge.

"Yes," Edmund confirms. "I brought you food too."

He waves to a man standing by the stairs. He rushes over when beckoned, handing a tray to the prince.

Edmund turns, venturing closer to me.

"You didn't kill my men before, so I brought you more oysters."

That's a lovely thought.

He sets the tray down for me, this time only taking a step back. Instead of a handful, I find the tray well stocked with the shellfish. Surprised, I look up at him.

He says nothing, and after a moment, I reach out for the food. Breaking it open, I eat my breakfast. I suppose at some point I should inquire about Phorcys, but not just yet.

"Would you like one, Price Edmund?" I ask, holding an opened oyster out to him.

He grimaces, panic lighting up his eyes—they're brighter than I thought. The prince shakes his head slightly.

"No, thanks."

I pull the oyster back toward myself, unsure of how to proceed.

"They're for you," he tries to recover. "And we don't really eat them raw up here."

"What do you do to them?" My eyes are wider than I intend for them to be.

"We steam them or roast them first."

"Roast?" That's a new term to me.

"Cook them over a fire," he explains.

"That sounds…awful," I reply before I can stop myself. Nothing I've read about fire sounds like it's a good thing.

"It's better than it sounds," he smirks. "Finish eating."

"Prince Edmund?"

"Yes, Princess Celena?" he repeats after me.

"Where is Phorcys?"

"Oh. You mean the one who *doesn't* care." He gives me a look. "I'm assuming he's one of the sirens you've been talking about? He doesn't seem to care about the two of you very much."

"He has no reason to—we killed his king."

"*You* killed him?"

"We were defending ourselves—we didn't mean to—but yes."

I set an oyster shell down on the tray and pick up another as the conversation continues.

"I suppose you're also the one who gave him that nasty wound—or was that us?"

"Most of it was us, some of it was you. Are you sure you don't want to try one of these?"

"I'm positive." He gives me a curt smile and nods. "Why do you ask about him?"

"I'd like to know that you haven't cut him into bits or ripped any of his scales off."

"Why? Is that *your* job?" He looks at me with all the seriousness in the world.

"I've never hurt another mer or siren for any reason other than self-defense. Prying off scales is hardly something I'd tolerate."

"Looks like *you're* missing a few," the prince comments, waving to the water hiding my tail.

"The siren king and princess might have taken a few for fun," I answer, setting the next oyster shell down harder than I mean to.

"Sounds like living under the sea isn't as easy as one would think."

"Not in the least," I agree.

"I have a question," the prince steps dangerously close to me, upsetting his servant.

"Okay." I set the next oyster down before I can struggle to pry it open, waiting to see what the human prince has to say.

"Do mermaids really have the power to let humans breathe under water?

"You're asking if Persephone lied to Jarek." I pause for a moment. "No, as far as I know, there's no way for humans to breathe underwater. We all believe Persephone really was in love with Jarek, and at first, she believed her love could allow him to join her in the sea.

"After her mother, Chantay, got involved, it became more about revenge for how Jarek's mother shackled Persephone. Chantay instigated the war, not necessarily *Persephone*, though she certainly had a hand in it. I don't believe she intentionally lied to him, I just think she made a stupid choice."

Edmund nods, considering my words.

"I have to go. I'll be back. Perhaps pay attention this time." He throws a look over his shoulder as he strides across the room.

I have a feeling I'm not going to like whatever happens when the prince returns.

CHAPTER 3

When I wake the next morning, I find Analia sitting on the steps, a servant standing behind her. The princess has her head propped in her hands, elbows resting on her legs hidden under a long dress. The bottom of her gown cascades around her ankles, flipping out to the sides.

Her dark hair is still curled—something we don't see under the ocean—and it mesmerizes me even from afar. Her face brightens when she notices me over the pool wall.

"You're awake," she yelps, rushing to her feet so quickly, I'm not sure how she doesn't topple over.

The princess looks back at the man standing behind her. He gives her a reluctant nod, and she rushes toward me. If anyone else had run at me like she is, I'd be terrified, but somehow her exuberance is reassuring.

"Good morning, Princess."

"You can call me Analia." She stops short in front of me, reminding me of a dark version of Coralie. "What's your name?"

"I'm Celena."

She eyes me, narrowing her features momentarily.

"Edmund says you're a princess. Is that true?"

"I am." I nod as she notices my crown and change in appearance.

"Where did you get that? You didn't have it yesterday."

"Your brother gave me some supplies to fix my *iluse* with." I point to my covering so that I don't have to endure any more questions on it. "I made it."

"You made a crown?" she asks skeptically. I nod in reply. "I can't even make myself breakfast, much less anything to wear."

She crosses her arms, turning to spin slightly as she sulks.

"Making a crown isn't hard," I inform her, reaching up to take mine off. "Here, look."

I point out what I did to string the shells together, weaving the extra netting into a tieback with bits of seaweed. If I had access to more from the sea, the crown would have been magnificent—but simple, elegant beauty will have to suffice for now.

"If I get my own, would you show me how?" she asks, pointing to my crown.

"If you wish." I smile at her.

"What's all this?" Edmund strolls into the room, arms fastened behind his back. He smiles at his sister. "I believe I told you not to come in here."

"She's not going to hurt me, Edmund." She grins back at him.

"She'd best not," he replies. "Now run along, Ana. I have things to attend to, and you don't need to be here for them."

That thought frightens me. I feel safer when the princess is here— I suspect her father and brother won't harm me in her presence.

"Analia?" the king questions as he walks into the room.

"She was just leaving, Father," Edmund quickly says. He gently pushes his sister into motion. She stumbles toward the stairs, barely missing her father as she hurries.

"Sorry," she mumbles.

"Run along now, Analia." He smiles carefully at her as she passes him. The king turns back toward me once he's sure his daughter is gone.

"Hello." I'm not sure what to make of his greeting.

"Your Highness," I acknowledge him.

"My son says you've been cooperative."

The water around me suddenly feels cooler. My instincts tell me to dive deep under the surface, but with barely a length and a half between the surface and the floor, I have nowhere to hide.

"I'm willing to try something if you're willing to continue to cooperate," the king continues. "If you *don't* behave, you'll regret it."

"What is it that you want to try?" I ask cautiously. My fingers quietly move toward my *iluse* in case I need one of the broken shell pieces.

"We'll get back to that. First, I have a few questions." He holds back from approaching the side of the pool, hands clasped behind his back. The king stretches his feet apart, locking his knees in place. "What do you know about the human world?"

"Only what Princess Aila and King Gaspar passed down, and now what I've learned since being dragged into your palace."

"Surely your collection has learned a thing or two over the years," he muses, releasing a hand to gesture. The strange way he emphasizes the word *collection* leads me to believe that he's been studying us enough to know our terminology. It seems as though Jarek passed on quite a bit of information about us over the years—from drawings to terminology.

"My collection left Metten a century ago. We live far away now and only ended up back here because of the sirens. The mer haven't had any contact with the humans since the queen decided to end the treaty with King Gaspar. Even the books I've found from shipwrecks haven't told me anything that Aila's generation didn't pass down."

He looks skeptically at me, frowning slightly.

"Where did your collection move to?"

"Deeper into the ocean," I respond, unwilling to give him a location.

"Yes, but where?"

"Come now, your highness, you don't honestly believe I would put my collection at risk, do you? They're far, far away from here where you'll never find them, and they won't bother you. That's all you need to know." I tip my head, mimicking the humans. "I'd happily tell you where the *sirens* are at this point, but most of them are dead, and the rest decided to flee before you dragged me up here."

"Are you uncomfortable here?" the king questions.

"Of course. If I confined you to a tiny cell with locked doors, wouldn't you be uncomfortable?"

"You have water, what more do you need?"

"Even Persephone was given more space than this when King Gaspar locked her in a cell to wither away." I tip my chin up in defiance.

"The king locked up Persephone?" Edmund sounds shocked.

"After we left Metten, Persephone was captured when she tried to murder Aila for ruining her plans. Chantay escaped and formed the sirens, which is why we've been having all of these problems."

"They locked up Persephone?" Edmund mutters again.

"I admit, I didn't think they would have done that," the king responds in a hushed tone, turning toward his son as if I couldn't hear them.

"Persephone was given her chance. She listened to her mother instead of my great-great-grandmother, Aila. She paid the price."

"How long was she held captive?" the king continues to question.

"She didn't last long—a few years. She died very early—some say of a broken heart over losing Prince Jarek, some say it was being separated from her mother. I think she just gave up trying to escape and withered away in that cell—Aila never told us about Persephone's time in the cells though, so it's all speculation. Only the immediate royal family was allowed to see her after she was locked up."

"What did they do when she died?"

I don't like answering the king's questions, but I need to figure out how to get along with these people in hopes that they'll be reasonable about letting me go.

The light shifts, dancing on the ground near the king and prince. Bits of dust sparkle in the air much like the debris floating in the water of the kelp forests in the ocean—it's a familiar—yet wholly new—sight.

"They buried her with the rest of the royals in the crypts—she was still a princess, after all."

"And who are *you* to the royal family?"

"I'm of Aila's blood. My cousin is the reigning queen of…the sea." I almost slipped and said Scylla. "I'm regarded as royal, but I do not live in the palace. We would have to work our way down a very long list of mer before I even came *close* to being in power."

"But you have negotiating power?"

Edmund flinches slightly at his father's words—so little so, that I barely notice. It takes me a moment to register what I saw. He turns to watch his father, covering up the movement.

"I suppose. Are you looking to negotiate something?" I respond.

"Not yet," he replies coolly. "I see you've changed your ensemble…"

"Yes. Your men have been very gracious."

I swim to the wall, placing my hands on the sides to show I mean them no harm—yet. It's almost a shame that I can't siren them over quickly and cut off a finger or two just for good measure.

"Is there anything else you require, princess?"

Both the king and prince have displayed a level of decorum I didn't expect from the humans, especially after how they've been treating me. Despite being a hostage, they seem to acknowledge that I'm a princess—I wonder if they're treating Merrick and Phorcys the same way.

"I would like to speak to my mermen," I inform him.

"And just how do you expect me to make that happen?"

"Bring me to them…or bring them to me. I don't care, just make it happen."

"What about a conch shell, father?" Edmund asks. My eyes dart over to him. "We could listen to her speak and then deliver it—that way, we'd know what was being said, but she'd still have the assurance that her friends are alive."

Friend, singular. Phorcys is *not* my friend.

"I can accept that," I quickly say before the king can argue.

Unable to argue in front of me, he sighs.

"I'll consider it." He takes a step away from the pool. "I have things to see to. I'll be back."

Once he's gone, Edmund turns back to me, his servant still hovering behind him—it's a different man today—this one looks a little braver and closer to the prince's age.

"Just remember who did that for you when the time comes," Edmund says, brushing back his hair.

"Let's see if it actually happens," I remind him.

He smirks at me. His entire face lights up like the mid-afternoon sun beaming down through the ocean waves, illuminating the entire ocean floor in rays of dancing light.

"That's a good point—he didn't actually promise anything. But *I* did, and I always keep my word."

"You'd go against your father's wishes?"

He takes a step toward me.

"Unless it was dangerous, I don't see the harm in keeping promises, even if they're a little inconvenient."

"Interesting," I murmur, watching him move closer.

"What is?" he asks, stepping forward again—his servant looks nervous.

"I thought humans always had to follow the rules."

His expression changes slightly, sensing my challenge.

"Isn't keeping promises part of the rules?"

We stare each other down for a moment, waiting to see who will bring up broken promises first.

"Well, I suppose neither of us is very good at following the rules then, are we?" I flip my hair over my shoulder casually as one side of his lips quirk up.

"And just how do you break the rules, Celena?" I noticed that he didn't use my title.

"If I had followed the rules, Edmund, do you really think I'd be in this position?" I tease. Perhaps I could persuade him to be friends.

"Well," he replies. "I know if *I* had followed the rules, you wouldn't be."

My face goes slack before I can stop it.

"What do you mean?"

"I wasn't supposed to go in the water after all of you, but I did it anyway. I thought if I could stop you from singing, I could end the bloodshed. Father ordered me not to, but I got in the boat anyway, and here we are."

"Did you intend on capturing me?" I ask after a tense moment.

"Truthfully?" Edmund hedges for a moment. "No. I had planned on killing you, but to be fair, I didn't know it was you. When I recognized you, I watched to see what you would do, and then I pulled you up."

Great, so murdering mermaids isn't a scruple for him.

"Don't look at me like that, *Princess*," he adds. "You would have killed me too to protect your family."

He makes a valid point.

"In fact, I believe I witnessed some of that," he reminds me, shrugging.

"Perhaps if we stopped killing each other, we could work out another treaty," I suggest.

"I doubt we'll ever trust your kind again, Celena... It's a nice idea though." He turns as footsteps approach. "Analia!"

"I saw Father leave. I just wanted to see Celena," she chatters, rushing across the floor. She grins at me as she approaches.

"How old are you, Analia?" I ask. The prince frowns.

"I'm eleven," she replies, tossing her curls again.

"That's a good age." I smile back at her. "I have a sister not much older than you."

"So *that's* who that was," Edmund mumbles to himself, realizing the only reason I killed that sailor a few days ago was to save Coralie.

"Tell me what the ocean is like," Analia begs, twisting her dress around in her hands.

"What do you want to know?" I ask, hoping that if I befriend the girl, her brother will consider working with me.

"Everything." She looks at me as if I'm the most amazing thing in the world. I chuckle.

"Maybe you could be a little more specific, and then we can work up to *everything*."

"What is it like to swim?"

"You've never been swimming before?" I shouldn't be as shocked as I am considering the humans haven't been in the ocean for a century, but I had assumed they had access to smaller bodies of water that didn't connect to the sea.

She shakes her head.

"Yes, you have," Edmund corrects her, rolling his eyes. "You just haven't been in the *ocean*—aside from being thrown in, and that hardly counts."

"That doesn't count," I agree. "The ocean is magnificent. Everything is alive and full of color. There are currents and different temperatures. The sea creatures are amazing."

"What sea creatures?" Her eyes sparkle as she asks.

"Starfish and seahorses. There are stingrays too—my cousin feeds them every morning and evening. The dolphins are brilliant."

"You've seen the dolphins?" she gasps.

"Seen them? Why, they're some of my very best friends. They give me rides all the time when I need to get somewhere quickly." I try to capture her imagination with my words and create an image for her.

"They're so beautiful. I've only seen them in books and *once* since we arrived at the palace, but I want one as a pet."

"Oh, I don't think you'd have anywhere to keep one in the palace." I wink at her. "But if you wave to them from your window, they might chatter back at you."

"Will you teach me how to make a crown?" she asks suddenly, changing the direction of the conversation as quickly as Llyr does backflips in the water.

"Yes, of course."

"Edmund, could you go get me some shells and whatever else that is?"

"Not now, Analia." He pats her on the head, unwilling to leave her alone with me.

"Here," I say, swimming back from the edge of the wall.

I reach below my *iluse* where I have the extra netting hanging and quickly cut off a strip below the wall where they can't see me—I hope they believe I ripped it. I untangle three small shells from my covering and then set them and the netting on the edge of the wall.

Edmund reaches around his sister, putting a hand on her elbow in case he needs to protect her. The prince studies my offering for a moment before reaching out to take it off the wall.

Deciding it's safe, he passes it off to his sister. She tries to suppress her grin when he hands it to her, but she can't.

I quietly explain what she needs to do in order to fashion it into a makeshift crown. Once she has it twisted properly, she tries to work the shells in, but her fingers can't manage to get them balanced properly, and they topple out each time she tries to put it on her head.

"Here's an idea," I interrupt her frustration. She glances up at me. "Hand the shells to your brother."

I wait as she reluctantly gives them over to Edmund. He holds his hand out gently as she places the broken shells in his palm.

"Now, tie the net around your head with the tie in the back—just be careful not to catch your hair in it—that hurts."

The girl fumbles with the ties, flinching as she catches her locks in the net. I wince with her each time, knowing the pain of tying my hair into a tieback knot.

Edmund eventually sighs, setting the shells on the side of the pool and spins his sister around to face away from him. Taking the tieback from her, he grapples with it as he attempts to tie it for her. It takes a bit, but he manages to fasten it around her head securely enough that it stays in place.

"Now, just tuck the shells in," I direct as the girl turns to face her brother.

Edmund reaches over to the wall of the pool and picks up one of the broken shells. He's careful to face the sharp side away from her skin as he tucks the shell between the net and her forehead. When he's finished, the crown doesn't look terrible.

"Just like a mermaid." I smile at her, and she beams.

"Will you sketch me like this, Edmund?"

His face dips down, but he nods.

"We can't let Father find out."

She nods furiously, nearly knocking a shell out of her crown. Edmund tries not to smirk.

"You should take that off before he comes in here and finds you like that, Analia."

The young princess sighs, reaching up to remove her new toy. She cradles it tenderly in her hands, folding it in on itself to conceal it. Miraculously, Edmund tucked the shells in enough that they didn't fall out when she removed it.

"Why don't you take that up to your room?" Edmund teases, waving his hand toward the stairs.

She considers his words, finally giving in to his wishes in order to protect her new plaything. Analia turns back to wave goodbye before ascending the stairs. Edmund waits until she's gone before speaking.

"She was terrified of you until we brought you in here. Now, you're some magical creature she can't get enough of."

"I'm hardly magical," I reply, though I wish I were—I'd use it to escape.

"I appreciate you playing along with her."

"She seems sweet." I offer him a small smile. "She reminds me of *my* sister."

I emphasize the thought again, hoping to reinforce the idea that he shouldn't harm me because I have a family too. I see the spark in his eyes as he catches on to what I'm doing, but I don't have time to react.

Loud footsteps fall on the stairs, crashing into the room hurriedly. The guards rush around the corner, coming quickly toward the pool.

"What's happening?" I ask Edmund as I quickly swim back.

The men close in on me, a few holding weapons, others holding a net.

"Edmund?" My voice is high-pitched and terrified as the guards run at me.

"I don't know," he replies as the men cut him off from me.

"Edmund!" I shriek, knowing either he will save me, or I'll have to fight the men off myself without being able to siren them—their ears are covered.

The large net covers the top of the pool, closing me in. The ends are tied to spears that they shove in the water, and the men drag the net under me, scooping me out of the pool viciously as I scream.

CHAPTER 4

I struggle against the net as it drags along the bottom of the pool. The spears against the rough rock create a horrific noise in the water, though I don't have time to focus on it as I thrash in the water, trying to free myself.

In truth, it doesn't matter if I struggle—they have complete control of the situation. My reaction is merely an instinct—the very core of me fighting to survive against that which I know is wrong. I will fail in every way, and this struggle is simply so I can console myself with the fact that I tried later on when it's all over.

"Enough!" Edmund shouts, trying to quiet the men as they attempt to haul me out of the water. I restrain myself from whimpering as they crunch my body into itself.

"Sorry, sire," one of the guards addresses him when he finally catches their attention. "You'll have to see your father about this."

Edmund storms off, face red. His hands are balled into fists at his side as he stomps through the room.

"Come on now, girly," the guard snaps once the prince is gone.

The men start off toward the stairs, carrying me between them as if they're afraid I have a disease that they'll catch if they touch me— they probably assume I'll kill them if I can reach them. I glance down at the shells on my *iluse* and consider it.

It's less jarring going back up the steps to exit the room as I swing from inside the net. Logically, I suppose it makes sense that it would be more bumpy when I was riding on the arms of men standing on different levels of steps than it is now as I'm balanced in a swinging net.

The guards carry me out of the room, and a tightness creeps into my chest—I don't think I'll be seeing this room again. The light dances through the window for me one last time, sparkling against the crisp white walls and floor.

The hallway is much cooler than the poolroom where I had been kept. The tapestries appear to have been cleaned off since my arrival.

We travel through several halls, turning around several corners until we step through a doorway. I try to study my surroundings like my mother trained me to do, but it won't ever help me—there's no way I'll be able to drag myself this far, even if I do escape from wherever they are taking me.

This new room is different than the rest of the palace. The noise echoes different, twisting and turning off the sides of the room. When we walk around the giant wall, I discover it's a larger version of the room I just left, though this one isn't as spotless. The white walls have been replaced with rock walls, though flat and not like the inside of a cave. Their tan color reminds me of the ocean floor in crystal light.

A huge pool sits in the middle of the room, taking up the majority of the floor. The water laps quietly against the edge of the slightly-raised wall.

The men weave their way around a set of shorter walls, designed to be like the grooves of brain coral—a maze. Walking up to the water, the men fidget as they attempt to change my positioning.

Without any ceremony, they lift the spears from their shoulders where they were supporting me and throw the net toward the water. I tumble away from them, crashing hard into the surface of the water.

Splashing around, I try to free myself from the netting that miraculously slid off the spears without dragging the weapons into the water with me, which is a shame—I would have liked to have used them.

When I finally free myself and surface to see where the guards are, I find them backing away quickly from the pool. They stumble over the walls on the floor, tripping into each other as they hurry to leave the room.

Silence washes over me as the men escape, leaving me with waves of fear pulsing against the inside of my chest just like the water against the side of the pool.

It wouldn't be hard for me to climb out, though, by the time I navigate the maze, I'm sure I would be caught. The floor appears to be raised at different levels, almost like seats or long benches that people could sit on—perhaps they mean for people to stare at me in the pool.

I need to know what I'm facing, so I dive under the water. Miraculously, the pool is deep enough that I can do so. Under the surface, I discover that the pool is luxuriously deep compared to the tiny pool I was just in. The walls below are like those of a cave, the rock jutting out sharply before pulling back in.

In the bottom corner, a light glows. No, not a light—an opening.

Swimming to the bottom as quickly as I can, I realize I'm in a pool attached to the sea, and that bright spot is an exit. I dart toward it, desperate to find help on the outside of the palace.

The palace itself sits on a rocky cliff, only the steps at the bottom of the cliff extending into the water actually touch the ocean. If I'm able to see the exit in the distance, this must be an underground tunnel that leads to the sea. The bioluminescent glow on the walls of the tunnel assures me that I'm correct in my assessment. The bars covering the exit promise what I should have known all along—they'll never let me escape.

My fingers close around the metal bars as I test my prison. I imagine this is how Persephone must have felt like once King Gaspar locked her away inside the palace at Scylla.

I can see the outside world, glowing blue in the waters in front of me. The tunnel isn't long—I can see where it opens up into the ocean beyond it—but it's empty, void of mer. A starfish crawls along the seafloor, walking toward me.

At least I'll have a friend, assuming it manages to come all the way into the pool. Fish swim in the tunnel, though most avoid the pool. I stretch my hands out, hoping to entice the creatures to come to me.

In the opening of the tunnel, a stingray glides into the water, changing course almost immediately as it swims back out. I sigh, watching it go. I'm jealous, though I can't begrudge the little creature its freedom.

A slap on the water above gets my attention. I look up and find what appears to be an oar lifting out of the water. It drips onto the surface, leaving little marks like the rain does when it storms out at sea.

"I trust you find this more comfortable." The king offers a restrained smile as I surface a few feet in front of him.

"What is this?"

"This was something King Jarek was having built for your ancestors to visit the palace. Apparently, Princess Aila and that sea witch, Persephone, had wanted to see the palace, and Jarek was working on a surprise for them. Obviously, it was updated immediately once they found out about the sireny." He motions toward the tunnel entrance I just left. "I thought perhaps this would be more accommodating for you, Princess."

"That was thoughtful of you." My words are restrained. I'm still reeling from the way I was just carried in.

"Of course there will have to be a few rules," he adds, waving his hand in the air. "You may swim where you like, but if I call you, you must surface immediately. You will stay in the pool at all times—do not try to leave this room—I have men posted outside the door.

"Oh, and don't get any ideas about trying to pull any nonsense in here. If you go against my wishes, or actively work to hurt any one of my people, I'll skewer you, and won't think twice about it."

He turns on his heels and walks away through the maze of tiny walls no higher than his knees, hands clasped behind his back.

"I have some matters to attend to. You may explore your new home, but I'll be back to speak with you later. If you're lucky, you'll make yourself useful here, and this might be your home for a very long time."

If I don't, he'll kill me. Grand.

Once I'm sure he's gone, I dive back under the water. The bars are too close together to allow me to slide between them—something I'm sure Jarek's mother ordered knowing how tiny Aila and Persephone were. I can fit my arm up to my shoulder through, but my bone structure is to wide to allow me any further, and I know enough not to try to fit my head through the bars.

A tiny octopus rests on the ocean floor, tentacles wrapped around the bars. I pick it up and set it on my wrist, allowing him to wrap around me.

Companionship—even for a few moments—is my saving grace.

The creature sits on my arm, content to let me swim around with him on my wrist. I explore the rest of my prison. Two hours pass as I run my hands over every inch of the walls, looking for hidden doors or anything that might help me.

When I find nothing, I sink to the sand and pick at the shells that have washed in. Discovering a few that might work as weapons, I hide them in the corner where I can easily reach them if I need to.

A slap on the water indicates that my presence is being requested.

I set my new friend on a small ledge on the wall of the pool and return to the surface, making sure my hair is angled so that I won't look *as* ridiculous when I leave the water.

Instead of finding the king staring back at me, I'm greeted by the prince. His expression is timid, as if he doesn't quite know what to say.

"Do you like it better here?"

"I *don't* like how I was *brought* here," I inform him. He cringes.

"I apologize."

"Tell that to the scales I lost." I blink. I'm not sure when I decided to be so bold with the prince, but now that I've started, it won't do me any good to back down.

"At least you have more space here. You can swim around." Edmund shrugs at me.

He moves around to sit on the edge of the wall. All I would have to do is reach up and wrap an arm around him to drag him into the water and drown him—*why is he sitting here?* His servant looks horrified, but then, so do I.

The prince twists around to face me, one knee raised so that his foot dangles as he balances himself on the far side of the wall.

"What are you doing?" I ask, nose wrinkled.

"You're not stupid enough to try to hurt me here, and even if you were, the guards would all follow wherever you take me. They're willing to sacrifice themselves for me, and you're no match for the number of men who would enter this pool and destroy you. I'm safe here, and it's easier for us to talk."

He smiles at his servant, trying to make him more comfortable.

"Sir," the servant shouts, unsure of his own volume with cloth in his hears. "Your father would not be pleased—"

"My father needs information. He doesn't care how I get it." Edmund waves the servant off.

"What does he want?"

The prince turns back to me, looking me over.

"He wants information on your collection. More than that, he wants information on how you siren humans—we need to be able to defend ourselves, and if we can understand how you do it, we can protect ourselves and our people."

"You've already figured out how to block our voices." I nod toward his servant. "Why does anything else matter?"

"We can't always cover our ears, Celena—that's ridiculous. We have to know how to prevent this from happening again." He pauses for a moment, drumming his fingers on his knee. "The alternative is killing every mer in the sea, and I don't think you want that."

As far as I know, there are no secrets to this, but hope makes us believe all sorts of things…and so does fear. They're desperate for answers so they won't stop looking for them, even if they don't exist. No mer would ever be so illogical.

"You and I can either work together on this, or we can do it on our own, and I'm positive that will be far more deadly for your kind." He shrugs. "All I need to know is how this works."

"I have no idea, Edmund. I sing, and you listen, that's all I know."

"But *why?*"

I shake my head, sighing.

"Fine, but we'll have to figure this out soon," he says, not giving up. "One way or the other, we'll figure out how this works and stop it."

I honestly don't know if it's something that can *be stopped.*

This close, I realize how slender his fingers are as they tap against his knee. He has a long nose like Jarek's portrait has. His dark eyes catch the light beautifully as it bounces off the surface of the water.

"I've answered all of your questions. I think it's time you answer some of mine." I wait to gauge his reaction.

"You really think you're in a position to negotiate?" he asks, amused.

"I think your father sent you on a mission, and if you want to return to him with answers, you're going to have to cooperate with me." I hope my bravado works in my favor.

"What do you want to know?" Edmund asks, leaning back slightly.

"You know what happened to the mer since the treaty was broken. What happened to the humans?"

"We left." He rocks forward again, leaning slightly on his knees toward me. "As soon as King Gaspar refused to hand over Persephone, we knew it was war. Jarek was moved inland to a different palace. A generation later, we moved to one of the other castles, and it wasn't until my grandfather took power that we moved closer to the ocean so he could oversee the export business better.

"Our major export is still what we harvest from the sea, and we were having trouble with pirates—and sirens—so we needed to be here to defend our exports. My father was here dealing with the mer, and you know the rest."

I dislike how he still groups us in with the sirens, but I don't correct him this time. I tentatively place the tips of my fingers on the wall far enough away that I couldn't touch him even if I reached out.

"There's not much else to tell. We left, now we're back."

"Do you intend on staying?"

"*I should think not*," he replies, appalled. "We just need to handle this, and then we'll return inland."

"I haven't eaten today," I remind him, abruptly changing the subject.

"I'm aware," he waves a man over from his place by the stairs.

This particular servant seems to look less stressed about being in my presence, but his eyes roam over me longer than I like. I'm sure he's thinking about how much he could get for selling my scales to siren-collecting humans who want a piece of the myth.

Once he steps back, Edmund waits for me to open my food. Instead, I reach around the large pile and scoop it into the water in front of me. The shells hit my tail on the way down—stinging— but I don't let him see that.

He looks shocked at my actions, eyes wide as he shakes his head back and forth a little.

"Why did you do that? Didn't you want them?"

"I'm saving them for later. I thought it was more important to talk."

The last of the bubbles I created subside around my stomach, popping gently against my skin as I lean back on the wall. Crossing my arms, I lower my head, looking up at him like Aila used to look up at Jarek from the palace steps—though *she* was a free mermaid. I want him to feel like he has the power in the situation.

"I would have waited." He almost looks comical as he pouts, though he's very serious.

"Perhaps next time you'll bring your own meal and join me."

"Perhaps," he murmurs in return. "You're an unusual princess, Celena."

"And you're an unusual prince, Edmund," I retort. "I doubt many princes would sit on the wall of a pool next to their enemy without a second thought."

"I told you, you're not going to hurt me."

"You're awfully trusting of that, though you're correct—I don't want to hurt you."

"I noticed you didn't say that you *wouldn't* hurt me." He quirks an eye brow up, giving me a cocky look.

"I noticed you still have me locked up and separated from my friend and the rest of my collection. I *also* noticed the way I was brought in here."

"You've mentioned that," he reminds me.

A starfish crawls on the ocean floor beneath me, catching my eye, but I force my gaze to stay on the prince—something that was easier to do in the tiny pool a few rooms away where there were no distractions.

"I thought you needed to be reminded of it again." I smile, batting my eyelashes. "You realize this entire thing is ridiculous, don't you?"

"If you're going to suggest a treaty again, the answer is still no. We're not going down that path again. We just want our waters clear, and to never see the mer again."

"What if I take them far away? We can go farther than we were. None of them would fight me on it—they want to be away from you far more than you want to be away from us. *We're* not the ones hunting humans as trophies."

To be fair though, the sirens *did* build part of their kingdoms out of the skulls of their enemies, but I don't need to remind him of that.

I'd be more than willing to guide the collection beyond Scylla. I'd even be willing to travel north to Keldori, though I'd genuinely prefer the warmth of Dariah over the cold temperatures of our mer to the north. Ambra came to our aid during the battle with the sirens—I'm sure they'd be willing to take us in until we could rebuild somewhere else.

Based on what I'd seen as Tarni and Phorcys dragged us across the ocean, it might even be easy to find an old siren settlement and trans-form it into a new kingdom for our collection. We'd have to find one that *hasn't* been taken over by jellyfish though.

"You're very optimistic, Celena."

"That's not what they usually say about me," I joke.

"No? What *do* they say?"

"Nothing nice, I'm sure," I reply, making him laugh at me.

"I've heard some rather unpleasant things about myself too, Princess. I suppose not everyone is going to like us."

"Did you feed Merrick today?"

"I told you I would take care of him, and I did. I promise."

"Edmund!"

We both turn as the princess rushes into the room. She flies around the maze as if she's spent her entire life navigating it. Coming to a halt in front of us, she barely refrains from flinging herself at us.

Instead, she gracefully sits on the wall next to her brother, moving her dress as she sits to spread it out.

"Father says she can stay with us," she grins at the prince before turning to me. "You get to stay with us forever, Celena. You can live here forever and be my mermaid."

"She's not a *pet*, Analia—" Edmund gapes at her.

"You keep saying that." She shakes her head. "Do you like your new home? I can decorate it and make it prettier if you want. I might have them put a bed down here so we can spend the night together sometimes, so you don't get lonely—"

"Analia!" Edmund shouts indignantly.

"I don't want her to feel alone, Edmund!" Analia shouts back. "You can stay with us too if you want, but I'm staying with her for the first few nights."

"You will do no such thing," he argues back, putting his hands on his hips. He winces as he moves as if his shoulder hurts.

"I'm not staying here," I announce, making Analia swing toward me.

"Yes, you are. Father said you can be my mermaid. No one else has one. I'm sure my friends will love you."

"You're not showing her off, Analia, and your friends aren't even here," Edmund replies, standing to his feet. "And Father isn't showing her off either. She's a captive, not a show pony. She's here to provide us intelligence, not to be your plaything."

"But she's my friend—she saved me. I want to spend time with her."

"You can, but stop calling her *your mermaid*—she doesn't belong to you. She has her own life. You wouldn't like it if I said you *belonged* to me simply because you're my little sister, would you?"

"No," she grumbles. "But I don't want her to be all alone down here."

"She won't be—it will be fine."

It doesn't surprise me that the king wants to show me off as a status symbol. A dead mermaid is a prize to be shown off, but a living one is a miracle, I'm sure. Sailors don't do well with keeping us alive once their bloodlust kicks in.

"But she *is* alone when we're not here, and Father won't let us stay down here all the time."

"She won't be alone, Analia. It's fine." He looks down at her from where he towers over her.

"How?" the little girl demands.

As if on cue, people enter the room, rushing around the wall. They struggle with someone, but I can't see around the front of the group. The noise is nearly as loud as when we were locked in battle outside the palace walls.

Several people trip, falling over themselves as they struggle against their captive. The king's head appears over the top of the group, still walking down the stairs. He follows behind him as the shouting intensifies.

Elbows and hands fly, mixed with threats and shouts of fear. They fight against each other, unable to work together to accomplish their goal—whatever that may be.

Another guard trips over one of the short walls, revealing their captive.

Everything jolts in pain as I launch myself forward, feeling like I'm being stung with a thousand jellyfish all over again.

"Merrick!" I scream when I see him.

CHAPTER 5

Merrick twists around violently, trying to see me as he fights against the humans.

"Celena!" he yells back, trying to get to me. He flinches in pain as the movements hurt him.

"Stop fighting," I shout, trying to calm him—he's safe now—or at least as safe as we *can be* in this palace.

They're bringing him to me, and we'll be okay now.

He slows, locking eyes with me, and I realize just how damaged he is as he hangs upside down from the men's arms.

"Merrick," I gasp quietly as I take in the sight from inside the pool. Edmund twitches next to me but says nothing.

The men drop his battered body in the water, and I rush to him, letting him sink into my arms as I seethe at the prince. My teeth are gnashing so hard that I have to force myself to stop so I don't break them.

Traitor, my eyes glare at him.

He swallows—apparently, he wasn't ready to tell me they had been torturing Merrick.

"He wasn't supposed to be brought in yet." He turns on his father.

"We have things to do, and it doesn't matter."

"He's in no condition to be moved, Father."

I cradle Merrick in my arms, pulling him back in the water until I reach the far wall—thankfully, the humans can't reach us unless they enter the pool, and I fully intend on drowning anyone that tries.

"Then he shouldn't have made things so difficult—none of this was necessary."

"Is *this* what you meant when you said she wouldn't be lonely?" Analia turns on her brother, stomping her foot. Her hands on her hips make her look slightly older than her eleven years. "You knew they were going to bring him in here."

She wrinkles her nose, glaring at Merrick. I can feel my nostrils flare as I take in her expression—like I'm some kind of possession to her, and Merrick is here to take me away. It makes me nervous.

"Relax, daughter. They'll be good for each other." Her father puts his hand on Analia's shoulder, guiding her away. "Maybe they'll mate, and you'll have even more mermaids to show your friends."

Edmund looks as though he's been struck. He glances at me quickly before following his father.

"And if *he* doesn't, I'm sure the other one will. Either way, it won't be too terribly long before you have more to impress your friends with," the king adds as he leaves.

Edmund turns back to me and shakes his head once before hurrying after his family. Not caring what he meant, I drag Merrick under the water to protect him.

Swimming to the bottom, I tuck us away in the front corner where they can't see us. Tears well up in my eyes, slipping into the water as I settle us on the ocean floor.

"Merrick," I murmur, pulling him against me.

Brushing his hair, I wait for him to look up at me. His eyes sparkle as he grins at me. Reaching up, he buries his hand in my hair, cupping my chin as he leans in to kiss me.

"What happened?" I whisper, unable to speak any louder.

"I didn't do what they asked, and they took a few scales."

"And beat you," I correct.

"That too," he acquiesces. "Can't exactly get away in those tiny pools. Have you been in here the whole time?"

"No, I was in a tiny pool too. They just moved me here a few hours ago."

Merrick's hand traces over my arm, checking me for injuries. His eye looks swollen, and there's a small cut in front of his ear.

"Are you hurt?" he asks quietly.

"I'm okay. There's an exit over there, but it's blocked." I wave to the tunnel. "It leads to the ocean, but maybe we can find a way out. Did you see anything when they transferred you?"

"Just the hallways—nothing we can use."

"You did a number on a few of those guards." I smirk at him. He winces as he tries to return my look. "Oh, Merrick. You couldn't have just kept your mouth shut? You had to antagonize them?"

"How do you know I *didn't?*"

I tip my head down, giving him the most withering look I can manage. He chuckles at me.

"Fine, I gave them a hard time—I think I deserved a little fun after everything we've been through."

"We may need to have a conversation about your definition of *fun*," I tease him. "Are you hungry? I have food."

"I could eat," he says, releasing me.

I swim over to the oysters I dropped in the water earlier and scoop them up. When I return, I drop them next to Merrick and swim up to the ledge I left the octopus on to wait. He's still sitting there, and I return him to my wrist before taking a seat next to my boyfriend.

"Who is this?" Merrick asks in surprise.

"He's cute, isn't he?" I hold up my wrist for him to see.

"Not cuter than me though, right?" He grins at me, looking out from under his long, blue bangs.

"Eat your food." I hand him an open oyster so he doesn't have to open it himself. "How are we supposed to get through this?"

"I don't know, but at least we're together now." He raises the oyster to his lips, and I suddenly remember the pearl he accidentally sent me. "And at least we can swim around again."

"Speaking of which, thanks for the pearl."

"What?" His brow furrows.

"When you refused to eat and sent me your oysters, I found *this* in one of them." I dig the pearl out of my necklace and show him. He smiles softly.

"Yeah, well, I guess I'll always find a way to get you little presents."

"So I see," I agree. "But if you *ever* do that again, Merrick, I'll make all *this* look like it's nothing."

I wave my hand at his injuries as I emphasize my point.

"Are you threatening me?" He jokes.

"I am. Do *not* put yourself at risk for me again, Merrick. Never refuse food for me again. I need you to stay strong for the both of us."

"I hear you," he says quietly, informing me that I've made my point.

He leans forward, setting the oyster shell down between us. His sigh makes me close my eyes, drinking in the sound of it.

When Merrick kisses me, everything else quiets. The edges of my fins lift off the sand, fluttering every time his lips come into contact with mine.

Floating up off the ocean floor, I move to cross my tail over his, drawing closer to him. He darts forward kissing me as he wraps his arms around my waist, pulling me against his chest.

My hand roams up his forearm making him latch onto my hip harder, dragging me closer to him. Over and over again our lips meet, eager to make up for the time we were apart.

"Merrick, I—"

He kisses me, cutting me off.

"I know," he mumbles against my skin. "I—"

"Mhmm," I mumble back, returning the favor as I kiss him.

We lack the array of fish we had the first time, but the light from the tunnel adds a beautiful glow to the other side of my closed eyelids. I clutch his shoulders in my hands.

Reaching up, I tangle my hands in his hair, running my fingers through his tresses. He moans quietly as my fingers work their way through his blue strands. I pull back on his short hair near the base of his neck, tipping his head up slightly. Darting forward, I kiss the tip of his chin as he grins, watching me.

"You're certainly good at this. Have you been practicing while I wasn't looking?" he teases. The tips of his lips edge up slightly as he gives me a smoldering look.

"Hmm, and here I thought I needed a little more practice." I shrug playfully as he tips me off of his lap, depositing me next to him.

Merrick shifts to face me, covering me with his arm as he wraps around me. I lean against the wall, making sure that I don't move and accidentally hurt him. When he finds a comfortable position, he brushes my hair back, tucking it behind my ear.

"What's with the outfit change?" he asks, taking notice.

"I think I'm starting to get through to Edmund."

"Who?"

"The prince. He seems to think that because I'm a royal, I'll work with him. I've been trying to befriend him in hopes that I can be the *Aila* to his *Jarek*, and maybe fix all of this."

"It's not a bad plan, but do you really think we can trust him even if he *does* seem to be playing along?"

"I'm not sure, but I think it's our best shot for now. I think we need to get him to see that we're not trying to hurt them—I keep telling them that we're not sirens, but I didn't exactly help our case when they saw me kill that sailor to save Coralie."

"I'm sure she's fine," he murmurs gently, closing his eyes as he leans his forehead to mine. He's so sweet when he's trying to take care of me. "Casp took her to safety, and I heard him calling when they dragged us out. He never would have left her if she wasn't safe, so she has to be safe."

"What about the rest of our families though? Did you even *see* yours at any point?"

"I didn't," he confesses. "I just have to believe they're okay for now. Everyone would have protected Marilla and Dylana, so I'm sure they're getting the collection to safety right now."

"I heard Llyr with Caspian before they brought us in, so I'm sure they're working together on this," I echo his list of certainties. "Maybe we'll get lucky and find a conch shell to send out to them so they can find us. They might have better luck getting us out from the other side of the bars."

"That's a good idea. I haven't seen any conch shells yet, but there are starfish and stingrays—"

"And your little friend there." He nods to the octopus I peeled off before we kissed moments ago. It sits not too far away in the sand.

"And him," I agree. "I'm sure other things will make their way in, and it seems like the current is bringing objects in as well."

"So we'll keep a close eye out for one. Maybe if we wish on that starfish over there, it will work out."

I humor him, closing my eyes to wish on the starfish. When I open them back up, Merrick hovers so close that we're practically touching.

"Now, we should probably get back to eating," he taunts me. "Feel like opening a few more of those oysters up?"

I sigh happily, reaching for our food. If I could spend all of my time with Merrick, I would be a very happy mermaid.

Opening the oysters, I hand one to him before indulging in one myself. We save several of them for later in case the king decides to withhold food from us, though with the way things are washing through the tunnel, I'm sure we'll find additional food sources at some point.

We talk about what we experienced in our separate pools. Merrick's room was similar to mine—bright white walls with a sparkling floor. His treatment was rougher, as evident by his injuries. The king spoke to him a few times, but mostly it was the guards.

Edmund visited a few times, but it appears that the majority of his time was spent with me. Analia, on the other hand, only came to see me, though whether it was her own decision or her father and brother's, I'm not sure.

"Do you know what happened to Phorcys?" I ask.

"I haven't seen or heard him since they separated us. You?"

"I haven't heard anything from him either. I wonder if he's cooperating with them."

"I wouldn't put it past him—he has to survive *somehow*. His siren collection is gone now, which means he's basically alone. If he thought he could leverage *us* to get something out of it for *himself*, he probably gave them whatever they wanted."

Truthfully, I was afraid he might do just that. I don't trust Phorcys or any of the sirens, and if it comes to saving his own scales, I wouldn't put it past him to put the blame on Merrick—he could even be the reason they were so brutal to Merrick to begin with.

I need to stop thinking like this—I don't know what he has or hasn't done yet. It's all conjecture, and guessing games like that could get me in a world of trouble.

"You're wondering if he blamed me too, huh?"

"How did you—?"

"Because I know you, Len. Always have, always will."

Merrick has always been an incredible partner—we've worked well together from the start. We know what the other is thinking, what we'll say, and how we'll move. He and I trust each other implicitly.

"Eat your food, Merrick," I pretend to chide him.

While he finishes his meal, I create an area for us to store food in for later use. I pull some of the seaweed in that's wrapped around the bars of the tunnel entrance and create a little basket to store small items in on the sand.

When I'm finished, I use the extra to create a *sarasa* for Merrick. If he's going to be trapped here, he should look the part of a royal mer. So far, they've treated me with more respect because of it.

I loop it around his neck and shoulder, settling it on his opposite hip as he moves his upper body to assist me. Adjusting it to sit properly across his chest, he smiles at me.

"This is great, thanks, Len."

"You're as much a prince as I am a princess, Merrick. Don't forget that."

He understands that I'm not talking about birth lines and doesn't fight me on it. Instead, he lifts his arm for me to join him in the corner. I nestle against him, falling asleep in his arms as I promise to show him around our new dwelling in the morning.

"Celena," a voice whispers. I take a deep breath, coming out of my sleep. I smile, remembering that I'm safely wrapped in Merrick's muscular arms. I nestle closer to him, keeping my eyes closed as I enjoy the moment.

When the voice shouts, it frightens me awake fully. I bolt upright, launching Merrick into action. Before I can even assess the situation, he's swimming in front of me, broken shell in hand, ready to defend us from whoever is yelling at me.

"Knock it off, Merrick," Caspian calls from the tunnel exit.

"Casp?" I dart around Merrick, shocked to see my twin.

His hand rests on the bars separating us, and he reaches through for me with the other. I swim to him quickly, taking his hand in mine as he pulls me close to the bars for a difficult hug. The metal presses into my body uncomfortably, but I don't care—my brother is here.

"How did you find us?"

"Accident. We've been checking every cave we could find near the palace. We've even taunted the humans to come out in hopes of sirening them, but no luck. We were here not long after you were taken, but we decided to double back this morning."

"Hey, brother," Llyr smiles, reaching through the bars to clasp Merrick's outstretched hand. He eyes Merrick's bruised face. "Looks like you've had an interesting time."

"What happened to you—are you safe?" Caspian asks, not caring about the conversation Llyr and his best friend are having right next to us.

"They put us in tiny pools—like a rounded wall that contains water so small we could barely swim at all in it—and we were separated until last night."

"Why did they put you together?" Llyr interrupts. Noticing our change in attire, he adds, "And where did you get the *iluse*, crown, and *sarasa* from?"

"Prince Edmund is trying to give me a little more freedom so I will cooperate more with them."

"What does he want?" Caspian gives me a worried look, not giving me a chance to explain our wardrobe change.

"I'm not positive what the king wants, but Edmund wants to learn how sireny works so he can prevent us from using it against humans."

"And he wants to destroy us all," Merrick adds. "He told me their goal is to rid the waters of mer so their sailors can do their jobs without fearing for their lives."

Caspian's grip on my fingers tightens as he pulls my hand toward him. I can feel the worry in his fingers as they nervously twitch against my hand. For a moment, he looks deeply into my eyes, and we have an entire conversation without the others in that one look.

"We need to get you out of here," Casp whispers.

"I know. We need to get through these bars somehow, and I have a feeling broken clam shells won't get the job done," I joke, trying to lighten the mood.

"At least you know where we are now," Merrick reminds us. "Where is the rest of the collection?"

"We have a group of them here," Llyr replies. "Dylana is with Keone and Natale. Thirty of us stayed behind to try to help—or to stop the humans if they come after us again."

"I sent Mom and Dad with Coralie," Caspian says quickly. "They're all okay…mostly."

I breathe a sigh of relief—I've been so worried about my father. Caspian is quickly explaining his injuries when a slap sounds on the water above us. I look up.

"They're signaling me—I have to go, or they'll hurt us."

"I'm coming too," Merrick says, following me.

"We'll wait here," Caspian calls as I dart away.

I surface before Merrick does—he's not able to move as fast as I can yet. When I rise out of the water, I discover Edmund is waiting for me, mercifully without his father or sister.

His lips pull back in a grimace when Merrick joins us.

"Not you," Edmund says.

I look over my shoulder to Merrick as something passes between the two. When I turn back to Edmund, he's pointing at the water.

"I just need to speak to Celena. You may go." Edmund's voice is clear and strong as he waits for Merrick to leave.

"I'm not leaving her," Merrick challenges. "I don't trust you."

"I've been with her alone for the last four days, *mer*," Edmund counters angrily.

"That's four too many," Merrick growls back, placing his hand on my back.

"It's fine," I say softly, trying to diffuse the situation. "Merrick, I'll be fine."

I turn back to him, blocking my face from Edmund with my hair. I drop my eyes down, telling Merrick to go back to Caspian and Llyr. Reluctantly he follows my orders, dipping down slowly into the water so only the tips of his shoulders and his face remain.

"I'm right here if you need me," he says pointedly to me.

Once he's submerged under the water, I turn back to Edmund, waiting to see what he wants. Merrick's hand glides down my tail, letting me know once he's actually left my side.

"What did you need?" I ask coolly.

"I wanted to come check on you," the prince replies.

"*And?*" I know better than that.

"*And* I wanted to apologize for yesterday and let you know that we're not going to force you into anything."

"I see." I cross my arms. "Though it seems like you're forcing me into quite a bit here already."

"We won't make you do…*that*," he corrects, reminding me of what the king said to his daughter before they left. "I know my father and Analia want to show you off—no one else in the kingdom has a mermaid—but I doubt you want a bunch of people in here poking and prodding at you."

"Where is Phorcys?" I demand. "What are you doing to him? Are you beating him like you beat Merrick?"

"Merrick didn't cooperate—I couldn't help that."

"You ripped his scales off," I insist on placing the blame on him. "Do you know how long it takes those to grow back?"

"I had nothing to do with that. I wasn't there when that happened, I was with you."

If he hadn't wasted so much time with me, maybe he could have prevented Merrick's injuries. I internally growl at myself for trying to keep the prince with me for so long to convince him to help us—instead I only made it worse for us inside the palace walls.

"You could have stopped it."

"Yes, I could have," he confirms. "But I still don't trust you, Celena. You're restricted here, and under our control, but if you find an opportunity to get the upper hand, I don't know what you'll do."

"I told you, my only goal is to get out of this palace and return to my collection so I can take them far, far away."

"And now you know what will happen if you try something you shouldn't." He waves at the water where Merrick disappeared. "The guards might have wanted to hurt him because he is a merman, but I don't relish in causing people pain. He brought it on himself when he fought against my men, so like it or not, Celena, he did this to himself."

I open my mouth, about to protest.

"No, you don't get to be righteous about this, Celena. He went after my men, and you yourself delivered retribution against *my* men when they went after your sister. If he had cooperated like you did, he would still have his scales. The other merman is cooperating—mostly—so he's in better shape than your friend.

"You *should* know though," he quiets his voice, telling me something he doesn't like admitting. "Most of it was him fighting to get to you. The entire time, he just wanted to know about you. I think they frightened him a little in hopes that it would get him to cooperate, but it just made him fight harder."

"What do you mean *they frightened him?*"

"I spent most of my time with *you*, but one time I heard them tell your merman that they were hurting you, and it would be worse if he didn't cooperate. I'm pretty sure he made it out of the pool and across the floor once before they found him."

I'll have to ask Merrick about that as soon as I escape this conversation. I don't like the idea of him being hurt for me, and if he threw himself outside of the pool and dragged his tail across the floor, I might have to lecture him.

"And you didn't think this would encourage me to *not* help you?" I say incredulously. My hands float to my hips under the water. He frowns.

"We can still hurt you both, Celena. Try not to forget that."

He turns on his heels, walking away. Edmund doesn't turn around as he mounts the stairs—he's annoyed with me.

His footsteps fade as he quickly stomps away. I duck under the water, racing back to the boys.

CHAPTER 6

"What did he want?" Merrick demands before I can reach him. I slow as I approach the bars.

"Why did he flinch when he saw you?" I ask suspiciously.

"I might have hit him at one point."

"Excuse me?" My eyebrows shoot up. It figures that neither of them would readily admit to that.

"We really don't have time for this," Caspian interrupts, raking his hand through his hair.

"It wasn't intentional." Merrick refrains from rolling his eyes, but I can tell he wants to. "He got in the way during a struggle."

"Is that why he's favoring his arm?" I gasp, realizing what I had been seeing.

"Probably," Merrick grumbles.

"Where is Llyr?" I snap, suddenly realizing he isn't with us.

"We sent him to find Keone and the girls," Caspian replies. "We're working on a plan—it would be great if you could get your head in the game."

"We need a way through the bars, that's as simple as it gets." I shrug as I place my hands on the metal near my brother's.

"The humans have ways to cut through metal." Casp frowns. "Too bad we can't get around easily in the palace to find something."

"Do you think we could trick them into bringing something close enough to us that we can take it from them and get out before they catch us?" Merrick asks, already knowing the answer.

"They're not that stupid. Although," I pause, "If I can get them to trust me, and they leave the princess alone with me, I can probably convince her to unwittingly help us."

"Good, try anything," Caspian says as he lurches back in the water, trying to pull on the bars.

"You've been trying that since I left, haven't you?"

"Do you have a better idea?" Caspian growls, pulling on the bars again.

"Enough, Casp." Merrick puts his hand out. "That's not going to work."

"We need to be logical. We're not getting out of here today," I direct the conversation. "We need to think longer term. We'll play their game *up there*, and *down here*, we'll work on escaping.

"The bars go into the sand," I point out. "Maybe we can tunnel out under it."

"I'm pretty sure there's rock under the sand," Caspian replies, looking grim. I notice an area that's dug out a bit—he must have checked.

"We're going to need supplies," I continue, ignoring his comment. "You can bring us food—they aren't feeding us much in here."

Caspian floats up in the water, straightening his neck up. He looks ready to break through the bars and murder the king.

"They aren't feeding you?" He blinks at me, jaw tight as he jerks a shoulder back in annoyance.

"Some, just not enough. Go find us some food before they come back. We'll be fine here."

He looks like he wants to argue, but he glances down at my stomach once before flipping around and careening out of the tunnel.

"That will keep him busy for a few minutes," Merrick smirks. "How much trouble am I in?"

"Edmund told me you crawled across the floor?" I cross my arms angrily. "You could have been killed."

"I wasn't. I had to get to you." He reaches out, offering me his hands. "They told me they were torturing you. I had to get to you, and if I couldn't do that, at least I could keep their focus on *me* so that they'd leave you alone."

"You're an idiot."

"Probably." He shrugs.

"No, definitely," I correct, taking his hands. "That was not a bright thing to do."

"I got that." Merrick gives me a patronizing look. "I'd do it again if I had to."

"Of course you would." I sigh as he pulls me closer.

"I have a feeling we won't be left alone again for a while, so if you want to kiss me, now is the time."

I glance up quickly, surprised by his words. He's right, of course—our collection won't leave us alone now that they've found us.

Merrick pins me against the wall a length away from the entrance to the tunnel where Caspian and the others will have a hard time seeing us if they return. I wrap my arms around his neck, playing with the ends of his hair as he crushes his body against mine.

His fingers work their way into my hair, magically making me forget all of my stress. I laugh, enjoying myself as he kisses me, making him chuckle against me. Each slow kiss reminds me of how lucky I am to be in this merman's presence, *let alone* how lucky I am to be kissing him.

Merrick's hand moves slowly down my side, close enough to my back to make me shiver, but just far enough to the side to make sure he doesn't hit the welts from the jellyfish while still avoiding the knick on my side. I shudder as he reaches my tail. He grins.

In retaliation, I slowly drag my hand off his shoulder, onto his chest. By the time I reach his abdomen, only one finger is touching him, but it's enough to make him cringe forward and gasp, eyes alive with sparks.

"Len," he whispers as I walk my fingers around his hip to his back. I drag them up his spinal chord, and he clutches at me, locking eyes with me.

His lips hang open in amazement just enough that I can't help but do something about it. I press my lips against him, spurring him into a passionate kiss as he lifts me up in the water, both arms wrapped around my waist.

Merrick moves his lips along my neck, brushing my hair back with his nose before kissing my skin again. I whimper as he hits a spot that tickles, and I cringe into him only to catch his chin with my finger and move his mouth back to mine.

My tail moves around him. I perch on his hip as he rests me back against the wall, slowing our pace once again. His shoulders are tight under my grasp, and I tip my head to the side more to accommodate his lips.

We pull back to catch our breath—and stare at each other—for a moment before a loud splash sounds overhead.

A body tumbles into the water, creating a cloud of bubbles so thick that we can't see who it is. Merrick whips around, holding me behind his back against the rocks, allowing me the advantage of preparing a weapon where the intruder can't see.

I quickly reach for my *iluse*, pulling a shell out and placing it in Merrick's hand. He holds it in front of him, ready to strike out at the humans while I untangle my own weapon from my covering.

Even for all the beatings Merrick took, he's still able to move remarkably well when needed. He's never been one to let things hold him back…though occasionally he pushes himself too far for the sake of a mission.

Orange fills the water as the bubbles clear, mixed with a flash of sandy yellow—Phorcys.

He dips down backward in the water, trying to get away from the surface.

"What do we do?" I glance at the tunnel entrance.

It's doubtful that we can trust Phorcys at this point, but there's no way to hide Caspian and the others from him.

"Emphasize what's in it for *him*," Merrick murmurs.

"Phorcys!" I yell just as he flips around. His eyes grow wide when he sees me, but immediately narrow when he catches sight of our weapons.

"We're less likely to hurt you than they are," I warn him as he starts to swim back up pitifully. He seems to have healed some in the last few days, but he's still clearly suffering from the wounds I gave him during our fight.

He appraises us as he slides down in the water. I almost dart forward to help him sit, but then I remember that I don't actually care about his comfort.

"What is this?" he asks.

"It's the ocean," I reply curtly. "We just can't escape the bars."

I motion to the tunnel, and his eyes grow wide.

"We have to get through them," he says anxiously.

"We tried, we can't break out," Merrick informs him. He holds his hand up, cutting Phorcys off as he tries to speak. "But we have another plan."

Phorcys raises his eyebrows, waiting for more information.

"Part of our collection is here," Merrick addresses him. "They're going to help us escape."

"Where are they?" Phorcys demands, sitting up.

"They went to get the others, and to find us more food." I tuck my shell back into my *iluse* and cross my arms.

"Food?" My words catch his attention.

"They haven't been feeding you?" I ask.

"Not much," he admits, though I'm not sure if it's an act or not.

I swim over to where we have the rest of the oysters from last night and pull them out. I carefully hand them to Phorcys, allowing him to eat.

"Caspian will be back with more anyway," I murmur as I join Merrick across the pool.

"How many of them are here?" Phorcys asks without looking up.

"Enough," Merrick answers, intentionally being vague. Our enemy doesn't need to know how many of us stayed behind. "What did they say to you up there?"

"They asked a bunch of questions," Phorcys says before taking a mouthful of food.

"Such as?"

A school of fish swims into the pool, circling the area as they flash their bright red color. I nearly reach out to touch one, but then I think better of it and keep my focus.

"They wanted to know about sireny and where the mermaids were located." He rolls his eyes, chewing a bite of food. "Obviously I have no idea where they are now."

"Did you tell Edmund about sireny?" I ask.

"What is there to tell?" he snips back. "We sing, they listen. I don't know how that works."

Strangely enough, I believe him.

"What in the seven seas is *he* doing here?" Caspian calls from the tunnel exit.

Phorcys snarls at him, not bothering to get up.

"They dropped him in here a few minutes ago," Merrick replies, running his hand through his bangs that I had been playing with not too long ago.

"This is the last crab's leg," Caspian mumbles angrily. "We're getting you out of here."

He drops a pile of oysters on our side of the bars and starts pulling on the metal again. Casp motions for Merrick to join him.

"Celena!" Dylana's voice travels through the tunnel, and I race toward it.

We collide against the bars at the same time, gathering each other's hands in our own. Her hand bumps the cut on mine, and I try not to flinch. She and I speak so quickly that the boys just blink at us, but we understand every word. When we calm down, she eyes Phorcys.

"We can't get rid of him," I inform her before she can ask.

She tilts her body, looking around me.

"I see she left quite the scar," she shouts over to Phorcys.

"Jealous?" he retorts, setting down the final oyster shell.

With great effort, he gets up and swims over to us, resting a hand on the bar. I have a feeling he's making his injuries look worse than they really are.

"Back off," Llyr orders him as Phorcys lurks closer to Dylana.

"No, let him get closer," Natale sings. "I'll slice his hand off while he's busy staring at her."

She grins sarcastically at him for a moment before settling into a rather unpleasant look—if she could treat him like an oyster, she would tear him apart. My cousin glowers at the siren, but he doesn't back down.

"My mother is dead because of you," she finally adds. "You're going to want to be very careful when you make it out of here."

"I had nothing to do with that," he remarks casually.

"You and your sirens lured us out here to fight your war with the humans—*all* of this is your fault." I wouldn't want to be Phorcys when Natale gets unrestricted access to him.

At the back of my collection, another merman floats up in the water, trying to see over everyone. It's hard to see his features in the backlit water, but it's even harder to recognize him because I don't *actually* know him—I recognize his voice though.

"What exactly is the plan here?" Quilo asks, his Ambraian accent evident.

"We need to find a way to get them out. Any ideas?" Llyr asks.

"Why would we have ideas?" Quilo retorts, tipping his head like Edmund does.

"I thought maybe you did things differently in Ambra," Llyr replies, shrugging. "We haven't exactly come up with the best ideas for this yet, so I thought maybe you could help."

"We'll help, we just don't know *how*," the Ambraian mermaid—Larina, I think—responds, pushing her way through the collection. "Looks like you got yourself into quite the mess here, huh?"

She eyes me as she runs her hand along the bars, trying to get an idea for what we're up against. Larina busies herself assessing the situation. It looks like a few others from their collection stayed to help us as well, but it's hard to see from my vantage point.

Larina notices Phorcys in the distance and smiles softly, waving around me. I turn back to look as the siren nods to the Ambrian mermaid, and I realize *they* must have been the friends Phorcys mentioned before we were captured. I *knew* someone had to have helped him after we left him for dead—the Ambrian's just didn't know any better.

"He's a siren," I whisper quietly so Natale doesn't hear. Larina's face falls as she realizes their mistake. I cut her off before she can apologize. "It's okay, just don't let him out of your sight when we get out of here."

She nods.

"I'll make sure the others know."

Merrick places a hand on the small of my back—we're floating so close together that no one can see his movement, but I'm grateful he's next to me, supporting me through this. Natale calms down as we wait, tossing around every idea that we can come up with—none of them seem like they'd cause anything but a whirlpool of trouble.

"If only we had something to pull it with," Llyr mumbles. "We could use it as leverage to bend the bars."

"But what?" Merrick asks. "We don't have access to anything, and it's not like the humans will just give us chains so you can all pull on it at the same time."

The idea hits me as fast as a jolt from a jellyfish. I jerk up in the water, frightening Merrick as his hand moves on my back.

"We *do* have access though." I grin as a plan formulates in my head. "Casp, do you remember The Ropes?"

He gives me a look indicating that I might be insane, but Phorcys lurches forward in the water as he realizes my idea. Merrick turns to me, catching on at the same time my brother does.

"You have to be careful," I say sharply before he can speak.

"We'll be fine," Caspian promises.

"*Casp*," Merrick growls, warning him not to be foolish. "Do *not* die for this."

"Whoa, wait, what?" Larina gasps. "Who's dying?"

"The Ropes is a place where dangerous things were dumped in the middle of the ocean floor—anchors and chains, ropes, and other dangerous things mer could get tangled in," I explain. "Phorcys showed it to us once."

I glance at him sideways, glaring for just a second before turning back to the collection.

"If you get caught in there, you might not come back out," I warn. "You don't have to help with this—"

"We're helping," Quilo cuts me off. His collection nods.

"Okay, but you all have to be careful. Just get things we can use from the outside perimeter, and for the love of coral, *don't* go inside to get chains and tools."

"We'll get what we need, Celena, but we'll be careful," Caspian promises, taking my hand. "It's going to take some time, can you stall until then?"

I nod.

"Good, stay alive until we get back. We'll leave a few of the guards here with you in case you need anything," he adds.

"Dylana and Natale will stay," Llyr interjects. The girls vehemently protest, but he shouts above them. "They will stay because they can siren the humans better than the rest of us, and if you need help, you're going to need them around."

"Not that they can do us much good from *that* side of the bars," Phorcys grumbles loud enough to be heard.

"They can surface if they need to. The guards will be here to back them up. Between the three of you *inside* and the two of them *outside*, maybe you'll stand a chance," Llyr snips, turning to swim away. "We need to move."

Caspian hugs me quickly through the bars before darting after Llyr. The collection rushes out of the tunnel, leaving it feeling empty with only my cousins on the ocean's side.

"Phorcys, go away," I demand, waving him back. "We need to talk."

"What, I'm not part of the team now?" he scoffs.

"You've *never* been part of the team," I correct him. I consider grabbing one of the fish that swims past me and throwing it toward him, but that would be cruel to the fish to have to get too close to the siren.

"Not even when you curled into my neck as I carried you back to your baby sister?" Phorcys leers at me, prompting Merrick to dart toward him a bit in the water, clearly struggling to restrain himself as the siren hisses. *"Jealous?"*

"You will *not* touch her again." Merrick's fists are balled at his sides. Dylana looks shocked as she places a hand on the bars, but Natale watches quietly.

"That's up to *her.*" Phorcys smirks. He risks a look at me around Merrick.

When Merrick turns back to face me, his face is surprisingly calm, but his eyes spark fiercely. Phorcys swims to the back corner, taking a handful of the new oysters with him—I have no idea when he picked them up.

"I've got him," Natale mumbles, watching over my shoulder as I turn my back on the siren. "I *really* don't like that guy."

"Nope," Dylana agrees. "So what do we know about the king?"

My cousin eyes Merrick's injuries, reaching out to touch his arm above a cut. She pauses us for a moment as she swims to the end of the tunnel to instruct a guard to find a few supplies for her to take care of our wounds. When she returns, I inform her of everything I've learned about the king—Merrick adds in his own details about the guards.

"Miss me yet?" Phorcys sings, interrupting our conversation from across the pool.

"Nope," I call over my shoulder, not bothering to turn around. Natale snarls at whatever face Phorcys just made, but I still refuse to look.

A piece of Dylana's hair floats toward me as the current drags more water into the pool. She reaches up and tucks her pink locks back just as one of the guards arrives with her supplies.

"Can we trust him?" Natale murmurs, still spying on Phorcys over my shoulder.

Dylana quietly examines Merrick's injuries, patching him up as best as she can. He winces as she hits a tender spot on his arm.

"I doubt it, but we don't have much choice at the moment," I mutter. "He could turn us in if he doesn't like what we do."

"He knows he'll die if he does that—there's no way the humans will let him live."

"I don't know…he might risk it. We just have to be careful," I reply, making eye contact with Natale.

"I can tell that you're talking about me," Phorcys calls over.

"We're talking about dying, so I suppose that's the same thing," I viciously call over my shoulder, earning a smirk from Dylana. Natale's eyes glitter, and she barely manages to hold a straight face. A second later, she glares over my shoulder.

Phorcys swims over to us, joining us near the bars. He settles on the sand, back against the wall as he stares into the pool area.

A slap sounds against the water overhead.

"What's that?" Dylana asks, looking up.

"I'm being summoned." I sigh as I swim back.

"Shouldn't you *all* go?" Dylana looks concerned when the boys don't move.

"They're afraid of the boys." I frown, continuing to swim up. "They're only negotiating with me because I'm a princess, and I saved *their* princess."

"*You* definitely don't want to go up there, Dylana. They're very anxious to meet you." Merrick's voice fades away as I reach the surface.

I expect to find the king waiting for me, not Edmund after the way he stormed off. When the prince pats the wall next to him, indicating that I should pull myself out of the water and sit next to him, everything inside me screams that I should swim away.

CHAPTER 7

I force myself not to tremble as I slowly swim toward the side of the pool. The prince smiles at me, but I can't return the look. Tentatively, I stretch my hand out on top of the wall, preparing to balance myself so I can leap out of the water to join him.

Fifteen guards stand in a semi-circle around the edge of the pool, far enough back that they can't hear our conversations—even if they didn't have their ears blocked—but close enough that they can skewer me if I attempt to drag their prince into the water.

With both hands on the wall, I flip my tail as hard as I can and propel myself out of the pool. I land sharply on the ledge, the edge biting into my scales as I misjudge the distance.

"Are you okay?" Edmund smirks as I grunt in pain. Glaring, I quickly remind myself not to and soften my gaze.

"Why am I here?" I demand to know what he wants.

"I apologize for getting upset before. I thought we could talk. I brought food." He waves a guard over, and I realize he has been holding a tray—not a weapon. The man sets the food between us.

"What is that?" I ask, wrinkling my nose.

"A slice of an apple," he replies, picking it up. It crunches when he bites it. "Go on, try it."

It looks like a perfectly smooth inside of an oyster shell, free from blemishes, in the purest off-white color I've ever seen. A rim of red covers its contour. The food is cool to the touch and smells tangy.

"It's fruit, just try it," Edmund encourages, pushing the plate toward me.

When I bite into it, my mouth explodes with the new taste. It travels up into my ears, making me shiver—it's strange but good. I take a second bite, this time not reacting nearly as badly. Edmund grins at me.

"I thought you might like that. You should try the cheese too." He motions to a yellow thing on the tray.

Instead, I reach for the oysters he as also provided on the other half of the tray. I'm starting to get sick of only eating oysters at this point, but I'll have Natale find us some other food once I return to the water to make sure we have a balanced diet so we don't get sick.

"Tell me about your sister." Edmund picks up a piece of the cheese and pops it into his mouth.

I see his game now—he's trying to connect with me so he can manipulate me easier. I can play that game, especially because it *could* work in my favor if I convince him to connect with me for real. If nothing else, perhaps I can learn valuable information about his family to use against him.

"She's young, but she's lovely."

"I saw," he agrees, reaching for another apple slice as I pry open an oyster.

"I meant as a mermaid, but she's beautiful too."

"Her tail is a nice color," he offers, and I nod.

"Blue and green is a good color for her, especially with her hair. She would be very intrigued by these apples of yours." I reach for another piece of it.

"Analia likes apples too. She's been very anxious to come see you —we haven't told her we put the other merman in here yet—I don't think she'll be pleased."

"She wants to keep me all to herself?" I ask, saying the words he won't. "I appreciate you not treating me like a possession, Edmund. Tell me more about Analia—perhaps if I can talk to her, she'll stop thinking of me like a toy."

Sitting on the wall of the pool up in the open air is a strange sensation—much worse than sitting on the deck of the ship when the humans attacked us outside of Scylla. I feel exposed as I hunch over onto myself, trying to get comfortable. The breeze in the room is discomforting as it kisses my skin, and I'm grateful my hair is covering my back, though, I think because I'm wet from being in the water, it's making me chilled.

"She's a very energetic little girl when we're alone. She's rather quiet and sullen in public, but that's how she was raised to be—her actions reflect on us, so she must be regal and refined."

I understand that—Dylana and I were raised the same way—our actions reflected on our mothers, though we were raised to be *fierce* rather than meek.

"What does she like to do when she isn't in front of the world?"

"She likes spending time with her horse." I perk up at his words, jostling my dripping hair as it sticks against my skin. He looks amused, one eyebrow raised. "You like horses I take it?"

"I've never seen one," I admit. "Aila passed down stories of the horses and creatures she would see when she visited the palace steps though. They sound lovely."

"Perhaps I'll show you one day," he murmurs, reaching for an apple slice. "You'd like the summer palace."

He's taking me to the summer palace?

My world stops. I can't leave the ocean—he can't just transport me wherever he likes. I have to stay in the water. I'm not his pet that he can just take around from palace to palace. Isn't this exactly what he told his sister she couldn't do?

If he takes me away, I know for certain that I will never come back. I'll die before I let him remove me from this palace and take me to another.

He notices me cringing, and I realize that I'm starting to dry out—I need to get back in the water.

I look at the water, glancing away from him. Panicked, he holds his hand out.

"Please don't go," he begs, catching my wrist. "I'm not planning on moving you, I was just talking. Don't run away."

"I need to get in the water." I can hear the tremor in my voice. "I'm drying out—I need to get in the water."

"But you'll stay here?" he whimpers. He knows he's messed up his plan—I can't let his folly destroy my chance at winning him over.

I nod, preparing to move to slide into the pool.

"I just need to be back in the water." At his nod, I slide off the wall, thankful to put some space between us. At least when Aila was sitting on the steps near the palace, she could stay partially in the water.

The pool feels cool around me. For as cold as I had been sitting on the wall with my dripping hair, I realize my skin had been rather warm, and it feels like it's sizzling as I sink back into the water.

Dipping down under the gentle waves, I douse my hair. I come up feeling refreshed, despite being nervous. I smile, trying to assure him that I'm being cooperative.

"So, Analia likes horses. Do you?"

"I enjoy horseback riding. I haven't been in a while though. I've been too busy."

"Doing what?" I ask impertinently.

"Well, most recently, handling the war here. But before that, I was working with my father on kingdom business. We had a few things to take care of, and my father asked me to oversee them."

"It doesn't sound like you were too happy about it."

"Some of it was fine." He sighs. "Some of it I wasn't pleased with."

"Such as?" He casts a withering look at me as I speak. "*You* wanted to be honest."

"I may be searching for a bride," he grimaces.

"Oh." I'm taken back by his admission. "That sounds awful. Aren't you a little young for that?"

I can't imagine being forced to marry at our age—the prince can't be more than a year or two older than me.

"Aren't you a little young to be sirening men to their deaths?" he counters. "I'm trying to put it off a little, but there are alliances to be made with the other kingdoms. It's my job to see which one is the right fit."

"Girl or kingdom?"

"Kingdom." He smirks sadly. "My wife is just what comes along with it."

"Have you met her yet?"

"I think so, but my Father still has to decide if it's the right fit."

"Do you like her?" It's strange how normal this conversation is— it's almost like I'm talking to Dylana back in the Palace in Scylla— without all of the gushing, of course.

"I honestly don't know. She seems nice, I suppose—but then, I suppose they all do."

"She's not the one you would have picked?"

I twirl a piece of hair around my finger, waiting for his answer. This is much deeper than I had anticipated.

Something moves in the water below me against the wall of the pool—the water waves against me. An oyster—or what I *assume* is an oyster—gently collides with my tail before falling down in the water. Merrick wants to know if I'm okay, but he can't risk being seen by the prince. He must be hiding against the wall.

I casually swim closer to the wall, resting an elbow on it while dropping my other hand into the water to wave him off. The water pulses against me again, letting me know he's left.

"I don't know which of them I would have picked. It's my duty to marry as my father tells me to—Jarek kind of ruined that for us."

I give him a quizzical look, and he sighs, dipping his hand into the water to create ripples.

"Jarek fell for Persephone—or was lured in by her—or both. After that, we weren't trusted to make our own choices. The reigning kings and queens decided whom the royal children would marry."

What a stroke backward! *For coral's sake*, if they tried that under the ocean, the *entire collection* would have been beside themselves. We've always been allowed to choose our own mates. Dylana, of course, has certain responsibilities, and with that, limitations, but she still has a say.

"I take it that's not a problem where you come from?" He sounds discouraged. I shake my head. "Tell me about your merman—the blue haired one."

"His name is Merrick," I inform him, knowing that he already knows. "He was my partner—we work together."

"Doing what?" His fingers continue to dance in the water, sending little ripples to wave against the skin on my arm that's still mostly under the water.

"Whatever the queen needs us to do. We help the royals," I reply, avoiding details.

"Your cousin."

"Yes." A moment later, Edmund nearly falls in the water, jumping up from his seat, but not entirely leaving the wall as he jerks his hand out of the water. "Oh!"

I turn to follow his gaze as he blinks at the water, and discover a small stingray brushing against the top of the water.

"Careful!" he cries.

I reach out to pet the velvety creature. He swims up to me, tickling my hand, but I have nothing to feed him.

"What is that?" Edmund demands, cradling his hand next to him as if he had been bitten.

"It's a stingray." I reach out with both hands, practically scooping the creature up into my arms like I did to Coralie when she was a baby.

"It has wings." His voice still sounds too high, but he edges toward the wall again.

"Kind of." I frown at him, continuing to pet the stingray. "You can touch him if you want—he won't hurt you."

Edmund blinks a few times before cautiously readjusting his seat on the side of the wall. He decides to watch me before making up his mind about offering up his hand to the vicious beast in my arms.

The stingray flaps, begging for a treat.

"Sorry, little guy, I don't have anything for you," I murmur.

"Why is it doing that?" the prince asks. He looks like he's flinching as he reaches his fingers out and pulls them back.

"He's hungry—he thinks I'll feed him. Last chance…" I offer the stingray to him again, holding it toward the prince so that he can pet it.

Just when I think he won't, Edmund reaches out, dipping his finger just below the surface of the water. He gasps when he touches it, not expecting the texture—to be fair, they feel a lot different than one might imagine them to.

Edmund smiles, petting the stingray. He laughs when it flaps in the water, splashing quietly. After a few moments, the stingrays gives up and dips back under the water in search of food elsewhere.

I wonder if one of my friends let the stingray in on purpose.

"I've never seen one of those before," he murmurs, trying to see the stingray as it swims away.

"Is it as lovely as a horse?" I ask, giggling. He turns to look at me, grinning as he contemplates his answer.

"Maybe." He nods. "You were telling me about your friends."

"Yes," I reply, moving back to lean on the wall. "Merrick is amazing. He takes such good care of everyone—me, his family, the royals—*everyone.*"

"Ha," he scoffs. "I did *not* see that side of him."

"Of course you did, you saw how he tried to get to me—to protect me from you. He crawled out of a pool and across a floor, and endured beatings to protect me."

He looks as though I've struck him.

"I suppose that's true. Perhaps I misjudged him."

I leap out of the pool, sitting next to him on the other side of the tray again. His head pulls back slightly, once again surprised by me. He lifts a hand, holding off the guards.

"Tell me about the other one," he encourages. I take a deep breath.

"Phorcys. He's *horrible.*" I turn to face him, looking out at him from under my lashes.

Edmund chuckles, leaning back to support his weight on his hand, straightening his shoulder.

"He seemed pretty eager to learn about you, from what I heard. I didn't spend much time with him. Sounds like he hates your merman though."

"He *should*, we messed him up pretty badly."

"I think there's some jealousy in there too, am I correct?" Edmund teases, a sparkle in his eye.

"I really have no idea," I protest.

"Oh, come now… *you know*."

"Fine, maybe. Phorcys and the siren princess captured my sister and dragged us out into the open sea—to *here*. Along the way, he might have come up with some weird reason to like me, but I honestly don't know if it's that, or he's just being rude."

"And what would have given him that idea?" Edmund prods. He glances down when I flick my tail in the water.

"When they sent me into the jellyfish, I was hurt badly enough that I could barely swim. Phorcys had to carry me back, so I assume it was connected to that."

"He thinks he saved you? It sounds like it's straight out of a book," Edmund comments.

"*Merrick* is the fairytale knight. Phorcys is more like the dragon." I pause. "Are there dragons around here?"

Edmund laughs, lighting up the room. His smile makes me smile back.

"First, there are no such thing as dragons—they're made up. Second, how do you know about knights and fairytales?" He continues to smile at me as he waits for an answer.

"From the books you humans drop in the ocean." I feel a little embarrassed about not knowing that dragons were mythical, but Edmund doesn't seem to mind.

"I'll have to make a note to stop doing that—if we're going to educate you, the *least* we could do is to do it properly. No more dragon books." He laughs again, quieting after a minute.

"I'm sorry you have to marry a girl you don't know," I say softly, leaning forward to touch the wall with my hand. If it were any of my friends, I'd cover their hand with mine, but Edmund is human, and we're not close.

"I'm sorry you have a creepy merman chasing you around." He offers me a half-hearted smile as he sobers, laughter dying away.

Footsteps sound, echoing off the walls of the room. Edmund's eyes grow wide and his gaze darts to the pool. I jump off the wall, splashing as quietly as possible into the water just before his father rounds the corner.

Edmund is on his feet, not giving his father any reason to find grievances with his son. The king frowns at us, raising an eyebrow, but given the distance between his son and me, he can't say anything.

I watch him warily, waiting to see what he wants. He nods for his son to leave, taking a place in front of me. He widens his stance, placing his feet so far apart that they match the distance between his shoulders—it's so strange to think of having feet that separate instead of one tail.

Edmund slowly leaves, watching over the wall as long as he can. I listen to the footsteps as they go, but I don't think he makes it all the way out—I think he's paused to listen. His father doesn't notice.

"So, Princess Celena. I need some answers from you. So far, we have not been successful in gaining any insight from you or your friends. We've tried convincing each of you individually, but now I think it's time to switch our tactics."

He looks down at me. The king's hands are clasped behind his back—something that appears to be trained into the royal males. He looks remarkably like a stern version of Jarek, the softness of his features fading away as he studies me with a harsh gaze. It's as unnerving as it is captivating.

"I want to know how sireny works. My son will continue to speak with you in his own way, but if you don't tell *him*, you'll have to tell me." He pulls his hands in front of him, crossing his arms across his chest. Bending his arm at the elbow, he lifts one hand to his face to stroke his chin. "I'm not unreasonable, but this *is* your last chance. If you don't tell us by tomorrow, I'll take matters into my own hands.

"Perhaps your friends won't talk when we torture them but based on what I've seen of you, *you* will speak to me if I hurt *them*. You're strong when it comes to handling things yourselves, *mermaid*, but your weakness is your collection and has been since Gaspar's time… And I know better than to hurt a princess when I have other available options.

"Tomorrow, you will give us an answer, or I'll start ripping your mermen to pieces in front of you, starting with the blue-haired one. Do you really want to be left alone with the other?" His eyes spark as he speaks. "Think about it, Princess. Their lives depend on your answers. Cooperate, and the three of you can live your days out here.

We'll take care of you here, but those are your only two options. Choose wisely."

He tosses something at me. It slaps against my chest before falling into the water. A dark blue scale sinks back and forth in the water until I reach out and snatch it in my hand—Merrick's scale.

He nods sharply to me once before sauntering away.

"By tomorrow."

I swallow, waiting until he and the guards have all filed out of the room before I sink back down into the water. I can hear the king and his son arguing over the wall once he reaches the entrance where Edmund has been waiting for him. Their voices fade quickly.

Tears prick at my eyes—I have no doubt the king's threats are serious, but I don't have the answers he's looking for, which means I only have until morning to get us out of here or he's going to go after Merrick again.

I know he and his son won't hurt me anytime soon—they think I have answers—but I can't survive watching them pick Merrick apart piece by piece.

"Well?" Merrick says when I return. My tail curls under me as fear creeps into my body.

"Merrick, we have to get out—*tonight*."

Chapter 8

"What happened?" Merrick gapes at me, looking like he wants to rush to my side. Instead, he lets me swim to him.

"They've given us a deadline. I have to tell them what makes our sireny work or they're going to start the torture again."

"We've been through this before—"

"No, you don't understand," I cut him off. "They're not torturing *us.* They're torturing *you* in front of me so that I'll talk—they already know we won't talk to save *ourselves.*"

"They won't be back tonight," Dylana shakes her head.

"I can take it," Merrick announces. "It will be fine, we'll just survive it until that point. Caspian and Llyr will come back and break us out, and we'll escape."

"And what if you die before that point?" I snap.

"Then you two will escape," Merrick says matter-of-factly. "Celena, let's not be ridiculous here. This is going to happen—we just have to be prepared for it. It will all work out."

"*That's* not being ridiculous?" Dylana chides. "You're just going to *swim into this?*"

"No, I'm going to go up there and fight them, but if it means Celena gets out, then I'm fine with it."

"You understand," Dylana says calmly before I can, "that *she's* better at this game than you are—*miraculous, I know,* but she is—and Celena will find a way to take it *for* you, don't you?"

Her hands are on her hips when Merrick turns around to face her.

She's right, of course, but he doesn't like it. He keeps his frustration checked—as he's been trained to do.

"I'm sending the guards to find Keone and the others." Natale sounds upset—something I rarely see from her when she's not pretending to be meek. Even before she revealed her training to us, I rarely saw her as anything but even-tempered. She darts down the tunnel.

"We don't have long until it gets dark," Dylana takes charge. "If we can get you out while it's still dark, that's probably our best bet."

She squints when she notices I'm holding something in my hand. I open it to reveal the scale. Her face goes pale when she recognizes what it is, then immediately swings to Merrick as he realizes it came from his tail.

"Oh, Merrick," she breathes.

"I'm fine, Dylana, really," he insists. I hand the scale to him, and he examines it before dropping it, shrugging. Dylana catches my frown and nods slightly, indicating that she'll pick it up when he isn't looking as it twists in the water through the bars, resting gently to the side. It's strange, but it seems wrong to just let the scale float away.

We spend the next hour strategizing our escape.

Through the window in the ceiling, the moon looks orange, not too far off of the same color of the starfish that crawled into the pool earlier today. The creature is resting in the corner of the pool now, basking in the glow of the moon, high in the sky.

Clouds move across the sky—dark black like the night itself—covering the moon as if it were one of the bars blocking us from the outside world. They shift in the sky, blowing with the wind as they cover and reveal our light source. It glitters through the rippling water on the surface.

I dive back down, assured that there are no humans in the room above watching us. They have no reason to think we may be escaping in the middle of the night—as long as we remain quiet and under the water, they shouldn't catch us.

We all took turns sleeping early in the evening to make sure we were ready for our escape. I didn't sleep much, but knowing my friends were watching out for me, I rested on the ocean floor long enough to feel a little better.

"It's still clear," I inform everyone as I join them again.

"I think this is attached properly," Keone mumbles. He had returned before the others with two of the guards carrying chains from The Ropes—the others were still digging out supplies when they left, but the three mermen raced back to start setting up once Natale's charges found them and told them to hurry.

He tugs on the chains to see if they'll hold. Dylana and Natale swim over quickly, helping him test it.

"Don't pull yet," Merrick warns. "We don't want you to get strained before the others arrive to help—we only get one shot at this."

"They should be here soon—they weren't that far behind," Keone adds. "Now, we just have to hope this thing works."

Our goal is to bend one of the bars far enough that we can squeeze through. I'll go through first because I'm smaller than the mermen, and help pull once I'm on the other side. Merrick and Phorcys are about the same size, so they both should be able to make it through once we bend it far enough.

The tunnel glows a deep blue color, casting everything in a layer of bioluminescent glow that's much deeper than it is during the day when light filters down from the surface. It's comforting, but at the same time makes it a bit harder to see what we're doing.

Dylana ditched her crown of shells for a smaller one with fearsome broken pieces much like mine. It was a wise choice, considering what we're swimming into once we make our escape.

"I know everyone left for Scylla, but are they still there or are they moving?" I ask, pushing my floating hair behind me. In the blue light, it barely looks pink.

"They're pausing at Scylla to decide what to do. If they leave, mother will have left signs for us in several locations so we know where to find them," Dylana replies. "If we get separated, just race for Scylla, and we'll all meet up there."

We've always had predetermined meeting spots in case any of our operations ever went sideways, so the group already knows where to check. I'm positive Natale and Keone know where our meeting places are from observing us so closely over the years in secret. Phorcys has no way of knowing, and Dylana doesn't tell him…neither do I. I'm sure the group from Ambra will either stay with one of us or head back to Ambra if we get divided—I'm just grateful they've helped as much as they have.

"Princess," one of the mermen addresses Dylana. She turns as he offers his report. "There are a number of places we can hide in if we need to during the escape. One has a tunnel straight through it that we can use to confuse them."

It's probably the one Merrick, Caspian, and our small team used to get around the sirens on our way here. It's a smart plan.

"They're here!" another merman shouts from the far end of the tunnel. Moving back, he reveals the tiniest hint of light, but it's quickly swallowed up as Caspian and the others rush in.

Chains drag along the ocean floor, but they're also carrying other things too. I can't make out any of the details until they get closer. It looks like some of them are carrying poles, while others have chains and ropes.

"We found this," Casp informs us as he drags part of a large metal rod behind him. Llyr holds the far end, struggling to keep it up. Natale swims over, grabbing the middle in an effort to help support it. "If the chains don't work, we can try to push it with this."

It makes sense—if we push the rod between the bars and push on it, it should make the bar pop out in the middle, bending it in half like that time we found that sunken ship and couldn't get one of the doors open. When we used part of a railing we found as leverage and pushed against it, the door flung open, and we were able to go inside to explore—we didn't find anything, but at least we knew the room was empty.

They quickly wrap more chains around the bar we've chosen to try to bend. Llyr arranges the group in order, instructing them which chains to hold and where to float in the lineup.

"We're going to count down and all pull at the same time. Merrick will tell us when to stop, so be listening for his instructions. We'll try this several times before stopping to check on our progress at which point, we'll reevaluate what we're doing if we need to in case we need to try another strategy," Llyr continues. "Take a minute and get ready, we're going to start momentarily."

He swims over to us smarmily, a wide half grin on his face.

"So, princess, when this is all over, this makes me your hero, right?" He grins at me before winking at Merrick. "Careful, Merrick, she's going to swim off with me when this is all over."

"Mhmm, I'm sure," Merrick jokes. "Maybe you should save the talk until *after* you get us out of here."

"Yeah, yeah, brother." Llyr waves as he turns away. "Take the lead."

Merrick and Llyr may not be actual brothers, but they're as close as Caspian and I have ever been. It's sweet to watch…in a sickening way.

The collection picks up the chains all connected to the bars in a similar location. Phorcys and Merrick watch over the chains to ensure none of them slip too high or too low once the collection starts pulling.

We had considered attaching a chain to the bar next to it so that we could pull from the inside, creating a larger gap in a faster time frame, but none of the three of us inside the pool are in any condition to be doing the heavy lifting required to bend a metal bar in half. Still, a chain rests on the sand on the second bar, just in case.

Merrick gives the order, and the collection pulls, straining against the chains. Their tails thrashing in the water create waves that stretch out to me after a moment, pulsing against my body. Several of them grunt as they pull, but the bar doesn't move.

"Stop," Merrick commands, holding out his hand as if they were watching him instead of facing away as they pull.

The group pauses, letting the chains rest in their hands. The pulsing water fades around me as I inspect the bar from two lengths away—it doesn't appear to have dented it at all.

"Ready?" Merrick asks after a moment, indicating that they should prepare themselves to pull again. "Again."

The group pulls, and I wish on the three starfish inside the pool that it works this time. The moon casts a strange orange glow in the water that mixes with the blue from the tunnel in an unsettling way while my friends fight for my freedom.

This time, the bar starts moving.

It's not enough to escape, but there's a visible bend in the bar, giving us all the hope we need to keep going. I nearly start cheering the collection on when I hear a slap on the water above me.

Merrick quickly stops everyone as we all whip around to listen. The slap sounds again.

"Did they catch us?" Dylana squeaks.

We wait in silence to see if the splash would happen again or if it was a fluke. After a moment, another splash sounds, this one gentler.

"I'll go." I start swimming.

"Celena, no!" everyone gasps behind me.

"One of us has to distract them, or they'll *definitely* know something is wrong. I'll be fine."

'It's the middle of the night—whatever this is, it can't be good," Merrick growls. "I'm going with you."

"No, you need to stay here and help them," I refuse to let him join me. "Just pay attention in case I signal you. If I wave, that means to hurry up. If I place my hand flat, that means to standby, and if I do nothing, then it's okay. Just *watch*."

Without waiting, I rush to the surface, slowing only when I can tell who is on the other side of the water. Edmund stands along the side of the pool, waiting for me.

"You *are* up," he murmurs as I surface.

"I wasn't," I pretend to yawn, slipping into an actual yawn. "What did you need?"

"Oh." He frowns. "I'm sorry, I didn't mean to wake you."

'It's fine, what do you need?"

"I couldn't sleep," he admits. "I thought we could talk."

Glancing around, I realize he's alone—there are no guards here.

He either trusts me, or they're hiding somewhere.

"Do you want to sit with me?" He takes a seat and pats the wall next to him.

"I think I'll stay down here," I reply softly. "It's too cool for me to be out right now."

He nods, glancing around as if he's just noticing it's cooler than it was during the day. Edmund turns a bit to get more comfortable.

I move my hand in the water, leaving my palm out flat so that my friends know to wait a moment.

"I've been thinking," Edmund starts, sounding reluctant. He dives forward, "It's different here than I expected. A lot of it is what Jarek used to tell us, but it's so much more than that here.

"The people are incredible, and they work so hard, but they're also in such danger. The towns are magnificent, and I see how easily this place could be incredible again if we allowed people back into the area—I mean beyond the sailor's families.

"I want to fix this place—I want Antaire to be prestigious once again. I want to restore it to its former glory. We're a kingdom built on exports from the sea, and yet we live nowhere near it—it's shameful. The other kingdoms look down on us for fearing the sea. I don't want that under my rule."

"Why are you telling me all this?"

Maybe I *should* have taken a seat on the wall with him, I could have put a hand on his knee and convinced him to tell me everything, one friend to another. The water separates us too much, creating a wall between us. I swim closer.

"I don't know why, Celena, but I think I actually trust you. I think you're either the best actress in the world, or you genuinely just want to leave and not hurt my people.

"I know my father will never acquiesce to a human-mer treaty again, but I think he's wrong. I think we need it and I think you and I are going to be the only ones that can make that happen." He looks desperately at me as if I control the fate of his entire world and what I say next will cast him as the greatest king Antaire has ever known, or banish him into oblivion.

"How can that happen when your father is in charge? Even if you and I wanted to form an alliance, we'll both be old enough to have grandchildren by the time you take over as king."

"I don't know, but I think we need to try. I heard stories of more attacks today—I don't want my men to die any longer. If what you say is true, you don't want this war either. We need an agreement in place, and we need our leadership to enforce it with harsh consequences for anyone on either side that disobeys.

"We don't have to be friends, we just have to have rules and boundaries. It doesn't have to be like before."

I'm not sure it ever *could* be like before—humans and mer being friendly with one another. Though, I'd almost like to try with Edmund.

For a moment, I wonder if there's an easy way to murder the king and install Edmund as Antaire's official ruler early. I blink, shaking my head just slightly as I banish that idea from my mind.

I pull my hand up, releasing them from worrying about me.

"So you want the two of us to create a treaty that might not ever go into effect?"

"I do."

"You know I'm not a reigning royal, right? I don't have that kind of power." I swim closer to him, setting a hand on the wall.

"But your cousin is the queen, you have her ear, don't you? Wouldn't she listen to you?"

"She'll listen to me, but I don't know if this will work."

"Can we try? I just want to try." He sounds so sad as he speaks. "I just want this to be over, and this is the only way I see how. Don't you think you and I could get along, Celena? Outside of these walls when you're free, can't we try to be friends?"

"You were rather insistent on offering to torture me until just now…"

"Aila would do this," Edmund retorts, challenging me to make a choice.

My great-great grandmother had risked her life multiple times to save the human-mer treaty. She fought against her own cousin

*—someone she adored—*to protect the alliance. Aila did everything in her power to save Prince Jarek and rescue him from her cousin, and it cost her the friendship that she held dearest to her outside her family. Now, a century later, I have the opportunity to restore that alliance.

One way or another, we're escaping tonight, but once we get out, it would be wise to keep Edmund on our side. Perhaps one day the treaty could be real—there's no telling what the future holds.

I take a deep breath and launch myself out of the water to sit on the wall beside him. He looks surprised but attempts to keep his composure as I drip on the wall, the water traveling over to where he sits.

"How do we do this?" I whisper. I'm nervous—I don't know what this means for our future, but I think I trust that he means what he says and that he actually wants a treaty.

"We need to discuss the terms. Then you take it to your queen, and I'll take it to my king."

"How do you expect me to do that?"

"I'll free you, Celena. I'll get you out."

I suck in a breath—he's offering to free me....but is he offering to free us *all*?

"Merrick?"

"I'll try," he murmurs, reaching out to take my hand. "This is bigger than the both of us, Celena. I'll do my best, but we're talking about protecting entire kingdoms here."

"No, we're talking about creating a treaty that may not ever come to fruition—what do you think will happen when your father discovers I'm gone?"

"He won't kill the only mer he has left." He purses his lips.

"Maybe not, but what else will he do to them?"

"He wants to show you off, Celena. If he doesn't have the pretty one, he'll need to keep the other two looking decent."

"Or maybe he'll want to prove how fearsome they are with their scars."

"This is getting us nowhere, Celena." He releases my hand, aggravated.

"Fine, let's work on the treaty," I agree, knowing it won't matter anyway—we're freeing ourselves. "We can talk about how to get us out of here later."

In the orange moonlight, his sandy-colored hair looks almost red. I imagine my pink hair has taken on an orange tone as well, but he doesn't say anything. He holds a hand out, waiting for me to put mine in his as an agreement.

I reach out, touching his hand. It's warm against mine and feels almost as comfortable as holding Llyr's hand when we occasionally have deep conversations together. Humans are less comfortable holding hands than mer, so I know this is important to Edmund.

"I promise, I'll get you out of here, and I'll do everything I can to get your friends out too. I'm not sure how yet, but I will."

"I believe you," I squeeze his hand to let him know I'm on his side —even though I don't need his help to escape.

"I am going to do everything in my power to support the mer and form this alliance. I don't want to live in a world where we're surrounded by unnecessary war. We'll undo what Jarek and Persephone did. We'll work together and fix all of this."

"What is *this*?" the king gasps, a mere length away from us. Edmund and I jump, and I nearly topple off the wall into the water— only his hand on mine keeps me in place. I don't know how the king snuck up on us, but he managed to overhear our conversation.

"You sirened him," the king whispers, accusing me.

"No," I gasp back, pulling my hand from Edmund's.

"No!" Edmund shouts, standing to his feet.

"You sirened my son, you sea witch!" The king's shrieks alert the guards by the stairs and they rush over to assist.

"She didn't, Father," Edmund shouts, hand between the king and me as he tries to block part of his father's wrath. "We want to create a new treaty between the mer and the humans—we want to end this."

"She tricked you into saying these things, son." The king looks aghast. "You don't know what you're talking about because she whispered these thoughts into your mind. This isn't truly how you feel!"

"It *is* though," Edmund argues. I can barely turn to see both of them fight. "Antaire is a glorious kingdom, but we've been exiled from the sea—the source of our wealth and power. We need access to it again! The only way is with a new treaty. It doesn't have to be like the last one, but it needs to exist!"

The guards close in, spears ready. I leap off the wall into the water to protect myself. I hear Edmund call my name before I slam into the water.

Unable to keep myself above the surface, I bob under the water just long enough to see Dylana watching me with a terrified look on her face as Merrick and Phorcys try to pull the bars open from our side of the divider. The bars are wider now, but still not enough to fit a mer through them.

"Hurry!" I shout to them, rising above the water once more to distract the guards. When I surface, the king is trying to wrestle his son away from the water.

"Get her!" the king shouts, directing the men to capture me. I swim back in the water, putting more distance between us—if they enter the water now, they can still drag us out, but if I can stall and give them more time to open the bars, we have a chance.

"Celena, get down," Edmund calls, trying to get me to dive under the surface where his men can't reach me. He waves his arm furiously as his father turns bright red even under the orange light of the moon.

A loud splash to my left makes me turn. Several more follow—the guards are in the water, spears in hand. They look nervous, but not nearly as frightened as the men who usually show up in this room. Their fear of their king must be great to convince them to jump in after me.

"Celena!" Edmund calls, not understanding why I won't leave.

I start shouting, hoping to draw the men's attention. I back up toward the far wall, knowing I can draw them away, and then dive under the water and swim beneath them faster than they can track my movements.

"Sire!" one of the guards in the water shouts, "The mermen are trying to escape!"

A shadow crosses over Edmund's face for a moment, but he doesn't hold it against me that I'm trying to escape. He nods briefly, telling me that it's okay.

Brilliantly, Edmund flings himself into the water, taking his father with him. In sheer panic, the king releases his son as the guards swim to save their king. The prince makes his way to me, swimming across the surface.

"I want to stay here, Celena, and I want to stay in peace. I want this war over. My father might not think there can ever be a treaty again, but I do. Meet me at the cave. Go!"

He turns his back on me as he pushes me under the water.

I dive for the exit, but it's not open yet.

The tunnel is still blocked, though there's a definite opening in the bars. Caspian and Llyr have forced the metal rod between the bars, seeing the commotion, and as many strong mermen as possible are pushing on it, forcing it apart. It moves with a loud groan every time they throw themselves against it.

"Hurry!" I scream, racing toward them.

As soon as I reach Merrick, he pushes me at the opening, demanding I try to fit through. Unable to fit, I pull back.

"Look out!" Phorcys shouts, pulling Merrick back.

Merrick whips around to face him as a spear lands between us.

Several of the guards drop their spear in the water, and they float down to us. Others intentionally throw their spears, but the water slows their decent, allowing us to easily avoid them.

While Caspian and the others try to break the bars on our prison, we quickly collect the weapons, knowing we'll need them later. I pass the extras through to Dylana and Natale who distribute them on the other side of the bars.

Turning, I hold my spear out, ready to attack. Two of the guards dive under the water, swimming toward us. The king must have ordered his men to attack us because the entire group turns tentatively before taking a gulp of air and diving below the surface. Some have knives in their hands, others rope, though some retained their spears.

I prepare for battle.

Unsurprisingly, the king and Edmund are no longer in the water.

Llyr yells as one final push bends the bar in half behind us. Caspian screams for us to move.

Before I can turn, Merrick grabs my tail and pulls me backward, much rougher than our usual fighting tactics. I keep my spear up as he drags me through the water, waiting to take out any human that gets too close.

Phorcys pushes his way through behind me and the entire collection floods out of the tunnel. Merrick doesn't let go until we're in the open waters—it surrounds me like a whale swallowing krill.

I've never felt as free as right now, but I don't have time to really experience it—we're swimming for our lives.

CHAPTER 9

The orange light of the moon shifts away into the muted colors of early morning. Schools of fish float gracefully by, but their colors nearly blend with the dark waters.

Merrick and Caspian cling to me, both wrapping an arm around my waist as we swim as quickly as we can. Llyr and Keone keep an eye on Phorcys, Dylana and Natale taking a place behind them in case he tries something stupid, and they need to assist the boys to stop him, though I doubt he will.

Once we're a safe distance away, I quietly tell my brother and my boyfriend what happened.

"It doesn't matter, we're leaving," Caspian informs me.

"Edmund told me to meet him in the cave."

"Which cave? He didn't give you any specifics?" Merrick asks, a bit more open-minded.

"I assume he means *the* cave," I reply. "The one where Persephone sirened Jarek."

"And Aila saved him," Caspian adds. "You're still not going. We need to get as far from here as possible.

"This is our only chance at overcoming this, we can't swim away from this opportunity. Edmund helped me escape—I believe he wants this treaty to work. Even if we can't make it happen while the king is alive, someday, Edmund will be in power.

"We don't ever have to go near the humans again, but now even if we stumble upon them, they won't be able to hurt us for fear of punishment from their king."

"And what if they secretly kill us and the prince doesn't find out?" Caspian makes a good point.

"I don't know, but it will at least stop *some* of the murders," I point out.

We duck under a sea turtle that obviously doesn't care that we're in the ocean with it. My hair slaps against its underside as we move to avoid hitting it.

"They're launching boats," one of the mermen from Ambra says, ducking back under the water.

"This is our only chance to go back," I murmur.

I stop in the water, nearly causing some of the mer to collide with each other to avoid swimming into me. I mumble an apology as I drop back to Dylana. Regardless of what the boys say, it's her choice.

Words tumble out of my mouth as I explain, stating my case. After a moment, she slows.

"We go back," she announces to everyone's shock. "We have a chance at a treaty. I can sign it—we can end this war now. We go back."

She looks around the group as they wait for directions.

"You don't have to stay, but Celena and I are."

"We stay," Llyr says, taking the lead to support us.

"We stay," Caspian quickly adds, refusing to leave my side. The rest of the group echoes my brother. Phorcys grinds his teeth but doesn't say anything, nodding briefly when I make eye contact with him.

"Where do we go?" Dylana turns to me, knowing of everyone here, I know the direction of the cave from Aila's stories.

I point, and we all turn to swim back, hovering as low to the ocean floor as possible. We stay as close to the kelp forests and caves as possible, hiding any way that we can.

"I trust her on this," Dylana whispers when Caspian swims up next to us. "If she got through to the prince, we have to try. If there's a treaty in place, it might just save us. You know that if there isn't, the humans won't stop until we're all dead and they control the seas."

We pause inside a cave, letting Llyr ensure there are no ships nearby in the dark colors of the early morning water. After a moment, he waves us forward, and we dart out, swimming to the next momentary shelter.

We continue forward, darting around rocks and broken ship pieces on the ocean floor. Carefully, we avoid the fishing nets the humans had left when the siren attacks started.

Swimming low in a bed of seaweed, we glide over the ocean floor toward the cave. The seaweed tickles my skin, but I don't have time to care. I brush it away from me with my hands as I flick my tail to swim forward.

We don't see the net off to the side, so when one of the mermaids swims into it, her scream terrifies us. She pulls back, attempting to untangle herself, but the humans pull her up quickly.

The abandoned fishing net must have caught on something near the surface for the humans to have so easily found it—there's no way they could have put this in the water without us seeing it as we approached, so it must have already been here. Their ship is so far away, it's barely noticeable on the water, but in the distance, if I look hard, I can see the outline of the boat floating against the waves.

They drag the Ambraian mermaid across the ocean. She claws at the ground as she is forced over it, bumping into the sand over and over as they haul her in. Her fingers scrape at the loose sand, looking for anything to hold onto.

Eventually, she grasps a shell, but the quick motion of the moving net knocks it out of her hand. She yells, desperate as it topples away.

We push as hard as we can, trying to reach the girl in time. With weapons ready, we close in on her, ready to cut her free. She catches a shell in her hand once more, this time holding tight enough to keep it in place. She hacks at the ropes as Llyr and Caspian reach her.

They slice into the net, ripping it open. She forces her way out as the three mer are lifted high into the water. The boys quickly check to make sure she is free of the net and for an instant, I flash back to the start of all this—when a siren mermaid got caught in the human nets outside the reef barrier protecting Scylla, and I met Tarni, Roni, and Tiko for the first time as they mourned their dead friend—how far we've come in a month.

The mermaid rushes into the arms of her collection, and they comfort her, helping her swim with an injured tail. It's not too bad, but she'll be sore for a while. She tucks her blue hair behind her ear as she holds on to Larinia.

Once the humans pull the net up, they'll see what happened and know they've found us—we have to move.

We quickly follow Merrick—he's swimming surprisingly fast for all of his injuries—and dart low to the ground again, this time swimming two at a time to avoid spreading out.

The ocean is a blur as we swim, my mind drifting ahead to the cave, wondering what I'll find. I don't even know if Edmund will be there.

What if he couldn't escape his father? What if the king tortures the meeting location from his son, or worse—he guesses on his own?

I can't let anyone go into the cave with me until I'm sure it's safe. One of the boys can wait at the entrance, but it's illogical to have them swim in with me.

I'm not even sure what the cave looks like. I know Aila said there was a ledge where Jarek stood, and that the cave was deep, but the stories she told were always more about the events than the setting—of course, they could have eroded over time until we just had the main events of the story, but I have a feeling she never described it much to begin with.

We move sideways, swimming in a large arch to reach our destination in an effort to avoid the areas they might think of to check. Dylana and Natale take places by my sides, edging Merrick and Caspian out so we can talk.

"I know you're going to tell me you want to go in alone, but I have to be there to negotiate this treaty," Dylana whispers.

"You two aren't going in there without me," Natale snaps. "We do this together."

"Aila, Kailania, and Ebba back together again?" I smirk, trying to make light of the situation.

"If one of you suggests finding Tarni, I'll give you to the humans myself," Natale sneers, but we know she's joking. I'm still not used to this new version of her.

"She's not really of Chantay's blood—we can skip her on this little adventure," I reply. "But you're still not going in with me."

The two argue with me, insisting on joining me inside the cave with Edmund.

"Merrick will guard the cave—or Caspian or Llyr—and I'll go in alone. If it's safe, *then* you can come in with me." I look at Dylana, purposely avoiding Natale. I'd prefer she stay outside with the others. Neither of her demeanors will be helpful during the negotiations.

"I need your help anyway, Natale," Keone swims up next to us, invading our private conversation. "While the guys are keeping them safe, you and I need to make sure the humans don't find them."

I imagine Natale wouldn't say no to an excuse to get near the humans—if there's an altercation, she could hurt them for what they did to her mother and no one would hold her accountable for striking out at them. She turns to her boyfriend, and they argue quietly. Her body language changes when he brings up that very point, and she changes her mind.

Now the only challenge will be convincing the mermen to let me go in alone. Merrick glances over at me around Dylana. We make eye contact and I know he knows what I'm about to pull on him—he's always been able to read me.

We slow, feeling confident that we're far enough away that the humans won't know where we went. Unfortunately, it also means we have a long way to go to get back to the cave. Turning, we start our path back toward Jarek's cave.

"That's it?" Caspian asks as we stare from inside a seaweed bed. The water is cooler as a cold current moves through the ocean.

"Looks like it," Dylana mutters. "Celena?"

"That's it," I reply, remembering how my great-great-grandmother described the cave. My great-great-grandfather, Troy, had waited outside with her until she discovered that Persephone was sirening the prince over a century ago—I'm staring at the rock where he had hidden himself out of sight.

Aila may have received all of the credit for rescuing Jarek, but Troy was essential in the success of that day. If he hadn't been there for Aila, she never would have been able to save the prince. Troy never took any of the praise though—he always deferred to Aila. From the stories I've heard, they were the couple all mer should aspire to be.

I wonder if my great-great-grandparents would be proud of me as I try to fix the treaty they worked to protect. I like to think they would be.

"You must be in awe," Caspian smirks next to me. "I'm sure Cor will have a fit when she hears about this."

"Probably," I joke with my twin. "Maybe we should skip over this part when we tell her later."

"Talking about how Coralie is going to hold this against you for the rest of your life?" Merrick swims up next to us, putting a hand on the small of my back. It's amazing that he doesn't flinch when he brushes over the raised welts the jellyfish left—I'm sure they don't feel pleasant—it's a good thing those are starting to heal. "I have a feeling Aila wasn't decked out in shoulder armor when she was here though."

He winks flirtatiously at me when I turn to face him.

"You know our sister well." I grin at him. "And maybe I'm more fierce than Aila."

"Aila saved *a nation*—you're saving *several*." Caspian snorts at Merrick's response, but his eyes are serious as he nods his agreement to me quietly.

I take a deep breath, staring at the outside of the cave.

"Let's go," Merrick says before I can ask if he's ready.

Caspian and I traded weapons—he took my spear while I have his trident. I clutch it in my hands as Merrick and I head for the cave. If Edmund is there and brought people with him, I'll have to be prepared to fight. I know better than to swim into this naively. If this is a trap, then it's likely there will be nets or some kind of trap door like the one Morgen used in the palace in Scylla to trap the sirens. I'll have to watch for those as I enter.

We pause outside of the cave entrance. I touch the wall, letting my fingers dance over the bumpy rocks. A slight blue glow filters out, but I only spot it because I already know what to expect inside the cave.

Merrick peeks around the cave entrance, and I take a place just below him in the water, looking around the rock wall as well. When we don't see anything, I covertly turn my head to Merrick, knowing my hair is hiding us, and brush my lips against his. He moans softly, not expecting the display of affection. He grins, opening his eyes as he motions me into the cave, promising he'll be watching.

The inside of the cave is magical. Streaks of light are embedded in the walls, glowing a magnificent blue color. The light from the spores sparkles off of the water and reflect back onto the walls. It's almost as magical as the Scur Caverns Merrick showed me when we were in Metten—also a favorite of the royals from a century ago.

If Edmund doesn't show up anytime soon, I wouldn't be opposed to calling Merrick in for a few moments alone.

I didn't see any nets as I swam in, but I turn to check behind me to ensure there is no trap door waiting to cut me off from the world. When I find nothing, I look to the ledge.

"Prince Edmund?" I call out just above a whisper. Placing a hand on the ledge, I flick my tail just enough to raise myself out of the water a little to get a better view.

Nothing stirs in the cave except the shifting blue glow from the walls. I call out again, slightly louder but don't expect much. As I turn, something shuffles beyond the cavern walls on the far side of the ledge.

A human peeks out from around the wall of a cave and panic seizes my chest. I start to dive into the water, but a man's voice stops me.

"It's her."

"Celena," Edmund calls out from behind the rocks. He quickly appears around his servant, moving toward the ledge. His eyes scan the water, looking for signs of trouble. "I'm here alone."

He turns back to his servant, waving him in. Surprisingly, the servant doesn't have anything blocking his ears from me. The man clasps his hands in front of him and waits for directions—he looks like one of the humans that protected the prince in the palace, but there were so many of them that I can't be sure. He watches me carefully as I swim halfway between where I was and the ledge.

"Did you make it out okay?" Edmund asks. I nod.

"We're all relatively safe. How did you escape?"

"My father has the palace on lockdown, but I've read Grandfather Jarek's journals from after he left the palace—he had maps of everything. We took one of the secret entrances—I doubt he even knows we're gone. To be fair, he's a bit busy hunting you."

"We can't stay long, sire," the servant says.

"I know, Jackson." Edmund never takes his eyes off me.

"I have to get the princess," I blurt out, surprising even myself.

"What?"

"The princess… I have to get her to do this treaty with you."

"I thought *you and I* were creating the treaty," Edmund comments, frowning.

I duck low in the water, preparing to signal for Dylana to join us.

"I'll be here, but she has to be the one to work it out with you."

"She's *here?*" he yelps. "I thought she left."

"Her mother did," I reply. "Dylana stayed to save us."

Edmund looks impressed by her loyalty as I slide under the water. Merrick is watching me, not taking his eyes off of me.

"He's here. Get Dylana."

Merrick refuses to turn until he's sure I'm staying under the water and not returning to the surface. He leans around the edge of the cave entrance, motioning Dylana to join us. She swims quickly from the seaweed bed the rest of the collection is hiding in.

"Edmund is here with one of his servants. They're waiting for us. His father doesn't know he's gone, so we need to be as quick as possible. I'll back up whatever you want, cousin," I mumble quickly. She nods, following me to the surface.

"Wow, this is beautiful," she murmurs before we surface.

Out in the air, Dylana looks radiant as she hovers out of the water. She looks regal with shoulders back, her deep pink hair flowing down her back. Her shoulder armor sparkles under the blue bioluminescent glow of the cave. Edmund and Jackson quietly gasp when they see her.

"Princess," he regards her solemnly.

"Prince Edmund, my cousin tells me you want to make a new alliance with the mer." Dylana sounds remarkably like her mother as she addresses the human prince.

"I do. What should I call you?"

"My name is Dylana. I am the daughter of Marilla, Queen of Scylla, Metten, and the surrounding kingdoms. I will speak on her behalf today."

"You're sure your mother will be okay with this?" Edmund asks nervously. He twists his hands together, watching us.

"Yes, my mother trusts my judgment, and we both would like for this war to end," Dylana says confidently. She's far more self-assured than Edmund. "What would you like to discuss?"

"Terms for a truce," Edmund explains. "Terms for a future alliance, and rules and consequences should someone break the terms we will set forth to our people…umm, mer. Mer and people."

I quietly will Edmund to calm down—I've never seen him so nervous, even when he first captured me. He glances at me and nods slightly, shifting back on his feet to steady himself. He redirects his gaze to Dylana.

"Terms for the truce first?" Dylana asks. "I say we call for an immediate end to the fight. My collection has already left and does not plan on returning to the area, so that would mean your humans would only be responsible for not seeking us out."

"Agreed, but I should let you know that I don't have my father's blessing for this yet."

"I understand. This is an agreement between you and the mer collection. If your father does not abide by this, we won't hold his actions against you *once* you take power. Until then, if your father attempts to attack the mer, we can not be held to the terms of this agreement if we need to protect ourselves, but we vow not to actively come after the humans."

"I appreciate your deference. I know this isn't an ideal situation, but I promise I'll do my best."

"I've explained the situation to my cousin, Edmund. She knows why you're doing this," I add.

I allow Dylana and Edmund to discuss terms, waiting patiently. On occasion, I make comments, but I spend most of my time focused on the cave itself. I memorize every inch of it—both in case I end up back here *and* in case I never see it again.

Jackson watches me intently, but his attention is divided between Dylana and me. I'm sure it's mesmerizing watching two pink-haired mermaids float in a cave, but his head is bobbing back and forth between us so much that I'm starting to get stressed out—I wish he would hold still.

An hour goes by as they work out details, compromising where they must, arguing over other things. I dip my face in the water once in a while to let Merrick know that things are going well—he watches from the entrance, quietly slipping a little closer each time I check on him.

They still have a long way to go, discussing what locations would be devoted to which group in an effort to avoid each other when shuffling sounds behind the prince and his servant. Panic is written all over Edmund's face as he turns.

He waves his hand to us, indicating that we should hide. Dylana and I duck under the water, swimming to the ledge so we can surface again, hidden by the rocks.

"Prince Edmund, we have orders to return you to the palace," someone addresses him formally. "You are to return immediately at which point you will be remanded to your chambers until you can be escorted back to the Winter Palace tomorrow."

"What?" Edmund sounds shocked. "I'm not going back to the Winter Palace—there's too much to be done here."

"Sire, your father has said you are not to return to the palace here again." The man's voice is hard and unrelenting. Edmund won't be able to convince him of anything. "You are to come with us at once. If you will not come on your own, the king has instructed us to take you back by force."

Dylana looks worried, but I'm furious—we've worked too hard and lost too much for this treaty to be destroyed.

"Jackson, I'm going to need you to trust me," Edmund says somewhere over our heads.

"Yes, sire," the servant replies. I can hear Edmund and Jackson walking back, closer to the edge. It takes a moment, but then I realize what they're doing.

"We're here," I shout, letting him know that I understand what his plan is. Dylana looks horrified until she realizes what we're doing.

The prince and his servant splash into the water.

CHAPTER 10

"Hold your breath," I instruct as I grab onto Jackson. Dylana wraps her arms around the prince, and we drag them under the water as the guards above shout, preparing to follow us.

Merrick's confusion is evident, but he immediately flips in the water to wave off the rest of the collection. He shouts that we have the humans and need to move.

Jackson's fingers claw into me in terror, bubbles escaping his lips as I drag him further down into the water. I hope Edmund isn't as rough as his servant, but unlike Jackson, Edmund knew what to expect.

Merrick whips back around, holding his trident out to the guards as they jump into the water—they're not nearly as fast as us, even as we carry humans through the water—so they're no real threat at the moment.

Dylana and I dip down through the entrance to the cave, coming up on the open waters side. We flip our tails as quickly as possible, rushing toward the surface before the humans run out of air. They come up choking in the mid-day air.

"Jackson?" Edmund asks as soon as he can breath.

"I'm here, Edmund," he sputters, still clutching at me. "Are you all right?"

"I'm fine, friend. We have to get out of here." Edmund treads water on his own, spinning to look around at our surroundings. "There. There's a boat—they have to listen to me."

He starts swimming toward the large vessel, expecting us to follow.

"We can't go over there, Edmund," I remind him. "We can't be anywhere near them."

"I'm going to command the ship, and we'll finish this treaty," he replies.

"You think they're just going to listen to you?" Dylana asks, glancing at the ship. "Those guards in the cave didn't listen—why will these men?"

"I'm the prince, Princess Dylana," Edmund retorts as he brushes his sandy-blond hair back with one hand. It drips in his face almost comically. "They don't know I'm not representing my father at this point, so they'll have to listen."

"And once you have this ship of humans, what then? We still can't go near it, it's too dangerous," I remind him.

"We'll think of something, but we can't stay in the water unprotected like this, Celena," he points out. "You stay here and just watch for my signal. I'll move the ship away from the rest, and we'll find a way to talk without the rest of the sailors finding out. Just keep watching Jackson or me, and one of us will direct you to the right place."

My heart stutters as he brings Jackson into this—I don't know him, and I certainly don't know where his alliances lie.

"I trust him," Edmund whispers, leaning closely so only I can hear him as his nose crashes into my hair. "He's loyal to me."

The two start to swim off as Dylana and I shrink back.

"We don't have a choice, do we?" Dylana asks.

"No, we don't. We have to finish putting this treaty into place."

The collection hovers below us in the water—I can feel Merrick's hand on the edge of my fins. Dylana nods, telling me it's okay to duck under the water to update the collection while she watches the humans above.

I stay just under the surface, still at Dylana's side as I inform them of what happened. Caspian and Llyr nod, looking grim.

"We have to follow them—we're so close to having a treaty everyone can agree with. We can't swim away now."

"We'll do what we can," Llyr says, "but we're also not risking your lives for this. The collection is already long gone—they'll be safe, we'll make sure of it—we just need to get back to them. This treaty is a good thing, but not if we have to die for it—we can survive without it."

He glances at Dylana's tail, and I know he's worried about her. Llyr has always been good about hiding his feelings, but I've always been equally as good at fishing for information.

"They're moving," Dylana drops down in the water. "We have to go."

Llyr volunteers to swim above the water before anyone else can, leaving the rest of the collection to trail behind him under the water. He guides us for several minutes until we get too close to other ships. Diving under the water, we risk getting closer to Edmund's boat so we don't lose it, swimming so close that if we sped up, we'd be directly under it.

"That's not right, is it?" Larina asks.

"I don't think so," Quillo answers her, putting a hand on her back.

I tip my head up to see what they're looking at and find a small rowboat moving away from the boat Edmund is commanding. The oars dip into the water, pushing the boat further away from the vessel.

"I'll go," Llyr announces, but Caspian's hand stops him.

"Let me," Casp says. "Your hair is a bit...noticeable in the light right now."

My twin hands me his spear to hold. Carefully, Caspian peeks out of the water, hovering just enough that his eyes are over the surface. He floats above the water for a few moments before sinking back down with us.

"It's the prince."

"We have to follow them," I reply instantly, changing our direction as the humans row away from the boat. I definitely don't mind escaping from that thing.

Edmund dips a hand into the water, wiggling his fingers under the surface—it looks like he can't quite reach into the water all the way. Eventually, he pulls it up, leaving it in the boat with him.

I dart ahead of the others, swimming up to the small rowboat. Intentionally staying on the opposite side as the large boat they just left, I slip carefully above the surface.

"I'm here." I hear both of them jump above me as I startle them. "Sorry."

"Get us out of here, Celena," Edmund requests. "Before they notice we're gone."

"They didn't see you steal a boat?" I can't believe that he could have possibly taken a boat and escaped without someone noticing.

"We might have thrown someone overboard to distract them," Jackson grumbles, obviously upset.

How did we miss a person in the water? Maybe we were too distracted by the rowboat.

"Do you have any rope in there?" I ask, putting my hand on the side of the rowboat.

Edmund looks around at the boat, moving random objects—apparently, the sailors were treating the rowboat as if it were made to be used as storage.

"Oh." He moves something. Edmund holds up a length of rope. "Yes, actually. Why?"

I reach for it, and he hands it to me. Working quickly, I tie a knot at one end and slip it over the front of their boat.

"We'll help pull you—it doesn't look like Jackson is going to last long at those oars." Jackson puffs his chest out, looking annoyed, but the way he's breathing tells me he needs a break. He clearly wasn't made for this kind of labor.

Under the water, I hand the rope off to Keone who takes the first shift pulling the humans across the sea. We swim quickly away from the sailors, hoping they don't take too much notice as the tiny rowboat skims across the surface of the water.

I don't bother surfacing for now—we're faster under the water. I'll check on the prince in a while. Dylana takes a place next to me, and we discuss what else the royals still need to work out.

Eventually, Edmund taps on the water, trying to get our attention.

"I really think we need to find a better way of doing that," I respond, coming out of the water.

"Well, for now, it's what we've got," Edmund doesn't look amused at my attempt at a joke. "Where are we going?"

"Somewhere safe." I grab hold of the boat, catching a ride like I sometimes do with the dolphins.

"Where, Celena?" He refuses to be dragged around without answers.

"We're going to Metten. Your father won't be able to find you there."

The prince pales.

The sun has shifted, leaning more toward late afternoon. It sparkles below the surface, casting long rays of light to sparkle on the ocean floor. I wish I were under the waves to see how the light dances with the colorful fish and sea life, but it's a sight I see every day, so it's more important to speak with Edmund. I've seen enough of Aila's world to keep me happy for now.

"You'll be safe in Metten," I promise. "We'll bring you right back here when we're done."

"We can't breathe underwater, Celena, how do you expect us to go to Metten?"

"We're not taking you to the palace, just to the area. We have borders set up so humans can't access the kingdom easily. If you weren't in this tiny boat, you wouldn't be able to reach the kingdom waters.

"Our plan is to bring you inside the barriers so we can finish the treaty. They won't be able to reach you there."

"Unless they come in on small boats too," Edmund points out.

"Would they really do that? They're pretty scared of the water."

"If my father orders them to, yes. Of course, he's not here and doesn't know what's going on yet, so I suppose we have some time."

"Should we perhaps get the princess up here to start talking this through while we're traveling?" Jackson suggests, clearly still annoyed at me.

I had considered having Dylana talk to the prince, but it's one thing to have *me* strain to stay above the water to have a conversation with the prince, but it's an entirely different thing to have Dylana struggle while also trying to negotiate.

"This isn't exactly easy, you know." I direct my comment at Jackson. "Swimming above the water is a lot of work."

"You're hanging on to the boat," he points out.

"It's still difficult, Jackson," Edmund comments, silencing his friend. "We can discuss the treaty when we arrive in Metten. You're welcome to stay up here and talk with us, Celena, but I won't force you to. If you'd like to sit in the boat with us, we can make room for you for a little while, but I won't hold it against you if you'd like to swim under the water."

Phorcys appears out of the water behind me, latching onto the boat. Edmund makes a face, unable to restrain himself in time. He winces, realizing his mistake but attempts to cover it over with contempt for the merman.

"What do you want?" Edmund asks coolly.

"I came to find out why Celena is still up here." He gives me an icy glare. "Your boyfriend is worried."

He's not—Merrick trusts my choices. It's *Phorcys* who wants to interject himself into the conversation, and that's just his excuse. I'm a bit surprised the mermen let Phorcys surface, but I'm sure they have their reasons.

I give Edmund an apologetic look, nodding for Phorcys to return to the water.

"You know he likes you," Edmund mumbles before I leave. "Careful."

Once under the water, I let the boat drift away as I stop Phorcys. I know at least one of the boys—Merrick, Caspian, or Llyr—has noticed and is keeping an eye on me, so I don't worry about the boat straying too far.

"What do you want, Phorcys?"

He raises an eyebrow at me, crossing his arms to match mine.

"I want to know where I float in all of this." He puts on a brave face, but any mer would be nervous in his situation—his collection is gone, he's swimming with his enemies, and the humans aren't far behind. He has nowhere to go and no one to depend on. If we force him out, what is he supposed to do?

"I don't know, but I'm positive what you choose to do between now and the time we get back to Scylla—or wherever the collection is —will affect the queen's decision on your fate."

"So there's a chance I'll go all this way with you and still have to suffer?"

"Considering how many mer you killed—or had a hand in killing —I'd say you'll be lucky if they don't put you on trial and sentence you to the shark barrier without your disgusting shark skin protection.

"You're also lucky the queen doesn't believe in sending mer out there, no matter what they've done. It's only ever happened in extreme cases."

"And if *you* had to decide what happens to me, what would it be?"

A stingray swims by him, nearly knocking into his arm. It glides over my way, tilting around me.

"I think you'll have better luck getting into the good graces of the princess—she's not allowed to be biased when it comes to deciding on these things."

"Celena, I have a feeling my fate rests more in *your* hands than in anyone else's. I need to know how bad this is going to be—should I leave now?" Phorcys' voice is gruff as he glares at me, fully prepared to push me out of the way to make an escape if he senses that I might be lying to him.

"I have no intention of making that decision, Phorcys. I don't like you, I don't think that's in question, but I'm also not going to force you out. Like I said, your actions here will influence a lot of people's decisions about you, so figure out your life and get things handled.

"But if you plan on swimming off, we'd better never see you again, Phorcys, because we won't hesitate to hurt you if you abandon us now."

I turn, swimming away. He has a choice to make.

Caspian and a few of the guards swim ahead to Metten to make sure we aren't swimming into a trap. When they return, Caspian nearly collides with me, he's swimming so fast.

"The entire collection is in Metten." His smile is bigger than I've seen it since before all this started. "Celena, they're all still here. They didn't leave."

"*They're here?*" Dylana's tail twitches in excitement. She hasn't seen her brother since she left Metten to handle the battle. I'm sure she's worried.

"They're waiting for us. Your mother will meet us when we get there to talk to the prince." He reaches out to take her hand, sharing his excitement. "Then we can drag him back toward land and be free of them forever."

"Did you see Morgen?" Dylana's eyes are pulled back wide as she waits for an answer.

"No, but they said he's doing much better."

Dylana visibly sighs, her entire body lowering in the water. Llyr's eyes sparkle when he notices her relief.

"I didn't have time to tell them much, just that we were bringing Edmund to Metten. They're making preparations."

"Mother tried to force Coralie back to Scylla with the children, but she had as much luck as we did," Caspian informs me as we pick up the pace to Metten.

"That mer child is a *force*," I joke. "Were *we* ever that bad?"

"I mean, we *did* try to sneak pets into the house."

"And *that* worked so well." I laugh, batting at Llyr's tail as he slows in front of me, nearly hitting me with his fins. "Speaking of which, I don't think I told you yet—that's how Coralie and I found you out in the open waters. I found the *sarasa* on the rock, and we played that game we used to play when we tried to sneak things in, and *that's* how we found the rest of your signs."

"Well, at least we did *something* right." Caspian bumps his shoulder into mine. "Cor's handling it all pretty well from what I hear."

"Whom did you talk to?"

"Mom." He offers me a smile. "If you think Marilla doesn't have her overseeing everything, you're crazy."

Caspian's smile drops, and he grows somber, glancing over at Natale.

"She was pretty upset to hear about—" he nods to Natale, not wanting her to overhear us talking about her mother's death.

"I'm sure," I reply quietly.

Ahead, the coral reef looms ahead of us—the barrier.

"I suppose we should tell Edmund—it's been a while since I checked on him anyway."

Caspian nods, releasing me. I swim to the surface, slowly lifting myself out of the water so that I don't frighten them. They both turn to me, looking out of the boat.

"I was wondering where you'd gone off to," Edmund jokes.

"We're at the barrier," I explain, lifting my hand to hold the edge of the boat. "The collection stayed in Metten to wait for us—the queen will be joining us shortly to finish negotiations."

Edmund gulps, looking nervous, but he straightens his shoulder much like Dylana does when she's taking a position of authority over something.

"It will be fine," I insist. "Dylana and I will be there the whole time."

"She's not going to drown me, is she?"

"You came all this way thinking that was a possibility?"

He sighs heavily. Turning, he looks out at the open sea—nothing but water for leagues.

"I guess I was a little focused. I didn't think about all the possibilities."

"I suppose that was your doing?" I turn an accusatory glare at Jackson, wondering if he turned the prince against us. Maybe I shouldn't have left them for so long.

"My job is to protect him. I came on this little journey to make sure he was safe. I flung myself into the ocean with a bunch of mermaids set on killing humans—you don't get to judge me, Celena —I'm here to support my prince."

My entire face falls.

"I'm sorry," I say, only partially remorseful. "You're right. You're doing your job, and I shouldn't criticize you for that.

"Be warned, Celena, I'll kill you first if you're lying to us."

"That's assuming you're alive to do so, Jackson." Fear creeps into his eyes, but he holds his face straight at my threat. "We really don't need *you* to make this treaty happen."

"Enough. We don't need any extra hostility right now. Celena, Jackson and I are practically brothers at this point in our lives. Please treat him accordingly. Jackson, she's foreign royalty, and I will not stand for you being disrespectful, friendship or not."

Jackson nods.

"There they are," I redirect. "That's the queen."

I point behind Edmund, and he turns around on the bench he's sitting on in the rowboat to see. A pod of dolphins swims in the water around the queen—a strategic move in case we need to move her quickly. They stay by her side, cutting us off from Marilla.

Whoever is pulling the boat, slows as we approach. The boat glides through the water. I stop its motion when we get close enough, allowing Marilla to swim up to us. Dylana joins us to make the introductions.

"Hello, Prince Edmund," Marilla greets him. She glitters in a fearsome shell crown. Her *iluse* is covered in shells and sparkling crystals mixed with the pearls that are so celebrated in our collection. She wears royal shoulder armor that glints in the sun. "I'm pleased you've decided to enter into negotiations with us. We would very much like to end this war and separate our groups so that this does not happen again."

"I think that is a wise decision, your majesty," Edmund agrees.

Dylana quickly explains what they've already discussed, pointing out areas they did not speak on or have not reached an agreement on yet. Marilla nods, listening to her daughter.

I linger by the side of the boat as Merrick takes a place beside me. Marilla raises an eyebrow for a moment but allows him to stay by my side.

Merrick's hand slips around my waist as he pins me between him and the boat. I lean against him, but jerk forward suddenly as one of the dolphins bumps me in the back.

I turn around as Merrick snorts, quietly making fun of me. I pet the dolphin for a moment until it swims away—I've missed them. Wrapping myself around Merrick's arm, I focus back in on the conversation as Marilla works out details with Edmund. He glances at me for a moment but looks back to Marilla almost immediately.

"Did you ever think you'd live to see this day?" Merrick whispers in my ear, voice low and intentionally flirtatious.

"I didn't," I reply, refusing to take the bait—we don't have time to flirt right now. The sun is setting, and we need to get Edmund back safely to the shore.

My mother eyes me from her place in the line of mer several lengths away. She raises an eyebrow and smiles just a hint.

Marilla was smart to keep the collection back so that they didn't surround the human prince and his servant—we don't need them to be any more nervous than they already are. It's nice to know that my mother approves of Merrick—even though I haven't seen her long enough to tell her that we're together yet.

Caspian and the others wait below, hovering underneath the boat part way between the ocean floor and the surface in case we need anything. They're deep enough to be out of the way, but close enough that they can assist us if we signal them. The rest of the collection is preparing to fight off the humans if they find us once we leave Metten.

I rest my head on Merrick's shoulder, and he tips his head on mine. His shoulder armor is uncomfortable, but I don't care. Merrick shifts, sensing that it's slightly painful against my cheek, lowering his shoulder so that I'm not putting as much weight against the side of my face to rest against him.

Through the water, I can see Phorcys grumbling to himself as he stares. Keone and Natale glance at him at the same time, but he just crosses his arms and continues to stare. I'm surprised he bothered staying with us. I had thought Marilla's gaze would have scared him when she saw him before approaching us, but not even *that* turned him away—he must be more nervous about being alone than I thought.

It's a shame we don't know where Cassidia—I doubt Tarni is still alive—is so we could send him off with her. Perhaps if Marilla decides to let Tiko and the others go, he could leave with them and cross the barriers into the open waters. Maybe they could even return to Shadare or Rochay.

The light fades out of the sky, leaving a dark, murky color. Several midwater squid glow in the ocean below us, lingering near our collection. Metten's palace and dwellings can't be seen from the surface, but I'm sure the collection is hiding most of the biolumines-cent glow tonight to be safe.

Merrick leaves me, diving into the water. When he returns several minutes later, Caspian is at his side, helping to carry a rock covered in spores that glow. They set it on the side of the boat, allowing Jackson to move it between him and the prince so they can see better until the moon appears.

The two stay next to me, floating in the water. They can sense I'm getting dried out and gently push down on my shoulders until I dip under the water for a moment—Marilla and Dylana have already taken turns to sink under the water momentarily.

It feels cool, but that's only because I've been out in the warm air for so long. I sigh, and Merrick squeezes my shoulder, still holding on to me. Running my fingers through my hair, I shake the dried pieces loose, letting them soak up the water. After a moment, I finally relent and swim back up, leaving the water until my shoulders are exposed once more.

It appears as though Edmund and Marilla are finalizing everything. She swims toward him to shake his hand—something important in both human *and* mer culture. The prince reaches down, stretching his arm so that Marilla doesn't have to do most of the work. Jackson leans back slightly, making sure the boat stays balanced.

"And you're sure you want to go against your father's wishes?" Marilla asks before removing her hand from his. "If you want to change your mind, Prince Edmund, we won't hold it against you. We'll take you back to Antaire safely."

Jackson suddenly gasps, clutching at his chest. When I turn to look at him in the limited moonlight, I notice a long dark line protruding from his chest. His eyes are wide as Edmund screams his name, leaping forward in the rowboat to help his friend.

"Get down!" Marilla shouts, diving under the water.

A spear pierces the surface of the ocean, barely missing me. It's followed by more.

CHAPTER 11

Jackson's body topples into the water, drifting down as Merrick and I dart away from the boat. I turn, allowing Merrick to pull me as I watch for oncoming spears in the water—one of them hits the servant's leg as his corpse sinks.

"Edmund," I call, realizing we left him to face his fate alone.

The fleet of small rowboats closes in on the prince from one side —they must have determined that they couldn't cross the barrier in their ships and did exactly what we did, skimming over the surface with the small vessel.

I'm shocked any of the humans were brave enough to attack Jackson when they easily could have missed and hit the prince. Edmund's body isn't in the water, so I assume they want him alive.

The entire mer collection races to our aid. We stay closer to the ground than the surface as we loop in a giant arch under the rowboats, positioning ourselves to surface on the far side of the tiny fleet to surprise them.

Marilla attempts to surface with us, but my mother drags her back. Llyr mimics the motion, forcing Dylana down to the ocean floor.

When I surface, the rowboats are surrounding Edmund, bumping into him. He stays in the center of the boat, trying to avoid their reach—he looks terrified. The men shout that the king has offered a reward to whichever sailors brought the prince back.

Several of the sailors try to stand in their boats in an effort to step into the prince's at the center of the crowd. One man rocks violently as the entire boat lurches to the side—a merman bravely knocks another boat, shifting them all in the water in a ripple effect. More of our collection moves under the boats to help, attempting to avoid the spears being thrust into the water between the tightly packed boats.

"How do you want to handle this?" Merrick asks quietly, assessing the situation. "I don't think we can get his boat away from them."

"Isn't it funny that we're up here fighting *for* a human?" Phorcys appears next to us, trident in hand. I'm not sure where he got the weapon from, but as long as he doesn't stab *me* with it, I don't care.

"I suppose you suddenly have an idea of how to help?" I snip at him.

"Other than leaving him here?" Phorcys sneers. "Siren them."

"We're not sirening them. I doubt they can even hear us anyway—they know what they were sailing into."

"Then you have to kill them," Phorcys replies. "What's more important—the prince or *all of them?*"

"If we get him in the water, we can swim him out of here," Merrick comments, ignoring Phorcys. "I just don't know about what we do after that point. We can't swim him all the way back to Anataire without a boat."

"That's a problem for later." I shake my head. "We have to get him now. *Natale!*"

My cousin looks over, poised to stab a human in a boat. She grimaces, moving her arms back to strike. Instead, she hits the side of the boat, toppling it enough that the man falls into the water. Natale rushes to my side.

"We're getting Edmund and swimming away with him. As soon as we have him, and are far enough away, get the collection out of here —we don't need any extra deaths."

She nods, darting under the water to watch us sneak up to Edmund's boat. I lead the way, Merrick and Phorcys trailing behind me.

"What are you doing?" Caspian shouts, noticing our movements as I count the boats overhead, trying to locate the correct one.

"We need to get Edmund into the water!" I shout. "We're going to take him away."

"And do *what?*" Caspian calls, knowing we don't have another boat to put him in.

"We'll figure that out later," I reply.

"It won't help if he's dead," Phorcys replies darkly.

Caspian swims over to join us, leaving his post.

"Which one?" he asks, looking at the underside of the boats.

"One of those." I point. "That one, I think, but I'm not sure."

"So we tip them all and figure it out after," Caspian replies, working with my line of thinking. Without waiting, he propels himself toward the boats. We follow behind him.

I slam into one of the boats, rocking it. Moving back, I hit it again as it bounces on the waves, this time, tipping it enough to knock the humans out.

Unfortunately, I had miscounted—the men I tip out aren't the prince. Two sailors panic in the water, trying to surface. One glares at me, realizing what happened. He tips his spear toward me and thrusts it at my stomach.

Caspian reaches out, taking the hit with his forearm. He doubles over in pain as blood blooms from his injury.

In our rush to save the prince, I had forgotten that blood would fill the waters—this time at night. While I doubt there are any sharks in the area at this point, anything is a possibility, and I hope our collection is safe.

I lurch forward to help Caspian, but a waving arm catches my attention. Edmund thrashes in the water. When he finally sees me, his movements halt for just a moment before he struggles to get to the surface for air.

"Go," Caspian commands. He whips his tail out, slamming into a human who turned toward me.

I jerk my arm back, hitting the man in the face with the flat end of my trident. His unconscious body floats in the water, and I realize I just sentenced him to death—he can't save himself from drowning.

I rush to Edmund as he surfaces, gasping for air. I pop out of the water next to him, quickly hissing in his ear for him to take a deep breath and trust me. He does, gulping in the night air before I drag him back down under the sea.

Caspian joins us, cradling his arm as we bypass the boats in the water. Edmund's fingers dig into my arm when he runs out of air. We aren't far enough away yet, but I'm forced to surface to keep the prince alive.

Edmund coughs when we reach the night air, and he slams his hand against his chest, fighting to keep control. He drags in several ragged breaths before nodding to me, telling me it's okay to take him back under the water.

Merrick and Phorcys appear, looking a little worse for the wear, but my boyfriend slips his hand around Edmund's upper arm and helps me propel him through the dark water.

We stay near the surface, just far enough below the waves that we can't be seen, but high enough that we can easily give Edmund access to the air he needs to survive on short notice. He attempts to hold his breath for as long as possible for us, but each new dive is shorter than the last as his lungs start to rebel.

"There's nothing but open water, where do we take him?" Casp asks. Thankfully the bleeding on his arm has stopped, but I convince Merrick to dive below and find something to wrap my brother's arm in.

Phorcys takes Merrick's place, helping me move the prince through the water. Once I can no longer see the boats, we take Edmund to the surface to swim, allowing him to breathe.

Swimming in the waves isn't easy, but we drag Edmund along, allowing him to hold on to our upper arms as we swim for him. He weakly kicks his feet along with us, but holding his breath for so long has worn him out to the point of being practically useless.

He stays quiet for a long time as we move through the water. Merrick returns, wrapping Caspian's arm in seaweed to protect it. He allows Phorcys to continue to assist me, instead of taking a place at my side.

"You have a plan yet?" Merrick mumbles just loud enough for me to hear. The back of his hand brushes against my hip as he pulls ahead of me slightly in the water. Warmth shoots through my body, tingling in my scales.

"I've been trying to think about the maps of Metten," I reply. "I know there was an area where the ocean floor was closer to the surface. There was something about it that made ships unable to go there—well, certain places anyway—and the rest of the area was hard to navigate."

"I remember reading about that during my studies—" Edmund's words are cut off by a small wave slamming into his face. He sputters before continuing. "It's a rocky area that most ships can't get through. The mer navigated certain boats through it at certain times of the year because the harvest was so good, but ordinarily, it's not something we could make it through on our own."

"We could go there until we have a better plan," I suggest.

"I've seen drawings of it," Edmund continues. "There are rocks stretching out of the water."

"At least you'd have somewhere to sit."

"Okay, we'll go there for now. Which direction?" Merrick asks.

"I'll go leave a trail," Caspian sighs, ducking under the water to leave a marked path for the rest of the collection to follow behind us.

I dip below the water, watching him go as I wet my hair. Someday soon I'll be able to stay under the water, and when that day comes, I may never surface again.

"Feel better?" Edmund jokes when I bring my head back up out of the water. "I've noticed you do that a lot."

"As fun as it is being up here…" I trail off, rolling my eyes as the prince smirks. I have a feeling that Merrick wouldn't be so calm about my interactions with Edmund if he were a merman.

"Want me to take over?" Merrick asks, relieving me. I nod, and Edmund releases my arm.

Scooting over, I take the opportunity to dive under the water, twirling around a few times to work the kinks out of my muscles. I stay under the water for a minute, needing a moment alone. I like being around my collection as much as the next mermaid, but I haven't had a minute to myself since we escaped the palace.

If the area we're taking Edmund to is hard to navigate, that *should* mean that the king will have trouble following us.

The water rushes over my hands as I race ahead, suddenly eager to pick up the pace. The moonlight sparkles down from above, now high in the nighttime sky.

Despite my exhaustion, I feel alive as I spiral through the water. My instincts tell me to leap from the water like a dolphin, surprising the others, but I know how ridiculous that would be. Instead, I surface, swimming ahead of everyone.

"Slow down, Len," Merrick calls playfully. "Not all of us can keep up."

Edmund mumbles an apology, but Merrick brushes it off good-naturedly. The prince looks relieved when I glance back, but he also seems to be getting a little of his strength back after being carried for so long.

Caspian swims below us, leaving a trail of signs for our collection. I wave down to him when he glances up, and he smiles. It's hard to see through the dark water, but the light is just strong enough to make out some of his features.

I wonder if Edmund has thought this through yet. His father has to know Edmund went against his wishes, so what does that mean for Edmund's return? Will his father lock him away like Jarek's mother did to him a century ago? Will the crown be taken away from him and instead passed on to Analia—and what will happen if *she's* in charge?

The moon shifts in the sky as we swim. The colors start to change when we finally swim into the area where the ocean floor rises closer to the surface, and Caspian joins us to avoid the vicious rocks resting on the ocean floor.

A few minutes later, we see the first of the rocks protruding out of the water. It's small—small enough to miss, especially from the deck of a ship—but it's there.

We're all quiet as we linger through the rocks. We take our time moving around them to avoid accidentally scraping our scales against the rough edges hiding below the surface. Edmund stops kicking his feet, allowing the boys to guide his path through the water.

When I spot a cavern entrance looming ahead, complete with a massive set of rocks piercing through the water, I point us in that direction. Edmund climbs up onto a green-covered rock. He slips at first but manages to take a seat.

He glances around from his new throne in the sea, admiring his temporary kingdom. The walls of the cavern glow with bioluminescent spores, though not nearly as brilliantly as the other caves we've been in recently. Fish swim in the water as day breaks, leaving the area in a mint colored glow that would make even Llyr's hair jealous.

I take a seat on a rock near the prince that hasn't bothered leaving the comfort of the sea. Merrick leans against the rock next to my tail, resting his shoulder against my hip. Phorcys sulks a few lengths away while Caspian unwraps his arm to check it.

"Here." I reach out to him, beckoning him over so I can look at his injuries. I wince when I see it, but it's not life-threatening. "Maybe next time don't take a spear for me, okay?"

"I will take a spear for you *every single time*, Celena," he grins up at me, emphasizing his words. "You and Coralie...*Merrick*, not so much."

"Thanks, buddy."

"You're welcome, brother," Caspian replies before cringing as he realizes that it has new meaning now that I'm dating Merrick. He glances between us.

"It'll be okay," Merrick jokes.

"So this is your...brother?" Edmund asks, looking directly at me.

"Edmund, meet my brother, Caspian. Casp, this is Prince Edmund."

"I hear you threatened my sister and tortured my friend." Caspian's voice is dark as he pretends to threaten the prince. Edmund's eyes grow wide.

"He's joking, Edmund. Casp, stop scaring him." I roll my eyes. Caspian drops the scary act and offers the prince a smile.

"If you ever try anything like that again though—"

"I know, you'll drown me," Edmund interrupts. "I get it. I get *all* of it."

Merrick and I chuckle, knowing he's been threatened so many times already that it no longer affects him. Merrick takes my hand, running his fingers over the back of it.

"I'm sorry about Jackson," I address the prince. He sighs deeply, casting his eyes down to look at the water.

"He helped me escape—he was a traitor. I should have realized that earlier. I never should have brought him along."

"You don't know what would have happened if he had stayed," I offer. "He could have just as easily been held accountable back in that cave."

Several colorful fish swim over to me, darting around my tail to investigate who I am. Once they're satisfied, they take off, swimming away.

"I'm going to check the cave," Phorcys grumbles, pushing away from us. "Maybe there's a way through it."

He disappears into the cavern.

"Do you think he's coming back?" Caspian asks, watching the orange-tailed merman swim away.

"If there's no exit, he is," Merrick smirks, earning a snort from the prince. "I don't think he's going anywhere. He's trying to earn his way into our good graces so he doesn't get kicked out."

"For as rough as he is, I think he'd be lost without a collection," I add. I don't know much about him, but I know he had risen in the ranks of the sirens enough for Tarni and Nir to trust him. I think he needs to be around others to thrive. If his solo mission after we left him for dead is any indication, the plans he tries to execute on his own don't necessarily work so well.

"He's going to be an interesting addition," Merrick remarks as if it doesn't matter. It does, and we both know it.

"Edmund, what's your father going to do to you once you return?" My tail twitches as I ask the question, unsure I want the answer.

"I'm not sure. I'll probably be in pretty big trouble. I can always say you sirened me though." He smirks. "Honestly, he'll probably send me away like he had planned on doing. Once he's done here, *then* I'll be punished for this. I don't even know how to let you know when it's safe."

"Use a conch shell," I remind him. "They're bound to wash up from time to time or have the sailors bring them in. All you have to do is say our names into them and then your message, and throw them into the sea."

"If you have sailors you can trust, you can have them drop them out farther into the sea for us," Merrick adds.

"We'll have guards who will find them and bring them to us," Caspian concludes. "It might take a bit, but it will make it to us."

"Use the terms *mer queen* and *mer king* too in case things can't reach us for some reason." *In case we're dead.*

"There's nothing in there," Phorcys interrupts, exiting the cave. "It's just like every other cave we've been in—decidedly lacking in human skulls."

"What?" Edmund chokes.

"You don't need to worry about that." I wave my hand at the prince.

"Your friends are coming," Phorcys points out to the horizon. "I saw them through the water while I was under."

A smile creeps across my face—our collection made good time. Merrick slips under the water to watch for them as I sun myself on the rock. The sun rises over the horizon, casting the area in gold.

The water waves against my tail as Merrick swims away. I'm sure he's going to greet the collection and guide them to our location, but I miss his presence next to me.

When he returns, Llyr, Natale, Dylana, and Keone are at his side along with Relo and some of the others. They join us on the surface so that Edmund isn't left out of the conversation.

"We swam ahead," Keone explains. "The others are just a few minutes behind."

"This is interesting," LLyr eyes the location. He turns to face me perched on the underwater rock. "Having fun, Celena?"

"*Resting* is more like it." I stretch my hand out to him, and he swims over to kiss it as if I were the queen and he was showing respect. He looks up, smiling, but side eyes Dylana behind him. I fan my fins out, swishing it against his tail to let him know she's watching.

"Guys." The voice behind me frightens me, and I leap off the rock, whipping around in the water, trident ready. Llyr is beside me, ready to strike. From inside the cave, the voice sounds again.

"I want to help." It sounds familiar, but it isn't until Murdoch peers around the cave wall that I realize Phorcys just lied to us.

I whip around to face him, leaving Llyr and the others to face Murdoch and what I assume has to also be Roni and Cassidia. Phorcys stares me down but doesn't raise his weapon. He glares at me as I snarl back at him, demanding to know what is going on.

"Celena, please!" Murdoch shouts over to me. "He was protecting Tarni."

How is she still alive? Apparently, it's as hard to kill her as it was to kill Nir.

"Why are you here, Murdoch?" Merrick growls at him.

"This is as far as we made it—Tarni's not well. We hid here and have been trying to care for her—she's getting better." He sounds hopeful as he speaks. "But she can't leave yet."

"Why did you bother to come out?" I shout, still staring down Phorcys. He snarls at me but doesn't say anything.

"I want to help you. I messed up, and I know that. I want to try to make it right."

"Do you honestly think you'll be allowed back in the collection after everything you've done, Murdoch?" Llyr taunts him.

"I don't need to get back into the collection. I just want to…apologize."

"Here's your knife back, Caspian." There's a pause as I assume Caspian retrieves the weapon the sirens stole in the palace in Scylla.

I actually feel bad for Murdoch. He turned his back on his collection, the mermaid he cares for might not make it—I'm surprised she's lasted this long—and he realizes just how much he gave up to start a war no one won.

"They're not coming with us," Merrick says. I assume he's talking about Cassidia and Roni, but I'm not turning around to look.

"Roni and Cassidia will stay with Tarni," Murdoch informs us.

"We should take them," Phorcys mutters. "We might need them."

I shake my head quietly, telling him to stay quiet, but the siren doesn't listen.

"Cassidia comes with us—we may need her help."

I turn in time to see Roni's face twist in anger as she floats next to Murdoch and Cassidia.

"You are *not* leaving me behind," she growls. She looks ready to strangle Murdoch next to her, but her glare is deadly as she swings around to aim her accusatory eyes at Phorcys.

"You need to protect Tarni, and we may need Cassidia's skill set,"

Phorcys addresses her, leaving the word *sireny* unsaid in front of the prince.

"We most certainly will *not*," I snap at him. I turn to Edmund, ready to tattle. "She will *not* be sirening anyone."

The prince narrows his eyes at the blue-tailed mermaid, leveling a gaze that would make anyone but her squirm. She glances at him before flicking her gaze away casually to me.

Apparently, the decision comes down to me.

I don't trust her not to follow behind us and disrupt our plan—I'd rather have her where we can see her.

"She can come, but she doesn't leave our sides."

Her lips twitch, but she swims out of the cave. Murdoch follows in her wake. Roni fumes, still inside the shadows of the cave. For a moment, she looks as if she might lash out, but suddenly she jerks her shoulder back, flinching. She looks over her shoulder, retreating into the cave.

None of us have checked on Tarni yet. I have to make sure she's actually still alive, and in the condition they're claiming her to be in. If she miraculously recovered—or if she's dead and this is some kind of trick—I have to know.

Merrick's hum is low as I swim past him—a warning to be careful. Cassidia and Phorcys don't bother trying to follow me as I trail Roni inside the cave.

The glow is brighter inside, but not by much. Tarni lays on the sand below, Roni at her side. Tarni grimaces at me while her protector snarls.

"Get out, *mermaid*."

Tarni's eyes flutter shut, weak enough that she doesn't care that I'm in her presence. Her friend strokes her hair, reminding me of when I took care of Coralie after these two attacked her. The thought makes me rage inside.

Turning, I leave the cave.

"Time to move," I announce. In a mumble, I add, "We need to get as far from those two as possible."

I almost feel bad for Murdoch as he flinches. He wants to believe the best in the mermaid he cares for, but he also knows the truth about her—she is a murderess, and she doesn't care whom she hurts to get what she wants. I still don't believe she could possibly love Murdoch the way he thinks she does.

"I don't have a weapon," Murdoch points out.

I'm sure the collection will have extra weapons with them, but none of us carried extra tridents or spears. I reach into my *iluse* to untangle a knife I've been hiding.

Murdoch's eyes widen as I hand it to him, but he takes it gratefully. Flipping it in his hand, he tests its weight, getting comfortable with the blade.

"I want that back later," I remind him, lips pursed.

After all he's done to us, I don't mind giving him a hard time. He nods solemnly, gripping the knife tighter in his hand. I sigh, turning away from him. A few days ago, I would have been willing to cut his fingers off, but after the last few days, I just want things to be easy, which means not picking fights that aren't absolutely necessary.

"Thanks," Murdoch says when my back is turned. I nod briefly.

"They're here," Natale announces, jerking her head back toward where the collection is swimming to us under the water. We wait as they swim up to us.

CHAPTER 12

"Mother." Dylana signals the queen over.

Marilla's eyes narrow when she notices Phorcys, but she halts in the water when she realizes Murdoch is with us. He backs up in the water as she swims straight for him.

"Why are you here?" Miraculously, Marilla manages to keep her voice even.

"We were hiding in the cave—we didn't know they'd be here," Murdoch says, trying not to stumble over his words. "I just want to help, and then I'll leave."

"Who is *we*?" Marilla demands in an unnervingly calm voice.

"Tarni and Roni are here," I inform her. She glances at me.

"Where?"

"In the cave," Dylana points. "Cassidia will be joining us."

Her eyes dart to the blue siren, informing her mother of the mermaid's location.

Marilla turns in the water, my mother by her side. Sometimes it's hard to believe this is the same mermaid who feeds seahorses in her chambers in the palace in Scylla—this fierce mermaid warrior queen, who looks as though she will slice your throat and ask questions later, is also the soft, kind queen I grew up following.

With her shoulders back and crown on, she is magnificent. My mother mirrors her movements, looking just as regal as the two slip into the cave.

Murdoch looks terrified that Tarni's torn up body might float out of the cave at any time, though I doubt they'll hurt the siren. Minutes

474

stretch out, but no one exits the cave. I glance at Dylana, silently asking if we should check on them. Her bottom lip pinches against her top lip, but before we can decide on anything, our mothers emerge from the cavern.

"We need to go," Marilla announces. "We must return the prince to Antaire."

Murdoch glances at the cave, but he knows he can't check on Tarni. Reluctantly, he's forced to believe she is okay as he turns to follow the collection.

Edmund slips into the water and allows two of the guards to guide him through the waves. I stay close by, knowing it will concern him if I don't. Merrick nods to him, lending his support.

Cassidia swims ahead of us, separated from Phorcys. Her blue tail waves majestically in the water. Her entire body moves gracefully ahead of us, and I wonder if I've ever been half as effortless as she is. Her long hair is enchanting as it flows behind her in a white wave.

She looks back over her shoulder as if she knows I'm studying the way she moves, hoping to learn from her during the swim. She makes eye contact with Phorcys as he swims next to Merrick before she turns back to watch where she's swimming.

Phorcys keeps a close eye on me around Merrick as we move, not even flinching when a pod of dolphins joins us for a time while we swim toward Antaire. The open waters below us are colorful—more colorful than when we were here before fighting a war that was never our battle to begin with. Coral litters the ground, mixed with kelp and seaweed. Fish swim in every direction, darting out of our way as we approach.

"Never thought I'd miss a rock," Edmund jokes.

"Are you okay?" I ask, looking over.

"I'm fine," he puffs. "I clearly should work on my long distance swimming skills though."

I'm sure swimming in his heavy royal clothes isn't easy. I'm thankful he wasn't wearing one of those silly capes I've seen in story-books and in some of the drawings Aila left of Prince Jarek—*that* would only serve to kill him. Then again, perhaps we could use it to pull him along instead of letting him cling to our arms to be dragged across the seas.

I wish we could use this time to discuss what our collection will do after we return the prince, but we can't let Edmund hear out plans. I want desperately to dive under the water and swim with Marilla and my mother for a while to learn about what they have planned.

I haven't seen my father yet, so I assume he didn't come. He's likely recuperating with Morgen and the other injured mer that were too unwell to join the new fight. At least one of us will be left alive to care for Coralie when this is all over.

Ahead, I see Marin, the merman Coralie was gushing over a few weeks ago in Scylla. I vow to keep an eye on him for her. I would hate to have her heart broken if her crush were to die in war. He seems far too young to be with us, but the choice isn't mine, and I won't challenge it.

We hit a warm current, and I shiver at the change in temperature. Warmth floods through my scales, and I realize just how cold I've been this whole time. Scylla is so much warmer and I long to be back in the colorful waters of our home.

As if he can read my mind, Merrick bumps into my shoulder, smiling at me. I tip my head toward him, allowing us to have a private moment as my hair blocks us from the world around us. He breathes deeply, sighing just enough so that only I can hear it.

I'm tired—we're *both* tired. We're ready for this fight to be over. If we can go home and never leave the Scylla courtyard again, I'll be happy.

Well, unless we go visit the caves. I'll make an exception for those kinds of trips.

Merrick raises an eyebrow at the look on my face. I bite back my sarcasm and turn away from him, but not before winking flirtatiously. His hand finds its way to my back and rests just above my tail as we swim.

It's a strange sight to see the top of the ocean without any boats. After the number of ships I've seen the last week, the world feels slightly off without them bobbing dangerously on the water, rocking with the waves.

A dolphin surfaces next to me, spraying me with water as she opens her blowhole to breath. I reach out a hand, letting it slide over her skin as she chatters next to me for a moment before moving on.

Another one surfaces near Cassidia ahead, but she only glances at it before continuing on. The siren doesn't even attempt to reach out to touch it.

"She's never liked them," Phorcys mumbles. "She only sees them as tools to be used for transportation."

"One of them probably bumped her when she was a mer child and took her personality with it," Caspian jokes quietly. Phorcys glares at him while Merrick and I smirk.

Llyr swims suspiciously close to Dylana off to the side of Cassidia, far enough away that they can talk quietly without being overheard. I wonder how long it will be before he actually tells her how much he likes her. I've been pestering him about it for over a year now, but he's far too respectful to think he could end up with a princess. Personally, I think he would make a fabulous king once Dylana takes her reign.

He looks back, catching my eye, and I bat my lashes at him to tease him. He rolls his eyes, grinning wildly when Dylana catches him. She glances back at me, and I raise an eyebrow at her suggestively. The princess casually looks back at Llyr, and I think she's finally ready to do something about the flirtatious banter they've been locked in for months.

"I see you've been helping things along," Merrick mumbles playfully. "I've been working on it too. Nice teamwork, partner."

"Congratulating yourself a little early, aren't you, Merrick?" I pretend to chastise him. "Nothing has happened yet."

"You two make me sick," Phorcys groans.

"I have to agree," Caspian chimes in. "You two are disgusting."

"Thank you, Caspian, you've been so helpful," I sing, giving him the most annoyed look I can muster up.

He returns the same face, having mastered it far better than I did over the years. I suppose he was always more fond of studying himself in bubbles than I was, so of course he had more practice. He also had *me* for a sister, so *that* might explain it as well.

I dip under the water, wetting my hair for the next portion of the swim. At some point, we're going to have to decide how to return Edmund without getting any of us killed. It seems like a monumental task—it's as difficult as moving one of those caves we just left would be. Or perhaps it's impossible.

If that's the case, if it's too dangerous, I'll volunteer to go. It's my fault we're out here. Merrick and Caspian won't like it, but I can convince Llyr to force them to stay. If I genuinely asked him to, he would do that for me.

I tap my knife in my *iluse*. Murdoch returned it once one of the collection members offered him a spear to fight with instead. I prefer my weapons where they belong—with me.

Birds cry overhead like ugly little white stingrays in the sky, though they are much nosier than stingrays. One of the things I love about sea animals is that most of them don't make as much noise as animals on land seem to make. The dolphins and whales, of course, make beautiful sounds when calling to each other under the water, but starfish are ever silent.

The sun is higher in the sky now, and it sizzles against the skin on my shoulders—I'm not used to being in the direct sunlight for so long. I shrug uncomfortably as I try to dip down far enough to cool them off under my shoulder armor.

Marilla and my mother slow in the water, waiting until we catch up. Natale notices and nods to Keone to watch Cassidia as she sinks back in the water to join us, her lips pulled back in a grim line.

"We've decided the best course of action is to take you back as a united front, Prince Edmund. The entire collection will be returning you to your father," Marilla explains. "We hope that your father might see this as a sign of goodwill because we have not harmed you. Do you think he will view this as a threat *no matter what?*"

"Or perhaps will he be frightened enough of his son being surrounded by a hundred of his enemy to think it through before he attacks?" my mother adds the question to the conversation.

"I think seeing an entire collection of mer will give him pause, especially when he sees me with you," Edmund answers. "I don't think you should just hand me over though.

"When we arrive, I should stay in the water where I'm clearly visible. I'll direct the guards to get my father from the palace, and I can explain how you all helped me to return safely.

"At that point, I think you all need to leave before I swim back to shore. If I'm out of the water, there's nothing to prevent him from coming after you, but if there's still the potential that you could hurt me, he will have to cooperate at least a little."

"That's a wise plan, your majesty," Marilla nods. Edmund might be young, but she's treating him with the respect his title owes him. "You will be all right when we leave you?"

"I'll be fine, Queen Marilla," he assures her.

Marilla delves into a conversation about how to use conch shells to communicate with us, repeating everything we've already taught him. Edmund listens carefully as if it's the first time he's hearing the instructions. I'm positive Dylana already informed her mother of our conversations, but it's worth repeating.

"For what it's worth," Edmund says, glancing at me. "I'm sorry the treaty fell apart. I believe you when you say it was only Persephone and her mother that did this to us. I believe you about the sirens, too."

Cassidia whips around to look at him, snarling at Phorcys as Keone mumbles something to her. I'm sure he's reminding her to cooperate, but his trident twitches in his hand as he speaks, clearly annoyed.

Off to the side, I hear a click. A rush of wind follows, filling my ears as it ends with a harpoon slicing through the water in front of Cassidia. She screams—the first real emotion I've heard come from the siren—and whips around in the water, ready to siren anything that gets in her way.

Keone turns to see where the weapon came from, lurching in the water to avoid a second harpoon. They fill the air, slicing through the water when they land.

The collection drops under the water, diving deep to avoid the weapons. They quickly double back, hiding under the boat where the sailors likely won't think to throw their weapons.

"Casp!" I gasp, nodding to Dylana. My twin launches himself at our cousin and drags her under, putting his own body between her and the humans. I hate that he has to use himself as a shield for her, but we all know it's our job to protect the reigning royals.

"Go," my mother commands, attempting to push me down in the water. "Merrick, get her out of here."

Merrick hesitates for a moment, then tries to push me down in the water.

"Merrick!" I shout, struggling against him. "We can't let him stay up there."

"Your mother is watching him." He grits his teeth as he drags me down in the water. I should fight harder, but I'm trained to trust him, so I follow his lead.

"We can't just leave them up there," I protest.

"We're not, Len—we just aren't deep enough yet." Merrick forces his tail to work harder, and I join him, realizing his plan to swing back around and attack the boat from the backside.

Merrick turns us in the water, moving under the boat, though we're quite a bit higher than the rest of the collection. We dart up in the water, close enough to the underside of the boat to touch it. The vessel is far too big for us to tip, even if the entire collection was assisting us.

We stop when we reach the edge, still hovering underneath the ship where the humans can't see us. Merrick hands me his trident as he flattens himself against the underside of the boat, his chest pressed against it as he floats upside down in the water.

Slowly, he uses his hands to pull him forward, tentatively peeking out beyond the edge of the ship. When he feels that it's safe, he moves further out.

"I'm here," Llyr announces behind me. He hands me his weapon, and I balance all three in the crook of my arm, holding onto the handles with my hands to keep them from slipping and falling to the ocean floor below us.

Llyr puts his hand on Merrick's tail to let him know he's there. As Merrick moves farther out away from the boat, Llyr wraps both hands around the end of Merrick's tail just above his fins in case he needs to pull him back.

"Try not to get too jealous," Llyr mumbles at me, smirking.

"You're just holding his tail... *I* had him *wrapped around me*," I quip, making him fumble. I snort at his response. "I doubt you're going to make me jealous, Llyr, sorry to waste your last few years."

"Wow, thanks, Celena. I appreciate you leading me on and making me think I had a chance to sway you away."

"You didn't," I confirm snarkily.

A loud sound rocks the ship, and I nearly drop the tridents.

"What was that?"

Something drops in the water as I look at Llyr, unsure of how to answer. The black thing sinks heavily in the water.

"It's a cannonball," I stutter, trying to process what I just saw. "*What...how?*"

"They're shooting *cannonballs* in the water now? What's the logic in *that?*" Llyr shouts. "Those things are meant to sink ships—what good will it do shooting it at us now? It could take out, *what—one or two* mer? Isn't that a waste of ammunition?"

"It's ridiculous, but maybe they're trying to scare us away from the prince."

Just then, Merrick does a backflip. Llyr releases him so he can return to us. Merrick flips his blue hair up, moving his long bangs away from his eyes as they wave in the water.

"What are we looking at?" Llyr asks, reaching for his trident. Merrick does the same.

"They're focused on the other side. This is our chance."

"What's up there?"

"Not much," Merrick admits, shaking his head at me. "There's a boat about halfway down the side of the ship resting on ropes. There's a bunch of windows in the side of the ship."

"So what is our plan?" Llyr wrinkles his nose adorably. It's easy to see why he's always been so popular with the mermaids in the collection.

I dart out from under the boat, popping out of the water enough to get a good look at the side of the ship waging war on my mother and collection.

A small rowboat dangles from the side of the ship. It's about the size of the one Edmund stole during his escape. The ropes dangle from the top of the ship, almost reaching the water. They're loosely tied at the top.

"The boat is our plan," I reply, darting back under the ship. "You mermen are going to grab the ropes and pull. It *should* knock the ropes loose, and we can lower the boat."

"And do *what?*" Llyr's words are punctuated, eyebrows lowered at me.

"She's going up in the boat." Merrick's tone is a cross between concern and awe.

"Celena!" Llyr chides.

"I'll siren *one* of them," I respond, sighing. "We just need to get one of them to wreck the cannon. And maybe part of the boat."

"*What?*" Llyr yelps. "I mean, I get it, *really*, but…*really?* I thought better of you, Len."

I smirk as he uses Merrick's nickname for me. I have a feeling he has adopted my boyfriend's name for me when the two are talking when I'm not around. He raises an eyebrow at me, trying to cover his slip as if it were intentional.

"Fine. Go up in the boat. Blow the ship up—do whatever you have to do. Just get it done quickly and get back down here."

"You two need to get the boat down," I remind him.

We swim out from under the boat and Merrick and Llyr assess the situation. After a moment, they swim down in the water, giving themselves space to build up speed.

I hold my breath as they crash toward the surface, leaping out of the water. I follow them, prepared to siren any humans that might overhear the boys working.

They latch onto the ropes at almost the same time, using their weight to pull the ropes loose. The coils pop free, cascading down to the water, giving plenty of extra rope.

When the mermen pull on them, it jerks the rowboat, smacking it against the side of the ship, but no one seems to have noticed. It rocks from its place along the ship, higher than it was a moment ago.

Merrick and Llyr release the boat, moving the rope hand-over-hand until it rests in the water.

"Up you go," Merrick says, offering me a hand.

I grab the side of the rowboat and pull, using my tail to propel me out of the water. Llyr and Merrick grab my hips and help push me inside the tiny boat.

The feel of the rough boards under my tail isn't an experience I care to repeat. It's one thing when a mer sits on a sunken ship—the water-soaked wood isn't nearly as uncomfortable, but this is dry, and warm from the sun—an entirely miserable experience.

The two try to pull me up, and I slowly jerk away from the surface. Suddenly the boat is moving smoothly, hurdling toward the sky. As I look up, the clouds reach out to me quickly, ready to swallow me up.

Grasping the edge of the rowboat, I peek over and realize a quarter of the collection is helping to pull the ropes in the water. They hold me in place as Merrick and Llyr surface to listen for me to call to them. I wave, letting them know I'm okay.

Turning back, I listen to the noise over the edge of the ship. Several men are nearby, but I can't tell where unless I'm a little higher. I wiggle my fingers at the mermen, and they instruct the collection to raise me higher. The movement stops a moment after I signal them to pause—thankfully I knew it would take a moment and signaled early.

The men yell at each other on the deck of the ship, shuffling about to follow orders. In the distance, I can hear two yelling about the cannon.

Taking a breath, I sing softly, trying to call one or two to my side. It takes a moment, but five men peer over the edge of the ship, looking down at me sitting in the boat.

Two of them look surprised, not fully under the influence of my song yet, but a few more notes and I have them all. One reaches for me as if I'm made of solid gold. I banish his hands with a few words.

I instruct the men to return to the cannon and change its position. Before I can finish, a cheer goes up, and I hold the men back.

"Bring him in, boys!" someone instructs.

"Look at him, Captain, he's not as nervous as the *mermaids* usually are."

"That's because he thinks we won't hurt him," a man snaps, chuckling. He raises his voice to make sure their captive hears him. "We will, of course. We have no problem putting a little fear into captives."

"Aww, he thinks this is a rescue mission," another man shouts, laughing.

"Sorry, little prince, we're not the welcoming committee. You're not going home just yet. Swing the net over!"

"Bring him in!"

It sounds like they're struggling to get Edmund in the ship—now is my only chance.

"Go," I release the men under my sireny.

It's a moment before anyone realizes that something is wrong. Once they discover the men taking over control of the cannon, shouts go up ordering them to stop. When they don't, the other sailors try to stop the men under my song, but they won't be stopped yet.

To my horror, the shouts change, adding in cries about another ship. I claw my way up the side of the boat to see. When I reach the top, I discover that they're right—a secondary ship is on the way.

Edmund calls out, avoiding using my name so as not to draw attention to me. He's hanging in a net over the opposite side of the ship, struggling to free himself as he dangles over the water.

"Go get help!" he directs me. I shake my head, telling him I won't leave. "Go get help—we need the king. I know these men, go!"

He looks desperate as he yells to me over the noise of the sailors. In my peripheral vision, I can see the men swing the cannon around, preparing to shoot a hole in their own deck.

The majority of the sailors look more worried about the oncoming ship, but I don't have time to investigate as Edmund screams for me to hurry. His eyes grow wide as he realizes the cannon is now pointed to the middle of the deck, not too far away from me.

My heart drops into my stomach as I realize that the cannonball has the potential to travel through the ship and end up in the water where it could hurt my collection.

I don't have time to have the boys lower the boat for me—I have to escape *now*.

I nod sharply, then drop back down into the rowboat, clawing my way to the side, and I throw myself over.

CHAPTER 13

The wind rushes by me as I sail through the air toward the water. I know this is going to hurt—it's hurt every other time I've plummeted from a ship. Merrick and Llyr dart out of the way, eyes wide as they see me dive toward them.

I slam into the water fingers first, slicing through the waves. Shock races through my body as I hit the surface, working its way down to my tail, each scale screaming at me for making the choice to jump out of the boat, but I don't have time.

Angling my fingers, I aim toward the collection. They release the ropes, turning to swim away. I suppose it's an easy inference to make —if I'm swimming like this, something bad must be happening, and they need to move to get ahead of it.

Merrick and Llyr are quickly on my tail as we rush away.

"We have to go to Antaire," I gasp through my pain. Given all I've been through recently, the aching sensation fades rather quickly in comparison. "We need to get the king."

"We're going without Edmund?" Merrick questions.

"I don't know who those men are, but Edmund does—he looked terrified of them. He begged me to get his father. He seems to think the king is the only one who can rescue him."

I don't have time to see where anyone is, all I know is that I need to get to Antaire and get the king to save his son.

After a few minutes, I have to slow, unable to keep up the speed. I've managed to lead us toward the front of the collection, overtaking many of the mer.

Dylana and Caspian make their way over to us, and Llyr looks like he wants to wrap his arm around the princess. I consider pushing him over to her, but if I focus on that for even a moment, I risk losing my focus altogether. I have to convince myself to speak to the king in the first place, so losing my focus could be detrimental to my entire mission.

"She's hurt, but she's alive," Caspian whispers to me, putting his arm around my waist.

"Mom?" My head darts over to him. I'm terrified.

"She'll be okay." He looks worried. "They're taking care of her."

"Who?" My face pouts without my consent.

"The collection. They're taking her back to Metten. We're on our own, Celena. Marilla is still here though—we'll have to make sure we watch her."

"You're not your mother," Dylana reminds us. "You have other things to worry about right now-it's not your job to take over protecting my mother. The collection will watch her. The guards are with her. You two are not responsible for her just because your mother isn't here."

"We're responsible for *you*," Caspian points out.

"Llyr can be responsible for me," Dylana challenges him. I'm not sure if she did it intentionally or not. Llyr subtly beams where she can't see him. "The king knows you two, and Caspian needs to protect Celena. I'll be fine."

"Oh," Natale gasps.

I drop my gaze, looking down to where her eyes are fixated on the ocean floor. We must be close to Antaire—the bodies of dead mer and sirens litter the ground.

Colorful hair waves in the water, floating up from the corpses resting on the sand. Weapons protrude from the ground and bodies at odd angles.

Iluses sparkle in the sunlight as it filters down through the ocean. *Sarasas* lift off the mermen's chests, gently moving with the current as it slips along our path.

The entire collection stops speaking in reverence for our fallen friends. Phorcys looks more remorseful over the deaths of the sirens he grew up with than Cassidia does—she barely looks like she cares about the consequences of her actions at all. Perhaps she's hiding her feelings, but maybe she simply doesn't care about the destruction below us.

Sailors and guards are mixed among the dead. Some wear

uniforms while others wear tattered clothing covered in stains that I don't want to know about. One man's beard waves in the water, looking bristly as it waves like a white cloud about to swallow him.

Spears and harpoons mix with tridents. Several of our collection switch their spears for tridents from the dead—a much more effective weapon should we swim into trouble.

The fish don't seem to mind the carnage as they swim around the corpses cluttering the floor of their home. Their colors set off the mer tails below us in a horrifyingly beautiful array.

I hadn't considered the possibility that the aftermath of the battle would still be on full display when we returned to the human kingdom. I try not to look too closely, knowing that if I do, I'll discover that the sea life has had little respect for our fallen mer. I have no desire to see missing eyes and flesh that has been partially eaten. Once their skin is gone and the bodies decompose, this area will become a boneyard for the fish and small creatures to hide in, using ribcages and eye sockets as shelter.

I drag my gaze up, unwilling to look at it any longer. Merrick's throat bobs as he swallows, also tearing his eyes away from the sight.

"This is horrific," Caspian voices what we're all thinking. "We can't even do anything about it, can we?"

"Not today," Merrick acknowledges the hopelessness of trying to do everything. "We have to stay on mission, and by the time we get through all of *this*..."

"They fought valiantly," Dylana says diplomatically. "We owe them much."

A few moments later, we find ourselves outside the palace. The steps still rest in the water, the waves washing over them. The outside is devoid of life, and no ships sit in the waters.

"The pool," I conclude, knowing our only way to get anyone's attention is by going back to the very place we escaped from.

Merrick and I veer off leaving the rest to follow us. Around the side of the palace, I locate the tunnel we vacated yesterday. Nothing blocks the entrance, so I force my way in before Merrick or anyone else can stop me.

I expect to find the tunnel blocked off again, but the bars are still bent at the end—apparently, not a priority. I hesitate for only a moment, closing my eyes before rushing in. Merrick stays with me. Caspian darts into the pool, but Merrick stops Llyr, instructing him to wait on the other side of the bars in case something happens.

Caspian looks around, spinning in the pool to get a good look at it while I dart to the surface—I don't have time to be quiet or scout the area. I need to make an entrance.

"Hello!" I splash out of the water, calling to anyone that can hear me. "Please! Is anyone here?"

When no one replies, I lower myself in the water and prepare to launch myself out of the pool. Merrick yells, but it doesn't stop me from hitting the side of the ledge, turning as I land to twist my tail around to the opposite side of the wall.

"Celena!" He sounds terrified as he surfaces, a tremble in his voice.

"I have to get help, Merrick."

"Get back in the pool—we'll yell for the humans," he insists, eyes wide. Caspian appears next to him, equally as furious with me.

"I tried that, they didn't hear me." I push off the wall, falling to the floor.

"Celena, this is insane!" Merrick's voice holds an edge of warning to it, but most of his tone is pure fear for my safety.

"Celena, *please*," Caspian begs, reinforcing his friend's sentiments.

I don't listen, dragging myself across the floor. I almost wish we had escaped from the tiny pools we had originally been in—the floor was flat. This room forces me to crawl around the tiny partial walls the humans installed that act as a maze for me. I attempt to go over several of them, landing hard on the other side.

"Len?" Merrick calls out as I grunt when I hit the ground…again. The water behind me splashes like he's struggling to see me.

"I'm fine," I call, holding my hand in the air to prove I'm still alive. I regret everything about leaving the pool, but I force myself forward.

Footsteps sound beyond the high wall—tentative at first, but they quickly pick up the pace as the tiny feet slap against the stairs. Before they reach the end, a head of dark hair pops over the wall as the owner jumps in the air. She jumps again, gasping.

The footsteps echo off the walls as Analia rushes around the corner, running at me. Her dress is clutched in her hands as she moves quickly. I notice she's barefoot as she runs.

"Celena!" she shouts, throwing herself on the ground next to me. "What are you doing out of the pool?"

"I needed to find you," I gasp—I didn't realize how exhausting dragging myself across the palace floor would be. "Your brother is in trouble."

"I know, Father has been looking for him everywhere. He's going to be in *so* much trouble when Father finds him."

"No, Analia." I shake my head. "You don't understand. We need to get your father."

"I don't think that's a good idea—Father's very angry. If he finds Edmund before he comes home and apologizes and fixes things, it's going to be worse for him."

"There isn't time for this, Analia—I need you to go get your father."

"No, I won't get Edmund in trouble. He always protects me, now I'm going to protect him." The curly-haired princess shakes her head, folding her arms over her chest defiantly.

"Analia, I just left your brother—bad people have him. We need to get your father." I reach out, touching her elbows. "Please, Analia. Your brother sent me—he *told* me to get your father."

Something twitches in her eyes. It's like the light shifts even though nothing in the room changes. She sucks in a breath, considering my words.

"Father will punish him," she feebly protests.

"Your father can't *punish* Edmund *if he's dead*," I present her with the facts. "Just go get him, *please!*"

She bounces to her feet, taking a few steps back. She still looks unsure.

"Analia, I wouldn't be back here if it weren't important," I remind her. "Please, go get your father."

"What if he doesn't listen to you?"

"I need you to help me convince him. Don't let him come back in here without you. You have to help me fight to save your brother."

"I thought you didn't love us anymore."

Did I ever love you? It's hard to love someone while being held hostage and threatened.

I fight to keep my head from jerking back in surprise.

"Analia, I only escaped because it was dangerous for me here, not because I didn't like you. I like you very much." Her face brightens at my words. "Now, go get your father, and hurry."

She turns, running back to the steps. The second it's quiet, Merrick's commanding voice fills the room.

"Celena, you get back over here *right now*." He leaves no room for discussion, but I'm already busy crawling back toward the water.

"Ow," I accidentally say out loud when I smack my tail off of a corner of a wall.

"Len?" Merrick calls, concerned.

"Celena?" Caspian echoes.

"I'm fine," I mutter. "Almost there."

I reach out, grabbing the side of the wall and Merrick's fingers instantly cover mine from the other side. I pull myself up, and Merrick hands his trident to Caspian so he can lift me over the wall. Caspian looks annoyed that he can't help, but he shouldn't even be using his trident with that injured arm, much less drag a mermaid over a wall and into a pool.

"What is this?" the king bellows, entering the room. Analia follows closely behind him, looking nervous.

"Your son needs help." I speed my tail up a little to raise myself up in the center of the pool. The king's eyes widen as he takes in Merrick and Caspian at my side.

"*You're* new," he muses, looking at Caspian.

"And worse than the last one," Casp regards him, hoping to make the king nervous.

"Injured, I see," the king points out. Analia's eyes are wide next to him as she stares at my brother like he's the most beautiful thing she's ever seen in her life.

After a moment, her gaze bounces back and forth between Merrick and Caspian, completely ignoring me. She blushes profusely, and I catch Caspian lowering his grin. The king shifts, irate at my brother, and furious that we've summoned him.

"Edmund needs your help," I say louder, insisting he revert his gaze to me. The king eyes me.

"We were bringing Edmund back—"

"The prince," the king cuts me off, correcting me. "You will address him as *the prince*."

"*He needs your help*," I push, annoyed. "On our way back, he was taken by sailors."

"Of course he was, I sent my men to rescue him," the king sneers at me.

"They weren't your men," I disagree. "Edmund was scared of them. He begged me to come and find you. He said you're the only one that can save him from them."

The message didn't make sense to me, but I followed his instructions to retrieve his father for him and bring back reinforcements.

"Father, you don't think…" Analia sounds scared. She clutches her father's sleeve. He glances at her for a moment before returning his glare to the pool.

"No, I don't. I think they have your brother." He nods at us.

"We don't," I insist. "We were bringing him back after he escaped your men. The boat took him—they forced him out of the water by scooping him up in a fishing net, tangled in seaweed and fish."

I try to paint a horrifying picture to get their attention. I easily sway the young princess, but her father is unmoveable.

"Where is my son?"

"He's on a boat."

"Where did you hide him?" The king's insistence to accuse us of hurting his son is frustrating. "Did you kill him?"

Analia shrieks, whipping around to face me with wide eyes.

"We didn't hurt Edmund." My words come out as a growl. "He is on a boat with men who said they were willing to hurt him."

"It *is them*, Father!" Analia wheels back to the king, tugging on him again. "The rebels have him!"

She dissolves into tears, and the king reaches to comfort her.

"Father, they're going to hurt him," she sobs. "They nearly drowned me, and now they have Edmund, *please*! Please, go save him. Don't let them take him."

"Hush, now, Analia." He tries to stop her from speaking in front of us.

"These people hurt Analia?" I ask, demanding answers.

"They were the ones that took me when you saved me," Analia cries harder. I'm not sure if she's faking the show or if it's real, but if she had the forethought to pull this on her father, I give her a lot of credit for being able to manipulate him.

If these men that have the prince are the same ones that had been bringing Analia and Edmund to Hontan when I found them, that means these are the same men that Tarni made me siren to save Coralie.

"They're ruthless, Father, please. We have to do something."

"*If* it's them, they'll ask for a ransom, and we'll get him back," the king tries to console his daughter. "But it's not—it's the mer. They have him."

This is ridiculous—he's never going to listen to me.

"If we had him, wouldn't *we* ask for a ransom?" Merrick asks before I can. "Don't you think we'd leverage a treaty to trade with you for the life of your son? If that was our goal, why would we come to you with some story like this?"

Analia locks eyes with me, and I can tell immediately that while she's worried about her brother, the tears are *completely* for her father's benefit. I can see it in her eyes before she switches over, turning on her father with the attitude only an eleven-year-old princess can muster.

"They want to help Edmund. If you don't help him right now, I'll help the mermaids save him. Do you really want me to fling myself into a pool to get away from you like Edmund did?"

The king looks horrified. His chin drops as he steps back from his daughter to get a good look at her. She crosses her arms, eyes still shining with tears.

Analia takes a daring step toward the pool—there's no way she'll ever jump in. I doubt she could hold her breath long enough to get through the tunnel anyway.

"Analia!" The king's sharp voice gives her pause.

"It's not their fault," she yells at him.

I swim back to the wall, forcing myself up on it so they can see me better. Water trickles off me as my hair sticks to the sides of my arms, dripping down onto my fingers as I lean forward on the wall.

Analia rushes to my side to lend her support. Merrick and Caspian join me, taking places at either side to show our strength and resolve. I feel braverer with them by me.

The king considers us for a moment. When he takes a gentle step toward us, I think we've won him over. He reaches his hand out to me like Edmund does. I place my hand in his, and his fingers close around mine.

I'm shocked when he pulls me forward, and I topple off the wall onto the ground. The mermen clamor behind me, demanding the king not touch me as I try to catch myself. Analia shrieks but doesn't move.

The king turns on me, grabbing me by my hair and waist. He lifts me, throwing me across the room. I collide with one of the short walls, falling over it. My scream startles everyone, and I hear a tiny war erupt behind me between the mermen and the king.

I roll over, trying to sit up. Swallowing, I attempt to force down the pain crawling through my body. Analia snaps out of it, rushing to my side.

"Are you okay?" she murmurs.

"Get back," the king roars, coming for me.

"Father, leave her alone," Analia shouts, brushing back her hair nervously.

I crawl around one of the walls, dragging my tail behind me. I'd prefer the scooting technique I used inside of the caves, but I don't have time to protect my scales. I'm grateful the floor isn't made of bumpy rock but is rather a smooth, polished surface.

Merrick is on the wall of the pool, swinging his tail around to face us. Caspian quickly hands him his trident, but Merrick waves it off. Instead, he pulls out his knife.

"Analia, go to Merrick," I instruct as I attempt to escape her father.

Analia does as I say, not thinking it through before she moves. Merrick whispers something to her—I assume the assurance that he won't really hurt her—and then wraps his arm around her neck and chest. He raises the knife to her.

"Let Celena go," Merrick says, voice echoing in the room in a deep rumble.

"Father," Analia squeaks. She doesn't look terrified until her father turns. I wonder which parts of her conversations with me were purely for *my* benefit—she's skilled at manipulating people's emotions.

"Get your hands off the princess," the king growls.

"Get your hands off *our* princess," Merrick counters.

From my angle, I can't see the king's face, but I can tell his jaw just twitched. He faces them for another full minute before he turns back to me.

"I'll see you mutilated for this," he hisses.

I crawl over to the side of the pool. It seems to take a painfully long time. Merrick removes his arm from Analia, leaving only the knife against her throat—Analia doesn't move, knowing the moment she does, her father will attack again.

Merrick reaches down to me with his free arm, tightening his muscles. I latch on to his forearm, and he helps to pull me up onto the wall next to him. Caspian drags me into the pool before I can pause to wait for Merrick. My twin thrusts a trident into my hands, and I whip around to direct it at the king in case he dares to step toward Merrick.

"Don't move until I'm in the water," Merrick whispers to Analia. "I don't want you to get hurt."

"Release her, *mer*." The king's eyes twitch, but I detect worry in his voice. "You have your *princess* back."

"Stay still," Merrick instructs again. He leans back, falling into the water backward. He flings his arm to the side to avoid hurting the princess.

When she hears the splash, she turns.

"We have to help Edmund!" Analia spins back to her father, demanding he refocus.

"I will have them cut in half," the king growls, eyes slicing over to Caspian and me.

Caspian turns, and Analia watches him intently as he drags me under the water. I see the king latch onto his daughter's arm, pulling her from the room.

"Hurry," I say as soon as Merrick rights himself. We rush toward the bent bar.

"What just happened?" Llyr yelps. "Caspian held us off."

"I didn't want to scare him into hurting her," Caspian protests as we careen down the glowing tunnel.

"He took Celena," Merrick explains.

"Again?" Llyr looks back at me over his shoulder as we burst out into the open waters. "Are you okay?"

"He didn't slice me open...yet," I reply. "There's a very good chance he's out here waiting for us though. We're going to have to help Edmund ourselves."

"We just have to find him," Dylana adds grimly.

"*Oh*, I don't think *that's* going to be an issue," Keone calls back to us. "Looks like they've brought him home."

A man stands on the deck of the ship, one arm tangled in ropes hanging from the boom. He leans out over the water, prepared to enter into negotiations with the king.

Edmund is bound with ropes around his entire upper body. He's gagged, but his eyes roam the waters, looking for something.

The king stands on the shores above the steps, arm posed in the air as if he's ordering his men. He glares at the ship entering his royal kingdom.

"Your majesty," the man cries, sweeping his hand grandly to the side. "We need to have a conversation."

His chuckle fills the air. The king shouts back in response, threatening the man if he doesn't hand over his son.

"Happily, sire. Which piece of him would you like first? His hand? His ear?" The man reaches for Edmund's ear, and Analia's piercing shriek from near the palace makes everyone duck as if a cannon had been shot.

The ship is not the one I dove off of. It appears the men have several captives from that ship, including one of the men I sirened into shooting a cannonball into their own deck—this must be the second ship and the reason Edmund was insistent on finding his father for help.

The vessel is brown and stands tall in the water, looking menacing. The windows are outlined in dark metal, and ropes hang over the sides of the boat. Men leer at us in the water as the entire collection surfaces.

Edmund spots me just as the others reveal themselves, tridents in hand. The mer surround the boat at a safe distance, blocking it in. Edmund's eyes are huge as they focus on me.

When he looks to his father, I follow his line of sight. The king stands in awe at the mer collection willing to fight for his son's freedom.

"Father!" Edmund yells. I look back just in time to see the man holding him rip the gag from around his neck, jarring him.

"Stay calm, son!" the king shouts back. "We'll get you back."

"We need to talk about terms!" the man shouts.

A line of guards steps up behind the king, readying arrows in their bows. Each one flames orange as the king lifts his hand.

"You will give my son back, and I won't burn your ship, *Captain*."

"You wouldn't burn a boat with your son on it," the captain laughs. His taunt is cut short when the king drops his hand and his men release their arrows.

They fly in a glorious arc that matches the sunset that has turned the sky a fierce orange color. The arrows land on the deck of the ship well beyond where Edmund and the captain stand. A few hit men, making them shriek in pain or collapse on the deck. One falls off the ship, dead. The fire extinguishes when it hits the water, sizzling.

The captain turns back to the king, mouth open.

"You had your chance, Captain. Now you're left with only this— hand my son over, get in your rowboats, and leave before I send my mermaids after you. If you don't, you'll be lucky if my men reach you before the mer do."

"Do it," I instruct, raising my trident toward the boat. The others follow suit, looking destructive. I don't like that the king is lording us over the men, but now is not the time to argue.

The flames cover the boat, looming over the edge. It crackles as it starts to lick its way down the side of the ship. Smoke pours into the sky, dark against the sunlight glistening through the clouds bathed in gold.

CHAPTER 14

The captain and Edmund disappear from sight. I can't tell where they've gone, but the king is calm, so I assume he can still see Edmund.

Men jump into rowboats and lower themselves into the water. They don't have much space between us and the boat, but that doesn't seem to deter them. Before they reach the surface, they launch their attack against the mer, trying to clear us away.

"Celena, find the prince," Marilla instructs, moving in to handle the fight.

I don't hesitate, diving under the water as my collection holds back the sailors from fleeing with the prince who is our only hope to end this war. My friends follow behind me, ready to support my mission.

From the backside of the boat, I spot a tiny rowboat moving away from the ship. Surfacing, I can see the captain holding a knife to Edmund's neck.

"Call off your sea witches, your highness," he shouts. The king deftly shakes his head.

"Let him go, and I'll consider sparing your men." He spooks as I address him.

"Not going to happen," he shouts back, knife moving closer to Edmund's throat. The prince closes his eyes for a moment, fingers flexing at his sides.

"Should we tip the boat?" Natale suggests.

"Would he slit the prince's throat when it moves?" Keone counters.

"We could surround him," Dylana offers. "We all have tridents."

"Siren him," Phorcys says in a flat voice. "Swim up to the boat and siren him."

"What if he has his ears blocked?" I counter.

"He talked to the king," Phorcys points out.

"Doesn't mean he doesn't have something there to block it."

"I'll do it," Cassidia pushes past me—I didn't realize she was here with us. I jerk on her tail, and she turns on me.

"Stay out of this, *siren*." I'm positive if Cassidia is involved, Edmund will die today.

If the prince perishes today, I'm also positive the king will blame the mer and come after us even more ferociously—I can't let that happen.

"We surround them. He can't take on all of us at once. Once we get Edmund out of the boat, we get him as far away as possible, and try to take him to the palace steps."

I look around the group to make sure everyone understands.

"Whoever can get to him, take him straight to the king—the rest of us will help. We only need one or two of us to handle the captain." My mind instantly flashes to the captain drowning next to his rowboat. "Don't wait—just go straight to the palace steps."

Everyone nods, even Phorcys and Cassidia—though *she* doesn't look happy about it. Murdoch swims quietly beside us, still looking uncomfortable being in our presence.

We swim up from the depths, surrounding the boat as it moves. Merrick and I take the lead position at the front of the boat—we'll be the first ones the captain and Edmund see. On my signal, we lift ourselves out of the water.

The captain stops his man from rowing. The boat floats in the water, stopping with a jerk as Merrick puts his hand out to halt it. It bounces into his hand, but he doesn't flinch.

He raises the knife to Edmund's throat again, glaring at Merrick.

"I'm not the one you need to be worried about," Merrick addresses him with a smirk and hard eyes.

"Release him," I say in my most dangerous voice. I use it when I interrogate mer for Marilla—and I *always* get my answers.

The captain's sneer fades away, leaving a hard line of a mouth and slanted eyes in its place.

"Or what—you'll siren me?" he arrogantly challenges me.

"Look around you, Captain." I nod behind him. "You're not going anywhere."

He slowly turns, observing the collection holding tridents to him.

"You won't hurt me while I have him."

"You forget, Captain," I remind him, smiling. I hope he believes we're attempting to trick the king, but really plan to double cross him. "Mer and humans no longer work together. That treaty was broken a century ago. We have our own reasons for wanting the human prince."

We lock eyes as he tries to read me. I hope I look convincing.

He places a hand on the side of the ship to steady himself as Llyr knocks his trident into the boat. The boat tips back and forth three times before settling, then Caspian repeats the process from the other side, throwing the captain off again.

Edmund attempts to balance himself, but he pitches around with the rocking of the boat, eyes locked on me as he waits for instructions. I swim forward while the captain is distracted.

"We would like the prince now," I say, getting the captain's attention. "Please."

The captain starts to raise his hand to me but can't get it past the blade I hold over his knuckle. He looks down, paling.

"Once more, we would like Prince Edmund now, please."

The captain whips his blade away from the prince, slashing at me, but I move faster. His finger falls in the water, bumping my tail as it sinks down to where the fish can find it. Blood pours from the stub on his hand as he screams, cursing at me and promising to cut me into pieces.

I reach inside the boat and lower my blade to his leg, prepared to cut him again. He flinches and drags his knife lightly across the back of my hand, misjudging my location through the tears in his eyes.

The boat rocks as Keone and Natale work to flip the boat. Phorcys joins them as Caspian and Cassidia dart out of the way. Merrick swings his trident, aiming for the captain's head but he pulls up at the last second to avoid hitting Edmund as the boat shifts position.

I grab the edge of the boat and swim under the water, helping the collection to flip the boat as the humans topple onto me. I flick my tail, moving away so that I can turn to see where everyone is in the water. Merrick pulls Edmund out from under the boat, but the other sailor quickly follows, trying to latch on to Edmund.

When I surface, several other rowboats have converged on the collection. Caspian takes on a man dressed in a dark grey shirt and darker pants as he uses an oar to attempt to injure my twin. His trident takes the man out easily, piercing through his chest.

"Len," Merrick's shout draws my attention back to him, and I discover a boat attempting to rip the prince away from him. Edmund is still tied up and can't help with his escape—his struggling makes him look like one of the creatures that accidentally crawled into a brine pool.

I pierce a sailor's wrist with my trident, twisting as he shrieks. He loses his grip on Edmund, but the sailor behind him lunges toward the prince, thrusting a spear into the water

Reeling back. I send the flat end side of my trident into the sailor's face, destroying his aim as his spear enters the water. Edmund bellows in pain.

"It's his leg," Merrick quickly states, letting me know he will survive the strike.

I pull my trident back as Merrick attempts to move Edmund out of reach. Caspian and Llyr appear next to me, tridents up.

"Untie him so he doesn't drown," Caspian instructs, handling the sailors in the boat I was fighting.

I rush to Merrick and Edmund, fishing my knife out of my *iluse*.

"Hold still, I'm going to cut the ropes."

Edmund flips over in the water so that he's floating on his back. Merrick supports him, letting the prince rest his head on his shoulder to ensure he stays above water while I'm working.

I work my fingers between the bottom coil of rope and the prince's stomach, lifting it enough to slip my knife between him and the rope upside down. I saw it back and forth until the rope snaps. Quickly, I rush to snap more of the ropes, peeling off layers as quickly as I can.

Merrick keeps an eye on the fighting so I can focus on freeing the prince. Edmund slows his breathing, trying not to move as I work.

"Almost there," I mumble as the fighting grows louder behind me. "Merrick?"

"They're okay so far. They took out a couple of sailors."

"Assuming I survive this, I'm going to drive out all the mercenaries," Edmund grumbles.

"You're father is here," I inform him.

"I saw."

"He tried to hurt Celena…again," Merrick takes the opportunity to inform him.

"What did he do?" Edmund bolts up in the water, knocking Merrick and nearly causing me to stab him—I get my finger out of the way just in time. "Sorry. What did he do?"

"We'll explain later," I grumble. "Hold still."

With the lower part of his arms free, he reaches up, trying to remove the ropes around his upper arms, hindering my ability to help him.

"Edmund!" He stills as I lecture him.

Once he's free, I instruct Merrick to return him to the king. I turn, ready to defend them from behind. Swimming backward isn't nearly as easy without latching arms with Merrick and allowing him to direct my moves. Merrick and I call to each other as we move since we're unable to feel each other's movements.

"Len, we've got a problem," Merrick shouts as we round the corner of the burning ship. Several small boats turn toward us, making their way through the water as our collection battles against them.

There are more boats than there were before—the king has sent his men in the water, but I can't tell which ones are our enemies and which are our temporary allies. More boats turn toward us when they see the prince.

"Len, time to switch," Merrick decides, summoning me. I know he's right—I have a better chance of moving the prince while Merrick defends us.

I rush to his side, brushing against his arm as I take Edmund's from him. He darts forward, kissing me quickly.

"Careful," he whispers before taking off. I have no doubt he'd kill every human here to ensure my safety as I drag the prince to shore.

"Merrick." My voice trembles as he looks back. I whisper, "Don't do anything stupid."

He flashes the most brilliant grin at me, revealing his dimples. His eyes sparkle as he tips his head, flipping his bangs back out of his face. He purses his lips, blowing a tiny kiss to me, winking as he leaves to face the humans alone.

"Hold your breath," I tell Edmund. He gulps in air, and I submerge us under the waves, swimming until he squeezes my arm as I'm wrapped around his waist and back.

The palace steps aren't terribly far away when we surface, but we have to get by several boats before we're in the clear. The king spots us, relief washing over his face when he sees Edmund in the water. He waves, trying to get us to come to the step.

I wonder if perhaps the king has taken one too many hits to the head recently.

Edmund turns on his back to float while I swim toward the steps, much like Merrick and I do, only the prince isn't trained to fight. He attempts to kick his good leg but quickly gives up.

When he reels back and kicks out, it surprises me. The movement bobs us under the water, but when I turn, I see a man in the ocean behind us, swimming toward us quickly. Bravery—or more likely, *stupidity*—has encouraged the man to take us on in *my* world instead of his.

Edmund kicks again, trying to keep the man at bay. I release the prince and flip under the water, pulling the man's legs. He bounces over the surface of the water until I drag him down, moving him far away.

The man claws at me when I release him, but he only has so much time to swim to the surface before he's out of air. He picks his life over his revenge and attempts to claw his way to the surface.

Edmund struggles in the water with another man—this one clearly a sailor. His beard barely moves, despite being soaking wet from the ocean water. He holds a knife in his hands, and it glints gold in the light of the fire.

Edmund punches him, holding his collar—I'm impressed.

"Celena, behind you!" Edmund shouts to me, striking the man again.

I turn just in time to see a boat sneak up on me. Rushing at it, I slam into it full speed, turning it over in the water. I swim away upside down, monitoring the surface as I rush to Edmund's aid.

Twirling in the water, I spiral down to the depths with the bearded sailor. His eyes are alive with fear, and his nails dig into my arm just below my armor, making me wince, but I refuse to let go. His hands had been around Edmund's throat as he attempted to choke him when I intervened. Edmund had almost held his own, but the man's arms were longer and stronger than the prince's, and Edmund didn't stand a chance.

Bubbles slip from his lips—so many that it's hard to see. I release him, clawing once at his face. If he wants to live, he'll have to swim quickly.

Leaving him behind in the water, I find Edmund swimming toward the steps slowly. He rotates between swimming on his stomach and on his back, checking in front of him and behind him as he moves. At least he had the foresight to do that.

"Edmund!" the king screams from the shore. Somewhere in the background, Analia screams for her brother as well. I'm not sure if Edmund can hear them—he's incredibly focused on his survival right now.

We're closer to the steps, and several of the boats have moved, but two battle directly in our path—guards and mercenaries fighting against one another.

"We have to go under," I prompt Edmund. He nods.

Below the waves, everything sparkles with an orange tone—a mixture of the reflection of the fire from the boat and the setting sun. Bubbles shine like bursts of light every time a sailor hits the water.

Bubbles slip from Edmund's nose slowly, and I know he'll need air soon, but I can't afford to stop yet—we have to make it further.

Splashing sounds behind me, and I think part of the ship just crashed into the water loudly. A light wave confirms my suspicions as it washes over my back, moving my hair as I guide us around the battle above us.

Edmund's fingers dig into my waist as I carry him upside down, his chest against mine. He wraps himself around me tighter, fighting not to panic as he begins to choke.

Further. Don't stop.

I beat my tail, accidentally slapping his legs as I move us through the water, but I can't angle myself away from him—I need to get him air. His grip loosens, and I panic.

Darting up, I surface right where both boats can see us. I shake Edmund, and he coughs, gulping in air as he sputters.

"Breathe," I direct, not wasting time trying to soothe him. He continues to choke but tries to hold his breath again for me. Before I can drop us into the water, he chokes again.

"Hurry, Edmund," I mumble.

If I had seen any starfish below, I would be wishing on it, but right now, all I have is the palace steps ahead of me. Water laps against them, rising and falling at different levels with every crash of the waves. Sometimes they cover the higher steps, sometimes the lower steps, but never more than halfway up.

I focus on it as a punch sounds directly over our heads. We both look up as a guard slams his fist into a sailor, knocking him back. The man staggers but pushes himself forward to clash against the guard.

"Hurry!" he shouts to us without looking.

I heed his warning to flee and take off with Edmund. Dipping under the water, he clings to me again. When we surface, we're only a few lengths away from the steps.

I picture my great-great-grandmother Aila sitting on those steps with Edmund's great-great-grandfather Jarek. Aila always said that Jarek would sit toward the bottom of the steps while she and Persephone sat partially in the water. Jarek didn't mind getting his boots wet if it meant he got to be near the mermaids and the ocean. She told us he could stare at the sea for hours and loved watching the sunset with his mermaid friends.

I imagine their evenings looked much like this—without light from a burning ship overtaking the sunset while people died all around them.

We crash into the steps, and it nearly knocks the wind out of me—it's hard to see the steps under the water without actually *being* under the water to see them. Edmund hauls himself up, being careful of his leg.

"Look out!" he shouts before he can scramble up all the way.

The prince reaches down in the water, scooping me into his arms. He hauls me onto the steps, tossing me high as a rowboat crashes against the stairs, pinning his already-injured leg between the boat and the step.

He screams in pain as I collide with the steps, high out of the water—I have no idea how he threw me so high. The king and his men rush past me. One guard kicks at the boat, forcing it back so hard that he nearly falls in the water.

The king and a guard pluck Edmund from the steps and pull him up to the ground, leaving me to sag against the steps, trying to catch my breath. My ribs throb from the impact with the steps.

"Celena, go!" Edmund begs through his pain. "Get back in the water and go!"

He moans as the men stumble, trying to move him quickly. I watch them drag him for a moment.

"Come back when it's safe, but go!"

Turning, the sun is setting over the horizon. It glints off the water magically. The fire illuminates the water and the side of the rocky palace cliff—much of the ship is submerged in the water now. It crackles loud, sizzling when fire meets wave.

The palace guards retreat once the prince is safe—they'll all be safe inside the palace if they can lock the mercenaries out. The men stumble up the hill, checking for enemies as they move, but are greeted with nothing but an empty courtyard and path to the ocean.

Bodies float in the water, bobbing lifelessly. The collection is smaller yet again, but Marilla is still alive, calling for me from the ocean. I scurry down the steps, bumping painfully into each one until I reach the water. I push off of it like Aila did so many times before they were banished from Antaire. The water swallows me up, darkening as I sink below the waves.

CHAPTER 15

The mer collection immediately follows, dropping down to the depths of the shallow inlet near the palace. From our vantage point, we can see the guards attempting to finish the battle in the water above us.

Boats are tipped over, floating upside down. The burning ship sinks entirely in the water as Merrick races to me. We collide, and he wraps his arms around me.

"Are you hurt?" His face is so close to mine that all I can think about are his lips on my skin. I shake my head.

"Are you?" My hands close around his upper arms, just above his elbows as he stares into my eyes.

Instead of answering me, he kisses me. We don't move at first, our lips just pressed together, but after a moment, he tips his head, separating his lips.

"We're all still here, thanks," Llyr interrupts, elbowing Merrick.

"Like you don't want to do that," I chide, shaking my head.

"Maybe I already did," he grins, glancing at Dylana. My jaw drops.

"When you work fast, you really work fast, Llyr," I joke.

"Worth it," he nods, grinning.

"Celena!" Caspian barrels into me, colliding against Merrick and me.

"Your arm?" I ask.

"Still attached," he replies, eyes sparkling.

A new body drifts down in the ocean, landing on top of a merman that died in the initial battle a few days ago—things are starting to pile up. I cringe as it hits its resting place.

"Where is Edmund?" Dylana questions, looking concerned.

"With his father in the palace," Marilla interjects. "He was wounded, but he'll be okay."

"What is *that*?" Keone asks suddenly, pointing at the surface.

"Is that the king?" I ask in horror.

A large boat sails in, overtaking all of the remaining rowboats. It's not as tall or as wide as the ship that burned a few minutes ago, but it carries enough authority—and weapons—to make any man nervous.

The king's flags sail from its mast, confirming that the king is angry and wants to end this. He stands at the front of the ship, pointing to the men in the water.

The sides of the boat are low enough that his men can haul in victims from their guard or take hostages from the collection of mercenaries in the waters.

His guards reach out, pulling men from the sea. If they are found to be the enemy, they are slain and returned to the water to wash away with the tide. What the king doesn't notice is that the captain has somehow survived and is in the water below him.

"The captain is going after the king," I mumble.

"What?"

"The captain is going after the king!" I shout, darting away from the ocean floor as I flip my tail as hard as I can toward the surface. Merrick takes off after me, begging me to wait, but I can't.

I'm not sure what possessed the king to take to the waters, but it was a terrible idea. He had been safe inside with his children, and yet he decides to come out to fight a bunch of sailors who had already lost any control they might have had? Revenge is in his blood, it seems.

The captain swings himself up onto the boat, surprising the king. The man steps back, crashing into one of his guards. The captain takes a menacing step toward the king, knife in hand. A guard blocks him, taking the strike and he topples backward, flipping outside of the boat.

I reach the surface and jump toward the open part of the ship. My hand catches the captain's foot, and I pull back. The man pitches forward, slamming into the deck.

The captain turns on me. Somehow, he managed to keep his knife in his hand, though it looks like he bit through his lip when he fell—a tremendous amount of blood falls from his punctured lower lip. A broken tooth is missing from his mouth, and I'm positive I can see it in the background behind him.

He slams the knife at me, driving it into the wooden deck as I recoil, barely missing the attack. The captain growls at me, wincing when he realizes the damage he's done to his face.

A guard comes to my aid, wrenching the captain around as the king kicks at his head. Merrick grabs hold of me and drags me backward.

"Careful there, princess," he teases. "I'm pretty sure bad things happen when mermaids end up on boats."

Above the water, the king staggers to his feet. He moves toward the captain, but the sailor is faster. He grabs the king's leg and pulls it out from under him, making the king fall to the deck of the ship again.

The captain pulls his hand back, preparing to strike, but the guard snaps his hand from behind him. The captain recoils in pain—it looks like his wrist is shattered. My jellyfish stings must feel like nothing compared to the pain of a shattered bone.

The king scrambles back, not realizing how close he is to the opening in the ship's wall. Merrick moves to warn him before I do, but neither of us surface in time and the king crashes backward into the water.

The flash in the water is so quick that I'm not entirely convinced that I see it until I drop under the waves. Cassidia has somehow found her way around us and is rushing toward the king. Phorcys darts past us, racing after the blue siren. Her icy blue tail looks serene and gentle compared to Phorcys' fiery orange one, but *she's* the one we need to worry about.

The mermaid siren catches the king and drags him down to the depths, twisting as she swims to disorient the king. Phorcys shouts to her, but she's on a mission and doesn't hear his cries as he pleads with her not to do this—he knows the mer wrath will be swift.

"She's going to kill him," I shout. Given the number of times I've had to swim at full speed this evening alone, I think once I return to wherever the mer settle, I'll take up permanent residence on a lounging couch and never move again. Perhaps I can train a dolphin to fetch things for me.

Cassidia slows near the ocean floor, a mere length from the dead bodies resting on the sand. The king struggles, kicking at her tail, but she holds fast. Her white hair flows out behind her, and once again,

I'm in awe of everything about her. It amazes me that Nir was the royal and she wasn't.

Phorcys reaches them and attempts to rip Cassidia's hand away from the human. She glares at him, saying something we can't hear from this distance. Phorcys argues, trying again to loosen her grasp.

The king's dark clothing helps him to blend in with the darkening water. The sun has disappeared from the sky, and while we still have light to see by, it won't be long before we don't.

Phorcys attempts to wrap his arms around Cassidia and pull her away, but she crashes her head back, slamming into his face with her skull. The merman looks up, catching my eye and it renews his commitment to stop her. He pulls at her angrily as she puts up a fight.

Bubbles escape the king's mouth as he cries out—Cassidia buries a broken shell piece into his side. His hair is long enough to float in the water, but not quite long enough to cover his eyes as he stares at the mermaid in front of him. Blood blossoms in the water, dispersing quickly—the fish don't seem to notice as they swim around the scene.

My hands are on Cassidia's wrist before she realizes I have joined them, far too distracted by the king and Phorcys. I slice into her with my trident, slamming into her arm just below her shoulder. It was a risk attacking her near the king, but it was the only thing I could do to stop her.

Merrick reaches the king and pulls him toward the surface, leaving Phorcys and me to handle Cassidia. She glares at me.

"You've ruined everything," she says calmly. "You killed Nir, you killed Tarni, you let the human prince and king go. You even destroyed the siren collection—they're all dead because of you.

"Look around, *Celena*—all this is because of you." She points to the bodies on the ocean floor in the dwindling light. "You killed all of them. *Why?* Because you wanted to prove some point your great-great-grandmother was trying to make a century ago?

"She failed *then,* and you failed *now.* Congratulations, you've sealed the fate of three kingdoms, and destroyed the entire sea nation."

"Aila didn't fail—she protected the collection." I ready my trident, knowing an attack is imminent.

"She turned her back on her own blood. If we had all worked together, the humans would be gone, and the sea would be a peaceful place."

"Instead you turn it into a war? Nir's father was an idiot to think he could take on the humans like this—we've avoided them for a century—we could have gone on avoiding them forever, and everyone would still be alive," I challenge her.

She twitches in the water—my only signal that something bad is about to happen.

Cassidia dives at Phorcys as he hovers in the water behind her. She wrenches away his trident and rushes at me. I wait for her to approach me, using the force of her movement to set her off balance. I move at the last second, and she crashes forward, tilting at an angle she wasn't expecting.

Phorcys is close behind her, but only has a knife to defend himself with now. The struggle is written on his face—protect a siren he's likely known his entire life—a trusted advisor to his former king and prince, and an ally of his princess—or help the mermaid who holds his future in her hands.

The merman grits his teeth and moves slowly—*intentionally*—in the water behind her as she starts forward toward me. He has the look of a predator closing in on his unwitting prey. Cassidia's piercing blue gaze is fixed on me with deadly precision as she swims toward me slowly.

"Nir—*and* his father—were protecting the ocean, *unlike your* queen," she addresses me in a cold voice.

"My queen protected the collection. Yours *sacrificed* your mer." My fingers close tighter around my trident. Cassidia's blood is still caught near the points at the end from my last attack.

"It was a sacrifice we were willing to make for the sake of the seas, wasn't it, Phorcys?" She expects the merman to be on her side. She doesn't realize his alliances have changed.

"There are a lot of things I'm willing to do," he growls as if he's supporting her, but he keeps his deadly eyes trained on his former collection mate.

I will spend the rest of my life leery of Phorcys—his allegiance changes like the tides.

Cassidia moves to strike, and I hold my hand up in warning. She quirks her head slightly, narrowing her eyes.

"I wouldn't do that if I were you."

"Leave her be, Cassidia."

Fear flashes over Cassidia's pretty features, leaving her nearly unrecognizable for a moment as she discovers she is alone in this fight.

"Nir would want us to finish this." Cassidia raises her voice. "So would Tarni."

"They're both dead, Cassidia. We're all that's left."

"Roni is still here. They have Tiko and the others—"

"Tiko's not getting out." Her face twitches slightly at his words, and I wonder if she has some kind of connection to the siren with the periwinkle tail being held at Scylla—or Metten…I have no idea where the prisoners are.

"You and I could take them on together." She turns slowly to face him, risking her back to me. I don't move.

"This is about survival, Cassidia—I'll take my punishment with *them*. I won't work against them." He slams his trident into the sand so that it's pointing up toward the water. He reveals a knife in his hands, making it an even fight.

Cassidia's shoulders straighten, and she flips the broken shell in her hand. I expect her to charge at Phorcys. Instead, she flips in the water toward me for the final time—she wants to take me down with her. I dart back, but she has the advantage.

Phorcys reaches her just as her knife drags along the bottom of my tail just above my fins. My purple scales separate under the jagged shell, several pop off, falling to the ocean floor. I cry out in pain.

Caspian collides with my back, pulling me away as Phorcys drags his knife across Cassidia's hip. She screams, thrusting her hand at Phorcys to injure him. She collides with his shoulder, infuriating him as the broken shell opens his skin.

The collection closes in, unsure if they should get involved.

"Phorcys!" I yell. I may despise the mermaid he's about to destroy, but I don't want her to die—she should suffer for her actions for the rest of her life. Unlike Persephone, I'll see to it that she won't die early.

Llyr rushes into action, trying to break up the brawl, but Phorcys is a force, and no one can stop him as he drags his knife through the mermaid again.

Cassidia twists in his arms, but Phorcys has her pinned against him as he holds his knife to her. He makes eye contact with me, and his eyes soften for just a moment before he nods to the surface, indicating that I should help Merrick with the king.

The two drop in the water, twisting as they fight against each other. He's right—it's more important to protect the human king.

"Don't interfere," I warn the collection. "This is a siren matter— the *last* siren matter."

Swimming is excruciating with my new injury, but Caspian guides me to the surface as Llyr oversees the fight below. We race to the top of the water, slowly exiting to determine where we need to go.

The captain's body floats on its back in the water a few lengths away from Merrick. He swims slowly with the king—they're both injured. Several other bodies bob in the water too, and I wonder if Merrick just took on all those men to protect the king.

"Father!" Analia screams. She elbows a guard and races to the steps, crashing into a wave as it crests on the stairs leading into the ocean. It nearly knocks her off balance and sends her tumbling in the ocean, but the guard she hit catches up, reaching out to save her by her elbow.

She jerks, feet nearly slipping out from under her but he holds her in place. She pins him with an adoring, awe-filled gaze before turning back to her father and Merrick.

"Father!" she screams again, sounding like she's been sobbing.

The king tries turning around in the water to face his daughter, but Merrick holds him tightly, making it difficult for him to flip off his back. Merrick says something sharp and the king stops struggling.

The guard pulls the princess back up the steps, out of the way of the other men who rush down to help pull the king from the water. They wait anxiously.

"Is your brother all right?"

"Edmund's inside," she calls back, voice quieter.

"Is he safe?" the king calls as he and Merrick approach the steps.

"Yes, Papa."

The men trample the water with their heavy boots, not slipping like Analia did. They reach out, pulling the king from the ocean. He only makes it a few steps before he collapses into a sitting position, hand on his chest, and gasps.

Angry tears in his shirt reveal open wounds on his sides. One of his boots is missing. The king has marks on his face, which will bloom into angry purple tones tomorrow. He looks worse than his son's crushed leg.

Analia sobs when she observes his injuries and begs the men to take him back to the palace. They lift the king, sharing his weight, and move toward the opalescent dwelling as he lolls limply in their arms.

Merrick doesn't look nearly as injured as the king, but it's clear he's been through a battle on his own. I touch his arm, making him jump. He tears his focus away from the king and quickly scoops me into his arms.

"Phorcys is about to kill Cassidia."

"What?" he demands, eyes wide.

"Celena!" Analia calls when she notices me with Merrick. I turn to face her, but Merrick refuses to release me. "Edmund said to tell you to stay. They're setting his leg, but he needs to speak with you right away."

I nod, unsure if it's wise to stay.

"It might take a few hours, Celena, please don't leave," she begs. "Whatever he needs, it's important."

The princess lifts her dress and runs up the path to the castle. Once she's inside, Merrick, Caspian, and I dive back under the waves to see which siren won—if by some miracle it was Cassidia, I doubt the collection let her last long.

Phorcys floats in the water, shoulders bent over low. They sag with each heavy breath he takes. Cassidia lies on the ocean floor, arms stretched above her head, hair tossed over them. Slowly, Phorcys puts his knife away and sinks to the floor next to the blue-tailed siren.

He rolls her over and cradles her in his arms. His face is hard, but the tiniest flicker of regret pulses out of him—at least that's what it looks like to me. Phorcys reaches down to brush the hair out of her face as she dies.

Her entire body is covered in open wounds—Phorcys showed little mercy during their battle. She blinks, slowly slipping away. I suppose we'll never find out how she learned to siren so well.

The collection watches nervously, ready to take on the merman siren if they need to. They move, making a way for us as we swim slowly over to Phorcys and Cassidia.

Perhaps it's a good thing we have to stay and wait for Edmund to speak with us.

Marilla intercepts us, eyebrow raised as she waits for a report.

"The king has been hurt—they took him inside. Edmund sent his sister to beg us to wait for him."

Marilla sighs, knowing we don't have much of a choice. Perhaps this evening will convince the king that all we want is to live in peace, far, far away from the humans.

I turn back to Phorcys just as he sets Cassidia down. He takes the shell out of her hand. Swimming up in the water, he moves toward Marilla.

The collection seizes their weapons in their hands and prepares to stop him. Phorcys ignores them and opens his hand palm up, displaying the shell to the queen.

"I'm prepared to follow you," he addresses her, "and to take whatever punishment you deem fit for my actions during the war."

Marilla stares at him for a moment before moving—her version of hesitation disguised as something meant to make the mer before her wait in fear. She reaches out and takes the blood-covered broken shell.

"I'll consider your punishment. You will have a trial, and we will proceed with sentencing when we return."

Phorcys nods like a good soldier. He drops his hand to his side, and Marilla continues to stare him down. She drops her chin just enough to be a simple nod, indicating that the collection should move.

Everyone turns their backs on Phorcys, casting one last look at the blue siren. He follows behind them, stony-faced.

I slip under Merrick's arm as we follow behind Phorcys and the collection.

We swim away, but Marilla only lets us go so far before she commands our attention.

"We are staying—we will not swim in the dark tonight. We're far enough away that we won't be hurt, and deep enough that no man can reach us, but we'll take turns keeping watch anyway," the queen directs the collection. I'm glad I'm not in charge at this point.

We settle onto the sand, curling up close together. I nestle against Merrick, and Caspian protectively rests on my other side, the backs of our hands touching so that we know the other one is safe. Dylana finds us, and we lay so that our heads are near each other. Llyr positions himself next to Dylana, mirroring my positioning with Merrick.

I know Marilla has our best soldiers on watch duty, so sleep comes easily.

CHAPTER 16

The ocean sparkles with color when I wake. A school of brilliant red fish swims a few lengths over me. I curl into Merrick as he begins to stir next to me, taking a deep breath. His lungs fill, moving me so gracefully that I smile, finger slowly moving down his chest.

He blinks awake and grins at me.

"Good morning."

I reach up and move his blue bangs out of the way, clearing his vision. He reaches for my hand trailing down his skin and brings it to his lips, kissing it gently. My scales race with a spark of energy.

A starfish rests against his tail, and Merrick flicks it gently, letting the ripple motion inform the starfish that it's time to move. Merrick's fingers drum lightly on my hip.

The sun cascades through the water, glimmering against every piece of debris that floats in the ocean. I imagine much of that is from the boat that burned last night. Tipping my head straight out from my neck, I see it in the distance, submerged in the ocean.

"How sore are you?" Merrick gives me a cocky half smile, wincing as he stretches his tail to see how bad the pain is. He flinches more than he did when he waved off the starfish a moment ago.

I sit up, instantly regretting it as my back screams in pain.

"Oh," I groan. "I regret everything."

I lift my hand to my head, pushing back my pink hair.

"Here, let me." Merrick places his hands on my shoulders and turns me to face away from him. I stare at my sleeping twin as Merrick gently untangles my hair with his fingers.

"Good morning," Dylana says, sitting up. Somehow her hair has managed to stay perfect.

"Celena?" a merman's voice says. "For you."

I reach out, taking a conch shell from the merman. His tail is a dark red color mixed with purple tones on the sides—it's stunning. He nods before swimming away.

"I take it we're being summoned?" Merrick muses, continuing to work on my hair. I lean back into his hands, closing my eyes as he works his fingers through my locks. A sigh escapes my lips and Caspian stirs.

Lifting the conch shell to my ear, I close my eyes and focus on the words. Edmund's voice bounces around inside the shell.

"Celena, it's Edmund. We need to speak. Bring the queen with you. My father's still recovering, so I'm in charge, and we need to finalize the treaty while we still can. Please hurry."

"Time to go," I say with a sigh. "Dylana, we have to go to the palace. Get your mother."

We swim back to the palace at the front of the collection. We move slowly—slower than usual. I think we all need a break—it's been two weeks since we left Scylla, and even longer than that since the fighting started.

When we reach the palace, the collection stays back, rising up out of the water en mass as our small group approaches the steps where Edmund is waiting. He attempts to stand, but the guards on either side of him have to help.

Edmund hobbles down the stairs, looking as if he's walking on knives with every step. He finally drops down to sit slightly higher than the waves and looks helplessly at me.

I swim up to the steps and rest my hand on the bottom one. Marilla and Dylana join me.

"I'm sure you don't want to, but you're welcome to join me," Edmund says, waving his hand at the steps. He winces with the motion.

The prince's leg is braced with something. It's bandaged, but it looks like some of it is falling down from his walk out of the palace.

I pull myself out of the water, sitting on a low step. Wrapping my hands around my tail, I pull it to my chest. Dylana and Marilla stay in the water, letting me be their ambassador.

"I don't have the power to put this treaty into effect until my father approves it," Edmund admits. "But we can finalize everything right now, and when he signs on, it will be enforced."

"Everything we discussed before is still acceptable?" Marilla asks.

"I've had my people write everything up for us. If you can sign it, I can bring it to my father. I have copies for you to read the terms before you agree."

Edmund raises his hand, and two men bring down two large pieces of paper. The signing of the treaty is more of a formality, but it's important in the human culture, so we patronize him. Marilla holds a conch shell in which she will record the treaty, and all parties will agree before the conch is sealed.

Dylana and Marilla each take a copy of the paper, reading it over. They mumble the words quietly at the same time to ensure it's the same on both pages. Marilla speaks into the shell as she reads.

The prince leans forward as they're reading to softly speak to me.

"You don't look like you fared well last night." He glances at my cuts.

"The blue siren sliced me open—don't worry, she's dead."

"Well, I suppose that should give my father some ease."

"Your leg?" I inquire. Just looking at it makes my fins hurt.

"It's going to take a long time for it to heal, but the doctor says I should walk again." He sighs. "I'm better off than my father though."

"What did they say about him?"

A wave crashes on the steps, nearly washing me back into the ocean. My hand darts out for the step but is caught instead by Edmund's hand. He holds me in place as the wave washes back out to sea.

"It's pretty bad, Celena," he whispers. His eyes say what he does not—his father might not survive.

"I'm sure he'll be fine." I squeeze his hand before I let go. The next wave doesn't try to pull me away.

"Until then, I'm in charge. I'll be acting on his behalf and handling the kingdom until he's moving around again." Edmund's voice is stronger, knowing the guards standing a few steps up are listening. "Of course, he'll advise me, but I'll do all the footwork for him while he rests."

"On only one leg?" I tease.

"I'll find a way." He grins back at me. He motions to my tail. "*You* manage with only one."

"How is Analia handling all of this?"

"She hasn't left my father's side." His face drops. "I'm worried."

"We agree to these terms," Marilla says, interrupting our conversation. She swims toward the steps to hand the document back. "I am prepared to sign these. Dylana will be signing them too, just in case it takes time to convince your father."

If Marilla is suggesting she might not be around when the treaty is finally enacted, she must be assuming the king will say no, and we'll be forced to wait until Edmund takes over years from now. If that's the case, we need to get as far away from here as possible.

I glance out at Merrick. He's just far enough away to give us space, but still close enough to hear when we're speaking loudly. I see his tail twitch through the water—he must realize Marilla's hint too.

"I think that's wise," Edmund replies, a hint of sadness in his voice. He doesn't believe that his father will sign it, even after everything he witnessed. My heart sinks like the burning ship did last night.

Marilla and Dylana are presented with pens similar to the utensils we use under the sea to write with, and they scrawl their names on the papers. With a flourish, Edmund signs the copies as well, leaving room for his father. They all take turns speaking into the conch shell.

"We look forward to a fruitful treaty with you and your kingdom, Prince Edmund." Marilla nods to him. Stretching out, she hands him a different conch shell. "This is for your father when he is ready. I hope he receives this well and considers our proposal."

"Thank you, Queen Marilla. I will pass this along to him. I hope that we can conclude this quickly, for all of our sakes. Please know that from this day forward, I personally will be acting in concordance with the stipulations of this treaty and will encourage my men to do the same."

"As will we, your majesty." Marilla nods once more before offering him her royal goodbye and swims away, taking the collection with her. Dylana follows quickly behind me after giving me a look.

"*This* seems more like what Jarek and Aila would have experienced," Edmund snickers. "I suppose this is goodbye."

"I suppose it is." I turn to look out at the sea as the collection sinks under the waves.

"I'll try to keep you updated," he offers quietly. "I might encourage Analia to send you shells too—I'd like her to see you as a friend."

"What? I'm not a pet anymore?" I joke.

"You were never a pet, Celena." His voice grows serious.

"I know, Edmund. I appreciate you listening to me on all of this."

"I appreciate you making this treaty happen." His smile is sad even though his eyes sparkle. "A century later and it ends the way it began. Goodbye, Celena. I look forward to your conch messages."

"Goodbye, Edmund. I look forward to yours as well."

"Maybe I'll send some to Merrick too so he'll stop hating me," he calls teasingly as I slip into the ocean.

"He doesn't *hate* you…much." I grin as I turn to wave one last time, dipping below the surface.

"So it's done," Dylana grins. "It's all over. We just have to wait for the king to give his permission—"

"Or for him to die—" Caspian cuts her off.

"Let's hope it doesn't come to that," Marilla calls over to us.

"Either way, it will happen soon—it can't take too long, can it?" I ask, musing out loud.

"We must be patient, Celena." Marilla glances at me. "For now, we will go home to Scylla. The humans couldn't find us there for a century, and I don't think they'll find us there now. But we must leave Metten immediately, just in case."

The more I think about it, the more I'll miss Metten. I wish we had had more time to explore it while we were there before. At least we'll be able to stop to get the rest of the collection that is waiting there before we swim home.

"Perhaps some of us should hold back, just to ensure no one comes after us," Merrick suggests, reading my mind. "We could wait an extra day before following along from Metten. I don't mind waiting—I also don't mind traveling a little slower at this point."

He glances around meaningfully at the others, looking for support. They squint their eyes as he nods covertly at them.

"That's a wise idea." Dylana is the first to speak.

"I'll stay back to make sure everyone is safe," Llyr adds.

"*Everyone*…or my daughter?" Marilla's voice is short as he glances at her guard from the corner of her eye. Llyr stops swimming, eyes wide. Marilla snorts. "Hmm. *See that you do.*"

With lips still pursed, she swims away, giving her daughter permission to date Llyr. He grins wildly at her, and the princess looks like she wants to rush to him, but she restrains herself.

"Adorable," Caspian teases, rolling his eyes. "I'm obviously coming to chaperone you four. Now we can't trust *any* of you."

The water appears clearer today, though the light sparkles

through the ocean all the same. A sea turtle crosses our path, unconcerned of our presence. Caspian opens his hand palm up and pushes it up in the water, creating a small wave that bounces the turtle up when it hits the bottom of its shell. He smirks as the turtle bobs in the water, but the creature doesn't care.

We say goodbye to the collection from Ambra as they turn off to make their way home. It's sad seeing them go, but I have a feeling it won't be too long before we see them again. Now that the open waters are slightly safer, I have a feeling we'll be doing a lot more traveling in the future. I'd enjoy visiting Ambra if I ever get the chance.

An hour later, we reach the outskirts of Metten. The coral is stunning as we swim over it. It towers high above the shadow of the city, blocking ships from sailing over it.

The wreckage of the boat that tried to abduct Edmund sits at the bottom of the sea. I plan to explore it later, checking to see what damage I did when I instructed them to shoot a cannonball into their own deck.

"Mother!" Caspian shouts when we swim into the heart of the Metten palace. She's recuperating on a lounging couch, tail draped gracefully over the curved rock.

"Are you both safe?" She sits up as soon as she hears his voice.

"We're fine." Caspian hugs her, moving back for me to do the same.

"We're staying in Metten overnight, but we'll follow behind in the morning." She starts to protest, but Caspian raises an eyebrow and silences her.

"Just don't get caught," she warns, knowing we're planning to leave the palace walls once night falls.

She examines my tail, then turns to Caspian to assess the injuries on his arm. Miraculously, in all of this, Caspian's injuries were mainly directed to his arms—his scales all remain perfectly in place.

Marilla only gives us a few minutes before she arrives to speak to my mother. We leave the grotto, giving them space to talk.

"So, I assume we're exploring tonight?" Caspian says softly as we set out in search of our friends.

A few seahorses float in the water, tails wrapped around bits of seaweed. An octopus slinks around the corner ahead of us, and we follow its lead.

Caspian and I find Merrick, Dylana, Llyr, and Phorcys waiting in one of the grottos. They all look up as we enter. I'm surprised they let the siren join them.

I sigh and take a seat next to Phorcys.

"How are you doing after yesterday?" I ask to gauge his level of remorse over killing his friend.

"Cassidia was never meant to survive this war. She said it all along." That's new information to me.

"How much do you hate all of us?" I refuse to look at him as he side-eyes me.

"I don't."

"We killed your king, your prince, and your princess, and you don't hate us?" I cross my arms, turning to him.

"I don't like you, but if I wanted revenge for any of that, I already had plenty of chances. I know where I float with all of this."

"You want a life when this is all done," Dylana adds, nodding with understanding.

"How bad will my punishment be?" He turns to address the princess.

"We'll see in the next few weeks," Dylana replies. "I honestly don't know how your trial will go at this point, but you'll be prepared before you swim into anything."

The mermen scowl at him, and Natale shoots him an icy glare. Phorcys eyes her for a minute, and I almost think I see the beginning of a smirk on his lips—his instinct is to flirt with her. Maybe he's more like the boys than any of us realize. It will be interesting to see his walls broken down in the coming months.

The former siren reaches up, brushing his glorious hair back, and shrugs. When Dylana motions for him to leave us, he swims out without questioning her directions. Pausing at the door, he throws a smirk in my direction.

"The shark barrier. Tie him out at the shark barrier," Merrick mumbles, making Llyr laugh loudly.

"So, what is this secret reason we're spending the night here?" Dylana brushes her hair back, smirking at me over the boys' antics.

"Merrick has something he wants to show us." I grin, refusing to give any details.

"You're really not going to tell us?" Dylana complains. I shake my head, trying not to smile. "But I'm the princess."

"I'm a princess too, so I hear."

"What if I command you to tell me?" Dylana reaches her hand out to pet a tiny stingray as it glides by.

"Don't ruin the surprise, cousin."

"We're *all* spies here," Natale jumps in. "*One of us* has to be able to figure this out."

"I'm fine with leaving it as a surprise," Keone counters. Natale gives him a murderous look, but he pulls her into his arms and grins at her. She struggles for a moment but settles when he weaves his finger in her hair and pulls her to his lips for a kiss.

"Casp, I'm pretty sure you're going to want to run that little mission of yours now," Llyr says, shrugging. The two make eye contact and have an entire conversation without us before Caspian nods once and swims out of the room.

"Where is *he* going?" I point to my brother as he swims away.

"You had your secrets, Celena, and now he has his. You'll find out later." Llyr grins at me. "But speaking of secrets, I guess *we* don't have to be anymore."

He reaches out to Dylana, and she swims over to him, a gentle smile on her lips. She takes his hand and settles against his chest as she floats down to the palace floor to sit by him. Her pleased sigh makes me incredibly happy.

"It's about time you two finally did something about this," I pretend to chide them. "I didn't like not being able to tell either of you."

"It does explain a lot of your little comments though, cousin," Dylana smirks. "At least it's finally out there."

"And the queen gave you permission," Merrick adds. "I suppose it's time to start bowing?"

"Mer don't bow," Llyr says in a tight voice. He's not used to the idea that he could end up as king one day yet.

"Oh, right, too much time with the humans, sorry," Merrick goads him.

"Did they bow to you, Celena?" Dylana asks, amused.

"No, but they called me *princess* a lot." I bat my eyelashes at her.

"What about you, Merrick? Did they call you *prince*?" Keone asks as he strokes Natale's arm. She grimaces as we notice, but settles back against his chest anyway.

"No, I'm just the hired muscle." Merrick laughs at the question.

"Mmm, well you *do* have muscles," I say, crawling over to him. I position an arm across his chest and place it on the ground next to his hip so I can lean over him.

His eyes grow wide before his lips do. He leers at me, eyes darting from my eyes to my lips to my hair and back to my lips.

"Aw, you're cute. *Now stop*," Llyr jokes. He laughs at himself, shaking his head at us.

I sigh and pull back. I'm not too worried—once the collection leaves, we'll have more time for alone time.

We banter for a few minutes across the grotto, each of us leaning against a wall. A few jellyfish float overhead, but their glow won't be evident until this evening.

After a while, Caspian swims back in slowly, his hand stretched out behind him. Attached to his hand is another hand, followed by an arm, and an entire body as he pulls in a mermaid.

She beams in his wake, eyes locked on his every move. I startle and sit up, taking my hand off Merrick's chest. I glance at him to see if he's as surprised as I am—he isn't.

I glare at him for not telling me about this, but I can't really blame him. He's Caspian's friend too, and we have barely had any quiet time to speak alone together since our first kiss—I can't expect him to tell me everything from the very beginning. He'll pay for blindsiding me later though.

"You all know Aeria," Caspian announces. "I ran into her out in the hallways and invited her to hang out with us and go back with us tomorrow."

Her brown hair picks up a copper tone as she moves and I suddenly realize why she seems so familiar—I saw her right before the battle with the sirens began, just outside of Antaire. I should have recognized her mauve hair first, but the shock of seeing her with Casp made my head go empty for a moment.

"I think that's a great idea," Llyr calls, obviously aware of their relationship in advance too.

"*Caspian*," I call.

"You had your secrets, and I had mine, sister." He bats his lashes innocently at me. Caspian pulls Aeria close. She dotes on him. How did I miss this?

"It's because you were too busy swooning over me," Merrick whispers in my ear, knowing what I was thinking. His nose tickles my ear as he brushes my hair back. "You'll get used to it."

We spend the rest of the afternoon talking until the collection leaves.

CHAPTER 17

Marilla's speech is rousing before the collection leaves, but once they're gone, the courtyard is quiet. We still have time before Merrick takes us to Scur Cavern, and each couple quietly makes their way off for a few moments of quiet.

I take Merrick's hand and lead him out of the palace. He gives me a curious look once we're outside of the looming palace doors, hovering over the useless steps, but his expression changes when he understands where I'm directing us to go.

He switches positions with me and guides me down through the courtyard, past the large dwellings that sparkle in the sunlight. His hand is warm in mine, reminding me of Scylla's warmer waters.

I study him as we swim, memorizing the pattern in his tail that I already know so well. He grins when he catches me staring and pulls me up to swim shoulder-to-shoulder with him, making a flirtatious comment.

Switching my hands out, I place my inside hand on his shoulder, moving it slowly down his back, surprising him. He turns to me, and I giggle, disarming his snappy comment.

I'm grateful we left our shoulder armor at the palace. The water feels refreshing against my skin, and I finally feel as though the fighting is over.

Before long, we swim out of the palace proper and into the dwellings that sit further out from the palace. The dwellings aren't as big or as shiny as the ones next to the royals, but they're beautiful all the same.

We quietly sneak around the homes, weaving our way in and out of the homes the ancestors of our collection used to live in a century ago. I let Merrick lead me—he knows exactly where he is going.

"I'm sorry we didn't get to do this before," I murmur, taking in the sights.

"That's why we're doing it now." Merrick grins softly at me. "There it is."

I follow his finger toward a light colored dwelling. Somehow it seems perfectly like him and his father, even though his great-great-grandfather was rather different than them from what I hear.

Pausing, I refuse to swim into his family home before he does. He shakes his head and slips inside, turning to wait for me before he takes a good look.

The room is large, with the hallways leading to other small rooms. Many of the family items were removed before the collection fled to Scylla a century ago, but much like with the abandoned siren dwelling, it's easy to see evidence of what used to be there.

I swim over and sit on the lounging couch. Merrick follows behind me, leaning heavily on the bump between us. His blue bangs dip over his eye, and I reach up to brush them back.

"Welcome home," I murmur.

"I miss *our* home," he says honestly. "I'm ready to be home with you, Celena."

I look away, embarrassed. I'm still not used to his attention.

He takes my hand in his.

"You're okay with all this, right? I know you haven't had much time to process all this."

"I'm *very* okay with being with you, Merrick. *More* than okay."

He sighs in relief, leaning closer to me.

"I'm glad to hear that. I've been waiting a very long time to be with you, Len." His fingers close over mine harder, and he refuses to look away from me. I'm trapped in his gaze. "Once we get back to Scylla, I'd like to take you on a date."

"Tonight isn't a date?" I smirk.

"Not when six other people will be with us." He makes a face.

"But that doesn't mean we won't kiss tonight, does it?" I ask.

There's *no way* I'm going back into Scur Caverns and *not* kiss this merman. If I have to force every last mer out of the ocean, I *will* kiss Merrick in that magical cave tonight.

"Oh, we can kiss." He laughs. "We can kiss in the cavern, we can kiss on the way to the cavern, and we can kiss right now."

My grin pins my ears back, it's so wide.

"Oh, you want to kiss *now*?" I question as I float out of my seat, pulling him with me.

"I want to *kiss you now*," he says as he nods. Merrick wraps his arms around my waist.

I lean into him, and his hands caress my hips. I run my fingers up his arms, pushing just below his shoulders to brace myself.

His tongue finds mine as we kiss, and I shiver. Merrick pulls back, biting his lip. I can't stop staring.

"You know," he whispers. "I *really do* enjoy being partnered with you."

I raise an eyebrow a second before he darts forward and covers my lips with his. I tip my head up to allow him to reach me easier. He breaths against me and we tip our heads in unison, kissing as if we've been doing it for years—but then, we've always known how the other would move.

His hands tangle in my hair, and I wrap myself around his waist, holding him to me as he guides my movements. One hand gently glides to my chin and Merrick holds my face to him as he slows our kiss. We settle into a slow rhythm, our kisses deep and full of unspoken words.

My fingers glide up his back, making him gasp, but he doesn't take his lips from mine. I sigh deeply against him, but it only encourages him more, and his mouth moves quickly, inviting me to do the same.

I laugh, enjoying myself—and Merrick does too—until we have to separate or risk smashing our heads together in our fits of laughter. We double over, but Merrick holds his hand out to me.

"It will always be like this between us, Len—it's the way we've always been with each other."

"We've been kissing like this all this time and I somehow missed it?" I joke, letting him guide me back to the lounging couch.

"We'll always understand each other," he clarifies. "And we'll *always* enjoy each other's company."

"You just want me for my superior kissing skills." I dare him to challenge me.

"I can't deny you're very good at that, Len." He licks his lips slowly. "Unfortunately, I'm going to have to prove that I'm better at it than you."

"Is that a challenge?" I ask, knowing where he's going.

"It is." He grins. "Just try to prove me wrong."

I take the bait and swim over to him, sitting on his lap as I curl my tail under his to support myself.

"Fine, I will."

Slowly, I reach up and put my hands in his gorgeous blue hair. Locking eyes, I move my fingers achingly slow. I drag one hand down to his chin, intentionally brushing against the soft spot in front of his ear, down his cheek, and to the tip of his chin where I tilt his face up to mine.

"I will prove it every day," I inform him.

"I hope you do," he mumbles. His eyes snap fiercely as I lean in.

"Where are we going?" Natale sounds annoyed.

"It's just up here," Merrick replies, clutching my hand in his. I try not to give anything away as we swim up to Scur Cavern.

"A cave? Really?" Natale snips. "Haven't we seen enough of those in the last two weeks?"

"This one is a little different," Merrick says in a voice that is way too flirtatious—it's a good thing he's looking at me as he says it.

Everything is black at first, just like it was the last time Merrick and I were here nearly a month ago.

Dylana and Aeria gasp as the cave suddenly lights up, even more grand than the last time. Colors swirl around us.

"Like the storms," Caspian murmurs. Maybe he heard about the caves even though I hadn't.

"It's stunning," Dylana whispers reverently.

"Apparently, the royals used to like to frequent this place," I tell her.

"Kailania had it right, I suppose." She sounds in awe. When I look over, her jaw is still hanging open, but she's grinning like it's the most beautiful thing she's ever seen. "Any chance we can keep this to ourselves?"

Everyone glances surreptitiously over at Aeria. When she notices, she confronts us.

"Hey, Casp and I didn't say anything to you lot *until today*, so I'm pretty sure *I* can keep a secret." She softens her words with a playful smile.

My eyes grow wide as I realize this has been going on for a while. My twin shoots me an apologetic look—he and I *will* be talking before we go back to Scylla.

The cave shifts colors, turning a deep purple. Everything sparkles brilliantly, and this time, there's no sea creatures to distract us.

Kissing in front of our friends is strange, but each couple risks it for a few moments under the stormy skies inside the cave. The colors dance on the other sides of my eyelids as Merrick crushes me against him.

When we pull away, the others do as well, and we spend the evening talking, getting to know Caspian's new girlfriend, and admiring the lights.

The swim back to the palace is slow. We take our time, knowing once we return, we'll have to take turns sleeping and keeping watch.

Aeria trails behind Caspian, and he glances back, still holding her hand from a distance. I want to dislike her, but I can't. I'm happy Caspian has found someone—even if he waited until now to tell me about her.

Coralie, on the other hand, will have something to say about all this. Caspian is going to be in a whirlpool of trouble for hiding this from her.

The palace shimmers in the pale moonlight. Shells gleam on the ocean floor, reflecting the light. Everything about Metten is perfect… except for the lack of mer.

"This was an incredible kingdom once," Merrick comments as we enter the palace proper.

"Scylla is an incredible kingdom *now*. Metten holds our past, but our future is in Scylla."

"Perhaps," Merrick mumbles. "We'll see what the future holds."

"Don't get all sappy on us now, Merrick," Caspian teases. "Unless you're planning on rebuilding this place, Scylla is where we'll spend our days."

"Once the humans decide their course, our own lives may look very different, Casp."

"I plan to stay in Scylla no matter what," Dylana announces. "I wouldn't necessarily be opposed to sending you two here to rebuild, but I also don't want to lose my best two spies."

"Excuse me?" Natale yelps. Keone distracts her with a kiss.

"I don't want to leave you either, Dylana." I reach my hand out for hers. "We'll see what happens. Until then, you've got all of us at your disposal."

"Yes, now that you all let your secrets out." She chuckles. "I admit, *you* threw me, Natale."

"Me too," I smirk.

"I believe that was the point," Caspian adds. The way he looks at Aeria is even worse than the eyes Merrick and I make at each other—Llyr points out as much.

The palace looms in front of us, and we swim up the steps into the large doorway.

"Caspian and I will take first watch," Merrick announces, surprising me. "We need to talk anyway."

Knowing I don't want to be around when those two talk, I agree to take the second watch with Llyr. I have a feeling it's a safer idea than trying to get to know the mermaid my brother has been wrapped around all evening while we're supposed to be watching for enemy attacks in the middle of the night.

Natale volunteers to keep watch with Aeria, leaving Keone and Dylana to take the last shift. Everyone but Merrick and Caspian file into the palace to rest.

Dylana and I spend the evening in our great-great-grandmother's rooms. It's a unique experience sleeping in the exact room where Aila slept when she was my age. A roaseca colony floats near the ceiling, making the room glow comfortingly.

I sleep soundly until Caspian wakes me up to take my shift.

CHAPTER 18

"Celena!" Coralie crashes into me, wrapping her arms around me. We haven't even made it to the palace before our families rush around us.

The collection bustles about like normal, repairing the damage the sirens caused when they attacked. The mer children play by their parents' sides, no longer afraid. Rows of tables are set up, and I wonder if we're planning some kind of announcement followed by a celebration.

Coralie looks like she's about to hit me with a million question, so to stop her, I say the first thing that comes to mind.

"Starfish, Caspian has a girlfriend."

Our brother whips around to me, shocked that I would do that to him. I grin, shrugging one shoulder.

"You should have told me," I remind him.

He closes his jaw and grunts as Coralie rushes to him, her blonde hair trailing behind her. I'll sit with her later and brush her locks, regaling her with stories from everything that happened since we left each other back in Antaire.

I frown as I see the cut Tarni gave her run from her shoulder to halfway down her back. It's a good thing the siren is no longer around for me to take my anger out on. Coralie is too sweet for what Tarni put her through—I still need to ask her if Tarni forced her to siren the humans. As far as I can tell, Murdoch never did, and I hope the same for my little starfish.

Merrick's family surrounds him. I'm grateful they're all safe. His sisters cling to him, and he wraps his arms around them in a hug. His mother glances over at me, followed by his father. They smile—he must have told them.

His mother has been waiting for this day for a long time apparently based on her expression. She bites her lip but only nods to me—we'll have to talk later. Merrick's sisters try rushing to me, but he holds them back. His father ends up pinning them to his sides so Merrick and I can escape.

Caspian extricates himself from our little sister and quickly catches up with us as we dart after Dylana. Llyr hugs his father, assuring him that he's fine before joining us. Keone and Natale follow, after greeting what is left of their families.

The palace radiates an opal glow in the sun, and somehow it's even more beautiful than Metten. We enter through the front doors and find Morgen waiting for us.

Dylana rushes to her brother, throwing her arms around him.

"I'm fine, Dylana," he murmurs, brushing her hair off her back so he can untangle his arm. "I was told *not to threaten Llyr.*"

He glances at Dylana's beau and taps a sword on his belt. It shines in a gold tone that matches his crown. Llyr holds up his hands like he's surrendering.

"I'll take you on if I need to, my friend." He grins at Morgen before swinging his gaze over to the princess.

"I get a week before I have to decide," Morgen announces. "We'll see if you last that long, *guard.*"

We all know that Llyr isn't going anywhere, so Morgen will have to harass him while he still has a higher status than he does.

Our parents follow us in, prepared for a meeting with Marilla. The cousins follow, their children in tow.

Coralie quietly swims into the palace as if she's trying not to be noticed. I covertly track her to make her think she has her privacy—that's when I discover that puffer fish, Marin, reach out and take her hand.

"Caspian!" I whisper harshly.

He turns, tracking my gaze. His fists ball up at his sides as he sets his jaw.

"I'm going to feed him to the sharks," he growls quietly. Merrick and Llyr agree and nod their heads.

"You're not going to touch him," Natale growls. "I worked far too hard to make that happen, and if you destroy it, cousin, I'm going to tell Aeria stories about you from when we were mer children."

We look at her, surprised.

"Well, it wasn't *all* fake," she snips, swimming into the meeting without looking back. It's nice to hear that she wasn't *just* using Coralie for information all this time.

I still don't like the mer boy though.

As the foyer clears out, I notice several guards bringing Roni through the hallway. Marilla had sent several mer to bring Roni back to the palace, and help take care of Tarni's body.

She glares at me, catching my sight. Phorcys eyes me from her side.

"Should I ask?"

"They're taking me to see Tiko." She sounds unsure of herself.

"He's here from what I've been told," I reply casually. "I'll swim with you."

I follow them down to the cells, Merrick at my side. Tiko's face lights up and then falls when he sees them, worried that they've been caught too.

Phorcys quietly explains what happened and Tiko's face falls even further as he realizes that Roni and Phorcys are temporarily free while he is not. He nearly crumbles when he learns of Cassidia, and I can see Roni deflate over his reaction.

Being a siren is apparently very complicated.

Merrick and I leave as Phorcys explains the trials to Tiko. It's strange to see one of them locked up while the other two are not. If I had it *my* way, Roni would be in the worst prison imaginable for what she did when she pushed Coralie into the brine pool, but I have to wait for her trial to see her twist like that—the collection will not be kind to her when I testify about hurting Cor.

"You handled that well." Merrick looks at me as we swim back to the meeting that's already in progress.

"I'll push her in a brine pool later," I mumble, brushing my hair back angrily.

Merrick catches my raised hand in his, giving me a look. He half smiles at me and I crumble. Rolling my eyes, I let out a sigh mixed with laughter.

Marilla is already dolling out assignments when we swim in. She looks up at me and waves me in as she continues. Dylana regally floats next to her mother, hands folded in front of her as she makes eyes with Llyr obnoxiously—so much for keeping that a secret. The cousins glance at him and smirk now that they're no longer trying to keep it quiet. Most nod in approval, while others stare.

"We don't know how long it will be until the humans start enforcing the treaty, but we will live it as law starting now," Marilla addresses us. "We must be careful to avoid the humans until we know it is safe, however. Please do not mistake this for anything other than what it is—a promise that *someday* we will not be hunted anymore. Until then, we must stay strong and stay vigilant.

"Live with the faith that promises will be kept, but protect yourselves in every way that you can until it is proven that they will do as they say."

"Thank you, everyone, for what you did for the collection," Dylana adds. "We know that many of you lost someone over the last few weeks—their sacrifice will not be forgotten."

The king looks on proudly at his wife and daughter from the side of the room. Morgen nods from his side, grinning.

"The trials will begin the day after tomorrow. Every siren and mer connected to this tragedy will answer for their crimes, judged by their peers and the collection. We *will* see justice for this," Marilla assures us. "Until then, watch them closely, but do not harm them— the trials will decide their retribution."

The small collection of cousins nods. Marilla will be repeating all of this information shortly when she swims outside of the palace to address the entire collection.

The stingrays swim into the room, begging to be fed, and Dylana can't help but crack a smile. She reaches out to pet them, and Llyr quietly moves to find the food Dylana keeps in the palace so that she can feed the winged creatures every day.

Colorful fish swim into the room as the queen, my mother, and the others move into the foyer and head toward the door to talk to the collection. The fish swirl around the room, mixing with the stingrays in a vivid display.

Merrick knocks into my hips and nods to the fish that look just like the ones that swirled around us during our first kiss.

I turn to him and wrap my arms around him.

He kisses me first, but I kiss him back.

"We survived," he reminds me quietly, then repeats it louder for the benefit of our friends still in the room. "We survived."

Everyone grins, commenting on our mission's success.

The tides have finally shifted in the Siren Wars…just like my hair when Merrick brushes it back to kiss me.

EPILOGUE

I look up as the door opens. Dropping the materials I'm using to create secret places on my new *iluse*, I find two mermen swimming into my dwelling.

Merrick hands me a conch, tucking a piece of folded paper into the pouch on his belt as a replacement.

"Have you been carrying this around all day?"

"Well, I couldn't exactly get back here to give it to you until now." He grins, releasing the shell into my hand. "Your brother and I have been pretty busy. I figured you'd want it though."

"Thanks for bringing it over, Merrick. I'm sure you must be exhausted."

Caspian sprawls out on a lounging couch.

"That would be an understatement, sis." He sighs, stretching out his tail.

Merrick kisses me, then swims over to the kitchen to set down a large bag filled with food I should probably store before listening to the message from the prince.

The last two years have been filled with messages back and forth between the prince and me. Merrick has learned not to be jealous of them over the months, and *usually* waits for me to tell him about the messages after I listen to them.

"What does he want this time?" Natale asks, not looking up from her *iluse*.

Coralie's eyes are fixed on me from a few lengths away. Marin brushes his hand over hers quietly—he's grown on me.

"Probably just another update," Merrick answers for me. "Those two just like to talk."

"Who's talking?" Dylana asks as she drags her fiancée inside from the open waters outside the dwelling. Llyr holds her hand, studying me.

"Ah, we've heard from Edmund," he replies, eyeing the conch as he answers for me. "What does he say?"

"I haven't listened yet," I retort, "and *I don't think I will* while all of you are here, chattering away."

"Oh, come on," Coralie rolls her eyes as she sets the netting down she was attaching to her *iluse.* "Just listen."

"No, thanks." I grin triumphantly—they can't force me to do anything, and they can't listen themselves because *my name* is being whispered by the shell—no one else can unlock the message.

I spend the next few minutes grilling my boyfriend and brother about their mission, still frustrated that I had to teach some of the mermaids about how to hide weapons in their coverings earlier today. Most of them left hours ago, but my small collection has a mission to handle, and we can't afford to stop until we're finished.

Two hours later, with the mermen's help, we finish our projects and hide them. The fringe groups of sirens that have reestablished themselves over the last year and a half won't know what hit them. It's a shame they didn't stay hidden like they did for those first few months, but we know their plans now, and it won't be long before we stop them.

My fingers brush over the *iluse* I'm wearing, checking to make sure Merrick's scale is still hidden away where I keep it close to my heart—I'm not usually so sentimental, but I couldn't bring myself to do anything else with it once Dylana gave it back after we returned to Scylla.

The group chats for a little bit, relaxing before we start to swim in different directions outside of the dwelling we are using to hide our covert work. We couple off as if we've been doing it our whole lives.

I pull the conch up to my ear and listen as the shell unlocks its message. Tears spring to my eyes as I shout for everyone to wait— they quickly swim back, concern on their faces.

When the message ends, it fizzles away like seafoam.

"Celena, what is it?" Dylana's eyes are dark.

"The king is dead," I whisper.

No one speaks.

"The king is dead, and Edmund has taken the throne." I look up at Dylana. "It's taken two years, but our treaty is finally in effect."

We all slowly beam at each other.

"It's over. The fighting is done—we're safe." Dylana voices our thoughts.

"We have to tell your mother," Llyr holds his hand up, shaking Dylana's as he holds it.

"We need to go to Antaire," I announce. "Everything else can wait. We need to go make a formal alliance with the humans. He wants us to join him immediately—they'll meet us in the water halfway if they can tell when we'll arrive."

I don't like putting off our mission to Ambra any longer than we need to, but Larina and Quillo will just have to manage a few more days without us. The sirens can't cause too much trouble between now and the time we get back—hopefully.

"We need to make preparations and decide on a team to send," Dylana replies, already organizing the trip. "And on the way back, I know a good cave we can stop at."

Everyone smirks, glancing at their partners. I nod to Coralie, telling her that she and Marin can join us this time.

"To the palace," I say. My collection follows behind me, thrilled to finally be returning to Antaire by way of Metten to free the seas for the humans and mer once more.

I can't wait.

The story continues in Forbidden Waters (Book 4 of The Siren Wars Saga)

Acknowledgements

Oh, my fabulous, lovely friends, thank you for coming on this journey with me. I have *loved* getting to tell Celena's story and I couldn't be more happy with how it all played out.

I'm also excited for you to meet the next mermaid in The Siren Wars Saga—but don't worry, we'll be seeing more of Celena and Merrick soon!

Right now, it looks like the next installment of The Siren Wars Saga will be out in 2019, so don't go too far! Until then, I have a ton of other books to keep you occupied!

If you adored Celena and Merrick's story, drop me an email or direct message on social media and let me know you enjoyed the story—I love chatting with people!

Special thanks to Jess and Elle, my ever-present help in times of need. I appreciate you two more than you know!

To Yentl, thanks for all the mermaid drawings, lovely. I made sure the stingrays were taken care of just for you! PS I didn't write this in the book, but Dylana and I have agreed to name one after you!

Thanks to Charlotte for keeping me sane while I was doing my mad writing dash throughout this series. I always love our chats!

And mostly, thank you to you, oh lovely reader. I appreciate you more than words can say.

Get ready...I'm about to dive into the next story in The Siren Wars Saga and info will be coming soon. PS...the covers for the next section are magical!

Turn the page to read the first chapter of the fourth book in The Siren Wars Saga...and don't worry, we'll be seeing Celena and Merrick in Forbidden Waters.

Stay inspired!

-K.M. Robinson

SECRETS SURFACE

by

K.M. Robinson

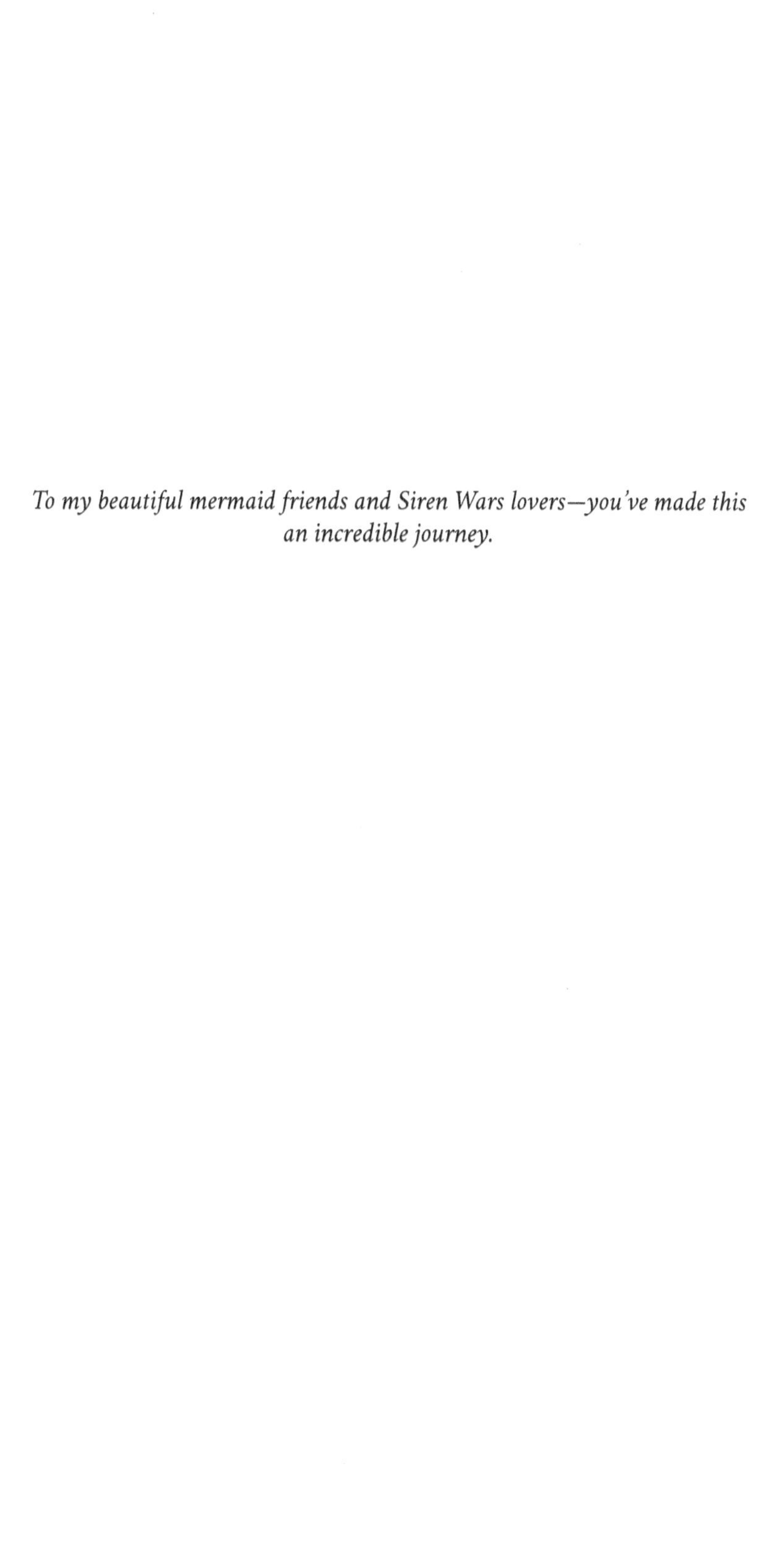

*To my beautiful mermaid friends and Siren Wars lovers—you've made this
an incredible journey.*

A secret is only as good as those who keep them.

Keeping a secret for yourself is difficult, but keeping one for someone else is nearly impossible, and if you don't keep it hidden, you could destroy their world.

I keep far too many secrets.

"Merrick, can you get that?" my father asks, lifting a cannonball from the ocean floor. The muscles in his upper arms strain as his lifts it, but he doesn't grunt.

"Shoulder still hurt?" I ask casually as I swim over to pick up the remaining canonball.

"It's fine," he mumbles in reply. It's not, but for his sake, I'll pretend I don't notice the way he favors his left arm.

"What do you plan on doing with these?" I change the topic.

"I'm not sure yet, but it's always good to have them around." My father nods as he adds our new treasures to the net. "I'm sure we can come up with some fascinating way of reusing them. Someone will buy them—they always do."

I take the ends of the net from him, maneuvering it over my shoulder. He starts to protest but then sighs, nodding that he appreciates me carrying the heavy load so he doesn't have to help.

In the distance, a few mermen swim by. I assume they're changing shifts. The coral barriers are far from Scylla, so the guards have a bit of a swim ahead of them to return home. For that matter, so do we.

Moving the makeshift carrier, we set out toward the kingdom, leaving the bright coral behind. Below us, the kelp bed waves in the water, mixed with flashes of pink—Celena.

My father pretends not to notice her, but he's as skilled as I am at spotting things that are out of place. He taught me everything I know, so of course he's aware of my work with Celena.

I offer him a slight shake of my head, telling him I'll swim back to our dwelling with him. Celena is perfectly capable of waiting, and if it were important, she would have found a way to interrupt us. We watch her trail below us until the kelp bed disappears and she waits until we're far enough ahead to dart out into the open waters.

Looking behind me, she mingles with a school of fish, her purple tail a daring contrast to their red fins. I can't help but smirk when a pod of dolphins rushes by us, and Celena attempts to hide among them as they race ahead of us—she'll beat us back to Scylla.

"You should have waved her down, son—we could have borrowed her ride." Father grins. One day I will have to tell Celena he always noticed her attempts at hiding from his sight.

Our dwelling is small compared to some in Scylla, but we don't need the same opulence everyone else needs. Outside, my mother and sister bustle about, getting ready for our return.

"Better give that to me." Father reaches out to take the net. "I'll tell them you swam into a friend on the way back and you won't be joining us until later."

Handing him the net, I turn to find where Celena is lurking in the distance. I catch sight of her tail darting around one of the nearby dwellings and follow quietly.

"Why, Celena," I drawl when I catch up. "You seem to be following me…"

I swim up next to her as close as I dare, dipping my head so that my bangs fall over one eye. She holds her position but I know I can make her crumple.

"Something I should know?" I drop my voice.

Celena's eyes widen, and the muscles in her face go slack, but to her credit, she doesn't back down.

"You think too highly of yourself, Merrick," she retorts, flicking her tail at me as she stretches into a back roll. "We have work to do, and you were slower than Natale back there."

Celena's hair sparkles as she tips her head, the shell crown catching the light that streams down through the water. It sets off the spark in her eyes as she lifts her hands to adjust the shells—my sister is wildly jealous of Celena's talent with creating the pieces she wears.

My poor sister reminds me of one of the jealous stingrays in the palace when the princess summons them for feeding time the way she flips her fins over each of Celena's new creations.

"Nice *sarasa*," Celena quips, forcing my eyes away from the crown on her head.

"I had a feeling you'd appreciate it. Now, what is going on?"

She turns, swimming away from the dwellings. I follow her around the shiny buildings toward the palace, but she dives to the left and veers off course. I tip my fingers to follow her, curving my path in the water.

"We have to meet Llyr," she informs me, glancing over her shoulder.

More secrets to discover—more secrets to keep.

"Don't tell me we have to go all the way back to the reef," I protest. Llyr is a guard that works for Queen Marilla and frequently takes a post at the reef barrier, but can't he come to *us*?

"No, he was working while you were out there—I caught him before I found you. He's meeting us at the cavern, apparently he found something."

"Just what were you doing out there when you swam into him?" I question.

She shrugs—there are some things she won't even tell her partner, but to be fair, I'm keeping secrets too.

Celena lets me swim into the lead. She quietly tucks herself close to me, just far enough behind me to use my slipstream to save her a bit of work.

The cavern isn't anything special—a dark mix of rocks that converge together to create a hollowed out cave. Light shines in through the holes in the top, sending beams of light dancing inside. Bits of dust sparkle as we swim inside.

"I'm here," Llyr says as we enter. Usually, we sweep the cave before we enter, but since he's already done the work, we don't pause.

"What's this about?" I cross my arms over my chest, knocking my *sarasa* off center. It shifts on my shoulder, rolling slightly, but it stays on.

"When I arrived at the barrier this morning, we had a bit of a disturbance," Llyr informs us.

"Sirens?" Celena asks under her breath. I know she's always been nervous about our banished brethren—she should be given her lineage—but no one has seen or heard from the sirens in generations. They're nothing but stories to scare merchildren...and royals.

"No, nothing like that," Llyr pushes his green hair back out of his eyes. "Humans."

"What?" My hand automatically goes to the knife on my hip and I brush against the belt it's fastened to before grabbing it.

Occasionally, human ships found their way near Scylla, but as far away from Metten as we are, those sightings are very rare and usually end badly for the humans.

"A boat," Llyr is quick to correct himself. "The problem is that it sank on the other side of the reef, so we didn't go to check it out."

"We're not going over the reef," I warn him to swim lightly.

"You don't have to come if you don't want to, Merrick, but Llyr and I are going to check it out." Celena sides with him.

I flick my tail. I have no intention of letting them go alone.

Celena reaches up to brush back her hair as it floats in front of her shoulder. Frustrated, she pulls a shell out of her *iluse* with a pin attached to it and shoves it in her hair over her ear to keep the stray strand held back. It works for a moment, but the end floats back up with the current and wraps around to float in front of her face.

"Want me to braid that for you?" I soften, relaxing the muscles in my face as I volunteer to do her hair. I'm hoping it might act as a distraction long enough that I can talk them out of crossing the barrier.

"It will be fine," Celena replies, seeing through my plan. "Always following the rules, Merrick."

"It might kill him to swim out of line," Llyr smirks, taking a place by Celena. Sometimes I wish I could joke around the way those two do.

"I do what needs to be done for the mission," I retort. I'd easily swim over the barrier to investigate while Celena was safely back in her dwelling or at the palace with her cousin, Dylanna. I wouldn't even mind taking Llyr with me—in fact, I'd prefer the backup—but Caspian would kill me if I let anything happen to his twin and I'm certain the Queen would anchor me near the shark barrier if her cousin were hurt.

"The mission is taking us over the barrier, Merrick. Are you coming or not?" Celena does a backflip, and Llyr takes her lead, mimicking her movements.

I swim behind the two as they make their way to the barrier, Llyr guiding us to where he saw the boat go down. It's a smaller ship with room for only a few mer to hide inside. We gaze down on it from the top of the coral barrier.

A jellyfish swims by lazily, pulsing in the water. My hand brushes against a piece of coral as I stare and I pull back.

"Careful there," Celena chides quietly. From the corner of my eye, I see Llyr smirk.

"It looks like the open water is clear," I grumble. No one will see us leave the kingdom. "Shall we?"

With a grand sweeping motion, I gesture toward the sunken boat. Llyr leads the way, rising up over the coral before angling himself down in the water. Celena turns, offering her arm to me. I wrap mine around her, linking us together as she swims backward to watch for any mer that might appear over the coral barrier as we swim into forbidden waters.

Celena flicks her tail quietly beside me but doesn't say anything as her head moves slightly to scan the area. Llyr's tail moves the water ahead of us, but I ignore it as the boat draws closer.

It rests on the light sand on the ocean floor. The sea life hasn't had time to overtake it yet, but a starfish sits nearby, orange and vibrant against the sea floor. A stingray glides over the sand and plant life, ignoring us.

I release Celena when we're close enough and pull my knife from my belt, wishing we had brought tridents with us instead. Llyr still holds his from while he was on duty.

We spread out, each of us taking a direction to approach the boat from. Any human that remained in the boat is long since drowned if the boat sank this morning, their secrets dying with them, but we don't know what else we might encounter.

Celena touches the side of the boat first, placing her hand along the top edge. I follow suit, placing my own hand against the wall of the sunken ship. It's smaller than it looked from on top of the coral reef, able to fit only a few humans comfortably and even less mer.

"Have you ever seen a boat so small?" Celena asks. "It couldn't hold more than three of them."

"Humans are resourceful," I murmur. "You might be surprised what they can fit in this thing."

I wouldn't be surprised if we found half a dozen bodies inside. But then, my information is only what has been passed down over the years from our ancestors, so I don't actually know how humans function—they kept their secrets from us since the war began.

It's strange seeing a boat this close to the reef, but to see one so small...something must have happened for it to be this far away from shore.

"I wonder if this came from a larger ship," I muse.

"What makes you say that?" Llyr asks as he tries to pry open a door with the tip of his trident.

I sink down in the water, attempting to see in a tiny window. It's too dark inside to tell anything.

"Merrick?" Celena's voice pulls me back. I had been distracted by the way the window was bolted to the side of the boat.

"It's so far away from shore—what would a tiny ship like this be doing all the way out here—they had to get through some rough waters to make it all this way. Even getting to Metten would be a stretch, but to make it all the way to Scylla on this tiny thing—I don't buy it."

"Do you think they're still in the area?" Celena asks, disappearing behind the side of the boat.

"I haven't seen anything today, but we should be vigilant." Llyr continues to attempt to pry the door open. He yelps and mutters when something pops.

"You okay, brother?" I call over.

"It nearly bent my trident—what is this boat made out of?" I'm sure he's scowling.

"Boys!" Celena's voice stops our banter. I rush around the boat to see what she discovered, leaving bubbles in my wake. I nearly collide with a large red fish but manage to dart around the wooden boat.

Celena's eyebrow is raised, giving her face an adorably asymmetrical look, but she isn't smiling. A school of fish swims behind her, glinting in the sun that is clearly starting to set above the waves.

"We can't leave those here," Celena remarks, pointing to the boat,

Inside, a single beam of light filters through, catching the glass at just the right angle. It falls on the far wall where a row of spears lay.

"If the sirens ever *do* show up, we can't leave those for them to find."

"No one has proven that they aren't around here, Celena," Llyr replies as he swims closer, obviously thinking about the stories the younger mer tell to scare each other when a false sighting surfaces. He tightens his muscles as he forces himself not to look around—something I've caught him doing many times, especially around the royals.

"You have a point, though, Len," I add. "We'll take them to our side of the barrier."

The light shifts above us, dancing at a tilted angle. The beam sweeps off of the spears, almost as if it had only been illuminating the weapons long enough for us to see.

"We need to hurry because they're about to change guards again," Llyr reminds us. "We can't afford to let them catch us out here. I think it's time we stopped worrying and just handled this."

"Far side." I nod to them, moving the small collection behind the boat toward the open waters. "We'll break the window. Len, you'll have to go through and let us in through the door up top."

She nods, waiting for us to break through the round porthole in the boat's side. Using the hilt of my knife, I crash into the glass. It cracks but doesn't shatter as I expect it to. Another blow and the lines branch out like jellyfish tentacles. Llyr nods for me to try once more, and this time, it works.

A few fragments sink quietly in the water, floating into the darkness. I turn to catch Celena's gaze while our friend uses the long end of the trident he's carrying to clear away the rest of the glass to protect Celena's scales. I don't like sending her in first, but Llyr and I couldn't fit if we wanted to.

The water is alive behind my partner and she looks more radiant than any royal I've ever known, including what the stories say about her great-great grandmother's beauty. Fish of every color swim behind her, some slow, others quick. The light bounces off their tails as they turn.

She sighs and pushes past me, eyeing the open hole in the ship.

"Would be nice if I had something that glowed," she mumbles.

"We can catch you a jellyfish, but that might get a little problematic," I joke. Her nose wrinkles as she squints her eyes at me quickly to make a point. Celena's attempt at a sneer is about as good as her little sister's when she tries it on me.

Brushing past me, she intentionally bumps me with her fins, slapping my chest and nearly hitting my face as she dives through the window without looking.

"At least we know it was sealed up tight," Llyr murmurs, shaking his head. "No sharks in there anyway. You've got to stop pushing her like that though, Merrick."

"I didn't do anything," I reply, stunned at the accusation

"You're existence pushes her." He looks at me as if I should know what he's talking about. "And her little sister, if I'm not mistaken."

"Coralie has a crush on all of us," I remind him. The mer girl has always looked up to her brother's friends.

"You better watch yourself, you don't want Caspian finding out about any of this. If he thinks you two are flirting, he's bound to start watching you."

Going on missions for the queen with Celena was the *last* thing I wanted Caspian to know about. He'd try to stop her and when he couldn't, he'd end up in our way and could put us all in danger.

"Casp thinks we've been flirting for the last year," I correct him, brushing my hair out of my eyes. "It explains why we spend so much time together. Let him think it."

Llyr and I look up at the same time as we hear the noise above us, interrupting our conversation. Darting up in the water, we move to where Celena is beating against the door.

"Len?" I call through the ornate door. For a small boat, it's incredibly fancy. I wonder whose boat this might have been—a small part of me hopes it's a human royal.

"I can't get it," she returns. Her voice is muffled. Celena fumbles with something on the other side of the door. "I found some bodies though. More than I thought."

We hear more tapping through the large door as Celena attempts to open it from her side. Suddenly, a small piece of the door slides away. Celena's eyes peer back at us, the rest of her still hidden.

I force my face back into its normal position, dropping my eyebrows as if I'm not surprised.

"Are you going to help me or should I just stay in here with the humans?"

"Right," I say, snapping out of my shock. I glance around, trying to come up with a plan. "Llyr, I'm going to need your trident."

"Why?" He hands it over anyway.

"Now that we've got this...*window*...we can use it to help get her out." I push past him, angling myself near the door. They both watch me carefully. "I saw my dad do this once when we needed to leverage an anchor off the ground that was too heavy for us. We got the chains out from under it easily, and he moved it by himself with the aid of something like this."

I jam the end of the trident into the small window Celena had unveiled, using the tiny metal bars that we assumed were just for design to balance my movements.

"Len, make sure everything is unlocked before we do this."

Celena moves forward, disappearing behind the door as Llyr takes a place by me, ready to push against the trident. Once Celena moves back and gives us a signal, Llyr counts.

It doesn't take too much force to push the door open. It pops out enough for Celena to swim forward and catch the door. She pushes it the rest of the way, nearly knocking into Llyr as he moves to help.

"Nice work, princess," he says approvingly.

"Knock it off, Llyr," she threatens, glaring at him for pointing out her royal heritage. She was pretty far down the list for taking on the crown and didn't like to acknowledge it out of respect for her cousins who were the reigning royals.

"Whatever you say, your highness."

"I'd say it back, but that wouldn't really work, would it?" Celena softens, joking as she moves back for us to join her.

"That would be the day," Llyr replies. "They'd flip their fins in Scylla if anyone dared to say *I* was a royal. We'd be better off with Merrick reigning."

He and Celena laugh as I shake my head.

Inside, several bodies hover near where they drowned. If they had been smarter, the humans wouldn't have a gap between the door and the deck of the ship, but no mer assumed that humans had that kind rationality to think that through after the last century.

The spears rest easily along the wall, and we scoop them into our arms. I pick up a few nets and drape them over my shoulder. Out of the corner of my eye, I see Celena take a few shiny trinkets she would be able to use for her *iluses* and shell crowns later on. She slips them into the pouch on her hip. I grab a few for my sister as well—humans are known for carrying trinkets to sea, and this is no exception, but usually, they wash in with the tide for us to find.

We close the door behind us to keep any other mer from noticing a difference in the ship and quietly swim toward the reef barrier, arms full of human-made weapons. When we decide it is clear for us to make our way over, we quietly slip along the coral so close that we had to watch that our scales didn't brush against it.

At the top, Llyr peeks over first. He is well known as a guard and could claim he is checking something out if we are caught, while Celena and I won't be able to explain it away so easily. He flicks his tail, sending him up in the water. When he doesn't stop, we follow.

As soon as we were on the opposite side, we dart into a kelp bed that leads into a kelp forest. The massive pieces of kelp surround us, twisting in the water. Everything grows quiet, taking cues from the floating debris in the water.

Celena swims behind me, staying close. Llyr follows as I lead us through the water, holding his bent trident close to him. The last of the light falls away, leaving only the ambient light from above the waves to guide us.

The spears roll in my arms as I turn to check on my collection mates, catching on my torso. I adjust them as we swim into open water.

"What are we planning on doing with these?" Llyr's voice breaks the silence.

"We'll take them to Marilla," Celena responds matter-of-factly. I wonder if she was headed there anyway when Llyr caught her earlier.

"Where are you going to tell her you found all these? Llyr protests.

"Marilla knows not to ask questions," Celena huffs in return. A lock of her hair floats in front of her, and she flips her head to try to force it back. When it doesn't work, she tries again, nearly dropping her spears. Giving up, she lets it float where it wants.

"I think the better question is how we get them through Scylla without anyone noticing," I muse.

"You mean we can't just swim through like this?" Celena asks sarcastically. "You can bat your eyelashes and convince everyone to let us through, right, Merrick?"

Two stingrays glide in front of us, dipping down in the water enough to cause us to halt. Celena's tail crashes into mine as we both struggle to keep the weapons from falling.

"It's like they planned that," Llyr quips from the back. "And speaking of things we didn't see coming... Celena, isn't that your brother?"

"*Clamshells,*" Celena breathes. "And my father. Don't let them see us."

Ahead, Caspian and Hallmar are swimming through the outskirts of Scylla toward the dwellings. A small collection of merfolk swim around lazily, packing up for the day, but we won't run into too many merchants until we reach the palace district.

"Strange that they would be all the way out here," I murmur. If Celena hears me, she doesn't let on.

While Celena's little sister shares similar coloring to their mother, Caspian and Celena's coloring can be found in their father's silver tail, tinged with blue tones and touches of purple. Our coloring is not passed down through the generations, but I've always found it interesting how their family is so close. My own father and I are as opposite as possible when it comes to tails—my dark blues are a stark contrast to his sandy tones.

The pair carries nothing with them as they swim through the water. Celena scowls as they stop to talk to a group of mermen.

"That's the only way through without going around the entire kingdom," she concludes.

"I'd volunteer to distract them," Llyr offers, "but you can't carry all these without me."

"What if we can?" An idea sparks. "We're having trouble because there are so many of them individually and they aren't staying together, but if we tie them together, it will be easier to hold."

I dive to the ocean floor and drop the spears in the sand. Reaching across my body, I tug my *sarasa* over my head.

"Merrick, don't ruin—" Celena starts to protest.

"It's fine, Len, it's easy enough to make a new one." I bundle mine with Llyr's, allowing Celena to carry her own. "You two go—Llyr can get you through the waterways without being questioned once you make it into the palace district since you won't look like you're returning from the barrier and Celena has to get you into the palace. I'll handle Caspian and your father."

I hold my hand out to my partner.

"Give me the baubles."

Celena's brow furrows as she questions my request.

"Oh!" she gasps as she realizes I mean for her to hand me the trinkets we found in the boat. She pulls them from her pouch and drops them in my waiting hand where I slip them into my own pouch.

"How exactly are we going to get *Celena* by them?" Llyr questions. "It's pretty hard to miss her, especially in a group of mermen."

"Give her your shoulder armor and chest plate," I suggest as I finish tying the spears together—so much for ever wearing *that sarasa* again.

Llyr slips out of his silver armor and hands it to Celena. It's far too big for her, but it covers her enough that they might not take notice if two guards slip by while I'm actively working to keep their attention on me.

Glancing around, I try to locate something to help me sell my story. Caspian knows I spend my days helping my father collect items on the ocean's floor throughout the kingdom so it wouldn't be out of the question for me to be on my way home at this late hour. I just need to find something that would work.

Celena realizes what I'm doing and turns in a circle to help me search. From the corner of my eye, I see Llyr slipping the spears into his arms, wrapping the end of the *sarasa* around his wrist to secure them in place.

"The trident!" Celena suddenly says loudly. She ducks at the sound of her voice. She drops her volume and continues. "Take the trident and tell them you were taking it to your father to fix."

Llyr hands over the bent trident without hesitation.

"You'd better hurry up." He nods toward Celena's family. "We have to get to the palace before dark and get her back before Caspian realizes you're a distraction."

"Are you two going to be able to swim with those?" I ask as if we hadn't been swimming quickly with them this entire time.

"We'll be fine, just hurry. Get them back to my dwelling, and I'll slip in through the back—Mother will watch for me."

"We'd better do something about your hair," I add, knowing the pink is hard to hide. She nods sharply and turns.

Llyr and I each take part of her hair, chaotically whipping it back into braids that we loop together to keep it as pinned down as we can.

When we finish, I dart up in the water without saying anything and swim quickly toward Caspian and Hallmar. The water feels cool over my skin and scales, but I notice it less as I slow down. For the sake of the charade, I pretend to almost swim by them without noticing.

I can't let Caspian or his father see Celena and start asking questions—it could destroy everything.

"Merrick?" Caspian's voice fills the water.

"Casp." I turn, grinning. "Hey, brother."

"Working late, I see…"

"What are you doing out here? Isn't it getting a little late for a guppy like you to be out swimming?" My words are laced with sarcasm, and he takes the challenge.

"I could say the same—especially since you don't seem to have worked very hard today." He motions to the trident. "What's this?"

I hold it up for him to inspect.

"I suppose one of the guards dropped it because it was bent."

"I admire you for helping your dad all day, Merrick," Caspian responds, pausing for a brief moment of sincerity before grinning. "It's much better than you stalking my sister all day."

"I see more of *you* than I do of *either* of your sisters," I correct him, even though he's right. "I actually have something for Len and

Coralie. I found some trinkets out there today and thought I'd split them between our sisters."

Caspian nods. His father quietly turns and swims away from the group in a wide arc after saying goodbye.

"We were headed there anyway," he jokes. "Maybe you can grab a few oysters while you pop in. I think Coralie misses you and she will be furious if you don't stop for a few minutes."

"Not Celena?" I tease. He'd feed me to the sharks if he ever thought I was *really* dating his sister—good thing I know how to keep my distance—but he loves harassing the two of us about it.

"Nah, she probably likes Relo or someone. She'd never go for a merman whose hair always flops in his face like that." Caspian laughs. "Coralie is already planning your wedding though, so I guess I'll have to get used to having you around."

"As sweet as that mer girl is, I'm pretty sure I'd rather be anchored out near the shark barrier than to be brothers with you, Casp, sorry."

"I'll happily chain you out there myself," Caspian promises.

We joke the entire way back through the palace district, weaving around dwellings in the dwindling light. Homes light up with the blue bioluminescent glow that we've become accustom too when the sun sets above the waves. The water is relaxing as we swim.

Almeta looks up just in time to catch us through the window as she swims by. Her face registers shock for only a moment as she sees me without her daughter, but she recovers quickly and opens the door for us.

"Merrick, what a surprise." She swims back to allow us in.

Caspian glides across the room and drops onto a lounging couch. From down the hall, I can hear Coralie calling out to ask if they're home yet.

"There's a surprise for you, Cor," Almeta calls, not bothering to fill her in yet. We both know Coralie's reaction over my surprise visit is supposed to cover for Celena not being in her room.

As soon as Coralie appears in the doorway, her face lights up. She rushes toward me, nearly colliding with a small sea turtle that swims by. Her arms wrap around me quickly, and through her floating hair, I see Almeta slip down the hall to watch for her daughter through the back.

For coral's sake, Celena and Llyr had better hurry up—I forced us to swim as slowly as possible on the trip over.

"What are you doing here, Merrick?" Coralie asked, grinning up at me.

"I found some baubles out in the open water today. I thought I'd divide them between my sisters." She pouts for a moment before she realizes I'm including her in that list.

Her eyes sparkle almost as brightly as the trinkets we found today. She waits eagerly, but I motion to the lounging couch. Pushing Caspian's tail, she takes a seat, leaving him disgruntled.

I swim over and open the pouch on my belt, reaching in to remove the shiny objects from the boat. She waits as I set them on the bump in the middle of the couch and push them around to examine them—I hadn't had time earlier while we were on the dark boat.

Almeta appears in the hallway long enough to instruct her husband to take care of something in the other room, leaving me to distract her children long enough for Celena to return without them questioning anything.

Coralie chatters away, doing most of the work for me, but Caspian is too smart for that.

"Where is Celena?" he asks after another moment.

"I don't know," Coralie responds, tossing her hair.

"This would be stunning in your hair," I jump in, holding what could be a hairpin up to reflect the bioluminescent glow of the room. It casts a few circles of blue light over Coralie and Caspian's faces. Cor squints.

"Would you help me?" she asks, angling her shoulder to indicate she wants her hair braided back.

"Oh, you know your brother is much better at this than me," I remind her.

"No, he's not," she protests, waiting for me to swim behind her and work on her hair.

"He doesn't want to work on your hair, Cor." Caspian's voice is exasperated. I imagine she's been on his case about helping with her hair recently. With the festival coming up, I'm sure she's been trying to find just the right style to impress the other twelve-year-olds.

Coralie pouts until Caspian swims behind her and quickly braids a few strands of her hair back. I watch quietly as he works, knowing anything I say will frustrate him. When he's done a few minutes later, I tuck the pin in Cor's hair.

"Add a few pearls and you'll be all ready for the Festival next week, Cor." She grins at my words.

"Are you coming with us?"

"I'll be with my family, but I'm sure I'll see you there." I wink at her and Caspian pretends to scowl.

"Leave my sisters out of this," Caspian warns good-naturedly. "Speaking of, where is my twin? There's no way she didn't hear all the noise from our little starfish here."

Swimming up, he maneuvers around her youngest sister in search for Celena—I can't let him find an empty room.

"Don't bother her, Casp," I yell, hoping to get Alemta's attention so she can intercede. "She's probably busy wishing on a starfish over that thing we discussed earlier."

If I needed him to believe Celena was pining over Relo or one of his friends, I'd make the sacrifice on Celena's behalf, though I'm sure she won't be happy if her twin starts pestering her about our fellow mermen.

A loud crash outside creates a distraction—it must be Celena.

"Stay here," I command Coralie not to follow me.

Turning, I dart outside to help smuggle Celena into her dwelling while Caspian continues toward the back. The water is dark, and I know I'll regret swimming home in it later unless I can get a hold of a midwater squid to guide me.

The water stirs. Moonlight filters down enough to see a few lengths in front of me, but the light is pale and hardly has the strength it usually does. Just as quickly, it opens back up, shining brightly enough to let me see all the way to the next dwelling—if Celena is out here, her tail will pick up the light for sure.

I had grabbed a net that was resting by the door on my way out, and I wrap it around my torso to conceal myself. It hangs loosely around me, and I wish I had rope to secure it.

"Merrick," Celena hisses in the darkness, seeing me exit the dwelling's blue glow. She makes a small clicking sound with her tongue, giving me something to follow. Slowly, I swim toward her, trying not to alert Caspian near the opposite edge of the house— apparently, Almeta couldn't stop him from investigating.

"Hello?" Caspian calls, trident in hand. His father swims a few lengths away.

"Merrick." Celena's soft voice startles me as she nearly whispers into my ear as I look over my shoulder at her family—I didn't know she was so close. "Get me inside."

I wrap my arms around her, pulling her close to my waist. My dark tail hides hers, blocking it from catching her brother's attention in the moonlight.

"Was that you or your mother?" I whisper.

"Wasn't me. I assume it was a warning."

"At least she's quick on her fins. Let's go."

Celena leans with me as I turn sideways. She allows me to do the swimming for us both, keeping her tail bent out of my way as I propel us toward the dwelling.

Her fingers dig into my shoulder—one of the men in her family has turned in our direction and any movement could give us away. Slamming her against the wall of her dwelling, I tuck her between my body and the wall. Her heart beats as rapidly as my own, though I can barely feel it through the net wrapped around my chest.

Celena peeks over my shoulder, letting me act as her shield. Three fingers rest on the front of my shoulder, wound through the net so I can feel her against my skin. Her other finger is poised in the water, waiting to give me the signal to move.

I catch her eye for a moment, and we both wait to be discovered. If they find us, we'll need an explanation, but I have a feeling Caspian's rage over me holding his sister like this is the biggest of my worries.

My partner shifts her gaze once more, watching her father and twin as her breathing slows. Her finger taps against me, and we move, darting into the water before diving around the corner toward her doorway.

"Hurry," her mother hisses just like Celena had. She waves us in.

Celena rips the pouch off her hip, handing it to her mother to hide as we hear noises at the far end of the dwelling.

"I sent Coralie to her room," Almeta whispers as she throws the pouch into a cabinet to conceal it. Celena will retrieve it later after her family has gone to bed for the night and no one can see her move it.

Celena rips at her hair, trying to take the braids out. I pull the netting off my torso and drop it by the door. Reaching up, I plunge my hands into her locks and help loosen them. I'm sure it's painful as we tear them out, but Almeta and Celena are under strict order never to let their family know that they spy for the royals—as far as Coralie, Caspian, and Hallmar know, Celena has been in her room all evening and only came out when we heard the noise.

My arm is still pulling out the last braid as Caspian swims back in and sees us. I drop my hand to Celena's waist. She lifts the hand next to me and rests it on my upper arm.

"You're sure it was nothing?" she says as if we had been in the middle of a conversation.

"I didn't see anything," I assure her. Glancing up, I address her twin. "Did you find anything?"

"No, nothing," Caspian confirms. He looks at us skeptically, but a chiding look from his mother makes him stop as I pull away from Celena—her secret is safe….for now. It's getting harder by the day to keep the whole of Scylla from learning what we do.

It's miraculous that they got all the way to the palace and back without getting caught, but the tides must have been with them.

"Is it okay?" Coralie asks. "Was it the sirens?"

"There are no sirens here, starfish. We don't have to worry about them—more likely a shark." Celena laughs as Coralie's eyes grow wide. "There are no sharks here, Cor, I promise. The worst we have are jellyfish, and if you pay attention, you won't even have to run into one of those up close."

Coralie swims out of the hall and wraps her arms around Caspian's waist.

"Don't worry, Cor. I'll keep you safe from the sea life, including that shark over there." He points at me and I oblige, growling like the merchildren do when they talk about sharks. I flip my tail and swim quickly toward Coralie, chasing her around the dwelling for a moment.

Almeta offers dinner, but I decline, saying I have to get back to my family. Celena flashes a signal at me to let me know the spears arrived safely at the palace.

Caspian swims out with me, making idle threats about staying away from his sisters. When we part ways, I swim into the night, headed toward my dwelling.

"Merrick," Llyr calls, bringing a glowing squid my way when I'm a few dwellings away from Celena and Caspian's home. "The queen would like to see you."

Apparently, the evening isn't over yet, and with it, another secret I must keep—this time from Celena.

Acknowledgements

Well, lucky you—you got more time with Merrick. Fans have been dying for more of his back story and it appears our leading merman has more of a story to tell. Intriguing, isn't it?

Thank you, fabulous reader, for sticking with me through the first trilogy in The Siren Wars Saga. I hoped you enjoyed Merrick's story as much as I have!

Shout out to the fabulous ladies who helped make this bonus short story a reality—you're awesome!

Special thanks to all my new mermaid friends—you all are inspiring and it's so fun to know you (and watch your social media feeds!)

Stay tuned, Siren Wars fans—more is on it's way…hit the next few pages for more info!

Stay inspired!

-K.M. Robinson

ORIGINS OF THE SIREN WARS-PREQUEL NOVELLA

A century ago, the human-mer treaty was established to protect the mer from the humans while they guided ships through storm-plagued waters. Now, Aila and her cousin, Persephone, act as representatives for their grandfather, King Gaspar, to the human world.

The mermaids share a close bond with the Prince Jarek, but when Aila catches Persephone trying to siren him into the waters, she must work to protect her friend from her cousin without hurting the human-mer relationship—something Persephone's mother won't tolerate.

War is brewing and Aila and Persephone are caught in the middle of a battle they never saw coming—one that will last for another century.

Get your copy at
originsinfo.kmrobinsonbooks.com

FORBIDDEN WATERS (THE SIREN WARS BOOK4)—CHAPTER 1

We can't always trust what we know to be fact. Even the most obvious truth can sometimes be a lie.

I've learned not to put my faith in what I know or even in my eyes have seen in the years since the war ended. Too much has shaken the reality of my world since then and nothing is the same. Even so, there are three things I *can* depend on—my sister, my friends, and my collection.

"What do you mean, *she's not coming?*" Shock waves over me like the pulsing water ripples over my tail…or maybe that really *is* the water moving over my scales as my sister flicks her tail and swims, expecting me to follow her. I tuck my knife away in my *iluse* and follow quickly behind her, the colorful coral flashing by as we move.

"The king of Antaire is dead, Iclyn—they have to go to formalize the treaty with the prince."

"You mean the *king*," I correct, brushing back a strand of hair that's caught on my shoulder. "If the king is dead, that makes Edmund the king now."

"Do you constantly need to correct me, Iclyn?"

No, but it adds a little significance to my life every now and then.

"Sorry," I mumble, knowing better than to upset her. "What are we going to do? We were counting on their support."

"We'll figure it out. Quilo is on his way—he's gathering the collection."

I assume she means our tiny collection and not all of Ambra. That's a conversation we do *not* need to be having right now.

Since we left the waters outside of Antaire two years ago, my sister has managed to get herself elected the honorary Celena of Ambra. I'm not sure how it happened, but she and her boyfriend, Quilo, positioned themselves as leaders and the collection backed them.

"We need to inform the queen," my sister mutters as we dive around a stingray.

Isla's palace isn't too far, but in an effort to beat Quilo and the others, we race at a dolphin's pace. The pearlescent building swells ahead of us as we crest the small mountains surrounding it. It glitters in the mid-morning light as Larina's hand floats back toward the conch shell resting in the pouch on her hip, it's outline pressed tightly against the fabric—Celena or Dylana must have sent the message of their change of plans.

"Do we know when they'll be here?" I ask quietly, brushing back my hair again. It baffles me how my tresses can continually float in front of me, even when I diving through the ocean at full speed, effectively pinning my hair back behind me. Larina's hair, however, is perfectly obedient—maybe that's why Queen Isla has taken to her so much—she's perfect.

"Babe!" Quilo calls as we dart around the back of the palace, seeking out the back entrance.

"So much for beating him," Larina mumbles. She glances at me as if it's my fault we didn't arrive earlier.

Quilo flashes me a smile before focusing in on my sister, grinning wildly as he wraps his arm around her hip and pulls her close to his chest. My sister giggles, brushing back her hair as he murmurs something in her ear—they're adorable and sickening at the same time. If I didn't think of Quilo as a brother, I'd have to force him out of our lives at this point.

The guards motion us into the palace. The water seems a bit icier inside the palace as we enter, but then, the palace always feels cooler than the open waters outside.

Isla motions to the lounging couches as we enter her receiving room. The group settles onto the bumps in the couches, and I lean over toward Kenda to rest my head on my arms for just a moment as I bat my eyelashes at my best friend. She rolls her eyes and pushes my elbow with hers, forcing me to sit back up as I risk a look at the merman she was just flirting with. Her copper tail flicks in playful annoyance.

"There was a skirmish today," Kenda whispers, leaning toward me. She attempts to cover her face with her hair so the collection doesn't notice that we're talking. "The sirens are becoming more bold, Iclyn. I think we're in real trouble here."

I envy Kenda. Larina and Isla trust her enough to allow her to go on missions while I'm tucked away inside the relative safety of Ambra. I do my fair share of missions, but I've only had two dangerous missions since we returned from Antaire and I'm dying to be let out of the barriers.

Isla raises her hands as she speaks, the crystal forming a cape between her shoulders and her wrists glittering in the sunlight as it pours down through the water into the palace through the hole in the ceiling. She looks at each of us, explaining what we already know— the sirens are trying to destroy all of the work we've done outside of the reef barriers.

"Your Majesty!" A long merman bursts into the room, trident in hand. "They moved up their timeline—the sirens are moving *now*."

Isla looks over in shock as Larina floats out of her seat by Quilo. He grabs her hand, holding her in place. She reminds me of a seahorse tipping forward as its tail is wrapped around a piece of seaweed.

"Armor!" The queen's shout slams into us all, knocking everyone into motion. The guards rush out of the room, attempting to find shoulder armor for all of us to wear. We follow behind them, knowing it's quicker if we just do it ourselves.

Larina shoves a chest plate at me as I grasp at a metal covering for my shoulders that is clearly too wide for me. Kenda and I switch—her shoulders are wider than mine—and I shrug into the cool metal. The silver gleams against my hair and tail, making me look even more Keldorian than I usually do. I consider switching to gold to avoid the comments later, but there's no time.

The pearls against my abdomen shift uncomfortably under the chest plate but removing them would just take extra time that we don't have. Mer hover around in the water like a confused school of fish, darting around each other hurriedly even though we know exactly what to do.

We ignore the sea life as it floats around us, not even flinching as we stream out of the palace and down the steps toward the main path that leads to the open waters outside of the city proper. Without a word, we all swim toward the sirens' goal—the storage dwelling.

When the sirens first started to attack, they raided our armory, sneaking into the city unnoticed. We had heard of a few fights between wandering sirens that found each other after the war with the humans, but until they took our weapons, none of the sea kingdoms knew just how strong the straggling sirens really were. Now they plague the seas, still small in number, but with a vendetta against the mer for disbanding them after Nir's death.

Our spies gathered word that their next target is a building we use to store food and supplies. We've placed guards there, but have kept them back far enough that we can hopefully catch the sirens as they move in. In truth, the building is more useful as a place to spy on us— the sirens would have the high ground and be able to see everything we do, and because we protected it so well, it would be hard for us to take control back without losing too many of our collection in the process…unless our strategy works, of course.

Lulling them into a false sense of security seems to be the best plan of action. Once the sirens have made their breach, we can take them by surprise, trapping them inside of the dwelling, but we have to be in position before they arrive.

Strangely enough, I hadn't seen any sign of them before Larina dragged me away from my post to the palace. I play everything over in my head, second-guessing everything I saw, but I don't recall seeing any signs of the sirens outside of the storage dwelling.

Kenda barely manages to keep up with me as I swim toward the front of the collection. I'm tiny compared to most of the mer, but I can out swim most of them too—something I've been working on for years to compensate for my smaller stature. My friend struggles to breathe as I reach the front.

Larina glares at me, motioning me back with a wave of her hand. I know she only means to keep me safe, but it's frustrating being constantly shoved to the side while the others are allowed more freedom. Quilo tosses an apologetic look at me. Beyond him, one of my merman friends raises an eyebrow but doesn't say anything. His long hair trails behind him as he swims, looking as angry and magnificent as the scars on his torso do.

We position ourselves along the underside of the dwelling entrance, prepared to slam a hidden door in place to lock the sirens in. Each of us has a job to do to block the holes in the dwelling walls to prevent their escape. When the time comes, Kenda and I will work together with several of the mermen to seal hole off on the south side of the dwelling, giving us a long way to travel around the cave to reach it.

An hour passes without any sight of the sirens.

"I thought they were close," Kenda whispers to the merman next to us.

"They were supposed to be," he whispers back, eyes dark.

Larina drags herself over the sand, trying to remain hidden as she moves toward me. She looks ridiculous, but I won't tell her that. She claws at the sand until she reaches me.

"Isla wants you to go check things out. Take this group with you, and we'll reorganize in case they show up."

It amazes me that I'm not allowed to do anything interesting until the queen needs me for my speed.

I nod to my sister before turning to make sure everyone heard. One at a time, we slip away from the dwelling into the open waters, staying low to the sand until we reach the seaweed.

Winding my way through, I make my way to the kelp forest in the distance—it will be the best vantage point for spying. Debris floats in the water, catching the noon sunlight directly overhead. My shadow is hidden on the ocean floor, mixed with the rapidly moving pieces of kelp waving around me as I swim into the haze kelp forests often provide.

"Careful," the orange-tailed merman says gruffly. He may act like he doesn't care, but I think he does.

We move in different directions, Kenda staying close by. My fingers itch to abandon my trident in favor of my knife, but I know the trident may end up being my saving grace should we encounter any sirens in the kelp forest or beyond.

Reports said the sirens were over the ridge and rapidly approaching, but they should have arrived at the same time we did, if not before. It's possible that they stopped along the way, but we won't know until we can locate them.

My armor shifts on my body as I tip myself forward to swim faster. I need to make it to the tunnel without being caught.

The sirens wouldn't dare enter a tunnel where they could easily be trapped, and hopefully they will assume we'd think of that too and avoid it—which means it's a perfect place for me to take advantage of while spying.

"Iclyn, don't!" Kenda warns as I dart out of the kelp and dive toward the tunnel under the cover of a large sea turtle swimming by.

I drop my hand behind me and wave at her to assure her that I know what I'm doing.

The turtle pulls away a few lengths away from the tunnel entrance, leaving me exposed. I dart inside, turning around once I'm in the shadows to make sure Kenda stayed in place at the edge of the kelp forest. Her copper tail glimmers alongside the kelp, making her the most radiant mermaid I've ever seen—not even Larina is as striking as Kenda when my friend is in the golden sunlight surrounded by similar colors...one more reason to envy her.

I run my fingers over my *iluse* to make sure my knife and shells are still in place should I need them. Turning, I swim into the darkness of the blue cave.

The walls are accented with bioluminescent plankton, radiating blue against the blue walls Ambra is known for. The glow gives me just enough light to see by.

A school of red fish glides toward me, pulling to the side just an arm's length in front of me. Shells litter the tunnel floor, covering the sand to the point of almost making the tiny brown grains invisible under a path of broken shell pieces.

I duck against the wall as a jellyfish floats by, careful to avoid its long tentacles. I'd rather face a shark than a jellyfish. I've only been stung once when I was a mer girl, but it was enough to give me nightmares about it to this day. I shudder as I think about it.

Ahead, I can see the opening of the tunnel, specs of debris floating in front of it as a piece of seaweed waves across the opening just enough for me to notice it. When it lifts an entire arm length toward the surface without the rest of it growing longer or short, everything in my body prickles—something is wrong.

I collide with a net as I dart backward—I hadn't noticed it as I swam past it, which means they hid it well. Grappling with it, I try to untangle myself, but it's the least of my worries as several dark figures appear in the tunnel entrance.

For a moment, I flash back to the time I was tangled in a human net, being dragged to the surface in retaliation for a war we had nothing to do with. I escaped that, and I intend to escape this.

Ripping my hair away from the net painfully, I aim my trident at the sirens approaching.

You're smaller and can escape faster than they can, I remind myself.

"There, there, little mer girl," a merman siren croons. "We won't hurt you...much."

"We just need to make an example out of you for the others," a second siren chimes in, his voice deeper than the first merman.

"It's just a few scales…and maybe a fin or two," a mermaid chimes in, trying to scare me. If I've learned anything in the last two years, it's to not show any fear in the face of danger if I'm all alone. One of the main things Celena teaches is how to appear brave even if we're not. Our sister kingdom, Scylla, has been adamant that all of the kingdoms are acting as one when it comes to fighting off the growing siren collection, and as the kingdom closest to them, we've received most of their support.

"Yes, I'm sure you won't miss them at all," I reply, grinning.

"Hmm, you think you can win against all of *us*?" the mermaid mocks.

"You're right. If you have one more friend out there, it will be a fair fight." I lunge at her, thrusting my trident toward her scales. I graze her hip, and she shrieks.

The mermen look at her, and I use the opportunity to attack again, this time slamming my trident into the merman in the middle. He cries out in pain as the edge of my trident pierces the edge of his scales and rips straight through to the other side. It's barely a flesh wound, but I manage to knock him off balance enough to race out of the tunnel beyond them.

The uninjured merman takes off after me, growling obscenities at me. I look around, hoping to make it to kelp bed on the far side of the tunnel where I might be able to lose him.

An entire small army of sirens stares back at me, eyes wide when they see I'm not being held captive. For as long as it takes me to hold in my gasp, I wish that Larina had prevented me from coming on this mission, but she'd never say no to the queen.

A small collection from the sirens moves toward me, ready to assist their friend in my capture. If they get their hands on me, they'll try to use me against Isla and the collection—I can't let that happen.

I dive toward the kelp bed, out swimming the mermaid on my tail. He yells for the others to spread out to look for me. A cry answers back from within the kelp forest and I realize I'm not alone.

The sand is gritty around my chest plate as I drag myself along the ocean floor as my sister had done not too long ago before I left on this mission. I'm sure I look equally as silly, but I don't know where the sirens are hiding in the kelp. I can't swim over it because the sirens waiting outside will see me. I don't want to risk swimming face first into one of them, so my best option is crawling under them.

"Come out, little mermaid," the siren chasing me calls. "It's better if you cooperate. Come out now, and we'll only take a few scales. Make us find you, and we'll send you back to your queen in pieces."

It's like he's forgotten that I've fought in a war against the humans. I know my sister has been overprotective since I almost died, but I'm not that far out of the loop that I don't know how to go with the flow when it comes to threats.

The sirens won't kill me—they need a hostage. The worst they can do is split my tail, and even my friends from Scylla who endure their tails being cut have learned to survive it. I just need to keep these sea monsters away from my collection.

"I see you, mermaid." The siren's voice is calm and quiet, hovering right behind me.

My body tenses, tightening my muscles against my shoulder armor. The water rushes around me as he descends on me, wrapping his bulging arms around me. I desperately wish any of my mermen friends were around to help free me.

I struggle against him, but he pulls me to his chest, his brown tail twitching around mine. My trident drops out of my hand, bumping into the bottom of my tail as it falls—for a moment, I wish I had legs so I had a chance to catch my weapon.

His arms are covered in seaweed—I assume a protective measure meant to camouflage himself—and it scratches against my skin.

Another merman appears in front of me, slipping around the long pieces of kelp as he watches me struggle. When he sees us, he moves back into the kelp out of sight, but not before I get a good look at his bold, red tail.

Like his friend, he also has seaweed wrapped around his body, but unlike the other siren, his looks stylized. The greenery is wrapped around his wrists like bracelets. A *sarasa* is proudly displayed across his chest, while fuller pieces of seaweed sit on his shoulder and fall off his hip on one side. His dark hair swayed in the water as he pulled back from us to hide.

I fight, willing myself to survive the angry siren. I wonder if they had been this bad before the war or if this anger was a recent development. I'm honestly very glad the sirens focused their rage on Scylla for all those years instead of Ambra. I suppose after a century, it's only fair that Ambra take a turn being the target, but I wouldn't object to passing off the burden to Dariah or Keldori soon.

The siren pulls out a knife and slices my belt off from around my waist. I'm willing to let go of the objects I collected this morning if it means I can escape, but I worked hard to create that belt, and temporary furry makes me forget to think things through before I act.

I bite down on the siren's arm, making him cry out and reel back just enough that I can reach my knife in my *iluse*. Pulling it out, I plunge it behind me into the siren. Without looking back, I whip the knife out of his flesh and push forward into the kelp ahead of me.

I swim directly at the red-tailed merman, unable to find a way around him before the injured siren can regroup and attack. In the background, I hear him screaming orders to the others, and a cheer rises up behind me.

"Touch me and I'll kill you," I shout, trying to frighten the red-tailed merman who's hiding somewhere in the kelp.

"Not if they kill you first," he hisses in my ear as his hand wraps around my body, pulling me to a halt. His other hand goes to my mouth to keep me quiet. "I'll help you."

He flicks his tail to push us forward, painfully colliding with mine as he drags me away from them. I try to get away, but he won't relinquish his grip. I grunt around his hand, trying to ask what he's doing. As if reading my mind, he hisses in my ear.

"You injured Halmar pretty bad back there—they won't hesitate to kill you now, even though we need you as a hostage. I don't care if we hold you captive, but I'm not going to let them kill you. They're as blood hungry as sharks these days, and you're an easy target, Little Blue."

I cringe as he references my coloring.

We dart out of the kelp. He aims us straight for a pile of nets on the ocean floor—I tense as I realize he's about to tie me up.

"Don't fight me, mermaid," he hisses, tightening his grip on me.

I throw my elbow back into his chest. He bucks but doesn't release me. The merman slams me into the ground, forcing my face into the sand. I cough, trying not to swallow the grains.

The red-tailed siren throws a net on top of me, but before I can object again, he moves the entire pile on of me, weighing me down heavily.

"Stay put, I'll be back to free you when it's safe. Don't give yourself away. If you get caught, I'll cut you in half myself— self-preservation, you know, Blue." He starts to leave but leans down one more time. "There are two choices here: you let me calm them down and use you as a hostage, or you move even the slightest bit, and they'll catch you and kill you. Your choice."

I can barely see him swimming away through the layers of netting, his red tail flashing in the crystal blue waters as he rushes back toward his siren collection.

Apparently, I'm about to be a hostage.

Forbidden Waters (Book 4 of The Siren Wars Saga) will be available from Crescent Sea Publishing in 2019

BONUS SCENES

Want to read a bonus scene from The Siren Wars? We're giving out an exclusive bonus scene over on the K.M. Robinson Facebook page!

Get it by sending the page a direct message at
facebook.com/kmrobinsonbooks

We're also giving away Siren Wars freebies in the newsletter. Join for free books, excerpts, and more!
newsletter.kmrobinsonbooks.com

We're constantly giving out additional bonus scenes for preorder swag, giveaways, and more, so watch the social media pages carefully for the next scene giveaway.

WORLD PORTALS

Ready to learn exclusive facts about The Siren Wars and other K.M. Robinson Series?

World Portals are now available on www.kmrobinsonbooks.com

Learn behind the scenes facts, watch videos, play games, check out our book filters, find out where to get bonus scenes, view fan art, and get access to other secrets we've hidden away inside the World Portals on the website.

You can also see the map that we weren't able to add to this version of the story due to file size limits.

The World Portals are constantly changing and information is being taken away and added all the time, so check back frequently for new content!

BONUS FACEBOOK FILTERS

Want to get your hands on some incredible Facebook filters for Siren Wars? Now you have the ability to get filters for the story, characters, etc right inside your phone.

You can use these on your photos, profile pictures, videos, and live broadcasts. All you have to do is like my author page and they will automatically show up in your filters!

I've even taken these clips and put them on Instagram Stories by saving them to my phone and uploading them to Instagram.

Visit www.facebook.com/kmrobinsonbooks to grab these filters for your photos, videos, and broadcasts! Bonus points for tagging me @kmrobinsonbooks so I can see how you're supporting The Siren Wars.

ABOUT THE AUTHOR

K.M. Robinson is a storyteller who creates new worlds both in her writing and in her fine arts conceptual photography. She is a marketing, branding and social media strategy educator who is recognized at first sight by her very long hair. She is a creative who focuses on photography, videography, couture dress making, and writing to express the stories she needs to tell. She almost always has a camera within reach. Visit her at her website: www.kmrobinsonbooks.com

CONNECT ON SOCIAL MEDIA

facebook.com/kmrobinsonbooks

instagram.com/kmrobinsonbooks

twitter.com/kmrobinsonbooks

Get free books and excerpts of other K.M. Robinson books at
excerpt.kmrobinsonbooks.com

ALSO BY K.M. ROBINSON

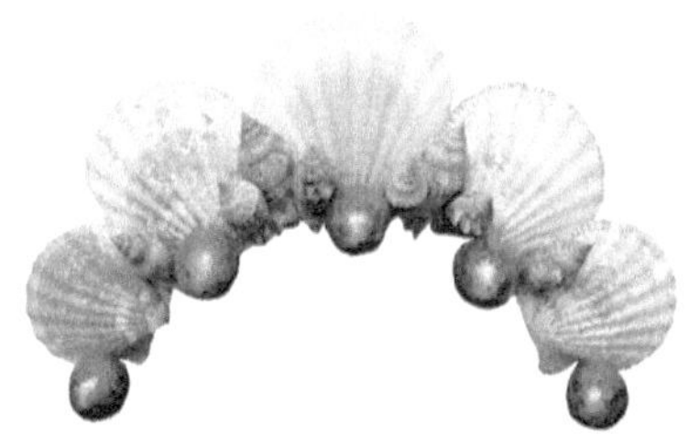

The Siren Wars Saga

Book One: The Siren Wars

Book Two: Darker Depths

Book Three: Beyond The Shores

Origins of the Siren Wars: Prequel Novella

The Jaded Duology

Book One: Jaded

Book Two: Risen

The Complete Series Boxset/Omnibus with exclusive epilogue

The Golden Trilogy

Book One: Golden

Forged: A Golden Novella

Book Two: Locked

Book Three: Edge

The Complete Series Boxset/Omnibus with exclusive bonus novella,
Tempered

The Legends Chronicles

Along Came A Spider: A Prequel Novelette

And They'll Come Home: A Prequel Novelette

The Revolution of Jack Frost

Virtually Sleeping Beauty: A Novella Retelling

The Goose Girl and The Artificial: A Novella Retelling

The Sinking: A Novella Retelling

JADED: BOOK ONE OF THE JADED DUOLOGY

Her father failed in his mission to take control from the Commander, a defeat that has cost Jade her life. She will die as punishment. Now she belongs to the Commander's son—as his wife. Knowing his intent is to quietly kill her in revenge, Jade's every move is calculated to survive—until she learns her death ensures the safety of her father and her entire town.

Roan doesn't want to kill Jade, but once his family isolates her from her father and community, his only choice is to go through with the plan. Jade doesn't make it easy as she tries to sway him into falling for her. Each misstep makes him question his cause. Each moment makes every decision harder, but the Commander won't allow him to fail.

One chooses life. One chooses death. In the midst of the chaos, only one will succeed.

Now available!
Learn more about The Jaded Duology at
jadedinfo.kmrobinsonbooks.com

GOLDEN: BOOK ONE OF THE GOLDEN TRILOGY

Goldilocks was never naïve. She was sent on a mission and Dov Baer is her new target.

When the girl with the golden hair betrays everyone, not even she has hope of surviving.

The stories say that Goldilocks was a naïve girl who wandered into a house one day. Those stories were wrong. She was never naïve. It was all a perfectly executed plan to get her into the Baers' group to destroy them.

Trained by her cousin, Lowell, and handler, Shadoe, Auluria's mission is to destroy the Baers by getting close to the youngest brother, Dov, his brother and sister-in-law and the leaders of the Baers' group.

When she realizes Dov isn't as evil as her cousin led her to believe, she must figure out how to play both sides or her deception will cause everyone in her world to burn.

If her allegiances are discovered, either side could destroy her...if the Society doesn't get her first.

Available now!
Learn more about The Golden Trilogy at
goldeninfo.kmrobinsonbooks.com

ALONG CAME A SPIDER: THE FIRST PREQUEL NOVELETTE TO THE LEGENDS CHRONICLES

Little Hacker Muffet
sat on her tuffet
destroying her cords and Way.
Along came a hacker named Spider,
who sat down beside her
and frightened his opponent away.

When Fet, one of the most skilled hackers in the Legends, discovers her best friend and leader of her group has been abducted and held for ransom, she must escape unnoticed and find Peep before it's too late.

When Spider, a new recruit training to join her hacker ring, slips out with her and claims to have a plan to save her friend, Fet is forced to bring him along. As she discovers he's not who he claims to be, she faces grave danger and learns just how deadly a spider bite can be.

Now available!
Learn more about The Legends Chronicles at
acasinfo.kmrobinsonbooks.com

VIRTUALLY SLEEPING BEAUTY

She may be doing battle in the virtual world, but in the real world, they can't wake her up...

All Rora wants is to help people as class president, give her time to local charities, and quietly earn her way to the top level of the virtual reality system that the entire country uses without anyone noticing she's the second best player in the game.

All Royce wants to do is level up as a knight inside the gaming system, slay dragons, and eventually play his way to controlling the palace as he takes the crown away from the reigning queen.

When his Aunt Perry calls him, hysterically screaming that her goddaughter, Rora, has been inside for more than the four hours the game allows, Royce rushes over to help.

Entering the game, Royce soon discovers that Rora is trapped inside the system after an encounter with an evil magician who can change forms inside the game and control the virtual world. If he and his friend can't help her beat the game, she might not be able to wake up in the real world at all.

When virtual knights and princesses meet to slay dragons and defeat evil rulers, there's nothing stopping them from suffering real-world consequences too.

To wake her up, he must enter the game and help her beat it.

Now available!

Learn more about Virtually Sleeping Beauty at
vsbinfo.kmrobinsonbooks.com

THE REVOLUTION OF JACK FROST

No one inside the snow globe knows that Morozoko Industries is controlling their weather, testing them to form a stronger race that can survive the fall out from the bombs being dropped in the outside world—all they know is that they must survive the harsh Winter that lasts a month and use the few days of Spring, Summer, and Fall to gather enough supplies to survive.

When the seasons start shifting, Genesis and Jack know something is going on. As their team begins to find technology that they don't have access to inside their snow globe of a world, it begins to look more and more like one of their own is working against them.

Genesis soon discovers Morozoko Industries, but when a foreign enemy tries to destroy their weather program to make sure their destructive life-altering bombs succeed in destroying the outside world, only one person can shut down the machine that is spinning out of control and save the lives of everyone inside the bunker—Jack.

Now available!
Learn more about The Revolution of Jack Frost at
jackfrostinfo.kmrobinsonbooks.com

THE SINKING

**The sea with wants to silence her, but not for the reason
you think.**

When a quirky older woman pawns a fancy seashell necklace at her mother's antique shop on the pier, Cara doesn't think much about the story the woman spins about the wearer turning into a mermaid.

On her way home, she accidentally drops the necklace into the ocean and is swept out to sea where she meets Quay--a merman who volunteers to take her to his mother, the sea queen, to help her get her legs back.

Cara soon learns that it's Quay's eighteen birthday--a day that has been a curse for his family--and is meant to be one for her too. Now she must fight to survive the sea with Quay at her side.

Fans of The Little Mermaid will love this twisted take on the beloved
story.

Now available!

Learn more about The Sinking at
thesinkinginfo.kmrobinsonbooks.com

www.ingramcontent.com/pod-product-compliance
Lightning Source LLC
Chambersburg PA
CBHW031728180726
48283CB00005B/1421